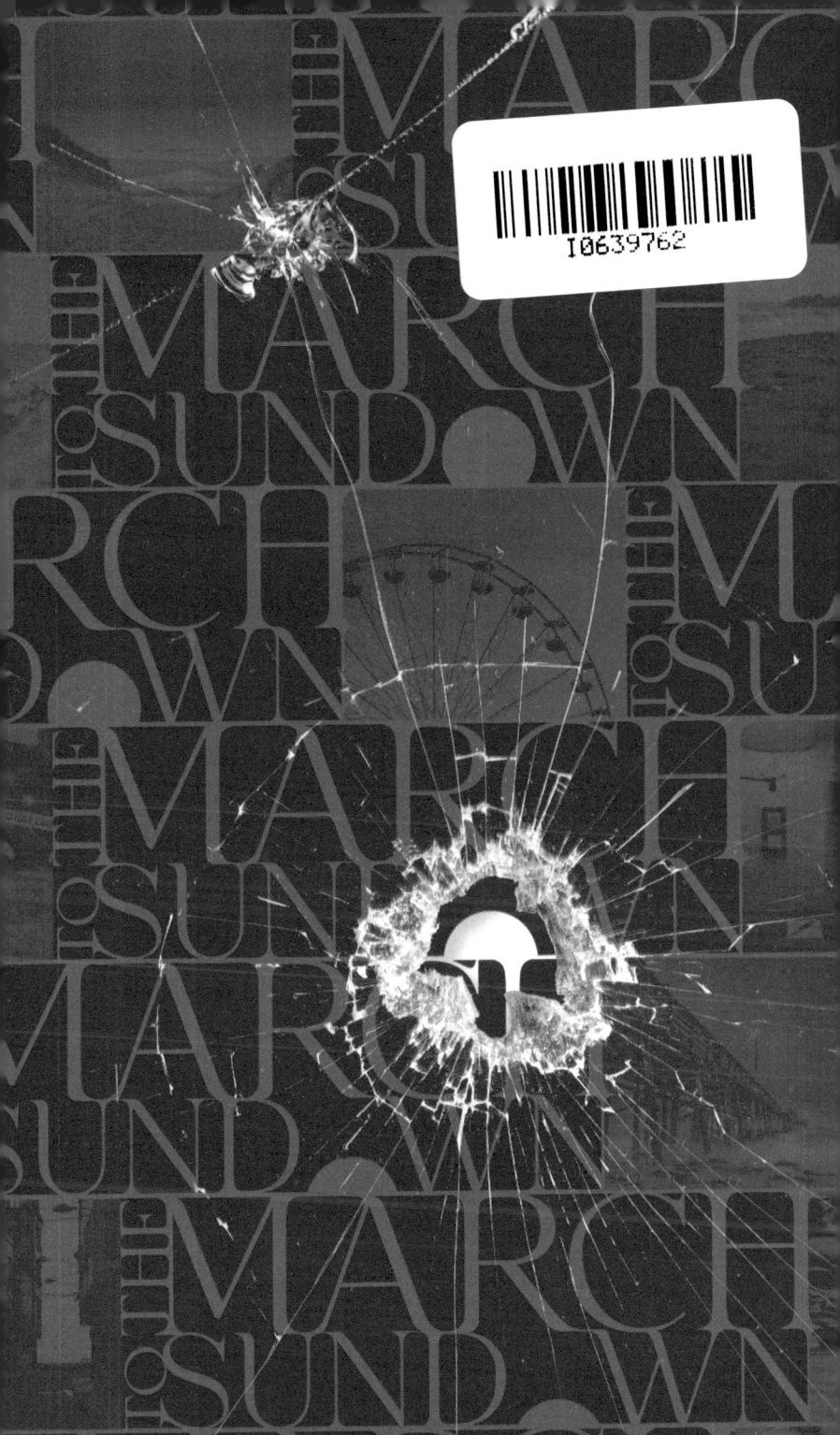

I0639762

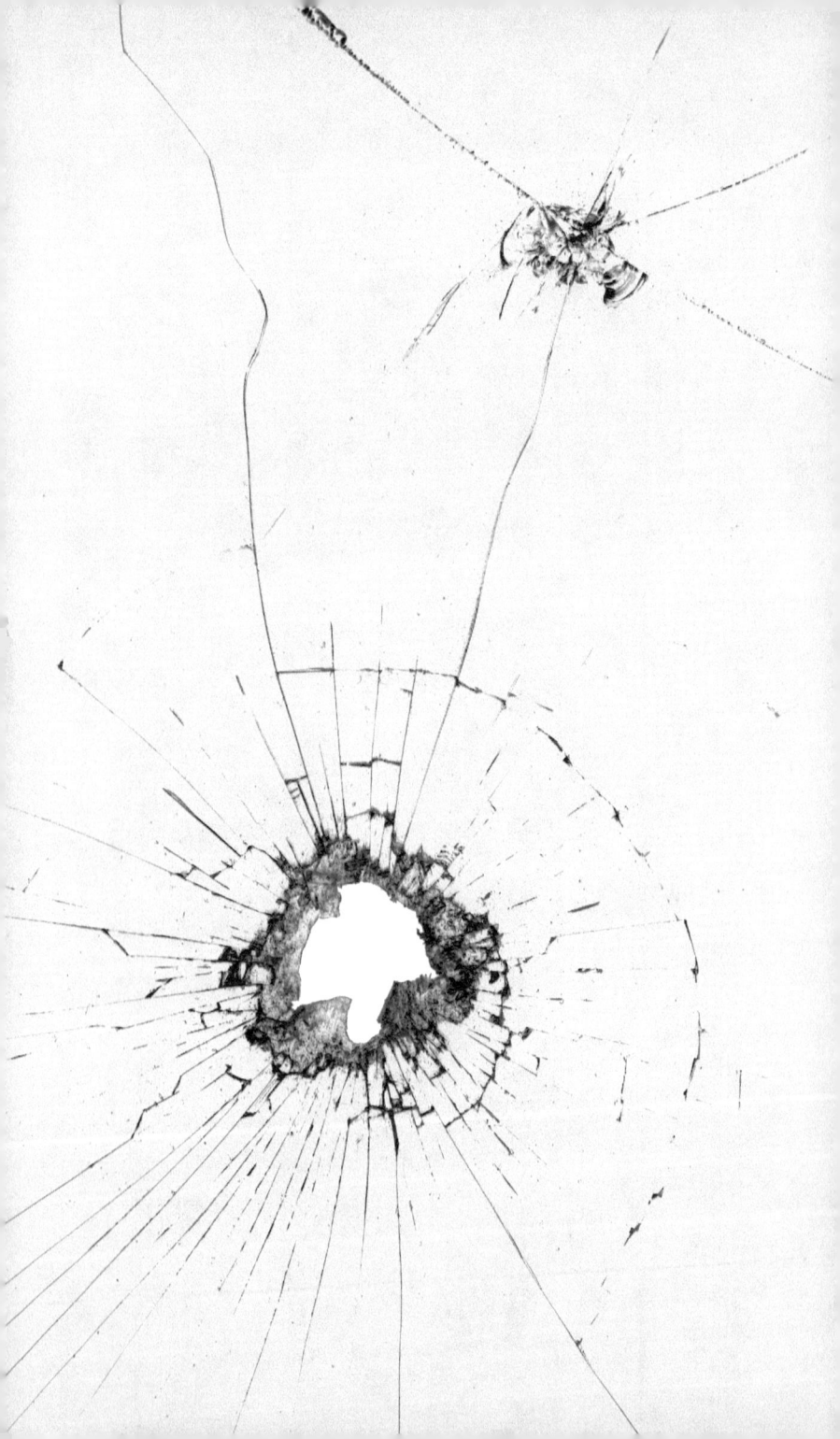

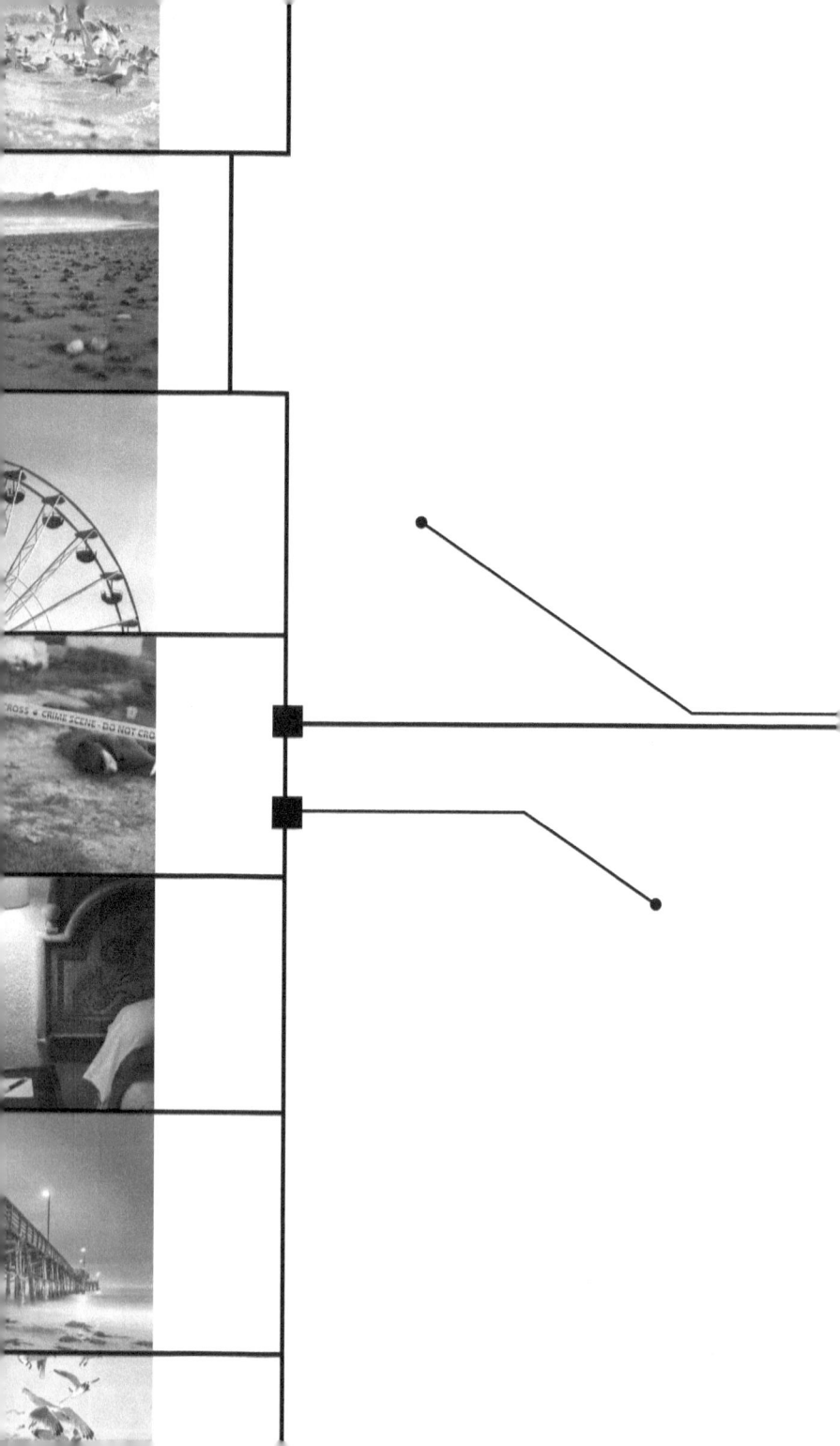

RED CLAW PUBLISHING

First Edition, September 2016
Written by Ellis Kross
Edited by Sidonie Lailler

ISBN: 978-0-9976453-1-6
Kross, Ellis, 1983—
The March to Sundown
I. Title. Fiction. Psychological Thriller

ISBN: 978-0-9976453-1-6 pbk.

Story by Ellis Kross
Book Design by Four Winds

CONTENTS

EPISODES (1-3)

Cont. Ep. 4 - 12 (PAGE V)

Figure 1

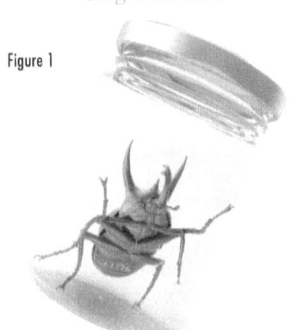

Fg. 1 Robert carries a jar that contains a *devil beetle*. Not to be confused with a rhino beetle, this beetle is believed to have psychoactive compounds inside its horns, which may produce what some users call a "killer trip" when cut with the popular street drug, lo-ro.

PROLOGUE

THE telling flame of the lighter that Rob swiped from the mister muncher man with "*Butt Hole eyes,*" as his wildly animated pen pal, Twiggy, or Twiggy's post-drugged alter ago, "Twigs," wrote in a venomous staccato-like manner, directed his eyes to one particular word, *snake*, which was buried underneath subtle (wink-wink) diversions in her unhinged scribbling that consisted of colorful slurs or nicknames for any meat who grabbed her reflective eye.

With his other hand, he used the scrub's pen to underline the notes "sight of the *snake*."

Another clue, he realized once he pieced together Twiggy's seemingly hyperbolic wordplay, like whacked out jigsaw puzzle pieces with each word serving as a marker in his very own escape guide; then, days later, after his verbal map was confiscated, he used the stolen key to sneak inside Harcourt's office.

Once inside, as instructed by those notes, he made his way directly to a morbid painting by Rhonda Abbott on the far end of the office. The painting was called "Dark Mountain," and below the matte read a quote: "*Beseech the O lord. Becometh who thou meant to be.*"

An electrical cord, he confirmed as his attention fell to the floor, not a snake. *Sneaky,* Twiggy.

Behind the miniature cube-shaped refrigerator underneath the Dark Mountain painting was a black cord lying in an S for Serpent-like pattern on the floor, unplugged from the nearest outlet.

With the *clip-clop, clip-clop* of footsteps sounding closer and closer, Rob kneeled down, placed his hand over the side of the fridge, which wasn't cold, in fact, it was room temp, and then decided to open the fridge.

There, Rob discovered the safe, as Twiggy's notes foretold. Those numbers were etched on his mind—How could he forget? He immediately spun the dial to the first number of the combination, number 8, then the next number, 43, and then, finally, the last, 11. Each number revealed as clues inside the notes.

"It's *not* bullshit," Rob said in a panicked tone. The beads of sweat dripped along the ridge of his brow and rolled down his cheek. He turned his shoulder toward a tall shadowy figure in the corner of the office and said, "See for yourself."

Once the combination was correctly entered, he pulled on the handle and cracked open the safe's door, revealing a bag of at least a hundred pills with an inscription of a winged dragon.

"Told you," Rob said.

Then, listened closely to the shadow.

Growing more upset, he said back to the shadow, "You're wrong. It changes everything."

After acquiring the score, Rob suddenly flinched from the *thud* of Harcourt's chatty Russian Blue leaping onto the top of the desk. He rotated his shoulder, only to find Igor crying for a treat. The delicate *jingle* of his metal nametag sounded with each pawing at Rob's shoulder, pleading "feed me, please."

As he continued to sweat, he tried to shush the cat, but his attempts were fruitless. He faced forward and pointed out the kitty bank-like container of treats called Purrcent on top of the refrigerator. He popped open the lid, reached inside, and then pulled out a handful of kitty treats, shaped like pennies—*right*, he finally caught on to the name of the bank, *Per cent, get it?*— and set them down next to the Russian Blue's paws.

The footsteps were right outside the office!

With his heart pounding, he closed the safe and as he was about to duck behind the desk, he thought that he heard Remi Rim Job and Bruno From The Planet Pluto arguing over what sounded like "red checker" pieces from the recreational room.

The footsteps came to a screeching halt and reversed, then trailed away from the office. Rob breathed a sigh of relief, but he knew that he wasn't quite out of the woods.

The book, he suddenly remembered.

Where was it?

Before exiting the office, he stopped by the only place that made the most sense, which was Harcourt's desk, and frantically rummaged through each drawer until he found a novel—*my book*, the map—in the bottom drawer.

With a bag of dragon pills, as well as the novel, in his possession, Rob did exactly what his pen pal instructed him to do within the PC Edition's Notes Section behind each chapter of the book, which was, after each distraction, trap, and poison, escape directly through the "FRONT DOOR!"

●

WHILE making his way to the Coast, Rob drifted deeper into his thoughts. He didn't know how these images manifested in his head—he wondered if he accidentally or deliberately swallowed one of Harcourt's experimental pills, or maybe it wasn't that at all, and he simply lost himself in the tedious highway, which induced a trance-like state—but when it reached a point where he couldn't escape them, these images, he was left with no other choice than to surrender to them.

While Thomas was out picking up milk at the local grocery store, Susannah phoned John Ruby, who just recently visited the Backers to discuss their next play. Fortunately for Susannah, he hadn't driven too far away, in fact, when he arrived shortly after the call, he told Susannah that he stopped by a family-owned restaurant Surf n' Turf, which had been in business ever since 1957, their once laughable, now trendy logo of a hotdog with a pair of Warhol-like sunglasses riding a surfboard recently gaining popularity on, of all places, the Internet— once Ruby and his former partner, who were in town to track down leads for a missing person's case, tried one of Surf n' Turf's famous pink hotdogs with chili and slaw ("Please do not ask about the ingredients," he'd tell his newly appointed health conscious partner) while taking a break, and the detective claimed it was probably the best wiener that he had ever eaten.

After Susannah invited Ruby into the house, she first apologized for Thomas's behavior and told him that he didn't mean any of those harsh things he said, especially the part about Ruby being a hack. The detective didn't take it personal, and with Susannah having married a cop, she was well aware that their skin, mainly the texture, as well as its remarkable thickness, was much different than the average person.

Once the awkwardness was destroyed by Susannah's warm smile, she returned to the folder of photocopies that Ruby had given her, the same ones that Harcourt copied days before the novel magically disappeared.

"When I was reading through these excerpts, one particular line stood out the most," Susannah said with a handful of photocopies of a novel in her hand. "This patient, the one who previously owned this book, mentions a line: 'Personal sovereignty.' Does this mean anything to you?"

She showed Ruby the line on the piece of paper.

"Based on your son's handwriting," he said as if he had read the book many times and already made his own mental cliff notes in his head, "it appears as if he has taken an interest in that one particular line. From what I read, I think this Twiggy character was trying to help your son escape."

"But why?" Susannah asked, as she walked Ruby into the living room, where he nearly tripped over a basket full of magazines, which warranted a word of caution from Susannah. Before he could answer, she followed up by saying with a more confused tone, "It doesn't make any sense (Twiggy's NOTES, not those magazines). How does she even know Robert?"

"Beats me—"

"Does she have a name?" asked Susannah. "I mean a real name, that is."

"I did some digging and found a patient named Medea Clout, her nickname is Twiggy."

"What kind of name is Twiggy anyway?"

"I dunno yet, but I'm looking into it."

"John—"

"I promise," he said and reassured Susannah. "I'm gonna get to the bottom of this."

A globe of silence filled the room.

"Before you left," she said abruptly, her words cutting through the soon-to-be tension, "I was going to tell you that Thomas and I spoke with Doctor Harcourt."

"And?"

"You don't trust him?"

"Not one bit."

Depressed, Susannah hung her head.

"He should've never been in that place to begin with."

Again, silence swelled over the conversation.

Susannah motioned for the detective to stay put.

"I almost forgot," she said and walked to the center of the living room where she grabbed a photograph next to stack of magazines on the coffee table. "I found a photo. Here. . . " she handed a Polaroid to Ruby, ". . . Take it. That's him. That's my little Moe."

"Which one?"

"The one in the blue shirt."

Ruby grabbed the Polaroid of her two sons.

"Whoever he became. . . " Susannah said over Ruby, as he studied the photograph, ". . . whatever he turned into, it's not him."

"But what if—"

"I don't care," Susannah cried out, her eyes glossy. "I've already buried one son. I'd be damned if I bury another. You have one job, Ruby: Find my son. Whatever it takes. Promise?"

Ruby hesitated.

"Sure," he said. "I promise."

"Ever since his brother. . . " Susannah's voice trailed off as she walked to the window and looked at the neighborhood street, where a neighbor was walking on the sidewalk in the front of the house while strangling a corgi with a yellow leash, his head buried in his phone as he scrolled through the news feed. "This is all my fault," she said over the silence. "I was the one who did this to him. I was just trying to make him understand all of the dangers out there and how unsafe it was, but instead, it backfired, and he started to resent me. I could see it in his eyes, the way he used to look at me—"

From behind, Ruby asked, "How do you mean?"

"Maybe I was too overprotective when he was younger. Maybe I wasn't protective enough. Maybe I was just an easy target. Or maybe I really did put hatred in his heart."

"You can't blame yourself, Susannah," he said. "He chose a path of violence, and there wasn't anything you did that set him on that path."

Teary-eyed, Susannah lets out an angry sigh. "I'm just worried sick about him." With her bloodshot eyes piercing through her own reflection in the window, she said indirectly to Ruby, "All I can think about is 'What's going on inside that head of his?' What's he thinking about right now?"

THE MARCH TO SUNDOWN

"I HAVE A BAD HEART.

Not like bad, as in what the stuck-up richies at East Providence call a well-executed nosegrind after deliberately eating a face full of asphalt to help cleanse the silver from their palates; or bad, as in poor condition, as if my heart runs off the jerry-built hand of a Doomsday clock ready to strike twelve; or bad, as in extremely unpleasant, so much that even a pride of ravenous lions picking me apart limb by limb would push around my foul heart only to get to my tasty bits, then save the leftovers for the hyenas; but bad, as in dangerously hovering over the darker side of wicked, as in devil without the d.

Every now and then, I catch myself thinking about what it would look like, my bad heart, if I sliced myself open with a scalpel, cut through all of the tissue and muscle and each vessel that kept my bad heart shackled to its maggoty prison, then held it in the palm of my hand before it inflated like a puffer fish.

What would it look like?

The only thing that comes to mind when I think of my bad heart is exactly that: a *thing*, not belonging to a he or a she but to some exotic creature, arcane by design as well as functionality, primordial, blacker than the ink of an octopus—that is, if there was even a color on the spectrum that was blacker than black, that would be the color of this vile, detestable thing—

and when it pumps dank sludge in and out of its spiny shell, it does so ominously through icy tentacles stretching like purple streaks of lightning across dark cumulonimbus clouds which consume my entire body; then the tedious process is repeated over and over until the blood stains everything it touches in the blackest of black residue.

I'm not sure why my heart turned corrupt, or if it had always been this way the moment I was brought into this cruel little existence, or if it gradually changed or evolved or even devolved from what people call a normal heart to a cold and poisonous one and now I'm finally feeling the irreparable side-effects of its gross and unstoppable transformation—one after another, each resonant throb casting ripples toward the desolate shores of my deteriorative sanity, and each and every echo stems from that slimy malicious *thing* that I have locked away behind a cage of bone and muscle.

If I had to guess when all of this crap really started, when the world around me started to shrink into peephole before my eyes, I'd say it began a couple of weeks after Jimmy's death.

PORN AND OTHER THINGS

E @ S T 2 W E S T.

watch the wet sand gradually sift through the cracks of my toes as the tide rushes back toward the open sea before me.

The force of the sea's mighty tug causes each toe—starting from my big toe to my pinkie—to sink into the sand as the tide rushes toward the shore; and every time the tide washes over my ghostly-white feet, the water climbs farther up my shins and shaves yet another inch from my height, and yet the only thing I can think about while I cradle Jimmy in my arms is what the car wash attendant said to me an hour ago—not how he said it, the tone of his voice shifting down an octave or the mannerisms that he displayed when he said it. What *really* bothers me the most was the quickness of the comment, a sneeze of a comment, as if the pudgy-faced jerkwad didn't give a second's thought about my situation—didn't put himself in my shoes, didn't even grasp what I had just experienced, the horror, the loss, the pain—then he spoke those words involuntarily from his little piehole, as if I was made of peppercorn or even worse, some kind of allergy. Peanut boy. That's all I was to him. A walking, talking peanut.

I can't help but wonder: maybe he has a bad heart too.

Or, worse, maybe William was right.

Or maybe this is all in my head.

I curb my frustration and focus on my toes sinking farther into the sand below me.

The clouds partially eclipse the rising sun over my shoulder. The sun eventually breaks free—and the sight of the sun gives me a sense of clarity, similar to the moment I first returned to Topside: driving along the always-busy Sun Park Highway, then crossing the Joaquin Bridge into Topside, then, as I made my way over that steep hill of anticipation, the land opened up and a horizon of water was stretched out like a blue desert before me, as if it was welcoming me back to a place that I once called home, reminding me who was in charge now. I knew, at that moment, that it was one of those moments that I'd never forget.

I bask in the openness of the Pacific, as well as the warmness of the sun, as I shield my eyes with my right hand—Jimmy now held in the other—and gaze at the last beams of sunlight dampening over the gunmetal sky.

The clouds, as rich and thick as the froth that cakes the edge of the tide like the icing trimmed along a birthday cake, blot out the sun in a minute-hand pace and finally, darken the sea with gloom.

A local told me the other day that these waters are infested with sharks around this time of year. She said that last year a high school girl named Deanna Wheeling (other surfers call her "Lil' Dee" because of her elf-like stature) was attacked by a Tiger shark—"fifteen footer," they said—while she was catching the break before a monster of a storm slithered its way around Mexico and made an unprecedented landfall through the southern half of California. They said waves were bad before the storm—*bad*, as in harmful—and the undertow, they said, was about as strong enough to drag the average man below, even if he was standing in at least three feet of water, but that sure didn't stop Lil' Dee. So they said. The shark pulled her into the sea—and apparently, she was much farther out than three feet—and then, after Lil' Dee managed to escape from the grip of the shark's jaws, the shark took a chomp out of her leg and swam away with a souvenir. Lil' Dee's name was in the papers, in the news, the headlines, all over the Internet like a deadly virus. She became a local hero around Topside—her name buzzing like a swarm of pissed-off bees throughout each bar along the beach—especially after she defied the doctors' orders and hit the waves the following year. They said Lil' Dee still comes out here every now and then—one leg and all—and surfs the break with a prosthetic.

Imagine that.

I listen to the song of the water singing in harmony; and for a moment, I can feel myself lying in my bed back home with my glazed eyes staring at the rickety ceiling fan spinning in circles overhead.

(I read in a self-help magazine—*First Time*, I think—that babies find comfort in the sound of a calm sea)

Must be the white noise or something.

The appearance of the water is soothing on my eyes as well, and I find comfort in how each wave scrambles past my body, as if the shore is the finish line; and then, once the waves make it across the line, they hurry back into the endless horizon, as if they have somewhere to be and I'm not invited. I like it here, in the water. I've always been drawn to the water. I think I used to like it here when I was younger. The beach. The feel of sand between my toes. All of the sounds surrounding the sea. I used to like how the waves flowed like a breath. The repetitiveness reminds me of this one drill my gym coach, Mr. Sanders, used to make us do on the basketball courts at the end of P.E., sprinting back and forth across the court, each time going a little farther out. The farther you go out, the heavier your legs get. Your heart beats faster. Your breath gets a little deeper. I miss that feeling.

I turn away from the water, glance at the beach behind me, and observe a couple of other stragglers walking on the beach, including a jogger squeezing in some cardio before work; but I don't pay much attention to them.

Instead, I turn back toward the sea and trudge forward until I'm about waist-deep in water.

As the water bobs all around me, I hold Jimmy closer to my sternum. I carefully remove the lid and clear away the clouds of ash, moving like these baby phantoms from the inside of the urn. Then, suddenly, a strange object catches my eye: a piece of metal glimmering like a nugget of gold within a mound of ashes. So clean and shiny, the piece of metal appears, as if it had been untouched by the flames of the furnace. I make sure to dry my pruned fingers along my sleeve before picking up the object. I hold the tiny thing close to my face, really close. The piece has all the right characteristics of a tooth filing, the hardness as well as the unusual round shape, but in my gut, I know the piece that I'm holding in my hand is *not* Jimmy's tooth filling. He never had one; in fact, Jimmy had the teeth of an actor. I remember he had braces when he was younger. Had an entire mouthful of colored metal worn across both his upper and lower teeth like one of those guard grilles on the front of a truck. But that's it. No fillings. The braces came off by the time Jimmy hit puberty. And by then, he was already on his way.

So, immediately, I'm way beyond intrigued. I'm floored as I realize that this very piece in my hand is everything.

It's my story.

Most importantly, it's Jimmy story.

I carefully place the metal fragment inside the breast pocket of my flannel shirt and embrace the cool breeze one last time by taking in a deep breath through my nose and tightly holding the breath inside my lungs before the creeping sensation of an impending doom enters my thoughts.

I tell myself it's *only* a thought, like any other cloud in the sky, and this thought, like the clouds, will pass just as any other thought.

I exhale through my nose. Every thought in my head fades into stark blackness. I tilt the urn toward the dark sea below.

Right before I dump the ashes into the sea, I witness the car wash attendant's face in the reflection of the murky water. He's staring up at me—stupidly—and I'm staring down at him. His chocolate brown eyes are fixated on me as well, like a dead man vacantly staring at the sky above, the water behaving no different than flexible mirrors as they distort his face in varying cycles.

As I try to make sense of his face, the very thought of how *we* ended up here comes back to me. . .

I look around the beach.

Confused.

I spot a man standing alone at the edge of the shore. He's much older than the car wash attendant—twice, even triple his age. Most of the sepia-like suit that he's wearing has been readjusted on his hunched body. Sport coat draped over his shoulder, index finger gripped underneath the collar. His other hand remains firmly planted in his pocket. He's also wearing his tie like a man who recently finished working a twelve-hour shift at a white-collar job. Something that involves cubicles and daily reports and a pest of a micro-manger. Both sleeves are rolled up to his forearms. His posture isn't that weak, though, not like a typical elderly man who spends the early part of his days wandering away the ache of old age. I'd say he's probably pushing eighty from the wrinkles and liver spots speckled on his skin; and he has a pink scar in the shape of a lightning bolt along one side of his face.

Why am I so interested in this old man?

Most importantly, why in the hell is this old man so interested in me?

I don't know. Don't ask.

The old man acknowledges me with a gesture.

I don't nod back.

I turn toward Jimmy.

I'll try again tomorrow, I tell myself.

I close the urn and walk back to the beach.

\\

MY appetite comes back to me by the time my jeans dry.

The past few days I've been scarfing down fast food in the musty confines of whatever car I can find and I can really use a decent meal—that's what Grandma Backer would say: *You look so thin, boy! You look like you can use a decent meal!* As of now, my car—you may be wondering—is a squashed cherry of a car, the repercussions of a hunk of metal that's been handed down by one delinquent after another. Besides a Toyota Camry or Prius, the Honda Civic F-Series happens to be one of the most popular vehicles in the Los Dementes area. So, as the kids at East Providence would say, "I'm mainstreamin'."

I leave my new Civic behind and stroll down a questionable sidewalk next to Main Street until I come across another elderly man.

Unlike the one on the beach, this guy looks like a character one would find in an Ernest Hemingway novel that's been updated—or dare I say, rewritten for my generation; his ring finger has the pale outline of a wedding band, which, strangely, is the first feature I notice about him, then the faded marks all over his body. I'd like to think most people carry stories in their eyes—you know, like that one saying, the eyes are the windows to the soul or whatever—this man, however, carries his in the tattoos along his arms: the name *Nancy* written in cursive over his forearm; a military emblem on his right bicep; a sword piercing through the armor of a scorpion on the inside of his left wrist, which—my first impression—is either militant or a brand of some kind of elite force that specializes in counterinsurgency or something of that nature. He appears much older than his lush hair shows, probably ten plus years than his age. His stony face is about as dry and craggily as a hand-me-down catcher's mitt—one would say a smoker's face, common to what *The Trail* may call "reverent masculinity" with his sleeveless powder blue dress shirt, exposing a brier patch of chest hair.

(I read somewhere, not in *The Trail* but in *Healthy Nut* magazine, that too much sun can lead to damaging of the skin, which will not only make you appear much older than your present age—maybe that's the whole point—but it will also make you a likely candidate for melanoma. That's skin cancer)

I ask him if he knows any good places to eat.

"A quiet place," I say, as I invisibly lasso in a trail of phlegm before it runs from my nostril.

He tilts his head in thought. I can't tell whether he's actually thinking about a good restaurant—a quiet place, as I told him—or wondering why I'm sniffling so damn much.

I follow with a higher tone, as if I'm posing a question without using the basic *who*, *what*, *when*, or *where* introductions of a question—"Non-touristy perhaps?"

He points to the end of Main Street, which is only a couple of blocks away, and straightens his ringless fingers into an arrow and aims them to the left—beachside.

"*The Cove*," he suggests. "Just around the corner. Best fish in Topside. It's a dive, though. If you don't mind."

I shrug, casually.

"I don't mind."

"Well, you'll fit right in."

"Thanks, man."

I walk away before he starts small talk.

I don't mind small talk; however, I'm afraid my stomach will probably do most of the talking.

\|\|\|

HALFWAY down Main Street, I come across a group of wiry people—a weird mix of both natives and tourists, a likely pair which is common around Topside—being escorted from the Main Pier.

I keep my head and scout out the scene from the corners of my eyes. Four cruisers are idling in a parking lot. Sirens flashing, however, switched to silent. Cops aren't saying much to the people, just guiding them away from Main Pier in orderly cop fashion while, at the same time, trying to maintain peace around the crime scene. Most of the spectators are more or less curious about all of the fuss, not fuzz. However, several spectators have their smartphones held steady in front of their faces, filming a couple of cops roping the entrance of the pier with the standard yellow CAUTION tape.

One guy—the surfer type who's dressed in colorful floral pattern swim trunks and a red dri fit T-shirt—is having a chat with another cop who looks about the same age as the guy.

Together, they're both laughing—and I'm extra curious as to why they're laughing.

Cop joke?

Maybe the guy used to be a cop?

Possibly an ex-cop?

Don't know.

I notice the cop is closely listening to the surfer-ish guy while jotting down his every word on a notepad with a pen. Could be giving a possible statement. About what, I don't know. I don't get all worked up over it, even though I can feel a slight stirring in my gut, not from the hunger but an overall sense of unease in queue. I remind myself that I'm in the clear. I'm okay.

I look around for any other activity. I don't see any re-porters or news vans yet, but I know any minute now, the en-tire scene's going to be swarming with media vultures.

They must've recently found the body, if I had to take a stab at guessing.

IV

BEFORE I grab a bite to eat, I decide to stop at an Internet café called Cyber Jaxx's for a cup of coffee. I log into each one of my social media accounts, first starting with Chatterz.

I type in my user name: CLUBHOPPER69*_*.

Ms. CLUBHOPPER69*_* is a smoking hot twenty-two-year-old stylist from Pensacola, Florida. Her real-life name is

Penelope Swearinger. During the day, Penelope works part-time at Version Hair and Makeup. Her sign is Scorpio. Her dating status is currently SINGLE, but, as Penelope's bio states, she's "☺ always lookin 2 mingle ☺." Penelope has blonde hair, blue eyes, tits like an established porn star—her hair is probably one of only two natural things about her, although she recently added purple highlights to her hair and got a tramp stamp of this cute fairy pointing a wand at the crack of her ass over the summer. She enjoys, like, "totally loves," hanging out with her bffs on weekends, and she gladly calls herself the ultimate "Weekend Warrior." Like some of the girls Penelope's age, she has experimented with the same sex, but she doesn't consider herself to be a bisexual. In her pro-file, Penelope also states that she's a vegetarian by heart who—from time to time—eats fish (Go save the dolphs!!!) and yet, a lot of her pics on MyCircle suggest that she's quite a meat eater (no pun attended, lol). Her guilt-food is "peanut butter and jellies" on a waffle. Favorite bands are *Blink 182* and *Green Day*, to name a few. She likes to shop at Victoria Secret, or as she calls, the "Secret." She attends FSU, the "best university in the whole wide world," where she's major-ing in political science. And, she absolutely *loves* to party. Like totally. She even has a MyCircle page with over 40K followers—that's *40K*, as in forty thousand, all unpaid for.

I don't even know a hundred people, including strangers. She frequently posts titty pics and selfies of herself standing in front of the mirror and chirps haiku poems.

In reality, CLUBHOPPER69*_* is *not* a party girl—at least, not anymore. And her name isn't Penelope Swearinger either. It's Penelope S. Shwin. She tied the knot one year after she graduated from FSU; and she recently had twins, two beauti-ful boys, Sonny and Wes, both named after her favorite TV show, *American Rebel*; and she's living happily ever after in Helena with her newly strap-on husband, Chadwick, or Chad, owner of a grocery store which specializes in organic food. She met Chad during a skiing trip with her older sister, Darcy, in Montana. Chad and Penelope dated for a few months, then that was all she wrote. Literally. She deleted all of her social media accounts. The pictures remained, though, even the good ones. For example, you take a picture. It'll last longer. That's true to some degree. But you post a picture online. It'll last forever—even worse, swallowed by the Internet, digested, then shitted out in the form of a pesky spambot. It's amazing, not only how people put themselves *all* out there, but also how many people will FOLLOW you if you post a picture of your asshole.

Sebastian Capello, aka "Flip," accepted CLUBHOPPER'S friend request after the first *five* minutes she sent it to him, consequently allowing his so-called "secret admirer" to gain access to all of Flip's PRIVATE accounts. Flip is from Newark, New Jersey, or what he tells CLUBHOPPER, "Jurzee." His grandparents migrated from Florence, Italy, to New York right before the original *Godfather* movies came out.

Flip's mother owns a bakery in Newark and from the pics Flip posts on his PhotoBag, or what Penelope calls, "PeeBee," she makes a really mean cannoli.

His father, formerly known as the infamous pro wrestler, "Speedo" Not Your Everyday Guido, is now retired. Speedo won the Light Heavyweight belt against "Tino Two Fingers," held the belt for about a month until he lost it to the high fly-ing Ukrainian, "Ivan the Incredible," in a brutal cage match, which was considered one of the greatest matches in the his-tory of professional wrestling (it was quite bloody—and I'm not talking about that fake shit either), then, a couple of years later after Speedo's reign, like most wrestlers, he disappeared from the face of the earth. Flip never followed in his father's footsteps. Most of the following he did was on the Internet.

That brings me back to Penelope Swearinger, aka CLUB-HOPPER69*_*. She and Flip have been talking for a couple of days now, mainly about clubs, dancing, and *Blink 182*. They've been sending each other pics as well. Occasionally, she'll send Flip a selfie of herself.

Flip will return the favor by sending Penelope rather sug-gestive pics of himself as well, including pics of himself party-ing it up at the "Palace," as he calls it, as in Crystal Palace, the nightclub formerly known as Daddy's Playground before it relocated from Old Town to the New Town area.

CLUBHOPPER69*_* knows what Flip likes to drink, whom Flip hangs out with at the popular nightclub, what he does for fun on a daily basis, what time he likes to go "down the shore."

Penelope basically knows everything about Flip, even down to his dick size.

As with Flip's social media accounts, the exclusive night-spot is super-private.

Members only.

Except for women, not just any guy off the street can join the club.

On the outside, the club is heavily secured—and more than likely, doubled with security on the inside.

In order to gain entry inside the club without drawing attention to myself, I need an "inside man," a guy who *knows* people.

CLUBHOPPER69*_* aside, even though Flip and I are nothing alike, we share similar stories in that he too followed his older brother out West.

His older brother is Shane Capello, a music producer who's put out as many records as *Dave Mathews Band* has put out live records. Shane moved from Jersey to Los Dementes way back when kids were wearing Reeboks, gold chains, and listening to Boyz 2 Men.

Not too long ago, he invited Flip to Los Dementes.

Like me, Flip ended up staying.

I pull up Flip's social media websites on the Internet: My-Circle, Chatterz, PhotoBag—PeeBee.

I check his latest posts, then the time.

His most recent post was posted on Chatterz fifteen minutes ago: He'll be "chillin' like villain" at a popular spot called Holes with his "crazy" crew this afternoon.

Next, I check out Flip's PhotoBag page.

He posted a pic five minutes ago with his friend, Wilt, whose hair is like a dorsal fin.

"On the way 2 pic up Chemo," the caption reads below the picture of the two in the car.

As I'm about to close Flip's PhotoBag page, a cute twenty-something struts past the café and I grow a stiffy.

Her tits are like small funnels underneath her tight pink tank top, and when she walks by, they skip the hopscotch.

I get back on the Internet, get halfway through typing the word *titty-* in the search engine before my stomach lets out a roaring bellow and I'm no longer melting in my chair.

I listen to my stomach, as I should, and my stiffy hides like a turtle's head in its shell. I leave the Internet café with a sense of great accomplishment.

D U H   F R Ø G   G Δ N G

M Y head is spinning from the caffeine by the time I arrive at the Cove.

The restaurant is packed, even before the antsy noon crowd arrives; and from what I gather, most of the place is occupied by the salty natives of Topside. Your everyday BINGO turnout minus sluggish reactions or dopey expressions; however, the only numbers being hollered out come from a sweaty behemoth of a cook reading numbers from orders on receipts rotating around a lazy Susan above the pickup counter. Random bursts of laughter spread across the main dining area, sending me into a state of alertness, which doesn't help with my momentary dizzy spell. Most of the laughter, I pinpoint, comes from a jolly party of five throwing back morning cocktails. They must be sailors. I find them to be strange creatures. Strange in a good way.

While I make my way past the vacant greeting stand with the sign that reads "Seat Yourself," I search for my exits, of course, then, lastly, the restrooms—something I've always been prone to do whenever I find myself in a foreign environment. Once I've located the restrooms, I spot several curious eyes moving toward my direction like tractor beams.

The laughter is taken down a notch, which makes me wonder if my presence has anything to do with the subtle change in mood—wouldn't be the first time—then, they ignore me as they always do and I ignore them.

They're just objects, I tell myself.

I arch my chin upward and take one last survey around the place, hoping to find an empty seat. My eyes cross a booth with my name on it tucked away in the back of the restaurant. I don't see any host or hostess in the area and therefore, I do as the sign states and eagerly grab a seat on my own.

A young waitress glides to the booth as soon as I enter. I wonder whether she's going to ask me to leave or ask for my order. She's holding a notepad, as well as a pen in her hand. I relax and greet her with a funeral smile. She's a couple of years older than me, I notice as she hands me a one-page menu: food on the front, cocktails on the back. She doesn't have any noticeable college fat—at least none that I can see on her face—although it's hard to tell what her body looks like underneath the loosely fitted *Guns N' Roses* T-shirt.

(I read in a magazine—can't remember which one—that most young girls gain at least ten to fifteen pounds during their first year of college. They call it "Freshman Fifteen")

The waitress tells me her name, I think, but whatever she says goes in one ear and out the other.

She waits for a response, the white of her Manga eyes slowly disappearing.

"Do you have shrimp?" I ask her before I draw any unwanted attention to myself.

She replies with a stiff nod.

"Best in town," she replies, sounding as if she's reading cue cards for an ad or something. From the way the volume in her voice spikes as if she's doing a mic-check, I know the words not to be her own but someone else's. Probably the owner, a colossal man frequently making pit stops at each table, making sure each customer is full and satisfied.

I go with the shrimp.

She asks me if I'd like the shrimp spicy and I tell her, "No thanks."

Did I mention that I have a bad stomach too? Not like bad, as in evil, but bad, as in poor condition.

The waitress smiles as she grabs the menu. Her hand grazes mine during the somewhat awkward exchange, and I make eye contact with her.

In return, she makes eye contact with me.

For a moment, I feel blinded by the radiance of her bubbly blue eyes, as if I'm staring at the sun or something incredibly bright, but I can only stare for a couple of seconds.

(I read somewhere that the color *blue* brings comfort to the human mind; however, I didn't feel the least amount of comfort when I looked into her eyes)

I remind myself she's only working tips. Maybe she has a boyfriend. Maybe she has a kid.

\\

WHILE the big guy's frying my shrimp, I pass the time by nibbling on a couple of hushpuppies as I read through a couple of magazines. One of them being *HOARDER*, a magazine primarily about modern day artists who draw inspiration from the culture of older time periods such as the Seventies and Eighties, even Nineties. Another: *Trucker By Heart*, which doesn't need any explanation. I skim through the trucking magazine. There's a sweet spread in the front of the magazine called "Greasy Gals of the Month." Each model has glam rock-sized hair and Junoesque-sized bodies. Basically, tall and shapely. Super-sized. I use the cuff of my sleeve and flip through the sticky pages until I come across a centerfold of an engine. I'm not talking about any ordinary engine. This baby is the crème de la crème of all engines, a Stower, and there's no mistake as to why it rhymes with the word *power*. I'm not sure if truckers get off on this kind of stuff—I mean, clearly, they like their gals as American as Frito pie—but, somehow, I'm drawn to the metallic image before me. I can't help but think of Jimmy.

I'm suddenly pulled from the pages by a strong smell, shrimp first, then coconuts.

I try to ignore the smells, both of them.

The waitress glances down at the magazine in my hand and smiles, as if she's waiting for me to say something.

"Here you go," she says as she places the food on the table. "Enjoy your meal."

I smile back, but the smile seems more like a nervous tick compared to hers.

I remind myself that she's working for tips.

The waitress walks away, but I end up checking her out when she's not looking. She's attractive, I admit, especially living in a place that thrives off sun—despite the unusually bad weather—*bad*, as in unpleasant. Her skin's smooth and creamy white, like a doll. My type. The backside of her body is toned as well, especially her legs, although it doesn't look as if she works out or anything. I bet she stays on the move. Like me.

Then, as I always do, I point out her flaws from the barely noticeable sag of skin underneath her chin to the slight dip of her shoulders. I concentrate on each and every flaw, as infinitesimal as it may be—I've always liked that word *infinitesimal* (I think I heard my algebra teacher, Mr. Hall, use it once in a sentence. He used to be a sucker for long words)—and blow each one out of proportion until she ends up looking like a troll.

I down two shrimp and cool my mouth with a sip of ice water and block out the waitress, knowing there's not a chance in hell she's interested in someone like me—and if she is, I remind myself that not only is she *not* attractive, but she's also working on tips. Why should I even waste my time on her? Plus, she's carrying a soon-to-be chin underneath her already naturally formed chin, and she hunches too; and in ten years, that extra chin is going to be like a double chin accompanied by other soon-to-be chins. A chin of chins.

It's nature.

And if there's one thing about nature, you don't fuck with it.

Never.

When you get older, you get colder. You get hairy. You get blubbery. You get ugly. I figure if I'm going to spend my time with somebody, she might as well look like a nine or ten before she turns into a four or five—at best.

I chase the remainder of shrimp with the glass of water.

Chew, swallow, repeat.

As I work my way through the third shrimp, I witness Anthony Foster's face: his chin dipped in dark blood, his yawning mouth like the black hole of a cartoon drawing, his tongue leaping from the penciled blackness and then ricocheting pinball-style against the roof of his mouth. All of the muscles around my stomach become all weird and all, and send a wash of panic over my thoughts. I try to practice what William taught me and ignore my surroundings, including the unattractive waitress. I ignore the graphic thoughts, turn my focus to my breathing, and think about the sea and how it made me feel a sense of serenity, if only for a while. The sea suddenly stains itself with a deep crimson red. My bad heart does this thing where it's trying to escape from its prison. And I can feel each pound. Each quake. Each thud. Each ripple throughout my body. A pale reflection in the water is brought forth before me, revealing these demonic black eyes. The eyes slowly roll over white; and as the vacant face emerges from the surface, the shrimp dances around my stomach and by the time, the shrimp trek from my stomach, my esophagus is like Mount Everest. Cooks are yelling at one another: *Needs more salt!* A cook yells at a waitress: *Order up!* A heavy set man sits with shoulders hanging over the table like an offensive line-backer, *sucking* down raw oysters from a shell, the oysters sliding down the back of his throat, fellatio-like. Each sound, each noise becomes louder, deafening. Three seats over, a cranky lady *coughs* out a laugh, which sounds like broken glass, the involuntary guffaw causing her dentures to clap against her gums like the shells of a lighthearted clam. A skinny man with a beak of a nose sits across from what looks like his wife and displays a boyish smirk. The gesture freezes in my mind and my thoughts are telling me to smile more, don't make a scene, like that one saying every concerned adult used to tell me when I was a child: "Poor dear, you should smile more." Or, even worse: "It can't be that bad, kid." Yes, asshole. It's that bad. A shy girl is complaining to her parents about how she's not hungry and she's pouting and I'm pouting too, and I tell myself over again to stop pouting, you pussy. Focus on the sea. My eyes turn to the glass of water before me and I see an imprint of a hand on the side of the perspired glass—and I think about that not-so attractive wait-ress's witch-like hand and now her hand is sliding down my pants. Why didn't you talk to her, you pussy? She was inter-ested in you. I start to have trouble focusing on one thing as the shrimp makes its inevitable climb. Approaching the sum-mit. All I see are faces all around me and the faces remain like snapshots in my mind. One still lasts for a couple of sec-onds, then another takes its place. An assembly line of stills, one after another. Focus. The sea. The sand. Seated in the booth behind me is an angry couple mumbling to one another. They're *scraping* their knives and forks along the glass plates as they pick through fried red snapper. The *clinking* sounds like some old school DJ scratching turntables and the sounds nibble away at my brain.

The *clinking*, the *screeching*, the *mumbling*, all of it coming to a rolling boil.

The sea. It's red again. A red wave comes crashing down on me and the wave is overrun with a thousand barracudas gnawing at my flesh. The prickly sensation makes its way to my extremities, and I feel sick all over.

I try to swallow, but I can't find any saliva in my mouth. I try to take in a deep breath, but it feels as if my lungs are deflated.

A layer of sweat swells over the surface of my skin, and the very tips of my hands grow tingly, as if my fingers are grazing that invisible fluff along the glowing screen of a TV.

The shrimp arrive at the summit.

Prepare for evacuation.

In five. Four. Three. . .

Before I reach one, I clench my jaw and exit the booth. I run to the last stall in the restroom. A person is drying a stain on his shirt underneath the hand dryer, but he remains nothing more than a blurry obstruction behind me. I vomit quietly too, years of practice. I keep my aim directly at the sides of the bowl—*cla-clum-cla-clum*. Then comes a round of dry heaves. I wait for the person to leave the restroom before I flush the toilet.

With my face now bloodless and my skin clammy, I exit the stall and wait until the facet water cools down before I splash my face.

I grab a paper towel from the dispenser and while I'm drying my face, I try to rub color into my cheeks. The color momentarily clouds into parts of my face before falling back to an ashen-like hue. The peach fuzz along the sides of my face stands up like goosebumps and becomes coarse. The texture of the hair feels peculiar to the touch, as if all of my five senses have been displaced.

Suddenly, one of the stall doors *squeaks* open!

In the mirror, I witness two legs covered in dark slacks underneath the stall as the door opens like some sturdy wooden door at the entranceway of an old castle.

Focus.

He's wearing caramel-colored wingtips; and he's whispering, too, but his voice is barely undistinguishable, like a muffled cyclone buzzing from one ear to another. The noise zips behind me, forcing me to rotate around. I see nothing. I face the stall once more and it's completely empty. Must've been the wind.

What else could it have been?

More curious about the noise than anything, I toss away the towel and walk over to the stall.

As I kneel down and glance underneath the remaining stalls, another door opens.

I stand up, only to find a local man standing next to the urinals.

I struggle to make eye contact with him as I cross his path.

"You okay, son?" he asks with a slack expression on his face.

I don't respond.

Instead, I exit the bathroom before I can give him a straight answer.

\|\|\|

THE waitress makes a pit stop at my table. I know the look on her face. Seen it a thousand times. The paleness has a way of bringing out worried looks.

She asks me if I'm done eating.

I tell her that I am.

Then, she asks me if there was anything wrong with the food. She's asking me this because I've hardly touched my food.

"No," I say shortly.

She grabs the basket from the table, only a few shrimp missing, and most of the fries and hush puppies have been pushed and picked through from what may or may not have been a bird.

"Would you like a bag or something?" she asks over a distant rumble coming from outside.

I turn to the noise because that's what it is, just noise.

Wilt cruises by the restaurant, windows down, the trunk rattling from the bass of what's supposed to be music. Flip is riding shotgun, smoking a cigarette and checking out girls.

"Sir?"

Flip shoots a glance at the Cove, his eyes cross mine; then he flicks his cigarette onto the street.

I hear the word *doggy-* over my shoulder.

Baffled, I turn to the waitress.

I open my mouth to speak and whatever comes out doesn't even sound like words.

"I said 'Do you want a doggy bag?'"

"*No,*" I tell her. "Can I have some more water? Please."

Her face melts into something slack.

I watch her walk away, but this time I don't check her out. Too embarrassed. I tip the waitress half of what the meal costs, grab my bookbag, and slide from the booth. Everybody is giving me the same look the waitress was giving me just seconds ago. I can't stand that look.

Hate it, actually.

IV

AFTER leaving the Cove, I feel much worse than I did when I first arrived. My throat feels as if it has the diameter of a straw, and like my throat, my chest is discernibly tight, and my breathing is shallow. And, I'm pasty now. More so than before. Lately, I've been feeling this kind of way, like my body is a little bit bent out of shape, as if it's all it knows anymore, being out of shape and misaligned, which makes me think if I've always been this way, even at birth when I was tugged from the womb. Can you even imagine that? Some slimy awkward thing—I mean, talk about given the definition of waking up on the wrong side of the bed—after being dragged from the darkness, slipping from the womb, all bent out of shape, like a twisted clothes hanger. I'd like to think that maybe one day I was a happy kid. Happy and carefree. Not a shiver in my bones or a quiver in my gut. A glad young lad. Now, it's just a whole bunch of shoulds or maybes.

As I make my way past the strip mall, I feel another attack creeping up on me, like a masked stalker in the dead of night, and the notion of a sudden attack is as tiny as a crack in a windshield in my mind and yet, at any moment, I know that crack has a prerogative to streak across the windshield, resulting in more cracks, more streaks until the glass finally shatters. These are the classic symptoms of what somebody may experience during coronary thrombosis—in other words, the other kind of *attack*, heart attack, not panic attack. I know these symptoms not to be the warning signs of a heart attack. It's just my body jonesing for a fix. So, I listen to my body.

I spot Flip and his crew hanging outside the popular donut shop, Holes, at the end of the Square.

As I head toward the group, I don't make eye contact with them. I keep them in the corner of my eye. All four of them. They should be in class right now getting a college education, and so should I—if they ask. I should be studying to be a nurse or something in the field of medicine. Susannah said I'd make a good nurse, in fact, one "helluva nurse," actually—her words—especially after putting everything on hold in order to take care of Jimmy.

I approach the group and get a better look at them.

Everything in my body relaxes, my stomach especially. They don't appear too socially "misaligned" from the way they interact with one another.

Then again, a picture doesn't lie.

I point out Flip, who, as suspected, happens to be the most vocal one of the group: slick dark hair; long sideburns that curl over his ears like the wings on Hermes' shoes; some tattoos on his chest—don't really care what they are—and he's sporting an off black hoody covered in cigarette burns and holey jeans, an outfit that clearly contradicts his nightly attire, but I take it—more or less—as a trend or whatever he's trying to bring back in style. He's also sporting a metal chain stretching from his wallet to his front pocket. Grunge kids used to rock the chain wallet back in the day, but I haven't seen any kids wearing them lately. Maybe Flip's bringing it back in style.

I overhear Flip talking to Chemo in his hodgepodge of North versus West accent, each vowel rounded down from spending years around laidback Cali accents; and whenever the conversation becomes more heated, certain vowels are drawn out. Flip's accent is hard to distinguish, to say the least, even when he uses phrases like "down the shore."

When we share eye contact, Flip flicks his head in a nod and says, "What's good?"

"Sup," I reply.

I'm not sure about the correct usage of lingo these days, and I certainly don't want to sound like a cop or anything. So, I use something universal and ask Flip and his friends if they like to party.

"You holding?" he says.

Not sure what he means, if I'm holding.

So, I keep it as vague as possible.

"Nah," I say. "Just looking."

He lets out a couple of croaking sounds from the side of his mouth and it's supposed to be a laugh, I think.

"Oh yeah?" He cocks his head and holds it there for a minute, as if he's striking a pose for the latest cover of *Toy Gangsters*. "You're in luck. We lookin' to party as well."

His laid-back friend joins in, "You a nark?"

"Nah," I tell him. "Are you?"

"A'ight, Rooty Tooty Fresh N' Fruity," he says. "No need to be all pushy—"

"—So, you trying to party or what?"

"Yeah, man," Flip says as he turns to his other friends. "We down to party. *So*, let me ask: Where you from, Party Boy?"

"I'm from Philly," I say confidently.

"No shit," he says with another croak of a laugh. "Long way from home. I hear they have a shitty ass football team this year."

"I think you mean Pittsburg, not Philly."

"Thought it was the same thing."

"Same state," I tell him. "But *not* the same. . . "

Wilt, the tall one in the group, asks me, "So, what brings you all the way from Philadelphia to the Top?"

Top, he said, as in Topside.

"Vacation," I say, "you know, a little R and R."

The frog laughs again. The other frogs join in.

(I read somewhere in *Finding Fit* that the French eat frogs; in fact, they consider frogs to be a delicacy)

I block out the sound of their laughter and yearn to feel the warm rays of sun against the back of my neck, but all I get is a cool ocean breeze.

"What's so funny?" I ask them, trying to be as kind as I can.

"Nah, dude," Flip says. "Nuttin'. Just the only people who come to this shithole are either a bunch of old-timey fucks or lost boys running away from something. And you don't look like an old-timey fuck."

I don't respond. Don't have the words.

"So, lemme ask: What's your poison, Philly?" Flip says, like a spokesman. "Uppers? Downers—"

"—I'm actually looking for some ah—some blow for to-night," I say hesitantly. "An eightball perhaps. Whatever you can find is cool with me."

"Okay," Flip says impressively. "I know a guy who knows a guy who's gettin' straight with some snow."

On the streets, cocaine goes by many other names: pow-der, sugar, coke, *snow*.

"But word is he ain't gonna be straight till later tonight, like eight or nine. . . "

"Damn," I say, disappointed.

He's talking about Cue, as in cue ball. CLUBHOPPER69*_* has seen many pics of Cue hanging around with Flip at the Palace. They've taken many selfies together, including one where Cue is standing like a Toy Solider with his bald scalp glistening like a disco ball as Flip photobombs him from be-hind.

I look around the donut shop. My hands start to shake a little, and it's not until I look down at them when I realize they're shaking.

I watch Flip's eyes trace mine.

". . . But you know what?" Flip says casually as he shoots a glance down at my hands. "I can find you some other stuff for the time being, if that's cool with you. Now, it ain't some, you know, Lois Lane, though, but it'll make you fly. It's like what I always be tellin' these fools here. . . " he points his thumb at the other frogs and laughs again, ". . . it's better than nuttin'."

I'm not sure if he means *nutting* or *nothing*.

Right now, it doesn't matter.

P A † † E R N   P R A C † I C E

K ERMIT and his merry gang of amphibians take me to the outskirts of Herald's Point, the town north of Topside. The Point.

As with the other towns surrounding the Topside area, the Point is a spit of a town with a population dwindling by the season. It is a town on the verge of extinction. A town waiting on a meteor shower called inflation. Not too long ago, the town filed for bankruptcy. Once, I mean, before the recession which left many businesses crippled, the Point was thriving with tourists. There was even this one joint, Early Bird, a local favorite that specialized in Asian cuisine fused with Latin American. It was to die for. Seriously, I'd give my left arm for their famous Vietnamese-style tacos—basically, shrimp topped with radishes and a sweet chili sauce, all stuffed inside a soft corn tortilla, which, by the way, were made in house.

When I was staying with Jimmy at West Harleton, we tried out different places around the area, one of them happened to be Early Bird. We went one afternoon during the peak of lunch hour, which was a terrible mistake. I tried the Vietnamese-style tacos. Jimmy ordered the stick-to-your-ribs short ribs. He was a sucker for meat, especially the red kind. The restaurant was even featured in the magazine, *Le Bon*. The article drew in hundreds and thousands of restaurateurs and chiefs alike from all over the country on a daily basis, as well as star-pitcher for the Salamanders and his no-good little brother. I remember every time we used to go we make sure to arrive an hour ahead of the lunch rush. Early Bird eventually relocated to Los Dementes after the riots. Last I've heard the business is still doing well. Like most local businesses, like Early Bird, all that remains of these buildings are these gutted boxes vandalized by looters and tagged by rival gangs. Once, there was life and stability in these buildings where the only motto was to eat well, be merry. There was nothing merry about these buildings anymore. Now, there was only rot and decay and the ghosts of a once modern world. The ones that are still scraping by just sit there like an unwanted child left to starve to death, a child unable to develop into its fullest potential. The beaches are unkept and riddled with garbage. They could almost pass as landfills. A while back, whistleblowers and finger-waggers pulled back the curtain of Herald's Point, revealing a string of murders and unrest: waves of police brutality, unlawful deaths, cops using lethal force against everyday bystanders. The stories made the national headlines. People were slain, then swept under a rug as if their lives didn't mean squat. Some of the people who died were innocent. Law abiding citizens. Good people who cared about their town. Just there. One minute, minding their own damn business. Then the next, you get the idea. Others were *not* so innocent. If there hadn't been a clear-cut divide between the citizens and the cops, then the incidents in the Point were one of the many straws that continued time and time again to break the camel's back. Nonetheless, cops were under heavy scrutiny by the media, by journalists, by whistleblowers and finger-waggers and social media organizations. The Point remained in the spotlight for a few months before the lights went out; and when they finally burned out, all that remained of the once eclectic town was a dead bulb that needed to be changed.

Nobody came around to change the bulb.

Nobody was really interested in buying a new bulb.

If the Point was a baseball player at bat, it struck out a long time ago. And the town stayed there at the plate. The game was already over. The stadium already cleared out. Yet, it was like the town was waiting for the umpire to escort it to the dugout. Somebody. Anybody.

"Take me to the batting cage," said the town. "Let me work on my swing."

Nothing.

Eventually, cops stopped patrolling the neighborhoods, the streets. They stopped doing anything, really; and the dauntless individuals who once cast a flashlight inside the dark closet of corruption had vanished into thin air. Like ghosts.

That's when the Point started to run amuck with the homeless, the squatters, the junkies.

That's when people stopped feeling sorry for the Point.

We ride farther inland in Flip's hatchback, which, except for being a manual, shares the same amenities as Fred Flintstones' footmobile—and I thought my Civic was a P.O.S.

Flip rides shotgun while I ride bitch. For about five minutes, he rambles on about this fine-ass "hippie chick" who stood him up the other day. The hippie chick's name is Sage, although he doesn't mention her name. She's more of a hipster. And she didn't exactly stand Flip up. Instead, she gave Flip an open invitation for him to pursue her further.

Sage attends HPCC—that's Herald's Point Community College. Her major is currently UNDECIDED. Most of Sage's classes suggest that she has a particular interest in art history. Doesn't have any social media accounts, except for PhotoBag, which is a private account.

She and Flip were talking about cars on PhotoBag after Flip posted a selfie of himself standing next to a Porsche 911. Sage made a comment about how she'd like to cruise the Strip with Flip and then she followed the text with a series of emoticons, which I'm not going to list.

And that was it.

\|\|

THE houses on either side of the street are shrinking smaller and smaller. I can't help but notice more junk scattered on the front lawns, from the cheap play sets to cheaper and broken play sets to even cheaper and rustier play sets that look as if you'd need a tetanus shot before playing on them; and the way Dale Earnhardt here is driving, I start to question why the hell I got in this prehistoric box on wheels with these four low-lifes to begin with. The driver, Wilt, doesn't talk much either. Whenever he does speak, he speaks in similes. For instance, it's "cold as shit" in here or that girl is "ugly as shit." I put the name inside the filing cabinet upstairs for future use. I've noticed that he doesn't have any social media accounts, either—at least none under the name Wilt. He doesn't act like the social-networking type, Queen of Hashtags like Flip here, although he has appeared in the background of the various pics that Flip has posted on PhotoBag. Like an extra in a movie scene, miming something or mouthing words.

Wilt: the name could be significant.

Right now, it means shit.

As Wilt takes another turn—this time more carefully—Flip tells me he'd be driving right now but pigs took his license after his third DWI—*pigs*, Flip means, as in cops, and I take offense to the comment, as the son of a former cop. I swallow my frustration in front of Flip and it goes down like a charcoal. I know Flip doesn't know any better. Somehow, I get the feeling that being locked up is the least of Flip's worries.

A couple of blocks before we arrive at the dealer's crib I can feel my stomach starting to eat itself.

I try to concentrate on something else like the grains of sand between my toes, anything other than eating frogs or puking all over the bald one's lap to the right of me—I'm not talking about a shaved head but bald, like Cue, as in head-like-a-bowling-ball bald—Chemo. I know. I don't care much for the name either. I wonder if the kid's really sick—and if he is, it's not funny—or if he's just scalping his head because it's the bad thing to do—*bad*, as in sick, as in you know what I mean—and if he is, I want to laugh in his face. I've noticed, like Wilt, he doesn't have any social media accounts. He's a vlogger who runs a video blog on "Conspiracy Theories & Phenomenons," which could make for an interesting conversation. He has over three thousand subscribers; however, he doesn't call them his "followers;" instead, he calls them his "disciples." But whatever.

I glance at Chemo without being overly suspicious and do a double take on the tattoo of a *barcode* on the side of his waxy scalp.

He glances at me.

I look to my left where a sickly kid sits with one of his legs bobbing up and down. I never catch his name, but it starts with an S, I think. He's nobody, a "What's-His-Name".

Flip opens the passenger seat and lets out all three of us, including What's-His-Name.

I stretch my legs in a discreet manner as I search for exits.

I do this only as a precaution whenever I find myself in the presence of aliens. Just in case anything goes down. Basically, whenever the shit hits the fan, I have an escape plan. There's a front door, which looks as if it's being held down by a screw and even that screw looks a little sketchy. I can't figure out whether the owner of this dump—they call the guy the "Apple Ripper"—lives here or, like most homeless in the Point, just squats here. I'm more interested in the name, though.

"Apple Ripper?" I reply.

"Yeah, man," Chemo says over my shoulder, "he's an 'eco-friendly' muthafucka."

"Dude gots the 'best drugs in town.' For real." Flip steps aside. "Anything you want. The Ripper Man gots it, except for the stuff you're looking for."

I can't help but think of what the waitress said at the Cove—the cue cards, the ad.

Flip shuts the door behind me, but the door doesn't close at first. He lifts upward on the door handle, aligns the door in its proper place, and rams his shoulder into the door. It closes.

Then, Flip and I share a strange glance before he slaps me on the shoulder and says, "After you, Philly."

I keep my guard up. Just in case.

\|\|\|

\| end up forking out forty bones for the drugs—*bones*, as in dollars. The Ripper man turns out being a squatter, as I suspected, the "eco-friendly" type. The man looks as if he hasn't showered or shaved in a three months. The house is equally as filthy, as if it had had somehow grown this man from the dampness of the air, like a weed or mushroom and some kind of fungus attached to the house. His hair is frizzy, too, and balled behind his head in a bun, and he has the arms of a golden retriever. Both of his eyes are pinkish in color, as if he's been battling a mean cold or some other sickness. And his breath smells like week-old kale.

Within the first few minutes talking to Apple Ripper—most of the conversation based around the evil forces behind the government, how they're eavesdropping on us through our smartphones, tracking us like tagged sharks, cataloging every click we make through our computers and whatnot and Chemo imposing his old ideas onto everybody else in the room (him and Chemo make quite the pair with their over-the-top paranoia)—I understand why they call him "Apple Ripper" from the homemade bowl, which is made from a black spotted Fuji apple. The center of the apple is hollowed-out; the stem has been replaced with a circular screen; a resin-ous pipe protrudes from the side of the apple. A couple of bright green buds with orange pubic-like hairs sit on top of the screen.

Apple Ripper asks Flip if he wants to take a hit from the apple.

I follow Flip's eyes to the flaming red sore along the side of Apple Ripper's mouth. The sore is so massive that it looks as if it has its own sore, like a sore of sores, a colony of sores.

Flip declines by saying "I'm still ripped from a minute ago." Which makes me wonder about Flip and if he's as real as he claims to be.

Apple Ripper asks me if I want a hit and despite that crea-ture-thing on his lip, I willingly take one for the team. I expect Apple Ripper to be bothered by the fact that Flip won't smoke his drugs. I know Apple Ripper's trying to be a good host. I know Flip's thinking the same thing I'm thinking: *What the fuck is that thing on his lip?*

Apple Ripper ends up selling me a half-ounce of swag, which looks like topsoil and smells like a Mexican's asshole. He opens a rusty lockbox, holding a handful of bundles un-derneath mollies scattered along the bottom like old crumbs. He throws in a handful of mollies as well—ten of them, two for each one of us.

"On the house," he tells us.

He thinks I'm a new addition to the crew. I keep my mouth shut and go along with whatever Flip tells him by mostly nodding, then repeating.

"He's new in town," Flip says.

"Yeah," I repeat. "I'm new in town."

"He's from Pittsburg."

I bite my lip and correct Flip, "Philly."

"Same thing," he says, waving his hand.

I glance at the mollies in Flip's hand, and they're a beigish-brown color—closer to the brown side. I don't sweat it because they're on the house. And I don't have much of an appetite for mollies.

(I once read an article in *Drug Culture* that the whiter the mollies are, the purer they are)

I've seen mollies back East—not Philly—and they were about as white as aspirin pills. The brownish color can either suggests the mollies are old, which, more than likely they are (how old, is beyond my scope of knowledge—a month? a year?), or they're from a bad batch (black market pharmaceuticals from Tijuana? Knock-off pharma? Who knows?).

Either way, I can't help but wonder how many dirty hands have handled these mollies before they wound up in the hands of some stoner-squatter who smokes his stash with an apple. A spoiled pimple popper from the burbs? A lazy freeloader from the projects? Or, even worse, a shady doctor getting kickbacks from pharmaceutical companies?

Anybody can make drugs if they acquire the right ingredients and, of course, have the quality time to make it. Right or not. You never see a junkie asking for a refund. The point: Without a maker, there's no supplier.

Without a seller, there's no buyer.

Except for a few mason jars containing a strange, murky liquid scattered around the kitchen, I don't see any laboratories in this rat's nest; and Apple Ripper sure looks more like Mad Hatter than Mad Scientist.

It's not Lois Lane, Flip says as he nods at the mollies, but "it's better than *nothing*."

Out of generosity, I break off two-blunts-worth—close to an eighth—and hand it to Flip.

He never says thanks. He just gives me a nod, which I guess is his way of saying thanks. I don't expect anything more from Flip. I remind myself it's just a finder's fee.

IV

WE leave Apple Ripper's nest with a bag of weed and these so-called mollies and cruise down Main Street. I ride window seat while Chemo now rides bitch. Not even an hour spent with these lowlifes and I'm already moving my way up from bitch to window. Burnouts can be your best friend when you're holding. I remind myself that I'm *not* one of them, even though I'm riding with them.

Flip and I decide to match each other's share. Sort of. I put in more, but I don't make a big deal about the matter. We pass the communal weed to Chemo, who grabs a *Bone Thugs and Harmony* CD from the floor mat, dusts off dry stems and seeds left behind from a previous roll, and pulls out a new box of Garcia Vega's from his oversized pocket.

As Chemo gets to work on the blunt, I check out the hot girls in bikinis strut their finely shaped tanned bodies they've been working hard on all summer—maybe some of them working too hard. Borderline anemic. Vampiric almost. Rib-cages showing. I believe Chemo's been working on his rolling skills all summer as well. He puts the final touches by running a long line of saliva along one end, then twisting the end into a sharp point. He acknowledges my disgust and says to me, "It's all good, Philly."

He takes his lighter and waves the flame underneath the saliva-drenched blunt without burning it, which makes the blunt crisper and easier to smoke.

Chemo does the honors and lights up the blunt.

Since I'm the one supplying most of the weed, Chemo flips around the blunt, sticks the lit end into his mouth, and gives me a shotgun. The smoke shoots out from the other end like a fissure in a scolding steam pipe. I manage to suck in most of the thick smoke, while the rest oozes past my cheeks like strands of white air. I swear I nearly lose a lung from the massive hit.

By the time I get done coughing, the saliva in my mouth is like water and my tongue acts like a dam. I crack open the door and spit as Wilt approaches a stoplight.

"You a'ight there, Philly?" Flip says amusingly as the others laugh at me.

"Yeah," I say and sit back in the seat. "Good—"

Once the cough settles and the fire in my chest eases into a steady and yet tolerable burn, the knot in my stomach loosens and the pain goes away.

Chemo takes a couple of more drags, then passes the blunt to Wilt, who takes a hit, then passes it to me.

I take a couple of hits, blow the smoke from the crack in the window, then keep the cipher going by passing it to What's-His-Name sitting next to me.

V

WE smoke the blunt down to a roach, then Flip suggests that we hit up Main Pier. He says it was crawling with broads earlier—and cops on top of that, but I keep the "cop part" to myself. He also claims to have some serious cottonmouth as well, and he says he can use a drink. I can really use one myself, something cold and refreshing, but I don't bring it up. Instead, I tell them I have to get going and that I got things to do. I make sure to leave Flip an open invitation without the emoticons or whatever by making a hint that I *don't* have any plans tonight. Flip gets thinking and I know exactly what he's thinking.

Once an addict.

Always an addict.

As Wilt drops me off at the popular donut shop, I place the stash back into my bookbag and just as I'm about to zip it up, I hear a voice over my shoulder, "Nice piece. . . "

The pain in my stomach comes back like a bull. I look down, hoping Chemo isn't talking about my revolver. But he is. Shit. I notice the red handle protruding from the side pocket. I look back at Chemo, his eyes still attached to the revolver as if he's never seen a gun before—not in real life, that is.

I say the only word that comes to mind: *Thanks*.

Then, Chemo begs, "Lemme see it."

"Maybe some other time," I tell him.

I know there won't be another time.

Some other time is my polite way of saying: "No. You cannot see my gun, you piece of shit."

"Come on, man," he replies in a state of betrayal, as if we're now good buddies and I've let him down. We shared a shotgun, which isn't considered a blood pact from where I come from.

He looks at me, not saying a word.

"Sure why not," I say under my breath. Then, I make myself clear: "Don't do anything dumb like shoot yourself in the face."

34

"Chill, Philly," Chemo says excitedly. "It's not like I haven't handled a gun before."

Liar.

I grab the revolver, turn it upside down—the barrel now facing the floor—then hand it to Chemo.

Then, I go over the specs with Chemo and the others in the car. Not for bragging rights. I make them respect the weapon because the weapon, junk gun or not, sure as hell doesn't respect them—at least that was what Thomas told me when he caught me in the act of stealing the cheap, junky revolver: a "four incher" made from what I believe is stainless steel; has a six round cylinder, which is maybe the truest thing about the gun; last but not least, made in the America.

He fondles it, then aims it.

"That's dope, man," he says.

Flip hollers out from the front, "You mind?"

"Sure, man," I say. "Whatever."

Chemo refuses and continues to fondle the revolver, as if it has a soul.

Then, Flip snatches the revolver from Chemo's hand.

"What the fuck, Flip?" Chemo yells out, his face slack and all. "You could've blown my fucking head off!"

I wonder if Chemo has even held a revolver before, knowing that the chamber is empty—even if he has seen a revolver before, I'm surprised he never checked the chamber.

"Relax, fool," Flip says, grips the revolver, and aims it gangster-style in the air. To this day, I still don't understand why people hold it like that. Flip, however, is no gangster. A clubber, maybe. But not a gangster. Not even a shade of one.

From the way Flip studies the revolver, Flip is somewhat experienced with the weapon—despite the way he holds it like all the wannabes do in the movies. He opens the empty chamber, then closes it. He inspects the barrel next, then tests the weight.

"Not bad," he says, bobbing his head.

Flip rotates around and hands me the revolver, handle-first.

"What's up with the tape?" he asks, nodding at the red tape wrapped around the handle.

I closely watch his eyes trace the large crack running down the side of the wooden handle.

"Better grip," I tell him.

I place the revolver back inside my bookbag.

Flip nods again. "So, what you planning on doing with it?"

I shrug.

"Nothing," I tell him. "It's just for protection."

Wilt asks from the driver's seat, "Protection from what?"

"Yeah, man!" Chemo says abruptly. "This is Topside. Not Sedgeville . . . although, Old Town might give Sedgeville a run for its money!"

A couple croaks of laughter bounce around the car.

"Old Town?" I say, as if I don't know the place.

Remember, I'm the idiot.

The out-of-towner.

Meet Philly.

"Richport, man," Chemo says. "The *err*-Port."

I act as if I don't know what he's talking about.

"About ten minutes inland," Chemo tells me. "South of New Town. Don't let the name fool you. It ain't a port."

"Yeah," Wilt says. "It ain't rich either. . . "

The inside of the car starts to sound like a swamp and before I get nauseous, I concentrate on the sand between my toes and how good it feels.

Flip lets me out, which helps loosen the knot in my stomach.

Before I walk away, Flip pulls me aside while the others remain inside the car and tells me about a club called the Palace. I act as if I know nothing about the Palace. Then, he says that his "boy" will be there—*his boy*, as in Cue, his hookup. I have no interest in this person, but I play along.

I tell Flip that I'm down to hang out later.

He asks me if I know where the "Dunes" are located.

I shake my head and tell him, "Nah."

He runs his hand along his chin and puckers one side of his mouth like Elvis and asks me if I know where Grier's is located.

Again, I shake my head and tell him, "Nah."

Remember?

I'm the idiot.

The out-of-towner.

Philly.

Then, Flip tells me to meet him at the same Chevron that we passed earlier—the one right before the Taco Bar—at nine.

Not sure why he doesn't include the other frogs in the conversation. Except for Wilt, I haven't seen the others in any of Flip's pics from Crystal Palace, which makes me wonder if he's ashamed to hang around them. I would.

Flip goes on to say, "And there'll be harder stuff there, too. Lois Lane," Flip tells me with a glint in his eyes.

I don't know what Flip's up to, but I know it's something.

C H Å S I N G   T H E   S U N

'M still pretty ripped when I part ways with my so-called "new pal." I'm high but not too high. I'm relaxed but not too relaxed. I'm just right.

I park myself on the side of a local clothing store along the Topside Boardwalk, still high and all. I pull out Chemo's wallet from my bookbag and sift through the contents of the wallet as if the wallet's some kind of a treasure chest. I come across two Trojan condoms well beyond the expiration date—in fact, three years old—a rusty *Pepsi* bottle cap, which appears about as old as my parents. I passed a pawnshop a couple of stores down. It could be worth a couple of bones? On the other hand, an item like this could have more of sentimental value to it.

I decide to keep the bottle cap for the time being by placing it inside the small pocket inside my pocket, the pocket's pocket.

Then, I search through each sleeve of the wallet. I can't find any credit cards, which isn't a surprise. Chemo doesn't strike me as a kid who has credit nor an address. The only cards I find are coupons: one being a FREE SUB at Sub Shop and the other a coupon for HALF-OFF ANY PAIR OF SUN-GLASSES at Sweet Tee's.

I glance over my shoulder and read the name of the store behind me.

Sweet Tee's.

Hey, what do you know?

I dig some more and come across twelve dollars.

I pocket the cash and coupons; then, as I'm ready to toss the wallet in the trash, I find a pack of matches. I pull out the matches from the side pocket of my bookbag and compare the two. I wonder if the matches were put here deliberately. For my eyes only. A higher power at work. Another sign. I don't know. I've never really been the type of person who believes in coincidences. I believe people have an uncanny way of looking for certain things even when they're not really looking for certain things, if you know what I mean. I'm talking about looking on like a subconscious level. I guess, in order to achieve that, you must have an open mind about everything— *open*, as in free from fear or judgment. Maybe it's just the weed talking. Whatever it is, it means something. I guess.

Except for a couple of matches missing inside, the pack is the *exact* same as Chemo's: pink pack with a stencil of a Bettie Page-wannabe gal blowing a kiss through voluptuous vermilion red lips. The name of the club reads: LEATHER N' LACE. I lose myself in the image; then, next thing I know, I look around and I'm no longer standing outside Sweet Tee's. . .

I'm on the edge of Main Pier and Anthony's face appears in front of me like a bad memory. Again, the horror drawn all over Anthony's face like the twisted scribble from a disturbed child's imagination, both of his fearful eyes shaking in their sockets as he presses his right hand against the laceration in his neck, the blood bubbling from the corners of his clenched teeth, the word *bob* escapes his mouth in a bubble of blood, then the bubble suddenly pops and the tiny droplets of bright red blood splash over his chin and I can't help but think about Jimmy and how he went out, his face, the horror, his face, the horror.

Hours before Anthony's neck found itself at end of my needle, he was like a rock star doing whatever rock stars do backstage. I guess Anthony was more of a burnt out than fade away type of rock star. He was taking one shot after another of Patrón in front of naked single mothers shaking their flabby tits and spreading their cellulite-ridden legs for him; and if it wasn't the booze, then it was doing pencil-thin lines of blow off the strippers' cleavages, then motorboats and slapping himself silly until his gums were as numb as the relics of war; then more shots, this time sucking them up from the strippers' bellybuttons; then dancing like an idiot; then obnoxiously singing songs by the band, *Foreigner*; then more dancing; then more celebration. If I didn't know any better, Anthony looked like an individual who didn't carry a single shred of remorse in his body.

But I remind myself that Anthony was no man. I'm sure at least one person will miss Anthony. He lived in a two-bedroom condo with his mother, Clementine Whitaker, off La Guardia Drive. After Anthony's father passed away from old timer's, she changed her name back to her birth name, Clementine Oleander Whitaker. Those who know her best called her Ollie. However, her son, Anthony, kept his father's name, Foster. Now, they'll have an eternity to catch up on all of the times his father smacked his mother around in front of him, all of the times he failed to show up to the important events in Anthony's life, like school plays, recitals, his first soccer game, birthdays, even marriage. Anthony followed in his footsteps and filed for a divorce six months ago from his wife whom he had been married to for seven years. Call it the Seven Year Itch. Call it whatever you want. Anthony was a gambling man who had debt up to his eyeballs. He was a loser. A thug. A disgrace to the human race. Not only that, he was a major accomplice to attempted murder. Except for the other members of the Circle, he didn't have many friends. Clementine may be one of the few who's going to miss Anthony, her sweet Tony, the innocent one who'd never do any harm, although I sincerely doubt it. He was lower than a prawn. He made prawns look like stouthearted hunters reigning on the top of the food chain. Mighty warriors.

Anthony Foster was food for prawns.

I pocket the matches and toss the wallet in the trash and as I try to rid Anthony from my thoughts, my high starts to wear off a little.

I block out Anthony and proceed down the boardwalk.

As I get about halfway down, I pass a majestic band of circus freaks entertaining pedestrians. I decide to stop and watch, as I've grown accustomed to doing.

The group is different from last time. A man covered in tattoos and piercings sticks an actual sword down his throat, then balances the sword inside his body without touching the sword. He removes the sword from his mouth, and I'm left in a state of awe. The blade remains the same way it did before he stuck it down his throat. Th guy even shows off the sword to the crowd. Even lets some booger-flicker touch the edge of the blade with his boogery finger.

Next to the sword-swallower stands a short Indian man with arms crossed in a glass display case. His face and body is completely covered in hair. The only skin showing—from what I can see—comes from the back of his eyelids.

The sign in front of the case reads, "Wolfman," but he looks more like Chewbacca.

I hang around the freaks and watch them perform their acts for the crowd—or "tricks," if that's what you want to call them. I don't realize that the crowd has dissipated substantially until I glance over my shoulder and find myself alone with the freaks. I end up talking to one of them during the intermission. He goes by the name, Nile, like the river, but his stage name is the Human Snake—says a movie-like poster next to him: "The Human Snake: He ssslithers, ssstrikes, and bitesssss! Ssssee for yourself at the Townss Sssquare!"

Most of his body has been augmented. He has scales covering his entire body, from head to toe, and he's wearing these yellow reptilian-like contacts. Turns out Nile's actually a charming fellow, despite his outward appearance or the stage name or poster or the fact that he's literally a walking, talking snake—I wonder if the owner of the freak show, an eccentric man with sallow skin worn tight over his face and a curly black mustache that looks as if it could be found at a local flee market, is looking for a new addition to his show. I don't know any tricks, but I'm always open to learn.

I ask Nile what brought him to Topside. He lets out a resonant laugh and points to the freaks behind him. They laugh as well. From the synchronization of their laughs, I can tell they're a tight-knit group.

Nile asks me where I'm from.

I tell him, "Just visiting from Philadelphia."

"Get outta here!" Nile says.

He has a British accent—I think—or it may be Jamaican. It's somewhere in the mix, elegant yet friendly. I guess you can tell a lot about people from their accents, how they talk, what words or gestures they use when they talk, where they've traveled, the people they've met along the way.

I feel a strange comfort in Nile's voice. I can't help but wonder what he thinks of my voice. It's not the least bit

Southern, but it certainly isn't Northern (most of the posers I knew who were originally from the Carolinas didn't even have Southern accents, mainly because most of the other kids like me, either from the West or North, tend to rub off on the drawl and refine their dialogue).

We talk more about Philly. Nile tells me his fiancée is from a borough outside Philly called Rockledge, but I've never heard of the place. But, of course, I act as if I do and nod my head a lot and say with maybe too much exaggeration, "Yeah! Rockledge! I know a couple of dudes from Rockledge!" Nile tells me his fiancée ended up leaving him and taking all of his money, and I muzzle my laugh.

I keep calm and talk to Nile for a little bit longer until another group of tourists pass by. I'm aware that he's considered to be on the clock, but the guy in charge of the show is laid back and looks as if he doesn't mind the freaks interacting with the public; in fact, I think he encourages it.

I say goodbye to Nile and follow the growl of an angry stomach.

\\

\ make my way farther down the boardwalk in search of something to eat.

I pass a strung-out musician playing an acoustic guitar and crooning about peace and love or something like that in front of a trendy record shop called Outfits.

When he's not paying attention, I reach into his open guitar case and grab a wad of crumpled ones. He looks as if he's jonesing for a fix, but I'm starved and I have to eat. Otherwise, I'll get a headache, and if I stand around here much longer listening to this clown, then there's no doubt about it that I'm going to get a headache.

Before he discovers the case devoid of loose pocket change, I'm already scoping out the menu at a concession stand called the Amazing Pretzel. It's not the Golden Corral. They have hot dogs, corn dogs, popcorn, and, of course, pretzels. Very simple; however, the pretzels are far from simple. They have these specialty pretzels: plain, salted or unsalted, savory or sweet, cinnamon, mild or spicy—basically, a flavor for every country in the world. They even have an Indian-themed pretzel with a chutney dipping sauce.

There's a sign out front: "Best pretzels in the world!"

I order the cinnamon pretzel, pay the cashier, thank her, and then leave.

I'm back on the boardwalk, minding my business and eating my pretzel when all of a sudden I hear the ding of cowbell next to me and before I can make sense of the noise, all of the blood charges through my veins and my body feel almost electric. I'm lying on the ground, half of my uneaten pretzel on the ground, as well. I look up, only to see that same girl who I passed in the Galatia the other day. She catches the gasp in the palm of her hand as she kneels downward. I notice some of her stuff has fallen onto the ground, as well. One item grabs my attention: an open sketchpad with some strange penciled drawing of a winged creature of some kind. She immediately closes her sketchpad the moment I lay my eyes on it. Then, she stuffs it back into her satchel. We finally share eye contact, both of our eyes locked in a sort of trance-state. Her face is put together like a poorly, disproportionate painting of a portrait. Her hair is rather short enough to question her sexuality, and she dresses as if she's into *Phish* or some jam band like that; yet, underneath the many layers of raggedy clothing, the girl takes good care of her body. If I had to guess, she looks a few years older than me, too young to be a tween, too old to be on the wrong side of twenty. I'd probably say twenty-one, if I had to put a number on it; but the girls today look much older than their age.

(I read somewhere that the hormones they put in milk or other dairy products make certain features on a girl's body look a lot "bigger")

The sudden bump somewhat ruined the rest of my buzz, but I still have a somewhat decent high and I don't want to come off as another burnout from the Point.

"I'm really sorry," she says after the shock has worn off. "Are you okay?"

"Yeah," I say and she helps me to my feet.

"You came out of nowhere," she says as she dusts off some of the boardwalk grime from my shoulders. She points at the pretzel on the ground. "Sorry 'bout the pretzel. . . "

I pick up the pretzel and dust it off.

"No worries," I say. "It happens."

"Lemme guess. . . " she says flatly, ". . . Amazing Pretzel?"

I turn to the stand not too far away.

"Yeah," I say and then hold up my smashed, disfigured pretzel. "That's right. Not so amazing anymore."

The comment draws a laugh from her, and when she cracks open up her mouth to laugh, her teeth are white and vibrant like a TV commercial.

"I'm really sorry, sir," she says again. "Lemme buy you another one."

She called me a sir.

Ha!

"No," I tell her. "Don't worry about it. It's fine. Really."

"Really?"

"Yeah," I say. "Really."

I try to think of something else to say. I have nothing, nada.

Then, she breaks the awkward silence, "Maybe it's not such a bad thing after all. You know, I read somewhere that hydrogenated oil can be bad for you," she says. "I read that it causes Alzheimer's. . . " she trails off, ". . . *or something like that. . .* "

"You like books?"

She shrugs, as if it's her natural response.

"Some."

"Same here," I say. "Well, I used to. . . *Periodicals*," I emphasize. "You know, magazines."

She tightens her lips together. She turns away in thought, as if she's thinking about responding but can't find the right words to continue a conversation.

"You like to draw, huh?" I say and point at her satchel.

"Now, where would you get that idea?" she replies with what sounds dangerously close to sarcasm, but I don't know the girl well enough to know what a sarcastic response would sound like coming from her.

One side of me is tempted to ask her more questions about herself, including the drawings in her sketchpad as well as that used whatever store where she works. Other side is tempted to walk away. I don't have the time or patience for her; however, I get the feeling that she feels the same about me.

"So, what—"

"—I gotta run," she says before I can even finish my train of thought, "Sorry. Again."

Three times she's sorry.

Not once do I get the impression that she means what she says.

She walks away while I search the ground below me once more, making sure I didn't drop anything during the collision.

I glance down at the limp pretzel in my hand, then toss it in the trash.

So much for that.

I look up and the artist is gone.

That's twice now she's done that to me.

THE

HIJACK

M ^ D   W O R L D

BEFORE I head back to my motel, I decide to wander through the Galatia, which is packed with both hard-core and first-time gamers alike. The place smells and looks like any other arcade: the savory yet sweet waft of processed food hovering in the air like an unseen mist; the brilliant glow of spastic machines, each casting a pale and flickering light over the goggled faces of both old and young beachgoers. A collection of tradition redemption games line one side of the wall: skee ball, claw machines, Whac-A-Mole. Nostalgia overload. Lounging areas line the other side. Most of the action, however, remains at the hub where the video games are located. The Galatia has a decent spread. Jimmy and I used to frequent arcades like this one around the time we were discovering our first pubes. I think I really enjoyed hanging out at the arcade, and I think Jimmy enjoyed it too. We didn't have to belong. We did our own thing, played our game, and escaped to whatever world awaited inside the game that we were playing. It was a special place to get lost in other worlds except our own.

I use the rest of Chemo's money and spend the better end of the afternoon playing video games.

Once the money runs out, I grab spare change from a pear-shaped brat with a Velcro wallet. Velcro is a much harder item to pick, mainly from that grating noise it makes when you peel it open or the flexible hooks getting snagged on your clothing like buttons and frayed material.

I take the brat's wallet to the restroom where I hear giggles coming from the last stalls.

I kneel down to the floor and find four legs: two with a pair of creased jeans around his ankles in the last stall and the other two bent like a catcher in the neighboring stall. One of them is making these wet noises, like he's sipping from a drink or something. The closer I listen I realize that the kid's *not* sipping from a drink.

I flip on the faucet to drown out the sound and take what I need from the brat's wallet. He has several twenties—three, I count—which doesn't surprise me. When I first arrived, I saw a Gucci-wearing, plastic-faced woman dropping the brat off.

Since I'm in a good mood, I take two twenties from the brat's wallet and leave him enough money to finish playing an hour's worth of games.

I carefully slip the wallet back into his back pocket while he's going to town on NBA JAM. I hit up Mortal Combat for about an hour or two, but I exhaust most of my time on Space Invaders. I used to play the game when I was younger, I think.

\\

I'M a zombie after spending the past two-plus hours killing alien warships. I check my eyes in the rear view mirror, and they're as red as the devil—that's devil with a *d*.

I make it back to my room without passing out—after all, it's only a five-minute drive and I've driven in worst conditions.

The room has been quiet so far. I haven't had too many interruptions. Occasionally, I'll hear someone scurrying past my room, screaming in gibberish without any consideration of the other guests. I guess it's not a motel room without its daily visitors. Mostly water bugs on a valorous quest to find water. With the drought and all. The mattress is as stiff as a brick and the comforter has an invisible film that's oily to the touch and I can only imagine if I were to shine a black light on the pillows what parasitic creatures I'd probably find. The toilet is crap too; and every time I flush it, it sounds like a particle detector picking up lethal amounts of radiation. The other day, I asked this handy man who looked like an over-weight version of Kevin Costner to fix it because it wouldn't flush. I think he only made it worse. But, I guess, it's either deal with the noise or let the shit pile up; and I'm not about to sleep in a place where I can't flush my own shit.

I close the curtains and lock the door behind me.

I stash my bookbag in the closet for the time being.

Close the door.

At that very moment, when I lock the door behind me, my stomach suddenly knots and the blood floods my head. I find myself getting roused from the anticipation.

(I read somewhere in *Finding Fit* that people read a book or watch TV or go for a jog or run or quick exercise or shoot a gun or even have a really stiff drink whenever they feel as if they're about to turn inside out)

I want to fight it. I want to read the pages I've dog-eared in my book, but I know I'm not going to be able to focus. I want to watch a TV show or movie—I swear I haven't seen a decent one since Red Pines—but I only get a dozen or so channels in here and I know there's nothing on that'll pique my interest because daytime TV is for either toddlers or old people who are about to kick the bucket and it's fair to say that I don't fall under either of those two categories—although, sometimes I feel like a seesaw moving from one side to another whenever things don't go my way.

Only one thing on my mind.

I know it'll come and go, as any other thought or feeling. I pace around the room and think about all of the other things to do around Topside but I come up short. I've already closed the curtains. I've already locked the door. I've already hid Jimmy. I'm already committed. I'm practically already there.

I go back to the closet. Pull out a September issue of *Busties* from the bookbag. I take the magazine into the bath-room. I flip through pages, the good ones; and while I work through the kinks, I can't help but think about the artist from the boardwalk.

\|\|\|

EACH day I'm going backwards. Even so, I find myself closer to the truth yet so far from it. Miles and miles of designated lanes left untraveled. I'm overwhelmed by the sense that one day I'll vanish without a trace, like all the others before me. The truth either left for someone else to uncover or, worse, left to disintegrate in the pendulums of time. When I'm no longer a part of this existence, I wonder what people will think about me, what I've done, what I was doing. The fact: I won't even be a glint in the minds of the ones I love. The only mark I'll leave behind in this cruel world is a sloppy inscription on the rickety door of a bathroom stall: was here. *Was.* Now, dust. Gone. At times, I try to put myself in another person's shoes and picture what I would look like through his or her eyes. The feeling I get is like the same feeling I get after I stub my toe on a piece of furniture, not the part where the initial pain sets in but the feeling afterwards, that radiating sensation coursing throughout my body. I can't escape it, the feeling. It forces me to think about my life, where I've been. I think about how I acted at East Providence, how "in control" I was. I feel like that was when I peaked, during those free and easy days where all of my troubles or worries about the future disappeared at the bottom of a drink. Nothing ever got to me back then. Now, my life is starting to feel like one *very* long prologue of the sequel to an autobiography about a youthful yet misguided kid who blew out his brains in the last sentence of a book. Now, here I am, stuck in this stagnant, repulsive cesspool. This is what my life has been reduced to: an introduction to not only the harsh repercussions of madness, but also the onset of madness. A life without any climaxes or resolutions. A life of jerking off. A life of driving down dark roads running through a forever night. A life of searching but not finding. Always one step ahead of me, the monster is; and each night, it pulls farther away from me, as that one feeling I once knew all too well.

If I don't find the monster soon, will I be lost in the darkness?

Cloaked by my own creation?

But is that the sacrifice?

Is it?

If you let yourself inside the monster's head, do you ultimately let the monster inside yours?

IV

As of lately, I've been having the same dream about the night of the shooting. The dream ends with the same: with the shooter pulling the trigger, a flash of lightning streaking across the black sky; then, I'm slowly sinking into the abyss. However, this time I don't wake after the shooting.

I'm standing on the same bridge in Old Town. It's raining. I'm shivering. I'm confused. My ears are ringing. I *feel* a trail of blood trickling from the gaping hole in my forehead. I turn to my left. The same strange men are standing with me, and I feel as if I'm like a child compared to them, as if they have lived ten lives and I haven't even lived half of a life. They're wearing jackets. Good leather. Expensive. Their hair is slicked back and black and glittery as wet asphalt. Their faces hold many secrets and shadows, many lives, many lies. One of them pulls out an eightball of cocaine and slips it into my pocket. I look down at my legs and yet, I can't see my legs for they're dissolving into the asphalt. My legs are there, though. I know. Even though I can't *feel* them. I wonder if me not feeling my legs has anything to do with why these men are holding me upright. The rain falls faster now. Piston-fast. It takes every single muscle in my body to lift my head. In front of me stands another man. A man taller than average. Slicked back hair with streaks of silver on the sides. The kind of haircut you'd see in the mafia movies. He's wearing a jacket as well, but it's not leather. I focus on the smoking pistol as he lowers it to his side. I *know* the gun. That exact one. A Glock 19. So many tiny lights along the handle of the Glock, festively dancing in the night darkness. Pellets of rain hit my face like splinters digging into my flesh. I blink my eyes like windshields wiping away rain. I trace my glassy eyes along the engraving on the side of the barrel: Gen4, AUSTRIA, 9x19. *Dad's Glock. . .*

I turn to my right and see a face in the darkness of the street. The face is narrow like a model's. The eyes are like the eyes of a cat.

All of sudden, I swim from the dream. Bolt upright from the bed. I look around the empty room, wondering what I'm doing here. How did I even get here? Is this even real?

I unpeel the collar of my shirt and breathe a sigh of relief.

I turn toward the windows, and it's darker outside.

As I breathe a sigh of relief, I hear the sound of thunder and it sounds as if the storm is directly overhead.

The rumble shakes the entire room and sends me into a state of high alert.

I listen closer.   More rumbles of thunder above, much closer together.

I roll out of bed, walk to the window, open the curtains, and find the same overcast sky.

I stand there for about a minute, inspecting a wash of gray cloaking the jagged skyline of Topside; and not once do I see any flickers of lightning.   No streaks.   No bolts.   Yet, the thunder still remains.

Weird.

I listen closely.   A distant screech of an animal.   Loud claps of thunder take a more distinct shape and form.

Feet, I suddenly realize, at least six of them pounding against the ceiling above me.   And this chaos goes on for about a half-hour. I try to block out the noise by turning on the TV. If I turn up the volume loud enough, it will dampen the noise. I flip to a channel playing movie trailers. I take a load off and turn up the volume to the max level. The pounding is still there. Now, I'm grinding my teeth—an old habit that I gave up before Red Pines. I try to stop, but each thud causes my teeth to run like a saw. My jaw flexes. I rush to the bathroom and blast water in the tub. It helps loosen my jaw, but the pounding is *still* there. Now, it's in my head—a subwoofer of blood pounding inside my head.

I grab the switchblade from my bookbag and exit my room.

As I arrive at the room directly above me, I get a strange feeling that I'm making a horrible mistake. My gut is telling me to turn back. Go back to your room, it tells me, or hit up the Galatia for about an hour; then, after you're done blasting away alien warships, head back to the motel and by then, it'll be time to get ready for the night.

And if that's not enough to release the tension, I've still got enough weed left to roll a joint.

My gut tells me all the *right* things.

The things I want to hear.

Yet, my bad heart tells me something drastically different.

I knock on the door and check my hands, and they're both as steady as a professional poker player's.

The door opens.

At the doorway stands a petite Indian man with a smile on his face. The upper part of his forehead is dotted with sweat.

"May I help you, sir," the Indian man says politely as he waits for a response.

I open the switchblade behind my back, making sure to keep it out of sight.

He cracks the door farther open and behind him, an entire family is lounging inside. Way more than six feet. Five adults are sitting at the table, as if they've been sitting there for quite a while. Two of them are as old as mummies. Three children are seated like monks on the floor, watching *Looney Tunes* with the typical youthful eagerness. All fingers point at the source of the sound, the heelwalker standing dutifully before me, Chief of the Thunderfoot Clan.

How can such a small person make so much noise?

I tumble my way into a numbing daydream which I had once wallowed in ever since I rented my first apartment. Bottom floor. Worst mistake ever. Above me lived some ditzy college girl who made it her mission in life to push my buttons. She was the type who had no consideration or respect, despite how many times I told her as benevolently as I could to turn the music down. She wasn't a heelwalker, like Chief here. More or less, a spunky thing that operated on batteries for days on end. I used to work in the hardware department at the Depot (*that's right, I used to have a job*—hard to believe, huh?); made enough money to afford a place of my own; and it was pretty nice, having my independence and all. . . but only for a while.

Throughout the day, I dealt with customers who were on a next-level of grouchiness (most of the men's wives had dragged them in by their ears like disobedient children or the men were sent by their ungrateful wives after they had been railed about "fixing that broken hinge on the door" or "making a spare key for the neighbor" or "hanging up that new picture on the wall" for the past month and they all came to me—husband and wife alike—in dire need of assistance and I was glad to help); then, after work, trying to melt away the complaints of the day, I came home to this little bitch blasting music above me, treating me as if I was an insect, as if she was waiting all day for me to come home so she could stomp all over me with her feet. She'd be up there without a care in the world, dancing to some Top 40 bullshit, the ceiling sounding as if it was about to cave in on top of me at any moment. Every time I went up there—I mean, *every* time—I fantasized about what I really wanted to do to her. My weapon of choice would be a bronze statue of an ape (Susannah bought me this statute of an ape with glasses reading a book as a apartment-warming gift). Little did she know that she *could've* been supplying her son with a possible murder weapon. First, it started out with the ditz swinging open the door, like the stereotypical ones do in the movies, chewing gum in the corner of her mouth, twiddling a loose strand of hair between her two fingers, rolling her eyes—You again! What do *you* want? I wouldn't tell her what I wanted anymore. I'd show her: first, I'd hit the bitch over her head with the statue; and once she fell to the floor, her legs still twitching even when I was straddled on top of her like a cowboy, bashing in her head, I'd toss aside the bloody ape and wrap my two hands around her throat and choke the life out of her until she started to smoke and sputter like a faulty piece of equipment. Then, I would assemble the machine back together, piece-by-piece, wind her up again like a clock, then continue to hammer away at her with my fists—

"Is everything all right, sir?"

I snap from my violent haze and turn my eyes to the Indian man. I turn to his children. The pounding stops.

Years from now, what would they think when the thought of their father popped in their heads? An image like that would never go away, an image constantly replaying in their heads.

I discreetly slip the blade into my back pocket.

"Ra—wrong room," I stutter. "Sorry to disturb you."

"No problem," he says kindly. "Have a good night."

"You too," I say and he closes the door as I leave.

I shamefully walk back to my room, wondering *what* in the hell has gotten into me.

William was right.

I am crazy.

THE SALAMANDER & THE SERPENT

WHEN I was as old as the number of fingers on my hands—that particular age where you don't know shit except for your own—I guess I was considered to be a firebug. I liked to play with fire. I liked to watch things burn—toys, insects, anything I could get my hands on. My parents thought it was an issue that stemmed way beyond pre-adolescent angst. When you're that age certain behavioral patterns spark much needed answers.

I had no answers for my parents.

And I think that's what frustrated them the most.

When I suffered from insomnia, I was watching myself burn. Slowly. Each flame like a tongue licking everything it touched until nothing was left but this charred nothingness. Each night wrapped in a blanket of flames. Every thought igniting over a carpet drenched with gasoline. The constant tossing and turning back and forth like a metronome. Waking to a dumb clock. Disappointed. Betrayed. Angry. The longing to fall asleep and wake up with the sun pressed against my face. If only for a moment, I felt as if I could turn into a delicate flake of ash, only to crumble away into a great oblivion. I remember what it was like to long. That was all it was, really, a distant feeling which bore the same significance as its meaning. The farther I reached for the feeling, the farther it pulled itself away from me. Times I've longed to fall asleep, only to never wake again. Eventually, the insomnia was treated with a little bit of tweaking. I was sleeping again. Then, after the shooting, the insomnia happened all over again, as if I had triggered it somehow; however, the insomnia didn't happen all of a sudden. This time, it felt as if I was building it, like the burning—*slowly*—during a crucial time in my life when I just wanted to live inside my dreams forever before they turned into nightmares.

\\

\ take a seat on the edge of the bed. Practice William's advice by closing my eyes, taking a deep breath through my nose, holding it inside my lungs, and then exhaling through my mouth.

Slowly.

This is the kind of spiritual meditation shit they teach you in yoga class.

It helps, though, according to my shrink.

I open my eyes, only to find a streak of red in the lower corner of my eye.

I look down at my hand and my wrist is smeared with blood. I turn over my hand—palm side up. I have a laceration running across the center of my palm. It doesn't appear life threatening, but it's deep. I may need stitches. I stare at the blood pooling inside my palm. I find myself drifting again. Into the blackness. A strange face comes forth. I realize, after steady concentration, the face is *my* face, and it's caked with blood. Blood is frothing from the corners of my mouth, like the edge of a red tide washing over my feet, staining my skin in dark red. I keep the face close to me and move my eyes from my bloodstained lips to my glazed eyes.

Before the face can take hold, I rush to the sink and wash the blood from my hand. I grab two Band-Aids from the First Aid Kit and place the Band-Aids in an X-pattern over my palm before the cut starts to bleed again. I splash cold water on my face with my other hand and look into the mirror.

For a moment, I don't even recognize the reflection of the person looking back at me.

For a moment, I see nothing.

I look down at my hands and can't stop staring at the calluses on my palms. Maybe the car wash attendant was right.

The attendant saw something that I didn't.

He saw right through me.

I exit the bathroom, trying to keep calm. I see a light in the corner of my eye. I turn toward the door and find that it's been opened. My heart suddenly anchors into my stomach, the blood fleeing from my now ghostly face.

I follow the grayish light onto the dark wingtips of a stranger. My eyes trail up his legs, his hands.

She's going to be a distraction—a voice rises from an aged wall of dust and the voice seems like miles away; yet, the voice inches across the desolate shores of what was once a sea.

You need to *get rid of her*, the voice feels as soft as a breeze, yet the words carry as far as a cave echo.

The stranger partially reveals its face in the dim light, crossing one leg over the other. He runs one of his hands over the coarse stubby hair along his cheeks. Moses. He skips through the foreplay and greets me with a *hello* and follows with a name, but I block out the name. He looks at me with a kind of predatory smirk on his face as he patiently waits for my response, his face no darker than a shadow.

Have you already forgotten why you came back here—

—What are you doing here?

You can't get rid of me that easily, Moses says.

The light shines over his suit, which matches the color of the sky, then the bottom half of his chin, the five o'clock shadow on his face. He dresses like a man who seems important. He looks good enough to eat—that is, if I was into that kind of stuff.

I thought we agreed to go our separate ways—

—You don't remember, he interrupts.

Remember what?

Our conversation last night, he says strangely. I didn't think you had the stomach to go through with it. Clearly, I underestimated you.

I don't know what Moses is talking about. Surely, he doesn't mean what happened to Anthony Foster.

What do you want?

Moses sighs.

I thought I told you.

You didn't tell me a goddamn thing.

Let me refresh your memory—

—What do you want?

I need to ask a favor, he says.

You came all of this way to ask a favor?

Moses nods.

I nod back, this time at the suit.

During the time we spent at Red Pines, Moses always talked about wearing a suit—a really nice one, like something a movie star would wear on the red carpet, the type who could pick up a dame with the magnetic lasso of his gaze. That, and what he'd do when he finally broke out, for instance, like catching up on lost time, seeing if the machinery still worked—*machinery*, as in, well, I don't have to explain. I'm not sure how he came up with the money to buy a suit. More than likely he stole it. I would.

Before I can put any further thought into how he acquired such a nice suit, I close my eyes.

I can hear William's words.

Take a breath, says William.

I do as he tells me and open my eyes.

Moses is still there even though I know he is *not* there.

Soon enough, I know, he will pass, as most thoughts tend to do.

I return by asking Moses the first thing that comes to mind.

It wasn't that hard to find you, Moses replies. All I had to do was follow the breadcrumbs. And if I can find you, then he can find you—

Ruby's not a threat to me.

Don't underestimate a cop.

Once a cop, always a cop. The man who's been on my tail ever since I left Red Pines: Detective John Ruby, like Thomas, is a decent man; and like me, he's persistent as hell. He's a man who started out with humble beginnings; and like Thomas, he's a man who came from nothing. After six years of being on the force as a police officer, Ruby became a detective for the St. Joanna's Police Department. He worked homicide before he decided to ride solo as a private investigator. Work started to lag. He mostly handled cases of infidelity: cheating spouse, an overprotective wife here and there, curious husband, the mysterious Jane Doe. Ruby did that for a couple of years before he focused his attention on *missing* cases. He's exceptionally good at what he does, too. He's never been married. Doesn't have any kids. Whatever's missing from Ruby's life, I'm certain that he's about to find it.

Not bad for a—

I already know the rest of what he's going to say before he even finishes his sentence.

—How'd you get in?

Moses points at the door.

You left the door open, he says. You should be more careful.

Once more, he intertwines his hands and then tilts his head downward.

Eyes like blades.

Breath cold enough to turn water into ice.

I look down at my hands and they're shaking.

You can't afford to make any more mistakes—What the fuck do you want from me?

A favor, he says casually, that's all.

I know it's *not* just a favor.

My thoughts turn to something pleasant, something lighter, a face.

Come back to me, he says carefully. Come back to the land of the living.

That's it.

Moses fiddles around with a pen on the table, mostly twirling it in fascination. A distraction.

I understand that you're having doubts, but you must remain vigilant. Is that clear?

The world goes shaky. My hands start to tremble.

Shut up.

I don't think you're in a position to be telling others what to do.

He says my name again.

I block it out.

Shut up, I tell him as I find myself pacing around the room.

He says Jimmy's name, and the anger swells over me and I can't control it anymore.

I do the only thing I was trained to do.

I react.

I grab the ice bucket on the dresser, feeling Moses' presence much closer to me now, his icy breath tickling the hairs on the backside of my neck.

Shut up!

I toss the bucket at Moses.

The bucket strikes the corner of the window with a piercing *bang*!

Moses is no longer sitting at the table.

He's gone, yet it feels as if he's still here.

Then again, he was never sitting there to begin with.

I pull my eyes upward from the sink below.

Before me, the mirror is shattered but still intact.

\\\

\ step out of the room for a breath of fresh air.

While I'm out, I grab some booze at Spirits—that's one thing I like about Topside, how they keep things simple.

The clerk asks to see my I.D., so I pull out the Philadelphia driver's license and give it a once-over before handing it to him.

I show the I.D. to the clerk, who, in return, studies it longer than I expect.

Henry Frick, says the name on the driver's license, is thirty-six years old—and in some countries, he could probably pass as my father. Henry's an organ donor—*was* an organ donor. From what I've gathered throughout my investigation into the shooting, he was a man who unfortunately shared the same fate as Jimmy. Worked as an insurance adjuster who handled property damage.

About a month before his disappearance, he was assigned to "CAT" duty—short for *catastrophe*, meaning floods, hurricanes, even fires. Henry was one of the many participants helping out with the deadly wild fires that had ripped through nearly the entire eastern half of Los Dementes, destroying thousands of homes, displacing families. Some were fortunate enough to make it out alive. Others, you get the idea. Several weeks later after Henry was done with CAT duty, he made another trip back to Los Dementes. It wasn't to help out with the wild fires. I had doubts about using Henry's I.D. I wondered if the name would draw any suspicion. Not too long ago, the name made its way into headlines around the country. Then again, how many people actually watch the news or read newspapers anymore? Exactly. You can thank social media. Anyway, despite our different views, Moses was absolutely certain that I was dealing with the type of characters who had short attention spans (*It'll work*, he couldn't stress enough, *in fact, it's quite poetic*, using the same name as the man who was murdered by the monster who shot Jimmy and then, like Jimmy, dumped in the Crux River as if he was a piece of garbage).

The clerk smirks as if he's impressed, hands me a brown bag containing my poison of choice and then the rest of my change.

In his Haitian accent, he says calmly, "Take care, my friend."

I want to tell him that I will, but I know I won't.

After I leave the liquor store, I use the free sub card and grab a turkey sub at Sub Shop.

I take the booze and food back to the motel where I eat in my room.

The booze helps.

It always does.

Always.

IV

THE last glimpse of sunlight shines through the parting clouds as the sun sets in the West.

I head back inside my motel room where I pull out the contents from my bookbag and line them across the dresser.

First, I start by digging through the side pockets and tossing away used candy wrappers.

I don't realize how much candy I've been eating lately until I pull out handfuls of sticky, week-old wrappers.

After I somewhat clean out my bookbag, I grab Jimmy and gently place the urn on the chest.

I place a crinkled paperback of *Joshua'ζ Tree*, as well as the partially torn and flimsy vintage mass-market paperback cover of the book, *The Art of Contortion* by hack writer Marty Erville, which I once used to conceal *Joshua'ζ Tree*, next to the urn. I set my revolver beside the urn, then my switchblade, then the two packs of matches—one of them once belonging to Chemo and the other once belonging to that prawn grub—then a key-chain holding the purple rabbit's foot that Susannah gave me during her last visit at the nut factory, Red Pines, as well as a key to my trunk, as in a large box, a glass jar containing the rust or "devil" beetle, the plate with the Volkswagen Beetle's

VIN number, and then, finally, the worn case holding my syringe, spoon, and band.

After all of the contents are laid out in front of me, I reach for the other side pocket and just as I'm about to grab the folder containing newspaper articles, as well as the photos of the Circle—the players involved in the shooting—I retract my hand and decide that it's best I find a more suitable place to settle before I start putting everything together. A nicer place would suffice. Nicer place means more money, which means more pockets to pick. I have my work cut out for me.

Next, I remove the nylon bag holding my Canon *Rebel XTi* with telephoto zoom lens that I recently picked up at the pawnshop.

I once owned a camera similar to this one, only less high-end. Susannah bought me one the same year Jimmy left for college. She said it'd give me something to do while Jimmy was at college. I used to take long walks through the woods and take photos of birds and things [northern cardinals, blue jays, finches, and even brown pelicans (there was a lake not too far from where we lived, Lake Beattie, and this one pelican used to hang out in the same spot everyday, hanging with the turtles on a protruding log in the cove)] and for a while, that was my thing until I later sold the camera for drug money.

Then, I pull out Jimmy's gold necklace with a pendant of a gold wing and place it next to the Cannon.

Lastly, I pull out the bullet fragment that I found in the urn from my breast pocket.

I grab a small pouch containing single-serving toiletries from the bathroom, empty it, and place the fragment inside.

I leave the magazines, as well as the smut material, inside my bookbag.

Where I'm going I don't need these things.

V

\ make the bathroom as comfortable as possible by lighting an incense candle, which helps me relax. By relaxing, it becomes easier for me to make sense of things, like Moses, the favor he asked me, why he came all the way out here to Topside. There is still one thing, however, I cannot make sense of. Even if I try.

I was with Patria the night before Jimmy died. When I try to think of a word to describe Patria, the only one that comes to mind is *pfft*—if that's even considered a real word. Patria wasn't my girlfriend. I wouldn't even call her a friend, really. There were some benefits to our relationship, but they were mostly one-sided. She was a girl whom I met during a night out in city of Elizabeth. I reached the point where I lost track of how many drinks I had consumed. Somehow, after several hours of hopping around uptown, Patria and I ended up back at her townhouse that she shared with a girl whose parents were filthy rich. I believe she was from Latvia or somewhere cold like that. I remember the first time Patria and I had sex. It was like trying to thread a needle with a rubberband. Not only that, she was as dry as the Mojave Desert, which didn't help either. Eventually, she came well before me—so she said. Before I passed out, I was wilting inside her like a dead plant. Patria happened to be the lucky one after I went through a long drought without having sex. I remember the sex was sloppy. I was a drunken mess. Out of rhythm, like a band rehearsal after years of hiatus. My dick out of tune. That night shouldn't have warranted another night with Patria. I actually deleted Patria's number—*twice*, I remember—as well as rid any artifact that was attached to her: a paperback by Italo Calvino that she gave me the morning after our one night stand; a crumbled receipt from a night of drinking; a bronze earring of a leaf that she had dropped in my car while we were making out before we stumbled into her townhouse, me half-cocked and ready to jump her bones, Patria, on the other hand, more hungry than horny. Three days later, she texted me: *What are you doing?* I had nothing to do that night. So, I responded to her text. One thing led to another. The second time around was better. Found my rhythm. The third time even better. I mastered my rhythm. The fourth time, like a volley of orgasms. Whenever we did it, her Spanish tongue would make an appearance, and I swear, at times, she sounded as if her mouth was made out of silk. It was like a hymn to my ears. We benefited from the sex so much that we both started to use each other. The extent of our relationship was strictly based around sex, lics, and manipulation. The only time we went out in public was to grab a drink or a coffee. Of course, the relationship ran its course like the flu. That was how long these "flings" usually lasted—if that's

what you call them.   Eventually, after a few weeks, we
stopped calling one another. I didn't care much for Patria as
an individual. She was on another level of crazy. Extremely
bossy. When I was with her, I never felt as if I could be a better person. She was the type who made my bad heart seem
decent. Maybe even good. She had this tattoo of Christopher
Columbus's ship, *La Santa María*, on her thigh. When I asked
her about the tattoo, she told me that her grandfather knew
the whereabouts of the ship's remains. She talked about the
treasures buried in the ocean floor, as if they were hers for the
taking. I asked her how she knew about this and she told me
that her father talked to ghosts. She said she acquired the ability, which was one of the many red flags that were raised during our brief time together. She was an artist, so incredibly
pretentious and self-centered. I bought one of her paintings
after she pulled out the sympathy card; then, after we stopped
talking, I tossed the piece of shit painting in the trash. Brutal,
I know, but it had to be done. She painted these strange be-
ings with facial features that were out of proportion. I guess
the only thing I liked about her was her body. And that warm
October night, I was all over it.   We were having lazy,
drunken sex, the kind where you're too wasted to come and
yet too tired to finish and the next morning, you wake up
ready to explode all over the person sleeping next to you. I
remember I was hitting all of her right notes when all of a
sudden she rolled over on top of me. I was pecking away at
her neck.   Then, I suddenly felt something cold pressed
against my throat—a bird's beak knife that she had kept underneath her pillow like a freshly plucked tooth for the tooth
fairy. I didn't know what came over Patria. It started with me
giving Patria a hickey, then my jaw might've clamped down.
Heat of the moment, I guess. Patria's eyes turned as black as
a raven's eyes, I remember, swollen and primitive, something
sinister inside them, something otherworldly. The left side of
her face was lit with the soft pinkish light from the marquee
outside the window. Her eyes, black. Face, evil. That night,
she slept as if she hadn't slept in years. I, on the other hand,
didn't sleep at all that night. Not a wink. *What kind of woman
sleeps with a knife under her fucking pillow?* I could've died, I realize. It wasn't until the next morning after my worse nightmare came true that I realized the face was the same one I
witnessed in the grease fire the night before Jimmy was shot

and left for dead—Was it the Devil's face? Or, was it something else? I didn't know if it was God warning me or if it was the Devil sparing my life. I'm positive Patria was neither God nor the Devil, but she wasn't herself that night. I believe someone or *something* was pulling her strings.

I shake away the thoughts from that one night and lower my head underneath the water.

As I'm *peering* at the ceiling, a silhouette of a body arches over the lip of the body!

My eyes flick open!

Not like open, as in I'm having a seizure or I'm fighting off unconsciousness, as if I have this annoying little eyelash caught in the pulpy flesh underneath my eyelid, the eyelash like a crab in a fisherman's net and I'm doing all I can to work it out by rapidly blinking my eyes, or like the same way an old fluorescent light bulb turns on after years of neglect, or open, as in a wobbly door with corroded hinges slowly opening, but open, like one of those creepy dolls opening her creepy demon-possessed eyes.

Once my world was as black as blood after oxygen gets to it and now, life.

Patria's face hovers over the water like a four-legged animal, her hand flat against my chest, smothering me. I can't help but wonder if Patria is really there or if I'm caught in a nightmare that I cannot wake up from.

I bolt upright along the bathtub, water splashing everywhere.

Gasping for air, I reach forward and unplug the stopper.

Once more, I look around the empty bathroom and realize it's exactly that, empty.

I use a dime to unscrew the panel to the AC.

I hide my bookbag inside and close the panel.

Then, I go to the closet and dress. First, I slip into a pair of gray slacks; next, a black v-neck sweater—sleeves rolled halfway up my forearms—then black wingtips. I place Jimmy's rubberband on my right wrist. On the other: the Rolex watch Thomas received after he stepped down from his tenure in Kuykendall, a microcosm of a town outside Elizabeth, which also happens to be the former residence of author Ellis Kross, who—according to an interview—said Elizabeth was one of his key inspirations for his novel, *Joshua'ζ Tree*.

I make sure to dress the part, watch and all, the clubber, with two scoops worth of hair gel in my hair. Slicked back. Ready.

After I finish dressing, I switch on a red heating lamp above and during that brief amount of time—one minute to be exact—I holster the switchblade on my leather belt, then the revolver around my ankle.

With red all around me, I stand in front of the shattered mirror, which looks like a spider web from where my fist connected with the glass, route my hand behind my back, and practice withdrawing the blade from my belt, and then opening the blade, and then holding it precisely where I think he's jugular will be until the motion from hand to blade to neck is quick and smooth, innate.

He'll *never* see it coming.

Once I find my stroke, the timer lets out a *ding* and the red light fades into the soft white light.

A staticky sensation suddenly rushes through my veins, my eyes flickering with confusion, trying to find something to hold onto, like an image or an object scattered around the bathroom.

I panic first, and then I hear his voice from behind.

Looks like it's going to be a hot night tonight.

Black attracts heat.

I focus on my warped reflection in the mirror before me, the blurry apparition coming forth over my shoulder.

Moses stands with his hands in his pockets, leaning against the towel holder as if he's posing for a magazine. He's wearing a different suit, I notice, a darker one.

I told you, I tell Moses. I can do this on my own.

I never said you couldn't. I know—

—What do you want from me, huh?

Just a favor, he says.

You know, I tell him. Fuck your favor.

One after another, I down three shots of Jose Cuervo; then, I roll a tight joint and smoke it until the voices finally fade away.

I mentally train myself to concentrate on the task at hand until the time slips past eight.

The alcohol helps me focus.

The weed helps me relax.

The other thing helps, too.

||

\ piddle around for another fifteen minutes until I gather the nerve to leave.

I make a quick stop at Cyber Jaxx's where I check Flip's online status.

CLUBHOPPER69*_* sends Flip a naughty message, just to let him know that she hasn't forgotten about him; then Flip replies immediately after, saying that he's been thinking about her and he wishes that she could come to T-Side and hang out. And he spells the word *come* cum.

I leave the Internet café amused from Flip's ignorance and decide to kill a couple of minutes by practicing my shot at the

Town's Orchard, which is located not too far from where Flip wants to meet. I use empty soda cans that I found in a trashcan and set them on the tree stumps of Asian pears.

I've lost my shot.

I can't hit a damn thing.

I'm *not* prepared.

After I leave the orchard, I drive past West Harleton. I drive around the campus for a few minutes.

After I leave the university, I polish off the pint of tequila during the drive to the Chevron and toss the flask out the window when nobody's looking. I'm fifteen minutes early, and Flip hasn't showed, but I got tequila pumping through my veins, and I'm feeling good (Besides, I expect Flip to be running late. He strikes me as the type who likes to make an entrance).

I just chill and smoke a Marlboro while I wait for Flip. I finish the Marlboro and light up another one with the lighter that I picked from a wino hanging outside Spirits. Flip pulls into the parking lot with his speakers blasting 2Pac's *Do For Love* for the entire world to hear. Most of the low end comes from a subwoofer that has no unearthly business being inside the P.O.S. hatchback that he's driving. The trunk and windows rattle like a maraca. The bumper wobbles and looks as if it's about to fall off the rear of the car.

Flip cranks up the song even louder, which brings more unnecessary attention to us. He bobs his head to the song as if he has a compulsive disorder while he mimes along with 2Pac until the song reaches the chorus; then, he turns down the volume to a more tolerable level.

He drags from a Newport, pops up his head.

"What's good, Philly," he says over the stereo.

"Sup," I reply and return with a nod of my own. "Thought you couldn't drive."

Flip waves his hand. I notice that he's dressed the part too, like a clubber.

"I'm straight," he tells me. "I ain't gonna be drivin' all night anyway. I'll probably leave my car parked at my boy's house."

He's talking about his friend, DRU2SCRU. His name in real life is Drew, as in Drew spelled with an *e* and a *w*. Last name McKee. Like the other burnouts Flip hangs out with, he's nobody. Flip sent him a chirp not too long ago, asking him if he was ready to tear up the dance floor tonight at the CP. Drew followed with a chirp, asking Flip if he was going to crash at his place tonight. Flip chirped back: Fo sho.

His words.

Not mine.

"So, you ready to party, Philly Cheese Steak?"

I don't know what Flip's on, possibly an addy, as in adderall, but he acts more hyper than he did when we smoked the blunt earlier today.

"Yeah, man," I say, catching a buzz from the cigarette. "So, what's the plan?"

"We gonna meet up with my hookup at the Palace in about an hour," he tells me. "He should be straight by then, but if not, it ain't gonna be hard finding sum shit there. Before we roll, though, I thought I get my get my drink on at this dude's house. He don't live too far from here."

He hawks and then spits a blue loogie out the passenger side window.

Just as I suspected.

"Is he straight?"

"Hell yeah, he straight, man," Flip says, his voice stretched out. "It's all good in the hood, Philly."

"A'ight then," I say.

Flip tosses his cigarette out the window and asks me, "You drivin'?"

"Yeah," I say. "I'm driving."

"Word," he says. "Just follow me."

"A'ight."

Flip drives away, and I follow him.

\|\|\|

THE more I drink, the quicker the night shrinks.

Two drinks later, I nearly put a crack in the shot glass as I slam it against Drew's countertop.

Like a domino effect, Flip follows suit, then Drew, grimacing from a rather smooth aftertaste.

If it wasn't for the turkey sub I ate earlier, then the shot of Lord® Vodka would more than likely be making a hasty climb up Mount Everest right now; and I reckon Drew's granite countertop would've looked like a graphic crime scene with CAUTION tape wrapped around all of the undigested mess.

I move my thoughts away from throwing up to a stark image of Mel Gibson dressed the part as the fearless warrior, the great Sir William Wallace, in the movie, *Braveheart*, Mel decked out in a raggedy Scottish kilt, war paint smeared across his face, a spear at his feet, anticipating an oncoming army of Englishmen as he yells out to his fellow Scots, "Hold!"

In a way, I feel like I'm the leader of my own resistance, urging my food to hold.

In a strange way, it works.

Then, my thoughts turn to the sea, each tide rolling into the shore, then, the tide freezes as it's about to crash onto the shore. I look forward to going back to the sea. The thought alone of the sea is like the icing on the cake and any notion of making a scene in front of my new friend is long gone. I'm much calmer, as well. My hands steady when I know they shouldn't be. We take four more shots, Drew passing on a couple of shots.

On the fifth shot, the base of my belly suddenly stirs with a ripple of nausea—*Hold!*

As before, I concentrate on the sea and any notion of vomiting immediately vanishes as I blurt out the words *one more shot*.

By the sixth shot, my words become sticky around each syllable, a precursor to what I like to call my drunken garble.

Before I enter the "blackout stage," we step outside and chill on this giant white ashtray of a porch and smoke cigarettes. Flip leans over a flimsy balcony, which leans slightly with his weight. I picture the balcony coming loose and Flip falling below. That would be a sight: Flip dropping two stories and landing on his face, his feet touching the back of his neck like a scorpion. I'd be lying if I said I didn't want that to happen, but I need Flip for one last thing. He asks me if I want to "match him" on a blunt and before I can respond—my mind mostly playing out different scenarios on how Flip will kill himself—Flip pulls out his share of weed leftover from earlier; and I match him just as much as he stuffs it into the blunt. He guts open the Vega. Then dumps the dried tobacco leaves over the balcony. The blunt is incredibly loose and messy; and when we finally smoke it, it hits three times harder than the tight one Chemo rolled earlier in the car. I'm already ripped and I don't think I can get anymore higher so I take a couple of baby-like hits, never holding the smoke inside my lungs like Flip or Drew, both of them taking massive hits and then holding their breaths, as if they're playing a game of "Who can hold their breath longer under water?"

After we smoke, Flip is itching to hit the club. Drew, not so much. He doesn't talk much either, not as much as he does online. On the Internet, DRU2SCRU's a social butterfly who frequently starts arguments on the comment boards of news articles and random forums. On the Internet, DRU2SCRU is an important person who has a voice—at least, that's what he thinks.

As I'm about to finish my cigarette, Flip smacks Drew on the arm and hollers out, "Yeah, man! You hear what happened to that muthafucka this afternoon?"

"You mean at Main Pier?"

"Yeah, man," Flip says with a girlish giggle. "I can't believe that shit!"

"Crazy shit, man," Drew says as he squints his red eyes.

"So, what happened at the pier?" I ask Flip.

Again, I'm the idiot.

Remember?

"Oh," he says abruptly, "you didn't hear about that shit?"

"What? You mean the accident?"

"If that's what you want to call it," Flip slurs. "Some muthafucka fell off the pier last night and busted his fucking head on a reef or some shit like that. They didn't find his body till earlier today. Crazy, *crazy* shit, man."

"Is he okay?"

"Nah, man," Flip replies with a weasel of a laugh. "That fool dead. . . "

I can't help but think about Anthony's face, all slack and all, as if gravity is pulling his jaw to the ground—then, a spray of blood bursting from the open carotid artery in his neck, then the thick strings of blood trailing from the corners of his mouth right before his world goes black—

" That's sucks," I say to Flip.

"Tell me about it!" he says loudly. "The muthafucka must've been drunk off his ass!"

Not drunk, Sebastian.

Just unfortunate.

IV

\ follow Drew to Crystal Palace.

We arrive at the club a little after ten. The place is unusually crowded for a weeknight. The parking lot is mostly full, except for a few spots near the front. I take note of the cruiser parked in the back of the parking lot, which, from my first assumptions, can only mean two things, really: either Conrad has gotten himself involved with people far more dangerous or Conrad has the cops in his pocket, like with Officer Daniel Ayker, the same cop who arrested Cedric Gaines, for surveillance or protection, mischief or mayhem.

Last I've heard Conrad was still hanging around Crystal Palace despite him handing the keys over to Bishop. He struck me as the type who didn't like to let go of things, even when they no longer belonged to him. A creature of habit, if you will. I can only assume that he's just as much a part of the scene as his son, Nico. Why? I don't know yet. I guess you can call it a hunch. Thomas used to be an officer of the law. *Used* to be. He knew all about hunches; and whenever Susannah was catching a nap before she worked the graveyard shift at Mecklenburg County Hospital, he'd pull Jimmy and I into the living room and tell us all about the hunch—a feeling, he'd say, like the kind you get when you feel a cold coming on in the winter—knowing when to spot a threat, and then after finding yourself face to face with the threat, learning how to stay calm. "*Danger doesn't take smoke breaks,*" he once told us, "or *it doesn't hold your hand while you're crossing the street* or *wait around to catch the bus.*" Once you spot the threat, the only person who decides whether you live or you die is your head (I can see Thomas now, standing barefoot on the front lawn during a Saturday morning with a perspired Coors in one hand, his other hand tapping on the side of his temple). I once heard about how if you don't use your dick, it'll fall off. "If you don't use it, you lose." I found myself wondering if that was the same with your brain. Thomas taught us to use our brains first. The fist was our last option, if it came down to that. I remember nights when he'd come home with a fresh shiner on his face. He'd go straight to the freezer and grab a bag of frozen veggies. We never asked how he got the bruise. And even if we asked, I don't think he would've told us. He never brought his job home with him, especially during the weeknights. That was the rule: the troubles of the day got wiped away on the doormat. Not once did he ever talk about all of the ugly in the world. Not once did he ever talk about the criminals, what they were capable of doing, or the brutality he saw day in and day out. As soon as he stepped into the house, he quit being a cop. He wasn't the type who talked about his job while we were eating dinner or watching the game either. In a way, home was his escape. He'd rather talk about the Yankees or ask about what we did at school that day. Thomas was an advocate for education and he'd always push us when it came to learning. He'd even give me five dollars to read a book and then, later, during dinnertime, he'd ask me what I learned from the book. He never paid us for doing chores. If you did chores, you were family. And he certainly didn't want to pay us for being a part of the family. And no matter what, he'd emphasize, treat your elders with respect. Even cops. Don't talk back to them. If you treat them with respect, they'll treat you the same way. It was the code of a cop, I guess. All of them had it. Do as they ask, obey them, he'd tell us, and get on with your life. I remember there were two times when I got in trouble with the law. The first time, I was at this senior's party, cops came, like they always did after word got out, busted it up, most of Jimmy's friends had already scattered like Canadian geese; I was snagged by this one cop, thrown in the back of cruiser like a criminal. I remember sitting in the cramped backseat—I don't exactly know why they make the backseat so damn cramped, but maybe that's the point. I was sailor-drunk, and I was carrying a bubbler in my pants—Sherlock was its name—and it looked as if I had a ragging boner. The cop—some young guy—called Thomas; Thomas showed up minutes later, disappointed. The cop let me go. Thomas didn't say a word to me on the way home; instead, he just sat behind the wheel as calm as a sensei; then, the other time, Jimmy and I were out way past curfew, and a cruiser was patrolling the area and he shined a spotlight on us, then we hightailed it through the woods. Two cops chased us for a while, then they gave up on us about two miles in. Till this day I don't know why we ran. But we did, as if our lives depended on not getting caught. We weren't really doing anything illegal or whatever, except smoking cigarettes and sipping from Kahlúa that one of Jimmy's regular friends stole from his parents. I guess, at the time, we thought we were breaking the law even when we really weren't.

Now that I think about it more, I know Thomas told us these things because he knew how *some* cops were, how some of them abused their power. What can I say? Thomas was a decent man but a lousy cop.

Drew finds a space behind the building. He pulls his golden Accord next to a fleet of sports cars parked in angles, like the car dealers park them in a showroom. Each one looks like something you'd see at an auto show, very upscale, tacky colors. I wonder if these cars belong to Conrad or Nico, or Nico's friends.

I park next to Drew and before I get out, I squeeze two drops of Visine into my eyes and then place my revolver in the glove box.

I tag along with Flip, who's instantly greeted by a clique of New Town pricks lingering around a sapphire blue Lambo: a Countach 5000 QV. I haven't seen one in person, only on TV. There's nothing special about it. It's just a car. It has a steering wheel and four wheels like any other car. Flip's friends gawk at it as if it's more than a car. I hang back for a second while Flip conducts his elaborate introduction. Drew hangs back as well, and acts as if he doesn't want to be here. I don't blame him.

As I always do, I look for my exits. I have many options to choose from. I spot a couple of back entranceways: a medium-sized man dressed in a black suit escorting an entourage of girls in dresses that appear painted on their bodies through an unmarked door; then, I find another door with a sign which reads, "EMPLOYEES ONLY;" and then, of course, the front door.

I hear Flip's voice calling out from behind, "Philly. . . "

I stroll over to Flip and the New Town pricks. It doesn't take me long to figure out they're *not* actually Flip's friends from the way they're talking down to him, treating him as if he's somewhere between the level of a dog and an ant. I feel bad for Flip. Almost. They're older than Flip, too—at least ten years. Flip's older brother is standing among the group as well. Gelled hair. Reeks of Old Spice. That's Shane, but I already know all about him before he even speaks his name. I decide to play along as if I don't know that Shane is a good friend of Nico's—not a close friend, but a friend, nonetheless.

Shane's posted many younger pics of himself and Nico on PhotoBag, pics of himself living the high-life, playing the part of a sheep (#ThrowbackThursday). I wouldn't go as far as to call him an essential part of Nico's inner circle, not the Circle. Shane's *not* a threat. I assume he's here for two things: the booze and the babes.

I greet the others by shaking their hands. Only one doesn't shake my hand. Yet, the guy stands there, glaring at me. I take note. I haven't seen his face before. His name is Chris.

Shane asks me how I know Flip and I tell him that I met him on the Strip. I tell him that he hooked me up with the chronic.

Shane replies, "That's my lil' bro for you. He's always *hooking* people up."

Shane's friend, the one with an eye problem, Chris, butts in by putting Flip on the spot. The comment is more of an indirect insult toward me since I showed up with Flip and now I'm considered to be tight with him.

"Hey, Sebastian," Shane's friend says, "why don't you make yourself useful for once and go to my car and grab my smokes for me."

Flip's cheeks turn cherry-red.

"Get your own fucking cigarettes," he says, gangster-like.

Chris slithers closer to Flip and wraps his slimy hand around Flip's shoulder.

I hear someone say the punk's name from behind.

"Damn, *Chris*," one of them says. "You gonna let him talk to you like that."

Chris squeezes his hand tighter around Flip's shoulder. Flip quietly turns away, struggling to look Chris in the eyes. All of a sudden Chris bursts out in a fraternity-like guffaw. Then, gives Flip a golf-like clap on the cheek.

He says, "I'm just fucking with you, Flipper."

Flip is shaking his head. He taps me on the arm. Nods toward the club.

As I follow Flip and Drew toward the main entrance, I turn my shoulder and notice the Chris guy eyeballing me. I remind myself that he's *not* a threat. He's just some guy picking on a kid much younger than him.

Maybe he has a bad heart too.

Then, again, worms technically don't have hearts.

V

WE make it to the front entrance where two men with arms as round as my thighs are standing like the Queen's Guard. Each one is wearing Secret Service-like earplugs in their ears and occasionally, one of the bouncers will touch the plug for a closer listen and follow with a nod, as if the person on the other end of the speaker is standing right in front of him.

Why the heavy security, especially for a nightclub?

Flip shakes one of the bouncer's hands and then the bouncer flicks his eyes toward me.

"You know the rules, Flip," I overhear. The bouncer's voice is deep like James Earl Jones. "Only one guest."

"Come on, *Zeek*," he says as he arches his head closer to the bouncer's ear. I can't hear what Flip's whispering to this guy, Zeek, but when Flip whispers in the bouncer's ear, the bouncer moves his beady brown eyes toward me and keeps them on me until Flip gives him a pat on the shoulder.

Zeek nods his head in agreement and then he opens the door for Flip and Drew.

Another bouncer pats down my pockets, as well as my ankles, and says, "Enjoy yourself."

VI

LIGHTNING storms of strobe lights dance throughout the dimly lit club as speakers secretly stashed away in each crevasse of the walls blast like a barrage of gunfire. Bass from the track sends shockwaves along the floor, inaudibly vibrating like the wings of a hummingbird. Droves of gorgeous women, all shapes and all sizes, nines, even tens, linger around an ice sculpture of a fountain, as if they're part of a buffet, while above a spread of glaciers shaped like Egyptian pyramids plays VHS tapes of avant-garde style clips with chicly dressed women dancing in grainy video monitors. The women lingering around the fountain look professional, I'd say. I try to keep my mind from the gutter. I look but don't touch.

Drew acknowledges an old friend standing at the other end of the club and tells Flip that he'll catch up with him later.

I rub my damp fingers together after running my hand over one of the ice sculptures.

"That's the real thing," Flip says closely as he glances at the long smear left behind from my finger.

We shoulder our way through the crowds. Most of the people—except for Flip and few others—aren't from Topside or the Point. They have that New Town waft of arrogance. And it's starting to feel a little stuffy in here. We break away from the crowds and prowl down a narrow hallway covered in red light. I can *feel* myself getting closer. The stroke of a hunch. The red light brings it out, that primitive side. The hunger. So does the music. I suddenly feel a twinge inside my stomach, butterflies ready to hatch.

We make it to the dance floor, which tiers downward into a massive amphitheatre-type room.

The redness dissipates, revealing a wall of soft blue light over a sea of flesh.

I direct my eyes above at a second level and see more people dancing. One side of the room consists of a lounging area, which is overcast with a cloud of dense smoke. All of the furniture is top of the line stuff and probably just as expensive as the Lambo parked outside. Women are everywhere. I haven't seen so many women. Flocks of women. All races. All shapes. All sizes. Take your pick.

Flip leans closer and says into my ear, "What the fuck did I tell you, son?"

"Damn," I say.

That's all I got.

I don't realize where the source of music is coming from until we walk down a small flight of stairs and stroll onto the dance floor where the carbon copy of a mask-faced DJ is playing IDM songs from a laptop. There's even what looks like to be a VIP section located outside the lounge; however, the area is mostly concealed with these flowing purple curtains suspended from the high ceilings.

I catch a glimpse inside the VIP where—to my surprise—two greasy individuals are doing lines of coke off a woman's stomach while she lays naked on top of a table. Most of the VIP is a sausage party, except for the women spread out on the table. The men are well dressed too, lots of jewelry; and there are more of them circled like a sex cult around the table. Watching. I crane my head above Flip and get a closer look inside the VIP, only to find two women playing with themselves. Each flicker from the strobe light brings out the orgy. I can't help but wonder if *all* of the women here are profession-als; and, strangely, I find myself getting somewhat aroused when I know I shouldn't. I remind myself of the task at hand: find Nico; and when I find Nico, I'll find Conrad.

I lean closer to Flip and ask him over the deafening music, "Is your 'boy' here?"

Flip checks his phone and then shakes his head.

"Nah," he says. "Not yet. He said he's on the way."

I nod to the bar.

"I'm gonna grab a drink," I tell Flip.

"A'ight," he says and approaches a group of women danc-ing on the dance floor.

As I head to the bar, I scope out the rest of the place. Two areas warrant the most attention, both heavily guarded with men dressed in black suits. One is a *red door* with the sign EM-PLOYEES ONLY, and the other, a darkly lit staircase to the right of the main stage, the stairs leading up to a secluded section; however, the only people I've seen accessing that area are mostly women. Professionals. Same women entering through the back earlier. Same escort. And the guards who let them through mean business. Definitely packing heat.

Why in the hell would they be strapped inside a fancy nightclub?

Only two reasons come to mind.

One of them has to do with the drugs.

Flip.

His boy, Cue.

Other stuff here, "harder" stuff.

I remind myself that I'm not going to do any blow. I don't like blow, especially when mixing it with booze. I had an experience after Jimmy's death (this was after I kicked the dope). I did a few bumps of blow. I nearly killed a guy.

I came home the very next morning covered in another man's blood.

The incident forced Thomas and Susannah to take action.

I guess they had enough of my behavior.

I don't blame them.

I grab a drink from the bartender and calm down once I see a group of girls around my age sipping from neon-colored martinis and nervously swaying to the music. They skittishly move pass me, and one of them smells vaginal. They move cautiously as well, as if they're inching through some kind of wake, paying their respects to the modern day disc jockey. Even when they giggle, it comes off as fake as a three dollar bill.

Maybe they're here to dance.

Maybe they're here for blow.

Maybe they're here to watch.

Maybe they're waiting in line to ride the train.

Maybe I need to stop worrying so damn much.

As I take a sip from my drink, a draft of potent cologne suddenly comes over me.

A rather handsome man in an expensive gray suit with a black dress shirt and black tie approaches the bar beside me.

The man doesn't even have to ask for his drink.

The bartender already has it prepared for him—a Tom Collins. He faces me, the gin drink nursed in hand.

Then, he nods.

"I've never seen you here before," he says smoothly.

The voice sounds familiar and yet the face appears extremely vague.

My bad heart becomes a thoroughbred, kicking away the restraints from its cage of bone and muscle. The muscles tighten throughout my body. I feel that fist tightening in my chest as well, and I want to snap. Everything about my body becomes tight. Like I have the jaws of a vise gripped around each joint, and I just want to pop each joint in my body, loosen them up for the sake of hearing things crack.

He waits for my response.

I muscle out the words, "First time. . . "

"Is that so?" the man says softly and raises his glass in a toast. "Then, we're glad you came out."

"Yeah," I tell him and then look around at all of the pretty faces coming in and out of the flashing lights. "Nice place."

"Thanks," he says.

He sips from his drink and reaches out his hand.

"Name's Nicholas West, but my friends call me Nico."

He's *not* Nico. He can't be Nico. I know that he's lying because I've seen pics of Nico on the Internet and he looks nothing like the man standing before me. Even if he's Conrad's son, he's changed dramatically. He's much thinner; his cheeks are sunken in like a fish; yet, he has the eyes of a shark right before it's about to tear its prey into shreds.

The left side of his face forms into a smile and all the skin on the left side wrinkles and shows his age.

I peer closer and see the old Nico, in his smile, in his eyes.

I keep my cool and shake his hand.

"Pleasure to meet you, Nico," I tell him as I cautiously ease my other hand around my back.

Then, the pale blue lights suddenly go red all around me.

And that's all I see before the madness begins, red all around me.

A L R E A D Y   G O N E ≈

I T'S happening again.
  The loss of control.
  The apathy.
  The blackness.
That's how it first starts out: I'm baptized under a moon-less night. I lose my handle. I slip into a void of blackness and free-fall through the hollow barrel of a gun until I finally ease into a bed covered in a thousand thorns as long as jave-lins.

I stop falling, eventually, when the feeling comes back to me; and I'm released from the thorny mess, my body perfo-rated like the lid of a cardboard box housing a mouse or ham-ster, something rodent-like, then I plunge with a thunderous roar into this pool of ice water, torpedoing my way to obliv-ion.

I surface, eventually, clawing my way through the gutters of blackness, through all of the muck and noise.

I find myself staring at a glint of light lost in the blackness. Softly twinkling like a star above me. A dwarf of a star. A mysterious, celestial thing curious of my existence.

Somehow, the light knows that I'm trapped and it acts as if it's making an effort to pull me from all of the blackness. I can't move, though. I'm locked inside a room covered in glossy black walls. Some strange liquid on the walls moving like warm molasses. *No* doors. *No* exits. Not one.

Then, suddenly, something is born from the blackness: first, fingers emerging from the wall, then a gnarly hand reaching toward me, as it remains lifeless. This arm appears as knobby as a tree branch, and a jolt of life runs through the arm, causing it to teeter closer and closer, shaking, convulsing.

The arm doesn't completely break the wall, though; yet, the wall stretches outward as if it's made of rubber. Both the wall and the hand inch closer. Another sense comes back to me, and now I can hear the wall violently screeching as it expands to the point of tearing.

I struggle to fight my way upright—doing everything I can to keep the black hand from touching me—but my body remains in a paralyzed state.

Then, the floor beneath me liquefies into this rich and heavy sludge.

I muster whatever strength I have left inside me and pull my arm from the sludge as it starts to consume my toes, my feet, my legs, each one of my limbs. My eyes move from the shaky hand to my own hand; and I realize the hand is *my* own hand. Lost in blackness. Sinking farther into the sludge below me.

Now, the sludge moves its way up my shoulder and neck and slides like wet mud across my chest.

I panic.

As sludge creeps into the sides of my mouth, the blackness washes over with red.

I taste the salt in the air. I feel warmth blanket my body as I crack open my eyelids, only to find the tide running toward the shore before me.

A *screech* of a flying creature cuts across a pale blue sky!

My eyes trace what looks like a seagull. I raise my head from the sand and witness three silhouettes standing in the beams of sunlight. They're looking down at me, as if I'm an attraction, a zoo animal, a freak.

I turn back toward the sea and wonder how I ended up on a beach.

For a moment, I don't recognize the beach, the ocean before me.

For a moment, I don't recognize myself, my hands, both of them powdered with grains of sand.

For a *moment*, I feel as if I'm actually dead, as if the flesh has been removed from my spirit, the bone and every single fibrous material attached to it, and all of the people gliding along the beach are either dead as well or alive, and they're oblivious to this imperceptible world.

Suddenly, a stabbing sensation splinters through the back of my eyes and burrows like a mole of pain into my head.

The silhouettes drift away as soon as I sit upright and wipe the sand and drool from the side of my cheek.

I watch the three materialize as they stroll farther down the beach. A man, I see, and two young boys—his sons?

I focus on my body. Study every inch. Down to the cuticle. I'm dressed in the same clothes as last night: black sweater, gray pants—*the club attire*, I vaguely remember.

I pat down my waist and then my pockets, as a cop would do. My switchblade is nowhere to be found.

I search through the hot sand, but all I find are footprints—much smaller than mine—leading back to a sun-beaten walkway behind me.

I pat myself down once more and touch a lump in my pocket. I pull out a wadded tissue stained with some kind of brown substance—*blood*, I realize, old blood. I open the tissue and cringe, but not in repulsion.

Before me: a smelly, pinkish condom balled up like a piece of fresh gum. I believe it belongs to me, as well as the DNA inside, but how I wound up on the beach remains a complete mystery.

As I search for saliva in my mouth, I taste a woman stained on the tip of my tongue. Not Yolanda, the girl who was hanging around Nico's infinity pool, but her friend, Nico's friend, Jamie. She neither had conversational skills nor a depth in vocabulary. She lacked personality, as well. At times, it was like talking to a slot machine and every word that came from her mouth was the same, only shuffled around in a different order; and her breath tasted like cheddar, I remember, really old, sharp cheddar—*old*, as in primal. The flash of an image comes to mind: circles, three of them; fleshy pink in color; blown up in size; and each one of them hung on the walls like paintings. One of the canvases was a close-up of a woman's lips, scarlet red and glittery and plump like the decal for *The Rolling Stones*. The other, similar lips, only vertical—a beautiful shaved clit, I remember, tight but extremely lippy, like packed deli meat. The third one, I can't remember, but I think it had to do with a woman's orifice.

And Nico, he *was* there—after all, I believe it was his house. Flip was there, too, but he never spent the night.

I retrace the events from last night: Flip and Drew following Nico and a group of people back to his beach house; a jockish man was driving my car. He could pass as a football player. He had shoulders as square as a fridge, no neck. I believe his name was Yoda or something like that.

When we arrived at Nico's, I remember being surrounded by more beautiful women than I'll probably ever see in a lifetime.

Nico hinted that they were *not* professionals, just "close friends of his," despite half of them strutting around with their perfectly cone-shaped tits on display once the party turned brothel-loose.

The lights dimmed to near black and out came these glow sticks, but they weren't exactly glow sticks. They were something else. I can't remember. I remember running into a group of strippers I saw earlier at Crystal Palace—I'm not talking about those from Old Town or the plastic-looking ones from Los Dementes. These chicks took extra special care of their merchandise. And that's what they were, really. They were no different than what we were at Red Pines. Products. Constantly being updated or taken apart for the sake of being updated or taken apart, being put back together again. Refurbished. Constantly serviced for a material world. Nico could sugarcoat the bullshit all he wanted, saying that they were his friends and all, but at the end of the day, somebody was getting paid. If not the women, somebody. I handed Jamie the two mollies Apple Ripper gave me, and she popped them like nuts, then we hooked up after the party was running as thin as a Motley Crew concert. Partygoers had already crashed, disappeared, or melted into the night. But Jamie stayed, I remember. And, so did I. I swear Jamie looked like a young Kate Moss. Face like a ten. Body like an eleven.

But what about Nico?

I remember Jamie, the both of us having sex in several spots. It all started while I was grabbing a drink from a wet bar next to the pool, her hand grazing mine. She asked me if I wanted to dance. So we did. I made a fool of myself, but Jamie was really into it. Guys were throwing me high fives as they shot glances at Jamie, as if they were congratulating me or something, like they knew something that I didn't. Jamie said that she heard I was holding mollies—could've been why she was so damn interested in me? I think she was talking to Flip for a while at the club. I gave her mollies. We made out in Nico's living room. She was wearing clothes too, and she wasn't with Nico.

But where was Nico?

Jamie's award-winning body straddled over my pelvis as if it was a saddle. Her hair, her lips, her scent, was all over me, like all of it had been infused with my body. We took our sex-capade to the pool. I've never had sex in a pool before. Last night was a night filled with many firsts. We continued our hump fest on the beach—*this* beach—the moonlight soaking our naked bodies in sickly paleness.

I lift up the waistband along my pants and find these serpentine-like red streaks running along the sides of my groin, as well as down my thighs from the sand rubbing against the flesh.

A dreadful emptiness suddenly washes over me like the tide before me.

I didn't pay her, though.

Or did I?

I spent my money on the Cuervo. Had a couple of drinks at Crystal Palace. I never spent any money on blow, either. That, I remember.

I quit thinking about last night. I fasten my belt buckle and gather the rest of my things from the beach.

A silver earring in the shape of a miniature hula-hoop digs into my left side—must belong to Jamie. Thomas's Rolex buried underneath my left butt cheek. Then, I find my smokes close by. Thank God for my smokes. I check the flattened pack, only to find one cigarette.

I pull out the loner, craving to smoke it in one single breath, but the squashed cigarette breaks in half.

My eyes graze a fresh bruise underneath my rolled up sleeve. I roll up my sleeve farther along my arm and follow the bruise toward my knuckles, red but not bloody. I stretch out my hand and then curl it into a fist and grimace from the soreness. The face, I see, neither Anthony's nor Nico's. . .

The face: narrow, well-groomed, blue eyes, hair the color of cheap Zinfandel. The face belonged to a friend of Flip's older brother, Shane. I forget his name.

Another faded image: Shane's boyfriend intentionally bumping into me while I was smoking from a glass sculpture of some kind. I accidentally broke the bowl, pipe, or whatever it was on the floor. The asshole spilled beer on my hand and shirt.

I take a whiff of my hand and then my fingers where the odor is the strongest, but I don't smell beer. I smell Jamie. Every inch of Jamie. I can't escape Jamie's scent. It's everywhere. On my hands. My lips. My body.

I concentrate on my knuckles and how they ended up so red and swollen. . .

The asshole aggressively came at me with four white knuckles—*Chris!* That's the asshole's name—No! Wait a minute! It wasn't Chris. It was Drew, Flip's friend.

I check the purplish bruise on my forearm and witness these nightclub-flashes of horror all around me. Each bright flicker of light throughout the darkness brings forth a face, then a still of action, then violence.

Red all around me as Drew swung at me. I dodged Drew's drunken punch, then countered with one of my own. I grabbed Drew's wrist and straightened out his arm across my body; and I didn't break, but obliterated his arm with a furious karate chop to the butt of his elbow. The bone pierced through his skin. An audience of cheers rang out behind me. *Ews* and *Ahs*. Music to my ears. To my surprise, the son of a bitch came at me again. I made sure it would be his last. I knocked him out with a hammering blow to his face. My fist curled tight, like the head of a hammer. Most of the pressure pushed to the meat of my hand. The bridge of his nose erupted, blood showering over my audience.

The flashes stop.

Flip and Shane and his other friends dragged Drew from the house while an argument was taking place. Then, Jamie. The infinity pool. Both of us like two horny mermaids.

Sand splashes over my shirt. I turn around and see a Frisbee stuck in the sand.

"Sorry, bro," a shirtless twenty-something says as he runs toward me.

I dust off my shirt and grab the pink Frisbee.

As soon as I stand to my feet, I immediately sway like a buoy from the smack of a dizzy spell. My ears close up shop and any noise coming inside them is thin and hollow. My vision starts to shrink into the circumference of a peephole. I can feel my own blood pounding through my veins. I feel each beat of my heart. I feel as if I'm about to faint.

Then, I hear a voice calling out beside me.

Hey, bro. . .

The sound of the voice brings me back, comforts me.

"Long night, huh?" he says as he approaches me.

I shake away the spell and hand the guy his Frisbee.

He looks me over and studies my condition.

"Thanks, bro."

"Yeah," I say with a wounded nod. "No problem."

He walks away and tosses the Frisbee to his friend.

The sight of the two friends playing Frisbee comforts me.

Everything feels normal again.

I'm somewhat relieved.

\\

\ toss the used condom in a trashcan and leave the beach.

I find my bearings once I make it to the road.

To my left, I spot a familiar house at least a quarter of a mile down the beach—Nico's house. Only three houses reside on the street. All three of them are separated by mostly over-growth of the sea. Two are ocean view, celebrity-style. I don't see much of any activity at Nico's. The place looks dead. As far as I know, Nico's dead too.

I breathe a sigh of relief as soon as I locate my car parked in the same exact spot where the Yoda guy parked it on the street earlier this morning. Still looking as ugly as ever. Only two or three cars remain on the street; however, they're parked closer to the house.

I grab the keys from my pocket and as I'm about to open the door, I step on a red plastic cup next to the back left wheel. Jamie was drinking beer out of a red cup. So was I? I think.

I open the door and immediately, I'm greeted by the smell of chlorine. I walk back outside and go directly to the trunk.

I open the trunk.

Empty.

For some reason, though, I know the trunk is not really empty.

lll

Two cruisers are parked in front of the manager's office of Seaside Heights.

I do a speedy U-turn around the median and park across the street and hang back for a minute until I can make sense of the current situation.

The manager, a hobbit of a man who walks with a limp, exits the main lobby and guides the two cops to my room, Room 102.

They stop in front of my room, which rests in early morning shadows.

With a flashlight, one of the cops inspects the exterior of the room: the windows, the panels, and lastly, the door. Then, the manager opens the door without even knocking, which makes me believe the little turd's already been inside my room. Has he gone through my things? Who is he? Is he working for Conrad as well? Has my cover been blown?

The cops follow Frodo inside.

After about two minutes inside, the cops exit and stand outside and talk. The manager uses his hands a lot when he's talking to the cops; and strangely, I know what he's talking about even though I can't hear him. I think of my next plan of action.

lV

It finally dawns on me what I need to do once I settle down at bit.

I go to the trunk and shuffle through the tags like a deck of cards. I find one for California. I remove the Arizona tag. Replace the tag with the California tag that I pulled from an abandoned Impala.

Next, I find the nearest payphone outside the parking garage and dial 9-1-1.

An operator answers first, asking me to state my emergency.

"I'd like to report an emergency," I tell the operator with labored breath, sounding as if it's dire, as if my life's in danger, as if, at any minute, I can die. I say it quickly too, all in a single breath. She remains extremely placid on the other end, robotic. She's trained properly. "There's a crazy man yelling and waving around a gun outside the Square," I say louder, more urgency in my voice, more everything. "He's threatening to shoot people! Help us! Hurry!"

I hang up the phone before she has a chance to respond.

I walk back to my car and watch the two cops from a safe distance. One of them excuses himself from the manager and listens to his radio. He nods at his partner, who steps aside. The cops stroll back to their cruisers as the manager holds out both of his arms with the common where-are-you-going expression; then, after the cops peel away, the manager callously waves his hand in utter disgust.

I sneak around the motel and peek inside the manager's office. He's chatting on the telephone. More cops? Don't know. Don't care.

I crawl under the window and keep out of sight; and when I make it to my room, I go straight to the AC. I grab my bookbag from the inside after I remove the panel. I check the contents inside, which remain the same way they did when I left them. I close the AC and wash up, as if, at any moment, the hobbit-man will return. I'm in desperate need of sleep; however, I can't stay here anymore.

Before I dip, I go to the bathroom and change shirts.

As I slip into a fresh tee, I find scratch marks on my back. I closely inspect the scratches. It looks as if Freddy Krueger went to town on me last night. The thought of the beach comes back to me. The feel of each grain of sand rubbing against my thighs. Jamie's nails digging into my back. Her lips. Her scent.

I run my hand across the side of my face and my skin feels coarse to the touch.

Did I really pay her?

V

I leave my motel with a sense of relief, even though my hangover is one for the records.

A few miles outside Topside I pull over along the side of the road and vomit. I don't throw up any food—at least none that I can see on the road, mainly just stomach bile—and for about a minute, my stomach feels as if it's leaping through my chest to kiss my uvula with each strenuous retch. By far, it's one of the worst feelings ever. I get back inside the car and check the rear view mirror, my milky white face coated with layers of sweat. I feel ashamed that I let myself get this wasted last night.

I drive to the Point and stop at a rundown convenient store, which appears to be closed. I make sure the place doesn't have any surveillance cameras before I decide to make a move toward the refrigerators in the back of the store. I grab a can of ginger ale, as well as a bottle of water.

Without the clerk noticing, I slip the drinks inside my back pockets and cover them with my shirt.

I stop at the checkout counter. The clerk is two generations older than me and possibly senile; and he's watching FOX NEWS on a boxed television perched next to a slushie machine when all of a sudden a news report scrolls past the TV screen.

On the TV a crane is hoisting a newspaper gray car from the heavily trafficked San Potosí Canal. A swarm of cruisers, as well as unmarked cars, are scattered around the junkyard, the crane pulling the vehicle above the round head of a blonde reporter who shares the characteristics of a Barbie Doll. I can't exactly hear what she's saying or mouthing. I don't need to listen to the news. I already know the news because I am the news.

The cameraman zooms in from a wide angle and gets a close-up of the waterlogged car, which happens to be *my* old Beetle.

The clerk turns to me and tells me that I look like I've seen a ghost.

I ignore him and ask if they carry "Pepsi," as if it's the only soft drink I drink. I already know they don't carry Pepsi, only some off-brand, but I ask him anyway in order to keep him distracted. He says no and then I ask him if there's a restroom I can use.

As he reaches for what looks like an ancient-looking spanking paddle attached to a key, I pocket a couple of snacks in front of the counter. He hands me the restroom key, unaware.

I ask him a couple of trivial questions while strolling toward the entrance (*Do you know how far Los Dementes is from here?* or *Know any good places to eat around here?*), mainly to keep his attention away from my pockets. He gives me a few places, which don't sound appealing to me.   Local dives. Places like the Cove.

I open the door and say goodbye.

As I step foot outside, I hear the clerk say over the cowbell, "Seems like you need to find a new hobby, young man."

I turn my shoulder and look him over.

"What I mean to say is that maybe you should try something else like getting a job," he says, as he removes his glasses and folds the newspaper over his lap.

I stutter for a moment.

"Go on, you hear," he says dourly, "but next time, it *will* cost you."

I exit in a hurry, more pissed-off than anything.   I skid away from the parking lot and then toss the ridiculous-looking restroom key out the window.

I drive roughly a mile until the very notion of the clerk calling the cops enters my mind; in fact, the old fuck's probably on the phone right now telling them about the make and model of my car.   I'm sure he didn't get my tag number.   I left in a hurry.   I switch out the California tag anyway and replace it with a new one or better yet, an older one.

VI

THE ginger ale not only helps get rid of the bitter taste of stomach bile in my mouth, but it also settles my stomach.

I drive south, stop in the small town of Los Alamosa, and rent a room from a shady-looking man at Lucky's, a shady-looking motel a couple of miles off the main highway.   The room's about as cheap as talent; and I only have enough money to my name for one night's stay, which is fine by me, although sleeping in my car would probably be more sanitary. The room at Lucky's is worse than bad.   Somehow, I can hear Thomas's words in the back of my mind: *You get what you pay for.*

Despite having the same salary as a teacher, I wouldn't call Thomas a cheapskate by any means.   He was what I liked to call a "saver."   Never missed a day of work.   Worked holidays.   I tip my hat off to the man.   He was a provider, through and through, the definition of a provider.   Most of the money Thomas made as a cop went directly into savings.   Whenever he did spend his money, say, for instance, on a washer—I remember it'd take him like weeks to pick one out—he'd buy the best of the best. He'd check out competitors or which one lasted the longest or which one would be the most efficient.

Whatever product he invested his money in he expected it to last forever.

VII

So many faces.

So many stories behind the faces.

That's how the dream starts out before it makes its ultimate decent into blackness: faces, *many* faces, all kinds of faces from human to animal to something unimaginable, all riddled by the frightening stories which consume them. Each one is made up of wax or something similar. Each one melts into another. This goes on for what feels like hours. So many faces. So many stories. I can't escape them.

The faces are crushed by a red darkness swelling behind my eyelids. Then, they're at it again, the faces, each one starting to morph into the next.

Finally—eventually—the detail of each face is brought forth in a better light and then sinks into the red darkness and then a new face surfaces with extraordinary detail, then the face sinks back into the red darkness. The cycle repeats over again. Each time these haunting faces morph into one another, detail magnifies: each mole, each freckle, each blemish, each wrinkle.

The faces.

I have seen them before. In person. Somewhere. Another time. Another world. I don't know when. Maybe another time. The past. Maybe another life, another realm. Each one is like ink stain on my mind. Snapshots lost in time.

Nico's face surfaces among the spiraling ball of faces. Then, Yolanda's face. Yogi's—that was his name, *not* Yoda—Yolanda's little brother. There was nothing little about him, though. His face was clean-shaven; however, he had this patch of hair underneath his chin, as if he forgot to shave the rest of his beard. Could be possibly setting a new look for men's facial hair. Not a goatee or handlebar, but the Yogi patch. Yogi was the one who drove my car from the nightclub to Nico's.

I visualize Jamie's face as well, then back to Yolanda's face. Her face morphs into Anthony's face. So many faces. So many stories. They grow more intense, meaner. Insect-like. One face drifts back into the red darkness. Nico's face. . .

I crack open my heavy eyelids. The room is bathed in redness. Neither night nor day, but somewhere in between. I look around in confusion, first unsure of where I am. I roll out of bed. Peel back the curtain. One half of the sky is lit with a lurid red.

(I read somewhere in a book called *Book of Phrases*: "Red sky at night, sailor's delight. Red sky at morning, sailors take warning.")

Maybe it's Jimmy's way of telling me to take the night off. I take the sky as—more or less—a sign of things to come.

So, I take the night off. I tell myself that it's for the very best.

THE

BIG FIX

UN SIR TAN
END DING Z

spend most of the night watching TV, mainly flipping
through channels while nibbling on peanut butter crackers. I
manage to hold down the crackers, which help relieve the
hangover.

As I go through another cycle of basic cable channels, I
come across a selection of pay-per view channels, which pique
my interest. I switch off the TV before my flesh starts to stir
and step outside for a breath of air.

I grab some change from my car and use it on a soft drink
at a vending machine.

I piddle around the lobby area—if that's what you want to
call it—and as I'm skimming through travel brochures, I notice the shady desk clerk is tracking me down with his droopy
eyes.

I can imagine the waste of flesh that he's staring at right
now, like something that just crawled out of an asshole.

"Is there anything I can help you with, cowboy?" he asks
me.

I step closer. I get about three feet away from him when
all of a sudden I walk into a wall of cologne. I do a double-
sniff. I pick up another stench hidden underneath all of that
other artificial crap. I examine the desk clerk's unusually
white eyes, then his two front teeth, which have been slightly
grinded down by his lower teeth. Then, I look over his shoulder and spot a glass of chocolate milk next to a partially eaten

Moon Pie stuffed with what looks like barbeque potato chips on his desk.

Takes one to know one, I guess.

\\

AFTER I hook up the clerk with the same amount of "pot" that I gave Flip—close to an eighth—which is more than he asked for, I head back to my room and order the movie *Debbie Does Dallas* from one of the many pay-per view channels called VV (the first V stands for Vintage. Don't ask what the other V stands for). Despite the ridiculous name of the channel, it gets the job done. According to the desk clerk, it's on the house.

I prop up a couple of pillows behind me and watch.

And I watch.

I watch until my eyes burn.

I never get hard, though. Not entirely. I should. The blood is there, throbbing inside my veins, but I don't get a hard on—at least not until I turn my thoughts to the strangely cute girl from the boardwalk.

Tent City.

I stay with her face, her ink-stained fingertips removing the black bra before me.

Undressing.

I focus on each dimple on her face, each curve of her bare chest.

I focus on her body, *not* Debbie's body as she *does* every man in Dallas, but the artist's beautiful black body.

I pull myself from my thoughts, now racing out of control, and I witness her face on the fuzzy TV screen—her mouth open, moaning—then her body on top of a hunky porn star.

Naked.

Both of them are naked.

Hard and drenched with sweat.

Excited.

She's straddling the actor, thrusting.

He switches positions, and he's on top of the black girl.

Thrusting.

And I keep going, and I'm angry too not for how pathetic I am to be fantasizing over some girl whom I hardly know, but for what the actor's doing to her. She likes it. He likes it. I like it, too, but I hate it. I like being angry. I hate being angry. I like watching the porn star do her the same way Dallas does Debbie.

All of a sudden, the actor turns his lecherous gaze toward the camera. A narrow beam of light shines like a masquerade mask over his sparkling blue eyes.

I gaze back at him; and I realize the porn star is the same guy from Lassie's—the girl's boss! And he's about to climax all over her. And he wants me to watch.

I switch off the TV before they climax; and as I always do, I finish my business in the bathroom.

\|\|\|

THE next morning before checkout I wake up to the softly spoken words *buenos días*.

A wall of sunlight slices through one half of the room, causing me to bolt upright.

I look toward the doorway where a stubby maid is standing outside the room. She's watching me. Waiting for a response. We both make eye contact. Then, she struggles to look my way as she excuses herself, as if she just caught me jerking off, and then shuts the door behind her. I throw on some clothes and go outside and tell the maid that I forgot about the time and I'm leaving right now and then she pushes her squeaky cleaning cart to the next room and goes about her business while I gather all of my things. I contemplate staying another night, but I don't have any money—and I prefer not to see that desk clerk again, especially after he sees what I've been watching all night on pay-per view. I leave Los Alamosa, still slightly hungover from the other night. Like I said, one for the records.

\|V

I drive past Topside and head north toward the Point.

Along the way, I drive through the one place I thought I'd never consider staying. I remind myself I'm already in it, waist deep. I've already met Conrad's son, Nicholas or "Nico," as he called himself, already hung out with Nico, already partied with Nico; and for all I know, I'm already as tight as crossed fingers with Nico—if Nico's still alive?

What other reason would he invite me back to his place?

I drive around Apple Ripper's neighborhood and find a couple of houses with FORECLOSURE signs. I've heard a lot of vagrants squat in these types of houses. I take my chances.

I remove my revolver from the glove box, check the chamber, and make sure it's loaded. Just in case.

I drive past a somewhat decent-looking house—*decent*, as in appropriate—and mentally mark it. I decide to abandon my car in the parking lot of a Dollar Store on the outskirts of Richport. Like Herald's Point, Old Town is a town that rests in the morning shadows of Los Dementes. A flickering bulb of a town that's no stranger to police corruption and brutality. Unlike the Point, Old Town managed to survive all of the media storms, the scrutiny, the vandalism, the chaos. The town's been limping on ever since. Not dead. Not yet.

Along the way, I work on the leftover snacks from the convenient store but I can only hold down a couple of bites before the nausea comes back. I make sure to stay hydrated.

(I read about dehydration in a *Finding Fit* magazine and how the blood can thicken when the body is dehydrated)

I reach the same house that I spotted a block away from Apple Ripper's crib. I don't see a soul in sight, only a stray dog with as many scars on its face as a mediocre boxer.

I check the windows first.

On the living room floor is a sleeping bag.

After a thorough study along the exterior of the house, I conclude that nobody is home.

I walk around and make it to the backyard—if that's what you call it. The yard looks more like a giant sandbox. The grass appears as if it's been scorched by the sun. The wooden fence that surrounds the yard in a perfect square has been picked through by both man or rabid dog; and a couple of planks from the fence lay scattered in the yard.

I keep my revolver close and sneak through the back door. Part of the door panel has been chewed up by what looks like an animal or even a crowbar.

I do a sweep through the entire house and conclude that the house is, in fact, vacant.

I move my search into the living room. Inspect the sleeping bag, which is covered in dark stains and smells like a used diaper. The trash is months-old, from what I can tell.

I roam around the kitchen. Shards of broken glass from a window lay forgotten in a sink. I've lost my switchblade, and

I need a sharp object for close quarter combat—if it comes down to that. So, I grab a piece of glass that closely resembles a knife and place it in my bookbag. I use the rest of the glass to my advantage and sprinkle the jagged pieces around the floors of each entranceway, first by carefully placing several pieces behind the front door, then laying down a heavy perimeter around the back door. Just in case.

After that, I grab a two by four from the hallway closet. This, like the glass, can be used to my advantage as well.

Then, I pass a torn curtain dangling from the window. I rip off the bottom half and take it with me to the bathroom. Cockroaches or water bugs or beetles or whatever insects scurry into the baseboards and holey caulking, which has as many cracks as a deadpan desert. I make sure to plug the drains. I find a used condom, all shriveled up, like a piece of cooked spaghetti had been thrown against the wall behind the toilet, then left to dry out. The evidence is missing from the inside, as if it somehow evaporated into this rare fertile atmosphere.

I check the cabinets next. Empty. I check underneath the sink, which is spackled with thick layers of mold. More insects, as well. It's not a Best Western, but, as Flip would say, it's better than nothing—or *nutting*?

I lock the door, wedge the two by four underneath the doorknob, and set my bookbag next to the bathtub. I've seen worse.

All of a sudden, the feeling of not knowing what will happen next strangles me and I can't release myself from its grip. I have trouble breathing and I start reaching for deeper, more laborious breaths. I'm tired of feeling like this, the lack of control, the lack of calm. I just want to end it all.

Is this me hitting bottom?

I mean, if this isn't Hell, then what is?

I do the one thing that I told myself I'd *never* ever do. I don't bother removing the contents from my bookbag. The only thing I remove is my revolver.

I empty the chamber into my palm. I grab a bullet and toss the others aside. I load the chamber with the bullet. Spin the chamber. Close it. I place the barrel to my temple. All in that order. Then, I squeeze my finger against the trigger and start to pull. My greatest masterpiece. My middle finger to a world that gave me lemons and then told me to make lemonade without a please or a thank you. I've decided to throw the lemons back at the world, tell it to go fuck itself. Is that all you got? Lemons? I say fuck your lemons. I gave you a chance, world, and yet, you didn't give a shit about me. Never will. So, this is my last retort.

When the jinxed coroners examine me, they'll gawk at each other in similar awe as the audience experienced when Beethoven performed Symphony No. 1 in C major in Vienna.

At the same time, they'll blurt out, "What a masterpiece?"

Every thought on display. A pastiche of light and darkness. How awfully wicked my masterpiece shall be. They'll even snap pictures before the cleanup crew arrives to wash away my savage little world. Afterwards, they'll catalog them in evidence lockers to later be discovered by young, aspiring sleuths; and when they gaze upon my masterpiece, they'll wonder: *What in the world was this kid thinking before he blew his brains?* I expect my entire world to be painted all over the jizz-stained walls. Lights! Camera! Action! *Boom!* My masterpiece. Instead, all I hear is the hammer going *click*, the piercing sound rattling my bones.

I check my body, then my head, my face, my eyes. Check the chamber. I was one more tug away from creating my masterpiece and the thought of coming "this" close to death causes the air to escape my lungs. I fling the revolver across the bathroom and reach down in the middle of my body for a breath.

I picture myself back at Red Pines, inside William's cozy office, listening to his words. I calm myself.

I check the window one last time. I take the curtain and ball it up as well and use it as a pillow.

I down the rest of the water in the bottle before I can wrap my head around what just happened and rest my head against the curtain inside the tub.

I tell myself: just an hour or two of sleep.

That's all I need, just an hour or two, and then I'll be good to go.

L I © E N S E D   T O O
S T E A L

I hear a *tapping* sound coming from the dark woods as I paddle canoe-style down a river inside an open coffin. I begin to sweat from the humidity of the swampy South. The clouds suddenly darken and swell up like foam above me; and next thing I know, I'm paddling through a downpour. The tapping remains, though, both in shape and rhythm. I move much faster down the river. My wooden paddle cracks, then breaks in half, and falls into the river. I have no control over where I'm going. The rain starts to picks up. And that's all I hear, the beating all around me like a flock of euphoric children dancing in unison. At that very moment, I realize the dream ceases to be a dream. Fuzzy lights build around me until the darkness is no more. I'm no longer in a river. Yet, I'm standing over one. It's nightfall. It's raining. Nico's dripping wet face remains blurry behind the Glock. His face is much younger, I realize after I focus on the ridges of his face. He carries that same silly smirk on his face too. The devil's smile. The rain falls harder—at times, slanting sideways. I direct my eyes upward, my face getting pelted by bullets of rain; and in a cold shower of rain, I find myself in the beam of a soft amber light.

I turn to my right.

A man.

All I can see are his hands, a row of stony knuckles that have recently pounded on something solid such as a person's face—Jimmy's face.

Pieces of raw skin have been shaved away while other pieces remain dangling from his red knuckles like shedded skin.

They're bruised and bloody as well.

I turn to my left where I witness another man standing next to me, and both of these men are holding me upright. My arms are numb. Same with both of my legs. Numb. They almost feel as if they don't belong to me anymore. The ache in my head lessens as a weight slips from my sinuses, like a sheet of ice falling from a glacier.

I pull my attention back to Nico standing on the edge of the street, lights glistening over each of his shoulders like fields of nebulas.

The rain continues to jab at my face. Harder now. Faster. Muffled claps of thunder rumble across the night sky. I anticipate the light. Soon, there will be light. Then, blackness.

Nico readjusts his grip around the Glock and says over the beating rain, "When you meet God, my friend, ask Him to forgive me." Nico pulls the trigger. A flash of lightning blinds my eyes, forcing me to open them. . .

The rumbles of thunder seep from the nightmare and send me into a state of alertness. I listen closely to the fading thunder. But it's there, *the sound*, less in intensity and yet constantly tapping like a woodpecker with a dull beak. At times, tapping sporadically.

I reach for my revolver next to the tub but my arms will not move!

I panic.

My heart rate rises. I look down at my arms. I see them and yet I cannot feel them. I bolt upright and bang them against the side of the tub. My left arm gains feeling but not before a rush of blood shoots through the arm and causes a temporary pins and needles sensation. I grab my other arm, as cold as a penguin's tale, and feverishly shake my noodle-like arm until blood rushes back into it and then that sensation runs through the arm yet again.

I remove the revolver from my bookbag. Check the window. I pinpoint the sound a couple of houses down. A roofer is nailing down a shingle with a hammer. The sun has hardly moved at all. Either way, the headache has lessened substantially. And that's all that matters.

Sleep can wait.

I gather my things and set a couple of booby-traps around the house by mainly stacking objects like empty cans, as well as standing twigs, against things that open or close such as windowsills and doors.

As I'm about to exit, a shiny object catches the corner of my eye. I want to keep moving, mainly due to my rumbling stomach, but my curiosity gets the better of me. A metallic object glitters in a beam of sunlight, twinkling like a distant star, begging.

I stroll through the living room and kneel down over the object. I pick up a small figurine. Hold it in the light for a closer look. It's a small pendant of an angel. The etching underneath the angel reads: THE SAVING GRACE SHELTER.

The sight of the pendant strikes a chord inside me. And I tell you, that chord resonates for what feels like a crescendo that never ends. The notes of a ghost hanging in space. I can't control myself any longer. I let it happen. I don't know why I've been getting like this as of lately, especially after long nights out of heavy partying. I can't rally a drop when I'm sober. When I go a day without a drink or a smoke, I'm like a jittery machine with a defective fuse; and yet, when I'm dealt with a hangover so excruciating that even the smell of alcohol makes me sick to my stomach, the tears come more freely. Like a wound that'll never stay closed. I don't know what the hell is wrong with me, why I can't gain control. It's like the pieces don't fit anymore. Before all of this crap started—I mean, before Jimmy's death—I was the king of my castle, priest of my church, master of my slave. Now, I feel like I'm less than a peasant. I feel like I'm dirt. It's been happening more often too—all of the crying—and there's nothing I can do about it. It just happens. The mornings after are the worst. When it rains, it pours. I guess. Sometimes, I wonder if there'll be a day when I can't cry anymore, when my tear ducts have been permanently sealed shut and all that comes out is dust. Like the same way I felt at Red Pines, me all doped-up, with that post-surgery feeling or lack of feeling draped over my body like a heavy quilt. Thomas went through the same crap after all of the riots and protests against law enforcement. That temporary numbness. Some nights whenever Thomas wanted to leave the job at the door and concentrate on being a father, the job wouldn't let him. Some nights, he couldn't escape the noise. Some nights, he couldn't hide all of his frustration. The badge that Thomas proudly wore had no longer represented a Hero of the community, a Mentor, a Guardian. The badge had been forever tarnished. Just another corrosive symbol of discord, something on the brink of abolishment. The word *cop* had become associated with a bigot, a bully, and a butcher, the world's most evil triplets. I remember he'd come home betrayed, abandoned by the very city that he fought to protect. Wouldn't say a word to us. We kept our distance, including Susannah. He'd never lay a finger on her. Never hit her, although, I'd be lying if I said that he never came close to striking her. I think the only thing that held him back was the thought of his father and the way he treated his wife, Grandma Backer. Thomas would shut down completely, as if his emotions were on sleep-mode. Nothing was getting in. And, if anything was getting out, I prayed for whoever was on the other end of his wrath.

After I stop being all dramatic, I perform an exercise of belly breathing before exiting the house. I make sure not to step on any glass on my way out. I avoid the pair of roofers and walk down a barren alley tucked away behind the houses until I reach a main road. The smell of cooked meat seasoning the air causes my stomach to speak not with a gentle roar, but, more or less, a boisterous ribbit.

Not too far away is a rundown strip mall, which looks both dead and alive. I pass what's known as a dive called Reuben's Ribs where a long line of people is wrapped like garnish around the front of the smoking hut-like structure. I seek out a couple of people waiting near the back of the line—one of them, I notice, chatting away on his cell phone. Pickpocketing is all about distraction. Similar, if not the same as a magician's trick. Most picks are done while the individual who's being picked doesn't even know he or she is being picked; otherwise, you'd come off as a mugger and I'm no mugger. I don't even bother distracting the guy. With him, no need. Instead, I do a "graze," which is in the vein of a "bump-and-grab;" however, it's way more subtle. I graze shoulders with the guy. He's a chubby fellow with love handles mushrooming over his belt buckle, covering his hips like a fleshy man skirt. The way I look at it: I'm doing the guy a favor. His cardiologist may thank me later. I grab his wallet and keep out of sight until he orders food—by then, he'll be redder than a rib eye and kicking himself for "accidentally" leaving his wallet back at the house. He may have been coming here for who knows how long. But hey, that's the guy's story.

I stroll along the strip mall—anticipating my latest score—until I stumble upon a comic book shop called *Heroes Vs. Villains*. The front is covered with a barrage of comic posters and all sorts of advertisements, a collage of chaos. Susannah used to take Jimmy and me to these types of places when we were much younger. Before comic books, it was bedtime stories. Susannah used to read us stories—and this was just a couple of years or so before I discovered the aesthetics of the female anatomy in *Playboys* or the other magazines that Thomas hid on the top shelf in the closet. I remember one in particular. There's always one, isn't there? Mine was Lewis Carroll's *Alice in Wonderland*. I'm sure most of you already know about this one. Not too long ago, I came across the book while rummaging through the reader's bin in the recreational room at Red Pines. This time, I read the story from front to back.

By myself.

I enjoyed reading about Alice and her adventures, but that's another story. After the bedtime stories, we graduated from having our mother read us stories to us reading on our own. Then comic books, then books without pictures. Jimmy was more of the bookworm. I preferred comics. The comic book store used to be like my version of the candy store. It used to be one of the highlights of my day. Susannah would let us pick out two comics each. Jimmy would always head straight to all of the parody comics. *Tick* was his favorite. He enjoyed those stories, even the many spin-offs. Me, I guess I was more drawn to the *Spawn* comics and stories of that nature. The darker stuff.

I step inside the store, and it's deserted, which is no surprise. I walk around the store until a strung-out guy with a black and yellow Batman shirt manifests from the back. He hangs behind a display case. He doesn't pay much attention to me. The guy looks how I feel, actually.

I take Porky's wallet to the *DC* section, gut the cash, and then slip the wallet behind a *Superman* comic book.

I browse through the shelves and occasionally take a peek at the hut next door. I stop at a graphic novel with a hologram on the cover, pick it up, and angle the cover in various directions. The holographic face changes from a masculine-shaped face of a Clark Kent-type character to a scaly, snake-like face with reptilian eyes.

"*HARD COPY*," I read the title to myself.

I glance at the clerk who's now rushing toward the back of the store. I can't help but think: *maybe he had a long night too.*

As I turn back around, I witness Porky storming toward his white Cady in a heap of rage. You're welcome.

\\

\ feel like Santa Clause when I make it back to the house.

I check each booby-trap. Each one remains undisturbed, as I suspected. I fortify myself in the bathroom and sit on the edge of the tub, feeling more comfortable than I did before.

I channel my inner handyman, rip off a piece of aluminum foil wrapped around the steak sandwich, unscrew the cap from the water bottle, and cover the top with the foil; then, once the foil is sealed tight, I poke tiny holes in the foil with the server's ball-point pen. Last, but not least, I burn a hole near the bottom part of the water bottle, take apart the pen until all that's left is a tube; and then, I insert the tube inside the warm plastic. I blow on the plastic until it's cooled and the tube is molded to the bottle. I make sure to seal any holes with a flame, warming the plastic first and then cooling it by softly blowing on the plastic. I sit back in the tub and place a pinch of weed leftover from the other night inside the holey piece of foil and burn it with a lighter; and, finally, I smoke. Eat that MacGyver.

I take a few rips from the homemade pipe and flip through *HARD COPY* until my appetite comes back to me. I eat one half of the sandwich and save the other half for later. I somehow finish the Pepsi before I swallow the last couple of bites. I asked the server for no ice yet she practically filled the entire cup with ice. I didn't say anything. I could've, but I didn't want to make a scene. Not my style. It's a good thing a bought another bottle of water on the way home; otherwise I'd be choking right now. I furiously wash down the rest of the food trapped in my chest. It's a condition, the results of having a bad stomach—*bad*, as in the only thing it's good at is throwing fits. It's like a bad child. The food gets stuck from time to time. Doctors told me it's from reflux. They gave it an absurd name like gastroesophageal reflux disease, but whatever.

After I finish eating, I doze off again. I don't dream, though. I don't have any nightmares. I fall into a dreamless sleep; then, a couple of hours later, I feel a ball of fire burning in my chest and I realize it's just a bad case of heartburn. I sit upright, which helps ease the burn, and as I'm I trying to focus on something else other than the acid eating away at my esophagus, I hear the sound of footsteps. I listen closely to the footsteps as I ease from the bathtub. Two shadows reveal themselves behind the doorway. I quietly grab the revolver from my bookbag. I keep the revolver aimed at the door until the shadows finally move away.

A *creak* chirps throughout the house followed by the sound of a person shuffling over broken glass. I hear the back door opening, then closing.

I exit the bathroom and rush toward the window and witness what looks like a homeless man—I think so—stumbling away from the house. Not sure if he's a bum. I'm not sure who he is, really. For all I know, he could've been squatting here. What I do know is his appearance. He's wearing a raggedy trench coat that stretches down to his ankles. The bottom part of the coat is frayed and faded and the coat itself appears as filthy as a straggly alley cat. He has holes in his clothes, not cigarette burns but the kind you get over time.

His greasy hair hangs over his shoulders like an old washcloth.

He's also carrying something underneath his arm, but I can't see what it is from where I'm standing.

I check the living room.

The sleeping bag is missing. That's it. That's what he's carrying. And that's my cue to leave.

DA GURL FRUM KNOW WHERE

WHEN I arrive at the pawnshop, some girl is trying to get a hundred bucks for a vinyl record player, which looks as if it's worth half of what she's asking for and that's really stretching it. The Russian, who, in fact, was the one who sold me the Rebel XTi, is giving her a lot of lip by telling her fifty, no more. I acknowledge the Russian.

He acknowledges me, his favorite friendly business partner; then, the girl turns a shoulder and I realize it's the same girl who bumped into me on the boardwalk.

My stomach suddenly lurches. My throat tightens. My palms become all warm and sweaty, and I do that untimely thing where I either want to fight or run and hide in a place of comfort. I'm past the point of no return. Not only that, she's already seen me; in fact, she's looking right at me.

I stay my course and keep walking toward the counter.

"Hey, the pretzel guy," she says abruptly and her face is glowing from my presence.

"Yeah," I say mindlessly. "That's me. Pretzel guy."

"So, how was your pretzel?"

I'm surprised she's talking to me when, just the other day, she couldn't get away from me soon enough.

"Not bad, a part from tasting like dirt," I say.

"Again," she says. "I'm sorry—"

Enough with your sorries.

"—A Conley."

I point at the vinyl player before her.

I do that thing where I call out observations.

A nervous tick, I guess.

Or, it's just my way of keeping the lines of communication open without having to venture into the territory of uncomfortable silence.

"Good product?" the Russian asks me. "Yeah?"

"Top of the line," I tell the Russian. I hardly know anything about the vinyl player, but I act as if I'm an expert on vinyl players. Screw that. I'm a connoisseur when it comes to vinyl players. I make sure to live up to my title by telling the Russian: "I have seen a player like that go for at least three hundred on the market, if you're lucky to find one as cheap as that."

I glance at her, and she's smirking at me.

"One twenty-five," he says.

The artist reaches out her hand and shakes the Russian's hand. He grabs the money from the cash register, counts it, and then hands it to her. Then, she tilts her head at the comic in my hand. She examines the comic.

"*The Amazing Spider Man*, the rare, nearly-impossible-to-find number five issue," she says louder than her normal tone, as her eyes widen with the kind of youthful excitement that never gets old. She knows her comics or at least I think she does. I'm surprised. She nods at the comic, asking me if I'm getting rid of it.

I can't tell whether or not she's returning the favor.

"Yeah," I tell her and again, decide to play along. "Why do you ask?"

She shrugs.

"No reason in particular," she says innocently. "That's worth a *lot* of dough."

"I've heard," I tell her.

"You know, its value will only increase over time. You sure you wanna get rid of it?"

"Yeah," I say. "I need the money."

As the Russian places the Conley on the shelf, he continues to eavesdrop on our conversation.

||

THE Russian gives me five hundred bucks for *The Amazing Spider Man*, which is still in mint condition. We could've kept haggling back and forth like a couple of dummies until I finally got the original price I was asking for—which was seven-fifty—but I didn't have the time. Plus, I didn't want to look like the King of all Dummies in front of the girl.

The artist and I leave the pawnshop with more money than what we had before we entered. Money certainly doesn't buy happiness, but it feels damn good when I hold it in my hand.

I secure the money inside the side pocket of my bookbag and stroll down the boardwalk. I think about all of the ways I can blow the money, most of those thoughts surrounded by booze and more booze, but I decide to hold onto it until I can find out what really happened to Nico.

As I'm about to part ways with my new partner in crime, she points to the pier.

"Say," she says curiously, "I have about a half-hour left until I head back to work. I was thinking about taking my lunch to the pier."

I already know what she's going to say. My stomach knots.

"You wanna join me, I mean, if you don't have any plans. . . "

"I should get going," I tell her.

"Why?" she returns, in similar taste. "You have somewhere to be?"

I come up short.

"You have a girlfriend?"

"Me?" I say stupidly. "Nah."

"Well then, what's the problem?"

Why is she so interested in me all of a sudden?

"No problem," I tell her.

She starts to walk away.

I guess I'm supposed to follow her.

"Sure," I say behind her. "Okay. I'll join you."

We leave the pawnshop and walk toward the pier—Main Pier that is.

She asks for my name and I tell her the first name that comes to mind.

When I speak the name, it rolls off the tip of my tongue as if it's foreign.

What about using Henry's name as my cover?

It's too late. I've already spoken the name. I can't change it now. Can't do anything but roll with the name. Jimmy was always good at adapting.

"Nice to meet you, Jimmy," she replies.

Then, she tells me her name.

"Jazz," she says.

I liked the name.

Jazz.

I ask her if she lives in or around Topside or if she's visiting; and then she tells me that she lives not too far away.

"How long have you lived here?" I ask Jazz.

"Too long," she tells me.

\|\|\|

THE wind starts to pick up from the west. The pier is still roped with crime scene tape. So, we find the closest bench next to the pier and soak in the ocean view while I ask Jazz questions about herself like if she has any siblings, does she live with her parents—she lives with her mom, she tells me. I ask her what's currently in her CD player, and she says that she doesn't have a car. So, then I ask her what's on her mp3 player. Some Mona's Arch, she tells me. On repeat. I'm a fan, I tell her.

About five minutes or so into the conversation with Jazz doing most of the talking we start to gel and the whole conversation picks up speed and fluidity and I find myself glad to have shared company with her despite her cat-like aloofness.

I'm talking more, too, which is something I never do, especially with a stranger.

Jazz tells me that she wants to stretch her legs—tells me how much she likes walking at night. She's been sitting behind the register for most of the morning, she says in a laid back manner. She's extremely particular when it comes to her diet. I like that about her, how she not only eats well, but she's also not afraid of the dark.

So, we take it nice and easy, like the old folks in their Golden Years of retirement do after a heavy meal.

While she nibbles from her spinach wrap—tofu maybe, but whatever it is, I don't think it had a name or even parents—I run through another list of questions.

I ask her what she was sketching in her notepad the other day—that winged creature, what was that thing? She dodges the questions and turns the conversation toward food.

Strike one.

Food is the universal language, I guess.

So, we talk about food for a while.

She's curious as to how I ended up in Topside—of all places, Topside.

"Just visiting," I tell her.

She nods and says with a half-smirk, half-nod, "Okay."

I feel as if she's going to reverse roles any second now and start asking me the questions. So, I cut Jazz off and ask her if there's anything to do around here to show her that I'm normal.

She names a few things that I already know about, although Jazz mentioning the arcade catches me off guard. She says it's like Paris at night.

I turn toward the end of the boardwalk and see the kids mingling around the Galatia.

"Say," Jazz says with a sigh, "you have a car?"

"Yeah," I tell her. "I have a car."

"That's cool," she says calmly. "I like cars. Most guys I know don't have cars."

Most guys?

She's *not* that kind of girl, I remind myself.

The blood suddenly rushes from my head. The pounding is back. The thoughts. The temptation. Don't screw it up, I remind myself. You've gotten this far. I mean, you're talking to a girl and you're not even drunk. Just keep listening and bobbing your head like a Bobblehead doll and you'll be fine, I tell myself. She'll like you more. No doubt. Whoever said anything about her liking me? I just met her.

I tell myself to take it one step at a time. Don't be too Frank. Don't be too Dick.

Jazz gets distracted by a daughter arguing with her mother. So, I cease the opportunity by shifting the bulge in my pants, then tucking it underneath my belt buckle.

I remind myself that she isn't that kind of girl.

"I'm not that kind of girl," she says after a long pause.

116

Her eyes are big and innocent, like a child's eyes.

Another pause develops over the conversation—more tense.

Jazz sneaks in another glance, as if she's waiting for me to talk.

I say the only thing that comes to mind.

"These *guys*," I emphasize. "Why don't they have cars?"

She does her typical shrug.

"I guess you don't need one unless you want to go into the city."

By city, I believe she means Los Dementes.

"You ever go into the city?"

She gives me a closed smile.

"Not really," she says quietly.

"Well, maybe I'll take you to the city sometime."

"Yeah," she says and smiles again, but this time wider. She fully exposes her front teeth, and they're slightly crooked. The first time I saw her I never spotted them, but now, they're clear as day. She has snaggleteeth on each corner of her mouth, very noticeable. I don't know why, but I never label them as a flaw. I notice them, but I unnotice them.

Then, before she catches me staring at her teeth, she shields her mouth with her hand, trying to cover any food that may be stuck in her teeth. She's fine, though. No leftovers.

She says finally, "I would like that."

I remove my hands from my pockets, slide them under the straps of my bookbag, rest them along my armpits, and ask the one question that's been on my mind ever since we began our little stroll, "What else is there to do around here?"

She shrugs once more.

"There's the Twin not too far from here."

"You mean the movie theatre?"

"Yeah."

"I passed that place on the way here. How is it?"

"It's nice," she says. "Every Thursday, they play old movies. I used to go a lot, but I haven't been in a while."

"How come?"

She shrugs, of course.

I look over Jazz's face and witness the same expression that I've been looking at in the mirror for the past several weeks.

"Don't have time," she says.

117

Her eyes glaze over with reflection.

"I remember the first movie I went to was the original *Hell-raiser*."

"Good movie."

"*Great* movie," she says as if she just upstaged me. "It was sometime around Halloween. Throughout the month of October, they play throwback horror movies."

I get the creeping feeling that she feels as if I'm much older than her.

"By the way," I say, "how old are you?"

"Isn't it bad luck to tell a person your age before you get to know them?"

"Never heard of that one before."

She shrugs again, as if it's her way of changing the subject.

"Just the other week," she says before the conversation drifts into silence, "the Twin was playing old Pal Viti movies."

"I haven't seen any of his movies, except for *Blaine's Move*, which was based on a short story by Dalivia Plaut."

"I love *Blaine's Move*," she says. "You haven't seen *Organized Criminals*?"

I shake my head.

"I don't think so."

"That's a good one," she says. "It's about the mafia taking over this publishing company that specializes in publishing children's books."

"I've heard about it, haven't seen it, though."

"What's your favorite Dalivia Plaut story?"

I pause for a moment.

"*The Snipper,*" I say, "Wait. I take that back. . . *The Red Wash*."

"Is that the one about the car wash that eats people?"

"Yeah."

Jazz rolls her eyes.

"What?"

"Nothing," she says, looking me over.

"What's your—"

"Personally, I like her less horror-ey stuff. Like *The Day of The Slaughter*."

"I like that one."

That was Jimmy's favorite.

I smile.

Jazz smiles, closed but warm, and directs it toward me. We keep on walking and talking at the same time.

I was never good at multitasking, but I'm getting really good at it.

IV

JAZZ and I stroll to her workplace, a thrift shop called Lassie's, where her boss is ringing up orders from customers while a few antsy people wait for help. Her boss is moving as if he's wearing skates, gliding back and forth behind the register, removing security tags or sensors or whatever from clothes with that staple gun thingy, then folding clothes, then bagging the clothes, then giving customers their change.

"Shit. . . " Jazz says in a rush, ". . . I totally forgot my phone. Do you have the time by any chance?"

I pull my bookbag in front of my body and zip open my bag. I read the time on Thomas's watch, turn my eyes to Jazz, who's nibbling on her lip. Her unblinking eyes are glued to the inside of my bookbag, which makes me wonder if her unsettled state is brought on from her being AWOL or from *what* remains inside my bookbag.

I turn my eyes below and see the urn protruding from my bookbag.

I zip the bookbag close and tell her clearly, "Two-twenty."

Jazz turns to the store.

"Eric is going to kill me," she says while trying to hold in her laughter.

"Eric?"

"My boss."

I momentarily feel a wave of relief wash over my body.

"You won't get fired, will you?" I ask.

Jazz gives a shake of her head.

"No," she says, now casually. "I'll just tell him I lost track of time."

She turns toward her boss, who acknowledges Jazz standing outside. The two share a moment, her boss glaring at Jazz while Jazz holds out her finger and mouths, "One second." Her boss, in return, shakes his head in disapproval.

I acknowledge Eric's distress from the way he moves frantically around the checkout counter. Jazz acknowledges this.

The whole crowd of customers acknowledges this as well. However, I get the feeling that Jazz will be fine.

"I better get going," Jazz says as she waits for me to respond.

"Yeah," I say. "Of course."

As she takes a couple of steps away, she stops and turns back around.

"Lemme see your phone," she demands.

"Ah—don't have it on me," I lie, as if me not having a phone on me could be the same as me saying, "I left it in the car" or "I forgot to bring it out with me."

Either way, she buys it.

"Well, you have a pen?"

I pull out one from the side pocket of my bookbag. All that remains of the pen are the guts; however, it still has ink to write. I hand the skeletal pen to Jazz. She'll have to make due. In return, she fishes out a clean napkin from her leftover bag of food. Tells me to turn around. So, I do without asking any questions. She places the napkin on my back for support. A wave of comfort slides over my body as she scribbles down her number. She hands the napkin to me. She catches me staring at the number. Quit staring. Act normal.

"Call me sometime," she says easily, as if she's used to saying the words.

I drift from my daze.

"Yeah," I say as I look into Jazz's glossy eyes. "Definitely," I tell her.

And that is that.

TECHNICALLY KNOT
ST@LKING

ACCORDING to the website Finder, Jazz's birth name is Samantha J. Caldwell—J, standing for Jasper, like Casper, as in that cute and friendly ghost, only spelled with a J, not a C. She lives approximately five miles from Cyber Jaxx's—in fact, 5.3 miles to be exact—in an apartment complex called Glendale Straits, APT.101, with her nonwhite mom, Rosa Caldwell, originally born in Panama City by the name Rosa Fuentes—as I've said, I've been wrong before. Wouldn't be the first time. Rosa moved to the States at the age of twelve, then "legally" acquired her American citizenship shortly after. Five years later, she won Miss Teen for the state of California but ended up losing to a blonde haired, blue-eyed gal from Texas in Miss Teen America. At the age of twenty-four, Rosa married Woodrow Caldwell, a local saxophonist who played in a band from Sinclair Leprieur, Louisiana, called *The Shift*. Probably where Jasper received the name Jazz—if I had to guess.

When Jazz was fifteen, her father passed from cardiac failure. I'll make sure to do more research on him, but for now, I focus on Jazz.

The last time she logged into her Chatterz account was two days ago—just moments before she knocked me flat on my ass.

The last chirp reads:

DRINKING COFFEE WHILE DOODLING ANGELS :)

—

Below the chirp: a partial pic that Jazz took with her phone's camera. The only visible part of the drawing—since half of it is cut off and most of the pic is the top of Jazz's hand holding a black fine point Sharpie—are two finely-detailed wings extending from the shoulder blades of what is supposed to be a sketch of what may or may not be an angel.

Jazz is an active user, as she mentioned during our recent conversation. She frequently goes on Chatterz and chirps about her job and takes marketable selfies with Eric at Lassie's, as well as random shots of her drawings or "doodlings". Her boss is Eric Knowles. Last year, he worked as an art instructor at Santa Anne, a middle school outside Los Dementes. He was laid off for inappropriately touching one of his students—*inappropriately touching*, as in he hugged one of his students. I don't really see what the big deal is, but whatever. The student's mother found out. Two days later, Eric was fired. Now, he sells used clothes. Jazz happens to be one of his employees; however, I'm sure he keeps his "distance" from Jazz. From his many pictures of arts and crafts abundantly scattered around his house, as well as the feminine man named Pablo seen in most of his pictures on his PhotoBag page, Jazz doesn't seem like Eric's type. If you know what I mean.

According to Jazz's profile on her website, she is a local artist who specializes in movie posters, which makes sense now that I think about it. She's talented, as in really talented, and has the skill to go all the way to the top—unlike some artists I've known. Most of her activity on social media is during the day. She also has a LINKEDUP page with over seventy-five connections, which isn't too bad for an artist. She posts artwork on her social media sites as well.

At night, though, Jazz is a ghost.

I scroll through her MyCircle page and search through her many photo albums. Most of the pics are decade-old Polaroids taken with her father, who's black. Most, if not all of them are tagged with the hashtag, Throwback Thursday, or #tbt; and the pics are from when Jazz was much younger— not even a teenager. Lately, she doesn't post many photos of herself. The last photo was posted eight days ago: a selfie of herself standing in front of a mirror, and from the way she's dressed, she looks as if she's spending a night out. She's wearing a rather skimpy lime green dress—see-through, depending on what angle you look at it on the monitor.

Jazz isn't showing her tits or anything, although she might as well be.

\\

I grab a newspaper from the dispenser and flip to the local ENTERTAINMENT section where I find the listings of movie times at the Twin Cinema. It's Thursday too. Just my luck. I remember Jazz told me a story about how she used to go to the movies on Thursdays. She'll like that I come off as a good listener when I'm far from one. Girls like guys who listen. After all, I don't know any girl who would turn down a movie ticket.

I skim through the times and find one at nine-twenty.

Two movies are playing tonight. The first one is *The Good, The Bad, and The Ugly*—which I've seen over a hundred times—and the other one is *Blood and Black Lace*, which I've heard of but never seen.

\\\

AFTER spending over ten minutes pacing around a payphone, I give Jazz a call. I ask her if she can talk and she says that she's just taking five, as in a five minute break.

I ask her if she would like to hang out tonight and her voice rises over the phone as she says, "Absolutely, I mean," she corrects herself. "Yeah. I would really like that."

Jazz tells me she gets off work at eight o'clock.

I tell her that I'll meet her a little after eight, near the Amazing Pretzel stand.

After I hang up with Jazz, I drive to the Twin and buy two tickets for the film, *Blood and Black Lace*, from the box office.

\\\\

I decide to spend the rest of the afternoon at the beach.

I seek out a quiet spot away from tourists and clean my revolver, which helps me relax.

After I'm done cleaning the revolver, I plant myself on the hood of my car and smoke from a brand new pack of cigarettes. I light up each smoke with a black Zippo with blue gorilla sporting a pair of Wayfarer sunglasses. I used to own a Zippo back in the day—that was before I lost it. Way back when, I lost a lot of things.

As I light up another smoke and place my new Zippo in the pocket within the larger pocket—the pocket's pocket—I realize that I've run out of room. My fingers come across a folded piece of paper underneath the bottle cap. I make my fingers into a pair of scissors and pull out the paper from the pocket. Unfold it. Nico's *name* is written on the paper, as well as a phone number—possibly *his* phone number.

I lean back and rest on the windshield and stare at the name, *Nico*. I now remember having a discussion with Nico about "old friends" at his house. Somehow, Anthony Foster's name found its way into the conversation. Nico said he hadn't talked to Anthony in years. He said they were no longer tight—*they*. Did he mean himself or his father? Anthony was much older than Nico. Or, maybe they, as in Nico and Anthony, had like a big brother-little brother relationship. Occasionally, they bumped into one another—Nico and Anthony, I mean. However, they never hung out together—or at least not like they did before when his father. . . I draw a blank. *His father what?* Nico turned really quiet after he mentioned his father's name. Changed the subject, actually. That, I remember. I never asked Nico about his father, even though the question was resting on the edge of my tongue. We talked about girls, I think. Then, I was sideswiped from behind. Drew threw a punch, then I countered and broke his arm in half. Nico was there when I was with Jamie, smoking cigarettes, watching. Nico didn't join us, did he? I remember the both of us were on the beach at some point in the night. I remember his moonlit eyes glowing through Jamie's hair, like two white marbles hovering in the night. Rewind to those moments leading up to the beach. I was hanging out with Nico. Correct. We were smoking. Correct. *But* not on the beach, though. We were walking on a street. Two cute girls—one, I remember, had a headful of red curls—whistled at us. They drove off, honking at us, screaming. Nico and I made our way to my car. . .

I sit up from the windshield and study the side of the driver's door.

Above the door handle, I find a mark about the size of an eyelash—Nico's hand once rested there. He was wearing a ring, but it wasn't a wedding band. It was something else, something important to him. I was standing in front of him, and we were talking in private. I can't remember what we were talking about, but we were talking all right. The both of us walked back to his house where most of the partygoers were calling it a night. A famished Jamie was stumbling about in the kitchen. I think the mollies were working their magic on her. She was feeling as hot as a firecracker. She looked so good, I remember, breasts swollen, eyes like hooks. Nico grabbed a pen, as well as a piece of paper from a drawer and then he handed me something just in case I dipped before he crashed.

I turn my attention back to the number in my hand—*this*. He handed me this piece of paper. That's why I hid Nico's number in *this* pocket, the smallest of pockets, the most valuable pocket where I hide things, especially things I don't want to lose.

Nico is alive.
I didn't kill him.
Or did I?

EPISODE 4

MORTAL

COMBAT

(L E A R N I N G   H O W   T O
K I L L)

I T doesn't dawn on me that the Twin is paying homage to "Giallo" films until I read the direct message sent by Flip.

If you haven't heard of the word *giallo* (Giallo—being a type of genre in Italian literature or film—which means "yellow," is based off a series of mystery novels called II Giallo Mondadori, published with a trademark "yellow" background on the cover whereas, in film, giallo has come to be known as murder mysteries, or what most people call "whodunits," which was popularized during the mid 1960's through the 1970's), more than likely, you've probably seen its influence in American slashers such as *Friday the 13th, Nightmare on Elm Street, Halloween*, basically, any film where some hottie is being chased around by some mask-wearing stalker with a knife or some other sharp object.

Every Saturday night, the orderlies used to play giallo films at Red Pines—bizarre, I know—but the crazies really got a kick out of them. There was this one crazy, a local. Buttons was his name. He was admitted to Red Pines three months before I arrived. The story goes that his mother walked in on him while he was making a smoothie out of their two-year-old Chihuahua, Lupe. So his mother claimed. After she scraped whatever was left of Lupe from the blender, the only thing she could recognize was the button on his collar. Poor Lupe. Buttons kept the button as a souvenir. Earned his name Buttons because he carried around these buttons. All types of buttons, too: shirt buttons, stud buttons, shank buttons. The kid liked buttons and, not to mention, giallo films, one in particular, *The Man with Icy Eyes*. Buttons wouldn't shut up about the film. I don't know why he was drawn to that one film in particular. He just was. Maybe he liked the story. Or, maybe he could somewhat relate to the icy-eyed man in the film. Who knows? You see, at Red Pines, you leave your questions at the door and your reason to the professionals.

At least that was the way they wanted the system to work.

I decide to minimize CLUBHOPPER69*_*'s Chatterz page for the time being.

I check Flip's PhotoBag page, which seems to be getting the most activity lately. He recently posted several pics, one being posted an hour ago. The other two posted the other night: one, I notice, was taken at the Palace. What do you know? I catch a glimpse of Moses standing among the group of clubbers. What the hell was he doing there? I can hardly recognize Moses. His face looks like a withered piece of fruit. He's holding up a glass of what looks like ice in one hand, and he's been moving about like a blind man from the way he stands sideways, as if the floor was made of quicksand or something wobbly.

I lean even closer to the monitor and see Nico standing in the background.

A momentary feeling of relief cleans my consciousness and for a moment, I feel as if I'm Baron Frankenstein shouting out, "He's alive!"

Flip was actually the one who sneaked up on me when I first introduced myself to Nico. My left hand was reaching for something—I think it was my switchblade—then I was ready to slice and dice. None of the slicing or dicing part happened, only the stabbing late to come that night. Flip slapped me on the shoulder, chirping like a finch, "What's good, Philly Blunt!"

I find another pic on Flip's page, the most recent one. Flip's feet are erected upright, his stubby toes curled inward like the legs of a dead spider. He's lounging on a crummy couch in his crummy apartment, watching an episode of *Seinfeld*. The one about the Soup Nazi. Flip's comment below describes exactly what he's doing in the pic, laying on the couch with a hangover, watching reruns of *Seinfeld*.

I reopen CLUBHOPPER69*_*'s Chatterz page and reread Flip's gibberish that he sent not me, I mean, "Penelope." Apparently, he wrote the message when he was seeing double. To sum it up in one sentence: Flip likes Penelope a lot—I mean, *a lot*—as if he didn't get his point across by sending her another dick pic.

I insert the USB flash drive into the back of the computer and scroll through each pic inside the folder named PENELOPE until I come across one that I haven't used yet: Penelope posing in front of a standing mirror in her cramped dorm room, flashing her fake, rubbery tits for the phone's camera. I send the tit pic to Flip. That should tie him over for the time being.

Then, I check out Yogi's PhotoBag page. I wouldn't call him a social butterfly like Flip or even Yolanda, Yogi's older sister, but there's no doubt that he shares the traits of a sheep. Occasionally, he'll post a pic of himself scuttling around town. He's part of Nico's circle, I learn. Nico can be seen in several of his pics, hanging, chilling, cruising. Yogi doesn't seem like a threat, though. According to Yogi's posts, he's a real softy. He actually got his name from the legendary baseball player, Yogi Bear. A soft bear, you can imagine. Like the one you want to cradle in your arms when you're still shitting in your diapers. His recent post is a pic of a strange device called *the* PleasureSaber™.

The comment below: "Got my lady a brand new present for her birthday!!!"

I type the words *Pleasure* and *Saber* in the search engine and find a business website at the top of the page.

The circles, I remember, on Nico's wall, each one depicting an orifice of the female body: mouth, genitals, you get the point. Nico and I were having a conversation about the circular paintings of the sex toys while hanging out on his raised deck, drinking skunky beer from a red cup, smoking cigarettes down to the filter. Huh? How about that?

I pull my thoughts away from the other night and remove the USB flash drive from the computer and smash it with the ball of the chair's leg. I brush the crushed remains into my palm and flush them down the toilet.

\\

PUTTING aside what happened at Nico's house, I concentrate on Jazz and pull up her MyCircle page.

The movie starts in less than two hours or so, which gives me plenty of time to get to know Jazz a little better—in person, that is. I'm not sure if I should tell her the real reason why I'm visiting Topside. She'll probably want to know what I plan on doing while I'm here, if I plan on kicking back and enjoying the beach vibes or if I plan on getting a job like a normal person would do. I can tell her that I'm on indefinite vacation. Playing it by ear. Day to day—

—Why don't you just finish what you've started?

I know Moses is right on the nose, as much as I don't agree with him. I should *finish* what I've started. Now that Flip is out of the picture for good, I should call the number on the piece of paper. I should pursue a friendship with Nico—if he's still alive, which, I'm certain he is—in order to acquire more information on the whereabouts of his father. And now with Anthony Foster out of the picture as well, I should investigate the other suspects involved in the shooting, the current owner of Crystal Palace, Luther Bishop, and the mysterious Smoker Man. I should be doing a lot of things, like straightening up my act or fulfilling Moses' "small" favor.

I should be doing all of these things yet somehow I always find an excuse.

I leave Cyber Jaxx's and walk to the boardwalk where I kill a good twenty minutes by roaming around a head shop. I arrive about ten minutes early at the Amazing Pretzel. Jazz is smoking a cigarette and staring at a sinking sun at the now reopened pier, Main Pier. The sight of the red sky brings me relief, and I can't help but think about Jimmy, again. I see that Jazz has changed clothes, which is a good sign. She's wearing a glittery sequined top with gold and black stripes and a pair of tight black pants, not leggings but tight enough to pass as leggings.

I play it casual and sneak up behind her without her knowing and give her a tap on her right shoulder. She turns to her right and finds an empty space next to her; then she turns to her left, wide-eyed and defensive, and finds me standing there with both of my hands open. Grinning like a goon.

"Hey there," she says and gives me a hug.

I embrace the hug.

She smells so good, like cotton candy.

When I ask Jazz about the smell, she tells me that it's coming from the perfume she's wearing.

"I like it," I tell her.

"Thanks," she replies.

As she leans back against the railing, she pulls out a pack of menthols and offers me one.

I pull out one of mine and smoke with her.

"Cool lighter," she says.

I hold up the lighter for her.

"You like it?"

"Yeah," she says.

"Didn't know you smoked," I say, pointing at her smoke.

"I don't," Jazz responds with a typical shrug. "More of a social smoker. I went through a phase where I smoked like a pack a day. I know it's terrible. It's like a double-edged sword. My nana smoked ever since she was like sixteen, and she smoked all the way up to eighty-four before she passed away."

"She died from smoking?"

"No," Jazz says shortly. "She fell down the stairs. Broke her hip. Never recovered."

"Sorry to hear."

"It's okay," Jazz says playfully. "That was a really long time ago. Anyway, I don't smoke that much anymore. Why? Does that bother you?"

"Nah," I reply and take a drag. "I'm not one to judge."

Silence.

Again.

I try to think of something to say, but I have nothing.

Maybe it's okay that I have nothing.

Jazz doesn't have anything to say either, which is okay, I guess.

I look Jazz over; and she's cool with me not having anything to say.

I think she enjoys my company.

I enjoy hers.

I'm glad I came out.

She interrupts the silence with a sharp exhale.

"So, what do you wanna do?" she asks.

I pull out the two tickets from my pocket.

"I was thinking about catching a movie. . . "

I show the ticket to Jazz.

"And you just so happen to have two tickets?"

"What do you say?"

She leans closer and reads the movie title on the ticket.
"I'm down," she says with a smile.

\|\|\|

SINCE the movie doesn't start until an hour and a half, we decide to kill time by hitting up the store Jazz works at, Lassie's, which isn't too far from the theatre. We spend a good twenty minutes or so hanging around the place, shuffling through clothes, trying on clothes from the different eras and whatnot. The place is dead. Except for the zombie playing on her phone behind the cash register—a twenty-something who, by the way, doesn't get along with Jazz, despite them being colleagues—it's pretty much just Jazz and me and it feels as if we're the only two survivors left after a fallout. I like the feeling with Jazz and me having the entire world at our fingertips. We'd make it a little less cruel. We'd make that our first obligation. Then, we'd kill all of the leftover zombies. Get them out of our hair. Then, from there, we'd make the world as big as we wanted.

A gang of hipsters and skater kids loiters outside the thrift shop, but they mostly keep to themselves—like the *Lost Boy* kids dressed in black, the ones playing billiards in the back of Galatia. Wanderers of the Free World, *my* world, our world. Jazz keeps prodding at me, insisting I try on these absurd outfits, one being an outfit from the Sixties: corduroy jacket, bell bottoms, a silky collar shirt that looks like the floral wallpaper in Grandma Backer's house, a neglected wooden box of house built in the wake of the Great Depression. The house reminded me of an animal that was tranquilized with a dart, then dumped off at the outskirts of an unnatural captivity filled with these cheap, low-income houses surrounded by corporate restaurants, cafés, and shopping malls. Last I've heard the house was scheduled to be demolished. I'm glad someone mustered enough courage to put the poor house out of its misery, but whatever.

I try on the outfits in the dressing room, then, with my "new" look, exit like some bashful four-year-old walking into a room filled with a bunch of unknown relatives. I shrug, as if I'm seeking approval, *her* approval. I make eye contact with Jazz, who's shaking her head not in disgust but more like disdain; yet, she seems almost amused from the permanent smile on her face. I think she gets a kick out of watching me make a fool of myself the same way a child laughs at a grown man being punched or kicked or hurt. I like the way her laugh sounds, a boisterous cry out to the world without any regard of her surroundings.

I swallow my pride and change into yet another outfit, like the one before, as quickly as I can, and then, like the one before, undress as quickly as I can. Jazz's hand grazes my shoulder as she helps me adjust the outfit. My eyes make contact with hers, both of them shrinking in curiosity as they fall onto both of my shoulders. She pinches the muscle along my neck, the trapezius muscle. Then, she squeezes. Really hard.

"You're strong," she tells me.

"I used to workout."

"Why'd you stop?"

I shrug one of my shoulders, a half-shrug.

"Don't have time," I tell Jazz as I drift in a trance.

I can't help but think about the time Jimmy came home from Rehab, as well as the long hours I spent building myself up into a perfect beast—shoulders and back, especially. I had Thomas's shoulders, like a sturdy beam running across my upper back. I felt like I was building myself into a piece of property, a structure that would be able to withstand an infinite number of natural disasters; and if it ever came down to me carrying Jimmy on my back, I had two finely chiseled shoulders to support him.

I hear Jazz's voice from a distance.

I suddenly snap from my daze.

Again, Jazz asks, "Are you okay?"

"Yeah," I mumble, unsure whether or not Jazz heard my answer.

We make our way to the checkout counter.

Jazz flicks her head into a nod toward the zombie, a Janis Joplin look-alike chilling behind the counter—according to Jazz, that "spoiled bitch," Melanie—and uses the money that she received earlier from the Russian to purchase a black jacket made of faux leather.

While she's waiting for Melanie to ring her up, she puts on a pair of bronze earrings of a lanceolate leaf and models them in the rotating mirror on the counter. In a way, Jazz reminds me of Patria, her carefree attitude similar to the kids from the Galatia; yet, at the same time, she's absolutely nothing like

Patria or any other girl I've dated. She reads the same books as me, watches the same shows as me—according to her My-Circle page, *Lost* happens to be one of her favorite TV shows of all time—which one would think that she would think the same way as me.

I decide to buy the earrings for Jazz, even though I know it's way too soon to be buying things for a girl whom I hardly know yet—that is, in person.

"Really?" she says, bordering rapture.

I nod *yes*.

She flaunts them in front of me, smiling from ear to ear. She doesn't even have to tell me that she likes the earrings. Her face speaks for itself.

"They look *great* on you," I say.

"You think?"

"Yeah."

I can afford to buy Jazz the earrings. I have the money, although I could've found other ways to acquire them.

IV

JAZZ and I are passing hipsters or skater kids—whatever they call themselves nowadays—when all of a sudden a guy wearing a red and black Los Dementes Red Devils baseball shirt stops me. He has the look of a person blindsided by nostalgia: dropped jaw, starry, swelled eyes. I can imagine a memory somewhere behind his eyes, blossoming. The guy claims that he knows me, that I look familiar—an old friend? Old classmate? Old lover?

Jazz remains speechless when I tell the guy that I don't know him and that he has me mistaken for someone else.

"No." The guy leans in closer, inspects my face as if I'm wall art. "*Jimmy*," he suddenly broadcasts. "It's me. Raúl." The guy holds out his hands as if he's inviting me into an awkward hug. "From West Harleton. Remember?"

His arms remain open. My eyes track the gold, chunky ring on his left index finger, which looks like a pimped-out Ringpop. The front of the ring reads, "NATIONAL CHAMPIONS."

Raúl Suárez, center fielder for WHU. The guy had an arm made of rubber. They used to call him Magnum, like the pistol. I don't know him, personally. Raúl was a freshman at

Richport High the same year Jimmy was shot. I remember Jimmy spoke fondly of the Dominican, his potential, his skills, his overbearing "swag"—Raúl was a cocky son of a bitch who thought he was the greatest ball player to step on the field. Not sure if he still carries the same attitude. Not too long after the shooting, the West Harleton Salamanders won the National Championship. Without Jimmy.

"Raúl Suárez?" he says, as if he's interrogating his own self.

"You got the wrong person, pal," I tell Raúl.

"Come on," he says. "It's me. Raúl."

"I don't know you."

"Jimmy—"

He touches me on the arm.

I push his hand away.

He holds out his hands again, but this time in surrender.

Jazz and I walk away.

I glance over my shoulder at Raúl. I overhear him say to his girlfriend, "I swear, he looks just like a guy I used to play ball with."

As we walk away, Jazz says closely, "Who was that?"

"I have no clue," I tell her.

Jazz doesn't need to know what Raúl Suárez has been up to these days.

Neither do I, really.

V

WHEN we arrive at the Twin, I buy the largest bucket of popcorn for Jazz.

"No butter please," she emphasizes to me, not the server.

I hand the server the money and tell him exactly what Jazz told me just as he's about to smother her popcorn in butter.

As we leave the refreshment area, Jazz asks me if I want any popcorn. I tell her no thanks yet she insists that I take a handful. After some convincing, I take a couple of bites and think of something else besides throwing up all over my date. The last thing she wants to take away from the date is her clothes stained with my puke. I desperately think about her earrings and how I have good taste in fashion, how they compliment Jazz's bumblebee-patterned shirt. I think about how good the earrings look on her as I breathe carefully, inhaling through my nose and then exhaling through my mouth without drawing too much attention to myself.

We walk down a long stretch of hallway covered in old movie posters. Jazz points out one in particular, a movie poster from the original *Terminator* movie.

The sign below says, "Next Thursday."

My stomach settles a bit. If everything goes smoothly, maybe I can take her next week.

"My favorite," she tells me.

"Yeah," I say. "Mine too."

"Not too long ago, I did a movie poster for one of their 'tbt' nights."

"Tbt?"

"Throwback Thursday."

Right. Throwback Thursday. I forgot. Silly me.

She scoops another handful of popcorn into her mouth.

"What kind of posters do you do?" I ask her after she finishes chewing, then swallows.

"Depends," she says casually. "I once did a poster for *Mad Max*."

"Which one?"

"*Beyond Thunderdome*."

Makes sense.

"So, you're an artist, like an artist-artist?"

"On the side—yeah," she says clearly for me. "I'd love to do it full time, but the competition is fierce."

"They don't call it 'starving artist' for no reason."

"Not me," Jazz says and takes another bite of popcorn. She says from the corner of her mouth, "A girl's gotta eat."

She goes on to say—after she finishes chewing—that the *Mad Max* poster was on display for about two weeks. The Twin paid her two-fifty for a copy of the print. They unveiled the poster at one of their "TBT" Nights. She says that the manager in charge of the theatre made it into a big deal. The whole staff was there. They made Jazz give a presentation, as well as a speech before she unveiled the poster. She tells me that she "hated" talking in front of crowds.

"There were only like ten people," she says, "but still, I was *so* nervous."

"I hate talking in front of crowds."

"I used to," she says. "I once took a public speaking course at HPCC. It was okay, I guess."

"Not me," I reply.

"Really?"

I shake my head *no*.

She shrugs.

"Maybe you hated giving speeches in a past life."

"*Maybe*," I say.

We arrive at our theatre. My stomach begins to tighten with nervousness. I hold the door open for Jazz, who, in return, says cutely, "Thank you." We walk through a narrow tunnel as dark as the night until we arrive at a dimly lit theatre, which is nearly full of people who are staring at us. Or, are they staring at me? I want them to stop looking at us. I want them stop looking, in general. I want them to mind their own business. That's when more tightness comes back, that relentless fist, starting with my throat and then my chest. I turn my focus to the sea, the serenity, the feel of each grain of sand between my toes as the tide rushes toward the shore. Tomorrow, I tell myself, I'll take a walk on the beach. I'll say my goodbyes to Jimmy. Maybe Jazz can join us, but then again. . . I've already spent enough time on her. And money. She has a job. She can afford these things. What has she done for me? What can she offer me? What does she get out of all of this? I don't need her. I'll get some action tonight. Then, I'll scrape her off my heel and be done with her. I have Jimmy. I have more important things to do.

And, Jazz doesn't involve any of them.

Suddenly, I feel a hand grab me by the forearm, but I close my eyes and I realize it's just my arm grazing the side of the railing—*did you say something?*

I look up and Jazz is staring at me.

"What is it?" she asks again.

I tense up for a moment.

"Huh?" I say.

"Never mind," she says and proceeds up the steps.

I nudge Jazz on the shoulder and tell her in a flat, mechanical voice, "I'll be back." She giggles, but it's not until I make it to the MEN'S restroom that I realize why Jazz was laughing.

I switch on the faucet and splash my face with cool water and practice breathing from my belly. My breath is like some kind of magical housefly disappearing from one passageway to another. I make the water warmer and dam all ten of my fingers underneath the water: a method I learned from a Chinese holistic doctor.

As the nausea begins to wear off, I turn my eyes toward the mirror.

The door opens behind me and I stop what I'm doing. In the reflection of the mirror, I see a man dressed in a gray suit walking to the urinal. I locate this pale scar on the back of his neck. I know that scar, which means I know the man.

What the hell are you doing here?

He doesn't respond. Instead, he starts to whistle something merry like "Mary Had a Little Lamb." I know the sound is coming from the faucet, the whistling. Go back to the theatre. Ignore him.

Moses finishes urinating, shakes it twice, and then turns his shoulder. Somewhere over his shadowy face, I witness a smirk. I look down at my pants to see that water has splashed over my groin. Shit. I dry my pants with a towel.

—You already know exactly where your relationship with this girl is going. Moses squares himself to me, and he's two shades beyond angry. The outcome isn't going to be pleasant. I'm going to ask you again. Why are you wasting your time on her?

You're jealous.

Do you hear yourself right now?

Do you?

All Moses cares about is himself and I voice my complaint to him, but he drowns out my voice by flushing the urinal.

Just as Moses takes another step closer, the bathroom door opens again.

An older man walks inside and nods a civil hello as he walks to the closest urinal.

I finish washing up and then head back to the theatre.

I've gotten this far into the night. I don't need him. I don't need a fix. It's all in my head. He's all in my head. . .

I'm back in the theatre, searching for Jazz. An arm suddenly stretches above the seats and waves at me. I track down the face underneath the hand. Jazz. I nod back. Somehow, she's found two seats in the middle—or, what I like to call the "sweet spot." She's smarter than smart. She knows her theatres. Either it's a coincidence that she found the sweet spot, or she is fully aware of the sweet spot. Very few know about the sweet spot. Not too close to the screen but not too far back. The sound is perfect in the sweet spot.

I find my way back to Jazz and sit down next to her.

More relieved.

"Good seats," I tell her.

"Yeah," she says. "The sweet spot."

I nod my head.

"Right," I parrot. "The sweet spot."

The lights darken and I quit thinking about all of the wrongs and focus on all of the rights. Right here. This is my right. Me. Right here. Sitting in a movie theatre with a sweet girl in the sweet spot. Forget about last night and the night before and the night before that. Forget about everything. This is as real as it is right.

Jazz pokes me on the arm with her elbow and offers me more popcorn.

I reach into the bucket, grab a handful of popcorn, shove the popcorn into my mouth, then chew and swallow before I can hold a thought in my head.

I calm myself as soon as I hear the drum roll of the film playing, a pale blue cloud billowing over the screen with the words *Gloria Film* pushing toward us.

The reel is old, from all the dust and scratches on the film. I like the way it looks: blemished with age, like an antiquity that only increases in value over time. Just like the *Spider Man* comic book: an investment. The Twin doesn't play any coming attractions. I don't expect the theatre to play any, especially from a film that was released decades ago.

Has it really been that long?

Jazz lifts the armrest and places the bucket between the two seats, and together we munch on popcorn.

Every now and then, our hands graze one another as we dig through the mound of popcorn and pull out handfuls at a time.

This is what normal people do.

It feels good to be normal, if only for a while.

VI

BY the time Inspector Sylvester closes in on the masked killer, I'm watching another film, not *Blood and Black Lace*. I turn away from the screen and peek over at Jazz, her slack face as still as a painting as it basks in the glow of the silver screen. I'm confused—at first—as to why Jazz's gawking at the film; then, every thought I carry inside my head becomes as lucid as the lines on the palm I hold before me. Jazz is not gawking, *not* watching. She's motionless, too. A body stuck on pause. A freeze frame. I look around and notice that the theatre is deserted, that only Jazz and I are sitting in the sweet spot of the last locale remaining on Earth, a solitary fortress of both amnesty and amusement to protect us from the beasts that roam the scorched wasteland.

Once more, I glance down at the palm of my hand and then at the other—my left one—which is locked with Jazz's hand.

Blood and Black Lace is still playing; however, it looks much different in quality. The film doesn't look as old as it did when it first started. I wonder if they're playing an extended cut or an alternate edition.

On the screen, the masked killer is pushing a woman's face into flames, her hands clawing at the sides of a furnace, screaming, fighting. She reaches around in a last moment of desperation, grabs hold of the killer's mask, and rips it off, revealing a face, Moses' face. Moses strikes her in the back of the head with a club—dazing her—then he tosses the woman into the blazing furnace and closes the door behind her.

The person being burned, I notice, isn't the woman from the movie. It's not even a woman at all. It's a man. The man, I realize, is Jimmy and he's trapped inside a box about the size of a coffin. We see the inside of the box, Jimmy hopelessly kicking and punching at the walls around him, trying to claw himself to freedom. During the attempt, his nails don't break off his fingertips. Yet, each one easily peels away like a stickie note. The flames rise from beneath Jimmy's naked body and cut through his blackened flesh, slowly turning it to ash. I can even feel the heat of the flames tightly pressed against my face. I'm sweating bullets. Godly sounds of thunder rumbling above, then the ceiling gives way to a night sky. I turn back around. The screen is gone. The theatre, gone. I'm back on the same bridge from my nightmares. Strobe lights of lightning flash all around me.

I'm dying again.

Besides me, two men are holding my body upright.

One of them is holding my hand—my left one.

I recognize his face, Anthony's pale, lifeless face. Strings of blood are gushing from his neck; yet, his grip around my arm is as tight as death. In front of me stands another man, *not* Nico. He looks like Nico yet he is much older than Nico. He is Nico's father, Conrad. I know this movie. This is it.

Jimmy's movie.

Jimmy's ending.

Jimmy's beginning.

I release my slippery hand from Anthony's hand and pull myself from Jimmy's body.

Now, I'm standing on the outside.

I'm no longer the victim of a crime.

Now, I'm the sole observer. The shadow watching the fate of my brother.

Flashes of lightning cut across the black sky, bringing out parts of Conrad's unhealthy face.

A smirk, I see, as he raises the Glock and points the barrel at Jimmy's head.

He speaks to him in a foreign dialect. Italian, I believe. I recognize the one word from his language: *Dio*, meaning God. When you meet God, Conrad says in Italian, ask Him to forgive me.

A bolt of lightning flickers across my eyes!

Then, I hear a gunshot!

I feel another hand shaking me on my shoulder. . .

My eyes flicker open!

Confused again, I look around and see people standing from their seats and then walking toward the exits of the theatre.

I turn to Jazz, still in a state of utter confusion, then I turn to the screen, the ending credits.

"Were you sleeping?" she asks me.

I look around the theatre once more.

"I must've dozed off. . . "

"It happens," she says with a shrug, "I guess."

She looks at me with that same look the cute waitress from the Cove was giving me the other day.

I hate that look.

"I know exactly what you need right now," Jazz says.

"You do?"

Jazz nods *yes*.

She does.

"What?"

She holds out her hand.

I grab it.

"Let's go," she says.

Hand in hand, I follow Jazz's lead.

We leave the Twin behind us.

VII

SOUTH of the Point is New Town, a snug city on the "other" side of the tracks. Jazz instructs me to park next to Ron's boat shop. I do as she tells me to. I park the car. She steps out of the car without saying a word. I follow suit, wondering what Jazz is up to, considering she's been acting strange ever since we left the movie theatre.

We walk through the edge of town for about a quarter of a mile until we reach the coastline. Each house looks like the silhouette of a baby mountain, alive in its own peculiar way with its windows like the eyes of a subterranean creature, so many of them and so bright.

(I once read an article in *Gossip* about a lot of actors and celebrities having houses in New Town)

It's one thing to read about it and another to see it.

Finally, after not being able to hold out much longer, I ask Jazz, "Where are we going?"

"It's a surprise," Jazz says as she leads me across a desolate street. "If I were to tell you, then that would cease to make it a surprise. Now, wouldn't it?"

I keep up with Jazz the best I can as she races down a steep pathway, which runs into a narrow strip of sand.

The nerves are like a web of hot wires tightly laced across my body. My stomach, like the beach mansions, alive as it makes all sorts of peculiar sounds.

I focus on William's *words*, as well as my breathing, and chase Jazz to the beach.

After I catch my breath, Jazz tells me that we're here, as she points to a massive edifice perched on a natural overhang. She acts as if she knows the layout of the house, as if she's been here before. I never ask Jazz if she has. Yet, I take it— more or less—as a sign that she's being spontaneous. We make it to the edge of the property. The lights are off, except for the pool lights, which cast a golden haze over the foggy ridge of the bluff.

I keep my mouth shut and follow her up a wooden pathway, which leads to the pool behind the house.

Jazz removes her new jacket and strips down to her undies.

"Jazz," I say suddenly, "what are you doing?"

With a shrug, she says calmly, "It's better than coffee. Plus, it saves money on utilities. *And*, not only that, it beats going to the public pool."

"Seriously?"

"Do I look serious?" she asks me.

She sets her clothes, as well as her phone, aside and doesn't waste any time jumping into the pool.

I scope out the place, make sure nobody is home. Last thing I need right now is being busted for trespassing.

Jazz surfaces from the water after several tense moments of ole me frantically scanning the area. She tells me the water feels great.

I tell Jazz to get out of the pool.

Her eyes sharpen, seductive.

"What are you. . . "

Then, the word rolls right off her tongue.

". . . *yellow*?"

I remove my shirt, then my pants, then my socks, then toss my clothes behind an azalea.

I clear all of my thoughts and stiffen up my body into a board as I step into the pool. Once I hit the water, it feels like a shot of adrenaline. The water is surprisingly cold, but it feels better than great. I make sure to tell Jazz that it feels amazing.

Her only response, "Told you."

We don't say much as we tread water. I swim closer to Jazz, shivering from the coldness of the water. I notice her makeup has washed off, which makes her look even more attractive. The nerves are gone as well, the nausea. I feel just right. Everything about the night feels right.

As I advance closer to Jazz—preparing my lips for a kiss—the lights inside the house suddenly turn on!

A nicely dressed man with a Herculean-like frame steps from the backdoor.

Jazz grabs me by the arm and ducks into the water before I can embrace one last deep breath before going under. We swim to the side of the wall closest to the house and keep out of sight. I keep my eyes open under the water and study Jazz's face. Her eyes are shut, both of them tightly closed as if she's bracing herself for impact. That's when my mind ventures to darker places: me placing my hand over Jazz's mouth, then slipping my other hand around her throat. Squeeze. Then, abracadabra! She'll be no more, dissolved in the water like an Alka-Seltzer tablet. It'll be as if God plucked her from existence. All that would remain of her is a memory, fading like a photograph over time. By then, it'll be as if she never existed at all. Her parents will miss her. Relatives or other distant family members. Who else? She says she "knows" guys, but I know that she's lying. What about her art, the movie posters? Will they be thrown away? Will they be tossed aside in storage, left to age ungraciously on the dusty shelves of an ancient world? Or, even worse, will they somehow smuggle their way into the vast wilderness of the Internet until finally being found by a desperate artist who'll photoshop Jazz's name and pass her art off as his or her own?

I shake the thought from my head and gently touch Jazz on the arm.

She cracks open her eyes.

Both of them.

Her eyes are like a cat, peering at me; and for a moment, she barely tilts her head, like a cat does whenever it's confused or intrigued or flabbergasted or whatever it is cats do—even dogs do for that matter—when they tilt their head to the side like that.

Again, my devious mind travels to dark places and I'm thinking about what she sees when she stares at me. I want to rip her eyes from the sockets of her skull and replace them with mine. I wonder what she would see. Then, I want to remove her brain from her head and replace it with mine. I wonder exactly what she would think. Would she love me?

I swim closer and the blood rushes down my body and I'm excited. I feel Jazz getting warmer as well. She stops shaking, squeezes me on the arm, as if she's about to run out of oxygen and she's ready to surface.

The lights suddenly shut off above us.

I draw my eyes upward and I surface.

Jazz surfaces shortly after.

I crane my head above the pool and watch the nicely dressed man walking back inside the house. I turn to Jazz, and what do you know, she's smiling at me.

VIII

AFTER we get out of the pool, we take our clothes and scurry back down to the beach. Jazz asks me to hold her things while she washes the chlorine from her hair. She can't remove the smile from her face as she rinses off. Neither can I. She cuts off the shower, shivering from the coldness of the water. I hand her things back to her, including her smartphone.

During the exchange, my hand touches a photo protruding from her purse. I can't help but glance at the girl in the photo. The girl is overweight, borderline obsessed, unattractive.

As I move my eyes from the photo, I find Jazz's eyes attached to mine as well. I don't ask about the girl in the photo. Instead, she tells me bluntly that it's her. I look closer at the photo.

"That's you?" I say in surprise.

She wrings the water from her hair, wags both of her hands, then dries them.

"*Was* me," she says, her voice deflated.

I don't have any words to say.

Jazz tells me, "I know what you're thinking. . . "

"So, what?" I shrug, as she would do. "You used to be fat. No big deal."

Her mood suddenly changes from carefree to uncaring.

"It was to me," she says sharply.

I've offended her.

Not only am I the idiot, but I'm also the asshole.

Despite being wet, Jazz dresses—struggling somewhat as she slips into her pants.

"I didn't mean it like that," I say, as I too quickly put on my clothes.

Jazz doesn't respond. Don't expect her to, really. Now fully dressed, she walks away without me. I don't bother washing the chlorine from my hair. Instead, I follow Jazz. We keep our distance as we walk along the beach. I hurry my way closer to Jazz and decide to break the tension between us.

"I'm sorry," I say closely. "I really am. . . "

"There's no need to be sorry," she says, her voice short and bitter as she curls her arms into her chest.

She sniffs the phlegm from her nose and it sounds as if she's been crying during our distance apart, but I can't tell whether she's insecure about herself or she's just plain cold.

"You didn't know," she says, her voice now more vacant.

"But I *want* to know," I tell her and stop in front of her.

With her head held down, Jazz takes a step around me, but I cut her off again. She stops. I face Jazz, and she slowly lifts her head.

"I want to know everything about you."

"You do?"

"Yes."

"Why?"

"I don't know," I say without giving any thought to my answer.

Wrong words, I know, but they're the right words.

She appears as if she's in shock. I don't know why.

"I know it's none of my business. . . "

I pause for a second.

What am I doing?

Stay out of her business.

Then, I ask Jazz, "I want to know why you hold onto something that makes you so upset?"

She uncrosses her arms, thinks for a moment as she stares at the dark sea, and then answers, "You got it all wrong, *Jimmy*. I don't hold onto it because it makes me upset."

The sound of the name punches me in the gut, but I hold my ground.

I focus on Jazz.

"Then, why do you hold onto it?" I ask her.

"I hold onto it because it reminds me."

"Reminds you of what?"

"It reminds me of who I was," Jazz tells me. She looks away, struggling to look me in the eyes; and each time she peeks over at me, her eyes are lowered as if the sight of me repels her. "I have regrets. I'm ashamed of who I. . . " she tears up for a moment, ". . . who I *once* was." She turns her gaze to the sea again and then turns to me with the same steely gaze on her face, as if she's ready to charge into battle, an animal ready to pounce, pupils swollen with blackness. "I need to remember as much as I need air in my lungs," she says, her voice raised with hostility. "It gives me strength. Purpose. Who are you to judge?"

"Jazz, I'm not judging," I tell her.

She gives me that same look again, not the one I'm used to, the one I hate, but one that sends me into a state of me wanting to know more about her. She cracks open her mouth as if she wants to tell me something personal, but she can't find the right words to say. I can see pain behind her eyes.

Right then and there, I know she's holding onto a secret as dark as my own.

IX

JAZZ doesn't say a single word to me as we leave the beach. I've only been on one date with this girl—technically, two, if you're counting the walk on the boardwalk—and now, I'm in the doghouse.

As I'm walking toward the car, I notice Jazz is walking in the other direction, as if she doesn't want to ride with me.

Since I insist on driving her home without coming off as a dick, she finally caves in.

Her apartment is located in a rundown area between Topside and the Point, and most of the people who live around here, I notice, are either illegals or poor retirees who have fallen victim to the last recession. That's our wonderful government for you: one day, they're taking a thick cut from your paycheck or jacking up the cost of your premiums in order to pay for freeloaders or, as Susannah would say, "lazy people," and then, the next forty-some years later, they're sending you a check in the mail with not even half of what they originally took out. You wind up living your final years with just enough money to buy pet food. All of the time you spent feeding the system for nothing. The government had their lubricated hand up your ass the entire time and they turned out to be the greatest ventriloquist of all time.

I continue to receive the silent treatment as I park in front of her apartment.

"This is it," she says as she turns to me in a somewhat fragile state. "Don't get me wrong. I had a great time tonight—"

"—Despite me falling asleep and then insulting you?"

"Yes," she drawls. A smile scrambles free on her face. The silence worked out in my favor.

I feel relieved from Jazz's smile.

"I had a great time too." I switch off the ignition and pause and think carefully about my next words. "Listen, Jazz, I understand why you were upset. I really do—"

"—Forget it," she says before I have a chance to finish my sentence.

She places her hand over mine on the gear. I turn my eyes to Jazz's. Then, she leans forward and kisses me on the cheek. No tongue. Just lips. Like her own little signature. She opens the door and looks back at me and says, "Who's Lamar?"

"What do you mean?" I ask as she steps outside and closes the door behind her. She leans through the open window.

Then follows, "I tried calling you earlier to tell you that I was going to be getting off work much sooner."

Technically, Jazz doesn't catch me in a lie.

As before, saying something as vague as "not having one on me" could pass as the truth, which is true.

I don't have a phone on me, but it doesn't necessarily mean that I don't own a phone.

I tell Jazz the truth about the payphone, about me not *owning* a phone—not even a landline—then I tell her about Lamar. I didn't exactly know the man's name at the time, but I remember him sitting there next to the payphone.

Each line or wrinkle on his aged face was like a depressing story and his breath smelled of an ulcer.

Another victim of a failed economy.

I bought three tacos from Pollo Picante, gave the guy one of my tacos, and I remember he couldn't thank me enough.

I expect Jazz to turn around, walk to her apartment, and be gone from my life for good, *but*. . .

She asks me if I'm some kind of alien in a joking kind of way.

"Not that I'm aware of," I tell her.

She smiles, again, as if me not having a phone doesn't bother her.

On the contrary, she finds it just as intriguing as me not being on social media.

"Well," she says, "I work tomorrow afternoon." She leans farther through the passenger side window. "Feel free to swing by, if you're not too busy."

"Yeah," I tell her through the window. "I might do that."

"And thanks for the earrings," she says.

"You're welcome."

They got her name written all over it. She was born to wear them.

"I'll talk to you soon then."

I tell her good night.

She repeats and strolls away.

As she disappears into her apartment, I pull out Nico's number from my pocket and hold it in my hand.

Decisions, decisions.

S I C D A Y

decide to go fancier, as in a slightly nicer room than the one at Lucky's. I have plenty enough money to stay at the Foreshore Hotel for at least a couple of nights.

The room is decent with a decent view of the Pacific—and by the way, much cleaner than where I've been staying for the past few days. It has your ordinary good coastal vibrations: powder baby boy blue walls, white wicker chairs, twin beds with a comforter patterned with palm springs, and not to mention, a kitchen.

My appetite is something fierce after spending a night with Jazz.

So, I grab a half-eaten cheeseburger and a plate of french fries, which have barely been touched, from a room service tray across the hallway and take it back to my room. The burger is as cold as the plate itself, but I've eaten much worse.

I kick off my shoes and socks and curl my toes into the shag carpet and watch a little TV.

I flip through the channels, but there's nothing on.

At least nothing that catches my interest.

From the nightstand, I grab the *TV Guide* with a current picture of Clint Eastwood.

I skim through a list of channels until I come across the pay-per view channels—the naughty ones that cost money.

\\

FoR about ten minutes, I pace around the hotel room and contemplate jerking off.

After another ten minutes fly by, and then another, I finally give in. I grab the issue of *Busties* from my bookbag and just as I remove the magazine, I come across a tube of red lipstick that I picked from Jazz's purse. I twist open the tube and take a whiff of the lipstick. The feeling comes back like a furious fleet charging directly south. I give in to the feeling and start to touch myself until I can't take it any longer.

I suddenly rush to my office, thinking about every inch of me being inside Jazz. I finish doing my business. Then, once the guilt phase passes, I lie down on the bed and close my eyes.

\\\

THE nightmares are gone.

I wake up to the sound of the angry sea by my side. I grab a cup of coffee from a continental breakfast downstairs and then I head back to my room. I drink about half a cup until the sweating starts and the coffee inches back up my throat. I rush to the bathroom and vomit and the vomiting is violent, too, as if I'm giving birth to ungrateful demon through my mouth. I end up vomiting whatever I put inside me, like orange juice or the apple Danish I pocketed while I was snooping around the lounge area downstairs, then dry heaving every thirty minutes for the next three hours, then lying in bed, unable to keep still, then sweating, then waiting around to vomit some more, then lying in the cool bed sheets before they turn all hot and wet again. I try to go back to sleep, to surrender myself to the black, but I feel feverish. I make sure to stay hydrated by drinking water, but even water is hard to hold down.

\V

\ wake up to the sound of a *gunshot*.

I jolt upright from the bed and check the door where I see a stubby-looking maid standing behind the peephole, both of her eyes bug-eyed and her head freakishly blown out of proportion like an image behind a fish lens frame. She knocks three times, then presses her ear against the door, listening carefully, waiting whether or not she should come in. No. Please don't come in. I check the time. It's already ten o'clock. Checkout was at nine.

Through the door, I tell the maid to pass as I try to pull myself together. I buy another night's stay; then, I go back to the room and sleep for the remainder of the morning.

V

\ dream about spiders of all shapes and sizes crawling on the walls, creeping on my bed, on my pillow, and cramming themselves inside every orifice of my body.

VI

IT'S already a quarter past four o'clock and Jazz is probably still at work.

I recognize that it's vital to eat, even though I have no desire to eat. If it comes down to forcing myself to eat, then I will. I guess. I used to get like this when I was younger, but that was so long ago. I'd lay, sit, or mope around my room all day, sicker than a squirrel with nut allergies, unable to play with the other kids outside, unable to eat, unable to do anything, really, but just lay, sit, or mope. Not in any particular order. Sometimes Jimmy and I would pretend to be sick, as in take a hot shower or run around the house like madmen before Susannah took our temperature, just so we didn't have to go to school. On those days when I didn't pretend, I felt like dying, like this was it, this is how I go, not fighting or, as I always imagined going out, in a blaze of glory, but shriveling away in my bed like some kind of neglected plant. At times, I felt like giving up. I threw up a lot, as if nothing was ever good enough for my spoiled stomach. I couldn't stand the physical strain of throwing up, yet I used to feel much better afterwards. Susannah used to call them bugs. I used to get a lot of them. A lot. I was a sex magnet for bugs. Jimmy, never. Of all the members of our family, he was the one person who never got sick. Never. For the longest time, I felt as if he wasn't human, as if he was made from some kind of material that hadn't yet been discovered by scientists, as if he was some kind of new organism or something like that, as if not getting sick was Jimmy's superpower. I remember I went a stretch for about four years where I didn't throw up at all. No bugs. Like Jimmy. I didn't even get sick in that stretch. Not even a cold during the winter.

If I don't eat, I'll be a sloth for the rest of the day. I need to eat without getting high, too.

I decide to stop at the nearest Burger Inn. I order the number four combo, chicken sandwich and waffle fries with a large Sprite, and I take the food back to my room and watch an episode of *Law and Order* while I nibble from the greasy fast food. I eat most of my food and manage to hold it down. I feel a little better now that I have food in my stomach.

After I finish eating, I relax on the balcony for about an hour and smoke cigarettes and watch the clouds pass by as the kids play in the sea below.

Another grueling hour passes and I get bored.

Most of the day has been a complete wash, so I make something positive out of it by stopping by Prehistoric Cave. I drive twenty minutes to Long Pointe, a small beach town outside Hillside. I walk around artificially damp caves and dwellings, which smell of fresh paint, and check out the waxed sculptors of cavemen and cavewomen and cavechidren. The whole time, I think about Jazz walking by my side. What would I say to her? What would we talk about? How would she react to the cavemen? If so, would she comment on them? I know she'd say something cute like: *What if cavemen have smartphones? Would they use text or emojis?* When I think about Jazz, all that comes to mind is her smile and that's what really keeps me going. I stop at one display of mammoths and sabertooths, both posed in positions that would suggest that these creatures about to tear into something living with their tusks and fangs. It's hard to believe that they actually existed. I've read all about these mammals in magazines and books such as *Modern Ice Age* by Kurt Van Burns, a prolific author who's right up there with greats like Steinbeck or Dickens. I've read about the violence of Mother Nature, the savagery when faced with survival. I can only imagine what it'd be like if these creatures weren't extinct. What if they were alive today? I can only imagine.

VII

WHEN I get back to the Foreshore after driving around for a couple of hours, it's already night and I'm feeling frisky.

I pull out two numbers, one being Nico's and the other being Jazz's, and lay them out on the nightstand.

I pocket one of the numbers, then dial the other on the hotel phone.

"Hello?"

I say hey.

Jazz's voice suddenly climbs over the phone.

"Hey, Jimmy," she says. "What are you up to?"

"Oh nothing much," I tell her. "I was meaning to stop by and visit you at work, but I've been under the weather all day."

"Is everything okay?" she asks.

"Yeah," I tell her. "Must've been something I ate."

"Really?"

"Yeah," I say, "but I think I'm fine now."

I lie down on the bed and make myself comfortable and talk to Jazz on the phone.

VIII

WE'RE about two hours in when sex enters the conversation.

Jazz was talking about an old high school boyfriend whom she ran into the other day on the boardwalk. She told me that he used to belittle her—he was even rough with her, not in bed, just in general, like in public or in the car. She asked me about the girls I've dated, and I only told her about the decent ones, which lasted past the normal month-ish fling. Basically, ones who were worth bringing home to Susannah. There were only a few of them. Maybe one or two whom I could've settled down with, if I put in the time and effort because that's what it really takes to be with someone, time and effort—not like I'm an expert on dating or anything. I decided to throw in a couple of other girls in the mix just to bump up my résumé. I didn't want to give Jazz the impression that I'm "inexperienced" or " not confident" when it comes to a person of the opposite sex. Yet, I've done this relationship thing before. Many times. Hell, I consider myself to be pretty good at relationships. Not to brag and all, but I think I've mastered the art and all of my breakups have been mutual—and not to mention, I'm still friends with the very same girls that I stopped dating. That sort of thing. Most importantly, though, I had to give Jazz the impression that I'm boyfriend material and not just some guy who sleeps around. This is the most important feature: self-control. The bells and whistles of a boyfriend. He has to be sensual and romantic and cuddly and a "good listener" and all of that other mushy crap girls like without coming off as some slutty dude-whore. Basically, he has to know when to keep his dick in his pants. I believe I've proved to Jazz that I could be that guy, the compassionate, sensitive, caring guy. One white lie won't hurt Jazz. I turned the question back to her and then she answered by listing off unusual encounters from previous relationships. For instance: "I once dated a guy who could turn his eyelids inside out"; or "I once dated a guy who had a pot-bellied pig as a pet"; or "I once dated a guy who drank his own urine"; or "I once dated a guy who collected cereal boxes"; or "I once dated a guy who went to Cosplay ever year dressed up as Tingle from *Legend of Zelda*."

I couldn't help but wonder what she'll be saying about me to another guy once she really gets to know me: "*I once dated a guy who was a full-on psychopath.*"

That was when things took an abrupt turn; and before I can even control myself, I'm sweating in unusual areas of my body.

Again, Jazz asks me about my sexual positions—doggystyle, missionary, reverse cowgirl?

Before I can answer, Jazz tells me her preferences.

My breath grows tight and labored and I find myself playing with myself yet again as Jazz starts to talk about how she likes it when the guy kisses her on her neck, just an inch or so below the ear—*softly*, she says, her voice soft as well, as if it's wearing a wool-knitted toboggan—then she says that she likes it when the guy *slowly* runs his fingers down her back, around the curves of her hips, and her words are slow as well, as if they're meant to draw arousal. And that's when I find myself growing, just when she's about to round second base.

Jazz says over the phone, "What are you doing?"

"Nuttin'," I say and quickly roll out of bed. "Nothing. Uh. I just spilled a drink on myself—"

"—Say, what are you doing right now besides spilling drinks on yourself?"

"Ah. . . nothing," I say again. "I'm doing nothing. . . "

"Do you want to do Facetime with me, if it's not too late?"

"Facetime?"

"Yeah," she says. "Facetime."

"I don't—"

"—That's right. I forgot." Deflation in her voice as she trails off, "Sorry. . . "

"No," I say without hesitation. "Don't be. What are you doing tomorrow? Let's hang out."

"I work again in the afternoon, but that's it."

"Say, why don't we get together tomorrow after you get off work?"

"Yeah," Jazz says. "I'd like that."

I feel Jazz smile over the other end of the phone and I find myself getting hard again.

piddle around for most of the day until Jazz gets off work. I give her a call with a burner phone that I bought at the electronics store off Park Central and tell her that I'll meet her at the same place we met the other night—near the Amazing Pretzel.

I drive back to the Foreshore and wash up. In the shower, I'm laughing and singing the oldie song "Book of Love" by *The Monotones* while I'm scrubbing the shampoo from my hair. For a while, I mean, for a minute or so, I'm not thinking about a damn thing and my voice sounds golden, as if I'm in a sound booth singing into a soap of a microphone as a well-groomed producer on the other side of the glass gives me a thumbs up. I sound as good as Sam Cooke—if not, ten times better—all thanks to the acoustics of the shower and halfway through singing the song, I hear two *thuds* against the wall from the guest next door. I just laugh it off. For a while, it almost feels like Fourth of July all over again. If only for a while.

I dress into fresh clothes and stop at Spirits to grab a drink. I take a step inside the store when all of a sudden I have a tough time picking out what I want to drink. So many to chose from. So many decisions. What kind of buzz do I want to feel tonight? Horny liquor buzz or laid back beer buzz? I stand in front of the whiskey aisle, still flustered on what to buy. The doubts start to swirl inside my mind. Each thought is telling me to turn around and leave and meet up with Jazz. Hang out with her sober, *not* drunk. I don't need a drink. My chest isn't that tight. Neither is my throat. My head isn't as foggy as it's been lately. I haven't touched a drink in a couple of days and I'm feeling like I'm at the beginning stages of that crucial process where I'm starting to get my shit together. I haven't felt like this in—honestly, I can't even remember how long.

I decide to leave the store and walk back to my car.

On the way, I witness a couple of lanky shadows slide across the pavement below my feet.

In the reflection of the door's window, two dark figures rise over my shoulder.

I hear a *click*; then I feel a barrel pressing against the backside of my head.

"Give me your fuckin' money, bitch," a bullet of a voice says from behind.

I turn my shoulder, but a black gloved hand suddenly forces my head the other way.

"Did I say 'turn around,' muthafucka?" the voice says.

I don't have a blade on me. I don't have my revolver either. I have nothing. Just my two fists.

This can't be how I die, shot in the back by some punk.

As I plan out my next angle of attack, I feel a rush of air over my ear.

Suddenly, the blood charges to my head. I stumble forward and ram my shoulder into the side of my car. I look up and see two faces underneath white bandanas with black paisley print. I can only see their eyes for they wear the bandanas like lawless bandits, and their eyes, from what I gather, have no color or life in them. The punks don't waste any time kicking me in the ribs. I defensively curl my body inward, tightening all of the muscles in my body, and shield my face. One punk is wearing this white cast, which runs from his elbow to his hand. He manages to get a good lick across my nose with the backside of the cast. I think I have a broken nose. I taste the tartness of metal on the back of my tongue and I know my nose is possibly fucked up. Maybe not entirely broken—I'm being rather dramatic—but it's bleeding badly. The other punk is tugging at my wrist, trying to grab the Rolex. I retract my arm and in return, I receive a swift boot across the face. Blood rushes away from the impact, sending a streak of pain throughout my body. Pellets of pain perforate my body. One jab after another. I feel like some lame character in a comic book with each exaggerated blow to my body letting a bold, italicized **CRRRK** or **KRRFPH!** The sounds of pain. In the midst of the pain, I feel Thomas's watch being yanked from my wrist as the winder scrapes along my skin and I try to find it but it's already in his gloved hand. As I make one last ditch effort to grab the Rolex, my head jerks back from another kick to the face. The blow hurts something awful. A mouthful of blood violently sprays from my mouth and hits the side of my car like a crushed egg. My world goes black for a moment and then a pale blue light shines over my eyes. I realize it's *not* the Light from Heaven—as so many of those survivors talk about on the TV or in the books—but the flash of a smart-phone. Somewhere below the blinding light, one of the punks is pouring a smelly liquid over my face. The liquid is strangely warm and yellow, too, as it pours over my face; and I don't realize what the liquid is until I get a better whiff of it.

Muthafucka.

I hear the *snap* of a camera!

Say cheese!

At the last second, I fight through the ache and raise both of my hands and block my face from the camera.

One of the punks sneaks in another kick to my exposed ribs, which are possibly broken.

I take note of his shoe and the feel of it pressed against my body, but the thought alone dissolves inside the gray haze.

The next sounds I hear are the footsteps of two punks running away followed by hooting and hollering.

||

THE two punks who jacked me ended up scoring two hundred and ninety-one dollars, not including the Rolex, which is probably worth triple of what they scored. Split all of that between two people and that's just over a hundred and forty-five dollars apiece, not including the price of the Rolex.

When I get back to the Foreshore, I'm more pissed at my-self than at the punks who jumped me from behind. I don't have any life-threatening injuries. Just a few cuts and bruises on my face and a banged-up nose and possibly a broken rib or two, but I'll live.

I wash the blood and urine from my face, put a handful of ice in a plastic garbage bag, and press the bag against my face. I lie down on the bed and relax; and as I'm replaying the past events in my head, I'm wondering what I could've done differently. It doesn't dawn on me that I'm supposed to meet up with Jazz until the thought of Jazz enters my thought—*shit!*

I pull the burner from my pocket, but I don't dial her number. I just stare at the burner, contemplating.

What do I even tell her?

Tell me.

\\\

\ open the sliding door to the balcony and concentrate on the sound of waves crashing along the shore. The repetitive sound helps me relax and makes it easier for me to retrace my thoughts to the initial point of impact—***CRRRK!***

I visualize the punk striking down at me, his dark eyes meeting with mine. Relax. Focus. Then, it suddenly hits me! *Not* the cast or his eyes. Instead, it's a moment of clarity.

That scumbag, that weasel, that lousy piece of shit, that goddamn coward. No wonder he jumped me from behind when I wasn't looking. No wonder he was wearing a mask to cover up his stupid face. Only superheroes with superpowers wear masks to hide their face in order to protect the ones they love, superheroes who stand against the tyranny of evil. He's no superhero nor is his weaselly friend. They're cowards. That's exactly what they are.

I hobble from one side of the room to the other, a constant back and forth, back and forth, contemplating my next move.

Why didn't I pick up on it sooner?

I'm extremely sore, but I clean myself up and throw on some clothes anyway. I drive straight to Cyber Jaxx's and log onto the first computer I see. If I know him like I think I do, the pic will already be posted. Sure enough, there it is. Posted exactly one hour ago on Flip's PhotoBag page. In the pic, I'm lying on the ground, my hands covering my bloody, urine-soaked face. The caption below: "*See what happens when you mess with the Crazy Cru.*" He's already received forty-three likes. The comments are divisive, to say the least. Some of the kids egg on Flip (*What a lil' bitch*) or point out the obvious (*Golden shower lol*). Flip replies to one of his many followers' questions: *"Yup yup,"* Flip writes. *"That's me taking a piss on sum lil' punk ass bitch who fucked with Dru Dog."* Some comments are followed by emojis. One troll comments on how much Flip is screwed up in the head. Then, Flip and the resilient troll go back and forth, talking shit to one another, a back and forth, like *I'll kill you*, then Flip's followers joins in by bashing the troll; then they start making jokes about each other's moms, and this and that.

I leave Cyber Jaxx's and make a stop at Spirits and pick up a bottle of Jose Cuervo. I pay the Haitian clerk. He doesn't say a word to me. Neither me to him.

I leave Spirits and drive to Drew's apartment. I find Flip's hatchback parked crookedly and taking up two parking spaces in front of Drew's apartment. Just as I'm about to open the bottle of Cuervo, I hear a *tap-tap* on the passenger window. I unlock the door. Moses steps inside the car with a grunt.

You following me—

—What are you doing?

With his posture weak, Moses sits in the passenger seat and waits for an answer.

What does it look like I'm doing?

You're not thinking clearly, Moses tells me. If you do this, you won't be the same. You hear me?

I hear him, but I don't answer him.

Are you willing to risk your life over some stupid watch—

—I know what I'm doing.

Do you?

I ignore Moses, open the Cuervo, and I drink until the light inside Drew's apartment goes off.

RE - PURR - CUSSIONS

THE next morning I wake up without a single memory of how I ended up back in my hotel room. In one hand, I'm holding a sticky bottle of Cuervo, which is bone-dry. My other hand remains curled inward like the arm of T-Rex next to my shoulder and when I finally uncurl it, a combination of pain and soreness runs through my knuckles. My ribs are extremely sore to touch, like buttons of pain scattered over my torso from just the slightest of body turns. I pop an aspirin from the bathroom, chase it down with some gulps from the faucet; afterwards, I splash my face with cold water. Even bending forward hurts like no other, the blood pounding throughout my head, like a vengeful driver making sharp turns after being detoured from one road to another. I sit on the edge of my bed and try to muster a thought from last, any thought, whatever, give me something. The fragmented memory of last night comes back to me as if my mind is a VHS tape on rewind (first, *guzzling away the rest of the Cuervo in my hotel room, then taking a hot shower, then paying the desk clerk for another night's stay from the wad of cash in my hand, then driving through the echoes of night, then leaving Drew's apartment, then drifting through the speckles of violence and grotesquery, then, lastly, towering over Flip as he sleeps on a couch with the glow of the TV flickering over the Rolex on his wrist*). I saunter my way to the table; and the memory starts to piece together as soon as I check out the score from last night: a 14 karat gold flat herringbone chain, which I can later pawn away for about two hundred dollars, give or take a few (I've seen them go for about two-fifty on the Internet, the real kind, *not* the fake-ass junk that makes your skin turn green); an antique ukulele, which, according to Drew, Mr. All-Talk, once belonged to his grandfather, which, at the time I grabbed it, looked as if it was worth some bones, but now that I look at it right now with much different eyes, I don't really understand why I grabbed it in the first place; three hundred and thirteen dollars both from Drew and Flip combined (which isn't really a score since most of the money belongs to me); and, finally, the Rolex, the glass covering partially cracked in half as a result of Flip banging it against the coffee table (again, not really a score).

\\

\ take another shower and wipe away the blood that I missed last night—mainly, scrubbing the cracks between my finger-nails and the areas behind my ear with a Brillo pad.

After I get out of the shower, I dress into something com-fortable and drag myself to the Russian, who ends up giving me four hundred dollars even for both the chain and the uku-lele.

After I leave the pawnshop, I stop by Lassie's and search for Jazz, but her boss, Eric, a petite man, very feminine like in his posts, *definitely* not into Jazz, as I assumed, says she's not working today. He says she called in sick.

I know it has something to with me, with her not showing up to work. I need to tell her what happened to me last night, but I can't let her see me like this.

I head back to my hotel room and rest until my injuries are fully healed.

\\\

Two days pass and I can't stop thinking about Jazz.

The nightmares are back.

I can't stop thinking about my fix.

IV

ON the third day, I run out of money for another night's stay at the Foreshore.

I pick up enough money from an older lady who needed help loading a bucket of cat litter into the back of her off-white Ford Taurus since the lot attendant was too busy texting or chasing around some imaginary pixie or whatever kids are doing on their smartphones. I use the money to buy a much cheaper room off Sunrise Boulevard.

V

I wake up bright and early from a vivid yet strange dream about partying at Crystal Palace and decide to hit up the Square, hoping to score some money.

As I step inside the car, I hear the *click* of my revolver right next to my ear!

You don't listen, Moses says. Do you?

I glance in the rear view mirror to find Moses sitting in the backseat with a sling around his left arm.

What the hell happened to you?

Fell, he says.

Moses flicks the barrel toward the front of the car.

Drive.

I put the gear in drive.

Where are we going? I ask Moses as I pull out of the parking lot.

You mean, where are *you* going?

For a moment, I don't know where I'm going. Just that I'm going somewhere. Right. The Square.

You have somewhere you should be right now, Moses says. Instead, you're off trick or treating with a girl you barely even know. He points the barrel to the right. Take a right here.

Right takes me to Main Street, which will take me straight to Topside Boardwalk.

So, why are you following me?

We share an icy glare in the mirror; then Moses turns to the window, gazes outside.

How many times have I covered your ass?

You know, I was doing just fine before you showed up.

166

Really? His voice sounds almost comical, as if I amuse him. Tied down to a bed at night? Forced to take medication. That's you doing 'just fine'? Moses points at Topside Board-walk, not too far away. Turn left at the stoplight.

I stop behind a car at the stoplight.

If I didn't break you out of that hellhole, he says, you'd still be there rotting away. That's the truth.

I glance at his knuckles, both bruised and swollen.

Sooner or later, you're gonna have to learn how to accept the truth for what it is.

The light turns green.

I turn into the boardwalk's parking lot.

Let me ask you something, I say. Why do you care so much about my business?

The sooner you find the rest of the suspects responsible for Jimmy's death, the sooner you can do me my favor.

So, what is this favor?

Moses tells me to park the car. I do. Then, he puts down the revolver.

He tells me I need a baseball cap, a pair of cheap sun-glasses, and a bottle of makeup.

Clearly, he says, he can't see you the way you are. Other-wise, your cover will be blown.

He, Moses says, as in Nico.

Then, the thought comes to me, and I know where I need to be.

Was that a dream?

Or, did it really happen?

I leave Moses behind in the car like an unwanted child and order a vanilla ice cream cone from the lively parlor, Sher-bet's, where Sherbet himself perches outside. He's a seven-foot tall statue of a chubby fellow as jovial as a jester who's dressed like a pimp with colorful Mardi Gras beads around the fatty layers of his neck.

I distance myself from Sherbet's.

Before the ice cream melts, I search for a woman carrying the largest purse and I act as if I'm eating when, in fact, I'm only pretending to eat.

I spot a flower child walking a rat-like dog, which nearly gets stepped on twice by bystanders. She's carrying a massive hemp purse around her shoulder, which looks more like a satchel. I realize the dog will make for good distraction; however, the girl doesn't seem like someone who wears a lot of makeup. More of the free spirit type. All natural. That sort of thing.

Next, I spot a shapeless woman with a purse. Lots of product in her blonde hair. Face like a clown. Let the magic begin.

I play the idiot and aimlessly wander closer toward her path and just as she's about to walk past me, I backpedal toward her direction and spin around. . .

Bam!

Her purse goes flying first. Then, next to fly is my ice cream cone. . .

Splat!

"Shit!" I hiss.

"Oh my god," the woman cries out as all of the personal contents inside her purse spill out onto the ground. "I'm so sorry. I didn't see you. . . "

"It's okay," I say bitterly as the woman glances down at the crime scene around the ice cream cone.

"I'm so, so sorry," she repeats as she redirects her attention toward the bruises on my face.

"It's okay," I repeat and kneel downward. "Really."

I help her with the things (wallet, ID, etc.) and hand them to her. My hand comes across a tampon. We share eye contact for a moment. I never touch the thing. It's like guy code or something: never touch a woman's tampon. Never. Her cheeks fill with the color of embarrassment as she kneels down on both of her knees and snatches the tampon from the ground and stuffs it in her purse.

"It's my fault," I say. "I wasn't paying attention. . . "

"No," she says, combing the hair from her face. "Don't worry about it. Lemme buy you another one of those."

"It's fine," I say, the bitterness lessening in my voice.

She asks one more time. She's not going to take "no" for an answer.

"How much did it cost?" she asks.

"Around three dollars," I guess.

She reaches in her wallet and hands me a five.

"Thanks," I say.

"My pleasure," she says. "Again, I'm sorry."

"Don't be."

She gathers the rest of her things and walks away. I pull out the case of makeup from my pocket. Bump and grab: first, it starts with an innocent bump or tap followed by a distraction (in this case, an ice cream cone).

Before I leave the boardwalk, I stop at Sweet Tee's and while I'm picking up a black Red Devils baseball hat and an off brand of sunglasses, I stop and think about what just went down. For some reason, I can't help but think about Jazz and the first time we met. No way. It can't. Really? Get out of here.

I shake the absurd thought from my head before it can gather any more attention and focus on the mission at hand.

When I get to the softball field off McDowell Park, I spot Nico playing cheerleader with the rest of the team.

The Dragons are dressed in carmine red while the other team, the Hairy, *Hairy* Scorpions, is dressed in desert orange.

Most of their fans look like—shall I say—porn stars and I start to wonder how Nico is able to pull these types of women.

I mean, seriously, I think I've actually seen one of these women before and I'm not talking about in person. I mean, on the Internet.

Her name is Lady Spitz, I think, or something like that. All I remember is that her name had a *Spitz* in it. Like most porn stars, it wasn't really her birth name. Just a play on words. Something suggestive. Like Jack Meoph or Mime Cumming or something absurd like that.

Not too long ago, Lady was one of the most popular porn stars in the industry. Starred in all kinds of parodies of TV shows or movies or whatever was currently trending at the time. She was best known as a squirter, as in she squirted a lot during sexual intercourse.

If it is "the" Ms. Spitz, I wonder what the hell she's doing here?

Nico tracks me down on the bleachers, breaks free from the other Dragons, and runs over for a quick chat. We slap hands and he says that he's glad I came out.

I shrug, as Jazz would do, and tell him, "I had nothing else going on."

He points at my hat and looks at me strangely.

"What's with the whole 'Stalker' look?"

I grab the bill of my hat. Raise it.

"Oh," I say. "This? Me and the sun don't get along."

"You take any acne medicine?"

I shake my head.

"No," I say. "Why?"

"I once had terrible acne when I was younger," Nico tells me. "Dermatologist put me on this medicine that made my skin extremely sensitive. Couldn't go out in the sun without lotion or a hat." He points at the Devils hat—this ridiculous thing. "That was a long time ago, though."

"Fair skin, I guess."

"Well," Nico sighs, "shit man, if you wanna ball, just grab a glove. I think Alfonso might have a spare. If not, you're free to watch."

"I'll just watch."

"You sure?"

I wave it off.

"Yeah," I tell Nico. "Besides, I twisted my ankle the other day when I was getting out of the shower."

He points to a cooler next to the dugout.

"Whatever makes you comfortable, man," he says. "We got some beer, if you want. Don't be a stranger. Seriously, feel free to help yourself."

"Will do," I say.

Nico runs back to the team who is tossing around the ball in the outfield.

I grab a beer from the cooler and talk to a couple of the girls. I remember a couple of the names from the Dragons; and when the game's over, I head straight to Cyber Jaxx's and look up the ballplayers on their LINKEDUP pages. Most of the ballplayers for the Dragons are software developers and programmers. According to a couple of their social media websites, they play for the company's team called the Dragons. I start making the connections. I dig a little deeper.

I research the company, VERSION DEVELOPERS.

I click on the company's main website and scroll down their client list.

There, I find Nico's company.

It all makes sense.

VI

THE next night, I step out of my room for a minute and finally, after spending what feels like forever, decide to give Nico a call. He's glad I called. He asks me what I'm doing tonight, and as he's speaking, I pick up an obvious slur in his voice, each word soaked in booze, or what I like to call swollen-tongue syndrome. He's not drunk—possibly tipsy—but there's no doubt that he's a couple of drinks away from being there. He tells me to stop by his place later. Says he's having a "few" friends over.

Nothing big.

Before he hangs up, he tells me that Bishop will be there.

Bishop?

"He's a friend," Nico says. "He's be wanting to meet you?"

Meet me?

Shit.

My cover is blown.

WHERE HAVE THE DECENT MEN GONE?

EPISODE 5

HROUGHOUT my life, I've felt like I was always that last one to show up at the party. I was always the "who's that guy?" Everybody had already been drinking on whatever, already drunk on whatever or halfway from being slinky-loose, and me, I was the uptight, uncomfortable one always trying to play catch-up, trying to blend in with everybody else, and by the time the night started to die down, everybody was already passed out and I was left wide-awake, partying alone, looming over all of the passed-out bodies around me.

It's still pretty early when I'm dressed and ready to head out for the night, which is more than a good sign. No more playing Mr. Who's That Guy anymore.

Before I go to Nico's party, I hit up the Three-Legged Stool, a hole-in-the-wall bar along the way. It's your typical bar with a nautical theme: fossilized jaws of Tiger sharks and other massive fish mounted on the walls; nets and spears and other fisherman tools hung on the walls as well; old men perched at the bar with cancerous faces glued to the TV playing the game (the baseball season winding down and closing in on the hunt for October); a group of immature college girls taking shots and acting animal-wild next to a jukebox; frat dudes playing darts, checking out the girls, wondering which ones they're going to take home.

I take a seat next to a lazy-eyed man with a ZZ Top-inspired beard at the end of the bar and ask the bartender for a shot of Cuervo. The bartender says they don't have Cuervo and there's no chance in hell that I'm going to order the house tequila. As you can tell, I'm very particular when it comes to my tequila. I tell the bartender to give me a shot of Jack Daniels. He doesn't even ask for my I.D. Yet, he dances around the bar for a minute, making a couple of fruity cocktails for the college girls, and then he finally pours me a shot.

I down the shot, knowing that it'll later catch up with me.

After I down two more shots, I forget all about the repercussions and pull out my burner and contemplate calling Jazz.

I do this several times: take a shot, feel the burn of Tennessee whiskey in my chest, then glance down at the burner.

Once I'm feeling loosey-goosey, ready to put Mr. Who's That Guy to bed, I seriously consider calling Jazz yet again. Actually, I dial her number and then press the END button. My thoughts go to even darker places—I'm talking horror dark—and I picture Jazz in the most hideous way possible— I'm talking train wreck-hideous—once I turn my gaze toward one college girl in particular: a red hair, twitchy-eyed, bouncy freshman with a famished vagina salivating for warm meat.

I hold the still image of Jazz's face in my mind—her snaggleteeth looking like the teeth on some grotesque Nosferatu-like vampire. Train wreck-hideous.

"He's right," I tell myself.

What the hell does Jazz see in me?

She doesn't even know me.

Moses is right.

As always.

||

WHEN I arrive at Nico's, the entire block is lined with cars.

I wonder how somebody is able to throw a party of this magnitude without the cops busting it up.

I walk for what seems like a quarter of a mile, passing a couple of cute girls dressed like professionals along the way. They appear as if they're just arriving, which, again, is a good sign. I can feel familiar electricity in the air, like something really good is going to happen tonight—or really bad?

I light up a cigarette.

An arched driveway of sports cars makes up the front of the house. In the mix of cars is Nico's blue Lambo.

On the third floor balcony, a couple of half-naked girls are leaning over a wrought iron railing and smoking cigarettes. One girl sees me looking up at her, but I realize, after a wave of people flock past me, that she's *not* looking at me. The girl flashes her tits and hollers at the group. They holler back.

I look for exits.

Old habit.

\|\|\|

THE slick bouncer at the door—or whoever the hell he is—lets me in without a problem. That's the moment when I realize I'm that guy now. The guy on the list.

I take a tour around the luxurious house. The inside is filled with cliques and pockets of partygoers. I remember being here. I remember certain places of the house while other places are new to me (like the miniature glass statue of the "Thinking Man" perched on top of a glass post next to the hallway bathroom—that's new—or the tank of epaulette sharks—that's new—or the theatre room—that's new, as well—in fact, most of the house is all new to me, as if I'm experiencing it all over again. I've heard kids call it different things: their goblin or demon or their party troll, living under the sticky bridges of the frontal lobe of your brain, waiting to emerge when you've had one too many drinks. I don't have a name for it. When you get blackout drunk, it's as if your mind takes a vacation and your judgment is replace with who gives a fuck—it's as if you switch over into a zombie, a thing without mind. Without reason. Operating on an innate hungry for flesh and all you really care about is satisfying the uncanny desire of all things red and holy. I guess, if I had to put a name on it, that's what I'd call it: My Zombie.

The living room is surrounded by a pane of glass and behind the glass sits a moonlit sea glimmering over the bodies scattered throughout the house. I've always dreamed about living in such a place. The elegance. The appeal. That *longing*. A constant view of serenity. Your backyard: the sea. Reminding you where you came from or where you're going.

(According to *Sci-N-Us*, the human body is made up of sixty percent water. That's sixty percent, as in the same percentage of large herbivores at risk of facing extinction)

I rub shoulders with fat cats and sugar daddies and wannabe actors, dancing to the same music from Crystal Palace,
and make my way to the patio where I light up a cigarette.
It's much quieter outside. It doesn't take long for me to
smoke the cigarette, as the sea breeze does most of the smoking for me.

I light up another cigarette.

What the hell did I get myself into?

From the patio, I watch partygoers dancing and talking
inside the house. I'm not the type to people-watch—never
really understood the gist behind it, why people go out just to
watch other people. What's the point?

The sooner I find Conrad, the better.

He's here.

I know it.

I *feel* it.

I stay alert and keep my eyes peeled.

I hear giggling coming from the side of the house, a mixture of men and women laughing in unison.

I move my way underneath a canopy, then pass a massive
fire pit where giggly partygoers are smoking from all kinds of
drugs. Then, I come across an infinity pool where a couple of
anorexic girls are skinny-dipping. I've been in that same pool,
I remember, with Jamie, my flesh pressed against hers. How
can I forget that? My thoughts turn to Jazz, both of us underneath the water like two aquatic mammals, those brilliant eyes
staring at me in both curiosity and confusion.

I shake the thought and grab a drink from the bartender
and light up another cigarette.

As I take a drag from the cigarette, I hear more giggling,
but this time much closer. The sea breeze swiftly gusts behind
me, causing all of the tiny hairs on the back of my neck to
shoot up like the quills on a porcupine.

I hear more laughing. Familiar. I turn my shoulder to see
Nico running through crowds of people. He's being chased by
a girl, who, by the way, is stark naked. She's also carrying
something on her wrist, but I can't exactly make out what it is.
However, from her calm demeanor, I can tell that she doesn't
mind being naked in front of strangers. They make their way
closer to me. I realize that "something" coiled around her
wrist is a ball python. And from what I can tell, she's not the
least bothered by the snake, as well. I get a closer look at her.

Her body is a ten, natural, no Botox or enhancements or any of that crap; her face is another story. However, I'd be lying if I didn't say it's the kind of face that may get better throughout the night. Like Jamie, she's about a four or five—five, at best, in the attractive department.

Nico waves me down. Runs over to me. Out of breath. He's drenching wet, too.

"Jimmy!" Nico says genuinely and uses my body as a resting post. "Glad you came out, brother. . . "

"Nice party," I say.

"Thanks, man," he says, catching his breath. Then, he looks around. "It's nothing big." Twice he's said that. There's nothing "not big" about the party. It's, by far, the biggest party that I've attended. "Sasha was chasing my ass around with that goddamn snake." He points to the girl whom I assume is Sasha. "I hate fucking snakes. . . "

He gives me a once over. Eyes widen.

"How've you been?" he asks.

"Good," I say.

Nico touches me on the arm.

"How's your ankle?"

"Better."

I look Nico over, as he does me. He's dressed more casual than he was at the club. He's wearing a white shirt with a splatter of black cursive lettering. I can't make out what the logo says. I think it's Spanish, but I may be wrong. The dampness of his shirt exposes the many tattoos on his shoulders and chest. As with the logo, I can't make out the tattoos. Only *one*.

"Well, glad you made it out," he says. "I can use a hand with the keg, if you're not busy. You mind giving me a hand?" He leans in closer. That patent queerness trapped in his eyes. "I'll make it worth your while. . . "

I think about his comment for a second. I don't exactly know what Nico means by that. *worth* my *while*. I've never been with another guy, as in I've never been inside another guy and a guy has never been inside me. I should tell Nico that I don't swing that way, but I decide to keep my mouth shut for the time being and act as if I'm open for anything and everything.

He steps aside and points to the three girls sitting poolside. One in particular.

"Yolanda was talking about you," he says quietly.

Yolanda. That's Yogi's older sister.

"Yolanda?"

"Yeah, man," he says. "You know, from the other night. She thinks you're—and I'm quoting her—a 'real cutie,'" he tells me. "If you give me hand, I'll introduce you to her. So, what do you say?"

I check out Yolanda. She's much older than me. Her profile on her MyCircle page says she's twenty-four but that's all bullshit. She's actually twenty-eight years old, but who's counting. She's cute. Sexy body. Sexier face.

I look down at the cigarette, now unlit from the lack of attention.

"Sure," I say. "Okay."

Nico pats me on my back.

"By the way," he says with a wink, "Jamie told me to tell you that she had a wonderful time the other night."

"Well," I say, "she's a lovely girl."

"Lovely," Nico repeats. "Tell me about it," he says, laughing. "And quite a handful."

I don't know what he means by that.

He slips his feet into a pair of sandals next to the canopy.

Nico walks me down a spiraled staircase, which leads directly to the garage below. I'm still baffled as to why he acts as if we're best buds when we've only hung out for one night. He tells me more about Yolanda and how amazing she is, but I already know everything about her. I wonder if it's either his way of feeling somewhat sympathetic toward me for showing up to the party alone or Yolanda possibly passing along a message. Either way, I don't think too much about it.

As we step into the six-car garage, Nico flips on a switch; and one by one, each fluorescent light above turns on simultaneously, except for one light, which noisily flickers like a bug zapper before staying lit.

We walk down another flight of stairs.

From my initial inspection—except for a fridge tucked away in the back and a row of cardboard boxes stacked against the wall—most of the garage is fairly empty. I'm more drawn to the shiny floors, which reminds me of an article I read in *Trucker By Heart* about "How to Epoxy" a garage.

I step farther into the garage and as before, I feel as if I've been here.

Nico says over my shoulder, "You good?"

"Yeah." I turn back around. "Why shouldn't I be?"

"I don't know," he says. "You seem distracted, man."

"Not distracted," I tell him. "I can't get over the size of this house."

"This?" Nico waves his hand. "It's just a house."

He points to a deep recess where over a dozen kegs are huddled together like an offensive line.

"Here they are, my friend," he says as he shows me the many kegs. "You can never have enough beer. Am I right?"

"*Right*," I parrot.

He turns to me and asks me, "What's your poison?"

"Poison?"

"Yeah," he says. "Your beer of choice?"

"I'm cool with whatever, man."

"No!" he chirps. "Go on, Jimmy! Name it!"

I shrug and say, "I don't know. Budweiser?"

"My man," he says pompously. "Budweiser it is. You know I was hoping you weren't going to say some light beer, but you don't strike me as a light beer kind of guy. No offense."

I push out a laugh.

"Nah," I say. "It's all good."

He searches through the kegs, pushing each one aside as he squeezes his body through a maze of kegs.

"I think we may just be in luck," Nico trails off, as he comes across the right keg, the Budweiser keg. "Here she is, good ole Budweiser," he says ecstatically. "The way I look at it," he trails off again as he reaches around the keg, "you can never go wrong with an ice cold Bud." I hear a *snap* and he hisses, "Goddamn it." He directs his attention toward the floor and then turns to me with a look of embarrassment.

"Need a hand?" I ask.

"Yes," he cries out with laughter. "Would you?"

I make my way to where Nico is kneeling. It appears as if the end of his sandal got caught underneath the keg.

"Just lift it up while I pull my foot out," he says as he kneels downward and exposes his neck for me.

Then, I get ready. . .

I lift the keg far enough off the floor for Nico to pull out his foot. He holds out his hand.

"Thanks, buddy," he says.

I shake his hand.

"No problem," I tell me.

His eyes light up for a moment.

"I almost forgot," he says and reaches in his pocket and pulls out my switchblade. "I believe this belongs to you."

He hands me the switchblade, his eyes never leaving mine.

"Thanks," I say and glance over the blade.

"I haven't seen one of those in years," he says. "Old school."

"Well, you never know when you might need one," I say and once more, glance over the blade.

"Better to have one and not need it than to not have one and need it," he replies.

"Yeah," I say. "Something like that."

"Well, from the way you handled that Drew guy—that fucking jackass—you're probably better off without it."

"How is he, by the way?"

"He'll live," Nico says as if he's not the least bit concerned about Drew. "Between you and me, I can't stand the prick. He's always starting trouble. I mean, *always*. Anyway, I'm glad someone finally put him in his place. Don't worry, though. That will be the last time he's ever invited over here. For real. And you won't need. . . *that* here." *That*, referring to the switchblade in my hand. "I like to think of this place as a place for lovers, not fighters. You feel me?"

"Feel you," I reply.

Silence grows.

I try to think of something to say, but all I got is a question.

"Say," I blurt out, "I gotta use the head."

"Sure, man," he says. "Bathroom's just down the hall. Stay to the right."

\V

\ exit the garage and make it to a dark, narrow hallway. I stay to the right, as Nico told me, but I don't look for any bathrooms. Instead, I do a little snooping. I find what looks like some kind of storage room toward the end of the hallway.

I flip on the light.

Inside is a stockroom full of cardboard boxes stacked against the wall, as well as organized on shelves. I step inside the room and get a closer look at the writing on the side of the box.

I suddenly hear a voice from behind: "Did you find what you were looking for?"

I turn around. Nico's standing at the doorway, staring at me.

I tense up for a second.

"The bathroom," I say abruptly and remove the tremble from my voice by clearing my throat. "Yeah," I say clearly. "I just got lost. That's all."

"I also see you've found my treasure of gold at the end of the rainbow."

"Oh," I say stupidly as I look around at all of the boxes, "*this*. It's none of my business what you do on your spare time."

"Don't be so naive, Jimmy," he says, entering the room. I'm cornered now. I have nowhere to run. "Sex," Nico says, "is my business."

He walks me to one of the many boxes.

The side of the box reads: "*the* PleasureSaber^{TM}."

He opens one of the boxes with a box cutter. Then, he hands me the box cutter.

"Hold this for a second, will you?"

I grab the box cutter while Nico pulls out a package from the box. He trades the package for the box cutter. I study the package, but I already know what's inside the package.

But Nico tells me anyway, as he opens the package for me.

"Two words," he says as he pulls out a strange device from a black tube, "sex sells."

"Interesting," I tell him as I look over the sex toy. "You sell this stuff?"

"Of course," he replies. "What'd you think I did for a living? Manage a nightclub?"

I don't respond.

"People, they can't get enough of this stuff," he says. "Seriously. I swear they sell like hotcakes. Originally, I was going to name it the 'Maneater,' but, you know, don't think Mr. Hall and Oates would approve."

"Dildos?" I say. "You sell dildos?"

"Not just any dildo," he untwists the end of the toy, revealing a sleeve of a vagina.

"Okay," I say in agreement.

"For her on one side," he says, "for him on the other."

"Like one of those *Fleshlighter* things?"

"Close," he says, "but not the same."

"You mean people actually buy these things?"

"Like I've said, sex sells, my friend," he says. "It's as easy at that."

I ask Nico, "What got you into the 'pleasure' business?"

"I'd say the money, but honestly, I mean, if I had one of these things when I was a kid, I probably wouldn't even leave my room." Nico's shakes his head, his eyes drift into thought. I try to think of something to say in order to keep the conversation from nose-diving into silence. Then, Nico blurts out, "And, between you and me—seriously, this doesn't leave the room—"

"Of course," I tell him.

"—I probably would've never picked up crabs from my high school crush, Charlotte Web."

"Charlotte's Web? Like the. . . "

". . . Like the book, just drop the s from Charlotte," he says. "It's a true story, man. Her parents must've had a sense of humor when they named their daughter after the children's book, *Charlotte's Web*. I remember after Charlotte I didn't touch a girl in like four months. Almost scarred me for life."

"Makes sense as to why you went into the business."

"Not only that," he says, "these things will help significantly reduce your chance at getting STD's or AIDS. Fucking AIDS, man! This shit will save people's lives!"

"Or destroy them," I say bluntly.

Nico doesn't laugh at first. Then, strangely, I start to laugh, which causes to Nico to laugh; in fact, he laughs over me.

"Nice one, Jimmy," he says. "So, have you tried one?"

"Nah, man," I tell him. "I haven't."

"Be honest."

I shake my head.

"If you close your eyes, it almost feels like the real thing."

"Seriously?"

"Serious," Nico says from the back of his throat. "I can't tell how many times I imagined trying to picture a girl naked when I was younger or even imagined what a girl's pussy felt like. I mean, for real." He hits a switch on the side of the sex toy and it lights up with a green light. "And," Nico says mischievously, "it glows in the dark."

I can't help but laugh at the sex toy.

I mean, seriously.

V

WE exit the garage with the keg.

As we make our way around the corner, Nico tells me about how he would've used the dolly, but the piece of shit broke on him.

"I swear," he says, "all of this money around us and we can't even afford a decent dolly. Ain't that something?"

He said *we*.

What does he mean by we?

"I think it was made in China."

"Doesn't surprise me," I say from the corner of my mouth. "I would say half the shit we buy nowadays comes from China."

"I know, right?" Nico says as we arrive at the stairs. "They really have us by the balls. I mean, don't they? When was the last time we actually built a product that genuinely lasted a lifetime? Fuck, a generation. Give me a product that can last *at least* a generation."

"Like the PleasureSaber," I tease.

"Hey," he says as we stop at the base of the spiraled staircase and rest a minute. "I can drop the saber from the Empire State Building and it'll still work like a champ. It's what I do. I make sex toys. The Italians make a great car. I'll give them that." He taps me on the arm. "Check this out: my grandmother, right? A great lady. She had this one sewing machine. I remember she would spend hours and hours on that thing. Even when I was a child I remember she'd be on that thing sewing her day away." He catches his breath, so I decide to light up a cigarette, since we've stopped working and all. "Anyway," he says, "I was cleaning out the garage the other day and I came across this bulky, ugly thing. I'm talking butt freaking *ugly*. It looked like some piece of junk you'd find in a dumpster. Turns out that it was my grandmother's old sewing machine. She must've accidentally placed it with my things or it got lost during a move. I don't know. Whatever. That's beside the point. Anyway, just out of curiosity, I turned it on, you know, to see if it still worked. The thing worked like a freaking champ!"

"No shit," I say.

Nico bobs his head, then his voice dampens close to a whisper. "I mean," he says cautiously, "it was corroded as ever. It's a good thing I had my tetanus shot; still," his voice climbs once more, "the point is, Jimmy: she's had this sewing machine ever since she was a girl and it still works to this day. Amazing. Her mother must've passed it down to her. Now, look at the shit we buy today. You buy some washing machine and four years later it has to be replaced or it needs new parts—"

"Or something better comes out, making the shit you just bought obsolete," I say.

"I know, right?" Nico exclaims. "Freaking ridiculous. What happened? You know!"

"Eventually," I say, "shit breaks, I guess."

He points at me and holds his finger closely.

"Not if it's built properly," Nico says passionately. "A hundred years from now people are still going to be using my PleasureSaber. I'll guarantee you—"

"—Okay," I say.

"I'm serious," he says seriously. "We used to build shit with our hands, Jimmy." He holds out his hands, shows them to me as if I've never seen hands before. "These were our tools. We built shit that would last forever, like my grandmother's sewing machine, like the PleasureSaber." He runs his hands in the air as if he's tagging a line, "MADE IN THE US OF A!"

I look closely at Nico and listen to the echo of my words coming out of *his* mouth.

"Now," he says, "look at us, we have a machine on an assembly line building it for us. We use cheaper materials. We take shortcuts, Jimmy. We've moved our manufacturing overseas all for incentives. Lower taxes. Cheaper labor. What's happened is that we've sacrificed quality for quantity. . . "

As silence builds over the conversation—finally—he waits for a response. I quickly think of something to say—possibly something that will calm the guy down a little. In a way, I admire his passion. We somewhat share the same views.

Somewhat. I just did the most work I've done all day and I'm dying of thirst.

"We're all fucked," I tell him.

That's all I give him.

That's all I got, really.

Not much of a joke, but Nico lets out a hearty laugh anyway.

Then, he taps the side of the keg and tells me underneath the trickle of a laugh, "All right, Double-0 Seven."

Double-0 Seven?

Why did he just call me that name?

"You know, Bond," Nico says, waiting for a reaction. "*James* Bond? Double-0 Seven? The Secret Agent?"

"Oh—right," I say. "I'm not really into movies."

"Whatever floats your boat," Nico says, nodding toward the exit. "Let's carry this bad boy upstairs. We don't want to keep Yolanda waiting around much longer."

We carry the keg up the stairs.

When we reach the top, Nico is greeted by another guy, tall, well built, and he's wearing a brown leather jacket with a blue shirt underneath. No tie. He has slicked back hair. His hair is thin too, and his face looks as if it's been cut off by a black market butcher, then dipped in wax, then tightly stretched over his skull. Parts of his face look painfully familiar, yet his face altogether looks freakish. I do a closer study of his face. I recognize the corners of his mouth—that criminal smirk creeping into his cheeks—and my palms grow sweaty. My throat tightens. Chest like a fist.

I hear Nico's voice next to me.

"This is the guy I was talking about," he says, as he shoots a glance my way.

Bishop?

"Jimmy," he says. "Am I right?"

I shake my head yes, then respond, "Yeah."

"Nico here has told me a lot about you," he says smoothly.

I don't answer. He holds out his hand, which glimmers in the moonlight. I don't shake his hand, though.

"Surely, you must have a name," he says, waiting.

"Jimmy," I tell him. "Just Jimmy."

"Okay, Just Jimmy," he says with the kind of arrogance that's worth stomping on. To make matters worse, he lets out a contemptuous snort from his mouth, which sounds in the ballpark of a *pfft*. "Like the artist—uh, what's his name—*Prince*? No last name. Just one name."

"Or Madonna," I hear from behind.

"I like that," he says.

I study the smirk on his face. I know that smirk, but it's *not* his smirk, the shooter's smirk—Conrad's smirk. Nico doesn't make any gestures to the man. Not even a twitch. Instead, he remains all business. Not Nico's style. I wonder why he's acting so serious in front of him. He's threatened by the man. Intimated?

He faces me and glances down at his right hand.

Finally, I shake it. Firmly. I make sure to feel each wrinkle and groove on his palm. His grip is tight, too, tighter than mine, and each bulky ring on his fingers press against the bones of my hand. I don't ignore the pain. Instead, I focus on it. However, I make sure not to display the least indication that I'm in pain in front of him. Instead, I keep my hand locked with his until he finally cracks open his mouth to speak.

"Luther Bishop, owner of the Crystal Palace" he says, but I already know the name, the story behind the name, his occupation.

He is the man from my dreams.

Like Conrad, Bishop doesn't have any social media accounts. To the best of my knowledge, he doesn't exist on the Internet. He's not exactly a ghost either.

But soon, he will be.

NEO - REΔNIMATOR

R EMEMBER Moses entered the frame.
  Remember, at the time, I had absolutely no idea who he was or why he was sitting behind me.

But soon, I would come to know everything about him.

He said something like "*So this is what happens to all the good boys*" over my shoulder or something along those lines.

At first—I mean, my first reaction—wasn't a reaction at all, but, more or less, an internal zap, like the center of my body had been violently woken up after an indefinite drug-induced nap.

At first, Moses' voice sounded like an echo without a source, a ghost echo. Then, his voice shrank in size, then materialized into this useable, tangible thing, something calm and reassuring, like an instant bond waiting to happen. We weren't friends, but I had a feeling that I was going to be seeing this man more often than none.

"Whenever you follow orders," he said more clearly, "they let you watch a movie. How nice of them?"

The movie that Moses referred to was the 1954 Japanese film, *Seven Samurai*.

Buttons—who had finally settled down after throwing one of his "fits" and now, he was really getting into the film, eyes never leaving the screen, a gaping mouth dripping with drool—turned to the strange man and held his index hand over his mouth.

"Do you mind?" I told Moses. "You're disturbing the lo-
cals."

He leaned in even closer, as if he was asking for a punch.

"What's his deal?"

"He's very particular about his 'movies.'"

"Right. . . " Moses said, his glossy eyes drifting to the side,
as if he just had a mental lapse, a common thing many had
experienced around here. A brain fart. "The giallo-guy," he
said under his breath. "Right. . . "

Buttons—who could call out the smallest disturbance during movie time—let out a slobbery *shsssh*, like a shush dressed
in a yellow poncho.

The noise had no effect on Moses.

Moses sat back in his seat for a moment, but only a moment, then he leaned over my shoulder once more.

"Is this the way you want to live out the rest of your life?"
he said quietly. "Trapped like a mouse?"

I turned around, fully.

"Who are you?" I asked him.

He ignored my question, at first.

"Follow me down the rabbit hole and I will set you free,"
he said.

The TV screen before me suddenly went black.

I studied the strange man's face, carefully.

He nodded toward the shadowy corner of the lounge; and
for some reason, I followed him.

At first, I thought it might have been from the water that
they shot in my ear the day before.

At first, I thought a lot of things. The one thing I failed to
grasp was that Moses wasn't just any other local at Red Pines.
He had been there long before me. However, he wasn't a
regular because even a regular must show his or her face every
now and then. Maybe a pop-in once a week, twice if he or she
was "good." Maybe even play a game of afternoon Checkers.
He was more elusive, the neighbor who never left the house.
The one who always kept the blinds closed and the lights on
during the late hours of night, and the neighborhood pack rats
had turned the enigmatic neighbor into a figure of many legends or myths. I remember seeing his face during my first
week. Just a glimpse. Heavily sedated. Gawking at me. He
was dressed like us. Yet, when I spoke to him for the first

time while halfway through watching *Seven Samurai* I realized he wasn't one of us.

How did I know Moses wasn't one of us?

I don't know.

I just knew.

Despite all of what William told me countless times during our daily sessions, I believe Moses was placed there. By what? I don't know. He could've very well been a figment of my imagination. A puzzler. Turning over all of the pieces. Constructing the frame. But, if he was a figment, a phantom, a thought, then who had placed him inside my mind?

Or, was Moses placed inside Red Pines for another purpose?

If so, who activated him? Was it the government? CIA? The Feds? Moses could've very well been a sleeper agent?

And, what is this favor he keeps bugging me about?

Then again, according to William, Moses *never* was at patient at Red Pines because, according to William, Moses doesn't exist in this plane of existence.

I don't know whether or not to believe William. Just like the orderlies, he was a person of transparency. He wanted to know where I was at all times, what I was doing, how I was acting—if I was behaving or misbehaving and if I was misbehaving, he'd readjust me according to my behavior. He liked me when I was as obedient as contestants at the Westminster Kennel Club. A good dog. Behaved. William's a good person and all, a family man who doesn't get paid enough, but he speaks in half-truths.

A loser disguised as a winner.

I guess I don't know anything anymore.

What I do know, like the air in my lungs, is that last night—if only for the slightest moment—I felt free.

Free from the pain.

Free from the misery, the longing.

Free from everything, including Moses.

And never has anything tasted so good.

\\

\ move farther out into the sea—skipping over each wave as it passes me by—and it's not until I look over my shoulder that I realize how far out I am. My toes are no longer touching

sand. I'm treading water like a seal, the soothing sounds of
the Pacific lulling me into a state of calm. I stare out into the
distant horizon and a distant thought suddenly floods my
memories. It's a thought that I once held inside my head
when I was younger. A thought, untouched and undeveloped.
Jimmy and I were treading in these same waters, staring at a
horizon that appeared as if it had no end. Jimmy never turned
away from the horizon, and it was as if his eyes were caught
in a spell. Then, he asked me about the world on the other
side, if they (the *Japanese*) thought about us the same way we
thought about them. Jimmy was fully aware that I had a thing
for the Japanese, the culture, the art—*thing*, as in an intense
attraction, like a crush that seems to never go away. Usually,
I'd be the one asking Jimmy these questions. Younger brother
picking the brain of the older brother. Never the other way
around. Whenever Jimmy did ask a question, I *usually* had an
answer for him. This time I didn't.

That's when the memories of last night piece together,
when I'm relaxed. . .

Her name was Kimberly or "Kim," but her colleagues
called her Greece, as in the country. She was born in Corinth,
an ancient city south of Athens. Then, her parents moved
when she was six years old to Rhode Island. She considered
herself to be a Rhode Islander, despite only living there for
eight years or so. Then, at the age of fourteen, her parents
separated. Her mother caught her father sleeping with a coworker, a much younger and attractive coworker. Her father
ended up keeping the house. The only thing Kim's mother
kept was her dignity. Then, Kim and her mother put Rhode
Island in their rear view and traveled west. According to Kim,
she didn't get along with her mother either. By the time Kim
was seventeen, she was spending the final years as a teenager
bouncing around the Midwest until finally settling in Los Dementes. She also attended the same university as Jimmy,
WHU; a graduate with a major in Marketing; and after she
graduated, she landed a decent job at an advertising agency.
How she ended up in flesh trade is beyond me. I never caught
her last name, only a brief synopsis of her background. Pillow
talk the morning after can be a great way to get to know a
complete "stranger." For me, one who I was exactly nine
inches and four centimeters deep inside the night before. I'm
not ashamed, though, for spending the night with a woman

who could've passed as my older sister. Wouldn't be the first.
I met Kim after Nico introduced me to the next man on my
list. I couldn't stop thinking about jamming my blade into
Bishop's throat and bleeding him dry. Then, there came Kim,
strutting along with her legs as long as stilts, hair like a wave.
I swear she looked like a painting. Bishop poked me on the
shoulder with his finger, telling me that if I didn't make a
move, then he was—I didn't break off Bishop's finger, if that's
what you're thinking, although I'd be lying if I said that it
didn't cross my mind.

As confident as ever, I cut in front of Kim, in spite of
Bishop claiming "first dibs." Kim and I chatted for a while,
but only for a while. Then, we parted ways right before Kim
was starting to become interested in me (this was a trick I
learned from Moses: leave when they're interested, then
they'll want you more). During the brief hiatus, I talked to
other women, including Yolanda (hoping Kim was somewhere in the vicinity, watching me from a distance as I created
the jealous factor). Yolanda turned out to be a conceited,
money-grubber, celebrity without the *celeb* part, popular on
social media and yet, a wannabe nobody in real life. Then, I
was back talking to Kim. Not the get-to-know-you chitchat,
more or less, just the two of us talking about our current environment—yes, I mean, people watching. I played along.

I swim back to shore, each wave reminding me of last
night as I bob up and down. Kim. Beautiful Greece. I trudge
onto the beach and stop in my tracks. I glance down at my
feet, and both of them are completely submerged in the wet
sand. I try to move them around, but they're cemented—
almost to the point of being completely stuck.

As before, I put aside the panic before it can take hold and
draw my attention toward the sky above. The clouds have
given way to a pale blue sky. The sun is also out for the first
time in a while. People are out too, enjoying the pleasant
weather. The breeze is cool and calm as well. And I'm still
running off a buzz from last night's high. I've made new
friends and allies (I even have a new nickname—*Can you believe that?*). I've made new beginnings. New endings.

I look ahead at my bookbag settled over the beach towel
and then glance down at my feet or my lack of feet.

\|\|\|

\ leave Topside feeling optimistic yet, at the same time, skeptical. Can you believe that? Me? Skeptical? I know, right?

A part of me wants to believe that I can truly put all of this crap behind me, for real. Put the shooting behind me, not to mention all of the crap that went down at Red Pines, Moses, the people responsible for Jimmy's death. Like the *former* Christian in me would say, "Reach deep down inside and find forgiveness in my heart." However, another part of me, the darker side, is waited for the right moment to kill every single one of them.

It's already one o'clock in the afternoon.

I kill about an hour walking around New Town until I build up an appetite.

I don't have that much money—at least, not enough to stay a few nights at a place like the Foreshore.

I only have eighty-seven dollars to my name and I'm saving up for a place later. I might have enough money to buy a sandwich or two, but we'll see. I have four airplane bottles of Tanqueray—Nico's liquor of choice—I pocketed without his consent from his wet bar before heading out, a couple of smokes, and the leftovers of an eighth of kind bud that I bought from Yogi last night. I should re-up soon.

\|V

\ head back to Topside Boardwalk and piddle around for about twenty minutes until I cross paths with two kids, a burnout hippie kid and a mooch, hanging around the Galatia.

I tell the kids that I have a half of an eighth for thirty.

We go to the very back of the arcade and the hippie pulls out these hand scales that appear like an insanely clever torture device from the Dark Ages. He tries to weigh the weed—*tries*. The weight's off, as it should be.

The mooch tells me to throw in a little more, then I tell him that I'll take off five bucks. I have to eat and I don't have time to haggle with a stuck-up hippie kid who's using his parents' hard-earned money to buy kind bud. I sell him the weed for twenty-five. He takes out a bud as small as a pea from the bag and asks me if I want to match him on a bowl.

I tell the kid no thanks, get the hell out of there, and use the money on two slices of spongy pizza and a thirty-two-ounce bottle of water at Rico's Pizza Parlor.

After my belly is full of pizza, I fill up the bottle with Sprite while the owner, Rico, is serving pizza to a customer and leave the parlor before Rico makes something out of nothing.

V

I should call Jazz, I tell myself over and over.

Call her, you idiot.

I search through my burner for any missed calls. I have only one missed call, which came from Yogi's phone, which—now that I remember correctly—I dialed last night from his cell to mine after he hooked me up with the weed. Another new ally, I guess.

I check my CONTACTS list, pull up Jazz's phone number, and contemplate calling her as I spend the next five minutes chewing a hole through the inner part of my lip.

Just dial her number and tell her the truth.

I can't tell her the truth. Not now, at least. If I tell her the truth, she'll have nothing to do with me. *But* that's the whole point, right? You have to let her go. Otherwise, you'll drag her down with you. She'll hate you. Is that what you want?

She's a distraction.

Remember?

Nile, who, like all of the other freaks, is dressed in an orange jumpsuit, very prison-y. He runs the blunt side of a blade along his Gene Simmons-like tongue for the sparse crowd of goggle-eyed tourists before him, then pulls the clean blade away, revealing a long slit in his split tongue.

Why are you drawn to that particular color?

You mean orange?

Soon, you'll be seeing a lot of that color if you don't get your head in the game.

I turn away from the chain gang; and from a distance, I watch Jazz assist customers inside Lassie's.

After I finally make up my mind, I leave the boardwalk; and as I'm walking back to my car, I take a sip from an airplane bottle and chase it with soda. It helps. I end up polishing off two bottles before I gather enough courage to talk to Jazz.

On the way to Lassie's, I hear a cell phone ringing and it's not until I remove my bookbag from my shoulders that I realize the ringing is coming from my burner.

I flip open the burner and see Nico's number on display.

Fuck.

I take in a deep breath.

Answer, "Hello."

"Yo," I hear a sheeplike voice over the other end. "What up, *Double-0 Seven*?"

Again with the nicknames.

"Sup, Nico," I reply, my voice remaining calm. "What are you up to?"

"Nothing much, dude," he says, laid-back. "What you doing right now?"

I try to think of something to say in return, but I can't find the words.

"You there?"

Say something, you idiot.

"Yeah," I say abruptly.

"Am I calling at a bad time?"

"Nah," I reply. "I'm just killing some time. And you?"

"What do you say we get up?"

Get up?

"Cool," I say, my stomach starts to churn.

"Where you at?" he asks.

"I'm at the boardwalk in Topside."

"Topside?" I sense disappointment in Nico's voice. Then, he says unsteadily, "A'ight. I'll swing by and pick you up."

I think about last night.

Twice I've spent the night out with or around Nico.

I don't want to give the impression that I'm a fucking mooch.

"I'm actually headed back to my place," I tell Nico.

"A'ight," he says. "Where you staying?"

I remember passing a fancy-schmancy hotel not too far from here. I should have just enough money to afford at least a one night's stay. Maybe two nights if I'm lucky. They might be running some kind of special deal right now, especially this time of year. I'm sure that'll earn me points: proving to Nico that I'm not just a vagabond-douche-moocher hopping from one place to another. Nico is the type who embodies—or at least attempts to embody—the characteristics of maintaining a stable yet, at the same time, a carefree lifestyle. I have to show Nico that I'm like him. I'm normal.

"The Palm Tree," I tell him.

"No shit?"

He sounds surprised—impressed, really.

"We actually had a convention there not too long ago," he says.

"Really," I say. "For your 'pleasure' thingy?"

"PleasureSaber," he corrects me. "Get it right."

"A'ight," I say. "PleasureSaber. Yeah. I got it."

"So, I'll meet you there then," he says. "Be looking for the Blue Dragon."

He means the Lambo, as in a Lamborghini.

"A'ight," I say and close the burner.

I place the cell phone back inside my bookbag and rush to an alley and wait until nobody is around the area; and once I have the green light, I jam my fingers down my throat and puke up the liquor, as well as part of my lunch.

On the way to the hotel, I grab a Gatorade from the closest convenient store and down the entire drink as quickly as I can. I pop two aspirins and keep the soon-to-be headache at bay. Then, once I'm feeling better, I drive to the hotel. I can't find a spot in the parking lot, which is *not* good, even though the sign out front reads, "VACANCY."

I drive to a somewhat rundown hotel next to the Palm Tree called Oceanfront, park in the visitor's parking lot, and walk to the hotel.

When I arrive at the concierge desk, a family of four is taking its good easy time checking in—some curious mother doing the whole small talk bid, mainly asking a variety of questions such as "Are there any good places to eat 'round here?" and then the not so hospitable clerk naming a list of restaurants in Carey, a town south of the Topside area, mainly a bunch of chain restaurants that he's memorized from a brochure: Applebee's, Chili's, Red Lobster (all of the wrong places that you'd want to promote in a itty-bitty beach town which thrives off local cuisine), and then the agitated father pinching his son's arm as he acts out of line while the other one, a bubble-wrapped kid who appears as if he's never broken a single bone in his body stays creepy-close to his mother as he reads a comic. The little bookworm reminds me of Jimmy, not that he used to carry a book around with him everywhere he went—which he did—but the way the kid clings to his mother, as if her boy is an extra appendage or something. Between Jimmy and me, he was the closest to Susannah. The quiet one who never acted out of line.

I start to grow fidgety, really fidgety. The guests are starting to detect me. Some of them are giving me "the look." I hate that look. Despise the look. I turn my attention back on the family. I want to tell them to speed it up already, but I don't want to make a scene—that is, if I hadn't already with my rattled state. I can't find any other way to ask the mother politely without coming off as an impatient asshole. Why is she even having small talk when there are other people waiting in line? Doesn't she know other people are waiting on her? I suddenly hear an engine roar from outside the hotel. A red sports car is driving down an entrance ramp. Not Nico.

As my temper starts to flare—the words crossing mid-tongue, now dangling over the tip and I can even feel them clattering against the backside of my teeth, *HURRY THE FUCK UP*—I hear a woman's voice over my shoulder, "Sir, may I help you?"

I don't even realize that I've said the words out loud until I witness everybody in the lobby gawking at me. Baffled. Disappointed. Frightened.

I turn back around and find another clerk at the desk. She's standing, shoulders squared, wearing a well-practiced smile on her face. A training-smile.

I walk over to the smiley woman and ask her if she has any rooms available.

She asks me how many guests and I tell her that it's just myself and the words feel like one of those toy racecars you'd find in a Happy Meal unwinding over my body.

Once more, she checks the computer screen before her and after a thorough study—her eyes dancing over the screen like ballerinas—she tells me, "We have one room available."

Ocean view?

"I'm afraid not," she says.

I should be even more frustrated, but I'm not.

I'm actually more relieved.

Now, much more calmly, I ask her, "What's the price for the room?"

She says, "Ninety-six dollars for one night, but. . . "

But I know there's a gimmick. There always is. I know she's going to continue to do her song and dance by trying to act professional and courteous, then, when it comes to me forking out the money for the room, she's going to put up a roadblock.

Then, she does it, her pitch about a special deal they're running for the weekend, but I don't have time to listen to it. Nico should be here any minute, if he's not here already.

I pull out the cash and count it. I'm ready to buy the room.

The clerk says, "I'm sorry, sir. We only take credit cards."

Roadblock.

"Credit cards?" I ask and show her the money. "But I have the money right here."

The clerk explains to me why they only take credit cards, but I already know the reasons why they only take credit cards and it's fucking absurd (*if* I trash the room or *if* I damage any furniture or *if* I take any cool beverages from the minibar or *if* any other incidentals have been made, then they can bill me through the credit card that they have on file—in other words, it's basically a whole bunch of "ifs"). They do this to keep people like me from staying in their fancy-schmancy hotel.

I turn away from the chatty clerk and spot Nico's blue Lambo parked right in front of the revolving doors.

How long has he been there?

I turn back to the clerk and tell her "thanks for nothing," and then storm away.

On the way to the entrance, I stop in the main foyer. I can't see if Nico is looking at me. The windows are tinted and definitely not street legal. "Fuck it," I tell myself and bolt straight to the restrooms next to the elevators. I splash my face with water, practice my breathing techniques, and then pull out the switchblade.

After several minutes of debating—mostly pacing around the restroom—I decide to toss the blade into the trash.

I zoom past the foyer, exit through a side door, and then walk back to the front of the Palm Tree where the Lambo is parked.

As I approach the Lambo from behind, Nico rolls down the window.

"Sup, playa," he says. He sounds excited. "I saw you talking to that chick."

What else did he see?

"Yeah," I say as I reach into my pocket, pull out Jazz's number on the napkin, and wag the number in the air. "Just got her number."

"Get outta here," he says.

I don't say anything in return. I just give him a shrug of my shoulders.

Nico waves me inside.

"Way to go, Double-0 Seven, my man," he says.

Then, I hop into the Lambo.

We ride off.

Together.

A MØØTUAL FRIEND

HILE we ride north along the windy Pacific Coast Highway, I frequently check the speedometer, which reads
well above the legal speed limit. Nico's well aware of
my uptight behavior, even though I try not to make it so obvious in front of him when, in fact, I'm flipping out. Seriously,
I'm about to jump my skin. He guns the Lambo around several cars and casually weaves in and out of traffic, as if the
road is like his own personal racetrack; and when he reaches
an open stretch of road, he leans close to me and says,
"Wanna hear her growl?"

Nico is referring to her, as in his Lambo, the Blue Dragon.

Even though my insides feel as if they're doing a number
on my body, I say to Nico, "Let's see what she's got."

Nico breaks a hundred in what feels like milliseconds.
How Nico hasn't already been pulled over by the cops is a
complete mystery. He barely eases off the gas too when we
approach a curve; instead, he hugs the curve well over what
the sign says on the warning sign. Other drivers give Nico an
earful by honking their horns. Nico doesn't appear to be
bothered by the other drivers. He acts as if he either enjoys
pissing off the drivers or he gets off on the rush. I can't quite
tell what the hell is going on inside that head of his. Maybe
it's best not to know.

Finally, Nico slows down once we approach more traffic.

We reach an intersection; then he hooks a left on Trader's Inlet and drives toward the coast.

"I always take her for a spin after a long night out," he says to me. "Sort of shakes the cobwebs loose, you feel me?"

I bob my head.

"I know exactly what you mean," I say, not missing a beat.

We pass a strip of million-dollar houses outside Laguna del Cielo. I've seen many pictures of these houses in magazines, but I've never seen them in real life.

Halfway toward the coast, we pass a congested group of girls walking down the side street. I can't help but check them out as Nico cruises by.

You can't get that in a picture.

As I did with the desk clerk at the Palm Tree, I don't realize that I've said the words out loud until I hear Nico reply, "You damn straight." He turns to me and asks, "How long have you been in Topside?"

"Just a few weeks," I tell him. "*But* it's only temporary."

"I hear you," Nico says. "Trust me. I've stayed in my share of hotels."

"Really?"

"Yeah," he says. "For conventions and whatnot. There was one a couple months back in Las Paraíso."

"Conventions?"

"For the PleasureSaber."

"I didn't know they had conventions for sex toys."

"Oh yeah," he says. "There are at least three I can think of from the top of my head. You wouldn't believe how many people show up to these things."

"Guilty pleasure, I guess."

"*That*," he says, "but most people go to see the women."

"I bet."

"So, you looking for a new pad or what?"

I don't want to impose myself on Nico. I need to show Nico that I have prospects on the horizon.

Therefore, "Yeah," I say, flexing my confidence. "I've had my eye on this one sweet-ass place right off Santa Luce. Two bedrooms. Garage. Ocean view. Nice."

"Well, I'm sure everything will work out," Nico tells me. "It always does, right?"

That same smile makes a sudden yet brief encore on Nico's face.

"*Right*," I parrot.

"Transitions. . . " Nico says as he starts to trail off, ". . . we all go through them."

"Right," I say again, as if it's the only word in my vocabulary, and then we ride in a weighty silence.

\\

NICO and I cruise along the coast until we reach a cozy spot overlooking the Pacific. That's when I get this knot in my stomach, when Nico parks the Lambo on the side of the road. My guard rises, and I get all defensive. I scan the area and check my exits. I don't really have any, but maybe that's the point. He's first to step out. I stay in the car, trying to make sense as to why Nico brought me here.

Through the door, I hear a voice: What you *waiting* for?

I snap from my daze and find Nico staring at me.

What am I waiting for?

I scope out the serene lookout and find two other cars—one being a Winnebago—parked not too far away. I see a couple—possibly out-of-towners—standing on a cliff, sightseeing.

As Nico walks to a steep cliff, I check the glove box on impulse. Tucked away underneath owner's manuals is the handle of handgun. I push manuals and papers aside and find a Beretta M9 in the bottom of the glove box.

"You coming or what?" Nico says, waiting for me to exit the car.

This is how it goes down in the mafia movies. I've seen it a hundred times. Some trustworthy friend drives the guy who's about to get whacked to somewhere remote or whatever. Nico wouldn't kill me in broad daylight, especially with people in the vicinity.

I close the glove box when Nico's looking away and finally exit the Lambo. I follow Nico to the cliff. He sits down over the edge of a flat rock. I don't sit, at least not yet. I'm still wondering why Nico is carrying a Beretta M9 inside his glove box. As far as I know, Nico hasn't showed me any signs of being a violent person. Yet, he acts as if he doesn't carry a mean bone in his body. Not once has he wished ill will against another person, except for maybe that punk, Drew, who got half of what he deserved. Nico is a businessman, an entrepreneur, a "lover, *not* a fighter." These are his words. In a way, Nico acts as if he's a collector of women. He likes taking care of women, the prostitutes, porn stars, models, likes the idea of having them under his glass house as if they're these figurines on the shelf of a display case, grooming them every chance he can find, hiding them from public view, accessing them whenever he wants—a womanizer, for lack of a better term.   I don't think that's a crime the last time I checked. Wrong, I know, but not a crime.

Nico turns to me with a strange, secretive look on his face, as if he knows something that I don't, then points to the bare area next to him.

"Take a load off, my friend," he says with a blasé attitude.

I admire that about him, his "Fuck it" way about him. I sit down next to him while Nico gazes at the Pacific before him.

"What a view," I say, turning my gaze toward the sea.

"It's something." Nico lets out a sigh, as if he's been holding it in his chest for a month. "Ain't it?"

"Yeah," I reply.

"The Pacific Ocean: the one thing that will *never* change," Nico says as he leans back and mounts his arms behind his back. "No matter how hard we try to screw it up with oil leaks, pollution, or whatever garbage we dump into it, somehow it will always find a way to bounce back and revert to what it's good at doing: staying blue. . . unspoiled. . . "

"Nature always has a way of balancing itself out."

"You got that right, Jimmy," Nico chirps.

Clearing my throat, I wipe the sweat from my forehead.

Nico asks, "You a'ight, man?"

I pull myself toward Nico, his beady eyes staring at me.

"Yeah—straight—why?" My voice cracks, as if I'm hitting the early stages of puberty. "Why shouldn't I be?"

Nico lets out a boxy laugh, which sounds ingenious.

While Nico's gazing at the Pacific, I study his eyes, his mannerisms.

"Too much liquid courage last night?"

"Better out than in, right?" I say, after I clear my throat a second time.

"If you need to hurl," he says as he points to the sea, "be my guest."

"Nah," I say. "I gotta stomach made of iron."

I expect him to laugh again or show some kind of reaction, but he doesn't.

Nico hangs his head, as if his mind is filled with all kinds of thoughts. Thinking heavily is not his style.

"Listen, ah Jimmy," he says, this time more seriously. The name *Double-0 Seven* nearly slips from Nico's tongue, but he corrects himself. "I know what it's like to start over. It's tough."

"It's a process, I guess."

"It's tough, though," he says. "You can be honest."

What does he mean by that, me being honest?

Did I say something last night?

If I did, did he catch me in a lie and now he's just toying with me?

Is this supposed to be an interrogation tactic? Nico, the good cop? He shares a heartfelt story. Then warms up to the suspect. Earns trust. Then let the confession begin.

"When I first arrived at Topside," I tell Nico, "I was just trying to get away."

"Get away?" he replies. "From what?"

I let out a sigh similar to Nico's just seconds ago.

"Family," I say. "Friends. I don't know. I guess I needed a change. New environment. New start, you know?"

"From Elizabeth?" he asks.

I must've slipped my tongue last night. Must've mentioned it to Nico when we were taking shots together.

Did I move from Philly to Elizabeth or the other way around?

"Yeah," I answer after a lengthy pause. "Elizabeth."

"Banking city, right?"

"Yeah."

"Never been there," he says. "I've heard many things about it, though."

"Well, I wouldn't recommend visiting," I say. "It's like a different world."

"How so?"

"For one. . . " I say, ". . . the people aren't nearly as friendly as they are here."

"I guess the 'beach life' gets rid of all that shit you pick up in the city." He quickly follows his own comment with a question: "So, how long did you live in Philly before you moved to Elizabeth?"

That answers the question.

Or, is it a trick?

"Just a few years," I say, wondering if Nico has caught me in a lie. I am lying, but does Nico know I'm lying? He doesn't follow up with anything. So, I beef up the story. "My father gotta job transfer," I say. "Then, we moved."

"So, what does your old man do for a living?" he asks.

"*Did*," I correct. "Insurance. He's now retired."

"I see."

"I like it here," I say, directing the conversation away from Philly's background. "I've been thinking about staying."

"Then stay," Nico says bluntly. "What's holding you back?"

I shrug, as Jazz would do.

"I think everybody deserves a chance to start a new life," he says, "to leave behind another one."

"Depends, I guess."

"Depends on what?"

"I guess it depends on who the person is and *what* they've done to want to start a new life."

He doesn't answer. He doesn't do anything for that matter, except listen to the soft whisper of a breeze.

"I remember when I was in my early twenties I stayed with my grandma in Montana for a hot minute," Nico says, as if he's never expressed this sequence of words before and they sound new to him as they fall from the cliff of his tongue. "She and my grandpa were separated, and it was just her and her boyfriend living in the middle of nowhere." He laughs but only for brief moment before he gets serious again. "No phone. No TV. No friends. No girl," he lists. "The first week, I almost went crazy."

"For real?"

"For real, man," he says. "All I had was air to breathe. Food to eat. A roof over my head. After a couple of weeks, I realized something about myself."

"What's that?" I ask, trying to put Nico's grandfather behind me.

"I *hated* myself," he says vigilantly. "Hated the person I was turning into. Even when I looked in the mirror, I didn't know who was looking back at me. I was trapped in this body that I couldn't recognize anymore."

He gets quiet.

I get quiet.

He stares at the Pacific.

I stare at Nico, discreetly.

"In a way, though," he finally says, "I wasn't really visiting my grandma. I think I was looking for him. . . "

"For who?"

I wait for it.

Then, he says it.

"*My father.*"

I clear my throat, this time more quietly.

"Did you ever find him?" I ask Nico.

He pauses yet again.

"Yeah," he says clearly. "I found him all right."

I expect Nico to tell me what happened to Conrad. As before, he doesn't. He doesn't do anything, really.

Over a strained silence, I ask Nico, "So, how's he doing, if you don't mind me asking?"

"He's dead, Jimmy," he says as soon as I finish my sentence. "That's how he's doing."

Conrad?

Dead?

He can't be!

I keep myself together, keep myself from unraveling at the seams, keep myself from displaying any kind of reaction. Most importantly, I keep playing the part. If Nico finds out the reason why I'm in Topside—or even how I "came back" to Topside—then the gig is up. I'm finished. Booted from the club. Ousted from the circle. All of the planning, all of the training, all of it for nothing. I tell Nico what he needs to hear. I make it sound like the car wash attendant, as if it's some kind of half-ass apology. A sneeze.

"Don't be," he says calmly as he fiddles around with a couple of loose pebbles on the ground. "He was a liar, a thief, a criminal." Then, he turns to me with amusement. "You know only three people showed up to his funeral. *Three,*" Nico holds up three fingers, "including me," he says. "You know you find out who really misses you once you're dead."

"Who were the other two?"

"I don't know," he pauses, "the people who found him. They said they found him lying against a redwood with a hole in the back of his head. They heard the gunshot. They said that every now and then, he'd show his face in town but nobody knew him because he kept mostly to himself."

"Where did he live?"

"They said he was staying in a cabin near Briar Canyon," he says but with hesitation in his voice. "Small town up north."

Briar Canyon.

Briar Canyon.

Briar Canyon.

After three times, the name sticks in my mind like a traumatic event.

"What a great way for your old man to go out, right?" he says gleefully, his eyes brimming with tears. "Eating a bullet. Like it was his way of saying the biggest 'fuck you' to me. Thanks for nothing, son," he says, trying to impersonate his father. "This is what happens when you abandon a parent." He flings another pebble in the sea and mumbles, "They blow out their brains and leave their children with questions that'll never get answered." Nico gets quiet again. I'm tempted to ask him more questions about his father, but I let him talk it out. Then, he looks at me: "If I didn't spend that time in Montana before I found out about his death, I probably would've never found out what I wanted."

I think for a moment and Nico waits for a moment, as if he's waiting for me to ask him the question.

I ask him, "What did you want?"

"*Closure.*" Nico's voice rises with muffled excitement, "When I found out that piece of shit was dead—I don't know—I started to think about all of the hate I was holding onto. I was a fool for thinking that it would all just. . . disappear." I search for Nico's eyes, but they're lost in the sea. "It was like his death left with a gigantic hole inside me, like I wasted so many years trying to repair a relationship that never existed. That's when I started the business. Work filled that void. Then, before I even knew it, the hate was gone. Like it was never there to begin with."

I listen carefully to Nico's words, about the hate. I find myself thinking about my own hate, where it came from, what it had become, and how to destroy it.

"I've done a lot of dumb shit in my life. . . " Nico says, shaking his head in disgust, ". . . bad, terrible shit." Then, Nico nods his head at the Pacific and says with resentment, "*And*, as much as I try to forget about all of the shit, it doesn't forget about me. Maybe that's why people come here. For this," *this*, Nico means the Pacific. "One second you're look-ing at the ocean and then the next, the ocean is looking right back at you. For me, at that point, it ceases to be an ocean anymore. It's a memory—same one each time—reminding me of all the shit I've done."

"Maybe we need to be reminded?"

"Maybe."

Nico waves it off as if his shit list is so long that he doesn't even know where to start.

I don't press him.

I don't do anything.

Then, Nico faces me: "The two things a man can *never* outrun are his past and his future. It's up to man to decide whether or not he's content with finishing in third place."

I think about what he says. He's right when he implies that the future is as inevitable as a sunset. The sun will always rise—no doubt—and, on the contrary, the sun will always fall. Nico goes on to say how the future will one day be upon me, and if I'm not making the best of the moment, then I'll be wondering where all of the time went because I was too busy thinking of the past *or* the future. I mean, unless you have superpowers, I don't think anybody can outrun time.

(I once read in the *Book of Quotes*—which was written by the same guy who wrote *Book of Phrases*—about time. The quote—and I'm paraphrasing here—went something like, "A rich man and a poor man are no different than any other man for they share the one common thing neither one of them can buy, and that is time.")

The past will always be there whether or not you'd like to admit it.

And the future will always be there too.

Waiting.

I can't outrun the future when the future hasn't existed yet. I mean, it will one day. Right? And when the future comes and passes you by, then it'll be the past before you know it. I don't put much thought into what Nico says after that, about being "content."

Nico doesn't seem too content about outrunning time at all, even though he acts as if he's already finished the race and now he's kicking back and watching the race from the sidelines.

Collecting.

I don't take much away from the comment other than feeling compelled to ask Nico what in the hell he really wants out of life. I ask him, but it's not quite the answer I expect.

"*Live forever?*" I repeat Nico's words. "I don't think any man wants to live forever."

"Sure they do," he says. "They'd be lying to your face if they didn't."

"Fuck that," I tell Nico. "I don't want to live forever."

Nico faces me once more and looks me directly in the eyes. Serious expression. No emotion. And he tells me with conviction, "Then, you haven't been living, my friend."

I glance down at my shadow sitting beside me on the rock and think about Nico's comment.

But that's all do, really.

I think.

ZERO ₃

TURNS out, Nico tells me a whole bunch of things after we leave Trader's Inlet. More than I expect, really. I'm not sure if he considers me to be a friend now because this is the kind of stuff friends do: they talk about themselves and express their feelings. He opens up about his grandpa, Grandpa West, the OD (original Daddy), and why he and Grandma West split—the OD was a metro (Elizabeth material) and she, a country girl. Nico tells me that his grandpa is a heavy smoker—or used to be—after I ask him how his grandpa developed a chronic—possibly fatal—lung condition after he handed down Daddy's Playground to his son, Conrad, you know, before it became what it is now known as the Palace.

I ask Nico a lot of things, maybe too much.

Surprisingly, Nico answers. Everything.

I ask him what his grandpa does nowadays and Nico tells me that he doesn't do much of anything, really.

I ask him if he's close to his grandpa.

Nico says he's "close" to his grandpa. He says his grandpa is a spark plug despite his old age.

"Once you get him going," Nico says, "he won't shut up."

I take note of his grandfather's personality. Then, I tell Nico that he should remain close to his grandpa, especially after everything he said about his father and how they didn't have much of a relationship. It's the right thing to say to

Nico. It's what a friend would say. I show Nico that I care. I mean, after all, his father was a total douche for the way he treated his son.

Nico tells me that he visits his grandpa every Tuesday afternoon at Grand Valley Estates, a home designated for the care of seniors.

I take a mental note of the retirement home.

Grand Valley.

Grand Valley.

Grand Valley.

\\

WE make it back to Topside in one piece.

Nico drops me off in front of the Palm Tree.

As I step out and close the door, Nico hollers out from inside the Lambo, "Yo!"

I lean through the window.

Study Nico.

"You know, I was thinking since you might be staying for a little bit longer, would you be interested in looking for work?"

I hesitate for a moment, then respond, "Sure. Of course."

"I know a guy who's been looking for an extra hand and I think it might be right up your alley," he says. "You interested?"

"Well, depends on the job."

"I can't go into any details right now," he says, "but I know him personally. He's a good man. Loyal. Extremely loyal."

"You're straight with mixing business with pleasure?"

"I don't mind at all, my friend," he says, smiling. "*Pleasure* is my business."

I don't know what he means by that. Surely, it doesn't have to do anything with what Nico does for a living, selling dildos or whatever he wants to call them.

"I'll think about it," I tell Nico.

"Sounds good, Jimmy," he says. "I'll be in contact."

I step away from the Lambo.

Nico speeds away and somehow I feel a sense of jealousy.

\|\|\|

I'M starting to wonder if Nico just said those things to get rid of me or to brush me off his shoulder like a piece of lint; and now, here I am, waiting around until the old black suit, Grim Reaper, knocks on my door. You're probably thinking that I can't stand the Reaper man—you know, being someone who doesn't want to live forever—but I don't. On the contrary, I respect the bag of bones. He's just doing his job. Of all the people whom I respect, the Grim Reaper is right at the top.

For the rest of the afternoon, I try to think of what I might've said back at Trader's Inlet that could've rubbed Nico the wrong way.

Did I ask too many questions?

No such thing as too many questions.

I pocket my burner and twiddle my thumbs until it starts to go out of style.

I can't stand waiting; in fact, I despise it.

\|\/

SINCE I've already worn out my welcome at Cyber Jaxx's, I decide to hit up the public library in New Town. There, I research the keywords *Briar* and *Canyon* and *Suicide* and narrow down my search from the day Jimmy was shot, the Thirteenth of April, to the days following the shooting. It doesn't take me long to find the name, CONRAD WEST, under the Briar Canyon County Death Records. I can't believe Conrad was there all along, like a ghost in the machine. So close yet so far away.

As I'm trying to dig up more dirt on Conrad, I find a newspaper article on a microfiche machine.

The article states that when cops first arrived on the scene, Conrad was already dead. A crater in his head. His brains like a mural on the redwood. Dead as dead. His "masterpiece." Days later, after Conrad was identified by his next of kin, Nico, they conducted an autopsy; afterwards, they ruled Conrad's death as suicide, just as Nico said at Trader's Inlet.

Why do I *not* feel a mountain of relief?

Why do I feel as if I've failed Jimmy?

I should've been the one to pull the trigger and witness that murderer's brain splatter over that redwood like a Jackson

Pollock painting. I should be feeling better now that Jimmy's murderer has been laid to rest. Now, I can somewhat move on with my life. I should be feeling better about myself. . .

But I'm not.

I don't feel much of anything, really.

I print out the articles, as well as the location of Grand Valley Estates.

If Conrad's father, Nico's grandfather, the OD himself, Valentine West, was with his son the night Jimmy was shot in Old Town, then he'll know what really happened that night. I believe Valentine is the last piece of the puzzle. He has to be.

V

I'M wiped. Literally wiped. I fell like an old dishrag. I find a rundown motel between Nico's place and the Strip—that way, if he calls, I'll be a hop and skip away from him. I buy a room for the night. I can afford it. The room is worse than bad, but it'll have to make do. The air smells like a dirty armpit that's been sprayed with cheap artificial fresheners. Next to one of the queen-sized beds is a dark, brownish stain about the size of a head on the beige carpet. Either it's from blood, vomit, or shit. I think it might be blood, but I could be wrong. I think maybe someone died in here. The bed sheets are dull-looking, too, and when I sit down on the edge of the bed, I nearly slip off from the slickness of body oil. I can only imagine what I'd find if I had a black light on me. I guess the less you know, the better.

After I get settled, I take a piss in the bathroom, which reeks heavily of Clorox. Then, I try to make myself comfortable by doing what I hate the most for hours, spending most of the time staring at my burner like a writer with writer's block—and even a writer—the good ones, that is, not those impostors spamming the Internet, *"Buy one ebook, get another one free!"*—will tell you that there is no such thing as writer's block and, even if such a phenomenon exists, which it doesn't (so I've read), the only cure is to write. Write anything. Doesn't matter.

I follow the writer's theory and write with my fingertips, flipping through the channels on the TV remote as if the up and down buttons were the keys of a typewriter, and as I'm flipping, *tap, tap,* tapping away, I come across a familiar face.

I go back to the previous channel—the local news, Channel 9—then turn up the volume. Anthony Foster's poor mug is plastered all over the TV, the reporter's speaking about his recent death. She's saying the coroner found "lethal amounts of opiates" in Foster's bloodstream; then, she concludes by saying the police ruled "Foster's death" as "an accident."

I feel somewhat relieved, knowing that—despite the falsity of the report—I'm in the clear for the time being. One less thing to worry about, I guess.

I make myself comfortable again and flip around until I find an infomercial on handguns. I watch the infomercial for maybe several hours—I don't know.

Before I even realize where the time went, the sun is already up.

I decide to stay another night in the shitty motel.

Why not?

I can afford it.

I spend most of the day hanging around the motel. I take a walk on the beach in the afternoon and contemplate calling Jazz a couple of times, once while I'm hanging out on the beach and another time while I'm walking back to my room; however, I never gather enough courage to make the call.

I rather just hang out in my room.

It's better this way.

VI

At nighttime, the tightness is back.

The tightness brings an unsettling feeling, which renders me into a continual state of uncertainty. My breath is getting more laborious, thoughts as well, like my body is warning me that I'm about to lose control. I find myself taking in deeper breaths throughout the slow night, constantly wondering when *or* if I'm going to be ripped from this very plane of existence at any moment. The more I think about death, the tighter the fist clenches inside me: in my chest, in my throat, in all my veins.

Since I'm strapped for cash and I'm currently staying in a location where most people are strapped for cash, I rush to the closest convenient store, a twenty-four hour Quickie Mart, purchase a six-pack of Miller Lite, spend the innocent side of nighttime in my room drinking beer and watching porn, then repeat in a different order until I'm red and swollen and afflicted with guilt. How much longer do I have to wait until Nico calls me? I start to wonder if this was his plan all along: to wear me down until I'm no longer in the picture. Maybe he thinks I'll forget? Maybe he thinks I'll get a job on my own? Maybe he thinks I'll leave once I realize that I have no friends here? If Nico knows anything about me, these ideas will never enter his mind.

After I down four beers, I stop being all pathetic and change into a pair of fresh clothes. Lassie's closes around nine or ten—I think—and maybe Jazz is working.

When I reach Lassie's, her gay boss, Eric, is flirting with two customers as he rings them up. I ask him if Jazz is working tonight—maybe she's in the back somewhere, taking five or using the ladies restroom; then Eric's mood suddenly changes in front of the customers and he tells me with a scowl streaking through his face that Jazz quit yesterday and he acts as if I'm predominantly to blame—but whatever, if that's what he really thinks. I ask him if she got a job anywhere else.

He shrugs, as Jazz would do, then plants his hand on his hip, then tilts his body in an angle, and says resentfully, "The hell if I know."

I go back to the motel and watch more porn.

I watch until its starts to go out of style.

And then I watch some more.

Like I'm beating a style to death.

VII

On the third day after Nico divulged the key information on his father, I cave in and contemplate doing the one thing I said I'd never do again.

For the first half of the day, I make sure to keep myself hydrated by drinking lots of water. I piss a lot, then shit a lot; and I make sure all of the booze is completely cleaned from my system—nothing worse than getting high with alcohol in your system. Look what happened to Anthony Foster. I guess everybody reacts differently to drugs, though, especially when mixed together. A cocktail of fun or a cocktail of death. I did it once a long time ago: shot up while I was drunk off my ass. Bad idea—*bad*, as in I nearly died-bad. If I didn't have a mother who used to be a nurse, then I wouldn't be here today. I'll never forget. She saved my life.

I pull out the case from my bookbag and lay it on the edge of the sink. I open the case. I cook the dope in a spoon; however, I botch the first cook. I'm still rusty, but I have more success on the second. It's not a perfect cook, but it'll do the job. I insert the needle into the dope and pull upward on the plunger. I find a vein in my foot. The needle, now dripping with dope. . .

I never shoot, though.

I think about it.

I even go as far as to place the needle in my skin.

I never shoot.

Almost.

Moses shows up at the door, disappointed. He's wearing another suit, an all-white one. He has dark bags underneath his eyes, as if he's spent the last three days wide-awake. He has so much anguish on his face. He tells me that I've come so far, that I've traveled so many miles, that I've hurdled so many obstacles. He tells me that if I shoot, then there's no coming back.

Seven hundred and eighty-one days, he reminds me.

And counting.

Think about *zero*.

I hate the number, yet at the same time, I respect the hell out of it. I respect its importance. I respect its modesty. It's fair to say that I need zero as much as it needs me.

I leave the motel and drive to Old Town where I find a thug hustling drugs on a street corner. I approach the thug and make myself known. He throws his head in a nod, exposing a mouthful of silver teeth. I ask him if he's holding. He snarls and looks me over as if he wants to either fuck me or do something strange to my body, then he asks me, "You five-o, white boy?"

I act like he's hard of hearing, which I know he's not, and ask him if he's holding again.

"You straight or what?" I say as I display dominance by puffing out my chest.

The thug gets close to me, real close. He smells like something died inside him, and for the life of me, I can't understand the next words that spit from his mouth. The thug tries to push a bundle on me but I tell him that it's not my thing.

I end up scoring a dime bag of weed, which is probably laced with PCP—that's phencyclidine, very nasty stuff that's also used in angel dust—as well as a thick wad of cash in his pocket, over a hundred: twenty of those dollars consisting of dollar bills and then the rest a fifty and a twenty.

I take the weed back to the motel where I smoke just enough to get me through the night.

VIII

By the fourth night, I sense the room getting smaller.

I'm aware that, if gets any smaller, I'm headed back to Red Pines.

Moses decides to hang around for a while, just to make sure I don't do anything stupid. He remains consistent on reminding that we're not going back to that hellhole, Red Pines. I don't want to go back. He doesn't want to go back. *We* can't go back. I check my cash the same way a solider does a shell count. I'm only left with twenty-three dollars and some change. I've stayed here long enough; and by knowing that, I know it's in my best interest to bounce.

I use ten dollars on gas, which leaves me with thirteen dollars, as well as a couple of dollars in change underneath the seats and floor mats of the car.

IX

I stop at Old Town Diner, grab a booth in the back, and order a cup of coffee. The waitress with squeaky tennis shoes giving me the tongue stops by the table and evidently she notices my fragile state and hooks me up with a slice of pumpkin pie. Then she goes back to the kitchen while the manager is off counting cash and sneaks me a bottle of *Reddi-whip* and tops off the slice of pie with a generous portion of whipping cream.

The waitress leans in close and tells me, "Our little secret."

I look closely at her nametag: AUTUMN.

The name comforts me.

I like the name Autumn. She looks as if she's well into her forties, and she'd look at least ten years younger if she had lipo done underneath her chin. I can tell she used to party back in the day from the rough edge in her voice, as well as the way she awkwardly gaits from table to table. I'd say she was either with Team Neil or Team Michaels when she was a teenager. I can see young Autumn with a monumental hat of hair sculpted with an entire can of hairspray, wearing a tattered jean jacket with lots of pink underneath. Showing some skin. Just enough to grab the boys' attention, like a bellybutton or a teaser of cleavage. She was once a princess cast from the days of glam metal.

I make sure to thank Autumn for the pie and then I tell her that her secret is sealed in the vault.

With her hands full, she points the coffee pot at the book, *Joshua'ζ Tree*, on the table.

She nods at the book, her eyes fixed on the VR hands.

"My nephew got me into that book," she says.

"Oh yeah?"

She nods again, this time in agreement.

"How old's your nephew?"

"He's a little bit younger than you." She tilts her head to the side, as if she's carrying a thought and the thought is starting to weigh on her. "I didn't quite understand the ending of the main story, not the epilogue or whatever." Then, she says in one breath, "Have your read it yet?"

"I have."

"Then, let me ask you, if you don't mind."

"I don't mind."

She leans closer.

"Was The Hate Train all in his head?" she asks me. "Like that one movie with that guy who started his own club. . . "

"No," I say, thinking. "Maybe. I thought the game was real, but the members who played The Train were not. In a way, they were all Joshua, each one representing the different sides of his personality."

"Okay."

"I read an interview with the author somewhere, and he said it was his intention to leave it up for the reader to decide, to make the reader think, not spell it out."

"Very interesting, *profound*," Autumn says with an expression which can only suggest she impressed with the words that came out of my mouth. She nods again at the book and says, "And the roadmap?"

Without thinking, I crack open the book and reveal a map of Topside, as well as the page full of handwritten NOTES.

"Just a bookmark," I say.

In a quick glance, she acknowledges, not only my hand-writing, but also the psycho-scribbling of those who previously owned the book.

"I guess I'll have to read it again, but I never thought about it that way." She pauses, surveys the rest of the diner with a drawn-out sigh. "Well," she says, "gotta check on other customers. If you need anything, just give me a holler. Name's Autumn. Like the season."

"Nice to meet you, Autumn," I say.

She smiles again before she walks away.

I eat the pie and before I know it, the entire plate is peppered with crumbs from the flaky piecrust.

She stops at other tables but somehow finds her way back to mine.

We share a conversation about burning the midnight oil.

Autumn does most of the talking while I do most of the listening. She reminds me a lot of my Aunt Gabriella—Aunt Gabby is what we used to call her. She was Thomas's sister, but it's fair to say that he didn't have much of a relationship with her. I don't even think they spoke to one another after she came out of the closet. Now that I think about it, I never really saw the two carry on a conversation; and if they did, it came across as contrived, even the time when we had her over for Thanksgiving. I remember she used to bring over the best sweet potato casserole. I swear it was like candy. I think she and Thomas weren't that close to begin with—at least that was the impression I got whenever the two of them ended up in the same room together. Aunt Gabby passed away some time ago from breast cancer. I used to visit her and her partner, Stephanie, all the time. I don't talk to Stephanie that much anymore; in fact, the last time we talked was at the funeral. I liked Stephanie. Liked her a lot. She was nice to me. She was somewhat shy, like me, a stargazer as well. Big into different galaxies and whatnot. We used to sit on her porch late at night and get baked out of our minds and point out the constellations. Whenever Stephanie spoke, she always had something deep or meaningful to say. She loved my Aunt Gabby. I think she loved me too even though Thomas wanted me to stay far away from her.

RISKY
BUSINESS

EPISODE 6

UNTOUCHABLE BUTT DESTRUCTIBLE

leave the diner and stop at Spirits to grab a pint of Cuervo.

As I'm about to checkout and blow the rest of my money on booze, the same Haitian clerk from before is staring at me with his arms crossed over his chest just like Mr. Hamilton, my ninth grade English teacher at East Providence, used to do whenever he caught me drawing storyboards in my Composition notebook while some teacher's pet was reading sentences out loud from some boring, outdated book that had absolutely no relevancy to anyone in the class, and I remember Mr. Hamilton, that spineless hack would be looming over my desk, that dreadful expression containing every word beginning with a prefix *dis-* engraved on his face like a memorial.

I hated that fucking look.

I glance down at the rest of the money in my palm.

"Sir?"

He tells me the price of the liquor once more with a tremble tone underneath his voice.

"Sorry," I tell the clerk and leave without putting the liquor back in its rightful place on the shelf.

I drive straight to Jazz's apartment. I don't even turn on the stereo during the drive. Instead, I ride in stark silence. Each intrusive thought running into the next. I focus my thoughts by practicing an inner dialogue on what to say to Jazz the moment I find myself face to face with her. How will she react to my presence? Will she act as if she's missed me?

Hey, Jimmy! It's great to see you! Or, will she hate me? *Leave me alone! I literally hate you!* Or, worse, has she already written me off? *Burn in hell, you jerk face!* I keep my thoughts as positive as I can, even though the negative ones try to squeeze in the final say. I find a middle ground, a state between positive and negative. The fact: I stood Jazz up like a clown. Plain and simple. We were going to hang out. I got beat up. I failed to take responsibility. What makes it even worse is that I didn't call her. *But* I feel as if Jazz deserves better than a phone call.

I park next to the curb and slap myself in the face a couple of times before opening the door. I exit the car and don't feel the nerves until after I knock on the door of her apartment.

When Jazz answers the door, she seems surprised to see me; in fact, she acts skittish, paranoid even, as she looks around the streets as if she's being watched, stalked, or whatever. Her state of shock leaves me in shock as well. I'm speechless. I have *no* words. Not one. Everything I role-played inside my head is all disarranged like a tightly packed deck of cards that have been dropped on the floor. Even when the words enter my thoughts, they don't quite reach my lips. Yet, they dangle on the edge of my tongue. Words not ready to leave the nest. *I want to be inside you*, I think, but I reckon my eyes do most of the talking as they trace Jazz's perfectly toned body. She's wearing black leggings, which should be illegal to wear in public, and a black *Dragonball Z* T-shirt, which is cut an inch above her innie belly button. I turn my thoughts to the sea and the thought of the sea prevents me from puking all over Jazz.

I keep it simple.

"Hey," I say.

"You shouldn't be here," Jazz says over a moment of silence. Her voice is phlegmy and scratchy, as if she's one holler away from going hoarse.

I don't respond.

She asks over my lack of response, "Jimmy, what are you doing here?"

I tell Jazz that I was just in the neighborhood—don't all the creeps say that? Just in the neighborhood, you know, watching you from a distance. The words don't come out as smoothly as I would like. Instead, the words leave my lips like ketchup being spanked from a half-empty bottle.

She doesn't respond.

The more I talk, the lesser I think about puking.

"I talked to Eric, your boss," I say. "He said you don't work there anymore."

"Yeah," she says with deflation. "It was only short term."

"So, what have you been up to?"

"Just working," she says shortly.

"That's cool—"

"—I went back to another job that pays better."

Jazz still looks antsy, like me. Still checks the streets behind me. Then she crosses her arms over her chest, like the Haitian not too long ago, like that mouth breather, Mr. Hamilton, something that I've never seen her do before, which is unusual. She gives me that look again, as if she's itching to tell me something but she's not ready.

"So, where do you—"

"—What happened to you the other night?" she finally asks.

She's been waiting for days to speak those words; and when they come out, the words are as keen as a blade.

I must tell the truth, not the entire truth, but I have to work my way up to telling her—like a runner training for a marathon. Each day increasing the length of a run. Building strength and endurance.

"I was jumped," I tell her, but she doesn't believe me at first. "I was too embarrassed to see you."

Jumped?

She studies my face. The cuts have sealed shut. The bruises faded to shadows along my skin.

"That's your excuse?" she asks, her voice slants with amusement. "You were jumped?"

"It's *not* an excuse," I say. "It's the truth whether you want to believe me or not. . . "

"Why would you feel embarrassed about that?" she asks me.

I look around the street, struggling to find the words. I tear up a little. Pull yourself together.

I turn back to Jazz and she's looking at me strangely.

"I don't know," I tell her.

Jazz acts as if she doesn't have much to say to me and the more I hang around, the more I sense that I showed up at a bad time.

She steps forward. Gives me a hug, but I know she's doing it out of sympathy. I've turned into that guy, the pathetic sap who keeps hanging around.

"I'm sorry," she says. "I was upset."

"You have every reason to be upset."

I've learned that the first rule in relationships is admitting to wrongdoing.

I apologize for not keeping her informed.

A shadow manifests over the wall behind Jazz. The shadow distorts, and then takes the shape of a person.

My stomach sinks a little.

Jazz's mother, Rosa, pokes her head from the kitchen. I only catch her eyes and everything up.

"Jasper?" she says in a sultry Spanish accent. "Who are you talking to?"

"Just a friend," Jazz says over her shoulder. Then, she blocks the doorway, as if she's shielding me from her mother.

She cranes her head over my shoulder and notices my car parked out front.

Then, she asks, "You wanna get outta here?"

"Okay," I say.

Before Jazz attempts to close the door, she says, "Give me a second. Will you?"

I walk back to my car and do the one thing I hate the most.

Three minutes later, Jazz hastily steps out of her apartment. I hear the voice of a woman yelling from inside. She speaks ridiculously fast, like one of those auctioneers prattling out prices to an audience of bidders. I can only assume her mother is upset from the sharpness of her voice, but I can only assume.

Jazz closes the door behind her and locks it, which dampens the woman's passionate voice. She walks away from the apartment. Doesn't look back. I notice that she's wearing the same earrings that I bought her—the lanceolate leaves.

I don't bother bringing up her mother whom I assume is upset.

Instead, I compliment Jazz's earrings as soon as she makes herself comfortable.

She smiles, a comfortable cat's smile, and says, "The guy who bought them for me has good taste."

I smile back and then drive away.

\\

SINCE I only have a total of fifteen dollars altogether, including all of the change I scavenged from the car, I tell Jazz that I can buy her just one hot dog. "*One is enough*," I tell her and she giggles at the comment. I can't figure out if she thinks I'm making an innuendo since the hot dog is in the shape of a phallus or I'm making a more insightful comment, such as a girl should only have one hot dog. More than one could possibly lead to extra pounds, which could lead to heart disease, which could result in death—or other things, depending whether or not Jazz's mind is in the gutter. Or maybe I'm not even telling Jazz these things. Maybe I'm telling myself without telling myself: One is enough, as in one woman. Maybe that's all I need; and when I've found the right one, *one is enough*. I don't know.

Either way, Jazz's laughter dwindles into the clearing of her throat. Her face absorbs in thought. I can help but visualize all of the thoughts like streams of data routing from one wire to another through the circuitry of her mind.

I wonder what she thinks of me.

I order the one hot dog for Jazz. *Just one.* When she asks me if I'm hungry, I tell her that I've already eaten and ask the server at the concession for a cup of water and then I turn to Jazz and she's left with a look that only one would get from a person trying to solve a puzzle: a furrow of the brows followed with a bite of the bottom lip. I like that she doesn't know much about me. I like that she's trying to figure me out. Not only that, I also feel a lot better knowing that I spent the money on a person whom I like sharing company with, rather than booze or whatever. I like the booze, but the thought alone of what can develop between Jazz and me is much more enticing and, fingers crossed, rewarding.

Jazz asks the server for a cup of ice, then pours the diet soda in the cup. The fizz from the soda brims to the top of the cup.

"Check this out." I run the tip of my finger along the side of my nose, place my finger inside the foam, and the foam quickly dissolves.

"How'd you do that?"

I tell Jazz that it's magic.

It's *not* really magic, just the oil on my finger reducing the surface tension of expanding carbonated bubbles—or what most people call *fizz*—causing the bubbles to collapse. It's science.

Jazz looks at her drink with mild disgust.

"Is that even sanitary?" she asks me.

Technically, it's not, due to bacterium called staph, short for staphylococcus—another one of those absurd words that some doctor or whoever came up with. And you probably don't even know that you have staph, but you do; and it's all in your nose.

I shrug, as Jazz would do, and tell her that I don't have cooties and she's safe.

"I thought all guys have cooties."

"Only the bad ones."

"And are *you* bad, Jimmy?"

I answer with a question of my own.

"Do you think I'm bad?"

She bites her bottom lip as she ponders the question. Her eyes narrow as if she's staring at a bright object or something and says, "Don't know yet."

"There'll always be good guys," I say to Jazz, "*and* bad guys. And the bad guys need the good guys as much as the good guys need the bad guys."

"So, which one are you?" she asks me.

"I guess I'm stuck in the middle."

"Nah," she says, shaking her head. "You're not bad. You're just an old soul."

As I think more about the comment, Jazz flashes a smile on one side of her face and the smile remains like a snapshot in my mind.

"Like me," she says coyly.

She nods at the Ferris wheel next to the carousel, which is swarming with kids and their parents.

"Wanna ride?" she asks me.

I shrug, again, and say, "Sure."

I've passed the historic Ferris wheel several times during the time spent in Topside. The Ferris wheel was here when Jimmy and I lived in Los Dementes. I remember we used to ride the wheel every time we vacationed on the beach. Several times I've been tempted to ride the wheel—purely out of nostalgia—but I never had anybody to ride it with. Not until now.

I treat Jazz the way every girl should be treated, and I decide to ride the Ferris wheel with her.

This is the right thing to do.

Keep telling yourself that, Moses says from the reflection of the warped mirror next to the carousel.

This *is* right.

Once she finds out exactly what kind of person you are, she'll run from you—

"—What did Eric say when you asked about me?"

"Eric?"

"You know," Jazz says, "my boss."

Right.

"He just said that you don't work there anymore, but I can tell he was pissed."

A hiccup of a laugh slips from Jazz's mouth as she takes a pinch from the bun of the hotdog and nibbles extra carefully, as if she's trying not to break a tooth or something.

"Tell me about it," she says with one side of her mouth full of bread. "When I told him I was quitting," she holds out her fingers inches apart, "I swear he came like '*this* close' from losing it. I could see veins in his forehead. His nostrils were flaring. It was *bad*." She hangs her head as she mumbles, "I feel bad."

"He doesn't have anybody else working for him?"

"Only two or three others," she says, "but I think they don't work there anymore. I haven't seen them around in a while."

"I'm sure Eric will find someone else."

"Yeah," she says as she steps inside the passenger car, Jazz first and then me. "He will, I guess."

The operator closes the door behind us and tells us to enjoy the ride.

I mentally run through the questions in my head and fire out one at a time.

"So," I say, anticipating Jazz's response, "you said you went back to an old job?"

As she takes another pinch from the hotdog, she clears her throat and then she washes the bite down with her diet soda.

"Yep," she says as she clears her throat once more. "It's like a modeling job."

She struggles to look me in the eye when she speaks.

"Modeling, huh?" I say, unsure whether or not to push the subject forward. "I can see that—I mean, you have the look."

In the background, a person is saying something over an intercom; however, I completely tune him out.

"It's okay, I guess," she says humbly as the car starts to lift. "The money's not that bad. There's a lot of upkeep, though, if you know what I mean."

"I bet," I say as we ride the Ferris wheel.

I stop and think of something funny to say.

"So, if like someone dyed your hair green and shaved your eyebrows while you were sleeping, I supposed that wouldn't be good."

Jazz suddenly leans back and looks at me in awe—a sort of "No, you didn't just say that!" kind of expression on her face.

"No!" she says, her laugh sounding like a melody. "Looking like a Chia Pet would most certainly not be good!"

I like it when Jazz laughs. She was born to laugh.

We make it to the top of the Ferris wheel, revealing the entire town of Topside, as well as the distant skyline of Los Dementes.

I turn to Jazz, who's putting aside the hot dog. I get a sense that she has lost her appetite.

"You should be proud of yourself," I go on to tell her. "I'm proud. . . "

Jazz turns her glazed eyes toward me. They look so far away yet they remain so close to me.

I know she's either hiding or dodging. Not sure which one. Either she's hiding behind the insecurity or she's dodging from something that I know all too well. I decide to leave it alone. I don't want to ruin anything between us—that is, if there is an "us" at all. I think there is. I think Jazz thinks so too.

\|\|\|

ONCE we finish riding, Jazz stops by a face-painting booth and tosses her empty drink into the trash. She wraps up half of the uneaten hot dog in the foil and tells me that she's going to save it for later. Then sticks it in her purse. I wonder what else she's got stuffed in there.

We walk around the carnival for a while and watch other festivities around us: the Horse Race game, the one with the water gun, or Drain-A-Hoop-Win-A-Prize. The games don't look that appealing, especially the one with the basketball hoop. I never was much of a shooter, as in I was never that good at basketball. I save myself the embarrassment.

Throughout our walk, Jazz is somewhat quiet—more so than before. I know it may have something to do with me telling her that I was proud of her.

As we idle past Sherbet's, the ice-cream place, a familiar face on TV stops me in my tracks. Daniel Ayker. What the hell is he up to?

I inch closer to the parlor and stare at the TV above the cashier.

On the screen: Ayker, everything about him reeks of a politician. He's wearing a watch similar to the one Thomas received as a retirement gift (a Rolex perhaps?). Behind him stand four expressionless men, two of them dressed in suits while the other two dressed in police uniforms, acting as if they're knights protecting their king as he preaches about how he wants to "get all of the guns off the streets" as well as solve the "drug epidemic" to a crowd of wired reporters and journalists gathered around like an ancient tribe circling around a chief in front of a courthouse. Nothing *new* here. Every election year the same subjects come up: guns, drugs, terrorism, and the economy. While one party spreads fear and uncertainty, the other one spreads false hope and broken promises. Yet, every election year, they, as in politicians, come up with cockeyed solutions to problems that will never be fixed. Ayker, being a cop and all, sticks to the two things he knows: guns and drugs. He sounds the same as any other politician, telling people what they want to hear, not what they *need* to hear.

I listen closer through the open storefront and he's now talking about his track record, how in the past six months *we*—and I don't know who he means by we (I'm guessing the Los Dementes Police Department)—have brought down over a dozen drug cartels in the Los Dementes County area, cartels pushing drugs that are "poisoning our youth" and "bringing mass corruption onto our streets." If you don't take a stand once and for all, he preaches, these drugs will keep pouring onto the streets and the cycle will continue to go on and on, like the Energizer Bunny—a juicy "sound bite" for the media (I can see the news immediately after the press conference with the tagline on the bottom of the screen reading: Ayker compares the drug epidemic in America to the *"Energizer Bunny that keeps going and going").*

A delicate voice over my shoulder: "Is something wrong?"

I should tell Jazz that nothing is wrong, but she's staring at me with confusion.

I nod at the TV; and out of the blue, I ask Jazz who the man is on TV even though I already know her answer.

She peers through the parlor.

"Which one?"

"That man," I say and point at the man inside the boxed TV.

"Oh," she says resolutely as she points to him. "You mean him?"

"Yeah," I reply. "The guy speaking. Who is he?"

"Uh, Ayker," she says, thinking. "Dan Aykcr, I think. I know he used to be a cop. . . he's the Sheriff of Los Dementes. *Was*, I think."

"What's he doing now?" I ask, trying not to draw any suspicion.

"I think he's running again for office," she says, clearing her throat.

"Huh?"

She too listens to what Ayker's preaching on TV. Then, after she picks up a line, her eyebrows rise about a centimeter into her forehead as if her shoulders aren't the only things she can shrug. She leans in close to me and says, "The only people who think there's something wrong with the world are the ones who are *not* living in the world. The world's just fine the way it is." Her eyes shoot at the TV, like *Superman* shooting red beams from his eyes. "Same shit. Different piles."

"Right," I utter, noticing that Jazz notices I'm focused more on Ayker than her. I can't help but wonder how much he has changed, dramatically. Another man who has aged significantly.

"Why are you so interested in him?" she asks me, as she furrows her brows.

A deflated shrug.

I don't respond to Jazz's question. I should, immediately. I shouldn't display any interest in this man, but I can't help myself.

As Jazz informed me, Daniel Ayker used to be a police officer employed by the Los Dementes Police Department. He was one of the many corrupted cops who disguised themselves as "honest" cops. I believe cops like Ayker was one of the reasons why we moved to the opposite side of the country. I never went to Thomas about Ayker after the shooting—even if I did, I knew he'd immediately change the subject or act as if he didn't want to hear what I had to say about Ayker. I'm not a cop, only the son of one, which puts me in the same boat as everybody else.

As a child—I mean, the age when I started to ask questions—I was shunned by the truth. Same with Jimmy and Susannah. Thomas and I lived so close to one another, feet apart, slept in rooms that were separated by a hallway; yet, we were complete strangers when it came to his job, as if an invisible force field was protecting him and everybody inside it, including Ayker. A Death Star of all things exclusive. I think everybody and their uncle knew Ayker was as crooked as a Kansas road sign. Even Thomas.

During the length of time I spent investigating Jimmy's case with Dwight, a close friend who played softball with Thomas on Saturdays and who, by the way, worked at the same precinct as Thomas before we became Tar Heels, I found out that not only was Ayker patrolling Old Town the same night Jimmy was shot, but he was also accepting bribes from Nico's father in order to protect Daddy's Playground.

Now, why would Conrad West need protection?

The answer: Conrad was conducting a prostitution ring, or a "racket," as cops call them.

Henry found out about what was going on inside the nightclub—the racket—the cops accepting bribes in order to protect the nightclub, then told Myrtle, as if she didn't know what was going on with her husband and his shady businesses. I couldn't dig up as much information on her as I wanted to, but I suppose she knew about everything that was going on. She had to.

According to Henry's sister, Bella, Henry told Myrtle about how he was going to bring down Conrad and all of his goons.

According to Bella, after Conrad found out about the affair between his wife and Henry, Myrtle was fluffed like an old pillow. Bella told me about the bruises and all on Myrtle's body. Henry even took a picture of them and showed them to Bella.

The thing I don't understand—still don't.

Why didn't Henry get out of there when he had the chance?

Henry had a life, a career, a home.

Why risk his life for a woman who was already married?

Henry had to know Conrad was onto him. Someone doesn't take a beating like that without spilling secrets.

As far as Ayker, he was never on my naughty list; in fact, I shelved him away along with all of the other crooked cops who were accepting bribes after I got wind of Conrad being the one who pulled the trigger. I wanted to hold Ayker accountable for the business he was conducting on the side with Conrad; but, to me, Ayker always came across as someone who was not only untouchable by the law, but also unreachable. Even though Ayker wasn't involved in the shooting, Ayker was *very* much involved. If that makes sense.

Jazz says my name again.

"Yeah," I say trance-like and face Jazz. "He just looks familiar. That's all."

"You okay?"

I nod my head.

Then, together, Jazz and I walk away from the parlor.

R O M A N - T I C   D R E A M S

W E leave the boardwalk.

Jazz grabs me by the hand and walks me to a tent near the beach and shows me a poster that she did for the annual "FREAKSPECTACULAR," which begins tomorrow and runs until the end of fall. She runs through every detail of the poster: how she did it—most of it created in photoshop—*why* she did it, what other software she used to create the poster, how long it took to make; and while she's doing this, she acts as if she wants my approval.

I look over the poster, which looks like something out of an old school horror movie, similar to the posters hanging inside the Twin. All of the freaks are in the painting, including Nile. I most definitely approve.

She stays humble. Not once does she ever play the sympathy card; in fact, Jazz doesn't even need the sympathy card. Screw the sympathy card. She's got skills.

"You're very talented," I tell Jazz.

And it's the truth, contrary to some—if not, most—people who tell artists that their work is good just to make them feel better about themselves.

She's good, as in she's going places.

I read the movie credits on the bottom. I see Jazz's name—JAZZ CALDWELL—next to the R rated sign.

I point at her name and say, "I know her."

"Yep," she says bashfully as she stays reserved. "That's me."

"Model by day," I say, studying the poster. "Artist by night. You're like a superhero."

I suddenly feel a hand slip next to my waist.

Jazz grabs my hand.

"Your hand is freezing," she says.

She's right. My hands are freezing. I'll admit that I have the hands of a dead man.

We share a glance until I win the game, *Who Blinks First*; and when she blinks, she does so distinctly, as if she's like a cartoon character; and I can just visualize her mascara-heavy eyelashes making that *blink*, *blink* sound. She turns her head to the tent, then faces me, and says to me, "Come on. I want to show you something. . . "

She has that same rebellious look on her face, the same one I woke up to after *Blood and Black Lace*: Jazz looking down at me, but this time she's eye-level with me, and she's telling me that she *knows exactly what* I *need*.

Jazz races toward the side of the tent. I follow closely. She finds a slit in the base of the tent and peels it open. She wiggles her body underneath the tent like a worm that's sur-facing after a spring shower. I do the one thing I hate outside the tent and stand with my hands inside my pockets.

What is she up to now?

I crouch toward the ground.

"Jazz. . . "

As I lift up the edge of the tent, Jazz's arm suddenly pro-jects outward!

I flinch and lose my footing and fall backward.

"Geez. . . "

She waves me inside, a hurry-up and follow-me kind of wave. I hear her voice whispering in the darkness, "What are you waiting for. . . "

I mimic Jazz and raise the base of the tent and slither my way inside.

As I stand to my feet, brushing the dirt from my shirt, I find Jazz drifting into a wall of darkness.

Jazz?

Before I can catch up to her, she vanishes before my eyes. I call out to her again, making sure to keep my voice lowered.

"Jazz?" I say yet again. "You there?"

I hear this dull cla-*clunk* inches away from me, then a canned light above me lights up the main stage, which has been partially set up earlier that day.

A pea green sign above the stage reads:

"WELCOME TO FREAKSPECTACULAR!"

On the stage are several contraptions, including the spinning "Wheel of Death;" a table holding a container of knives; then, next to that, a coffin-like box, which Jazz claims is used for the classic "body-splitting" trick, or that "Sawing a woman in half" trick or whatever you call it.

Jazz guides me to a gaudy mirror standing against a secured mount. The frame is lined with brass, as tarnished as an aged saxophone. Each corner of the frame is designed with a lion's paw, and on the top center of the frame is this statue of a lion's head with its eyes shaped with pink crystals, and I swear it's like something you'd see in a B-rated horror movie from the Eighties. I've been here before, I tell myself. I don't know when or how, but I have been here before. I can feel it in my bones.

I walk to the front of the strange mirror and examine its design. Jazz stands next to me, more curious than myself.

As we look into the mirror, I raise my shoulders into a steep shrug and say, "It's a mirror."

"Not just any mirror," she says, her tone teetering to the side of wicked. "Legend says that this mirror has the power to look 'inside' you. The mirror has the ability to see *what* you feel, *how* you feel, *how* old you feel, even *how* young you feel. And when you look at your reflection in the mirror, you see exactly what the mirror sees."

"Hmm."

That's all I got, really.

The noise only a dumb person would make.

She nudges me on the shoulder.

"Give it a try," she says.

I look at my reflection in the mirror. I only take a glimpse at my reflection. I don't look older or younger. I look the same as I've looked for years. I turn to Jazz and tell her that I look the same.

"Well," Jazz says with a shadow of a smirk arching across one side of her face, "you're not looking *hard* enough."

I look at the mirror once more.

Again, I see nothing.

I leave it at that.

"Your turn," I say, turning to Jazz.

Jazz faces the mirror. Stares at her reflection.

"So," I say, "what do you see?"

She continues to stare, her eyes unblinking. In return, I turn to the mirror and see Jazz's reflection and it looks the same as it did before. I ask Jazz again what she sees, but she doesn't answer. Yet, her eyes glaze over, as if she's about to start crying or something. She rapidly blinks her eyelids, now fluttering, like that old fluorescent light turning on after years of neglect, blinking its way into consciousness.

With a sudden gasp, she pulls her eyes away from the mirror as if she can longer look at her reflection and stares at her open palms in awe.

I ask Jazz again, but this time more quietly.

"What do you see?"

"The same as you," she says vacantly, then clears her throat and puts her hands down to her side.

Jazz walks away from the mirror. I follow her to the end of the main stage where a glass jar rests over a wooden post as tall as myself.

Inside the jar floats the head of a corpse in what looks like dirty floodwater seasoned with typhoid. The head looks like a dummy's head, mummified, older than old, like prehistoric old. My stomach suddenly lurches from the sight of the head. Shit. Think about something else, anything! I turn each thought to the sea, me paddling my way out to sea, the saltwater splashing in my face as waves crash down on me; somehow, Jazz finds her way in those waves, both of us now fighting our way through the turbulent water. The nausea fades, as does the hazy suspicion of me somehow being here before, right here in this very tent.

Without thinking, I tell Jazz that it looks like the real deal.

I think more about what I said—the part about it, the head, being the "real deal" and the more I think about what I said, the more I realize I wasn't entirely speaking the truth. I really have been here before. . .

"Déjà vu?"

I follow the voice and stare at the confused face behind the voice.

"I thought you said 'déjà vu,'" Jazz says to me.

I'm too confused to respond.

Jazz asks, "Are you okay?"

I face Jazz before nodding a *yeah*.

Without answering, I point at the head and ask Jazz, "What's this supposed to be?"

"Uh. . . " I find her searching for words, as if she momentarily has one of those brain farts, ". . . Ivory," she says, trembling her head. "Her name was Ivory."

Ivory, huh?

I study Ivory's face more closely, like Jazz's poster, gathering every detail, every shade, every fiber. Ivory has *no* eyes, I realize. Both have been gouged out and all that remains of them are two small voids inside the eye sockets. She has scales on the side of her face—partially chipped, cracked, or torn away from the dark decay of age—and each one appears like the fungus-riddled fingernails of a bum. Her hair appears like shoelaces too, very old shoelaces—like before-television kind of old—dangling from her scalp; and when Jazz tells me that she, as in Ivory, used to have snakes for hair, I peer closer at her scalp and see delicate skeletons of snakes. They lack any skulls or ribs; only the vertebrae of each skeleton are still fully intact.

Jazz tells me, "Her gaze used to turn men into stone."

"Is that so?" I say as her hand slips next to mine once more.

I turn to Jazz, who's now wearing little to no expression on her face. Her eyes are glossy, as if she's about to cry again, but the lack of expression contradicts her eyes. I clear my throat as she leans closer. I follow suit and lean closer as well. Our lips finally touch, my bottom lip pressed against her upper lip. It's a dry kiss, at first. A signature. I block out the grotesque imagery in the corner of my eye and kiss Jazz again, but this time with my tongue. Our tongues wrestle, her tongue grabbing aimlessly. Eventually, we find a rhythm and the kiss becomes more fluid. I start to get aroused as I feel each muscle of her grabby tongue, each groove, each bump, each tiny cluster of taste buds.

I slip my arm around her now warm body and her tits swell against my chest, nibbles harden. She slips her arms around my ribs and caresses my back.

As I make out with Jazz, I can feel the entire world around me crumbling away in an apocalyptic-style annihilation: Ivory, the stage, *the tent*, all of it gone, wiped away into oblivion, as if a nuclear bomb has been dropped miles away from us and a shock wave has reduced every single thing to ashes—except for us, of course—and the gray hell rains down on us, and we're standing in the ruins of a fallout, holding onto one another, my bad heart growing a little less black as Jazz forges her will upon mine. Her breath grows warmer. So too does her body, now as warm as a space heater.

I slip my fingers underneath her waistline. I unbutton, then unzip her pants. Jazz grabs a hold of my hand and guides it farther down her lower abdomen until my fingers are inside her, both middle and ring finger stimulating her flesh; then, as I get knuckle deep inside her—Jazz's body growing warmer and wetter, her breath much heavier—I hear a snappy voice from behind: *What are you kids doing in here?*

I suddenly remove my hand from Jazz. She coils behind me in defense as she zips up her pants.

I turn toward the voice. The man behind the voice points a flashlight at us. A small and glittery hexagonal object is the first thing I see, then a few inches above the object—which, I soon realize, is a badge—a round, doughy face with a mustache.

I grab Jazz's hand and we take off toward the beach.

The security guard chases after us, but we're too fast for him.

\|\|

WE jet through the crowds. Jazz is right next to me every step of the way, my hand never letting go of her hand as I maneuver around each buoy-like body.

As we finally make it to the beach, we lose the security guard. I loosen my hand over Jazz's, now that we're in the clear. She removes the black uggs from her feet and sets them down in the sand. She grabs my hand and places it over her chest.

"My heart is racing," she says, out of breath.

I feel her heart throbbing like a rave against her chest.

"Mine too," I tell her.

I switch hands with hers. Place her hand against my chest. She stares into my eyes, as if she's staring at something from a distance, like a star in the sky, not a person but something. She doesn't seem as fascinated as I was when I placed my hand over her chest and felt every beat of her racing heart. She looks the opposite.

She studies my face—now closely—as I did with Ivory.

The color suddenly swims from her face.

I can't help but wonder what she sees when she looks at me.

\|\|\|

THE whole time during the drive from Topside to Jazz's apartment all I can think about is that overly peculiar reaction Jazz made when she placed her hand over my chest.

Did she know something that I didn't know?

Did she witness the same thing the car wash guy saw when I first arrived at Topside?

Before I can understand her expression, I hear Jazz say next to me, "Here we are."

I turn off the ignition and show Jazz my new cell phone—the burner.

"I was meaning to show you earlier." I hand Jazz the burner. "It's not a smartphone, but it's better than nothing. Right?"

She looks it over, opens and closes it, and then hands it back to me.

"It's ah—nice," she says with one of her overly conspicuous shrugs. "Simple."

I know somehow I'm giving her the same look she gave me when we were riding the Ferris wheel.

I put away the phone.

"I had a good time tonight," I tell Jazz.

"So did I," she says as she reads my face.

"I'm glad you came out."

"Me too."

She makes the first move by leaning over the center console.

We kiss again, and that's as far as we take it for the night.

IV

I find a decent neighborhood in New Town and park my car underneath an oak tree that stretches over the street like an awning. I recline the seat and gaze at a wedge of the moon peeking through the branches.

I text Jazz, "Good night."

She texts me back the same message, only with one of those emoticon things. I can't help myself. I'm laughing out loud, not at the text, but the emoticon of a smiley face. I wonder if Jazz is smiling right now as she tucks herself in bed with the glow of her phone's screen gleaming over her beautiful face.

I can only imagine.

I smell my fingers, and the smell of Jazz all over my fingertips puts me at ease. A feeling washes over, similar to the one I used to get when I was a boy ready to attend my first day of school.

V

As I'm about to dose off into a dreamless state, I hear a hollow *thud* of a car door closing behind me.

I bolt upright and check myself first, making sure my body is still intact. I sneak a glance at the rear view mirror, now glowing with light.

A parked car—can't tell the make or the model—is burning its headlights behind me, and the lights are blinding for a moment. A dark figure walks through the beams of headlights and approaches my car from the side.

I quickly grab the revolver from the bookbag.

Make sure it's loaded.

As soon as I open the chamber, Moses is standing outside my window.

Waiting.

I breathe a sigh of relief and roll down the window.

You scared the shit out of me.

He nods to the car behind me. I step out of my car. Moses is walking toward *his* car, which, after second glance, I realize is a black SUV—a Toyota *Highlander*.

He stands next to the passenger's side. Flings his head in a nod toward the driver's side.

Get in, he says.

I stand my ground.

You've wasted enough time on this girl, he says. I'm not going to tell you again.

I get inside the SUV.

I leave my car behind and drive away.

VI

WF leave New Town and drive east of Los Dementes.

Moses doesn't say a word to me during the drive, except for the utterance of an occasional "take a right" or "left here," indicating for me to make a turn.

After about three "rights" and "four" lefts, we finally arrive at our destination: a wastewater treatment plant, which is located on the outskirts of a Sedaris Valley, a stepchild of a town northeast of Los Dementes.

Moses tells me to cut the lights before I park the SUV.

I do as he commands and cut the lights, revealing a glowing haze of lights before me. I park next to a telephone pole. Then Moses tells me to turn off the engine next.

I turn off the engine.

Then he grabs a pair of binoculars from the glove box and steps out without saying a word.

I follow suit without command and follow him to a small hill overlooking the wastewater treatment plant.

The smell in the air is enough to burn the hairs from my nostrils.

Moses tells me to breathe out of my mouth.

It helps, he says.

I focus breathing through my mouth.

It helps a little, but there's no escaping the repulsive stench.

We stand on top of the hill and watch a motorcade of cars pull into the facility. I count three cars, all the same make and model, black Suburbans, tinted windows, very politician-y.

What the hell is going on here?

Why are we here, I ask Moses.

He doesn't answer.

Instead, he peers through the binoculars. I turn my attention to the motorcade, now parked in an open piece of land outside the facility. A familiar group of men dressed in black suits steps out of the SUVs. Two of them drag out what appears to be a man. He's naked and weak, too, I can tell, and feverishly shaking. Other men are pushing him around, causing him to stumble and fall. He's panicked and he's looking around and waving his arms as if he's lost in pitch black. One of them kicks the back of the fragile man's knees, forcing him to the ground.

Moses turns to me and hands me the binoculars.

Watch, he says.

I grab the binoculars and peer through them. I get a better look at the sick naked man. He has a thin beard and he's got all kinds of cuts and bruises over his ribcage. He appears to be of Latino descent. And he's crying, too, and yelling at someone for sure. I carefully pan the binoculars from right to left, trying to find whom the upset man is yelling at. I find two of them. Both men are approaching the naked man. One of them is wearing a dark brown suit. He's as slender as stick figure and he carries no expression on his face. The man's dressed too nice to be a cop. Plus, he's not in uniform. Obviously. I get a closer look at his face. I've seen him before at the Palace—Bishop's guy! The other man, I can't quite make out his face, for the other men are blocking my view. He's wearing in an overcoat, gloves. Everything about him is black and very mysterious and he moves with a certain grace that only someone in the limelight can master.

Then, as he looms over the frightened man, now begging on his knees, I catch a glimpse of his face. Ayker. . . What the hell is he doing? I remove the binoculars from my face. Turn to my right.

Watch, Moses says clearly; and he's staring at me as if he's already seen what's about to happen next, like he's catching the rerun of a show, and now, he just wants to see my reaction for his own personal indulgence.

I force myself to look through the binoculars.

Slender Man pulls out a gun from the holster along his side and shoots the naked man in the head. His head violently jerks away, as if his neck is attached to a swivel. A faint cloud of red mist shoots in the air above his head. His lifeless body flops to the ground.

I turn away, too grossed-out to watch "what happens" next.

Why are you showing me this?

Why?

Moses steps closer, acting as if he's insulted by the question.   Why?

You need to get your head out of your ass.   You *need* to know who and what you're up against.

I look up from the ground below and look Moses directly in the eyes.

As with Jazz before, right then and there, I know he's holding onto a secret as dark as my own, one that can very well cost me my life.

How did Moses know Ayker was going to show up at this particular spot at this particular time?

I don't know the answer nor do I even know where to begin.

Right now, I don't know who or *what* to believe anymore.

Right now, I know nothing.

THE KNIGHT OF

PICTURE me trapped inside a dream: I'm speeding down a steep hill, pumping the brakes of a car without any brakes. I'm dodging one obstacle after another, like a raggedy lady pushing a cart full of empty cans or a stray dog wandering into the street or a group of children playing hula-hoop on the sidewalk.

I know the dream is a dream. Yet, it has all of the characteristics of a memory. It's that special transitional time of the day where the light doesn't know what it wants to be. It's day and yet, it has all the sentiments of night. A storm is coming, I realize, and soon, it's going to rain. . .

I'm falling deeper inside the dream. Level by level. Straight down the barrel. The squeeze of the trigger ignites a spark, and I find myself cowering on the slippery linoleum kitchen floor of Jimmy's three-bedroom apartment off College Street, a pillar of flames rising from a pan of piping-hot oil, taking form as it towers over my curled body like a man on fire. I know this is *not* a recent memory, rather an earlier one, a far more distant one, the night before Jimmy was shot.

I keep falling through black and white memories; however, it's now a painfully slow fall, any slower I'd be going in reverse.

Jimmy and I have the munchies of all munchies after smoking a joint. Jimmy's acting extremely paranoid, which isn't like him. He thinks Coach Bernard is going to give a pop drug test, which is issued by the Athletic Department each year, but I tell Jimmy not to worry. Why would the coach advocate drug testing one of his best players on the team? He wouldn't. Not like they randomly chose your name from a hat or, like, from one of those lottery machines. Pop drug tests are like urban legends. I put him at ease and tell him that I'll handle the food situation. I go to the kitchen, grab a pack of sliced American cheese from the fridge, a can of chili from the stockpile of canned food in the pantry, and then, finally, a bag of fries from the freezer. I place the chili in a pot and let it simmer while I empty the fries over a pan of oil on the stovetop, but I don't know—at least not yet—that the oil is piping hot. The fries, like icicles, hit the oil, then flames suddenly burst into the air, scorching my eyebrows first, then forcing me backward!

I slip and fall onto my backside and as I attempt to slide the pan from the stove, the flames shoot up once more, causing me to backpedal!

A *face*, I witness, emerging from the flames, eyes like voids, a mouth opening and revealing layers of black teeth. I reach up to grab hold of the counter, but I end up clawing my way through walls of ice. The kitchen floor beneath me is gone, and now it swells with cave blackness. I desperately climb along the rocky surface until I can't feel my fingertips, my hands. Every muscle in my arm feels as if it's on fire.

I release my hands from a crease in the wall and fall into the blackness; however, I realize, after my body goes weightless, that I'm not falling. Instead, I'm rising. The memory becomes much closer, more vivid.

Now, I'm driving through Richport, like Topside, a town that remains frozen in time, structures remain without pulse, without hope, and yet, the inhabitants who occupy these stillborn establishments act as if they have neither nothing to lose nor gain.

Twilight has faded now. It's dark outside, but I'm guided by two headlights, each one like an eye cutting through darkness. I tell myself that a storm's coming. Soon. I check every old alley, every old corner, every old block. I'm frantically searching the streets for Jimmy. I know he hasn't been himself lately. He's been thinking about giving up the one sport that he's been playing ever since he was wearing diapers. I know that I have something to do with his indecisiveness. I

know the day hasn't been itself either. Something's been hovering in the air. Something strange. Like a warning or pre-
monition. I'm worried, especially after witnessing that thing
last night—whatever it was—the one who visited me in the
flames.

What was that thing?

Now, it's well beyond nightfall and I'm still driving.

The campus can pass as a ghost town. Most of the students have gone home for spring break. Jimmy and I stay, as
we always do. The only time we ever went back home was
over the Christmas break. We never go home on the weekends either, as most students do here. I've been thinking a lot
about enrolling in West Harleton in the future. That way, I'll
have a reason for staying here. With my brother. With
Jimmy. I've set my sights on getting a bachelor's degree in
Film. I've heard WHU has an outstanding film program. I've
given serious thought about focusing on post-production
(sound design, editing, visual effects).

Ever since I was younger, I've always been fascinated by
the process of how movies were made from beginning to end.
The magic. Jimmy and I used to be "filmmakers"—I mean,
by rule, we couldn't legitimately call ourselves filmmakers,
definitely not in the same category as the Hitchcock's or
Spielberg's, because Jimmy and I hadn't actually made any
profit off what we had made (I believe that's the deal with all
crafts, right? If you can't make some bread off what you've
created—I'm talking about some real bank—then it's just a
glorified hobby). So, having said that, Jimmy and I were
technically hobbyist—or "aspiring" filmmakers. We lost the
films that we made during the third and what Thomas bitterly
called his "final" move—the one from Elizabeth to Kuykendall. We still owned the camcorder and all, a Hitachi 8mm
video camcorder VM-E530A with rapid reflex 16bit D.S.P.
Very groundbreaking stuff back then. It even had a LCD
color view finder. Like I said, groundbreaking stuff. Still
worked like a champ and everything. Most of the time, I did
the camerawork stuff; but whenever we needed an extra hand,
one of our neighbors, Turtle, a socially awkward kid who
lived two houses down from us, would step in and fill my
shoes—but, of course, after much convincing. The 8mm
tapes, on the other hand, were all gone. Each and every one
of them was lost in transition. One minute, they were packed

in flimsy uHaul boxes, then the next minute, poof. Just the thought of our movies somewhere out there was like this lingering taste on the back of my tongue, like after you eat something with raw onions and that oniony taste stays with you several days after. Just imagine that taste always being there, hidden underneath other tastes or smells. I could only assume the movies were either in someone else's possession or, far worse—the idea I always tried to avoid—they were in a landfill, being piled away with all of the other garbage. There were a lot of them, too, over fifty movies: parodies of the show, *Cops* (Jimmy playing the Chicagoan cop with his Mike Ditka impersonation; he'd cruise around the neighborhood; I'd be playing the part of a strung-out crackhead causing mayhem throughout my wanderings; Jimmy would chase me down and then arrest me—but, of course, I wouldn't go out without a fight), then all of the horror movies—the Creature Features—that we filmed while the parents were in bed (I remember I used to make fake blood earlier that day, a concoction of corn syrup and red food coloring), even the action movies (one time, in the movie, *Johnny Love's Revenge*, the action hero, Johnny Love, who was played by Jimmy, leaped out the window while the charming mastermind, Mr. Megalopolis, played by yours truly, grazed Johnny Love in the arm with one of his "mental bullets" and then, yours truly, who was also the special effects guru—I wore a lot of outfits—blew up the house, not really, but I made it appear on film as if I really did blow up the house when, in fact, I lit a newspaper on fire and then held the flaming paper underneath the lens of the camera, making the shot look as if the house was on fire when it really wasn't), then parodies of that one popular MTV show, *Fanatic*—you know, during that time when the channel actually stood for the letters implied—where I, the hysterical fanatic, met my favorite celebrity, Johnny Love (Jimmy), then came all of the ridiculous backyard wrestling junk (Jimmy, aka Too Smooth, then me, Captain Crunch—one afternoon, Susannah caught me swan diving off the deck onto Jimmy who was spread out on a wooden table in the backyard, all of her dishware and whatever we could find around the house scattered in the lawn, dented or destroyed, then her face would turn demonic-like followed with Susannah barking our full names in utter rancor). I couldn't possibly come to grips that all of these saved memories were being passed from one hand to another as if they were mollies or, far worse, reduced to landfill particles. All of the memories we shared together, the ones we had captured on film, were nowhere to be found. Each time I tried to access the memories—the many *Johnny Love* movies—they grew just a little murkier; at times, they'd be as fresh as a piece of ripe fruit, the colors vivid, then they'd vanish into the murk I created for myself.

What frightens me the most is that one day, they'll be gone, the memories; eventually, all of the murk washing over them, leaving nothing more than the fragments of lost time. It'll be as if they never happened.

Pellets of rain strike the roof of the car with what sounds like baby mallets.

I drive to the dorm, each *thud* or *smack* on my roof getting closer together.

I check both the student and staff parking lot, but Jimmy's Accord is nowhere in sight.

I check the dorm. I ask students if they've seen Jimmy and all I receive is the same response.

I leave the campus and drive through the night.

Searching but not finding.

I can feel a knife in my gut, starting to twist.

My knuckles growing whiter.

Heart blacker.

Jimmy's upset at me for nearly burning down the apartment with a pan of hot oil last night. He never voiced it at the time when he came rushing into the kitchen, grabbing the flaming pan and placing it safely in the sink. He was glad I was okay. I know he's pissed, though, not from last night, but from a whole accumulation of things. I know he didn't mean what he said to me, but it's somewhat true—I do envision myself being great, an important person one day; yet, at the end of the day, I fall short and I fail to live up to all of the expectations I've created for myself. Most importantly, I fail Jimmy. On top of that, he found out about Heather, a girl whom I hooked up with last weekend. Jimmy liked her, I think, used to talk about her. Mentioned her name a few times during conversations. Heather liked bad boys. Jimmy wasn't bad. I don't even remember Heather's last name. I was drunk. I'm always drunk.

After I exhaust my search, I park the car in an abandoned industrial park and think about the fire and what it was trying to tell me last night.

Suddenly, a couple of knocks on the window pull me from the fire. The beam of a flashlight shines over my face. I shield my eyes with my hand and see a rent-a-cop standing outside the car. He tells me to get out of the car; then he knocks once more on the window.

That's when I rise from the dream and open my eyes to the sound of *knocking*, wondering whether my reality is slipping into my dreams or the other way around.

I turn to my left and find the same large oak tree next to my car.

It's daylight too, and I've caught at least seven hours of sleep, which is the most sleep I've gotten in a while. I hear the *knocking* sound again, but this time it's coming from the windshield. I roll down the window and extend from my head outward and look up.

A squirrel scurries across the tree branch and drops an acorn on my car!

I ignore the feisty squirrel, the sound that the acorns make as they randomly drop onto the roof of my car—*knock, knock!*

I look in the rear view mirror. Then, I fully turn my shoulder and look behind the car. The space is empty behind me, and I find myself furrowing my brows into a twisted *V* from the sight of the empty space. I face front and spot a police cruiser pulling into the neighborhood street. I start up the car and slowly drive away. I pass the cruiser as I clear the blur from my eyes. I look into the rear view mirror; and as I arrive at a stop sign and make sure to come to a complete stop, the cruiser does a brisk U-turn.

The cruiser drives around me and then, once it finds open road, it switches on its sirens.

\\

\ stop at a sleazy-looking truck stop off Gallivant Highway to wash my hands. I leave dirtier than I found myself before I first entered the restroom. I think about the shooting last night—the guy who was killed, Ayker, then his minion shooting that guy in the face.

\|\|\|

\ retrace my footsteps. The first thing I remember is dozing off. Smells come back to me, like, first, that new car aroma. Then, somehow, I can see myself ripping off the neck of the steering wheel and playing with wires. The engine starts. Score. From there, pieces start to come together: Ayker, his minion, the guy from the TV, the shooting. It really did happen.

Before I run into the rush hour of morning traffic, I'm back in Sedaris Valley, back at the same wastewater treatment plant. I park in the same spot as last night, then I get out. I check out the place. It's dead quiet. I can smell the death in the air. I can even the distant echoes of gunshots. I go to the same spot where that guy was shot and carefully inspect the ground. I check for the tread of tire tracks. There are no tire tracks, no footprints—only mine—no blood, no body.

Nothing.

It's like it never even happened.

\|\/

AFTER I leave Sedaris Valley, I cruise around Richport for a while until I stop by what used to be Daddy's Playground and get out and walk around. Nothing much remains of the old nightclub, except for a gutted building, which speaks in suppressive coughs or sniffles or a distant, hollowed-out echo that has all of the familiarities of a groan. I keep my hands steady and keep an eye open for any local wildlife. All kinds of debris is scattered over the floor, including broken malt liquor bottles, crack pipes, and needles. It reminds me of a place that had not only been forgotten, but also a place that wanted to forget.

I leave the abandoned nightclub and drive through the rough parts of Richport—or should I say, the rougher parts.

I arrive at the location where Jimmy was discovered by an old fisherman the morning after he was shot, the upper half of his body on the shore while his legs remain submerged in the water. The fisherman looked as if he was pulled straight from the pages of a Mark Twain novel: a black man with a hunchback, dressed in raggedy overalls, straw hat, and a piece of some long narrow leaf or stalk or grain hanging loosely from the corner of his lip. According to the reports I acquired from Dwight, the only thing preventing Jimmy's body from sinking to the bottom of the Crux—or worse, being swept into the Pacific, which could possibly happen but it was very un-likely—was an industrial pipe that had taken root along the shore. Jimmy's necklace got caught around the pipe. Who knows how long Jimmy remained chained to that pipe. Pos-sibly all night. Then, his body was found earlier that morning. How Jimmy even had air in his lungs is—to say the least—a miracle or a curse depending how you look at it. I bought Jimmy the necklace for his birthday the year before everything went to hell. At the time, gold was a hot item—*hot*, as in trendy, not trending #gold (that was, of course, before silver came along and ruined the party). I was more into silver. Jimmy, gold. That was when I had a job to buy things like necklaces with my own money. I bought two of them, one gold and the other silver, one for Jimmy and the other for my-self. At the end of each chain was a pendant of a wing, one gold and the other silver. When Jimmy asked what the wings represented, I told him that one of the wings represented him and then the other represented me. I told him that no matter what happens between us we'd always have our wings. We'd always fly together. No matter what.

I pull onto the side of the road and tramp through all of debris tossed aside from the road until I reach the bank of Crux River.

The morning Jimmy was discovered is a moment of my life that I wished to forget and yet, as much as I like to forget it, the image remains like a stain of mustard on my mind. I don't remember the words I spoke. Nor do I even remember if I spoke any words at all. When your body's in shock, you can't remember a damn thing what comes out, such as words or noises, but you sure remember what goes in. The smells. The tastes. The images. I wondered, though, whether my body was in shock or, over time, my body had become desen-sitized by all of the violent movies or TV shows we used to watch or make, you know, being film hobbyists and all, and somehow, I was stuck inside an episode of some poorly acted dramedy that had some morally-laced "message" at the end of the story. Jimmy and I were raised by TV. Instead of spend-ing most of our youth playing outside with the other kids, ex-cept for playing ball or exploring the woods or the backyard wrestling phase, most of our childhood was spent in front of a TV screen with our eyes sunburned with radiation or making our own movies. The only downfall: reality becomes boring. I mean, really, *really* boring. Whenever we experienced a loss in the family, like when Aunt Gabby passed away, Jimmy and I knew what lines to say to grievers because we had already experienced the emotions through the movies or TV shows that we watched or made. We knew what kind of emotions to convey, what to say and what *not* to say, as if all of these cues were pulled from the dog-ears of a screenplay. Or, whenever Jimmy and I found ourselves in a predicament, like one time Susannah caught us leafing through Thomas's *Playboys* like spies going through TOP SECRET documents, we were like these recycled clones transported from the TV world (a blushing Jimmy pointing at me, *He made me do it!*). Thomas kept the best issues on the top shelf in his closet. Clearly, I couldn't reach them on my own. Too short, *always* too short, too short to ride Thunder Road, too short to play football for East Providence, too short to touch the rim, too short to kiss senior, Amy Shaffernak, on the lips. After a while, everything just seemed better on TV than in reality, as in the image was much better, the sound was better and much more clear, and everything that we experienced in the "other" world was mediocre or, dare I say, a cliché, as if we've seen it all before, as if we've seen everything before.

Like when a person says after experiencing a dramatic event: "I swear it felt just like a movie (or TV show)."

The morning after the shooting, I don't exactly know what I felt. The helicopter was ripping through the sky, like one during a car chase or a suspenseful scene in an action movie, but I had to tell myself, "This wasn't a movie." Far from one. Jimmy *always* called if he was going to be late or if he was going to stay at a friend's house. He *always* kept me in the loop. That's why I knew the helicopter was for him. An intuition, I guess. If it was any other day, I wouldn't have paid any attention to the helicopter. I would've just thought: Hey, *there's a bird, there's a plane, there's a helicopter*. Seen it before. I left the apartment, my gut balled up like a ball of yarn. I raced with the helicopter, trying to keep up with it without running into any oncoming traffic. I was stopped by a roadblock: two cruisers, two cops standing in the middle of the road, diverting traffic. I told them I was looking for my brother. So, they let me through without questioning me. Which was weird. I sped down an empty, eerie street until I came across a crowd circled around the bridge. The helicopter had already landed, kicking up all of the trash that Crux River gobbled up. The crime scene packed with cops, paramedics and firemen included. Seen it before. Everybody had a special role, except me. Other cops were barricading the other side of the street— and later, when I first arrived at the hospital, they told me the nurses pulled an eightball off Jimmy's person; but the doctor later informed me they found no drugs in his system, which was one of the many clues that I'd later uncover and then cops hanging around Jimmy's hospital room during odd hours of the day. By law, whenever a patient has been shot, the hospital is supposed to report it to the authorities. For Jimmy, it was as if they sent the entire precinct. Cops claimed it was a "drug deal gone bad." Yet, I knew a supposed drug dealer, like Cedric Gaines, didn't have the capacity or the knowledge to get rid of a body. It just wasn't his style. So, I knew from the get-go that the story was bullshit. Jimmy wasn't a junkie. Wasn't a drinker. Jimmy was as clean cut as the son of an abusive alcoholic. The type of guy who'd give you the shirt off his back. That's the type of person he was. A part of me thought it may have been because Thomas used to be an officer of the law. An attack on one cop or one cop's family is an attack on all of us. Another part of me thought it was odd—of course, it was odd—to see so many cops hanging around the hospital. Either the cops really wanted to catch the person responsible for shooting Jimmy or they had something else on their minds, like covering their own asses. One thing was for sure: the cops *knew* something I didn't know; and like me, they were waiting for Jimmy to talk.

The seventy-five thousand dollar question: What was Jimmy doing the night he was shot?

The million-dollar question: Did Jimmy *witness* something that he shouldn't have witnessed?

Paramedics and firefighters were pulling his body from the river by the time I reached the crowd. I never got a chance to see him in his entirety, the extent of his injuries, only the helicopter as it flew away. I raced through the scene—cops tugging at me, treating me as if I was less than zero. Cold and calculated, they were, like serial killers. I knew they were just doing their jobs. Thomas was like that. At the Academy, they trained him not to wear his heart on his sleeve. Never show emotion. Emotion exposes you. And criminals sniff it out as if it carried certain pungency. One lady was telling me not to look as paramedics were securing Jimmy in the helicopter before Jimmy was airlifted to the hospital. I remember she said that this shouldn't be the last image you'd want to remember. Last image, she said, as if he was going to die. I never showed any emotion; however, there was one emotion that was gradually building, like a mason spreading the mortar along a foundation, spreading the mortar and then stacking a brick, spreading and stacking. Day by day. *Slowly*. I sped to the hospital without a cop escort. When I arrived, the nurse told me that Jimmy was still alive. She told me that he was shot in the head and yet, despite the traumatic brain injury, Jimmy's heart was still beating. The words alone—about my brother being alive—turned out to be the best news and yet, at the same time, the worst news I've ever received. The best, being that Jimmy wasn't dead. The worst, being that when or if he recovered, I knew he would *never* be the same again.

The days following the shooting were, by far, the hardest days of my life. Painfully slow days. Unable to sleep again. Unable to eat any solid foods. Your thoughts do most of the eating. I remember we were taking shifts at the hospital. We even slept there, depending on Jimmy's condition and whether or not he was stable enough to make it through the night. It was a "waiting game" all over again, waiting for answers, results, prognosis, recovery. They, as in the doctors, told us time and time again that a brain injury was one of the most unpredictable injuries. We all wanted Jimmy to start healing, but we knew that it wasn't going to happen overnight. While playing the waiting game, I was thinking (I couldn't even imagine what Thomas was going through, what he was thinking. I was pretty sure he was thinking the same thing: *Who did this to Jimmy?* Who was involved?). While thinking, the self-betrayal sunk in like a hypodermic needle followed by the blame, the grief; and it was always there, an overall feeling of malaise, like *a bad ache*, inside your gut, your bones, your thoughts. A tapeworm absorbing all of the valuable nutrients inside you. No matter what, it will always take more than half of what you put in. Even words rolled off my tongue with a different rhythm and pitch. I practiced a lot. Practiced how to wear a smile on my face. Practiced how to be normal. When all of that failed, I was forced to interrogate myself: *If I hadn't* hooked up with Heather, *if I hadn't* placed that bag of frozen french fries into a pan of hot oil, *if I hadn't* gotten into an argument with him the night before, none of this would've happened. As soon as you entered the game, your world became a monogamous series of "ifs" and "whens." The game, however, never came without a prize or some kind of buzzing sound to remind you that you were *still* in the game, waiting. Each time the phone *rang* whenever I wasn't sitting at Jimmy's bedside, I experienced the one emotion that I never learned to conquer. That was fear. And every time I heard that awful sound, I always feared the worse.

I pull my eyes from my blurry reflection in the rippling water below and stare up at the bridge above.

I trudge up the hill, stroll along the bridge, and look down at the river below.

This is where it all started.

This is where it's all going to end.

Right here.

Right now.

V

As I'm about to get inside my car, I hear a commotion a couple of blocks away. Crowds of people are circling the corner of an intersection. As each second goes by, the crowds grow in size. Not too far is a grocery store. People drop whatever it is they're carrying—groceries and whatnot—to check out the commotion. Their cell phones and smartphones drawn like knives, ready and willing to capture a moment like the cameramen of a news team rushing to a scene of a crime.

Out of curiosity, I walk over to the crowd. Unlike everybody else, my burner remains in my pocket, as it should be. I shoulder my way through the dense, staticky crowd until I reach an opening.

I stop from the sight of the contorted man lying on the street. Holy shit.

I continue to proceed forward, more curious. On the pavement below is a man wet with fresh blood. His legs are bent ninety degrees in the opposite direction the same way a child recklessly steers the legs of a leaden action figure. His hips appear to be out of place, possibly broken or even worse. A

A thick and bubbly stream of bloody is seeping from the man's nose. Two men are kneeled beside the lifeless body. One of them is applying pressure to a deep incision along the right side of the man's ribcage with a wadded shirt. The other is wiping away blood from the injured man's mouth as he administers CPR. He acts as if he's done this sort of thing before—an EMC, possibly, a lifeguard?

The Samaritan checks for a pulse, but he says to the crowd that the man's not breathing.

I don't think the people care if the man's breathing or not. They seem as if they're too occupied filming and then posting the video on the Internet.

I ask the old lady next to me what happened.

She tells me that some lunatic hit this poor guy with a car as he was crossing the street and then the lunatic drove off.

I get a closer look at the bloody man by arching my head over the Samaritan's shoulder.

She asks me if I know the poor man.

I witness Moses' face covered with strings of dark blood—his glazed eyes fixated on me as I loom above his body. He looks terrible. Twice his age.

I tell the old lady that I don't know the poor man and walk back to my car.

VI

WHEN the first responders arrive, Moses is already dead.

It doesn't take them too long before they place a white sheet over his dead body. The police get statements from anyone who witnessed the hit and run while Moses lies like human road kill on the pavement, ready to be scooped and tossed away. I overhear a couple of statements. Some people said he had a pudgy face with short hair, like a crew cut and he looked like actor Sebastian Birch while he was popping pills. Others said he had a narrow face, sunken cheeks, scraggly hair, Aviators, like Sebastian Birch, post-drugs. I never give a statement to the cops. Never saw the driver's face. With that said, there was no need to give "my side" of the story; however, I wonder if Moses' death had anything to do with what we witnessed—or didn't witness—last night.

I leave the scene and walk back to my car, thinking about who may have either accidentally or *purposefully* killed Moses.

I don't know whether to feel relieved that he will no longer bother me or depressed from his passing.

I feel neither, really.

But what was the favor?

I guess I'll never know.

As I get back inside my car, I get a call. I check the number; and the sight of the name makes me forget about Moses.

"Hey, Jazz," I answer the call.

"Hey," she says.

Her voice sounds rejuvenated.

"I had a good time last night," I tell Jazz.

"Yeah," she says, her voice as soft as a lullaby. "I did too."

She asks me if I have any plans today.

My stomach churns with butterflies, the good ones. I know what she's going to ask me next. I'd normally decline and wait till I had a drink or two before I'd even consider going out with her.

I tell her that I don't have any plans today, anyway.

Then, she asks me if I want to have lunch.

I tell her, "Yeah. Sure. I'd like that."

As I leave Richport, I pass a royal blue campaign sign: VOTE AYKER FOR SHERIFF.

I do a double take at the sign on the side of the road.

What if it really was all a dream?

SOUTHERN
REGIONS

BEFORE I meet up with Jazz, I decide to make a pit stop at Topside Boardwalk, which is packed with tourists. It must be a new national holiday or something. Not only does "picking" calm me down by taking my mind off the upcoming "date" with Jazz—if that's what you call it—as well as what went down outside Sedaris Valley last night and Moses' death (I can't believe he's dead!), but it also gives me time to work out the kinks from sleeping in my car. I don't score that much, but it's better than nothing.

I leave the boardwalk with fifty dollars: forty of those dollars picked from a well-dressed man with hair like James Dean and then the remaining ten from a kid wearing a Lacoste shirt and khakis.

After Topside, I stop at a convenient store where I pull out the syringe case. The thought alone of zero forces me to break the needle over the curb without any hesitation. I toss the broken pieces in a trashcan, as well as the case.

I dump the bundle of dope, as well as the dirty weed, down a sewer drain.

The thought of not holding terrifies me and yet, at the same time, liberates me.

I think I can walk on my own now.

I don't need my crutch anymore.

All I Need Is Jazz.

I swear the line sounds like a bad lyric sung by a barber-shop quartet—*bad*, as in something that would eventually get muted or, even worse, swiped to the left.

I figure the more I say it the more it'll grow on me.

One more time: "All I Need Is Jazz."

\\

\ meet Jazz at the Eiffel Café, which is situated just off the Strip. She's waiting outside on the patio, sucking down a cigarette and sipping from a cup of coffee. She gets up from her seat as soon as we make eye contact and we hug.

I ask her if she's been waiting long.

"Just got here," she says.

She's jittery, and her voice is shaky, possibly from the caffeine or the butterflies—the good kind.

I ask her if she wants to hang out here or if she'd rather go inside.

"It's nice outside," she says, looking around the patio.

"Well, let's hang out here," I say as I pull out the seat for her. She sits down and I sit across from her.

The waitress stops at the table and asks me if I would like anything to drink.

I order a coffee with a little cream and a little sugar.

\\\

THE earlier half of the afternoon passes without any hitches—I mean, not one—which is unusual.

After Eiffel, we burn off our lunch by taking a much-needed walk on the beach. I don't realize how far we've walked until I find myself standing in Northside, the beach north of Herald's Point. It's much nicer here, the water seems cleaner, the sand finer—like sugar—the people, way more attractive. I can really care less, though, about the people or how they look. I'm more intrigued with Jazz. Any other day I'd be drooling like a mastiff right now at all of the tan flesh around me. I know that seeing Jazz like this, now a handful of times, the last time ending with a kiss, is going to catch up with me.

(I read somewhere in *First Date* that most of the serious—as in long-term—relationships start during the first week of seeing each other and then, after the second week, you build a connection)

I don't check out the other girls.

All I Need Is Jazz.

I don't tell myself that I can do better.

All I Need Is Jazz.

I don't come up with things to say to Jazz.

All I Need Is Jazz.

I don't even catch myself thinking.

And then, out of nowhere, Jazz tells me that she's never been out this far.

I tell her that I haven't either.

I tell her that we should go a little farther.

And we do.

IV

WE make a stop at Reed's Aquarium.

Jazz does most of the talking as she points out each fish. The girl knows her fish like I know my birds. She tells me that she thought about pursuing a career in a marine biology at one point in her life.

We stop in front of the shark tank and share a kiss in front of a school of nurse sharks swimming in circles.

V

WE finally make it back to Topside after leaving Reed's Aquarium outside Northside.

So far, the entire day feels like a dream. The nerves don't creep back in until Jazz asks me if I want to come back to her place. She clarifies that her mom's at court. I ask her if she's in trouble with the law. She laughs at the comment, tells me that her mom is a "stenographer," another fancy word for court reporter, but I already know these things. Jazz calls her "Quick Fingers," matches her quick tongue. My mind goes in the gutter and I find myself getting hard by the idea that somehow Jazz picked up the talent as well. We stop talking about her mother. Jazz tells me that she won't be back until later this evening. Jazz really, really wants me to come back to her place. I know what happens at her place. I know I should be a gentleman. I know I should call it a day. I had a "great time" with Jazz. One of the best dates I've been on since high school. Now, I know, it's time to go. I know I should take it slow. I know sex, especially at this early stage in what can be a "long-term" relationship, can screw everything up. I know these things, and I don't need to explain how I know all of these things. I've done these things. Lots of times. Too many times. It happens all of the time. We have sex at the beginning, then we keep having sex until the relationship becomes entirely based off sex and that's as far as it goes, where we leave very little room to emotionally grow. Either the flame burns out or it burns way too bright and someone gets burned. Someone *always* gets burned.

I wait next to her sea green Corolla that she recently bought with the money from her new modeling gig and think about the invitation. She makes it incredibly easy for me as she leisurely walks her two fingers down my forearm and her hand locks with mine.

I always find a reason to screw it up.

The butterflies are back—the bad kind—and they're wreaking havoc on my insides, the nausea, the tightness, as well as the paleness; it comes at me all at once.

I tell myself over and over.

All I Need Is Jazz.

Yeah.

Keep telling yourself that, idiot.

VI

I manage to hold in my lunch as I walk into Jazz's cramped bedroom. The walls are bare. The bed is messy and covered with a spread of bikinis and an army of stuffed animals lined over her pillows. A juvenile-sized desk is tucked away in the corner of the room. I walk over to the desk, observant of each product. On top is a fairly new Apple computer, which has been left in sleep mode. On the monitor cycles a screensaver consisting of movie posters, which—after I ask—Jazz tells me that she made a long time ago. Next to the monitor are empty boxes of various photo editing software stacked Jenga-style. Each software runs for at least a thousand dollars, even more. I'm not sure how Jazz can afford the software, especially from just working at a thrift shop. I don't ask her. Not my place. Next to the keyboard is a pair of Bose headphones. The Bentley of headphones. Next to the headphones is a seven-inch tall figurine of *King Kong* holding a yellow stickie with the line, "The world is yours," which, I believe, came from the movie, *Scarface*. Next to the desk sits a stool with vinyl records on top, mostly from the pre-disco era. On top of an old Monotones record sits a novel of *The Complete Poetry* of Edgar Allen Poe. I pick up the book, only to find more books on the other side of the room while I'm reading the back summary. I check her bookshelf and from a quick study, I find more authors whom I'm into as well, ones whom she hadn't mentioned over her MyCircle page. She has a ton of zines by Dalivia Plaut and various horror writers, which isn't a surprise. She's also into past writers as well, including King, Lovecraft, and Steinbeck.

"I take it you're not into ebooks?"

"Ebooks?"

"Yeah," I say, "you know, like *electronic books*?"

I glance over my shoulder and Jazz is trembling her head.

"I like the feel of a book, the texture of each page, the smell of it when you open it, you know. . . "

Her voice is trembling as well.

"Who doesn't?"

Before I can take another look at Jazz's mini-library, I feel a hand touch me on my waist. I rotate around and find Jazz arching herself closer to me.

First, she gives me a soft peck on my lips. Her lips are as soft as fruit well past ripe. I return with a more aggressive kiss. Jazz backpedals toward the bed.

With one sweep of her arm, she slides all of the stuffed animals onto the floor and grabs me by the belt and tugs me closer as she falls to the bed. We make out for a good five minutes, me moving my hand into her blouse and squeezing her tits and fondling her hardened nipples while she dry humps my pelvis.

With her breath labored, she whispers in my ear, "Why don't you finish what you started last night?"

I pull away—my body straddling Jazz's hips—and ask her as she bites her bottom lip, "Are you sure you wanna do this?"

She responds with a child-like bob of her head.

I finish what I started last night.

Afterwards, Jazz returns the favor.

APPARENTLY, Jazz has a cat named Bob.

I don't find out this information until the little white furball jumps onto the bed and my insides do the speed-up rendition of the honky-tonk.

Jazz exits from the bathroom, and she's giggling at my startled reaction.

While Jazz's cat bathes himself at the other end of the bed, I ask Jazz why she named him Bob. She corrects me by telling me that it's a she, *not* a he, and says the name is short for Bobbie.

I like the name, I tell her, "Bobbie."

"Well," she says, smirking, "apparently, she likes you."

Jazz places the washcloth aside and slithers into bed.

As she cuddles close into my side, I turn to the picture frame on the nightstand. I pick up the picture. I already know who he is from the old pictures Jazz posted on her My-Circle page, but I ask her anyway. The man is Jazz's father, who has wide shoulders, wider smile. He's wearing a fireball red collar shirt, tight black pants, and black wingtips buffed to a mirror shine. He could literally pass as Herbie Hancock's twin during his heyday. Standing next to her father is Jazz, a skinny tween with a mouthful of braces.

"That was my dad," she says quietly.

I know that exact tone in Jazz's voice, and it suggest that he's either dead or her parents are divorced. I know what happened to her father; however, I want to hear it come from her mouth, not the computer's.

I decide not to ask about her father. Yet, I let it come out naturally.

Then, she says it—*the words.*

"I'm sorry to hear," I say as I clear my throat. "How?"

"Heart attack," she says. "My mom was there when it happened."

"Where were you?"

She doesn't respond.

"I'm sorry," I tell her.

"He used to take me to the Twin all the time," Jazz says, trying to smile as if the thought of her father makes her smile; and yet, the thought of his death smothers her smile. "In fact," she says as her voice elevates slightly, "he was actually the one who got me into drawing." Her voice falls like a rock falling from a cliff, occasionally hitting the side during its descent. "He just left us *without* any warning; and it felt as if someone *pushed* this big 'red' button and then he was gone—"

I wonder if by "someone" she means God?

A child playing with his action figures—us being the action figures—contorting them, burning them, smothering them with hot glue, tossing them off ledges, tearing off limbs, drowning them, burying them, doing whatever He wants with us.

I can't help but think about our tragedy and then the calamitous ripple it cast throughout the family: the shooting, the news, the recovery process, and then, the end game, the inevitable yet *tragic* ending. I remember hearing about tragedies happening to people I knew—or didn't know—the car accidents, the murders, overdoses, suicides, but not once did I *ever* imagine our family going through one. I heard about them, and that was all it was really, just hearing, not experiencing. I can't say Jimmy checked out the same way Mr. Caldwell did, by "someone" pushing a big red button and then, *bam*, you're dead! Jimmy checked out the most brutal way any man could go: a ruptured artery from all of the suctioning and respiratory treatments he received on a daily basis, as well as the drugs that he was taking in order to stay alive. His body was compromised, riddled with clots, like death in waiting. When Jimmy checked out, it was as if, like Jazz said, "Someone," as in either God or whoever, had taken a nail and popped his balloon and all of the blood inside him came gushing from his face, including the tracheotomy tube which had been inserted into his neck after the shooting. A quick yet inevitable death. All of the blood kept coming, as if he had an endless supply of blood, and it was thick too, like syrup, bubbling along the corners of his mouth, seeping like red streams from his nostrils. There was nothing that could've been done to save him—at least nothing we had at our disposal. Two ways he could've survived: one, if a world class surgeon was on sight to cut him open and stop the bleeding; or two, a miracle. Even then, that was beyond a long shot. Like the flu, it just had to run its course. Jimmy was going to die. I don't think he felt any pain, but I just don't know. Everybody was scrambling around. Doing all they could. Everybody had a specific role: firefighters pumping oxygen into Jimmy, the aide trying to clear his air passages, Thomas playing coach, Susannah on the phone with the emergency operator. As for me, I felt as if I didn't have a role. I just watched Jimmy fall farther and farther into the great oblivion and I held him in my arms and told him to hang in there, to keep fighting even though I knew he was already venturing to the other side of light. His eyes stilled on mine. That's when I knew he made it to his destination. His life was over.

As much as I try to block out the very last image I have of my brother, it's an image that is stained on whatever soul I have left.

"—*After he passed*," I hear Jazz say next to me, "life hit another button and I didn't move forward or backward. Like everything around me was moving in slow motion. I didn't want to be like that anymore." Jazz stares at me and I stare back at her. "It was time for me to hit *play* again," she says to me, "this time without my dad."

"You sound like you were pretty close to him."

It makes sense, Jazz once being overweight, her putting on the weight, her losing the weight.

"Yeah. . . " she says as she grabs the frame and stares at the photo with a softness in her eyes, ". . . we were."

"How about your mom?" I ask her. "Are you close to her?"

"I am," she corrects, "Well, *was*. We used to be best friends, but after Dad died, she. . . "

Jazz makes an expression that has the similar traits of a pout, but I know she's way too old to be pouting.

"You know how it goes," she says.

"Yeah," I say, trailing off.

I face Jazz and she's giving me that look, as if she wants to tell me something.

Then, she does.

"After the heart attack," she says, "I remember she'd come home from work and pour herself a glass of gin. She wouldn't say a word to me. She treated me as if his death was my fault."

"Your fault?" I say. "Why?"

"I don't know." Jazz seems deflated from my remark. "She'd watch infomercials all night. A couple of days later, just as I was about to go to work, I'd find these packages addressed to her on the doorstep. It was her way of grieving."

"We all grieve in different ways," I tell her.

She reaches over my body, uses my sternum as an armrest, and places the photo back in same spot on the nightstand. Even shifts the frame around a couple of times and then angles it until it's just right. Then, she wipes the greasy smudge from the glass case, which, I believe, is a partial of my fingerprint. She does all of these things meticulously, putting the photo back the way it was, as if it's some kind of museum piece.

"How about you?" Jazz asks me, as she crawls back over my body. She rests her arms, as well as her chin, against my chest, as if she's waiting to hear a bedtime story. "Have you lost anyone close to you?" she asks me.

"No," I say after a long pause. "I haven't. . . "

Jazz unpeels her arms from my chest and brushes a strand of hair over my forehead. She studies my face and then my body, as if she's a doctor. She finds ancient needle marks dominoed like dull freckles along my forearms. She traces her index finger around each dot. I notice several bruises, days old, now purple and yellow, along the inner part of Jazz's wrists. I ask her about the bruises, where she got them. She shrugs them off, tells me that she bumped into the wall. She's "a clumsy girl," she says, but I know she's lying from the sudden change in her voice.

Why would she lie about these bruises?

She quickly directs the focus on me, my arms, my marks.

I grab Jazz's hand before she can make sense of the dots— each one like an elegy but in its own fucked up way, each one telling a story which I prefer not to tell, at least not right now. I rake her hand over my chest and run my finger over the dark streak of mascara smeared down the corner of her eye and I tell her, ". . . They remind me of who I was, *not* who I am."

I gently cup the lower part of her face and we make out until our lips grow tired.

VIII

JAZZ'S phone rings.

She answers the call.

She talks for a moment, mostly responding in guttural tones.

Then she hangs up.

Shortly after, I'm being rushed out of the apartment as if I'm an unwanted guest, a problem. She tells me that she'll be here any minute, as in her mother, Rosa, and that I "must" leave. I don't take offense as to why Jazz doesn't want me to meet her mother. I know it's all about timing and *now* is not the right time. I kiss Jazz goodbye and everything seems fine.

I drive away with an incredible buzz, one that I haven't felt in a very, *very* long time.

IX

I can't take it much longer, doing the one thing I hate. I did this when I was younger, the waiting, planning the next move, then sneaking around the parents' backs, then more waiting.

I find myself back at the public library, going through photos of Jazz on MyCircle.

As I'm about to logout, I come across a BREAKING NEWS REPORT on the library's LNEWS homepage and read Ayker's name in the headlines. I hold my breath as I click on the report. I'm taken to another page where an article talks about how Ayker's been working closely with LDPD on bringing down these drug rings scattered across around the Los Dementes area. Cops recently conducted a "massive" drug seizure in Mt. Avery. I scroll to the bottom of the page with related topics.

In other news: *Another* American found dead outside León Viejo, a town south of the Mexico border.

I skim through the article: Local farmer found an American dangling from a bridge with the insides removed from his body. What else is new?

I wonder if any of this has to do with Ayker's campaign.

What if all of these latest drug seizures have anything to do with what happened outside Sedaris Valley?

What if there's a connection?

Lots of what ifs, but no real answers.

.

TILTING
THE TIDE

EPISODE 7

GHOST INC.

A day passes, and I'm all sweaty again. I try to keep myself hydrated, hoping it will alleviate the creeping tension in my chest.

I check the time on the dashboard:

11:18

I've only been asleep for about twenty minutes or so and yet, somehow, it feels as if I've been asleep for twenty hours.

I hate eleven-eighteen with a passion. I stare at the time until it reaches twenty-three minutes past eleven.

Another five minutes pound away like a kick drum before I finally gather the nerve to call Jazz. Her phone goes straight to her voicemail. She's probably sleeping. A young woman sleeping at this hour of the night? I decide to give Jazz another call, anyway, but this time I leave a voice message. I'm not good at leaving messages. Never was. On the message, I tell her that it's me (I think we know each other well enough now to be giving each other the "it's me" during the opening line). I tell her that I was thinking about her and then I mumble a couple of transitional words or phrases and then start talking to myself. That's when I hang up the phone, when I come off as a blabbering idiot. I think about calling Jazz again, but I don't want to come off as the "that" type.

I put my burner away, let it chill for the time being. I drive past Nico's house. The inside of the house is dark, except for a TV-like glow coming from the aquarium inside his office, which is located at the farthest left corner, the spleen of the house. It's freakishly quiet as well, except for the soothing waves crashing over the shore at a distance. I don't hear any women hollering out drunken slurs or hoots or open cackles. No back chatter or crude remarks. No wavery pulse of EDM. No party. No Nico.

After I kill about an hour or two driving around the Square, which is sparse with people, my eyelids feel as if they've put on some extra pounds and I finally get to the point where I need to sleep. Otherwise, I'm going to hurt myself or even worse, hurt someone else.

I find a secluded area in an open stretch of land along the coast and the thought alone of Jazz wrapped in my arms puts me straight to sleep.

\\

I wake up to the sound of *knocking*. . .

Only this time the noise is coming from an older man knocking on my window.

No acorns showering the windshield or squirrels tap-dancing on the hood.

No cop.

No Nico.

My eyes readjust to the sunlight. Not too far stands another older man standing a stuffed shark upright—a seven footer?

I rub the blur from my eyes and realize that the shark is *not* a shark at all but a gray kayak perched upright.

I turn my refreshed eyes to the slumped figure standing next to the car. He doesn't look too pleased from my presence despite my well-being. With his right hand covered in pre-coffee bruises, he's motioning for me to roll down the window. So, I crack the window halfway.

"You're on private property, young man," he says.

I scan the field from left to right until I come across a mansion of a house about the size of a Monopoly piece from where I'm parked.

"I didn't know," I tell him. "I'm leaving now. . . "

"Please do or I'll call the cops."

I roll up the window and drive away.

He's seen my face.

I'm slipping.

My hands are shaking, and I haven't even had my coffee yet.

All I Need Is Jazz.

\\\

\ use the leftover twenty-seven dollars from yesterday and buy a pack of smokes from the convenient store. I smoke three cigarettes in a row as I do the one thing I hate.

With the car door open, I sit on the side of the driver's seat, as if I'm sitting in a waiting room: hunched forward, head down, one leg rapidly bouncing up and down over the cracked asphalt as I frantically shuffle from Nico's number to Jazz's. I'm a complete wreck.

As I pull up Jazz's number, I hear a croaky voice beside my ear!

His voice. . .

I move my eyes toward the rear view mirror—*Shit!*

My insides flex into a ball. I turn into jello.

You're—you're dead, I tell Moses.

He looks worse than terrible, like he's just been shitted out. He's aged significantly, more so than before. He's deathly frail, too, as if he'd shatter to pieces if he dropped on the floor.

You thought you could get rid of me that easily?

What the hell do you want?

Are you ready to get back to business or are you going to sit here, playing with your dick?

I shut my eyes, wishing away Moses.

I open them.

And he's gone.

Just like that—easy.

Over and over, I tell myself that if I can make it through the day without watching porn or having a drink or having a snort or a hit, then I know I'll be okay. And when night comes along, Jazz will come. I will come. Everybody will be coming like New Year's Eve. Everything will be okay. I tell myself these things over and over, about how everything is going to be okay when I know it's not. Somewhere strewed

275

among the blackness of my thoughts someone else is telling me: *As long as you hang around Jazz, nothing will be okay*. Never in my life have I longed for the night like I long for it right now.

White knuckles.

Black heart.

As I ash my cigarette, I feel a pain chewing at the pit of my stomach. It has all the traits of an ulcer. My chest feels like one of those Happy Meal toys, that racecar, all wound up and ready to peel away, swinging and screaming. My bad heart is trying to tell me something. I don't know exactly what that may be, but I know it's serious.

I patiently do the one thing I hate until the poor ole farmer tends to his first customer of the day. I pick a banana from the fruit stand on the side of the road.

Without the farmer knowing, I sneak the green banana in my pocket.

Along the way toward Topside Boardwalk, I eat the fresh banana—from pocket to mouth—which helps ease the pain in my stomach for the time being.

When I arrive at the boardwalk, I notice that it's somewhat sparse like the night before. Vacation season is winding down. Lately, the nights have been getting cooler. The days have been getting shorter. The crowds have been getting thinner, which doesn't help me out. Thin crowds are more challenging.

I stop at a booth in front of the "FREAKSPECTACU-LAR" tent and approach the owner of the freak show—the eccentric guy with the funky stache.

I ask him if they have any more tickets available for tonight's show and when I speak, he turns his head to the left, his ear in line with my mouth, like he's hard of hearing or something.

He tells me in an upbeat voice, "You're just in luck, son. I have exactly four tickets left."

"I'll take two then."

"If you can find two more friends, I can you sell you these right here for a discount."

He holds in a hiccup. Swallows it. I pick up a whiff of alcohol on his breath, which causes my stomach to tighten.

"Just the two please."

"You sure?"

He holds the tickets in front, as if he's trying to seduce me. I don't respond.

"Ohhkay," he drawls. "You owe me twenty dollars even."

I hand the man the twenty, which is all of I have left in my pocket.

He rips off two tickets from a roll and hands them to me.

"There you go," he says with a loose smile on his face.

"Thanks."

"You're very welcome."

I leave the boardwalk and find the nicest restaurant, the Flying Mackerel. According to the *Daily Point*, it's one of the finest five-star restaurants in Topside. I stop by the restaurant and ask the hostess for a menu. They have salmon filets, double what I paid for the tickets; Ahí tuna, which runs well over thirty dollars; the Catch of the Day, which has a starfish icon by it (I locate the starfish icon at the bottom of the menu: *Customer Favorite*).

Jazz mentioned the Flying Mackerel during our walk yesterday. Her face was like Prom when she talked about the restaurant; and at that moment, I swear she looked like the most beautiful woman I've ever seen. She said her mother took her there two years ago for her birthday—I'm guessing that was probably around the time of her father's passing. I'm straight with going out for burgers, though—and I'm not talking about the pancake-shaped ones at fast-food joints. I'm talking about a plump and juicy burger dripping with fat, like ones I saw at that local joint, BLT's—craft burgers, as the younger, much hipper natives call them—and they cost as much as the ones at the fast food places. Burgers also mean fewer pockets to pick. The fewer, the better. I think Jazz is well aware that I'm not trying to impress her; and for all I know, she's totally straight with grabbing burgers too. I'd rather eat a "craft burger" with Jazz at a hole in the wall, than rub shoulders with the swanky assholes at some five-star restaurant.

I tally up the price of the meal and then round up the number; then, after that, I make a reservation for seven o'clock.

I drive to the one place I hate more than going to the dentist: Seaboard's Place Mall.

It's your typical Saturday crowd, a picker's "Paradise."

I seek out someone who looks as if he's carrying around a lot of dough, as in cash. He happens to be a super prick: Calvin Kline model type wearing a dark blazer over a white tee and treating his girlfriend—or sister, I'm not sure which—as if she's six feet beneath him. I want to puke whenever I see a man talking down to a woman (it's how I was raised: *always* hold the door open for a woman, *never* curse in front of a woman, especially your mother, *always* treat a woman with respect). Ruining that nice blazer of his would be extremely rewarding for me, *but*. . . I think of Jazz, and the thought alone of Jazz, puts any indulgences I'm having at the moment straight to bed.

I do an easy pick, a "bump-and-grab."

Normally, I excuse myself after the bump. I don't give the prick any "instant gratification" and my head is swirling and my senses are heightened from the rush of adrenaline. I swear it's like poetry in motion. He'll never suspect a thing. Not at first. He'll be waiting in the checkout line at Narcissists-R-Us, thinking about how good his hair looks as he shows off his new do for other shoppers. The sight of the shoppers admiring him makes him *Rocky*-hard; then, when he goes to pay for his new loafers with his exceptional and yet average-sized hard-on, he'll reach for his gator-skinned wallet in his back pocket and all he'll find is a fistful of nothing.

As I round the jewelry stand, I hear a voice shout, "Hey! He stole my wallet!"

Fuck.

I try not to make a scene as I duck my way through a crowd of young trendy kids dressed in pink and black—a mix between punk and hip-hop.

I peek over my shoulder and see the ballsy prick chasing after me.

I part from the crowds and then take off.

I cut around a couple of booths, hoping to lose the prick.

He still remains on my tail, yelling out to others, "Stop him!"

One guy—some burly man in a wife-beater—actually steps in front of me and tries to grab me, but I remember the training and drop the guy on his ass before he can say, "Deinstitutionalization."

IV

AFTER I finally lose the prick in the parking lot, I drive off. I'm hammering my hands against the steering wheel and all of my anger is directed at that guy who tried to stop me in the mall. Not the slick-haired prick, but the guy who possible suffered a broken collar bone. I slammed his ass pretty good. Something broke inside him. I didn't hear him break, but I felt it. He was grabbing his upper chest area after I dropped him to the floor. In a way, I wish I did more to him.

I decide it's best to lay low for the rest of the afternoon. So, I drive south to Emerald's Lookout. I hang around a lighthouse and wait for Jazz to return my call.

As I'm waiting, I check out my recent score: thirteen dollars. I count again just to make sure I didn't miss any larger bills. T-H-I-R-T-E-E-N dollars. The wallet is filled with credit cards—mostly credit cards from retail warehouses. I find one of those black American Express cards—if the owner is smarter than he looks, the cards have already been canceled.

I pocket the money and toss the gator-skinned wallet out of the window in frustration.

I turn my eyes back to the wallet sitting in the gravel.

I get out of the car, pick up the wallet, and run my finger across the skin of the wallet.

V

I take the wallet to the Russian who hooks me up.

I expected at least a hundred dollars for the prick's wallet, but we ended up closing the deal at seventy-five.

VI

I decide to call Jazz, again.

It's already a couple of minutes past four and the show begins at nine. I've already planned out the night: we have dinner at the Flying Mackerel at seven; then, after we eat our fish and drink our top-shelf wine, we walk off the delicious meal, head over to the boardwalk before nine; then, after the show, I round third base—possibly go for an inside-the-parker.

That is, if everything goes right.

I get a ring this time, which gives me a sense of relief. The phone rings four times before going straight to voicemail.

I leave a message. I make sure to take my time by telling Jazz that a friend gave me some tickets to Freakspectacular tonight and ask her if she wants to join me. I tell Jazz to call me if she's interested. I hang up, feeling more frustrated than before.

Once it reaches five o'clock, I drive by Jazz's apartment and don't see her Corolla. I don't see her mother's silver Camry either. I don't remember Jazz telling me that she had any plans for today.

Or did she?

Maybe something unexpected came up. Maybe she's doing a modeling gig.

Maybe there's another guy whom I'm not aware of.

Maybe.

I don't know.

L ° W T I D E

EIGHT o'clock rolls around. I'm already tipsy from the Cuervo—*tipsy*, as in not drunk enough to be slurring my words but not sober enough to give a damn. I drink and listen to every shade of metal on the radio—the perfect playlist for being stood-up, screamo, thrash, death, all of it sounds the exact same: someone's screaming, someone's hurting. I do this for about thirty minutes until my mind is consumed with violence, a recipe for disaster; then, after I'm well lubricated with booze—the violent thoughts somewhat tamed—I go to the show by myself.

When I get there, a line is stretched around the tent; however, the line seems to be moving fast. I hang around and try not to make a scene. I'm not shitfaced drunk, but I'm about two drinks away from getting there. So, I keep my cool. I get about ten feet inside the tent when an obnoxious asswipe bumps me from behind, forcing me into a stern elderly lady who appears as if she has about year or two left before she kicks the bucket. Next to her is a younger woman—the daughter possibly? They turn around and glare at me with sheer repulsion, as if I'm the worst "thing" that has ever walked the earth. I tell them, especially the older one, "Excuse me." They keep their eyes attached to me, their eyes narrowing—the younger one shaking her head in disappointment.

I hear the asswipe giggling over my shoulder.

I discreetly turn around, only to find a good-looking blonde, very sporty, standing with a tall, puffy-chest man chewing on a piece of gum. To make matters worse, he's giving me a fuck-you smirk. I suddenly hear this *click* inside my head, as if my blood has turned metallic. The tightness grips me—in fact, it strangles me—my hands curl into fists; the blood stampedes through my veins like molten lava; my eyes become all twitchy and crazy as if they're about to pop like corks from my head. . .

At that point, I feel everything.

I hear everything.

I see everything.

Everything in my body is squeezed tight, not only my fists, but inside my chest, my gut, my jaw, my muscles, my bones, and even my eyes, which are like these tiny magnified glasses honing in on every single detail around me. Then, all of a sudden, my vision shrinks. All I see is a soon-to-be dead man standing in front of me and everything around him is soaked in black. The sweetest temptation swells over me, a feeling of euphoria. His smirk shrivels back into his shiny, handsome face. I map out my attack: first, me knocking this asswipe's teeth down his throat, each perfectly white tooth until he's left with none.

For me, that sounds like a great time. That sounds like the time of my life, destroying something that I cannot have.

Right when I'm about to snap, I feel a papery hand touch me on the wrist. I rotate around, only to find the same elderly lady looking at me. I look down at my wrist. I don't see a hand on my wrist. I turn my attention back around; and right then and there, I witness the misery in her face, *not* from what I've done, but from what I'm about to do.

Miraculously, I ignore the asswipe and keep moving with the line until I find a spot near the end of the bleachers where I not only have a decent view at the stage but also a decent view of the asswipe and his bimbo of a date.

About five minutes into the show, I can't stop thinking about that asswipe who bumped into me earlier and what I'd like to do to him after the show is over. Away from people. Just him and me. Alone. I take a couple of sips from the bottle of Cuervo that I sneaked inside; then a couple of minutes later, I eliminate any idea of committing violent acts against the asswipe and focus on the show.

The show is entertaining—somewhat—despite having seen most, if not all of the tricks on stage, whether it's from Nile cutting through the nontoxic glue on his already split tongue to the bearded lady being cut in half. One trick, however, is new; and it leaves me scratching my head: the mirror trick.

A behemoth of a man named Cyrus, also known as "The Tallest Man in the World," who stands well over seven feet tall, trudges onto the stage, waving to the audience, his hand twice the size of my head, like one of those colorful hands you get at a sports game, the ones holding up the number one.

The emcee, I realize after a thorough study, is the same half-deaf man with the mustache who sold me the tickets. He asks Cyrus to stand in front of the mirror of all mirrors, "The Lion's Paw," the emcee calls it.

As soon as Cyrus stands in front of the mirror, a pink triangular eye lights the center of the lion's head. A puff of smoke clouds over Cyrus and then, once the smoke dissipates, Cyrus is no longer looking at his own reflection in the mirror!

In front of Cyrus stands a reflection of a little person. They look identical and they're wearing the same clothes, same shoes, same hairstyle.

For a moment, I actually believe it's real.

The crowd roars with great excitement.

I realize there's nothing magical about the mirror.

All the same, it's just another illusion.

\|

AFTER the show is over, I give Jazz yet another call.

I receive no answer.

Instead of leaving a message, which I've already done, I decide to shoot her a text.

WHAT R U DOING?

I wait outside a coffee shop where people are staring at me and talking about me. I do my best in trying to ignore them, but they keep looking at me. I wait around for about an hour and I sober up a little. Jazz still doesn't return my calls or my texts.

What did I do wrong, Jazz?

\|\|\|

\| get sick and tired of people staring at me as if I'm some freak. I decide to stop at a nightclub off the Strip called Belew where there's a decent turnout.

At the front entrance, the bouncer asks for my ID. I pull out Henry Frick's driver license and hand it to him. Then, he looks me over several times with suspicion. Finally, after the back and forth eye-job, the bouncer hands the ID back to me and lets me pass. I head straight to the bar and order a beer that's on special—a "lite" draft that tastes like toilet water. The Cuervo wore off too, and I'm feeling much more nervous than I was before I entered the club.

When I'm anxious, I drink more. And when I drink more, I do shit that I normally wouldn't do.

On the fourth beer, I grow extremely agitated with the whole club or bar scene—whatever—especially the music. They're not even playing EDM or music anyone can "dance" to; instead, it's mostly crunk or pop songs consisting of a bunch of morons who sound like automations singing over the same generic beat.

Except for a few cougars acting wild on the dance floor, the ones who are dancing aren't really dancing; instead, they're like placeholders, wannabes trying to act cool or something. I really don't know what they're doing. They act like extras in a music video, and most of the guys standing around look like deadbeats waiting in a buffet line, licking their chops and sniffing out the sloppiest drunk.

One wild cat breaks from her hungry pack—possibly a ladies night out—struts toward the bar, squeezes herself in between me and some blowhard from the city. She orders a cranberry and vodka and while she's waiting for the bartender to fetch her drink, she grabs my hand without asking permission and glosses over my fingernails. She displays the same fuck-you, *not* fuck-me, smirk from the length of my fingernails. I'm aware that I haven't cut them in a while—they're not freakishly long but long enough to slice open an envelope—but it's none of her business. I know what she's thinking from the squint in her eyes, like her thoughts written in bold lettering over her eyes. Why does this woman care where I stick my fingers? She's about twenty years older than me—maybe even more—and from her thorough examination of me, she appears as if she's sizing me up, my nails, my body, my wallet, my ass, my dick. I used to go home with these types of older women all the time when I was a part of the whole scene. Not old enough to be my mother, but old enough to get what they want. From the way she's sizing me up, she's a woman who gets exactly what she wants. Like the others, she falls under the recently divorced or currently separated category because either a) my husband is a controlling asshole who treats me as if I'm a punching bag or b) my husband is a spineless wimp who can't get it up anymore or c) my husband is a raging philander who can't kept his dick in his pants or d) all of the above. I'm not proud of those nights, the blackout nights, the nights that crossed over into morning, waking up not knowing what happened the night before or how much I drank before I started to lose count or who I fucked or, better yet, who fucked me. At times, the days after the long nights were saturated with tremendous guilt—numbing, in some way or another, like I betrayed myself, like I've always been betraying or lying to myself. Each time I had opened myself up to these women, the greater the craving had become. I craved their attention. They craved mine equally—sometimes, twice as much. Each time, I raised the threshold of the extreme. I felt like I was in charge, like I was the one steering my own vessel through the flesh and chaos. I felt as if I had the strength of seven men—if only for a night. The funny thing: luck didn't have anything to do with it. After a few drinks, it's remarkable how the mind turns against you and a woman—average looking, even ugly—can become not only an attractive woman, but also the "right" woman. You never point out flaws. You never judge her for *who* she is or *what* she does. You look past the layers of makeup, the wrinkles, the blemishes, and you see how attractive she "used" to be or, even how attractive you "wanted" her to be. You want to be inside her no matter what the cost. For a night, it feels as if you can really settle down with this woman—I mean, really. The next morning, you swim from the haze, half drunk, half hungover, half stupid, your memory partially erased, wondering if the shards of memories were your own or someone else's—or implants? This ain't science fiction. It's reality. I remember those mornings and I'd do anything to unremember them, the way I was brushed aside as if I was dust (even a duster didn't receive as much attention as I did). But I brought it all on myself, like I knew the ending to the book, yet I decided to read the book anyway. For a while, it seemed as if I had craved the rejection, *not* the attention. I was nothing more than a particle and after a while, I felt as if I had grown into something parasitic that grazed off the bacteria cast from the last remaining inhabitants of a gray-heavy earth, something that only came out at night, a nocturnal creature, a leech.

Is it even worth it anymore? Jimmy's shooter is already dead. I should demonstrate that I've made the initiative to turn my life around, that I'm *not* just some kid taking up space. I should prove not only to myself, but also to the ones who doubted me, especially Thomas, that I am worthy of a second chance. God knows all of the bullshit I put him through. He deserves better after all of the years he took it on the chin. I should be heading back East to the Carolinas to take care of my aging parents, especially after the physical and mental strain of providing for a disabled son. I don't know what you'd even call them. I mean, they have a name for when a man loses a wife or a woman loses a husband. They, as in society, have a name for when a boy or girl loses both of his or her parents. They have a name for a child who is born out of wedlock. They don't have a name for a parent who loses a son or a daughter or even a name for a sibling who loses another sibling. I'd say they're good at a lot of things, except for putting a label on us.

In a way, I guess they never should have a name for us.

I survey all of the people inside the stuffy club: the phonies dressed like their beloved TV characters scanning the scene for the drunkest girl; the winsome server, who'd clearly rather be somewhere else, rolling her eyes at a snappy drunk complaining about his order; the owner of the club standing post with a couple of his associates who look like members of the Russian mafia; the wasted twenty-something making a fool of herself on the dance floor; Ms. Twenty-Something's obnoxious friend, beyond-wasted—in fact, a sip away from turning into a zombie—carrying a monumental arrow pointing directly at her vagina as she stumbles toward the bathroom.

I turn my gaze toward the drink in my other hand.

What am I doing? Why am I still here?

A woman's sultry voice tickling my ear: *I don't know—*

She's still standing next to me at the bar, still checking out my hand, still waiting for me to make a move.

"—Why are you here?" she says, her voice turning sour.

"Excuse me," I tell her and release my hand from her grip.

I give the woman the shoulder and take a sip from my piss-warm beer and when I turn back around, the woman is looking at me as if she wants to sink her teeth inside my neck.

She struts back to her loud friends, mumbling the word *faggot* under her breath.

It wouldn't be the first time someone's called me such a derogatory name. Kids used to do that back in the day when you weren't really a faggot. It was just a word that closet homosexual kids used to toss around so freely, mainly the football kids, the ones who acted as if they were tough when they weren't really tough; and they'd use the word if you didn't go along with them or if you didn't agree with them.

Like all faggots are skinny and single and wear gel in their hair.

I swear people and their goddamn stereotypes.

IV

AFTER I down my fourth beer, I spot another twenty-something standing alone at the end of the bar. Not as wasted as the ones on the dance floor. She has bleached blonde hair, marketable face, a TV face. I walked past her earlier in the night. That was when I was draining the lizard—I believe it was during my second beer. Second one usually gets the bladder working. She was talking to some black suave dude who was coming off a bit too abrasive; and about five minutes after I left the restroom and ventured back to my post, she was no longer talking to him. I saw him not too long after our eyes crossed paths, and he was talking to some white suave dude, who was also thin, by the way, and single, from the way his eyes were oscillating like a sprinkler around the club, and, of course, wore gel in his hair. But who's judging? Most of the girls or women here are either interested in big spenders or well dressed black dudes standing around the dance floor, looking important, waiting. Or, it may be the other way around minus the girls—or women. But, like I said, who's judging? I didn't dress the part, clearly. I left my Men's Warehouse suit, as well as my go-fuck-yourself loafers, in the car. I have no business being here, I tell myself again. None whatsoever. The place is as slimy as a swamp, and I've been telling myself more than on one occasion that I don't belong in these types of places anymore.

I can only imagine Henry hanging around a place like this, but I'm not like Henry. Not anymore.

Instead of standing around the bar, I order a shot of whiskey after I share a glance with the blonde hair girl across the bar. I huddle over the bar, shot glass in hand, and map out the next plays: first, I down the shot and let it sit for a while before I decide to approach the blonde across the bar; second, I ask for her name and if she's the least bit interested in me, she'll give it to me, no problem, and then, if she's really interested in me, she'll ask for my name; then, I'll buy her a drink and I'll make sure to show her the money in my wallet when I spread it open to pay the bartender (the girls who come to these places like guys with money); not only that, I'll make sure to show her that I have a particular knack for spreading things open and maybe I'll make a pun about it when I pay the bartender for our drinks; and finally, after we drink and talk for a little while, I'll ask her if she lives close by.

After I swallow my shot, I approach the blonde from behind. She turns her shoulder, sensing my presence, her heavy-lidded eyes beaming right through me. The first thing she asks me is what I do for a living—*do*, as in how do I afford the organic gel in my hair—which is an immediate red flag. I'm tempted to tell her—like the lecherous cougar before—it's none of her business what I do for a living, but I think of what any normal person in or around Topside would say. I tell her that I'm a screenwriter. I make sure to keep my words clear and friendly, easy to understand. I make sure not to come off as a drunk. There's nothing fun or interesting about one. They're boring. They have nothing to say about anything, really. She laughs, and if I really was a screenwriter, I'd probably take the laugh as a slap in the face, an insult, really. I like the way she laughs, though. It reminds me of Jazz's laugh.

"That's original," she says, sipping from droplets of melted ice from her drink. "So, you're broke. . . "

"Well," I say, "the only thing that separates me from other screenwriters is that I've actually written a screenplay."

"It got picked up?"

"Sold the script to Universal Brothers," I say humbly. "The movie is scheduled for pre-production next year."

She looks me over, more fascinated.

"So, are you here alone?"

I nod my head.

"There's nothing wrong with that."

"Whoever said there was?"

She recoils and starts to look a little less cute.

I'm tempted to ask her why she even made the comment to begin with, if she didn't feel as if there was anything wrong with coming "here" alone. The words are there, but they don't make it to my lips.

I glance around the bar scene, the talking heads, the wandering eyes.

A gap of silence develops in the conversation while I search for the next thing to say to her. The blonde acts as if she's waiting for me to answer my own question. I'm not good with people, especially people who don't think before they talk. I know. It's a condition. I'm a walking contradiction.

I point at her drink, which looks like it cost a lot of money.

I ask her, "What are you drinking?"

"Sex on the Beach," she says in a vampish manner.

I order her another sex on the beach.

V

Two drinks later, the blonde and I are having her favorite drink.

Halfway through, she acts as if she's fucking me out of charity and she begs me to come for her.

When I finally finish all over the flat part of her lower back, she dresses immediately and lets out a loud sigh of relief, telling me that she has to run.

I ask her if I can get her number.

"You don't even know my name," she says as she gives me a hard kiss on the lips.

What's Her Name holds her gaze close to mine and just as she's about to kiss me again, she gives me this soft pat on the cheek as if she's the one who got the better end of the fuck, the last laugh, and I'm just another lousy sucker.

"That's what I thought," she says sharply.

I tell her, "Of course, I do."

She stops dressing and gives me a worn expression.

Her name starts with a P, I believe. Or is it a B? I remember she told it to me once at the bar and then a friend that she met that night blurted it out a couple of times when they were grinding on each other. The more I think about her name, the more my head starts to spin.

"Are you hungry?" I say before she takes off. "We can get something to eat. . . "

"Good luck on your *little* movie," she says scornfully as she lifts up the yellow CAUTION tape stretched around the bottom of the pier and walks back toward the boardwalk.

After I slip on my pants, I notice the low tide underneath the pier.

Nothing has changed and yet everything has changed.

I check my wallet and pull out two dollars.

I'm still broke.

I check the stains on my pants.

I'm still an asshole.

I check the yellow bruises on my knuckles.

I'm still a loser.

T H E   E N T E ®   V I E W

THE tendons in the back of my hands look like white cords tied around Jazz's neck. I'm urging myself to please wake up; in fact, I'm screaming at myself. Wake up! Please, wake up! I can't. I don't want to. I like it here, in the red haze. I watch each vein in Jazz's purple face swell. Her eyes are like these two delicate glass balls ready to shatter. Coldness rushes into her face, causing her red eyes to wash over with panic. She desperately tries to claw at my face, but I block off each attempt with my shoulder and elbow. The life runs rampant inside her, every single band of fibrous tissue in her body tightening as tight as a corkscrew. She finally succumbs to my grip—her muscles now loosening. Her wet eyes fixate on mine. I look down at my hands, both as pale as a scar, and they feel as if they don't belong to me. Then, all of sudden, I hear that awful sound. . .

The first person who comes to my mind when I wake to the sound of *ringing*: Jazz. I search the car until I locate my burner wedged between the sticky tracks underneath the seat.

I grip my burner with my two fingers and studiously pull it from the seat as if I'm playing *Operation*. I hit the sides of the seat and drop the phone (Bzzzzz! Ruptured artery). I have more success on the second attempt. I do a double take: first reading the name on my burner, then looking at myself in the rear view mirror. Normally, he'd have something to say to me right now, something sarcastic like "I told you so" or even something violently elegant, "You should've gotten a good night's sleep before the massacre begins."

He doesn't say a word.

Not one.

\\

\ gather enough loose change inside the car for a fast breakfast.

I eat in my car; and after I finish eating, I pop an aspirin for the headache. The coffee helps too.

I drive to the nearest beach and use the shower to wash up.

\\\

NICO sets me up with a "meet and greet" in the ballpark of two o'clock with a guy who calls himself Mars. I'm a little nervous about meeting the guy, but I'm constantly reminding myself that he's just a guy. Nothing special about a guy. A guy is just like any other guy who eats, shits, and sleeps. If I don't land a job, then so be it. There'll always be another guy, another job. And that's how I go into the job interview even though Nico never really called it a job interview per se. Nico didn't say much at all on the phone except for giving me the name, Mars, and telling me that Mars is looking for an extra hand around the shop. The shop, I research, is called "MARS: TOUCH UPS AND REPAIRS."

When I set foot inside the pristine garage at precisely two o'clock, I notice a couple of sports cars hoisted up on the lifts: one being a red Porsche Boxer, another a black Porsche 911, then a Ferrari but not any Ferrari, a 458 Italia with a V8 engine.

I scope out the place, mainly looking for exits—you never know—then I come across a familiar blue Lambo parked at the other end of the garage. I realize after I get a closer look that it's Nico's Lambo—the Blue Dragon—but I don't see Nico anywhere around.

Then, a scruffy voice echoes throughout the shop, "You must be *Double-0 Seven*!"

The reflection of what looks like Quasimodo is walking toward me in the passenger side window of the Lambo.

I turn my shoulder and face the hunched man.

"Jimmy," I correct him.

"Jimmy it is," he says.

He calls himself Mars. "Like the planet," he says, exposing his tea-stained teeth. "Nico said you'd be stopping by."

I tell Mars that I like his name and he returns by saying that it's short for Marlowe. His mother, who was an immigrant from Ireland, was sick and tired of wasting her breath on yelling her son's name. She cut off *Lowe* and put an *s* on the back of *Mar*.

"Nice to meet you, Mars." I shake his oil-stained hand. Everything about the guy is stained—teeth, elbows, hands especially.

"You look a lot older from what Nico told me," he says.

"Is that going to be an issue?"

"Of course not," Mars replies with an ugly smile. "If you can get the job done, then we'll get along just fine."

When the sun shines through the shop, the sunrays bring out the red highlights in Mars's moppy dark hair. His face is the color of a scorched desert and covered with the leftover scars from years of acne during adolescence; and the jumpsuit that he wears looks two sizes too small.

I ask Mars if Nico is here and he tells me that he just dropped off the Lambo about an hour ago because it needs a little "touch up."

He asks me if I know my cars and I point out each car in the shop and name each one of them, as well as each tool.

Two invisible strings slowly pull that hideous smile across his chin and he bobs his head.

"You'll fit right in," he says amusingly.

I look around the shop and find myself mimicking the same expression on Mars's face.

IV

MARS gets me a job as an auto mechanic—actually, Nico gets me the job, but still. Mars tells me the job description, which consists of me doing oil changes, tire rotations, cleaning the brakes, checking oil level, the coolant, changing the battery, as well as the bulbs in the headlights: basic car maintenance. And last but not least, making sure the shop stays as clean as a virgin's pussy. Mars is extremely particular on keeping a clean shop.

He tells me that he let the last guy go because he was a slob.

Then, Mars asks me if I'm hungry.

I tell him that I'm starved.

V

WE have lunch at Old Town Diner.

The waitress first takes our drink orders as she's pouring us glasses of water from a pitcher.

Mars orders a glass of iced tea.

I order coffee, black.

I don't even realize that I'm shaking until Mars points it out for me.

"Looks like you've had enough coffee as it is," he says as he nods at my hands.

I glance down at my hands and place them underneath the table.

"You can never have enough coffee," I tell Mars, who laughs from the remark.

The waitress is about to leave when Mars throws up his hand and tells her that he's ready to order the food, then he points to me in approval.

It feels as if I've been put on the spot, but I don't make a big deal about it. I skim the first page of the menu and the first thing that catches my eye is a BLT sandwich.

I order the BLT with avocado, as well as a side of canta-loupe, and hand the menu back to the waitress.

Mars orders a salad, stressing to the waitress not to put any onions in the salad.

I search the diner for the waitress—Autumn was her name, I think—but I can't find her.

When I pull my eyes back around, I catch Mars checking out the waitress—not Autumn, but our waitress—as she walks away. He tells me that he's trying to watch his cholesterol. After his last check-up, he tells me, the doctor, who he calls the "quack," told him that he needed to cut out cigarettes and red meat from his diet. And he makes it clear to me that he's not one of those salad eatin' guys (*wink, wink,* you know what I mean). He says that he's trying to make life changes for the wifey. I don't see a ring on his finger, though. Not even a pale outline of a ring.

"Jimmy," he says and takes a sip of water and smacks his lips together as if he's never drunk water before in his life, "what's the best car you've ever worked on?"

"The best?"

"The best," he says, more exuberantly, "just name one, anyone. . . "

I think of one car, really, the *only* car I've ever worked on and that was a 1955 Ford Fairlane. Thomas took out a pinch from his pension every month until he had enough money to buy the Fairlane online. When we picked it up from the original owner a few days later, it was in bad shape. I told him that he'd take the Fairlane to his grave. It was *that* bad. One of the neighbors, Mr. Tapper, a former accountant for one of the corporate banks in Elizabeth, would pitch in and help out Thomas with the Fairlane. I didn't know any of the other neighbors, just their names, except for Ms. Niddleson who lived in this scarily perfect house to the right of us—I remember she used to call Susannah by the name "Suze," which Susannah hated; she'd go to lunch with her once a month, then the next time I'd see her after the monthly outings, she'd cite scripture to me, as if Susannah treated "going to lunch" as "going to confessional," and Ms. Niddleson knew everything about me; she'd always try to get me to go to church or introduce me to "better," more Christian people who were about as square as Rubik's cubes. Besides Mr. Tapper, who I considered "okay" in my book, I kind of wished I didn't know any of the neighbors' names. That way, if one of them kicked the bucket, I could be like, "Hey, that poor ole bitch next door finally croaked. It's about fucking time." Instead, it was more like: Poor Ms. Niddleson passed away last night. Bless her heart. She was always so nice to me. She used to always wave hello and ask me how I was doing and I'd tell her that I was doing fine even when I wasn't.

Neighbors aside, all the other expenses Thomas spent on the car came from a side-job as a consultant.

Since Thomas used to be in law enforcement, he'd help big *and* small businesses with their security systems, making sure they were up to standard. For Thomas, it was easy money. Not only that, it kept him busy during retirement.

Finally, I tell Mars with conviction, "A Fairlane."

"What year?"

"Nineteen fifty-five."

"Get outta here," Mars says surprisingly.

I tell Mars that my father worked on it for a while after we came back home to the Carolinas and then later I gave him a hand and helped him finish the job. We literally gutted the entire car until nothing was left but a shell; and then we installed a new engine, new seating, new paint job—Mr. Tapper, a car enthusiast like Thomas, helped him out with the engine. Jimmy was there as well. He'd sit in his wheelchair at a safe distance, his eyes moving back and forth like *Pong* as he watched us work. Even though he couldn't get his hands in the mix, Jimmy was just as essential to the process as the people who were fixing up the car. I put together a rainbow of colors that we all liked and printed them out on a piece of paper and then had Jimmy pick out the best color. Since he couldn't speak, he couldn't tell me what color he wanted the car to be. Instead, he showed me. And he happened to pick out the one color Thomas didn't like. Aquamarine. Jimmy's choice. That was the color we went with. After we breathed life into the Fairlane and got it running again, it was like our Frankenstein.

My parents always wanted a grandchild, but a Fairlane was what they got.

I thought that was what we *all* needed at the time.

Most importantly, it was what Thomas needed.

I don't entirely go into detail as to why we fixed up the Fairlane. I just tell Mars that we wanted to take something old and make it new.

Then, Mars tells me that an automobile is no different than you or me. "Like any human being," he says, "a car will not go forward or backward unless it is told to go forward or backward. Every part of the engine—straight down to a chrome molly piston ring—has a purpose, and without one part, the engine won't function properly. Each and every single part of a car is like a vital organ in the human body. If one organ fails, the car will no longer operate at its fullest potential. It's as simple as that. The question, however," Mars says, more carefully, "say, if a car part doesn't work properly anymore and it gets to the point where it is completely inoperable, 'how do we find a way to compensate for that part without having to replace it?'"

I never give Mars an answer. As far as I can tell, he doesn't expect one from me. He just wants me to think about the question. And I think about it, for a long time.

Next, we talk about Stower engines, then our food arrives not too long afterward; and then, before I even know it, I look down at the plate and the plate is covered with crumbs and I'm full.

VI

BEFORE I get into my car, Mars asks me if I can work tomorrow.

Without any hesitation, I tell him, "Absolutely."

We shake hands, a firm handshake, business-like.

He tells me what time I need to be at the shop in the morning.

I tell him I'll be there and he drives away.

After he leaves, I check the messages on my burner. I have a missed call and one message and they're both from Jazz. The message says that she got my message this morning and that she was sorry. She was returning my call and wants me to give her a call whenever I get the chance.

I call her immediately after I listen to the message.

She's glad that I called. She tells me that her phone ran out of juice last night and that she's really, really sorry about it.

Surprisingly, I'm not too upset about it.

I ask her if she's doing anything today.

She says, "No."

"Do you want to get together?"

"That sounds good."

"Great," I reply.

Not too long after we hang up, we meet at the boardwalk and go for another long walk on the beach and watch the sunset. I do most of the talking. I tell Jazz about my brand new job, and she's excited for me. I get excited because she's excited.

When I ask her about last night, she tells me that she had a modeling gig.

I know Jazz's lying, but right now, I just don't give a shit.

I ' M - P R O V - I S - A - T I O N

I'M going straight to Hell—that is, if there is a place.
    You may be wondering what kind of person would be-
lieve that he or she is so wickedly evil that he or she deserves
a one-way ticket straight to Hell. I'm talking about eternal
damnation, a crowded lobby filled with fire and demons.

Once, I mean, in another life, another realm, really, I used
to think about Hell, about Heaven. I used to think about how
I'd go out before I find myself face-to-face with my Creator.

Not go out, as in go out for the night—*Would I drive, take
the bus, or hitch a ride with a friend?* The friend scenario less
likely. What I mean to say is "How would I go out, as in how
would I die?" The universal language: food and death, two
things we all can relate to or agree on. No politics. Something we find ourselves fundamentally speaking with raw in-
stinct if it's from having confronted death to witnessing death
in all its graphic, unapologetic glory. Something we hold inside us, as if our deaths are like these small boxes of treasures
where its riches merely mentor the essence of the holder.

I used to think a lot about death—*a lot*, as in probably too
much. I used to think about all of the pending questions attached to death: Where do we go, as in where do our souls
go—that is, if we do have souls? Do they end up hanging out
with other souls? Is there a place primarily designated for the
soul? And if so, are they segregated from pure to putrid?
Most importantly, what "other" world is waiting for us on the

other side? Is it one similar to our own? Do we transcend up or down or do we continue to exist in the same plane where we were first spawned? Is it like some kind of secret society? A fraternity for the wicked? Or, darkly, is it a place far worse, a place forever stained with blackness? If we do have souls, something beyond parameters of reality, something that can't be physically touched or seen yet something that moves like air whenever the body dies, does the soul find itself a new host? An incarnation? Or, does the soul simply go where its vessel goes, back to the earth or the sea which kept it bound, only to explode into endless particles of pollen, each one sowing like seeds among other souls, pollinated into another form of life?

Once, I couldn't go through an entire day without thinking about death, about dying, about surrendering myself over to the great unknown, to—without question—life's greatest mystery.

Once, I actually wondered if I was already dead. That would be something, really, being dead yet knowing you were dead. Drifting around. Head to the ground or, even worse, stuck in a phone. Oblivious to the universe. Like something eternally just "getting by" in this fucked up existence filled with the merciless and the mundane. Then, you die but you don't really die. You keep floating along. Then, you keep dying as if it was your only purpose in life.

Once, I felt as if death was this microscopic entity perched on my shoulder, so small yet so astronomical, like the Lord of all Mighty Lords, easy to access yet so extremely difficult to breach.

Whenever I'm with Jazz, all I can think about is what to do next with her—Where will we hang out? What will we do? How will *we* go out, as in go out for the night?

The thought alone of death is—dare I say—starting to feel foreign again. Like a really, really old friend, grade school-old. I swear, if I didn't know any better, it's starting to feel as if I've been given a chance to put together all of the pieces, which have been recklessly scattered before me in the wake of tragedy; and now, I can redesign and format these old, blemished pieces to fit a new and improved version of myself.

\\

JAZZ and I are officially a couple.

It didn't exactly happen as I had initially planned when the idea first originated in my mind: Jazz and I being an item. Even the thought alone of what both of our names would sound like together was enough to warrant a laugh—I mean, it was pretty funny, like Bennifer (Ben and Jennifer) or the other ridiculous names for couples being branded by tabloids in order to make for racy headlines.

It started out around mid-morning with a text from Jazz:

WHAT R U DOING TODAY, JIMMY?

As giddy as a boy, I waited a few minutes before responding to the her text—I didn't want it to look as if I was at Jazz's beckon call—then, during my lunch break, we grabbed a bite to eat close by; then, after we ate, we went back up at her place, which wasn't too far from the garage; and then, from there, we went to the park, which wasn't too far from Jazz's place).

Throughout our brief time spent at the park—I only had like twenty minutes before I had to be back at the garage—I thought about inviting Jazz out for an upscale dinner later that night. A place where adults went to eat like that one restaurant, the Flying Mackerel, or somewhere where they had white clothed tables and French waiters that constantly kept your glass full or a place where the guests seemed important and dressed as if they were attending a fundraising or something that was going to better the world. Then, we'd have a great dinner, in fact, one step closer to bliss, the kind of meal you'd want before you die. Like a Last Supper. The food would be so delicious that we'd leave the restaurant lopsided with our bellies as fat as sandbags, occasionally excusing our flatulent selves from burping or farting, then we'd drive down to Topside Beach, remove the shoes from our sore feet, and take a well-needed walk on the beach. Marathon-long. Then, we'd stop somewhere quiet along the shore when our feet became blistered. The ocean breeze blowing in our hair as we peered out into night darkness. The stars like miniature spotlights glimmering down on us. Then, with our toes tucked in the cool sand, I'd ask Jazz if she'd wanted to take the relationship to the next level.

That, of course, never happened.

Instead, Jazz calls me over to her place after I get off work. She says her mom is spending the night out with a friend yet again. A dentist she met on some online dating site for older women. Apparently, they've been seeing each other a lot lately. He's nice, Jazz tells me with a thoughtful pause when I ask her about her mother's so-called "friend." And that's all Jazz says about him.

Then, I destroy any silence between us by asking her what she wants to do tonight. *But* I already know the answer, as soon as I catch sight of the stack of DVDs on the nightstand. Movie night. I believe Jazz owns every romantic comedy movie—or *rom-coms*, dramedies, whatever—that's ever been made, starting from the early Eighties to late Nineties. I notice that Jazz doesn't own any movies from this decade—at least, no physical copies. Instead, most, if not all of them are "in the cloud," so she says. I go through her library of movies. She's into a lot of cheesy romantics from the Eighties, movies that one would probably find in the five-dollar bin. She even has a section dedicated to all of the John Hughes movies: *Ferris Bueller's Day Off; Sixteen Candles, The Breakfast Club; Uncle Buck*, etc.

I skim through more movies, all arranged in alphabetic order: *Look Who's Talking, Mystic Pizza, Overboard, Romancing the Stone, Roxanne, Say Anything, Scrooged, The Princess Bride, When Harry Met Sally, Working Girl. . .*

I retrace my finger back the S section and come across the spine of one DVD in particular.

"Scrooged?" I turn to Jazz. "You own Scrooged?"

With her mouth closed, Jazz responds with an *uh-huh*.

Jazz picks out the movie.

We turn the lights out and get comfortable.

Then, it happens just like that: one minute, we're sitting on the living room futon with TV glow illuminating our faces as we watch the movie, *Big*, the one with young Tom Hanks who, after making a wish, turns into a thirty-year-old man-boy.

The next minute, Jazz turns to me and says, "I bought you a toothbrush."

\|\|\|

AFTER putting in over eighty hours of backbreaking work, Mars orders me to get away and go somewhere "nice" for a few days.

I take Mars's advice and head back to my motel where I take a warm shower to ease the soreness in my bones. I call Jazz after I wash up. She tells me that her mom's at court today, a new murder case; so I stop by her place. She's working on a poster for a "client," she says, a renowned author who's hired her to come up with a dark cover for his new mystery novel, *The Guilty Hand*, which will be available in stores before people head out to the beaches next summer. She says that she's received a couple of gigs from the poster that she made for the Freakspectacular. Other artists interested in doing projects with her. One happens to be a brewmaster who's in the early stages of building a new brewery at the Point. He wants Jazz to create some artwork for the label on their bottles. She's also currently putting together a portfolio for an agent. Jazz's thinking that, if she has an agent who can represent her, she has a much better chance at "making" it. The Internet can only take you so far.

We go back downstairs and as Jazz grabs some food from the fridge, I unpeel an older photograph of Jazz's mother from behind a CARL'S PIZZA magnet—a "throwback." If I had to take a stab at guessing when the photo was taken, I'd say when grunge music was peaking in pop culture and every kid in America was dressing like Kurt Cobain or Eddie Vedder. Parts of Jazz's face are revealed in her mother's face, her lips especially. Rosa has voluptuous lips. So does Jazz.

"That's my mom," Jazz says from behind. "My madre."

"You speak Español?"

"A little."

Jazz rotates her hand from front to back in a so-so gesture.

I point at the photo.

"This is your mom?"

Jazz nods a *yes*.

I recently saw a current photo of Rosa and she looks nothing close to the young starlet on the fridge.

Jazz places the orange aside, walks through the living room, opens a chest, and pulls out a photo album about as dense as a chemistry textbook. She brings the album back to the kitchen where she opens it up for me. I point at one photo in particular as Jazz turns each page. It's a photo of Jazz playing in a bathtub filled with bubbles. Naked and all. Her yellow "duckie" gripped in hand. A drunken smile over her round baby face.

"*This* is a better one," she says as she pulls out a photo taken of her mother.

In the photo, Jazz, six years old at the time, is holding hands with her mother, still glowing with beauty, both of them standing outside the ranch house where her mother grew up. Their hair is wavy and still with the wind.

"Where was that taken?" I ask her.

"My grandparents' house," Jazz answers. "This was taken—I think—a year before my poppa passed away. This was maybe a few years before she became addicted to pain-killers. It had gotten so bad that she had to go to these clinics to receive shots. Eventually, she had a pump implanted in her back."

I know all about these "clinics" that Jazz mentions. I went for shots of morphine, which helped me kick the dope. I think about *zero*, and how much I hate the number zero.

Then, I ask Jazz how her mother hurt her back.

"Taking care of her mom, my nana—I mean, my nana on my mom's side, not my dad's—" Jazz says quietly. "I remember she had trouble getting in bed. My mom used to lift her up a lot. I guess all of the lifting took its toll on her."

"Was your mom a nurse?"

Jazz shakes her head as she closes the photo album.

She asks, "Do you have to be a nurse to take care of someone you love?"

I follow suit. Shake my head.

"Of course not," I say.

The pause in the conversation gives Jazz an opportunity to peel the orange.

The pause forces me to think about other things, mainly the number zero.

Then, I finally pose the question: "Do you want to go somewhere for a couple of days?"

Jazz doesn't reply as she throws the orange peel in the trash.

She takes a bite of the orange and follows with a shrug.

I imitate Jazz by joking in an exaggerated kind of way.

"What does that mean?" I ask, referring to the shrug.

She feeds me an orange wedge.

"Where did you have in mind?"

"I don't know," I say. "Somewhere nice."

"Really?" Jazz says as a smile grows on her face.

She arches her body closer to mine.

"Somewhere north?" I suggest.

"The North Pole?"

"The North Pole, huh?"

"Why not?" Jazz says innocently as she kisses me, her lips covered in juice. "We can go visit Santa's crib."

Just the sound of the name, *Santa*, rolling from Jazz's tongue, warms my insides.

"I was thinking of somewhere a little less cold."

"Oh yeah," she says. "Like where?"

I reach around and grab her smartphone from the counter.

"How do you work this thing?"

"Here."

I hand her the thing. She types in her four-digit pass code. Hands it back to me. I pull up the GPS and scroll north of California until I reach Oregon. I find the town. I remember reading about it once in *Finding Fit*. Shies Lodge. They have these lake cabins, which look as if they were plucked from a Jack London book. They have spots where you can fish or hike or do all sorts of outdoor activities. I map out the time. An entire day's drive—at least. We could take the Coast Star-rail, which runs up and down the West Coast, and that would certainly cut the time in half; but it'll probably end up costing us more money. Time, we have. Money, we're somewhat limited. And even if we did drive, we'd be wiped out by the time we arrived at the cabins. Jazz and I would spend most of the time in the car.

On a whim, I type in Las Paraíso. Shorter drive, I realize, no more than three hours.

"How about Paraíso?"

"Paraíso?"

"Have you ever been?"

"No."

"Never?"

She shakes her head.

"Nope," Jazz says. "But I've always wanted to go there."

"What do you say?"

"Today?"

"Why not?"

"Yeah, okay," she says, smiling from ear to ear. "Lets go to Paraíso."

I place her phone aside and we pack for Las Paraíso.

IV

TWO hours into the drive, Jazz's mother calls, asking about Jazz's whereabouts. I overhear Rosa on the other end and she sounds pissed, royally "pissed." Right about now, she's probably reading Jazz's note that she left on the fridge. Rosa repeats exactly the same thing Jazz wrote in the letter—that she went camping with a friend, Amy, in San Dierno, and she'll be back on Thursday. Rosa asks Jazz who this "Amy" girl is and how long she has known her. Then Jazz tells her mother that she's a close friend who works with her. It wouldn't be the first time Jazz has lied. Rosa still thinks Jazz works at Lassie's.

V

ONCE we cross into Nevada, we make a pit stop in Grimm.

I find a gas station and fill up the tank with regular.

I pay the clerk for the gas, as well as a few bottles of water.

As I'm walking back to the car, Jazz pokes her head out the window and asks me if I'm hungry.

"I can eat," I tell her.

We hit up a King's Jr. Jazz asks me if I have any King's Juniors on my side of the coast. I naturally tell her that we do—since she thinks I'm from Philly (I figure now is not the time to come clean about me *not* being from Philly)—but they're called Marty's, not King's Jr. I order the number one combo. Jazz orders the same. We find a booth in the back. We hardly say a word to one another while we satisfy our massive appetites by stuffing our faces with greasy hamburgers and french fries and then chase it down with artificially flavored soda. Jazz tells me with a ketchup stain the size of a teardrop on the side of her lip that she can't remember the last time she's had a hamburger. She'd gotten so used to all of that veggie and low carb stuff that she almost forgot what a hamburger tasted like. I wipe away the ketchup stain with a napkin while Jazz patiently smiles. She doesn't have to say thank you. She doesn't have to say a single word. She doesn't even have to open her mouth. I can hear her speak even when she's not.

After we eat lunch, we decide to burn off the food by walking around a fashion outlet just next door to King's Jr. The place is filled with high-end designer stores, which never see the likes of me. It's packed too, especially for a Monday. We hop from one store to another. At one store in particular, Jazz asks me to try on a pair of shades. Posh and expensive. I glance at the price tag and hold in my laughter. I jokingly model them in the mirror. Jazz tells me that they're "so you," then she insists on buying them for me. As we wait in the checkout line, we ping pong back and forth on who should pay for the sunglasses—of course, I keep telling Jazz that I should be the one to buy them. Jazz tells me that she wants to buy them for me. I take it as a gesture of goodwill. So, I let her. Then I toss out my old pair.

VI

WE have about an hour or so left of daylight when we arrive in Paraíso. We drive around the main drag. Check out the many prestigious hotels: Silver Castle, the de Rio, Grigio, Oasis, Brea Inn, TNT Grand, Wisp, and then, that one with a rollercoaster, the Azure. Then we head to Tremont and check out one casino after another. We cruise around the downtown for a good thirty minutes, including the art district, which I swear is something you'd see in a Memphis Black movie (for those of you who are unaware of the eccentric director, he uses what *Reel* magazine calls a "rich palette" for his films—in other words, the guy's like Gilliam meets Scorsese—his sets are bright and lurid and yet his characters are incredibly dark and dysfunctional); after we see a decent portion of the city, we decide to search for a place to stay for the night. A special place. Not some shithole away from the main drag. I remember Jazz mentioned that not only does she want to one day visit Paris when, *not* if, she gets enough money, but also how much she adored the French culture, the food, the countryside, the simple way of life. . . the men, Jazz told me in a playful manner even though I know she was trying to get me going, which she did. She was good at twisting my knobs and pushing my buttons.

I spot a luxurious hotel, Planet Bollywood, next to an Eiffel Tower, not *the* actual Eiffel Tower, but one that looks close to the real thing. Who would've thought that we'd have any luck finding a room? The local rag, *The Insight,* said Planet Bollywood is known for having one of the best Indian buffets in Las Paraíso. They don't require credit cards either, which is a bonus. I end up having to put down a hundred dollars cash deposit, though.

Once we finally get settled in our room, it's already dark outside and Jazz is anxious about hitting up the casinos and participating in the many nightly activities Paraíso has to offer.

I tell Jazz to put on something "nice" while I step out for a minute.

Since I've been wearing the same handful of outfits for the past couple of weeks, I decide to hit up *HIDE*, a men's clothing store just a block from the hotel. The place is about as empty as a record store, which makes it easier for me to roam. I scan the store until I spot *my* color. I try on the outfit in a dressing room. I don't bother changing back into my old raggedy clothes. Yet, I stay as cool as Cash and glide back to Planet Bollywood.

When I make it back to the room, Jazz is stepping from the bathroom. I swear she looks like a centerfold. She's wearing a short red dress that matches her lipstick. It's remarkable what a fresh outfit can do to a person's mood.

"You look handsome," she says as she struts toward me as if the room is a catwalk.

"This," I say as I once over my Johnny Cash-like attire.

I shrug.

"Thanks."

Jazz runs her hands down my collar.

I gently kiss her on the lips, trying not to ruin the masterful artwork on her face.

"You look amazing," I tell her.

Jazz carefully rubs the shade of lipstick from my lips as we look into each other's eyes.

I don't even have to say another word.

Neither does Jazz.

DOUBLE LIFE

EPISODE 8

B A C K W A R D
C O M P A T I B L E *

THE knocking is back.

My eyes spring open like a doll's eyes.

I listen carefully to the silence of the room. I don't hear any knocking, only Jazz snoring to the right of me.

I hear the knocking once more, this time it's thunderous and causes the door to rattle.

I turn to the left: *chaos*.

Trying not to wake Jazz, I untangle my right leg from her left one, slip from the silky bed sheets, and inch my way toward the now *still* door and the whole time, I can't help but wonder what flavor of monster waits behind the door. My mind ventures to much darker places, the kind of places drenched with molasses where pariahs dwell and lurk about, and the only possible thing that could be waiting behind that door is something so wicked that the likes of our world has never seen before. I still my head and close one eye as I hone in on the peephole with my other eye, as if I'm peering through the scope of a long armed rifle. I don't see anybody behind the door.

I keep the chain attached to the door while I crack open the door. Again, I don't see anybody at the door.

I remove the chain and unlock the door, this time fully opening the door. I step into the desolate hallway, peering down one end of the hallway and then down another.

The brown pattern along the orange carpet moves like water moccasins.

Is this a dream?

If it's not, then someone must've slipped something into my drink last night?

How the hell did I end up here?

I rub my strained eyes and peer closer at the carpet.

The lines return to their normal crisscross pattern.

What the hell is going on with me?

Why can I not remember the last three days?

I walk back into the room and yet, it still has all the qualities of a dream, the empty blackness, the monsters lurking throughout the shadows.

I quietly shut the door behind me and make sure to lock the door.

While Jazz remains in a deep sleep, I stumble to the bathroom and spend the next five minutes praying for urine (I never thought I'd ever think of those words, *pray for urine*). My dick is red and swollen, I notice, and it feels like a warm smoked sausage dangling in my hand.

When I finally manage to squeeze a few drops, the stream is like a small statuette of a boy angel driveling water into a fountain. I spend what feels like an unusual amount of time pissing—an unhealthy amount, like I need to pay a visit to the dick doctor in the near future.

I flush the toilet and wash my hands in the sink and after I've wiped the sticky sweetness of what smells like maple syrup from my hands, I splash my face with water, taking in cat-like sips of faucet water from the palm of my hand. I check on Jazz in the reflection of the mirror. She's still sleeping, despite all of the racket I'm making. Then, I continue my investigation by searching for any signs of disease or worse along my groin area, mainly rashes or bumps.

After a thorough examination, I don't find any out of the ordinary marks or blemishes that pique my interest. The only discovery I make is the dried ejaculate covered over my genitals.

I run my fingers through my pubes, which are stuck together with semen. I dampen a piece of toilet paper and after I clean myself, I slip back into the bed. Jazz stirs a little by repositioning her lifeless arm across my chest. I watch her carefully as she moistens her lips, as if she's speaking to some invisible person right next to me. Her eyes remain closed, though, lips plump and shiny from the Paraíso nightlights outside the window.

I stay still and calm while Jazz traces her hand down my belly and shuffles around my genitals as if she's blindly playing dice. Then, she goes straight back to sleep with her hand cupped over my privates.

I prop two pillows underneath my head and rest my eyes until the sun rises. My hangover has significantly mellowed by the time sunlight greets my eyes with a drill sergeant-like hello.

I can't say the same about Jazz.

\\

"Jazz," I say as I tap on the bathroom door, "are you okay?"

Jazz doesn't respond.

She's been in there for too long.

Something's not right.

I decide to inch my way into the bathroom. I crack the door farther open, only to discover Jazz crouching beside the toilet. Her hands gripped along the sides of the bowl, as if she's clinging onto a life preserver. I hurry over to her and hold her damp hair over her scalp as she vomits.

After she's finished, Jazz, with her forehead now dotted with beads of sweat, crawls to the corner of the bathroom and cries.

I stroke the top of her head and hold her clammy body in my arms. I tell her that everything is going to be okay.

\\\

\ never understood what people meant when they said, "Whatever happens in Paraíso stays in Paraíso."

Not until now.

Over time, I've learned that a person will speak from either two places when he or she is under the influence of alcohol: one is from the heart and the other, the ass. I doubt Jazz was talking from her ass. Although she seemed so convincing, I must—and I can't stress enough—*I must* take in account that Jazz was completely shitfaced. I've never seen her like that, so distraught, not by me, but by someone else. Paraíso is a city that entices you to create memories. It's a city that holds your memories for you, a keeper; and behind each empty façade of Old Paraíso, remains a secret place where—if you listen closely enough—you can hear the dead speak through paint-chipped walls and musty corridors soaked in bleach and turpentine. Las Paraíso may as well be the greatest thief of all time. The Houdini of all thieves. However, on the other hand, it's a city that allows you to unburden yourself, if you want. Was Jazz trying to unburden herself? Or, did she accidentally say those things? A slip of the tongue?

Lynda Lynx.

Who are you? *What* are you?

I'm not sure of who or what this Lynda is and—considering Jazz's current state—I don't plan on asking her.

I play nurse until it's time to check out by giving Jazz a foot massage while we're lying in bed. I try to lift her spirits by poking fun at her. Trying to make a serious situation less serious—something Jimmy used to do to me whenever I was sick or feeling down in the dumps. I ask her if we got married last night.

"Did we?" I ask her, this time more seriously.

"Haha," she mumbles with her face buried in the pillow.

I ask her if she can eat anything solid, and she says that she doesn't think so. I step out of the room for a minute, buy her a pack of crackers from the vending machine, and make sure her body stays hydrated. She eats a couple of bites and takes a couple of sips of Gatorade before she gets nauseous again.

Jazz tells me what everybody says after a long night of partying: "I'm never drinking again."

An hour after we leave Paraíso, I pull over to the side of the road for Jazz. I race around the car and hold back her hair as she vomits yet again. That's four times now, I think.

I stop at the next convenient store and pick up a ginger ale for Jazz (that always helps me whenever my insides are throwing temper tantrums). She takes two sips as if she's sipping from hot coffee, places the drink in the cup holder, then touches me on the hand as if she's thanking me or simply letting me know that she's going to be okay without having to open her mouth. For her, even that seems excruciating. Did I push her to drink more than her body could handle last night? Or, was I subconsciously extracting *something* from Jazz? The truth? What was really going on with me? Was I myself?

The only thing I receive is a stark image of Moses' silvery face in the distorted reflection of a napkin dispenser while Jazz and I were shoveling eggs, bacon, and hash browns into our mouths, as if we were two famished carnivores who hadn't eaten in days. Later, just hours before the angry eye in the sky brought us back to life, we worked off the heavy breakfast and all of the alcohol back in our hotel room. Sloppy, rage-filled sex. The kind you'd see on the *Discovery* Channel with two animals really going at it. The first time should always be a memory that you should never forget; however, for some particular reason, I want to *forget* all about last night.

I let Jazz get this hungover.

I should've known her limit.

Yet, I pushed her.

In a way, I feel responsible.

I hear a fragile voice next to me.

"You okay?" Jazz asks.

I pull my eyes off the road for a second and shoot a glance at Jazz, who's curled up against the seat, one eye half-shut and the eye that's open is extremely bloodshot.

"I'm fine," I tell her.

But I'm *not* fine. I'm far from it.

IV

LYNDA Lynx?

Where the hell have I heard that name before?

While Jazz is catching some shuteye, I let the open road do exactly what it's good at doing. Everything is mostly a blur, the fragments—memories, nonetheless.

Except for the first night when we had dinner at Leurre, the last two nights spent in Paraíso feel like speck-like jewels submerged in black sludge. Right now I can visualize my mind rolling up its sleeve, reaching deep into that heavy sludge, wiping away all of the filth in a wax on-wax off motion until the memories reveal themselves. A mind working tirelessly. I remember the first night started off with drinks at a vibrant place, TUG, a social lounge located on the top floor of Planet Bollywood. Jazz and I polished off a fifty-dollar bottle of Cabernet Sauvignon, which tasted like a ten-dollar bottle any wino could buy at a local grocery store. We left TUG with a fairly moderate buzz and galloped to a hotel

called the Chateau. We reserved a table for two at Leurre.
Our designer-shaved French waiter was professional, I remember, yet he came off as some smug know-it-all. I ate a
filet mignon tender enough to cut with a fork while Jazz had
the duck, which was more rare than I thought it ought to be.
For the remainder of the trip, we mostly ate at small diners
during the day and buffets at night. Nothing too high-end like
Leurre, I remember—and we were fine with that. It wasn't
like we were tight on money or anything. Jazz and I were
well aware of how a place like Paraíso can rob your ass blind
if you weren't careful. The high-end shit wasn't for us, really.
We had a couple of glasses of Pinot Noir at Leurre—each
glass costing twice as much as a bottle of Cuervo. Next, we
headed to a place called Knight's Bay where we played slots
for about an hour. Not sure how long. We didn't spend too
much time in one spot. Didn't bring home the lottery either.
We spent just as much money as we won. Then, after
Knight's Bay, it was Silver Castle where we played slots and
threw back more shots. Then, it was blackjack. Jazz raked in
over three hundred dollars on Roulette that night, then she
blew it on blackjack the next night at the Diamond. We
bounced around three other casinos after Silver Castle: the
TNT, Grigio, and de Rio. I don't remember too much after
Charades. By then, I was starting to venture into the Twilight
Zone. My zombie making his unwelcome appearance. I
remember Jazz being turned off from my drunken state. Who
would've blamed her? Later that night, I threw up my fancy
dinner. A newly engaged couple invited us back up to their
room while Jazz and I were playing 5-card draw of poker. I
knew they were swappers from the start—or "swingers," or
whatever the fuck you want to call them. It makes weird look
normal. I mean, seriously. Who in their right mind would sit
back and watch another person do his or her spouse? Where
the fuck do these people come from? The woman character
kept touching Jazz on the forearm and her husband—I
think—kept checking me out, as if the guy wanted to play
cock swords with me in the MEN'S restroom. I came like
"this" close to telling Mr. Hungry Eyes that I had a gun and
was willing to use it if he tried anything on myself or even
worse, on Jazz, but I didn't want to ruin the vibes for the sake
of my pride. Jazz seemed to be having fun. I think I had fun
too. We spent the next day at Red Rounds, I remember, trek-

king up boulders about the size of two story houses, sweating out all of the poison consumed the night before—or should I say, that morning. The rest of the afternoon was spent walking through the canyons. I don't remember much that night, only that Jazz and I crashed early. We ended up going back to Knight's Bay the last night in Paraíso since we had so much fun the first time around. I didn't drink as much as I did the first night or maybe I did, and Paraíso, like my own personal weight trainer, helped build up my tolerance for spirits. Something was up with Jazz. She didn't seem like herself. She excused herself a couple of times to use the phone. She got over a dozen calls. I listened in on one call and heard her talking about prices; and when she finally moseyed back to the bar, I asked her about the call. She told me it was her agent. Not once has she ever mentioned her agent before. Said that she needed one to help out with work. She corrected herself and said she needed to get a "new" agent to replace her "old" one. The old one, she said, was getting her work as a model or whatever. When I asked her what her agent wanted, she told me he was informing her about a modeling gig. I knew it was all a lie. One humongous lie. And the thought alone of Jazz lying to me again made me angry. I never showed my anger in front of Jazz. Instead, I was left breast-feeding it like some kind of neglected mutation stranded in the woods. Even if I did show a little bit of the anger—like a half-snarl or even an evil eye—I don't think she ever picked up on it. If she did, she would've told me. She never said a word. At that point, I knew she wasn't a model. Frankly, I didn't know what Jazz was really up to or what she was trying to keep secret behind my back, although I had an idea. I knew that she wasn't being completely honest with me.

I knew something was going on behind the scenes.

V

DON Henley from the *Eagles* is singing about the boys of summer on the radio.

I turn up the volume, trying not to wake Jazz; however, I turn it up just loud enough to drown out the sound of her snoring. She mumbles something in her sleep, but I can't make out what she's saying.

As she falls back to sleep, I can't help but pull my eyes off the road and glance at her legs.

How many men have been in there?

What have I done?

Most importantly, what have you done, Jazz?

VI

ABOUT ten minutes outside Los Dementes, I give Jazz a nudge on the arm, letting her know that we're almost home. She suddenly wakes with her wide eyes riddled with panic, both of them looking me over as if I'm a stranger. She turns to the view outside, still confused. Then, she finally turns her eyes to me. She looks better than she did this morning. Her eyes, much whiter. Her face has more color. She feels a little bit better, she tells me. She's able to hold down the rest of her ginger ale.

We don't talk much for the remainder of the trip.

VII

BEFORE the trip comes to an end, I ask Jazz if she has anything planned for the rest of the day. She struggles to look me in the eyes when she tells me that she's probably going to sleep for the next two days. I really want to ask Jazz about last night, about those mysterious phone calls, about *Lynda Lynx*, about that one bizarre comment she made about the streetwalker when we were stumbling down the main drag.

I want to ask Jazz a lot of things—all of these things!—but I don't want to ruin what we have.

And I know we have something.

I decide not to bring up last night. Instead, I act as if everything's normal when, in fact, it feels far from normal.

I kiss Jazz goodbye and drop her off at her apartment.

As she opens the passenger door, I ask her once more, "Are you sure we didn't get married last night?"

She holds one leg outside, cracks a smile: "I don't remember anything about last night, but I'm pretty sure we didn't get married." She holds up her hand, looks over her bare fingers, then displays them for me. "I'm not wearing a wedding ring. A girl has to have a ring in order to get married, right?"

"Only if the girl wants to wear a ring," I say.

Where did that comment come from?

Jazz bobs her head, sighs.

"Someday, I guess."

She gets quiet.

Sighs again.

"I had a good time," she says.

"Me too," I say. "We should do this more often, now that I have a job and whatnot."

"Yeah," Jazz says, thinking. "We should."

She leans over the center console. We kiss again. Then she steps from the car and gracefully swings around the door and as she turns her hips toward me, I suddenly realize where I heard that name before. I heard the name on the same night Nico was having one of his infamous "saber" fights. Kim. That's the one. She mentioned the name to me. "Lynda Lynx," Kim said to me. The new girl, I remember. Then Kim continued to say that this new girl had "hips *like a twister.*"

Jazz leans through the open window and says, "I'll talk to you later."

I don't realize how pale I am until I see Jazz's eyes sharpen beneath her beetling brows.

"Everything okay?"

"Yeah," I tell her and turn on the ignition. "I just need some rest."

She smiles.

I like her smile.

I *hate* her smile.

"You and me both," she says and walks to her apartment.

VIII

I use forty dollars of the remaining money I have left from the first two weeks of work and buy a motel in San Ricardo, a town about seven miles away from Topside, where I catch a nap.

IX

AFTER I change into some decent clothes freshly washed at the nearest laundromat, I power through the mild hangover with a shot of Cuervo.

Once I'm starting to feel more relaxed, I swing by the public library and research the name, Lynda Lynx, on the Internet.

I find a couple of MyCircle and Chatterz accounts under the same name, but none of the faces bear any resemblance to Jazz.

I scroll through several other pages until I come across a RESTRICTED website.

I click on the link and a security page pops up on the screen, warning me that I do *not* have access to the ADULT CONTENT on this page.

There's only one place that allows you to access this kind of material.

Before I can logout, I'm already out the door.

X

AT Cyber Jaxx's, I grab the computer in the back corner of the café, away from curious eyes, and type the name, Lynda Lynx, in the search engine. I scroll to that exact same page as before.

Below the link is Lynda's description, which matches Jazz's description: similar height, similar weight, similar hair, similar eyes, similar everything.

I take in a deep breath and open the porn site, *Forced Entry*. I don't realize exactly what the title of the website means until I scroll through a gallery of videos. The caption below one of the videos reads, "Lynda Lynx doin' forced blowjob." Another caption: "Lynx takes it up the ass." Another: "Lynx goes hardcore." Another: "Lynda Lynx ruff doggystyle."

I grab a pair of headphones from the table and scope out the café and make sure nobody's looking. Except for a group of kids sipping on lattes and chatting up a storm about *Warcraft* across the main room, the place is reasonably quiet.

I slip on the headphones and pull up the first video, "Lynda Lynx doin' forced blowjob."

I take in another deep breath.

I press play.

The video starts with a POV, as in point of view.

Through the cameraman's POV: two legs crossed over a desk that looks like something you'd find in a Rooms To Go catalog. The legs belong to a man wearing loosely fitted khakis. There's a knock on the door (*tap, tap*). Letting out a mumble (something like *about time*), the man behind the camera tosses the magazine on the desk—I can't tell what he's reading. Maybe it's a Rooms To Go catalog. Who the hell knows? The man stands up, walks through a well-lit yellow room sparse of any furniture, and peels back a fine beige curtain. He opens a door, revealing Jazz. . .

My heart starts to race and I have trouble breathing.

She's wearing black-rimmed glasses, dressed like she works the 9 to 5. Not once have I heard Jazz mention anything to me about wearing glasses.

The camera pans down Jazz's body, down a white dress shirt worn with the top two buttons unbuttoned, down a black skirt—again, worn tightly as well—down her pantyhose covered legs; the camera settles on her black stilettos, then pans up her body and right then, I know exactly where the video is going; and yet, I continue to watch even though I don't want to watch.

I force myself to watch.

The cameraman's voice is deep and throaty, disguised. He guides Jazz to a brown leather couch, which appears to be the only piece of furniture in the room. Jazz sits down in the center of the couch—both legs pressed together, hands folded in her lap, polite.

She tells the cameraman her name, "Lynda Lynx," when he asks her.

I pause the video and look closer at the woman on the couch and conclude that it is Jazz, not a twin or a look-alike.

Then, I press play.

Jazz explains herself, telling the cameraman that she recently graduated from WHU with a degree in accounting and now she is currently looking for work as an accountant.

Halfway during the interview, the cameraman runs his ringed fingers over Jazz's thigh and then moves his fingers underneath her skirt. The next twelve minutes of this supposedly "fake" job interview are extremely hard to watch. I force myself to watch the entire video from start to finish.

When the video ends, I watch it again and then once more. The third time I fast-forward to the climatic scene where Jazz is forced to give the cameraman a blowjob.

During the scene, she's gagging and vomiting all over him, as if it's somehow scripted and yet, it appears as if he's really "forcing" Jazz to blow him. She's struggling, too, occasionally pulling away her head. Then, the cameraman yanks her head back over his genitals in a whiplash-like speed; then he toys with Jazz, tossing her around the room as if she's worth less than spit. In return, these violent acts cause Jazz to let out groans and yet, I can't tell if she's either groaning with agony or moaning with pleasure. She appears as if she's in pain yet—I don't know—the video appears staged.

An act maybe?

Then, the cameraman forces Jazz back to the floor where he pins her face with his knee, forcing her to slurp up her own vomit.

I pull my eyes from the screen and I don't realize that I broke the keyboard until I hear a couple of loose keys hit the floor.

I pause the video by clicking on the button with the mouse and look around the café. The other kids are still talking about *Warcraft*.

I watch another video and then another video where Jazz is wearing the same jacket that she bought at Lassie's. The black one.

In this one particular video, "Lynx goes hardcore," the same cameraman as before does a bump of coke from her cleavage with a hundred dollar bill. Then they have sex in a missionary position; then, the cameraman finishes all over her jacket, as she lies bound on her back with her wrists restrained by rope.

I watch another video where Jazz is being strangled until she's purple in the face. Most of her face is slimy and covered in a mixture of smeared mascara and what looks like spit or vomit. At one point in the video, Jazz suddenly *whoops* with laughter, as if she's enjoying what's being done to her.

After stomaching yet another video, I notice that the choking appears to be a pattern with this man. In one video in particular, he puts the camcorder aside, revealing himself in a black *balaclava* mask. He walks over to a tottery Jazz, floundering on the couch in a heighten state of disorientation. The *man in the balaclava* gets on top of Jazz and chokes her and starts slapping her across the face. He repeats this over and over: the choking, the slapping, the abuse. Then, Jazz screams out in agony while he's gives it to her. Really gives it to her. He treats her almost as if she's a device, like something he can easily throw away after he's done using it. He finishes all over her face, blinding one of her eyes. Then struts back to the camera. Still raging hard. He zooms in on her swollen face; and he's now laughing, like some pompous jerk who gets off on abusing women. Her cheeks are cherry red from each slap. Her eyes are bloodshot. Two glossy trails are painted on Jazz's face like the trails left behind a snail from where she had been crying. She acts as if she's in serious pain. From the tormented etched on her face, I know she's *not* acting anymore. I know she's hurting. Badly. Then, right before the video fades to black, Jazz looks up at the camera with these droopy cartoon eyes—her face red and messy with bodily fluids—and lets out a cute, child-like cackle from the corner of her mouth.

Why Jazz?

Why are you doing this to yourself?

I stomach another video—more choking, more rough, violent sex—and each time I watch this man—this animal, *this thing*—toying with Jazz as if she's his own personal toy, I feel that knife stabbing me in the gut. Twisting. Painfully deep.

I watch another one until I can't watch any longer.

As I close the videos, my world starts to spin.

I remove the headphones and turn my shoulder, only to find Moses sitting right next to me. He's different; his gray skin, along with his weak and frail posture, make him appear much, much older.

Don't you see now?

I wipe the tears from my face.

It's time to let her go. Time to finish what you've started.

Moses reaches out and as he places his hand over my shoulder, I push his arm away.

Get the fuck away from me!

People inside the cafe are staring at me. I want them to stop looking at me.

I didn't say it was going to be easy—

I stagger past the *Warcraft* kids.

Once I find myself away from people, I rush inside a bathroom that looks like a janitor's closet.

I try to hold the vomit inside my mouth until I can reach the toilet, but I end up vomiting all over the sink instead.

I take the second round to the toilet until I can't vomit anymore.

As I'm kneeled on the floor—my jeans tightly pressed against my legs—I feel a protuberance along my hip.

I stand upright and pull an object from my jean's pocket and hold it close to my face. The object, now as dry and powdery as a block of chalk, happens to be Jazz's phone number, yet after the recent wash, the paper is now a ball of nothing. I peel open the ball and only make out a 7 and 4.

The memory of Jazz's face, I witness in my mind's eye, as she hands me her phone number before she heads back to Lassie's. Did I do this to her? Or, was she like this before she met me? What have you done, Jazz? What have I done?

Somehow, I manage to clean off the sink with a handful of towels that I grabbed from the dispenser.

As I'm splashing my face with water, I lose it.

Niagara Falls.

Eventually, I pull myself together and drag myself back to the computer where I pull up *Forced Entry* and watch the first video over again.

I rewind the video to the very beginning, where the cameraman hears a *tap, tap* on the door.

I pause the video once his hand enters frame—his hand peeling back a beige curtain.

I partially see the cameraman's right hand. He's wearing silver rings on two of his fingers, two on the middle finger and two on his ring finger, the four rings are connected too, which make his two fingers look like one finger, like brass knuckles; and it appears as if he has only three fingers, not including his thumb.

I know *that* hand.

I've shaken it before.

HIS whole time Moses was doing all he could to steer me away from her, but I chose to ignore him.

Where are you now, Moses, when I need you the most?

He doesn't answer, and I don't expect him to answer.

However, if Moses did, I know he'd say that I've gotten myself into this mess.

He's right.

Only I can finish it.

I drive past the Palace and notice the same cops camping out in the parking lot, which is no surprise.

I can't help but think back to when I first went to the night-spot after my first couple of drinks at the bar after I had introduced myself to Nico.

A couple of girls were being escorting up a staircase. Two guards were standing at the base of the stairs.

Maybe that's where all of this happens.

Maybe there are more women.

Like Jazz.

More victims.

I bumped into two of them later that night and one of them was moving like the ocean while the other one—a tall brunette with legs as long as my own—was walking away like a pen-guin.

Kim?

Was it, really?

What the hell have I gotten myself into?

‖

ONCE I make it back to the motel in San Ricardo, I realize that I need to go to the Palace tonight.

I pace around the room, thinking about calling Jazz.

If I ask her about the videos on the Internet, she'll know that I've seen them. Obviously.

Either she'll be too ashamed to see me or she'll tell me that it's none of my business. I don't know what to do. I don't know much of anything anymore.

There's only one thing I do know.

‖‖

BEFORE I can make sense of the whole situation, I'm back where I started: hanging out at the Town's Orchard and I'm shooting empty cans off tree stumps well into the night.

I use the Civic's headlights for light, and I don't leave until I get my shot back.

I don't leave until I'm the best goddamn marksman in the state of California.

I end up going through two entire boxes of ammunition.

Eventually, though, I get my shot back.

Eventually, I remember why I came back to Topside.

And that's all that matters.

For now, that is.

‖V

AFTER thoroughly cleaning my revolver, I change into the same clothes I wore the first night in Paraíso.

I dress like the night.

I'm equipped to kill.

I'm ready.

V

BEFORE I leave the motel, I give Nico a call.

When he answers, he's surprised to hear my voice.

He tells me that he's busy at the moment and is very short with me.

We talk just for a little bit, mainly about my new job at the garage.

He says Mars really likes me and enjoys working with me.

I tell Nico that I like Mars as well. I'll admit he's a good man, Mars is, a "decent man" who makes a decent living; and someday, as in whenever all of this crap is finished, I'd like to be like Mars.

I thank Nico again for hooking me up with the job, but I try not to draw any suspicion.

Before he hangs up, I ask him if he's going to be at the Palace tonight. He tells me that he has some things to take care of and he won't be going tonight. He asks me if I'm going. I tell him, "I was thinking about it, but we'll see."

He tells me not to do anything he wouldn't do.

He tells me to stay out of trouble.

I tell him, "I will."

But I know I won't.

I have to get up early for work tomorrow, I realize, but I decide to hit the club anyway.

Tonight, I have another job to do.

VI

WHEN I arrive at the Palace, the bouncer doesn't let me in. I tell him that I know Nico. I tell him that he's a friend of mine.

"Sorry," the bouncer says.

I pull out a twenty and slip it into the bouncer's hand. He crumbles the twenty and tosses it on the ground, as if my money is not good here. I pick up the twenty and walk back to my car. I look around the club for any exits. A kitchen worker is tossing out garbage in a dumpster out back. It's the only way. Not the best way. But I *must* get inside.

Right before the kitchen worker steps back inside, I hit him in the back of the head with the butt of my revolver and grab the door before it closes. I apologize to the kitchen worker as he lays unconscious on the ground.

He'll thank me later.

"Just business," I tell him while he counts sheep.

I conceal the revolver underneath my belt and make my way through a lively kitchen, which, like the front entrance, is

heavily guarded with security guards; however, it's much easier to evade them with all of the cooks and waiters scurrying
around. I move quickly too, but I don't make it obvious that I
don't belong here to the other employees in the kitchen. I pat
one of the several cooks on the back as he tosses a hot pan full
of shrimp; and in Spanish, I tell him to add more spice to the
shrimp.

He feverishly nods his head and does as I command.

I leave the kitchen, enter the dance area, and find two
guards standing at the base of a staircase across the room.
Same spot. Same suits. Same heat.

I check out the other spot. The red door.

As before, the door is guarded by Bishop's sleaze balls.
They appear as if they're packing heat as well.

I weigh my options. I'm outmatched, I realize, outgunned.
I'm screwed. I need to find a way to divert their attention.
So, I work my way through the club and as I reach the end of
the bar, I pass an ice sculptor of an angel, which stands over
seven feet tall with its wingspan stretching at least double its
height.

I hope the angels are on my side tonight.

Once more, I look around the club.

The only option I find is the most *obvious* one.

It will work. It has to work.

After I pull the FIRE ALARM, each clubber, one by one,
does the whole deer in headlights thing, gaping around the
club as if they just got caught doing something they weren't
supposed to be doing. The guards leave their posts after
checking their earpieces and escort the clubbers from the
dance floor in a rather orderly fashion. And that's when I
make my move.

Without the guards noticing, I sneak my way up the stairs.
I reach the top, revealing a dimly lit hallway with three doors,
one of them glowing with light.

I check the first door on the right. Flip on the light switch.
It's a cramped office. It doesn't look out of the ordinary. On
the wall is a work schedule with employees' daily shifts; a coffee brewer sits on top of a filing cabinet; the coffee inside is
lukewarm; the inside of the filing cabinet is nothing out of the
ordinary either, mostly filled with manila folders holding employees' records. Everything looks ordinary. Maybe too ordinary.

Suddenly, I hear a noise coming from behind—*giggling*.

I switch off the light and duck into the office before the door opens across the hallway.

Two exit from another dark room.

I see their shadows dance across the floor, one of them saying to the other, "It's probably nothing."

Bishop.

He tells the other shadow to follow him.

"Kitchen fire?" says a woman with the voice of a chipmunk.

"The hell if I know," Bishop says. I sense aggravation in his voice.

The door closes, then I hear the sound of footsteps trailing farther away.

I crack open the office door and watch the two goliath-sized shadows against the wall getting much taller and wider as they move down the stairs. I don't waste anytime checking the other room—the room parallel to the office. It's unlocked. The room turns out to be a surveillance room with a couple of nice-looking leather couches scattered throughout. Not the same couch from the video. The walls are painted gunmetal gray, a complimentary color to a dungeon. A large pane of tinted glass is covering the wall. I walk over to the glass and behind it is an entire view of the club. The best view of the club. I track down Bishop and some dense floozy who are walking through the club. I leave the surveillance room. I check the last door at the end of the hallway—the one glowing like a door in a horror movie.

I open the door, revealing a beige curtain, same one from the video!

I brandish my revolver and glide into the room where I find the same couch from the video against the yellow wall. Then, I find the same cheap-looking desk from the video.

This is where it happens.

Right here.

I feel sick to my stomach knowing what goes on inside this very room. I check my exits and only two doors are what I find.

I check the first one: a bathroom which carries all the smells of a girl's bathroom with perfume and fruity soap and all sorts of girly stuff lined against a vanity. I check the next door. Locked. I look around the room—*the desk*.

I check each drawer, starting from the bottom to the top. I find a key underneath a stack of delivery receipts. I pocket the key. Then, I continue to sift through all of the junk inside the drawer, mostly porno mags and lubricants. Then, as I'm about to close the drawer, I see Jazz's face first; then, after I pull out the photo from the drawer, I see Bishop's face. The photo appears as if it was taken a couple of years ago. I'd guess that Jazz is probably around eighteen or nineteen, but I'm not completely sure. She's sitting with a glossy-faced Bishop on one of those couches from the surveillance room. He has his arm wrapped around Jazz's shoulder. Strangely, they don't look like they're a couple or anything; yet, it's more like a father-daughter type of relationship. I pocket the photo. I hurry to the door and insert the key into the lock and pray that it's the right key.

What do you know?

I turn the key. The door opens. The room is a closet, I conclude, but there are no clothes inside. No exits either. Only an entire collection of videos. Hundreds of DVDs organized like books on a bookshelf. Looks like Bishop graduated from conducting prostitution rings to making porn.

I search through each DVD. Each one is catalogued according to a date, as well as a name labeled on the DVD casing. So many names, I find, so many girls.

I search through recent dates and I find a few with the name: LYNDA LYNX. The videos are labeled just the same as they were on the Internet: *Lynda Lynx blowjob*; *Lynda Lynx anal*; *Lynda Lynx hardcore*; *Lynda Lynx doggystyle*.

I come across one that I haven't watched. Part of the sticker on the side of the casing has been peeled off. I can only make out the first three letters, *Lyn*; however, the rest is spotty, dried residue from the adhesive of the sticker.

I decide to pocket the DVD and leave the others behind.

Before I exit, I stumble across a wooden trunk similar to the one I left behind in Kuykendall.

I open the trunk and what I find stabs me right in the gut.

"You motherfucker. . . "

I shuffle through all of the sex toys, butt plugs, rubbers, dildos; then the toys get sharper, surgical: whips, chains, jumper cables, needles, bondage shit, all sorts of torturous instruments. I wonder if he used any of these on Jazz. I wonder if he's planning on using them on Jazz.

As I'm about to close the trunk, I suddenly hear two people talking across the hallway!

As I exit the "yellow room," I spot a guard strolling into the surveillance room.

I sneak past the guard who's carefully watching the surveillance monitors and quietly make my way downstairs.

As I'm making my way toward the kitchen, I hear a voice of a robust man from behind.

"Hey!"

I turn around. Another guard.

"You deaf, pal?" he says over the blaring fire alarm. "Evacuate the building!"

I do as the beefy guard says and slip through the front doors as the fire trucks park in front of the club.

As I head toward my car, I spot someone else: Nico standing among the crowd outside. He's staring at me with a vacant expression.

I stare back at him, but only for a while.

I get inside my car and take off.

Nico said that he wasn't going to be here tonight.

Yet, there he was.

Like he was there the entire time.

What if Nico knows about the shooting?

THE next day I decide to act normal by going to work.

The last thing I want to do right now is to draw any attention to myself.

Nico could've had a last-minute change in his plans last night. The Palace probably—I take that back—more than likely they have me prowling through the club on their surveillance videos, pulling the fire alarm, sneaking upstairs, although I never saw any cameras on the second floor, only the first floor.

Either way, I don't think too much about last night other than two things: the photo of Jazz and that unmarked video, which, may or may not, be important.

As far as I know, it could be another sex tape.

I don't know yet, but soon, once I gather enough courage, I'll find out.

On the way to the garage, I run into Mars outside.

We talk a little about my break.

I tell him that I went to Paraíso for a couple of days.

He asks me if I took a "hot date" with me, but I tell him that I went by myself.

We talk a little more about my time in Paraíso, Mars asking me what I did for fun—casinos, bars, hookers?—but I jokingly tell him, "Whatever happens in Paraíso stays in Paraíso."

He gets the picture.

||

\ stop by Jazz's apartment during my lunch break. Just my luck. Her car isn't parked in her spot. Rosa doesn't come home from lunch either—more of the brown bagger type when it comes to lunch. So, I'm not too worried about her knowing that I won't run into her. However, it's Jazz whom I'm mostly worried about, especially with her being so damn elusive all of the time.

So, I decide to park behind Glendale Straits. That way if Jazz does come home, then I'll have an easy getaway since the side of her apartment backs up to another neighborhood surrounded by a small grove. Jazz doesn't have a security system either and her neighbors have already seen my face around here, which can be both good and bad—*good*, as in they won't think nothing of me if they see my face and *bad*, as in they'll have something to talk about with Jazz the next time they see her, like "Hey, how's that boyfriend of yours doing? I saw him outside the apartment the other day." So, I take my chances knowing that if somehow they do see me, they won't call the cops. The other stuff, I can worry about later. For now, I use the spare key underneath a flower vase on her patio and break into her apartment. I make sure to clarify that she's not home by calling out her name, and then, in return, receiving a high-pitch *meow* from her cat, Bob. I search every square foot of the apartment before I investigate her bedroom. That way nobody sneaks up on me and mistakes me for a burglar.

Once the coast is all clear, I search through all of her things, going through drawers and shelves and whatnot. I don't know what I'm looking for. If she is close to Bishop, then what else is she hiding from me? I need to know. I move my search to her desk. Search the drawers. I don't find anything on Bishop, no photos, none that suggest that he's a father figure in her life or even worse, an old boyfriend. I mean, what kind of "father" figure would do that to a young woman? My point exactly. *Not* a father figure. If he were an old boyfriend or lover, why would he keep an old photo of Jazz? I take a step back and stop for a moment by getting a wider angle of the room.

What am I doing?

Why am I here?

I turn toward the chest. Search the top drawers first. I find panties and bras. Just the sight of Jazz's underwear makes me somewhat aroused. Focus, you idiot. I keep searching. I reach the bottom drawer. I find some paperwork on various schools, a textbook-thick curriculum packet from the community college that she attended—HPCC.

Lastly, I find a pink and blue folder from a Better Tomorrow clinic. Inside are guides and brochures on the three options the clinic offers: *abortion*, *adoption*, or *parenting*. Most of the information: "in-clinic" abortions, as well as the "abortion pill."

I keep flipping through the folder and find some more stuff on abortion, how safe they are, what to expect, where one can be done; then, I find a couple of bills for a "termination" dating back two years ago, as well as instructions after the abortion has been done.

I check the address on the bill: 347 Seascape Drive.

That's in New Town.

|||

LATER that afternoon, I find a moment while Mars is dealing with a customer and get on his personal computer in his office. I do a little researching. I pull up the website, Finder.

I type in the address from the abortion bill, *347 Seascape Drive*.

Just what I thought.

|V

I haven't eaten much all day and I've been working up quite an appetite.

After a brutally long day of work, I decide to grab a bite, hoping that it might help calm the nerves. I read in a magazine that sometimes eating something that tastes good, like guilty food or something fried or covered in a heavy sauce, can relieve anxiety. There's only one comfort food that comes to mind. I remember passing one of those "Wok" places on the way to work. I decide to check it out. I order the usual: Sweet and Sour chicken with white rice. "Extra pineapples," I tell them. It only takes them a few minutes to make it; and when my food arrives, it's glimmering with MSG.

The petite cashier asks me if I'd like any fortune cookies or soy sauce.

I tell her, "Chopsticks. And a fortune cookie, as well."

Then, she slips them into my bag and sends me on my way.

I grab two cokes from a soda machine outside the main lobby of the motel and take the food and drinks to my room.

As I approach my room, I bust open my fortune cookie and eat the whole thing all in one bite.

I read the fortune out loud: "Endurance and persistence will be rewarded."

God, I hope so.

Once I down the fortune cookie, my chest suddenly does that thing again and I'm find myself in a state of frenzy; and before I can think of something else other than scoring a fix, I'm gulping air. I move my breathing to my belly. In through the nose. Out through the mouth. I embrace the unrest inside my body. Everything around me intensifies. The ambience of traffic sounds like white noise in my ears. Even the lanterns on the walls make little hums. I hear the sound of someone beating the hell out of a drum set. I realize it's the sound of my bad heart, giving me a heads up. I continue to usher the breathing to my gut. Eventually, the drumming softens, the panic; and both of my hands feel like feathers moving through the air.

I see everything.

I take note of the cracked open door.

I take note of a lot of things: the sour men's cologne hovering in the air, the TV playing the game two rooms down (the *crack* of a bat striking a baseball, then the commentator yelling into the headset: *Back, back, back, it's outta here!*), the *squeaking* of a bed with a broken spring coming from young hipsters screwing in the room next to mine.

I place the bag of Chinese food on the ground, as well as the drinks, remove the revolver from my bookbag, and creep toward my room.

As I swing open the door, I'm forced back around from the piercing *screech* from tires melting over asphalt!

I check the room and it's empty. I turn back around at the street outside.

All I catch are two tiny red lights drifting farther away into in the night. The sound, however, is as clear to me as an audio engineer sorting through glitches or pops or unwanted noise in a poorly produced song. The engine sounds identical to a Porsche 911 Carrera 4S, and there's only one person I know who drives a Porsche 911 Carrera 4S. It can't be a coincidence. I go back inside the room. I lock the door behind me.

V

I borrow a DVD player from the desk clerk downstairs and contemplate watching the video from Bishop's secret stash. There may be nothing on the DVD—possibly just another sex tape or something incredibly perverse—but since I have it in my possession, I might as well see what's on it.

Finally, after pacing around the room for several minutes, I decide to watch the DVD. I unscrew the AC unit. I can tell the panel has been messed with because a screw is somewhat loose.

I pull out the bookbag from the AC unit. Open the bag.

The DVD is gone. I check the room, the drawers. Maybe I put it somewhere else. I check underneath the bed; and as I'm doing all of these things, the searching but not finding, I notice little things scattered around the room have been shifted around, like the Bible from the nightstand, my clothes, the bed sheets, hand towels in the closet. I find the impression of a handprint on the carpet next to the bed. Someone was looking for the DVD. A certain someone found it. But what the hell would he want with the DVD?

I gather all of my things, bookbag, clothes. I need to confront Jazz.

So, I decide to leave the motel.

Just as I step out of the door, my burner rings.

Why is he calling me?

I answer the call.

It's Nico, and he's telling me that he wants to meet up.

"It's important," he says.

I go back into the room, grab the revolver from my bookbag, and make sure it's loaded.

Then I leave the motel with a sense of urgency.

VI

EVERYTHING in my gut is telling me to turn around once I reach Strand Island. Everything feels so wrong and yet, I don't know, everything feels so right, like this is what's supposed to happen. I cross a poorly built bridge, which feels as if it hasn't been used in years, then drive about a mile until I reach a sign, Roads End, a bumpy two-lane road surrounded by marshes. I stay on the road until I reach the dead end. I step out of the car and find an unpaved road to my left, which leads to a beach at a distance. A cloud of hazy lights bloom over the man-high beach grass. Nico. But not just Nico, though. He's brought friends. I walk back to my car, let out some air from the tires, get back into the car, and drive down the side road.

When I arrive at the beach, Nico and Yogi are standing in a ring of headlights. I park my car outside the other cars—at least nine cars, I count, but I only see Nico and Yogi. There are other people, but they're as dark as shadows. I check my right hand—as I always do when things are about to go south. The squeezer remains steady. I check my eyes. They're clear and white, not bloodshot. I take in a deep breath, slip the revolver behind my back, conceal it with my shirt, and step outside.

I approach Nico. He doesn't say a word, not even a sup. He doesn't even *acknowledge* me. Instead, he turns toward his right and nods at one car in particular, a black town car with tinted windows. I can't see more than that, though, from the beaming headlights. The backdoor opens. Bishop steps out. Walks up to me with that same silly smirk on his face.

"I'm glad you showed up," he says strangely. "I believe we have a lot to talk about, Mr. Backer. . . "

I feel a presence lurking over my shoulder.

How did I let them get so close to me?

I look down at my shoes nestled in the sand below and catch two disfigured shadows breaking away from the hazy night and stretching across the sand; and just as I'm about to spin around, a black bag is thrown over my head. . .

I attempt to remove the bag from my face, but a swift kick to the bend of my knee causes my legs to give way.

I stumble backwards and fling my arm outward, trying to soften the landing. I attempt to stand, but I can't see a damn thing. A mitten-like hand presses down on my shoulder, which forces me to the ground. I search through the holey blackness. Two manly figures, I see, dark and bulky, loom over me. Their faces unrecognizable from the headlights. Cold. Dark. All around me: just cold darkness. Hands—four of them, I feel—are groping me. They push my arms closer to my back; then, they fasten my wrists together with a zip tie.

In a feverish manner, they work their way to my ankles. Fasten them as well; then, once I'm all tied up, they drag me from the beach and toss me inside the back of some van.

As the van speeds away, I roll onto my stomach, trying to feel for my revolver. It's gone. They must've grabbed it while they were carrying me from the beach. Then, I fall into that survivalist mode, searching for sharp objects, but I can't find anything. My eyes start to fail me. World spinning. *Blackness.* I turn into an ice-cold glass of water sitting on a table on a summer afternoon in the South. My chest tightens again. Then, throat. All I see is utter blackness. All I smell is aftershave. All I hear is the sound of my breath pumping like a rusty piston inside my black, shriveled lungs. All I taste is metal. All I feel is the vibration of four tires humming a song, which closely bares a resemblance to a note as grim as death.

F R O M   T H E   G R a V E

THE ride ends the same way as it started, with the van speeding over a bumpy, unpaved road, which I can only assume is in the middle of nowhere. The ground is much harder than sand too. Small pebbles or rocks get stuck inside the grooves of the tires as the van begins to reduce speed and grate along the road below like teeth grinding. We hit a couple of shallow ditches before finally coming to a stop.

It happens all so fast: a shooting star bolts across the sky, the only glimmer of light that I've seen in the past twenty minutes. We're officially out there, as in we're in the fucking boonies. At that moment, I realize that I'm not dead but I'm not much alive, either. I don't know *what* I am, really.

All I know are the sounds: the wet brakes *squeaking* over the worn tread of tires rolling over a ground covered in gravel; then one sound trails after another sound like falling dominoes; more cars; the passenger door opening; a gear slamming in park; more squeaking sounds from what appears to be from the slick tread of a sturdy boot; another door swinging open and then closing, causing the van to rattle; and then, finally, a heavier and much louder door opening behind me—the van's door!

A pale light cuts through the blackness veiled across my eyes, a snake of light, bending around my feet below. The hairs on my skin are erect as well; and that's when I know that I'm alive, when I feel the goosebumps spring upright along my arms from the wind blowing its cold, eerie breath over my shaky body.

The same aftershave from before comes over me, only more filtered and less potent.

Two familiar hands hook around the armpits like a butcher's meat hooks and then yank me from the van.

The cold air hits me as I'm dragged through an open field. My feet desperately try to find support, but my attempt at standing is a fruitless endeavor. I wonder what I look like right now: a drunken tap dancer who's lost his step.

Once I realize that the whole kicking thing isn't working, my legs go numb and my heels are like two plugs on an aerator digging through the parched earth. I don't fight them anymore, the men. Neither have the strength nor the will.

My body jolts backward as we come to a sudden halt. One of them kicks me in the back of my knee, causing me to flop to the ground.

Then, the fuzzy blackness is suddenly stripped away from my face like a piece of the tape and when the cold air hits my sweaty face, it almost stings.

Before me, headlights shine over a headstone.

The name on the headstone:

CONRAD ARTIMUS WEST

I hear the *snap* of a tree branch!

As these strange men drift back into the night, another one with glowing eyes strolls from the woods behind the headstone. He gradually exposes the parts of his body in the headlights—his black gloved hands first, then a black overcoat, then a miniature valley running through the center of his cleft chin, then his smooth jawline, his tall, defined nose, his reptilian eyes. Ayker. He pulls his eyes toward the headstone below. His mannerisms are solemn and reverent, which, I know, is for show. He doesn't give a shit about Conrad? Why would he? Why would anybody give a shit about Conrad?

Ayker runs his gloved hand along the top of the headstone. Part of his sleeve pulls upward over his wrist as he stretches out his arm, revealing a watch that closely resembles a Rolex—same one from TV. Every cop receives one when they retire. Thomas did. The moonlight glimmers over the watch and the pale light gets trapped inside the circular glass casing as if the moon teleported into the glass. Now it looks like a pocket-sized moon on Ayker's wrist.

Not too far away stands a reserved Bishop.

Behind Bishop stands another man, a fidgety man who stays close to the shadows.

"Two types of people in this world," Ayker says expressionlessly, "people who go out looking for trouble and people who go out asking for trouble." He shoots a glance at me, an icy expression frozen upon his face. "I still haven't quite figured out which one you are, Mr. Backer. . . "

I expect Ayker to be the kind of mustache-twirling villain one would see in the movies, but he's not. He's just a guy.

The same man from before hands my revolver and wallet to Ayker.

"We found this on him," he says.

"This is it?"

He returns with a military-like nod and then retreats back to the shadows while Ayker looks over Henry's license from front to back.

"So, what name are you going by these days?" he asks while he skims over the license. "Philly? Jimmy. . . Henry?"

Ayker tosses the wallet, as well as the license on the ground before me, then studies the red tape wrapped around the handle of the revolver. He lets out a noise under his visible breath, not a moan or a sigh, but somewhere in between.

I look around and see other silhouettes in the shape of bodies, all circled around me like a death cult about to sacrifice a living thing.

Ayker empties each round from the chamber into his palm. Pockets them.

"Nice piece," he says quietly as he studies the revolver once more. "You know," he says as he paces around me, "when I first heard about Connie's death, I knew his demons had finally paid him a visit, especially after that terrible thing he did. *Then*, just not too long ago, I heard about what happened to Anthony Foster. The 'apparent' heroin overdose."

I know where he's going with this and I want him to shut up, but I realize I'm not in any position to be telling people to shut up.

"I knew it couldn't have been a coincidence," he says. "Tony was not a junkie. As long as I've known Tony, I've never seen the man touch a drug in his life. Not one. A drinker. Yes. The man used to drink like a fish, and he certainly wasn't exactly a 'law-abiding citizen.' I'd say he probably did more harm than good, but still," he turns to me, his eyes narrow, "he wasn't exactly a monster. With that said, I couldn't help but wonder, 'If he's going after every single person responsible for his brother's death, how would *he* try to get to me—you know—me being a former business partner of Connie's?'" *He*, as in, I think Ayker means me, although he's pointing at Bishop. "Bishop finds *him* snooping around his club, going through all of his personal possessions." I turn to a glaring Bishop, who's standing like an icicle. "Is *he* trying to find something to use against Bishop? If so, for what purpose? If *he* killed Anthony Foster, then who will he kill next?" Ayker kneels down in front of me, revolver still in hand. "Since you think you know everything about what happened that night, why don't you tell us? How exactly were *you* going to destroy us, Mr. Backer?"

I don't give Ayker anything, or Bishop. I don't do anything, really.

This is how I die, by not fighting, not begging.

I was never a beggar.

Why should I start now?

I keep my mouth shut.

"I have to say, Robert," Bishop says as he steps forward, "I admire your persistence. Pretty clever." He turns to Ayker and then someone else in the crowd. "Using his brother's name as cover. Not bad."

"Not bad at all," Ayker replies, as he traces his lecherous eyes across my body. I want to snatch out his eyes and squeeze them to a mushy pulp. That's the first of many things I'd like to do to Ayker. Don't get me started on Bishop and what I'd like to do to him.

Bishop tells me that he was just like me when he was my age, as if by him relating to me will help soften the blow.

It only makes it worse.

"All dick and no brain," he says and turns to his left, nods to one of the silhouettes standing outside the beam of headlights.

I follow both Bishop's eyes and find a familiar shape standing among the others.

"You may have fooled Nico, Mr. Backer, but *not* me," Ayker says. He faces me. I can feel his breath pressed against my face like a sheet of ice. "Nico informed me that a detective paid him a visit a couple of weeks ago," he says, referring to whom I believe to be Detective Ruby, as in the detective who has been on my tail ever since I broke out of Red Pines. "He showed Nico a photo of you. Asked him if he had seen you before. I got some of my men to do some research. Then, all of a sudden, it hit me. *Bam*," Ayker mimes his hand into an explosion, a fist turned to a high-five. "After all these years, Thomas Backer's no-good son finally did something that his father could never do. . . " Ayker leans closer, too close, ". . . he grew some balls—or as my amigos across the border would say, '*Cojones.*'"

The comment stirs a couple of laughs from the people surrounding us, including Bishop.

Ayker stands to his feet and the sound of my father's name stabs me right where I kneel.

"Don't mention his name *ever* again, you piece of shit," I tell Ayker, but he acts as if he doesn't hear what I say as he paces around me. "You don't know what he's been through. . . "

Ayker gives me a casual shrug.

"I know enough," he says. "He was weak. You, on the other hand, I remember Tony mentioning your name before—this was years ago, back when you and that one officer friend of yours—what was his name?"

"Dwight Arlington," Bishop answers for me.

"Arlington, right," Ayker says. "How can I forget that trader? You two on your little self-righteous vendetta. Last I heard that coward was enjoying early retirement on Lake Henderson. Like he matters?" He looks me over, eyes narrowed. "He can rot, for all I care. We all knew you two weren't a threat." What does he mean by we? Does he mean *we*, as in the entire Los Dementes Police Department? If Ayker does, then there were more people involved in the shooting, in the cover-up. How many innocent people like Cedric were framed for a crime they didn't commit? Ayker pats himself on the stomach, tells me, "You guys had no stomach—*no cojones*—but now," he shrugs, as someone I once knew would do, "well, you filled into your fullest potential." He stops pacing for a moment, looks at me in the corner of his eye. "You know, Robert, I heard you escaped from a mental institution," Ayker says fatherly, as he shakes his head as if he's disappointed in me. "If I knew your brother's death was gonna drive you insane, I would've made it a lot easier on you and done you myself. Perhaps your brother could've saved you the trouble."

Ayker turns to the others, smirks.

"What the fuck does that mean?" I seethe.

Ayker lets out another sigh. I can feel the chill in the air, on Ayker's breath, but then I soon realize the chill is coming from my breath. He looks to the bright sky, squinting and thinking, speaking, "I can't wrap my head around what that must've felt like once you heard Conrad was dead."

I wonder how long Nico knew about me—the day at Trader's Inlet.

That has to be the day.

Ruby must've paid Nico a visit right before Nico picked me up at the Palm Tree. Something seemed off about Nico. He was acting as if he had something on his mind. Nico had *me* on his mind. That's why.

"I mean," Ayker says, this time more patiently, "if someone killed my blood and later, I found out this certain someone took his own life," he kneels back down, closer this time, as he taps his tongue along the roof of his mouth, looking me over with amusement, "I guess I'd be pretty upset too. I mean," he turns to the others, still amused, "who knows how far I would've gone to avenge this loved one who abandoned me. Would I even go so far as to murder another man, even if he was innocent?" Ayker turns to his left. "Would you, Tony?"

Not one of the many people circling around us in the shadows budges an inch or even replies to Ayker's question for that matter, at least not until Ayker throws his hand up in this come-here kind of wave.

Finally, another strange man steps forward in the light. The man shares similar features as Anthony Foster, the same height, same weight, same built. The man could possibly pass as a distant relative, twin, double, look-alike, clone, even doppelganger. I know he's not Anthony Foster because Anthony Foster is already dead. I watched him die with my own eyes.

"I don't believe you two have met," Ayker says, pointing at the strange man. "Anthony Foster met Robert Backer."

"Anthony Foster is dead," I tell Ayker.

"Yes," Ayker drawls. "There was an Anthony Foster that did die a few weeks ago; however, not the *right* Anthony Foster."

He's lying.

Ayker poses a question: "Did you know there are exactly *thirteen* Anthony Fosters who reside in the Los Dementes area?"

I don't answer.

"Looks like you happened to pick the wrong one." He looks me over again, something in his eyes. "I swear, you Backers are something else."

What Ayker is telling me can't be true! I looked up that scab on the Internet. Even followed him around for days. I watched his every move. I was convinced that he was the *right* Anthony Foster who was involved in the shooting.

I don't realize that I'm speaking out loud until Ayker extends himself into my range of vision.

"Think again," he says.

"He's telling the truth, Robert," Foster tells me, as he steps closer. "I was at the club with Conrad on the night your brother was shot. I'm sorry for your loss, but that was all Conrad's doing. Not mine." He points at Ayker. "Not Ayker's." Then, he points at Bishop. "Not Bishop's. . . "

"There you go, Mr. Backer." Ayker closes his hands together. "Straight from the horse's mouth."

He waits for a response.

I don't give him one. Not yet. Too shocked.

"If Conrad shot my brother," I say finally, "then why'd *you* arrest the wrong man?"

"Why—Because I could," Ayker answers without missing a beat.

I don't realize what I've even said until he lets out a hearty laugh, a booming *ha* in my face.

"Kill you?" he says. "I'm not going to kill you, Mr. Backer. Connie, on the contrary, that man would kill you if you looked at him wrong. But I'm not Connie. Foster is not Connie." He faces one of the many silhouettes, a man with a face as pale as a possum's in the faint moonlight. "And *Nico* is not Connie," says Ayker as his eyes fall back onto me. I turn away from Ayker and hone in on the other man's face. I'm not sure if it is really Nico, but it's somebody important. I hear Ayker talking again, as if that's all he's good at doing, talking, like some chatty, insecure villain who wants to justify every reason why he should kill you before he kills you. He goes on to say that killing me would only interfere with his business. I feel somewhat relieved, knowing that I'm not a dead man just yet. Ayker leans in closer, again, too close, but I don't feel as threatened by the closeness as I did the first time around. "If you ever try to interfere with our business again," he says, eyeing me first and then the empty grave to the left of Conrad's grave, "well, you're a smart man. You get the idea. . . "

"Why Jimmy?"

I make it loud and clear for Ayker.

"I'm afraid, Mr. Backer," he turns to the headstone next to the massive hole, "that's just something you have to take up with poor ole Conrad."

The shooting can't be from the ramifications of Jimmy witnessing something he shouldn't have seen. Wrong place, wrong time. That story's been played out before. Many, many times. There has to be more.

"*You*," I acknowledge Foster just as he turns away, "You were there that night. Tell me. Why did Conrad shoot my brother?"

He doesn't answer, at first.

Foster faces me.

As he's about to speak, Ayker places his hand over Foster's chest, causing him to hold onto his words.

I try not to break in front of him.

I stay persistent.

I want his words.

Give them to me.

Ayker eyes the revolver in his hand.

"I'm sorry, Mr. Backer," Ayker says, his voice lowering to a villainous tone, the mustache-twirler, "but if you want to talk to Tony, well, you know what to do. . . "

Without delay, he aims the barrel at Foster's belly.

Pulls the trigger!

Foster jolts backward from the sudden gunshot, every inch of his body wreathing toward the area of the blow. He staggers to the ground in a similar kneeled position as me. His face is slack and heavy as he looks up at Ayker, who empties the round from the chamber in a laid-back manner.

Foster then turns to me with the same lengthy expression on his face, then gawks at the other people surrounding the gravesite.

"You shot me, you son of a bitch," he says, his bloody hands cupping the bullet wound in his gut.

With a vacant expression on his face, Ayker kicks Foster in the chest, forcing him backward.

Foster rolls onto the ground and falls into the empty hole in the earth.

Ayker turns to me, snaps close the chamber of the revolver, and tosses it at my feet.

"There you go, Mr. Backer," he says, nodding at the hole in the ground. "Happy?"

I'm left without any thoughts, without any words.

Ayker doesn't waste anymore time on me as he walks away.

The others follow Ayker and walk away as well.

Then, lastly, Bishop walks away.

"Sleep tight, Robert," he says over his shoulder.

Something comes over me.

I have more questions. I *need* more answers.

"What's on the DVD?" I ask him.

Bishop stops in his tracks. Faces me.

"You didn't watch it?"

He seems surprised.

I don't answer Bishop.

"Why don't you ask your friend?" he says. "She'll tell you."

Then, he walks away.

I have nothing.

No questions.

I look around at all of the bodies drifting away from me.

One of them stays.

Everybody else gets inside the vans and other cars, but that one remaining person is staring at me.

I stare back until he hangs his head—like Ayker before, disappointed—gets back inside a black car, and drives away.

I pick up Henry's license from the ground. Pocket it. Then, I pick up revolver. I notice the weight of it. It's off. Really off. It should be empty. I open the chamber and notice one bullet inside. I know whom the bullet is for and it's not for me to finish off Foster. I tell myself over and over that I'm not going to do it, even though the idea is at the very front of my mind.

It would be so easy.

Wouldn't it?

One squeeze of the trigger and maybe I'd get a solid answer as to why Jimmy was gunned down.

I remove the bullet from the chamber, place the bullet in my pocket, and then I slip the revolver in my other pocket.

Before I leave the cemetery, I pass Foster who is curled in a fetal position. His glossy, moonlit eyes draw upward at me as I loom over.

"Please," he begs from the bottom of the hole, "help me. . . "

Why the fuck should I help this man who had *everything* to do with Jimmy's death?

Foster had a voice. The least he could've done was prevent an innocent man from being locked up. He could've let people know what really happened that night. He had a chance to turn a wrong into a right. Anthony Foster chose not to speak up.

I don't say a word to him.

The silence speaks for me.

"I had nothing to do with Jimmy's death," he cries. "Please! You have to believe me!"

I can either end Foster's misery or leave him here to die.

I decide to do the one thing I should've done from the very start.

I walk away from it all.

EPISODE 9

ONE STEP
AWAY

F Y R E W A L K ' E R R

GUIDED by the moonlight, I walk miles and miles down a gravel road with the erratic sounds of nature all around me.

At night, it's almost as if nature becomes something else entirely.

Like it has nothing to lose.

I walk for at least another hour and rest my legs for a minute. I hear something moving in the woods, and it sounds like something larger than myself stalking closer. I don't bother interacting with it. I've seen too many movies to understand that nothing good happens in the woods at night. I remind myself that the night isn't as forgiving as the day, and I pick up the speed of my pace and keep moving along the road until I finally hear the sounds of manmade things. Never has something so polarizing sound so good to my ears. Through the woods, which are now sparser than before, star-like lights twinkle through the gaps of naked trees. I realize they're streetlights.

I cut through the woods and reach a highway. I walk along the highway for a short while until I pass One-Way, a dining car next to a 24/7 gas station. I see humans inside. I decide to stop.

A heavyset waitress is first to greet me. She tells me that the kitchen is closed. I look around and there are a couple of stragglers and truckers sitting in the back of the diner. They're shoveling down the final bites of their food.

I take a load off at the bar and tell the waitress, "Just water please."

She looks over my current state with great concentration. I haven't looked at myself in the mirror and I'm sure I look like I'm at death's door.

"You got it," she says over a concealed sigh, grabs a pitcher of water from the counter, and pours me a glass of water.

"Thanks," I tell her and then take toddler-like sips from the glass.

"Would you like anything to eat, dear?" she asks. "We still have some cold cuts leftover from earlier today."

"No thanks," I say, struggling to look her in the eyes.

My hands are shaking, I realize, so does the waitress.

I'm crying, too.

That's when it creeps into the back of my throat, the defeat, that acidic taste of failure, unable to be scraped off or washed away.

I realize I've become another Henry, another "other" that has been swept under the rug or, as in Henry's case, dumped in the river; however, instead of swimming with the fish or, in my case, squirming with maggots, my life has been spared. Why? Why did he let me go after everything he just told me? I know—and they certainly know—that my story will never see the light of day. In their eyes, I've been forced to the shadows. Threatened and reduced to a sheep. Now voiceless. Like a victim, even though I'm anything but a victim. I'm pretty sure this is how Myrtle felt when she wanted to start over. New life. New man. To get far away from whatever fucked up love triangle she had created for herself. Even Bella. When she told me about the two detectives who had visited her the day after they pulled the remains of her brother's body from the marsh along the Crux, I didn't *want* to believe her that Henry's life was in danger or that, on the very night he disappeared, he was fearful for his life. Fearful of what Conrad, Bishop, Foster, or even Ayker may do to him. I mean, what kind of person could make another live in fear? Bella also told me about the two detectives who visited her house and how they didn't look "right." Her words: "They were threatening me (Bella) without having to threaten me (Bella)."

I shield my eyes, hoping the waitress doesn't see me. I break like glass. I don't look up, but I know the waitress is still standing there, watching all of the drama unfold.

"*So. . .* " she says as I wipe away the tears.

I look up and the waitress plants one hand over her hip and shifts her weight to one side of her body.

". . . You gonna give up that easily?"

I don't answer.

I don't do anything.

"Well," she says sternly, "are you?"

"I was thinking about it," I say, my voice cracking.

"Well, thinking about it is one thing," the waitress says. "*Doing it* is another." She places the pitcher aside. "It's none of my business what sort of mess you've gotten yourself into, but from your looks," she looks me over again, "you don't strike me as the kind of *man* who rolls over for anybody."

"You don't know me," I say, trying to keep my voice down.

"Oh, I know you," she says as she leans back. "I knew who you were the moment you walked through that door."

I make eye contact with the waitress.

I ask her, "Who am I?"

"You're a survivor." Her eyes move around the diner. "Look around you. What do you see?"

I don't answer the question.

"Survivors," the waitress says for me. "And any survivor can get knocked down. Even happens to the best ones. What turns them from good to *great* is they always find a way to get back up before the ref counts to ten."

I think about what the waitress tells me.

Before I can think about it any longer, she leans against the bar and says quietly, "You see that man right there."

I follow the direction of her nod to the back of an older man dressed in camouflage. He has broad shoulders and hair draped like an oily black flag with tattered ends from underneath a fishnet hat.

When he takes a bite of the pie and washes it down with sips of coffee, he does so like a saint reading scripture.

"That there is 'Big Joe,'" she says. "Big Joe was involved in a brutal car accident some years back. Driver pulled out in front of him, causing his truck to serve off the road. The driver drove away and left him there to die. The doctors told Big Joe's family to prepare themselves for the worse. After spending years in the hospital, Big Joe woke from his coma and surprised everybody. Took him about two years to get his stride back. Now, look at him," she nods outside. "You see that big rig parked outside?"

I turn my shoulder and look at the rig parked next to the gas station.

"That belongs to Big Joe, and every night, Big Joe drives the *Long Road*, but before his journey, he stops in here for a slice of apple pie and a cup of coffee. Right there is a survivor. There," she points to another scrawnier man, "and another and another. And like all survivors, they don't rest until the job is done."

\\

THE waitress calls a taxi for me.

I tell the driver to take me back to San Ricardo.

\\\

WE'RE approaching Topside when all of a sudden the fuzzy glow cast from the hotels that line the beach sharpens into a wall of flames. I wipe away the condensation from the back-seat window with my sleeve, thinking maybe there's a stain on the window or something; then, as the flames grow higher over the distant cityscape, I rub my eyes, thinking maybe I have something caught in my eye, like a piece of debris or a bug I picked up while walking through the woods. The fire remains strong, like lungs filled with flames; each window, recess, or vent of the buildings is like orifices of a face exhaling billows of black smoke. My stomach acts as if it's some kind of a beacon; and a call of numbness ripples throughout my body, starting from my stomach to the edge of my fingertips. My veins feel as if they're stuffed like feathered pillows. Prickly sensations spread into each one of my thoughts; then my eyes widen as if a crater has opened inside me. I don't know what's happening to me, if I'm having what William called a seizure. I've never been prone to seizures, but what-ever this is it's not normal. Every thought I carry can be seen dangling before me, like a montage of all things bad. The flames lick across the small coastal town, reducing it to ash. Yet, the smoke above remains cloaked for the sky is too black.

I pull my thoughts from the fire, calm my breathing. Patches of a distant city light fall back over the night darkness.

I turn my gaze to the driver's familiar eyes and they're aimed directly at me.

Right then and there, I realize what needs to be done.

IV

THE taxi driver drops me off at my motel.

He tells me the fare.

I pull out the remaining cash from my pocket.

Count it out.

I'm a few dollars short, and I make sure to tell the driver that I have the rest of the money in my room.

He grabs the crumpled money from my hand and tells me to forget about it.

Then, he drives off.

V

MY body speaks to me in various ways through aches and pains; and sometimes my body will not speak to me at all but rather show me through rashes or hives.

The body will always find a way to get its point across.

My body informs me all about a soon-to-be pounding headache.

It has all the characteristics of one for the records—I'm talking about a real killer.

My feet feel dead. Every muscle in my body is burning.

My knees are throbbing and I have a deeply-rooted twinge in my gut that just won't go away without a good night's rest without any interruptions.

My body is definitely getting its point across.

And tonight, it's screaming at me.

I listen to its screams and decide to call it a night.

VI

THE following morning, I pay the desk clerk for another night's stay and end up spending the first half of the day in bed.

In the afternoon, I take a walk on the beach and think about everything that went down last night.

I think about Ayker and wonder if he really is the devil himself.

I wonder how honest he was with me.

I think about Bishop and the DVD—*If I had only watched the video before I went to work.*

I mostly think about Anthony Foster, wondering if he's still stuck in that empty grave. I do everything in my power not to think about the other Anthony Foster. The thought of that man alone makes my insides tangle in knots and sends cold sweats down my spine. It's a hard thing to swallow, knowing that I may have murdered an innocent man by mistake. I know that if I think about it for too long, I could wind up back at Red Pines. I put the thought to the side and think about other things.

I leave the beach and take a taxi back to Strand Island where I pick up my car.

I check my things, my bookbag.

Jimmy's urn.

My camera.

Everything is there.

I decide, after much debate, to drive north until I reach the same unmarked cemetery from last night.

I arrive at the hole next to Conrad's grave—or lack of hole.

The hole has been filled and packed with fresh dirt.

No sign of Anthony Foster.

The only thing I find is a trail of blood leading back to the gravel road, as well as an empty airplane bottle of Tanqueray lying in a ditch.

I pick up the bottle and closely stare it.

There's only one person I know who drinks Tanqueray.

VII

WHEN night arrives, I disguise myself and drive by the Palace.

The same cruiser from earlier is parked not too far away from the club, which, again, is no surprise. The parking lot is full, as well; a line of partygoers is wrapped around the building, mostly young women.

All it takes is for me to see a group of hotties who are dressed in next to nothing before I find myself craving a drink.

VIII

IN a room painted black, I'm choking Nico to death.

Before his eyes fixate on mine, I wake up on the floor of my motel room, and it feels as if the memory fairy paid me an untimely visit last night. The last images I have of the dream are my hands, both of them tightening around Nico's throat, Nico's veiny face turning red, and he's mouthing the words *you're dead*.

I wake up with carpet in one side of my mouth and a leftover dream fading into the red haze. Only bits and pieces of memory remain intact from last night. That's all. *Bits* and *pieces*.

I believe Jazz not returning my calls last night had something to do with me overdoing it last night. I was a hot mess—*hot*, as in out of control—a victim of my own destruction.

I stagger to my feet and bump into a few obstacles. I'm half-dressed. Mud stains are dotted around the room. I check my shoes, and they're not muddy. How did the stains get there? That's the obvious question. I have no obvious answer. I undress and hop into a cold shower. My heart is treating my sternum as if it's a speed bag; and it feels as if it's about to explode from my chest like that alien baby in the movie, *Alien*. Something's not right. I feel off, way off. I let cool water run over my sore eyes and try to rake the doom from my thoughts by focusing my mind on something pleasant like the sea, the waves, the shore, the beach. It helps for a minute, but only for a minute.

As much as I try to block out last night, I find myself retracing the events that left me in such an excruciating state. My insides flex, exposing a rare glimpse at my closet six-pack. I suddenly gag. I feel everything inside me trying to escape. I know I'm about to erupt like Mount Vesuvius. I peel open the shower curtain.

I lift my leg from the tub and lift the toilet seat to vomit; and as I lurch forward, my legs give out underneath me!

I'm falling.

The blood races through my veins. I hear a loud smack from my flesh hitting the floor; however, I continue to fall, through the *smack*, through the hum of pain, through the slippery laminate floor, through a grungy pit of blackness.

I can see myself falling too, as if I'm watching myself from the outside, like the observer; and I'm watching a poor kid irrevocably plummet to his ultimate demise.

I'm no longer the observer.

Now, I'm flapping my arms around like a dove with clipped wings, searching for something as simple as air to grab before I crash straight through the fiery Gates of Hell.

My hand scrapes along sharp, rugged debris.

I stretch my arm outward, my hand siding across what feels like a wall made of whiskers. My fingers graze the coarse roots. I grab a root, a sturdy one. My body jolts upward. I hold on for dear life. Please, pray for me. . .

Engulfed by the incoherent whispering of prayers, I witness firsthand my own stream of consciousness: I'm doing a couple of lines of blow between the shoulder blades of a naked body. I can't make out whom the body belongs to—a man or woman—for the right side of my face is pressed against cold flesh. I pull my face from the shoulder blades and see a gray face turning over a pointy shoulder. The face carries no expression. No eyes. Only two black holes where its eyes should be. The face belongs to Jazz. *My* Jazz. Her perfectly shaped body feels soft and grainy. Like sand. *Not* Jazz. Now, I'm running on the beach, crying and screaming to the top of my lungs, cursing at the night sky, at the God who has forsaken me. I curse at Him. I let Him know how infuriated I am. He ignores me. I ask Him, "Why? Why do you not give a shit about me? What did I ever do to you to deserve this?" I scream, "Why? Why goddamn it!" And this makes me even angrier, when He ignores me, and I want to die just so I can finally face Him. Fire races through my veins, and my arms and legs lighten. Like feathers. I feel violent, animalistic. An ancient being lost in a world which he does not understand. I witness gray buoys in the corner of my eyes. I want to keep running. I want to keep screaming. I want to feel the fire, the fury.

I turn to the sea where rows of ancient bodies line the frozen tide. They're staring at me without any eyes. Only black holes. The sight of these eyeless creatures forces me to run faster. I embrace the fire, the fury.

One of the creatures breaks the line and grabs my arm with its stone-like hand and yanks me into a sea made of slush. I thrash and fight off the creature by striking it in the face. The creature's jaw fractures after I throw a godly left hook. The side of its face caves in and its skin is as delicate as papier mâché. The creature loosens its grip around my arm—it's deformed jaw now hanging like an old and putrid insect hanging from the destroyed web constructed by a spider.

As the creature falls back into the sea, I feel a warm sensation swelling over my shoulder.

I turn.

A thin woman dressed in flames is standing on the beach. Her body is charred. Her eyes, however, are bright and vivid, familiar. She's not struggling and waving away the flames. Yet, she stands there, as if the flames are a part of her. She's mouthing something, but I can't understand what she's saying.

Patria?

Suddenly, the same creature from before leaps from the water, grabs me by the leg, and tugs me into the sea!

Now, I'm falling through glass.

I'm falling through a dark abyss, through the icy water.

Through *blackness*.

Toward the fiery Gates of Hell.

I hear a delicate voice inches away from my ear, moving like a breeze. . .

I find myself lying on a stiff bed in a moonlit bedroom with walls covered in oil paintings from the Romantic era, and it all happens in the span of a blink.

One blink: I'm on the beach, drowning, dying.

Then another blink: I'm lying next to an attractive woman, drowning in sheets made of silk.

She tells me to remove my pants over the distant sound of waves crashing against a shore.

The eyeless creatures are nowhere to be found.

Nico struts from a dimly lit bathroom.

He's not wearing any clothes.

The bed shifts next to me.

Kim, I discover, is the woman lying next to me. And she's not wearing any clothes either. She's missing eyes too.

I turn back to Nico. His eyes are glistening in pale moon-light, two white marbles hovering in the night.

I'm not the least frightened by Kim and she's not the least frightened of me, despite not having any eyes.

I tell Kim I met someone special. I tell her that I really like this girl, and she seems intrigued as she carefully walks her fingers along my arm.

The bed shifts once more as Nico sits down on the corner of the bed and crosses his legs and says to me, "Tell us more about this girl."

I tell them her name—Jazz—and they both look at one another as if they know her.

"Lovely girl. . . " Kim says, facing me, ". . . very dead."

I don't believe she's talking about *my* Jazz.

Right now, I don't believe anything.

IX

DEAD?

That's the first word I hear.

Then, "Is he dead?"

Once more, I hear the desk clerk's urgent voice above me: "I don't know."

I open my eyes. A dense red all around me. Figures in the red reflection. One side of my face is lying in a puddle of blood. I believe the desk clerk is kneeled down over my body. Over his shoulder slumps another blurry man.

"Should I call an ambulance?" the blur says.

They both look down at me, both of their faces now materializing.

"Are you okay, son?" the desk clerk asks me.

The only words I can find: "Where am I?"

"You're in a motel room," he says. "Room number 23 at the Highway Inn."

The desk clerk helps me sit up while the other guy, the maintenance man, grabs a dry towel from the closet and drapes it over my private parts. He turns off the shower behind me. I try to make sense of the puddle of blood pooling around the base of the toilet. Next to the toilet is an overturned toilet brush. It too is covered in blood.

"We received a *complaint* about a loud noise coming *from your room*," he tells me. "You must've *slipped* and fell. . . "

I try to make sense of his words, but they're fading in and out.

"It's a good thing we found you when we did, otherwise—
"

"Oh you hush, Francis," the desk clerk says to the other guy. "He doesn't need to hear that. Do something useful for once and grab the first aid kit."

Francis, the maintenance man, leaves the bathroom.

"Do you want me to call an ambulance?" the desk clerk asks.

I start to see two desk clerks, then three, then four, five. . .

R E C Ω N s i l l y A T I O N

I wake up with the tide washing over my bare feet.

Strangely, though, I don't feel as if I'm on a beach.

I don't know where I am, but it's somewhere stale and boxy, like I'm in a film studio or something and, at any moment, some prop guy is going to pull away the backdrop of an ocean, revealing an entire production crew.

I summon whatever strength I have left inside me and manage to sit upright.

Two nuns move by me as if they're on Segways and continue along their way down the strange beach.

Where am I?

The tide washes over my feet once more, this time rising to my shins. The water feels much cooler than normal, especially for this time of year. People are out, I notice, enjoying the beautiful weather. Their dogs are with them, running around, fetching things. I even catch a white longhaired cat chasing after the seagulls. The air is somewhat strange as well because not only does it not have that briny smell to it like you'd smell on a real beach, but it also feels almost like recycled air blowing directly above me. The sky is creamy white. The beachgoers are running around in a hypnotic frenzy, as if they're being controlled by another force except their own.

Wondering what the time may be, I try to find the sun in the sky. I can't find a sun or even a round dot in the sky or what may look like a sun. The entire sky *is* the sun, a wash of light, which stretches across an endless horizon.

Suddenly, I feel an insect crawling over my forearm. It looks like a tarantula at first. I look closer. It's a baby hermit crab.

I reach toward the crab. It pinches me just as I'm about to grab it.

I brush the thing from my arm.

"You little. . . " I say.

The words come out like a paste, as if they're being brushed aside as well.

Finally, I stand to my feet and look down at my clothes and they're covered in damp, sticky sand.

I brush away as much sand as I can from my shirt and pants before the world starts to blur.

I've noticed that I'm doing a lot of brushing. Brushing away sand. Brushing away crabs at my feet. Brushing away the synthetic air. Even brushing away the blur.

Then, I hear a *smacking* noise coming from behind me.

I turn, only to find a boy—no older than seven years old—tightly packing sand over a three-feet tall sandcastle with a plastic blue shovel. I've seen the boy before. But where? Here. On the beach or whatever this place is.

I peer closer and yet, he looks stranger than fiction. I can't help but stare at him, his face.

The boy turns to me; and now, he can't help but stare at me. His fetal face has no emotion, blank. Like a canvas. A painting in utero.

We share a long, drunken stare before a petite woman races over to the boy and grabs him by the forearm.

"Come on, Robert," the woman says to the boy. "It's not polite to stare at strangers."

She looks nearly identical to Susannah, a twin, and yet, her voice sounds like a stranger's voice.

"Mom?" I say foolishly.

The strange woman stares at me with the same expression as the boy. . .

A hand touches me on the shoulder.

"*Sir*," the same delicate voice says to me—a stranger's voice.

I crack open my eyes and see Susannah's face.

She says again, "Sir, can you hear me?"

Her voice turns deeper, rougher.

The woman standing before me doesn't look like Susannah anymore. She has similar brunette hair like Susannah, even the way she carries herself is just like Susannah, a caring, sweet and scrappy air about her, as if she's made a lavender and grit, but I realize, after close examination, the woman isn't Susannah, only an impostor.

She waves a pocket-sized flashlight over my eyes, and as the light drifts in and out of my vision, I see her green eyes and the sight of her eyes soothes me.

Next, I see the stethoscope around her neck.

My senses come back. She smells like watermelons.

"My name's Deborah," she says. "Do you know where you are, sir?"

I look behind the nurse and see other nurses and interns in blue scrubs moving through the EMERGENCY room like ants scattering from an anthill. Every now and then a person wearing a white coat and carrying a clipboard rushes past the bed.

I look back at the nurse in confusion.

"Conrad," I say.

"Excuse me, sir?" she says, confused. "Conrad?"

She leans closer as if she's hard of hearing.

I don't even know I say the name out loud until she asks me again, "Who's Conrad?"

"Ah," I mumble, my lips are as parched as a hardpan desert, "I'm not sure."

"Do you have anyone we can contact?"

"No," I say, moistening my lips.

"You suffered a mild concussion," she tells me. "There was a man here not too long ago. He brought you here after he discovered you lying unconscious in your hotel room. You lost a lot of blood. You're very lucky to be alive."

She touches my arm.

"Where am I?" I ask her.

"Saint Mary Medical Center," she replies.

I look down at a tube running from my arms, as if I'm being cultivated for next spring. I follow the tube to a machine holding a bag of clear fluid with a drip-feed.

"It's intravenous fluid," she tells me. "Just think of it as Gatorade."

"When can I leave?"

"The doctor wants you to stay overnight for observation," she says. "If he sees nothing wrong, then he'll discharge you."

She waits for me to respond.
I nod my head.
That's all I got.
Just a nod.

\\

THEY move me into a room.

I turn on the TV and make over a dozen passes through the channels. One crappy show after another. One infomercial after another.

Hours pass.

At times, I'm not sure whether I'm awake or still dreaming.

\\\

AFTER dozing off several times during "quiet time" and then being awakened by the never-ending hallway noise or yet another nurse checking up on me, I can't hold it in much longer.

I manage to roll out of bed under my own will. I cling onto the machine with the drip-feed as if I'm clinging onto the side of a cliff, unlock the wheels with the butt of my heel, and roll my way to the restroom. My muscles are incredibly stiff and sore from the lack of activity and when I work through the stiffness with each pounding step, it feels as if a mound of fire ants has been forced from a colony and now they're marching and biting their way through my veins. I feel like I'm going to collapse at any second from all of the physical strain, but I tell myself that I've been through worse.

"This is nothing, *Robert*," I rally myself.

By the time I reach the bathroom, I've worked up a sweat. I lift up my gown and take I piss. Fire ants, again. The tip of my dick feels like it's on fire and even though they may be keeping me hydrated by pumping me full of what the nurse referred to as "Gatorade," even though I know it's not really Gatorade but some solution with lots of electrolytes, I make sure to take note of my urine and how dark and smelly it is. That can't be a good sign. That's never a good sign.

After I finish urinating, I rigorously wash my hands. I check myself in the mirror. I can't even recognize the person looking back at me or as Susannah once said, the Stranger.

I leave the room and walk down a ghostly hallway stretching all the way into a flickering darkness. If you listen close enough, you can almost hear the ghosts speaking to you. Susannah, being a nurse and all, was never into ghost stories. She wasn't that religious, either. Perhaps spiritual, I think she once said. I remember she used to *always* call it the "night shift" followed with a heavy, oppressive sigh, as if she dreaded going to the hospital; yet, at the same time, it was something she had to do. She'd tell us while putting away the dishes, "I gotta work the night shift tonight." Then, of course, came that wolf's huff of a sigh, ready to blow down our doors. She used to say there were many perks to the night shift. For instance, she'd tell us when you work the night shift, you see another side of life, a side that only comes out at night. Believe it or not, people do the "darnedest" things at night. She used to tell me and Jimmy stories about her night over breakfast the next morning. Sunday mornings always consisted of the best stories primarily because, unlike most weeknights, Saturday nights were always filled with the occult or the bizarre, like an episode straight out of the *X-Files*. Unlike Thomas, who wouldn't go so far as to utter a peep about how his day went at work, Susannah never held anything back. She was like an open book. She was never ashamed about who she was or what she did. She even showed us pictures of what she looked like back in the day, especially during her "rebellious stage," she said. Those *Father Knows Shit* days. She wore bellbottoms, the kind with holes in them, drove a peach-colored Volkswagen van that broke down all the time, and, of course, she did the whole Stockwood, flower power, peace and love, whatever thing. She never admitted to taking brown acid, so she said. She was just a kid back then, probably no older than myself. I think it was her way of telling us that she was once a "cool girl," that she wasn't always so "square." That was actually where my parents met, at Stockwood. Thomas arrested Susannah at the hippie festival, but that's not the only thing he arrested. That was my parents' soppy love story, their modern day romantic tale of the World War II solider bringing home his soon-to-be French bride from the battlegrounds of France (reference *Joshua'ζ Tree*), only except for crushing the evils spawned from the grip of tyranny, he was warding off hundreds and thousands of stoned, rebellious bohemians. Even after Susannah retired from nursing, she still had the uncanny ability to tell a story. However, instead of telling stories about her wild nights as a nurse, her stories turned to the humdrum of daily errands or outings or an occurrence that she encountered at the grocery store, like *some* "person" almost running her over on the road. Susannah would go on for what felt like eternity rambling about how much money she saved on groceries that day, what was on sale that day, or the discounts—she was a fiend for weekly coupons—yet, somehow, the stories that she told always found a way to veer back around and evolve from the overly annoying minutia to a somewhat amusing story, as if, at the end of the story, there was always something to take away from it. I wonder what the nurses are telling their children or significant others about me.

I ride the machine back to the hospital bed and watch reruns of *Law & Order*.

IV

THE next morning, an Arabic doctor stops by the room and asks me if I want to hear the bad news first or the good news.

He has that look on his face. You know the look.

He's holding a clipboard in one hand, his other hand stuffed in his left pocket. I'm pretty sure that whatever is on that clipboard is nothing good.

I tell the doctor to give it to me straight, no chaser.

"Your liver function doesn't look good," he says grimly.

What else is new?

"Frankly," he says, "I'm surprised you're still alive."

The doctor tells me that if I don't stop the drugs or drinking, then my next stop is going to be at the City Morgue. He tells me there's still a chance for me, as if he truly cares about me.

If there is *one* thing that I've learned about doctors, they *don't* care about you. I know he's just putting in the hours, acting as if he's important, as if he's saving lives.

He hands me a brochure with the words HAND OF DAWN on the cover.

"What is this religious crap?" I ask him.

"Not religious, sir," he says. "It's an opportunity to get control over your life."

I open the brochure and see all kinds of smiling faces of men and women of all races and creeds and all of that fake propaganda nonsense.

"You want me to go to AA?"

"If that's what you want to call it," he says. "It's your choice. It's not like anybody's sticking a gun to your head."

He tells me to give it a try.

I look down at the brochure and try not to laugh.

V

As I'm changing out of the silly hospital gown and slipping into some outfit that a volunteer worker gave me—a lime green shirt with the words *KIWANIS Club* and a pair of pink running shorts and worn Reebok sneakers that are too small on my feet—I hear a *knock* on the door before it cracks open. A familiar face inches around the door, and for a moment, I think I'm still dreaming.

"Nico. . . " I say surprisingly. ". . . what the hell are you doing here?"

"That's no way to greet a friend," he says as he steps inside the room.

"Friends?" I say. "We're not friends. Now, get the fuck outta here. . . "

"Please, Robert," Nico takes another step forward, this time more cautiously, "let me explain myself."

As he closes the door, I secretly slip the brochure into my pocket.

"Did he send you here?"

"Who?"

"Don't play with me," I say. "Ayker?"

"No, Robert," he says. "I came on my own—"

"—So, you know about everything now? Why am here?"

"Yes."

"Did you know what they did to my brother?"

"I heard."

"You heard?" I say. "Yet, you continue to hang around these people?"

"They're my friends, Robert."

"They're murderers."

"Listen, Robert—"

"—How'd you know I was here?"

"I swung by where you were staying," he says.

Where I was staying?

It was either he or Bishop who snuck into my room the other night. Now, I'm starting to lean more toward Nico, *not* Bishop. After all, that was Nico's Porsche 911 that I heard speeding away before I met him at Strand Island. I doubt Bishop was driving. Nico is not the type of person to let others "play" with his toys. Perhaps he's the one who's more interested in the DVD. What if he's on there, doing those things to Jazz? Or, Nico could be just doing Bishop's dirty work for him.

"Your landlord said that you were hospitalized," he tells me. "He said you slipped and busted your head open."

I keep quiet and let Nico do most of the talking.

"When I first heard," he says after a brief silence, "I thought Bishop might've had something to do with it. I confronted him. We got into a heated argument. Let's just say Bishop and I are currently at opposite ends, if you know what I mean."

I ask Nico, "So, why the fuck do you care what happened to me?"

"Why do you think I went out of my way to get you a job?"

I don't answer.

"I feel no different about you after I found out who you really were," Nico says as he takes a step closer. "We all have a past—"

"—What do you want?"

"Listen," Nico hesitates, "I just came by here to tell you that I played absolutely no part in what happened to your brother. I am truly sorry for your loss. I am. But you have to understand that *I'm* not the bad guy here. I'm on your side, Robert."

I don't say anything to Nico.

I don't have much of anything to say to him.

"What you said at Trader's Inlet, about how you wanted to stay here, were you for real?"

I don't answer.

My thoughts turn to Ayker, him mentioning Nico's name. He did so casually, as if they weren't just friends. They were good friends—*tight*, in my book. I already know Ayker and that animal, Bishop, are in cahoots with one another. Could be drugs? Another sex ring? Who knows what else they're doing together? As of now, I'm not a hundred percent sure about Nico and his role in all of this madness. One thing is certain: Nico was there the night Ayker shot the "real" Anthony Foster in the belly and left him to die. I just know it. I feel it.

I never bring up Foster's name.

Maybe another time.

"I hardly knew my father," Nico says as he walks over to the window. "He may have been blood, but we didn't sing on the same page, if you know what I mean. Whatever he did to your family, whatever debt he owed, whatever made him take his own life, I *know* he deserved it."

Again, I don't respond.

"Fine," he says shortly.

Nico gets the idea and walks away.

Halfway toward the door, he stops and turns around. "Mars asked about you this morning," he says. "I told him what happened. He specifically told me to tell you that his door will always be open for you. You just have to be willing to put all of this behind you, Robert. I already did. Now, it's your turn."

Nico stops at the doorway, opens the door.

"Is it really true what the cops said about you?" He turns his shoulder. "Are you crazy?"

"No," I tell him.

"That's what I thought," he says and then, just as he's about to leave, he steps back into the room. "By the way, the detective who came by my house—Ruby—he said that your parents were looking for you. He said they were worried. Thought you'd like to know."

Then, he offers me a ride back to the motel.

I tell him that I'm fine and he leaves, disappointed.

1   D A Y   O L D

O UTSIDE Saint Mary, a kind man hails a taxi for me.
I leave the hospital with a mixed bag of feelings. I can't
stop thinking about what Nico said about my parents. I
like to think the shooting made them more apprehensive.
During Jimmy's senior year at East Providence, they
didn't want Jimmy to go back out West (even though college
was out of state, he was given a full ride to West Harleton
through an athletic scholarship—Jimmy was *that* good, a
scout's wet dream). Strange, I always thought, because they
were *less* apprehensive about Jimmy jaunting all over Europe
for a senior trip than him living out West. Jimmy traveled a
lot. I wasn't jealous. Maybe a little. In the back of my mind,
I felt like I had a lot of catching up to do, like I was missing
out on another side of life, a side that could only be seen and
experienced in reality, not on TV. I've always dreamt about
traveling (I heard an adult once say if you don't leave the
country before you have children, then you will never leave—
or something like that). About a year later—this was around
the time I was rooming with Jimmy during his freshman year
at West Harleton—I seriously considered traveling overseas.
Europe. The same countries Jimmy had visited. Japan, of
course. As far back as I can remember I've always fantasized
about visiting Japan—Tokyo, primarily. Egypt. Spain. New
Zealand—*Lord of the Rings* country. The shooting happened,
and put to rest any notion I had about leaving America. The

shooting not only brought me back down to earth, but it also brought Thomas and Susannah closer together. They were speaking like they did when we were much younger. I knew Thomas would never leave Susannah, even though Thomas spoke about leaving Susannah months before the shooting, as if it was his own little tagline on how miserable marriage had become. Husband and wife living underneath one roof, however, two different houses. When I saw Thomas over the Christmas break before the shooting, he appeared as if he had become a man trapped. The man who always threatened to leave for good but never had the courage to never come back. The man whose stride had become the slow meander of a pet. The man who didn't say much at all to anyone at all. The man whose shoulders had become just a little heavier. Then, the shooting happened. All hands on deck. The long days together spliced the family back together. Somehow, I knew Thomas would never leave Susannah. Most importantly, I knew Thomas would *never* leave Jimmy. And now, after listening to what Nico said, I know Thomas would *never* leave me. I know he stills loves me in spite of everything I did to him.

When I arrive at the motel, I pay the taxi driver; then I pay a visit to the front desk.

The desk clerk doesn't charge me for another night's stay.

I can't thank him enough for helping me the other day and he responds by telling me that I had someone looking after me.

I head back to my room.

Everything is pushed back in its proper place—the furniture, including the dresser, the table. There's even a new flower vase on the dresser.

I check my book bag inside the AC unit. Everything is there. Jimmy's urn. The camera.

I check the bathroom. The floor is spotless. The air reeks of Clorox, which burns my eyes. I flip on a ceiling fan and crack a window to air out the room. My clothes are neatly folded on a chair as well. I find the burner in my pant's pocket. It's dead. I charge the battery.

After about five minutes of charging, I turn it on and check my voicemail. I have a message from Jazz. The sound of Jazz's voice is comforting. She tells me to call her as soon as I get this message. There's something she needs to tell me. The message doesn't sound pressing, yet it sounds undoubtably pressing—if that makes any sense.

I decide not to call Jazz.

I'll call her when I'm ready.

So, I relax on the bed, pull out the brochure that the doctor gave me from my pocket, and read it over from front to back.

\|\|

My hands are shaking when I arrive at the address on the brochure. The doctor told me that this would happen. He gave it an absurd name, of course, delirium tremens—you may know it as the "shakes." I've heard about people who suffered from the shakes. I've been through withdrawal a few times and I've never experienced the shakes—at least, not this bad, as in, you get the idea. There was one time, but it only lasted a couple of weeks.

I park the car not too far from a shady building in the rough parts of downtown Los Dementes and focus my mind on something else.

People are hanging outside.

Drunk off caffeine.

It's a fairly mixed crowd from what I can tell.

Young.

Old.

A diverse group.

They're all talking to one another: the old talking to the young and the young talking to the old.

I wait until the group enters the building before exiting my car.

The sign outside the doors reads, "Follow the arrow."

So, I follow the arrow to a room at the end of a dank hallway. The room stretches as far as I can see. Not one window on the wall. The room is lit up with fluorescent lights that occasionally flicker as if the bulbs are about to burn out. Reminds me of the hospital. The room feels claustrophobic, too, despite the wide space of the room. The ceilings are unusually low, the walls are painted with a sickly gray, and the floor is made of hardwood, which murmurs in shrill *creaks* when stepped upon. The same group is mingling around a table with an aluminum pot of coffee and boxes of every flavor of donut on display.

A debonair man dressed in a caramel colored sweater approaches me from behind.

"First time?" he says.

His voice is deep and resonant, like a voice over actor.

"Am I in the right place?"

"Are you here for *Hand of Dawn*?"

"I guess so," I tell him and pull out the brochure from my pocket.

"Of course," he says with a black Mona Lisa smile. "You're in the right place."

I look around at the others. They nod at me. One of them acknowledges me with a welcoming smile. Surprisingly, I don't feel nervous anymore. The trembling in my hands stops. I feel ready.

The kind man touches me on the shoulder.

"Welcome," he says. "My name is Jeremiah."

"Rob," I tell him.

"Make yourself comfortable, Rob," he says and points to the spread of donuts. "Feel free to help yourself to some coffee and donuts."

"Sure," I say. "Okay."

I pour myself a cup of coffee.

A slender half Asian, half whatever girl around my age slides in next to me. She has the whole Goth meets gamer thing going on. She's dressed in dark clothes and dark makeup—everything about her is dark, except for her pallid skin. She has a lot of piercings, ears like some African tribal woman, silver balls scattered along her lips and nose. She has a few tattoos. Barbwire tattoos for eyebrows. A tattoo of the tail of a scaly monster-looking thing runs down the side of her neck. I can only mentally picture the rest of the tattoo covering her torso.

I glance down at her green and black *MISFITS* shirt underneath her spiky black leather jacket and tell her that I like her shirt.

She responds with a soft "thanks" and then a swift nod. "Let me guess," she says, "you a newb?"

She's definitely a gamer.

"Yeah," I say. "You?"

I can also tell the girl's a tweaker from the way she jitters and jives, itching to scratch an itch.

"Second time." She does most of the talking with her hands. "Haven't quite cleared my newb status yet," she says unsteadily, "but I'm getting there."

"You'll get there."

"Really?"

"Well, I guess everybody starts out a *newb*. Right?"

"Right," she says, smiling. "So, you nervous?"

"Nah," I say after some thought. "Not really."

She shrugs and her shrug reminds me of Jazz.

"So, what's your drug of choice?" she asks me.

I shrug, as Jazz would do, and tell her, "Whatever I can get my hands on."

\|\|\|

\ listen to all of the junkies and former alcoholics and bingers share their R-rated stories to the group. Mostly depressing stories, tragedies. One man in particular, Jorge Calvini, shared a disturbing story about his wife who had multiple affairs. Before all of the truth came out, Jorge knew all along that his wife was two-timing him behind his back, but Jorge didn't do anything about it. His wife, Clarice, who had been married to Jorge for eleven years, had started secret relationships with inmates who were recently released from prison. While these inmates were locked up, she'd write letters to them. In return, these inmates would send suggestive pictures to her. These relationships went on for years—*two years exactly*, said Jorge. She'd even mark the calendar with various appointments such as monthly checkups or mammograms at the doctor's office or dentist appointments or car inspections on the days the inmates were released. Later, Jorge found out that Clarice never showed up to one appointment. Clarice was living a lie. While her husband was working at the factory (Jorge was an operations manager at a local potato chip factory in Hillside), she'd meet up with these certain inmates at hotels or halfway houses, then she'd take them out for a good time, wine and dine them, then, afterwards, she'd have sex with them. One night when Jorge came back home from work, he found Clarice sprawled out in the bathtub, butt naked, raped, bludgeoned to death. Many years of sex, lies, and deception, all funneled down to an inevitable outcome. Then, Jorge turned to his only friend: alcohol. He binged a lot, went through several days of drinking, then he'd stop, take a break, let his body heal, then he'd binge again. The drinking had gotten so bad that he'd have a drink the moment he woke from being drunk the night before. Jorge told us that he couldn't live with the fact that he "was" the one responsible for his wife's murder. Not inmates. The judges. The penitentiary. The lawyers. He was never there for his Clarice, he said, to take care of her. Instead, he ignored her, abused her, abandoned her. That was just one of the many stories shared in the group; and most—if not all of them—had some sort of underlying issue, which either stemmed from the sharers' childhoods, like there was this one guy who said he molested when he was seven years old, or it was something that developed over time.

Stacey, or "Jiggy Pop," or just "*Jig*," as her friends call her—the fidgety gamer dressed like Lydia Deetz—shared her story to the others. She mentioned to me that during her first meeting here she got a case of cold feet and wasn't going to share until after a couple of more visits. Her drug of choice, Stacey shared, was meth—that's short for methamphetamines—you may know as "crystal meth." Stacey was introduced to the drug after she was raped during her sophomore year in high school. She said that she was passed out drunk at a party and a kid stuck his penis inside her—and not only that, the kid filmed it as well, then posted the savagery on the Internet for everyone to see. The kid was tried in a court of law, she told us; then he was sent to a detention center outside Los Dementes. The incident screwed up Stacey, mentally and physically. On top of that, Stacey's parents were hard on her. Which did *not* help. They pushed her. She said she used to have a 4.0 GPA. By her senior year, she was addicted to meth and her grades were slowly sliding and starting to speak the alphabet. She said she felt "like some kind of fossil, hiding in the dark, *waiting* to be discovered." She said she cut a lot, too—and when Stacey said cut, I thought she meant like cutting class, which I was guilty of doing myself. She actually meant cutting her wrist. She was a "cutter." She liked to cut. She said it made her feel better. A friend of hers who was on the streets at one time mentioned *Hand of Dawn*. She decided to give it try. She was glad she did.

When I'm asked if I want to share, I don't know what to say at first.

Jeremiah tells me that I'm in a "safe space."

My heart starts to race. I can feel the blood swimming in my veins. I'm sweating, too, my forehead, armpits. Even my mouth starts to get wet. I find myself looking for exits. I see Stacey's face. I stop looking for exits. I take in a deep breath. I remember someone talking about taking a leap of faith.

"Where do I start?" I say as I glance down at my shaky hands.

"Start by introducing yourself."

I strangle the shaking of my hands and hold them in my lap.

"My name's Robert," I say with a tremble. "Rob," I correct.

Everybody in the circle welcomes me with hellos.

"Hey," I reply, more easily.

Jeremiah asks, "What brought you here today, Rob?"

I blow out a short, cigarette-like puff of a sigh.

"I'm ah. . . I'm an alcoholic," I tell him, the words coming to me more clearly now. "Drug addict. I pretty much do anything I can get my hands on. I guess. . . I guess I came here because, I don't know. . . "

I shake my head.

I can't tell them.

They're strangers.

"It's okay, Rob," Jeremiah says. "You can share whatever's on your mind. This is a safe space. Remember?"

Once more, I look around at the other people, at Stacey and she's nodding at me. So too are the others, throwing nods my way, as if they're encouraging me to share with them, like parents urging their toddler to take that first step—*you can do it.*

"I keep having this dream, right," I finally share to the group. "My girlfriend is in *this* dream. I guess you can call her my girlfriend. We met not too long ago, which I thought would never happen to me. We went to Paraíso for a couple of days. Not to get married or anything like that. We had a good time, though. I think I'm starting to like her, but. . . I don't know. We'll see, I guess." I take in another deep breath. I relax. "So, anyway, in this dream, I'm. . . I'm. . . "

"Take your time, Rob," Jeremiah says but his voice sounds distant.

". . . I'm. . . I'm choking her," I tell the group. "I'm choking her," I say clearly. "She's struggling. Kicking me. I know
she's struggling too, because I feel the muscles in her body
tightening. Then, I feel this. . . knot and it's swelling against
the butt of my hand where the air from her lungs is balling up
inside the base of her throat, and it's as round as a baseball—
this tiny *ball* of life. The only thing keeping that ball from
traveling through her airways is my hand, my fist. All I have
to do is let go, but I can't. I wanna let go. But I can't. And
she wants to be a part of me. Yet, it's like I want nothing to
do with her anymore. Something's keeping my hands around
her throat, something deep inside me, this force. . . then, she
dies and I wake up and then I have the same dream
again. . . " I don't even look around the group anymore. I
ignore them, each and every one of them, as if they're not
even there. Then, I speak, as if I'm talking to myself. "You
know I've always believed that your dreams were like these
doorways to your inner feelings," I tell myself. "I read once
that certain animals in your dreams represent this type of emotion. I remember I used to dream of sharks. Like the *Jaws*-
type. I read that sharks represent fear or something like that.
I mean, I'm not saying I was scared. Maybe at that time I was
scared. But anyway. . . " I pull my eyes upward and look at
the group once more, at their long faces, their dark eyes,
". . . I had that dream the other night. Same one. But. . . it
wasn't my girlfriend who I was choking. . . It was myself.
Maybe, I guess, that's why I came here. That's all I have to
say. . . "

One by one, each member of the group claps, and it's unsteady at first, like a beat lacking any rhythm. More claps.
The rhythm steadies. Jeremiah thanks me for sharing.

A weight releases from my shoulders, not the whole
weight, but a piece of the weight.

Day one.

IV

AFTER the meeting, Stacey stops me before I get inside my car.

"Rob," she says behind me. "Hey. . . "

I face Stacey and give her a nod of hello.

"I just wanted to say. . . " she sticks her hands in her pockets, ". . . you're a good guy."

I don't know why she's telling me this, but I know it possibly has something to do with what I shared.

"You're wrong, Stacey," I say after a long pause. "I'm not—"

"—Sure you are," she says. "You just don't know it."

Stacey curls her dark hair over her left ear and bats her eyelashes at me. Her eyes, wanting. I know the look. I adore it.

"So," she says finally as I'm about to open the door, "where you headed?"

I gaze around the street. I can't find any words to say to Stacey.

"I don't know," I tell her. "Just headed back home."

"And where is home?"

"San Ricardo," I say, then correct myself, "for now, at least."

"Well, I was thinking that maybe—if you weren't doing anything—you'd want to hang out or something. Grab some coffee? It's up to you—"

"—I can't," I say, "I would love to, but I can't."

Stacey hangs her head.

I know the look.

Hate it.

"I see," her voice trails off into a mumble.

I walk over to Stacey. She's shaking like a pet left outside in the rain. I lean forward and hug her. She doesn't know exactly what to do at first when I hold her close to me. Instead, she just stands there in her wilted flower stance.

I hear a sniffle next to my ear. Stacey wraps her arms around my body and holds me tightly.

We hold each other for a few seconds, a tight hug, in between a bear hug and a long-lost relative hug.

I lean back and look into Stacey's glossy eyes. I know her eyes. I've seen those eyes before. I can't explain when or where or even how. I've seen them.

V

As Stacey departs, I peek over my shoulder and watch her walking away with white ear buds in her ears until she fades into the streets.

I grab my burner from the glove box and call Jazz. She picks up. I can tell from the tone in Jazz's voice that something is terribly wrong. She says that she's been trying to get a hold of me.

I tell Jazz that I'm soon going to have enough money to put down on a new apartment and I'm ready to get serious with our relationship.

There's a moment of silence in the conversation before Jazz's voice comes back over the phone. She doesn't say anything directly. The speaker rattles with Jazz's breath. She doesn't even have to speak another word. I already know where the conversation is going.

I just wish I saw it coming.

VI

THERE'S always someone gunning for you whether it's in plain sight or in the shadows.

I call these adversaries "gunners."

I'm a gunner—*was* a gunner.

You're a gunner.

We're all gunners.

Your gunner can be your worst enemy or your best friend. Your gunner will either keep you alive or ultimately destroy you.

No matter what, you have to be one step ahead or else you'll be dust.

Most often, your gunner wants the same thing you want. Maybe it's the job promotion that you've been tirelessly working on. Your gunner wants *your* promotion more than you do, and that's just something you have to accept: that's there's another someone out there trying to take what you want. Your gunner: working "that" much harder, staying up "that" much later, making the sacrifices when faced with the big crunch.

I once had a gunner, the big cruncher, and the only thing getting in my way from what I truly wanted in life was the greatest gunner of all time.

VII

I'M standing in front of a shelf of Mason jar aquariums and staring at my warped reflection in the glass.

I move my eyes away from the reflections and look down at Jazz's number on my burner, a constant flux of thoughts replaying the recent events in my head, wondering what I did wrong, what I said or didn't say, wondering if Jazz found out about me, who am I, what I was, and how I've been spewing lies, wondering how close she is to Bishop, if they're still doing these videos together, wondering if she's doing these videos against her own will or if she gets off on making these disturbing videos.

All I can do is wonder.

I can't eat.

I'm not sleeping, again.

I'm having more and more panic attacks.

Maybe they were right about what they said about me.

Maybe I'm *never* going to change.

Maybe I'm no different than Jimmy post-shooting, his painfully redundant life after he left the Step Down Unit. I remember it was like a series of baby steps. Each step *slow* and wobbly. Each one wasn't accomplished without a fall; however, he didn't even get as far as a single baby step. After he was stable enough to fly back East, he spent a short time at a nursing home where he received treatment, both speech and physical therapy. Eventually, he was able to continue therapy at home (Jimmy had a lot of setbacks, hospitalized for weeks at a time—even months—due to infections, pneumonia, other complications). We stayed optimistic and positive that he'd recover, even though the idea that he may never recover was slowly starting to set in like a debilitating disease. Jimmy's caseworker, I remember this young and arrogant, patronizing bitch with way too much schooling. She reeked of government. Even the words that she used sounded slippery. She'd check up on Jimmy every couple of weeks, taking notes on her government issued notepad with her government issued pen, jotting down everything about Jimmy and his progress—or lack of—and everything about this bitch was slow and robotic, like the government. I questioned myself whether or not she was human. I know Thomas carried that same trait with his job—a cold and calculated feature—but still, if I looked hard enough in Thomas's eyes, I could see a soul in them when I talked to him. With this lady, I saw nothing. She was ready to write off my brother the moment she introduced herself to him. Her voice, I remember, was raised to a near shout as she talked to Jimmy as if he was either deaf, dumb, or blind. The bottom line: it was going to take way *too* much work and effort to get my brother back on his feet again. And people didn't want to work beyond their means or even go that extra mile— at least *not* with Jimmy. Therapists also recognized that he wasn't making progress so the insurance company stopped his therapy. Cold turkey. Whatever money was spent on therapy had come straight out of pocket—Susannah fighting tooth and nail trying to get the insurance company to cover the therapy; but the insurance company wanted results, and Jimmy wasn't giving them any.

Customers and tourists alike surround me, but I do a decent job at blocking them out. They act like floaters in the corners of my eyes, useless things, really, moving objects. In my way, *always* in my fucking way, always watching me, always there. Why won't they just go away?

I momentarily remove my eyes from Jazz's number and get a closer look at the people. They turn their unsteady eyes to me—worried, these people appear, frightened like children. They're dressed like commercials; and they waddle throughout the shop, swaying lethargically from side to side as if they're working off the dead animal that they recently stuffed in their bellies; and when they speak to one another, their voices sound like beetles rustling through dried leaves.

My finger hovers over the CALL button.

As I'm about the push my finger against the button, I feel the same prickly sensation opening inside me, a familiar voice telling me to *let her go.*

"How?" I say, my eyes falling to the floor in thought.

Finish what you started.

I raise my head from the floor and mindlessly pick out a Mason jar with a toy scuba diver figurine at the bottom.

In one hand, an aquarium. In the other, my burner.

All I have to do is press the DELETE button and just like that, she'll be deleted from my world forever, and it'll be as if I'm erasing her from my existence—and even if she ever infiltrated my world ever again, she'll be no different than a stranger. One minute, she's a part of my world. The next, she's an object.

I take the aquarium to the checkout and pay for it. I look around the shop. A young couple—a couple of years older than me—is standing against the shelf of a book aisle. The guy has his arms locked around his girlfriend's hips like a handcuff and they're making out. I want to tell the two to get a room. I want to smash the jar over Romeo's head and watch strings of blood run down his face.

I hear a voice and it's the clerk asking me about the weather or something like that. I ignore him. I tell the clerk to keep the change, grab the aquarium, and rush from the store before I feel sick to my stomach.

I stop before getting inside my car, take the aquarium, and toss it against the side of the building in a heap of rage.

The water suddenly splashes everywhere: on the ground, my car, my pants.

I watch the people scurrying away, occasionally looking over their shoulders with alarmed expressions.

I ignore them, as I should; and then, eventually, they'll ignore me, as they always do.

They mean nothing to me.

I stand over the jagged glass and pinpoint a scuba diver figurine among the debris.

I carefully brush away the pebbles, the tiny pieces of slate, aquatic plants, and pick up the figurine.

VIII

As soon as I make it back to the motel, I stop at the doorway and look around at the emptiness of the room.

A cockroach scurries across the baseboard!

I slip into the room like a furious gust, squash the cockroach, and wipe my shoe on the concrete outside the doorway. I shut the door behind me, causing the motel to shake like a tremor. I go the bed, sit down, and practiced my breathing.

Have I hit bottom? Not like before, but for real this time, as if I'm no better than a cockroach scurrying my way to freedom. Living on the bottom. In the gutters. In my own hell.

I turn on the TV and flip through the channels, trying to put my mind on something else besides doing something bad that I might regret.

All I want is to see her face once more before everything gets lost in the fray.

I know, though, as much as I want Jazz, there's a grim possibility that I'll never see her again.

As much as I try to occupy my mind with something more positive, like telling myself that "everything is going to be okay," things will get better, all I can think about is Jazz, me not being with her. The rejection. My whole life has been like one giant "no thank you" or "not interested."

I flip through the channels and think about all of the times that I wanted to be famous, wanting to be on TV or in the movies or magazines like all of the celebrities, wanting to be somebody who people admired, like a highly-respected director who won an award at some kind of prestigious award show, giving a speech in front of millions, first thanking my mother or father for all of their support and then putting in something thoughtful that had the power to change the world for the better of mankind, wanting to be a rock star playing for the masses singing the lyrics of my very own songs, wanting to be somebody "important," someone who proved to all of the people who doubted me or rejected me that I was someone important, I was famous, and yet, at the end of the day, I turned out being someone not evolving into much, just another body, another object, another obstacle in the way, something *always* in the goddamn way.

I throw the remote against the wall, like the aquarium before, in a sudden heap of rage. There's nothing on TV. It's daytime. There's nothing ever on TV during the daytime. I reach into my pocket, pull out the scuba driver, and stare at it for the longest time. The first person who comes to mind is *not* Jazz or Bishop or that cute gamer girl from the Hand of Dawn, Stacey, who appeared more interested in me than Jazz. Only one person on my mind.

I grab my bookbag from the AC unit and remove Jimmy's urn from inside. The sight of the urn causes me to break. I'm glass shattering into a thousand pieces and every inch of me hurts.

I suddenly fling the urn against the far wall, smashing it to pieces. Clouds of gray ash shoot up into the air in a magician-like poof and rain down over the shattered remains like mist. I drop to my knees, frantically searching through the ashes.

I don't know what I'm searching for.

I don't know anything, really.

I end up finding nothing.

Only dust.

The urn is broken beyond repair and that's when I finally let it out.

I run my ash-covered hands over my soggy face. I can't remember the last time I've cried so freaking hard—not under the influence, either. I'm sober. I hate being sober. Yet, it feels so good to cry, to let it all out. It feels good knowing that there's still a part of me that feels something other than anger.

KILL 4 U

I never *always* hated Fourth of July.

Once, I think I used to be as patriotic as Uncle Sam. I flew red, white, and blue with the highest esteem. I used to be your typical slice of the everyday kid who was raised in a strict, conservative household where "most" of the time I did exactly what my parents told me—and even if ever questioned them, the only answer I received was "because" *they* "said so." I remember I used to play baseball, but I didn't come close to being as good as Jimmy. I could've been, if I kept at it and practiced and all, but my heart wasn't into whacking around some ball and running around bases. It wasn't for me, and I'd say if you're going to spend so much time doing something, you might as well do something that you like. Thomas was actually the one who introduced us to the sport. He too played baseball before he joined the force. I remember he'd always be plopped behind home plate in his frayed blue lawn chair and study me as if I was an owner's manual; and whenever I was at bat, he'd yell out what I was doing wrong with my swing in front of all the other parents—*For God's sake! Quit dropping your left shoulder!* It was embarrassing, and it was pretty obvious to everyone that we didn't get along too well, especially during my childhood. Why? We were just too much alike. That's the best answer I can give you, at least for now. I used to root for the White Sox. Thomas didn't like that, being a Yanks fan and all. I liked that Thomas didn't like the things I liked. I used to proudly wear the colors of my favorite team—still do. Used to collect things such as trading cards or comics or hats, whereas Thomas was the type who disposed of things. If it was old or faulty, then it was either getting fixed or going straight in the trash. Used to go to church every Sunday. Thomas's orders. Not only did he encourage education, he encouraged faith. "A man without faith is not a man," he used to say. Used to go to *Fantasy World*—that was whenever Thomas could get away from work and even then, we were scrounging pennies in order to afford the trip since it was so damn expensive. What a rip-off? Used to celebrate each holiday, even Easter. Used to celebrate Christmas back when it was called Christmas.

It's fair to say that I used to be a "normal" kid.

Once—and when I mean *once*, I mean that certain time in a person's life when he or she doesn't try to make sense of anything—I think I might've enjoyed Fourth of July.

Whenever that special day came around, Jimmy and I never went all out like the other kids—*all out*, as in clearing out the entire store. We'd hitch a ride with one of Jimmy's friends' parents and drive past the South Carolina state line and buy bottle rockets and Roman candles, nothing too extravagant. More than anything, we liked watching the bright colors illuminate the sky as we walked around the neighborhood. I was thirteen when I smoked my first cigarette and it happened to be on America's birthday, as well as the same year Mona's Arch released their debut album, *Rule or Be Ruled*. Jimmy scored the smokes from one of his friends' older brothers. We waited until our parents went to sleep and smoked them inside the garage as the distant crackles of fireworks trailed off into the night sky like choked thunder.

Two Julys later, I drank my first beer with Jimmy. He wasn't much of a drinker. He drank a beer here and there. He never touched drugs, not until college. Even then, he hardly touched them because of baseball. Everything that happened later in life with Jimmy was *because* of baseball. Can't go out tonight. Why? Because of baseball. Can't smoke that. Why? Because of baseball. When we were younger, we never thought about the repercussions for any of our actions. I, on the other hand, didn't have friends whom I could genuinely call friends like Jimmy did when he was growing up. I mean, I associated with kids in my grade—sometimes—but they were *never* my friends. They were run-of-the-mill posers who thought their shit didn't stink. Plus, I knew most of Jimmy's friends, and I was much closer to them than the other posers my age. Jimmy didn't mind me hanging out with them. They called me Jimmy's "Little Shadow," but I didn't mind. I was his shadow, and I was little. The one problem was that Jimmy knew when to stop, whereas I didn't; and at times, he was forced to play older brother. I remember we had the house all to ourselves that Fourth of July weekend, which was rare. Thomas and Susannah never traveled. Thomas never took any sick days. They trusted Jimmy more so than me—so much they held him responsible for taking care of the house, as well as his good-for-nothing brother. One of Jimmy's friends, some kid from New York—can't remember his name—scorched his khakis clean off during one of our Roman candle wars. Except for the kid's pride, he wasn't injured. It might've been one of the greatest nights ever. A night of legends. I also received head from Becky Embers. That's Embers, as in the coals burning in a smoldering campfire. Becky was three years older than me. My first. You never forget the first person who steals your virginity. It's like one of those moments of enlightenment forever deeply embedded in my brain. I can remember the senses, how it felt, what the air smelled like, what I was thinking at that exact moment—it all came with the package of a memory. Afterwards, I remember, it felt as if I was committing a crime, as if I did something I shouldn't have done, and the thought alone made me feel as if I was unstoppable. All the girls hated Becky Embers because they all wanted to be Becky Embers. She dated some preppy tennis player who was not invited to the party. He was a poser. I'm sure I had something to do with Becky breaking up with the Sampras-wannabe at the better end of summer. Becky ended up going to a community college not too far from me. We were good for each other, I think. All of her friends said that we'd make adorable babies. I took it, more or less, as a compliment, considering most babies are these smelly, hideous things. Being with Becky was like the best drug in the world. At the time, I hadn't experimented with many other drugs, except for alcohol and weed here and there and shrooms a couple of times and then acid one time (had a bad trip after I did a couple of drops at a party, which was a really bad idea, as in what the sheep would say, *baad*. Most of

East Providence's football team was there. A couple of fights broke out between the jocks and wannabe thugs from a rival school, South Trenton—not the friendly, peaceful environment to open up one's mind. Instead, I was hallucinating dragons and demons in the bedroom darkness as my trip was wearing off. That night felt like an eternity, staring at a ceiling of horror. I just wanted it to end). Of all the drugs, though, Becky was it. She was my fix. Each time I spent with Becky required a new and more extreme potency in order to achieve the same high. On our first date, we went to the mall. We kissed. Second date, we went to a movie. I fingered her. Third date, I went to her house while her parents were in Cancun. She blew me for the second time—and it was way more climatic, considering I wasn't numb from drunkenness. On our fourth date, we went camping near Blowing Rock for the weekend. It wasn't a date—more or less—a mini-vacation. I pitched a tent. Literally and figuratively! We had sex that night in the woods. It was her second time in the sack. My first. Each date was greater than the one before. Each date forced me to be *that* much more. I had to work *that* much harder. I had to be *that* guy who everybody both loved and hated. By the third month with Becky—*with*, as in we were a hot item who were no longer going on dates but actually outings together—I was helping her parents with dinner. Becky made me better as an individual, in general. Dare I say: *A contributor to society*. One weekend I did volunteer work in the projects. Helped build a playground for the kids who were less fortunate. Becky and I were together for over a year until she took the Leap across the country to pursue an acting career. Never heard from her ever again.

Maybe she got that big break she always talked about.

Maybe she got married to some hotshot producer.

Maybe she spat out a baby or two.

Maybe she got a job waiting tables for a living.

Maybe she fell ass backwards into porn.

Or, maybe she died.

Who knows?

I think about her every now and then. And that's all it is, really, me just wondering what happened to her.

What became of my high school crush turned girlfriend, Becky Embers? How's Becky doing?

I wonder if Becky thinks the same about me from time to time.

Most importantly, I wonder if Becky found a person in her life who reminded her of the same way I once felt about Fourth of July before it lost all of its substance, sound, and even, color.

Before everything turned to gray.

\\

AFTER the recent score, I lift up my hand, flatten it, and hold it in front of the rear view mirror. My hand is as steady as a flatline. Damn, it feels so good to be back. Feels good to have my swag back, my confidence.

I leave New Town, drive the black Infiniti Q50 to a side dirt road off the main highway, and change the tags.

I swap out the California tag, which reads, "**2HOT4U**," with the Washington State tag.

After the tag is secured and mounted, I drive back to Topside and pay the Russian a visit.

I tell him, "Christmas came early this year."

I take the Russian out back and unload the truck.

"New car?" he says.

"You like?"

His entire body shrugs, including his facial expressions.

"Not bad," the Russian says as he looks over all of the gear in the trunk.

Flat screen TVs with surround sound systems, watches, jewelry, paintings which look as if they have been taken straight out of the Louvre, gold and silver things, shiny things—I even found a glass egg the size of a football which looks like it's worth a fortune—basically, I grabbed anything that looked as if it cost a lot of money. The Russian unloads it all from the trunk. I help.

All of these valuables belong to Eugene Russo, also known as "G'no." And that's a long *G* with a sharp *no*! Like the wannabe rapper, Penny, when he says his name at the beginning of every track, Peeeeeeeen-*knee*! You probably recognize Eugene from those over the top commercials where he's flexing his average-sized guns for the camera over some cheesy synth-wave music, telling you, the viewer, to get off your lazy butt off the couch and pump some iron with him. Eugene owns a chain of fitness centers along the southern part of the West Coast called Top Fitness—and from the size of his house, I can tell Eugene lives like a king.

I finally put two and two together the other day when I was mulling over where I went wrong with Jazz.

During my mulling, one tidbit came to light.

The night Jazz and I saw *Blood and Black Lace*: we sneaked into a swimming pool behind a luxurious house in New Town. My intuition was right about Jazz knowing Eugene. I did some research and discovered that Eugene's a regular. I managed to get a hold of Nico's friend, Kim, and she informed me that Jazz knows Eugene. She said Eugene paid her twice for her services. Said Eugene liked them young, even much younger than Jazz, she told me. She even mentioned that he was into "freaky" shit. Jazz met Eugene through Craigslist. I think about what Eugene might've done to Jazz. Kim never went into any details, but I can only imagine.

‖‖

I hand the keys to the Infiniti Q50 over to the Russian. Apparently, he knows a guy who knows a guy who runs a chop shop. I end up leaving the pawnshop with enough money to last me for the rest of the year. I say my goodbyes to the Russian and thank him for the business. He drops me off at the garage. Mars isn't working today. So, I should be in and out. I end up going with the Ducati Monster 1200 S with a Testastretta engine, L-Twin, 4 Desmodromically activated valves per cylinder, liquid cooled. I think the bike belonged—or least once belonged—to an actor or something. Mars mentioned his name once. I can't remember, though. He was like in a boy band or something. Singer turned actor. The dopey type who can't act worth a shit, but somehow, some casting director dumped him in movies for his charming looks. That type. Either way, the bike looks nice and it sure as hell rides nice, too.

Once I required a nice ride, I stop at the local pharmacy and hand over my memory card from the camera to the film developer behind the counter. He's a pasty-skin man with milky hair and an expression as solid as one on a bust; then, without anyone looking, I slip him a hundred dollar bill and tell him, "Between you and me."

He slides the hundred back my way.

"We don't look at customer's photographs, sir," he says.

I slide the hundred back his way.

He moves his eyes around the pharmacy, and that's the only part of his body that moves, just his eyes, both of them wigwagging like a flag caught in a flurry of wind. He has the mannerisms of a robot, and I start to question myself whether or not I can trust him.

Then, he says, "Fine."

The word comes out as sharp as its very meaning.

He leans forward and secretly grabs the money.

"Do you have a number I can reach you at?" he asks.

I give him the number of my burner.

I piddle around for a while until the film developer gives me a call and tells me my photographs are ready for pick-up.

IV

WHEN I make it back to my room at the resort, Plank's End, I begin the process of tacking the photos as well as the activities of each person of interest on the wall, starting at the very top of the chart with a photo of the fifth man of the Circle, Valentine "Smoker" West, who's sitting comfortably inside his cozy suite at Grand Valley Estates.

After Valentine, I place a thumbtack over a photo of Valentine's grandson, Nicholas "Nico" West, snip off a piece of red yarn, and string the yarn around the thumbtack over Valentine's photo. Even though Nico wasn't involved in the shooting—no evidence has come forward suggesting he was involved—Nico's photo still goes on the wall. He's a pawn, more or less; however, still associated with the very men responsible for Jimmy's death.

I sort through other photographs with other suspects interacting together, such as Nico hanging out with Ayker at the Northside Docks, preparing for a fishing trip or whatever (turns out they're extremely tight after all; in fact, Ayker acts like a father figure to Nico by the way he touches him a lot, poking at him in a joking manner or putting his around his shoulder like a father would do with son), as well as Bishop and Ayker shaking hands in the desolate parking lots in Port

Clifton, possibly making deals; then, after I'm done tacking the photos, I string yarn around each thumbtack.

Near the center of the chart is a photo of Luther "Bishop." I took the photo while camping out at the Palace. A long distance shot of Bishop exiting through the back entrance, sipping from a smoothie or some protein drink, looking as if he's up to something. The man always looks like he's up to something.

Underneath Bishop, I tack two more photos: one of Officer "Rodriquez" and then the other, Officer "Malone," the two cops who frequently hang around the popular nightclub.

After Bishop left the Palace, I followed him to a steamy, dark alleyway between Third and Price, located in the rougher side of Richport. I managed to get three shots: one of Bishop getting inside the back of Malone's Lincoln with his partner, Rodriquez, sitting in the passenger seat; then one of Bishop handing Rodriquez an envelope; then another one of Rodriquez counting the wad of cash inside the envelope. All I needed was Bishop spitting on his palm and then shaking the cop's hand. Talk about a money shot. It didn't prove that the two cops were involved in the shooting; nonetheless, it proved that they were involved in possibly taking bribes, possibly protecting Bishop's Palace, possibly doing something that's against the law.

I kept my eye on Bishop for a majority of my time, following him around Topside, keeping tabs on him, where he ate lunch, where he worked out, where he went to get a massage or steam or salt bath. One night, I followed Bishop back to his luxurious beach house, the one off Seascape, similar to Nico's in its contemporary interior design, only much bigger, twice the size, actually. The back of the house was more than revealing, considering the entire backside was made of glass windows, which covered the walls. He had minimal furniture inside his house and whatever furniture he owned was low to the floor. He even had a fireplace housed inside a silver column in the center of the living room. I managed to capture him performing—let's say—rather suggestive acts to a much younger woman than him, even possibly younger than me—wouldn't go so far to call her college material.

I don't tack those photos on the wall. Don't see the point, really. I already know Bishop, like Nico, is a collector of women, a man who treats women as if they are dolls. I haven't seen any signs of Nico being "abusive" toward women, although I could be wrong.

Next to Bishop's photo is a photo of the "wrong" Anthony Foster, which I took when I first arrived in Topside.

I mark a fat question mark over the photo with a red Sharpie, the question mark indicating that the "real" Anthony Foster's either on the run or food for maggots. I'm leaning toward the on the run part.

I place another photo on the other side of Bishop's. It turns out Slender Man has a name. His name is Argento Gonzalez. I do research on him and find out that he's one of Bishop's assistants. I check his background. Check for any priors but don't find any. He's a former Marine with extensive military training; was honorably discharge four years ago. He's definitely not to fuck with.

I construct the rest of the chart with the other photos, from "Flip" and his "Merry Band of Strung-Out Frogs," including a photo of "Drew," "Chemo," "What's His Name," and "Wilt," to the truck driver who calls himself, "Rooster." I place Rooster's photo smack dab in the middle. Rooster is the secret ingredient to Bishop's business, and without Rooster, the whole business would fall apart.

Every Wednesday, during unusual times of the day, Rooster makes pick-ups behind the nightclub in a white AL-PINE TRANSPORTATIONS truck.

Later, I researched the name, ALPINE, and discovered that it's an independent company that makes deliveries throughout the West Coast. Whatever Rooster's picking up at the nightclub, it has something to do with whatever's behind the red door.

Has to be.

After Rooster, I decide to tack two photos of "Jazz" since she is now involved with Bishop: one of the photos, an older one I took from a distance while she was working at Lassie's and then, the other one with her and Bishop, the one I stole from the yellow room. She's neither a suspect nor a victim.

Right now, she's just there.

Next, I place a photo of Jazz's boss, "Eric."

Why not?

Then, I construct the rest of the chart: Nico's girlfriend, "Jamie;" Nico's close friend, "Yogi;" Yogi's sister, "Yolanda;" Jazz's friend, the prostitute, "Kim;" then two cutouts from old newspapers, one of "Cedric Gaines," who's behind bars for a crime that he did *not* commit (if only I had Ayker on record admitting to Cedric's innocence), and then the other of "Henry's skeleton" being pulled from a marsh, his femur protruding from a fisherman's net like a broken twig.

Next to these articles, I tack an old Polaroid of Henry and his sister, "Bella."

I stole the Polaroid from Henry's sister, Bella—the photo was hidden in a cardboard box containing Henry's things in a storage locker outside Philadelphia. The last time I talked to Bella she said that she kept her brother's possessions as a reminder of how great of a man he was and that one day when or if she ever had children—Bella leaning more so toward the "if" part—all of Henry's "things" would be there for them; however, minus his driver's license.

After Bella, I tack a photo of Conrad's ghost of a wife, "Myrtle," who has been "missing" ever since, not only the night of the shooting but also the same night of Henry's disappearance, which—if you've gotten this far—you're aware means *dead*.

Last but certainly not least, I tack a photo of the cop who arrested Cedric Gaines, Officer Daniel Ayker, or shall I say, Los Dementes County's soon to be incumbent sheriff, Sheriff "Daniel Ayker." Started out as a police officer for the Los Dementes Police Department, then went up in ranks—climb the ladder, if you will. Next it was detective, lieutenant, captain, commander, first assistant chief, deputy chief, chief; and then, finally, he was elected sheriff of Los Dementes County.

I look over all of the photos tacked on the wall.

And it's like my own perfect work of art.

Like every artist, it took me lots of time and patience to construct each layer. But like every piece of art, sometimes it has to be destroyed. To make it imperfect. *Wabi-sabi*.

I grab Valentine's photo from the wall.

When Valentine falls, they'll all fall.

Like dominoes.

THE MOST
DANGEROUS
GAME

T H E § M O K E R

O UT of curiosity, I use my new cheap off-brand laptop that the Russian gave me and search through Jazz's social media pages. I use several search engines, thinking maybe the Internet is down or the hotel's wi-fi signal isn't up to par as it should be. I check the connection, and it's good. I search yet again for Jazz, and I realize that she's deleted all of her accounts, even her MyCircle and Chatterz account, all of it has been taken down and the only pictures that remain of her on the Internet are old ones, nothing recent.

That feeling is in my gut again—the one that I got the morning after Jimmy was shot, with me trying to piece together all of the moments before the shit hit the fan. My mind goes off and does that thing again where it tries to figure out all of the signs. What did I see earlier today? I drove past a dive called Lookout Patio. Was it a sign? What does it mean? Is danger coming my way? I think about all of the signs, even the frivolous gestures people made during the day, like that one older black lady who accidentally bumped into me at the office supply store while I was about to check-out. She placed her hand over my shoulder and the warmest smile crinkled along her face. She told me that she was sorry, and I remember feeling like I had known her before and wasn't the least bothered by her. Actually, I felt comforted by her presence.

I wonder if Jazz has a page under the name Lynda Lynx?

I search LYNDA LYNX and—what do you know—I find a new Chatterz page.

I read her last two chirps.

The first one reads:

"IN THE GREENEST OF OUR VALLEYS
BY GOOD ANGELS TENANTED,
ONCE A FAIR AND STATELY PALACE—RADIANT PALACE—
REARED ITS HEAD."

I read Jazz's second chirp.

"LIKE A GHASTLY RAPID RIVER, A HIDEOUS THRONG RUSH
OUT FOREVER,
AND LAUGH—BUT SMILE NO MORE."

I don't know what she means by these chirps. They sound like verses from a poem.

I decide to do some research on the Internet. I type the first chirp into the search engine and Edgar Allen Poe's poem, *The Haunted Palace*, pops up. Could Jazz be referring to Crystal Palace? Does she think it's haunted? What other reason would she be posting these cryptic verses from a poem whose title includes the word *palace*? Are there any correlations between Poe's morbid poem and the Palace?

I read the entire poem. Both of her chirps were taken from the same poem.

I pull up the porn site, *Forced Entry*, even though I swore to myself that I'd never go on the website ever again. I have to find out what's going on with Jazz.

I type in Lynda Lynx's name in the search bar and the results show two NEW videos posted not too long ago.

One was posted nine days ago and another video was posted exactly three days ago.

The first video is labeled, "Lynda vs. the Machine."

The other video, "Lynx Gangbang Rape."

I locate a date underneath the video's title.

Nine days ago.

I minimize the page and open Lynda's Chatterz page. Her last chirp was three days ago. Her second to last chirp was exactly "nine" days ago.

I close her Chatterz page, take a deep breath, and watch the videos.

The first video: Jazz is in the same room as before, the yellow room; however, the lighting is much different and more professional. The room is dimmer with an eerie red light shining over her naked body. More production involved as well. Jazz is lying on a wooden table: gagged, blindfolded, her wrists are bound by two large wooden cuffs that appear medieval. In front of her sits this bulky-looking machine, *the* machine. A long prosthetic arm is extended from the motor, and at the end of the prosthetic is a metal dildo about the size of baby's arm, and it's violently penetrating her to the point where she appears to be in pain.

Halfway through the video, I press stop.

I can't watch.

I don't really want to watch.

After I gather myself, I open the other video, the second one. The video starts out with the backs of two shirtless men standing in front of a work light. They're wearing *balaclavas* similar to the one the cameraman—Bishop—was wearing. They're both shaped like black bears. From the position they stand in front of the light, their bodies are covered in shadows. The cameraman zooms in, partially revealing one of the men. He's Latino, remarkably familiar.

I pause the video and pull myself closer to the screen. He has a mole the size of a pea right below his left nipple.

I know that mole. I've seen it before. . .

Yogi.

I open his PhotoBag page and scroll down to the pic of him and his so-called "lady," posing on the beach. The caption below reads: Taking break with my lady @TIGERBUNNY91 at Pearl's Island.

I compare the two moles: one from the still of the video and the other from Yogi's PhotoBag pic.

What do you know?

A match!

I close Yogi's PhotoBag and study the other man's body—the black guy. He has a tattoo of a diamond on the side of his neck. Between the two kneels a mousy Jazz, her eyes pointed up at the burly men.

I watch the video, trying not to crack my teeth in the process. Other men—at least four more—manifest in the video;

however, I can't identify them for they're *all* wearing balaclavas. Not once does Jazz appear as if she's "getting off" on what's being done to her, being thrown around, shoved, strangled, slapped, gagged, kicked, punched. Objects are being forced inside her. One of the objects—a cop's baton, I believe—is rammed so hard inside her that it draws blood. Not once does she show any signs that suggest that she's doing all of this for the sake of entertainment, as sick and disturbing as it may be.

After a while, I can't distinguish one from the other due to the red haze. My eyes are consumed with red. All I can see is red. The red special all around me. Smothered and suffocated by all the red. I can't watch it anymore. The title explains it all. Doesn't it? I don't need to explain anything, anymore. I think you get the picture. Don't you? What else is there to say?

I slam shut the laptop and get away as far as possible from the device. The sight alone of it makes me ill. I'm tempting to throw it against the wall and take my heel to it and turn it into something that would likely see the bottom of a dumpster. I do my best to hold onto the flames, the fury, and keep it at bay.

I remind myself it's not the laptop's fault.

It's not the Internet's fault.

It's *my* fault.

I pick up my burner and call Jazz, but she's already changed her number.

Somewhere, I can hear a thought in the back of my head telling me, "I told you so."

\\

\ spend the next hour or so emptying my bookbag, as well as all of the items obtained from the Russian, including a Beretta Px4 Storm Sub Compact, a "ghost gun" that I bought from the Russian's friend, a private dealer named Oscar—*ghost gun*, as in the gun is untraceable and not linked to any murders or crimes. It's the ideal weapon for not only a criminal, but also a person who wants to do what good cops can't do. The gun's extremely hard to find, but they do exist. They're out there among the underbelly of society. You just have to know the right people.

First, I place the Cannon on the table, then a 2-Speed Tape Recorder, two blank MC-60 microcassette tapes, a tie-clip microphone, which I will wear underneath my shirt, as well as two blank compact discs (CD-R), mainly for copies of the interrogation, my revolver, which I'll use as backup, a box of ammunition, including the one bullet that Ayker left for me at the gravesite, the newly acquired butterfly knife, Jimmy's urn that I jerry-built from the hotel's ice bucket and a lid with several plastic garbage bags sealed with duct tape, and then, last but not least, the pouch containing the bullet fragment lodged in Jimmy's brain.

\|\|\|

I wait until nightfall before I make my move.

First, I drive by the Palace, park at a reasonably safe distance, and make some minor touch-ups to the chart.

After I leave the nightclub, I stop by the same pharmacy before they close.

The robot says that it won't be ready till morning.

I hand him two hundred dollars and tell him, "It'll be worth your while."

He stays well after closing and then I leave with the new photos.

I hightail it back to Plank's End and place the photos of the bouncer guarding the Palace right next to Bishop's photo. He goes by the name, Darius Winslow Junior, dubbed "Babyface." The name speaks for itself.

Next, I move Yogi's photo from the bottom of the chart to the top and tack it to the left of Babyface's photo.

\|V

MORNING arrives.

I take a jog on the beach. I do a hundred push-ups back in my room.

Then, after the quick workout, I'm out the door.

I stop at Old Town Diner and I eat like a king. My breakfast is a hearty meal consisting of a bowl of oatmeal with scrambled eggs, hash browns, fruit, two glasses of orange juice and three cups of coffee to go along with the meal.

V

AFTER breakfast, I stop at the local video store called Fanboys. I browse through the science fiction aisle.

I pass the DVD, *Aliens: Resurrection*. There's this one particular character in the movie, I recall, a real tough S.O.B. who carried a contraption similar to what I'm looking for—in fact, it's exactly what I'm looking for—then again, the movie takes place in the future and I suspect the materials used in the movie will be exceptionally hard to find in any local store in Topside.

I place the DVD on the shelf and browse through the horror aisle.

I pass one movie, *Videodrome*, starring the actor, James Woods, released in 1983; it was directed by the master of "Body Horror," the great David Cronenberg; and if you've ever seen one of his movies, it's either one you'd like to forget or one you cannot forget.

I look over the back of the DVD for a couple of minutes and then I draw my attention to my hand.

I shape my hand like a gun and then shake my head.

Wouldn't work, I tell myself.

I continue to browse through the wide selection of DVDs—the store even has imported films from Japan, everything from anime to spaghetti westerns; and they even have a section dedicated to *Giallo* films.

How about that?

I make my way down the thriller aisle and head straight to a sub-aisle called "Psychological Thrillers."

I browse through the DVDs until I come across Pal Viti's *Prophet Pusher*, starring George Sorrento.

I pick up the DVD.

I skim the back summary of the DVD, even though I've already seen the flick many times before, despite what I've told Jazz.

I pay for the DVD.

VI

I leave Fanboys, head straight back to my room at Plank's End, and watch the scene where George Sorrento's character, Ash Trey, assembles a special contraption to holster his gun from the public eye. I've seen a similar contraption in several other movies—I'm convinced these other movies were inspired from the "original" concept used in *Prophet Pusher*. I do my homework. Thoroughly study the scene from beginning to end. I watch the scenes at least twenty-five times, maybe more. I make notes on a piece of paper, write down each idea. I note how the gun will slide from my wrist without piercing my hand. I even draw out a sketch of how the contraption should look, how it should fit along my wrist, what materials I can use without costing me an arm and a leg.

They'll never see it coming.

It's, by far, the perfect concealment.

VII

I stop at the hardware store and pick up the supplies I need to make my contraption.

The materials for my project end up costing a lot more than I expected.

I don't mind, though.

I have the money.

VIII

AT lunch, I eat like a prince. I make sure to stay away from the onion soup and the clam chowder. I stay away from all soup for that matter, or any food with any heavy cream or sauce. I eat a roast beef sandwich without any mayonnaise—I can't stress "no mayonnaise" enough to the waitress—and a side of oven baked macaroni. Oven baked foods are the toughest for any incendiary of the food industry, especially since the food is encrusted with a layer of piping hot cheese. That's enough to kill anything, even the bacteria in bodily fluid.

IX

FOR the rest of the afternoon, I build in my hotel room.

During one occasion, a vague-faced man dressed in a gold tie and carrying a walkie-talkie knocks on my door and tells me that they, as in the managers downstairs, received several noise complaints from the guest staying in the room next to mine. I apologize to the man; then he tells me to keep the noise down. And I do. When he leaves, I get back to work. I use the cordless drill with short, controlled bursts; and when it gets too noisy, I place a pillow over the drill, which somewhat helps reduce the noise.

X

WHEN dinnertime arrives, I decide to eat like a peasant.

While I'm eating, I check out Lynda Lynx's Chatterz page as I've been doing periodically throughout the day.

No new chirps.

I do the one thing I hate the most.

After I'm done waiting around, I head back to my room and spend the remainder of the night withdrawing the Beretta from my newly built contraption in front of a mirror until it becomes natural, like tying shoelaces.

XI

THE next morning, I try the continental breakfast downstairs.

There's nothing light about the breakfast. They have spongy scrambled eggs and fatty bacon and waffles stacked like piles of pamphlets. I eat like a king.

After breakfast, I head back to my room and with my knife, I file X's into each jacketed soft point bullet since I couldn't find any hollow point bullets for my revolver. I wasn't about to waste time searching ammunition shops in Topside for hollow points when I can dummy my own.

Not only will I been carrying the perfect concealment, but I'll also be carrying the perfect backup.

I need to prepare myself.

XII

I work off breakfast at Town's Orchard, testing out my contraption by carving up trees. The Beretta doesn't release as quickly as I configured. The contraption does a decent job by projecting the handgun from my wrist to my hand, but my enemies will see it coming. It's slow and clunky. It needs to be quicker and much more leaner.

After Town's Orchard, I'm back at the hotel, making minor modifications to the contraption by tightening coils and greasing the track along my forearm.

Once I'm finished putting the final touches on the contraption, the Beretta shoots out like a switchblade. I practice using the contraption until my appetite comes back.

As I'm about to head out the door for a bite, I suddenly receive a notification from Lynda Lynx's Chatterz page. I open my laptop and check out her latest chirp.

The chirp reads:

> "IN STATE HIS GLORY WELL BEFITTING,
> THE RULER OF THE REALM WAS SEEN."

I close the laptop and look over the chart on the wall. I draw my attention to one man in particular, the man at the top.

I grab the things I need for Valentine.

Then, I'm gone.

XIII

BEFORE I head to Jazz's apartment, I stop at the closest bookstore and pick up a copy of *French Guide*—a book on how to properly speak French, as well as a map on the many attractions and restaurants to visit while visiting France. I highlight the places I'd like to visit with Jazz; and I write a note on a piece of paper, fold the paper, and stick it on Page 37, next to an explanation on the history of the Eiffel Tower; then, lastly, I prop the book against the door of Jazz's apartment.

As I get about three steps away from the apartment, the door opens behind me.

Then, I hear a woman's voice: "Excuse me."

I turn my shoulder and see Rosa standing at the doorway and she's staring at me.

She squints her eyes, then leans down and picks up the book from the doormat.

"Can I help you?" she asks, looking over the book.

Her tone is sharp, almost angry.

Everything about her seems sharp and almost angry.

"That's for Jazz," I say, pointing at the book.

"And who are you?"

"I'm ah—Rob," I tell her.

"Rob?"

"Yes."

"She hasn't mentioned any Rob to me."

"Well," I say, "just make sure you give that to her."

As I turn and walk away, I hear Rosa say from behind, "You know a man named Bishop?"

I stop and face Rosa once more.

"I know Bishop," I say.

"You do?"

Her eyes widen, breath more labored.

"Yes."

"Well, the next time you see him," she says, her tone sharpening, "why don't you give him a message."

"What message?"

"You tell him that he needs to show a little more respect. . . "

"What happened?"

"Oh," she says, now speaking a lot with her hands, "he came in here and he was ugly to my daughter. I told him he couldn't just come in here and start barking orders at Jasper—"

"Did he say where he was going?"

Rosa shakes her head.

"No," she says. "He grabbed Jasper and they took off somewhere. He was driving like a maniac."

"Thanks," I tell Rosa.

"The next time you see him—"

"I will," I say and storm back to my bike.

This changes everything.

XIV

I'M screaming at myself for not killing that piece of shit when I had the chance.

I ride away from Jazz's apartment. Now, I'm stuck with two options. I look for Jazz (only two places she could be, the Palace or Bishop's house). Or, option number two, I stick to the plan. Get Valentine on tape. Make two backups on CD, one for leverage just in case things go south, then the other for Dwight. In return, Dwight will give the CD to Ruby, who will use it to bring down Ayker. Then, after Ayker is exposed, and Ruby looks like a hero, *then* I'll send Bishop back to where he came from.

I decide, after much deliberation, to make the drive to Grand Valley.

XV

ALTOGETHER, the drive from Topside to Grand Valley and back is two hours and twelve minutes according to the MapStar, which leaves me about an hour—two would be really stretching it—to get Valentine on tape and then, from there, after I get him singing a confession, hand over the tape to Dwight. It'll take some convincing—Dwight is probably one of the most stubborn men that I've ever met—but I can count on him.

XVI

I stop at a convenient store just outside Grand Valley. I attach the tie-clip microphone to the backside of my shirt, just between the collar and the top button, the part where the shirt forms into a letter *v*. I position the mic accordingly, making sure it doesn't move a hair when I walk, turn, or make any abrupt movements; but, still, I try to keep it concealed from my target. I test out the mic by speaking first, then making noises around the bathroom, then stop the recorder, then listen to what I just recorded. The mic is rubbing against my shirt a little.

I remind myself that in order to get Valentine on tape I have to remain as still as possible.

I'll make sure to sit extra close to Valentine.

Just to be safe.

XVII

I end up going through three cigarettes, lighting one after another; and during the whole toking session, I'm shaving away all of the leftover residue from the dry glue until Henry Frick's face is clean and presentable. I never knew Henry, personally. However, from the way his sister, Bella, talked about him with a look of glowing reminiscence, he seemed like a good man— a *decent man*. I couldn't help but wonder how much she reminded me of myself when she spoke about her beloved sibling, that glow. I can only imagine Myrtle felt the same way about Henry.

Was a man really worth dying over?

The same went for a woman.

Would you kill for love? Or, would you die for it?

With my mind made up, I put down the kickstand to my bike and make my way toward the retirement home.

When I step inside and that awful gassy stench hovering just underneath a heavy aroma of potpourri greets me with an air-smack across the face, I'm left in a momentary state of dread. It hits me, just like the stench, the memories, the promises, pain, so much pain. I can see myself, standing in a place like this in what feels like a lifetime ago, but I'm not that much younger—only a few years, give or take—and I'm telling myself to "never ever" come back here. I thought I'd *never* find myself in a place like this ever again. Now, look at myself. Here I am. In the one place I swore I'd never step inside. Let alone, visit.

After Jimmy came home from Vista Springs Rehabilitation Center outside Derry, a college town about two hours north of Elizabeth, I made a promise to Thomas and Susannah that I'd never put Jimmy back in "one of those" places—even if it had a five-star rating or top of the line accommodations or around the clock, one hundred percent satisfaction-guaranteed care from the best, most qualified staff in the world. A promise is a promise.

During my sophomore at East Providence, I worked at one called the Fountains. It was a part-time job. Nothing too special. Put your few hours in, then split and get high. I got a couple of kids from school to tag along and little did I know at the time what a mistake I was making. In all honesty, it was a so-so job that occasionally had more perks than it had flaws—and the pay wasn't anything to gripe about and much better than working at McDonalds, I'd say. Plus, we got like over an hour break where we could eat leftovers from dinner rush, then, after we'd eat, we'd find secretive screened-in patios in the residence, chill, and smoke until the dishes came back to the kitchen where we cleaned them. I didn't work there that long. About a year or so. The first several months by myself went smoothly, but nothing good ever lasts. Eventually, some asshole shows up, something happens that ruins everything.

Eventually, people come. People conquer. Then, people destroy. Overtime, I started to *see* things, bad things, really bad
things: the residents being abused and mistreated, being talked
down to, as if they were these two-year-olds who were only
good at making messes. I never tried to stop them. I knew
my role. I was the server who prepared the meals before I
loaded them up on the carts. I never ratted on them. And if I
did, I knew there was a chance that I'd lose my job. I had two
options, really: keep my mouth shut or do something about it.
I chose to the first option. Then came along the other kids
from East Providence. They heard I had a good thing going
for me at the Fountains. Good pay, easy work, free food.
What more could you ask for? There was one kid, Spence
was his name, short for Spencer, last name Bowling, like the
sport, but kids called him Jay, as in Jay Gatsby the name
taken from the *Great Gatsby*. He was more like a gangster version of Gatsby, dressed in baggy Nautica clothing, a blinding-
bright Polo shirt for everyday of the week, wore bean-sized
diamond earrings and a chain the size of a dog chain around
his neck, and he drove a souped up Mercedes with these gold
rims to school. Spence's father was loaded up to his eyeballs.
Owned an air-conditioning business, I think. Self-made type
who started from the ground-up, then struck gold, moved to
the Country Club, then turned as stuck-up as any privileged
socialite in the uppity-up class. The Bowlings lived in a mansion of a house three times the size of ours. Every four years,
he voted for the candidate who blew the most wind. Shot big
game strictly for sport, then stuffed the heads of their winnings
and mounted them on the living room wall like trophies.

I hated going over there. Every time.

One day, Spence thought it'd be funny to hawk a loogie in
one of the residents' soup. And Spence did. A bud-sized ball
of nastiness, a bastard offspring of the *Blob*; spat the lumpy,
mutated thing into a bowl of French onion soup prepared by
none other than yours truly. It was like a dollop. Even stirred
around the snotball with a spoon while the other kids laughed.
I wasn't laughing. I wasn't doing much of anything but standing there, watching some stuck-up, wannabe gangster rich kid
spoil some poor schmuck's onion soup. I know what you're
thinking: coward. Worst than a coward. A disgrace. My
mind ventured off somewhere else and I was no longer standing with a cart of food inside an elevator. I was wandering

somewhere in my thoughts, conceptually directing and per-
fecting a scene that *should've* happened that night: me luring
Spence to my car to get high after the others bounced from
work, then, once he was as stoned as a Rastafarian, rapping
out lyrics to a jam on radio, me beating the living shit out of
Spence—literally, Spence soiling himself in his khakis that his
mommy pressed that morning while I puked down his throat
as he screamed and cried for help—turning his handsome face
into a medley of vegetables, cheeks into red potatoes, nose
into an eggplant, then, once I was done gardening, I'd squash
that freakish face of his like a pumpkin.

The beating would become all Spence ever knew—the
sound of me breaking each bone in his body—and every time
the spoiled brat heard the sound of a *creak* or *crack*, he'd think
of my ugly mug.

After I was done with Spence, he'd look so hideous that
he'd make the Elephant Man look like George Clooney.

That should've happened to Spence.

But it never did.

Kids like Spence don't get beat up.

When they grow up, they run for President.

Or sheriff.

I shake away the thought and head straight to the front
desk and after I wait for a couple of minutes for the reception-
ist to return from the bathroom, I tell her that I'm here to see
one of their residents, Valentine West. The unsmiling, underpaid lady has me write my name on a sign-in sheet. I make up
a name. Then write it down. Shortly after, I smell throat lozenges in the air. As I'm about to pinpoint the potent stench,
another unsmiling, underpaid caretaker sneaks up behind me
like a spider and escorts me to Valentine's room.

Along the way, we walk down a couple of hallways—one
of the hallways reeks of a baby's diaper.

I tell the unsmiling, underpaid caretaker to point to Valentine's room while she tends to more important issues like taking care of the accident.

She continues to suck away on the lozenges and obnoxiously makes these *clicking* noises from where the lozenges
bounce off her teeth like a hockey puck, then she waves her
hand as if she's waving off my comment, and tells me it's just
Mr. Peabody.

"He'll be fine," she says nonchalantly.

There's nothing "fine" about a grown man lying in his own shit.

I never tell the caretaker.

I take that back.

She doesn't deserve the title, caretaker.

Undertaker is more like it.

I think about what I told myself a lifetime ago.

So many years have passed, and yet nothing has changed.

People are still people.

As we approach Valentine's room, the smiling, overpaid undertaker acts as if she's interested in my visit and asks me how I know Mr. West.

I put on a *Monopoly* dollar smile on my face in front of her and I keep it short by telling her that Mr. West is an old friend.

She doesn't respond.

Yet, she continues to wear her smile the way I wear mine.

We finally arrive at Valentine's muggy room, and thankfully it doesn't smell of anything awful.

Without the undertaker looking, I press the red RECORD button on the tape recorder along my belt, then conceal it with my shirt.

"You have a visitor today, Mr. West," she says, her voice now stern and domineering.

I follow the undertaker inside the stale, stuffy room, which is about twice the size of any ordinary hospital room. It's cluttered with newspapers so old that the papers have already started to turn brown in color. It's also furnished with a couch with two cushions, a queen-sized bed, a TV as old as *Jeopardy*, a shelf of yellow *National Geographic* magazines, and a puzzle table.

The undertaker walks me to the old man who's staring out the window and starts calling out orders in a near shout. It has no effect on him. She does her best at displaying dominance by puffing out her chest, squaring her shoulders, and raising her tone even louder; but he doesn't give her the satisfaction.

"I'll take it from here," I emphasize. "Goodbye."

She looks me over as if I just smashed one of her toes and leaves, mumbling something under her breath the same way a tween would do after throwing a fit.

He's dressed in a pair of plaid pajamas. A portable size oxygen tank is hooked up to his wheelchair and a spare tank is close within reach. He has tubes running from his nostrils. His hair, like the film developer, is milky white; however, incredibly thin. Each remaining strand is tightly pulled over his dry, pink scalp like wires. His once bluish green eyes are now murky; and it's hard to tell if there's any soul behind them.

He's a slow mover, the Smoker is; yet, he acts as if he doesn't have to move for anybody. He has people to move for him, like Foster, like Bishop.

Spark plug, I tell myself. You can't start an internal combustion engine without a spark.

"Don't worry about Wendy," Valentine says as he looks at me through the corner of his glassy eyes. "The thing about Wendy is that she knows she's a bitch. Being a bitch is about the only thing she's got going for her."

I pull out a flimsy chair from the poker table and place it in front of Valentine, who, in return, gives me a once over.

"So," he snaps, "what took you so long, son?"

"Do you know who I am?" I ask him, as I take a seat.

He waves his hand as if he's brushing off my question.

"Nicholas paid me a visit just recently," he says. "He told me *all* about you."

He stretches out the word *all*, as if Nico told him everything about me.

"Did he now—"

"—Are you not Tommy Backer's son?"

Spark plug, I tell myself.

I act as if we're starting from the very beginning—fuck what he knows or doesn't know—I ask Valentine, "How do you know Thomas Backer?"

"I know every cop," he leans in closer, "*every* single one, although Tommy and I, we didn't exactly have the greatest of relationships. I'll give it to him, though, for doing his job. I swear the man must've been colorblind. He saw everything in black and white. . . "

He looks me over once more as I remain at a loss for words.

"You know you look like him," he says, "your daddy."

Again, I have nothing.

"Why are you here?" he asks.

I turn to Valentine.

"I think you already know the answer to that question," I tell him.

I peel open the bottom half of my shirt.

I show him my revolver.

His eyes trace the steel, and he smirks.

"Doesn't fit you, son," he says without expression.

"You people keep on thinking you know me when y'all don't know a thing about me."

Valentine turns his eyes to the window.

"Maybe you're right, son," his voice trails off into a murmur. "Maybe I know nothing." The old man faces me again, this time carrying more color in his cheeks. "So, tell me, what's Tommy up to these days?"

"Why do you care?"

He frowns.

"I don't." He suddenly lets out a phlegmy sigh, as if he's stirring around a wet knot in the base of his throat. "Lemme guess, you're either here to kill me or you're here to find out why your brother was shot and left for dead?"

"You're getting warm."

He sighs again, this time it's long and burdensome and less phlegmy.

"You know," he says, "a memory is no different than treating an infection with antibiotics. Once that medicine starts to work, you start to feel better. You feel like your old self again. You're healed. All your problems gone. Your mind is ready to put the old memories aside and willing to experience new ones. If you stop taking the antibiotics halfway through the round, there's a chance the infection will come back and when it does, it comes back with a vengeance. Same goes for a memory. You have to treat it. You have to keep it from spreading."

Not bad for an old man.

"There's not a day that goes by," Valentine says, as his eyes glaze over, "that I don't feel sorry for what I did *or* what I didn't do. Forget about da'whole 'life is like a box of chocolates' bullshit. Life is anything but sweet, son. Life can be nasty and violent. And savage, at times. If you keep *drifting* around as naive as you are—"

Valentine lets out a bull's snort.

Nico's been talking a lot about me to him.

I wonder if all of their latest conversations have been mostly about me.

What else has Nico been saying about me?

"—One day, this world's going to eat you up and spit you out like a sunflower seed," he says. "You have to realize that we did the things we did *not* because we wanted to. We did them because we *had* to."

"He didn't have to shoot my brother," I tell him. "He had a choice. *You* had a choice."

"Sounds like you've been talking to Daniel Ayker."

I don't say a word.

Then, Valentine says for me, "Nicholas told me."

"Let's just say Ayker and I have some unfinished business."

"Yes," he says. "Nicholas told me all about your little run-in with him. From the looks, he didn't exactly get his point across. Did he?"

I swallow the dry lump, which feels like the size of a baseball, down my throat. Keep it together, Robbie.

"I came here for answers," I tell him. "That's all."

He looks away for a second; then he studies me with caution.

"You're right about Connie," he says, his voice much calmer. "He had a choice. I had a choice." Then, his voice rises again, angrier. "But if James—that was his name, right?"

I'll give him credit.

His memory is sharp for an old man.

I nod a *yes*.

"If James wasn't out *that* night at *that* particular time at *that* particular moment, then you wouldn't be here. Would you?"

I don't answer at first. I let the old man speak, hoping the silence will draw out any knowledge he has about the shooting.

"Why was my brother shot?" I ask him.

"Your brother was shot because he got himself involved in another man's business."

"Involved?" I repeat. "What do you mean 'involved'?"

"You open one door, son," he says, "that door opens another. Sometimes what you find on the other side can be darker and more disturbing than what you found behind the first one. Life has many doors. Many secrets. Why even open the door at all?" His eyes darken, like two little clappers belling my insides. He says bitterly, "Tell me, son. What makes you any better—"

"—I'm not any better," I say speedily, "but people deserve to know the truth."

"The truth about my son?" he says. "About your brother? About you?" He points his crooked little finger at me. "Should people know the truth about you? What *you've* done?"

I don't answer. Valentine looks me over again. Studies my eyes, my face. Then, turns away, saying, "Some people deserve the truth. *Some*. Not all people." He faces me, his jaw flexed. "In the olden days, you'd be fertilizer right now for prying into another man's business. Like your brother. . ."

A wave of silence builds over the conversation.

He stares out the window again, shaking his head from my presence.

His lips moves, but no words come out—at least none that I can understand.

"In some way or another, we all lives separate lives," he turns to me, something in his eyes, "your brother had a secret, Robert. We *all* have secrets."

"What the hell are you talking about?"

"Well, he was there that night and it wasn't the first time I had seen his face," he says. "I remember all the faces that came into my place. Never forget them. Their eyes. Their pain. You have your brother's eyes. He was there all right."

"How you know?"

"I was there," he says grimly. "I saw him."

"Jimmy would never go into a place like that," I say. "Plus, it never mentioned anything in the police report."

"And why was that, Robert?" he asks, but I don't answer. He shakes his head, almost amused. "You think we just hand over surveillance footage to the cops or let witnesses talk? When you buy something—or someone—you expect to get your money's worth, right? Otherwise, why even buy it at all if you know that, down the road, it's not going to work?"

Sounds familiar.

"The great thing about buying the cops is that you get to pick and chose who goes to jail and who stays home."

"Like Cedric Gaines?"

"There are plenty of 'Cedric Gaines' doing time for crimes that they didn't commit," he says with a tremble in his lips, the veins swelling over his flaky forehead. "You going to save them all, Robert? Huh? Why don't do yourself a favor and save yourself while you still can. You actually think people like. . . Cedric Gaines change? Well, they don't," he tells me, his breath grows heavier, hands now doing most of the talking. "People like Cedric Gaines don't deserve second chances. You think he gives a shit about you? About your brother?"

"Things break," I say. "*People* break."

His eyes narrow.

"Only the soft ones."

I don't respond.

Instead, I think about all of the families like mine, so many of them, families who lost loved ones due to acts of violence, broken families raked through the gutters of hell, used all for political gain or popularity or hashtags.

Again, I keep quiet.

"That's what I thought," Valentine says and lets out another snort, this time drenched with phlegm.

Again, I keep quiet, my thoughts doing most of the talking. What if he's right about Jimmy? It doesn't change a thing. So what? Maybe he was there trying to blow off steam. Maybe he did have a side to him. I knew Jimmy, though. If anybody knew Jimmy, it was me. He had a *good* heart.

"Let me ask you a question, Robert," he says more clearly, as he faces me. "You believe things happen for a reason?"

"Are you talking about fate?"

"Fate," he says. "Destiny. Whatever."

"No," I lie. "Not anymore."

"But you did?"

"Once," I say. "Maybe."

"It wasn't a coincidence that James was there that night."

"What are you trying to say?"

"I'm saying your brother killed Henry Frick," Valentine says, my blood runs cold. "Shot him in the chest."

"And why would my brother shoot an innocent man?"

"The same reason you shot Anthony Foster," he says, a smirk growing somewhere behind his vacant face. "Accident."

I reach my hand under my shirt and grip the handle of my revolver.

"Start making sense, old man," I tell him.

"You want the truth?"

"Yes."

"The truth: my son was a coward," Valentine says, thinking. "He couldn't face his own problems. So, he chose to run away from them." He points at my chest and holds his gnarly finger there like a witch's wand. "I can't tell you how many times people came to me, looking for Connie. I knew he was in way over his head, with debt, with Myrtle—"

"What does Myrtle have to do with any of this?"

"Myrtle has everything to do with what happened to James."

"Are you saying *Conrad* didn't shoot my brother?"

The old man looks at me. I see truth in his eyes. His breath is shallow: a telltale sign.

"Connie was a lot of things, a bad person, bad husband, bad son, but he wasn't a killer."

"Ayker says he was."

"And you believe him?"

"Ayker sounded pretty convincing," I say. "Why wouldn't he tell me the truth when he had his chance? Instead, he chose to lie? Why?"

"Yes, well. . . " he says, more casually, ". . . he's a politician. And like all politicians, they'll say or do whatever they need to in order to protect their ass."

I need the name for the recorder.

Just a name, and I'm golden.

"Who shot Jimmy?" I ask. "No lies."

His eyes drift in thought. He wants to tell me. I know it. He looks as if he's been carrying around a burden for a long time, too long. He's ready to unburden himself. I'll take it, his burden, because I can. Hand it over, Valentine. I stay strong, relentless. Come on, Valentine. Spit it out—

"When I first met her, I knew she was trouble," he says. "I warned Connie about her, but he didn't listen. That night, they got into a fight, which wasn't out of the ordinary. They always fought. I remember Henry was there at the bar, waiting to make his move. He confronted Connie as Myrtle was leaving. Connie and Henry went out back. James must've followed them." Then he says from the corner of his mouth, like a side-thought, "You Backer's, always trying to do the right thing."

"What happened next?" I ask him.

"Connie pulled a gun on Henry," he says. "They fought. Then one thing led to another. James wound up with Connie's gun. James shot the *wrong* man. He dropped Connie's gun, rushed over to check on Henry. Myrtle must've heard the gunshot before she got back into her car. She came running, found James standing over Henry's body. Henry didn't have long. Maybe a couple of minutes before he drowned in his own blood. I don't have to tell you what happened next. You know what happened—"

"—No," I say, holding in the fire, the fury. "Tell me. . . "

"Myrtle, she picked up Connie's gun and she shot James," he says, his eyes unblinking. "You *know* the rest of the story."

If he's telling the truth, then it proves that Ayker was lying to me. Same with Foster.

What if Valentine is right? If he is, then everything that I've worked on has been for nothing.

How about the man from the sewage plant? Was he someone like Jimmy? A guy caught in the wrong place at the wrong time? A guy who stuck his nose in another man's affairs?

I turn my attention back to Valentine.

"Myrtle West shot my brother," I say clearly for the tape recorder, "then Daniel Ayker covered it up by pinning the shooting on Cedric Gaines?"

"That's the truth, son, whether or not you believe it."

He takes in a deep breath, points at a chest, and asks me to reach in the top drawer.

I open the drawer and find a pack of Pall Mall cigarettes.

"Would you mind?"

I pull out a cigarette from the pack. Hand it to him.

I wonder why he still holds onto the pack when Nico told me that he quit after he developed issues with his lungs.

Valentine stares at me with guilty eyes. Waits for me to hand it over. He never asks the obvious question. The cigarette isn't going to smoke itself.

"I'm not *that* far gone," he says finally, squinting his eyes. "I can smell it on you."

I reach into my pocket and pull out my gorilla lighter.

I tell him to keep it.

He holds out the lighter and places the cigarette in the corner of his mouth. His eyes ease downward in thought. He removes the cigarette from his lips.

"How about Anthony Foster?"

"Which one?"

"You know which one."

"You mean the one you killed in cold blood? That Foster?"

I might need to do some splicing.

"The other one," I say before he can utter another comment. "What was his role in the shooting?"

"Foster was nothing more than a petty thief."

"Was he there the night my brother was shot?"

He hesitates.

I ask again.

"Yes," he says over a swallow. "He was there. He helped Myrtle get rid of your brother's body."

Just the sound of what he's saying sends thorns through my veins.

"How about Conrad?" I ask him, trying my best to keep the seams together. "Where was he?"

"He was cleaning up his mess with Henry."

"What about Bishop? Was he there?"

"Who?"

He gets ready to smoke the cigarette.

"*Luther Bishop*," I clarify for the tape recorder. "The owner of Crystal Palace. The man who took over the club after you."

"You mean, the man who took over for my son," he corrects. "You think I'd hand over my life's work to that piece of shit? If I knew that man was going to take over after me, then I would've burned that place down to the ground."

"So," I say, "let me get this straight. Luther Bishop wasn't there the night of the shooting."

"No," the old man replies. "All Luther Bishop cares about is Luther Bishop. He and Ayker make quite the pair."

As of now, it doesn't change a thing.

Bishop's still a dead man.

"*Why*," I say as I sit back down in the chair, "why didn't *you* come clean sooner? Why now?" I emphasize. "*You* could've put the right people behind bars. . . "

He lights the cigarette, takes a drag, savors the smoke.

"The way I look at it, son," he says amusingly, as columns of smoke flow through the corners of his mouth. "I'm already in prison." He shakes his head, as if he's more disgusted by his own actions than the actions of others. "I've been in prison ever since the night your brother was shot. I just wish you found me sooner." He waves off his own comment, looks me in the eyes—his eyelids are heavy, eyes red and watery.

Then, they wander once more, his eyes, like a toddler's eyes, not in thought, but almost in confusion.

I place the flap of my shirt over the revolver, stand up from the chair, and pull out the driver's license, which once belonged to HENRY FRICK, from my pocket.

"It wasn't our destiny, Mr. West," I tell him as I look down at Henry's face on the I.D.

I look over the license one last time; and while the old man sucks away on his cigarette, I place the license on the armrest of his wheelchair. He picks up the license and looks at it as if the image of Henry's face somehow hurts his eyes.

"What really doesn't make sense," he says, squinting the left side of his face, "is why your brother—a star baseball player who had his entire career on the line—wasted it all on some greaseball who was sleeping around with another man's wife."

"I don't know," I lie.

As I'm about to leave, I hear a voice over my shoulder, "You have no idea what you're getting into, *Robert*."

I stop at the doorway. Turn my shoulder.

He's holding up Henry's license.

"Is this how you want to be remembered?" he asks and tosses the license on the floor. "Just another picture?"

I don't respond to his comment.

As I'm walking down the hallway, I hear Valentine shouting from inside his room, "You leave my grandson out of this," he's shouting to the top of his lungs. "You hear? Nicholas had *nothing* to do with what happened to James!"

He says my name again, but I continue walking, listening to a series of phlegmy coughs exiting the room.

I don't feel like gold right now even though I should.

P R E P / A / R A T I O N

leave Grand Valley with a heavy heart and clear mind. Myrtle being the shooter changes everything, and yet it changes nothing. Ayker pinned the shooting on Cedric Gaines, *not* Myrtle—but what happened to Myrtle? What if Valentine's right? About everything? Jimmy accidentally shooting Henry, and then Myrtle, out of moonstruck rage, shooting Jimmy, then Foster helping Myrtle dump Jimmy's body. She had to skip town—had to!

All fingers put to the grave, but what if she's still out there?

Or, maybe Valentine's playing me as a gullible fool and he's making everything up in order to stir me away from the truth.

Maybe he's right. Maybe I have no idea what I'm getting myself into.

I decide to stick to the plan. I've gotten this far, I tell myself. Why walk away now?

I transfer the confession onto my laptop and burn two copies, one for myself just in case things go south (like a condom, it's better to have leverage and not need it than not have leverage and need it), then another for Detective Ruby. Then, I prepare the artifacts for Dwight, an envelope filled with all sorts of goodies: a copy of Valentine's confession; the pouch containing a fragment from the same bullet used to shoot Jimmy; the keychain holding both the rabbit's foot and the key which will open the trunk with every bit of intel I have gathered after the shooting; the interviews with Henry's sister, Bella, who had informed me all about the affair between Henry and Myrtle, who may or may not be alive—I'm leaning toward *may not*—as well as residents who lived in the Old Town area (I even have one resident on file stating that she saw a midnight blue 1997 Chrysler Concorde, which happens to be the same make and model as the one Myrtle drives—I didn't think too much of it at the time; figured Conrad borrowed her car for the night), including one of the key witnesses, Detric Wright, the kid who claimed that he was with his boy, Ced, the night Jimmy was shot, but, of course, his statement was thrown out in court due to minor discrepancies (like Valentine said earlier, why buy something if you know, down the road, it's not going to work); the patrolling logs from Dwight; finally, a personally written letter informing the detective of the room number to my hotel room at Plank's End.

Over the payphone, I tell Dwight to meet me at the same location that we met a couple of weeks before Jimmy was transferred back home in North Carolina. In a way, it's poetic, if you think about it, us meeting in the same exact location where it all started—full circle, if you will.

I can remember the last time I was here, Hope's Pier, an old, forgotten pier, which used to be a haven for sailboats until it was shut down due to lack of upkeep. It feels as if it was just yesterday we were standing on the creaking pier, same overcast sky. It felt as if the clouds were shielding out the sun and the heavens. A strange calm before the storm.

I hold onto a photo of Bishop handing the cops an envelope of money in my sweaty hand.

I chose to bring this particular photo because I need Dwight, since he's a visual guy and all, to understand that his people are involved in something bigger—*his people*, as in cop people.

Eventually, Dwight shows. He's late as usual. He gets out of the Silverado truck. Doesn't say a word.

"I didn't think you'd show," I say as we stand feet apart.

He steps forward and gives me a hug.

"Damn," he says as he embraces me in his arms. "It's good to see you."

"Good to see you," I tell him.

He leans back and studies me.

"You've lost some weight."

"A little."

And he's put on some weight from the cushiony hug.

Secondly, he looks down at the photo in my hand.

"What's that?"

I show him the photo of Bishop.

Dwight grabs the photo, carefully looks over it; and again, he turns away.

"Déjà vu all over again," I tell him. "I don't know what he's up to, but it's big."

"Robert," he says over a heavy sigh, "I told you I was through with all of this vigilante stuff. I moved on with my life—"

"—It was Myrtle."

"The wife?"

"Yeah."

I grab the envelope from my bike.

"It's all in here," I say, showing him the envelope. "Got Valentine West telling me that it was Myrtle who shot Jimmy."

"And you believe him?"

"I do."

"Why the hell would she shoot Jimmy?"

"Jimmy accidentally shot Henry," I tell him.

"Jimmy shot Henry?" he says, confused. "That doesn't make any sense."

"It was an accident, Dwight," I say. "It's all in here."

Dwight places his hand over his mouth, looks away, thinking.

"It's not the news I was expecting," I tell Dwight. "But it still changes nothing."

"It changes everything, Robert!"

"Ayker," I list, "Valentine, Bishop, Foster, they were all involved. They *still* are."

I push the envelope toward Dwight, but he doesn't grab it. I keep it there until he finally grabs it.

"What the hell do you want me to do with this, Robert?" he asks. "I'm out of the game."

"I want you to give it to Ruby."

"But Robert—"

"You're a good man, Dwight," I say. "You were a good cop."

"Don't start with this—"

"You were a *good* cop, Dwight.

"No, Robert," he says. "I wasn't."

"Sure you were."

"I did the one thing I vowed never to do."

"What's that?"

"I *broke* the law."

"You stood up against corruption," I tell him. "Isn't that why you joined the force to begin with, to end corruption, the police brutality? It's our time now, Dwight. We have an opportunity to turn a wrong into a right. Isn't that what you want?"

He doesn't answer. I don't expect him to.

"Bishop has my friend," I tell him. "I think she might be in danger."

"Who?"

"Doesn't matter."

He steps closer with barred teeth.

"How many more people have to die for you to realize that, whatever's happening to this country, all of the killings and the unrest and divisiveness, it's greater than you, Robert. By going after these people is going to change everything? Did you ever stop to think that maybe you're a part of the problem, not the solution?"

"—What the hell happened to you?"

"I woke up."

"No," I say. "You're just like the rest of them. Go hide, bury your head in the sand. If we don't stand together, Dwight, than we don't stand at all—"

"—Ruby," he says, "the detective working your case. He paid me a little visit the other day. Thomas was with him."

What?

"Thomas," I say. "You're serious?"

"Of course, I'm serious," he says. "You have to turn yourself in, Robert. You're in too deep. You need to help—"

"—What did they say about me?"

He's shaking his head, and he has tears in his eyes.

He's doing something really, *really* bad.

"We all lose ourselves at one point or another." He looks at me, something in his eyes. "Sorry, Robert. . . "

"What did you do?"

My heart starts to race, something's going down. I can feel it in my bones.

"You have ten minutes before they show up," Dwight says.

"Ten minutes before who shows up?"

"It's just your father and John Ruby," he says, as he takes a step closer. "They just want to help you, Robert. . . "

I get on my bike.

"Robert," he says before I peel away, "she better be worth it."

I nod at the envelope in his hand.

"Watch your ass," Dwight says.

"Make sure you give *that* to Ruby."

I put on my helmet and leave Hope's Pier.

\|\|

WHEN I make it back to Topside, breaking every speed limit on the road, I stop at the nearest men's clothing store. I realize that I'm pressed for time. So, I grab the first thing that catches my eye. My Sunday's best: a black leather jacket, black jeans—tight but not too tight—a black dry fit shirt. I notice the jacket won't work due to the right sleeve. It can work, if I make minor readjustments in order for the contraption to work properly.

I stop by the store, Lines and Linens, and pick up an out-door screen lined with magnets, like the ones I've seen adver-tised in those corny infomercials with the voice-over sounding like the host of a game show.

I head back to my room where I cut off the magnets from the screen. Then, cut through the right sleeve with scissors and hot glue the strip of magnets on both sides of the inner sleeve.

I test out the contraption by releasing the Beretta from my wrist. The sleeve opens smoothly. The Beretta shoots out with perfection. I lock the Beretta back into place, the sleeve snaps together, like the screen, by magnetization.

Once I'm all suited up and ready to go, I peel open the lid of the jerry-built urn, releasing a mushroom cloud of dust motes. I reach inside and grab a handful of Jimmy's ashes. I smear the ashes over both of the sweaty palms; and after care-ful consideration, I decide to leave the rest for Thomas.

Next, I peel Bishop's photo from the wall; however, I can't help but notice the other one, the one of a much younger Jazz and Bishop posed together like a happy couple, like the kind of couple that would make great kids. Forget about all that other nonsense from before, about them having like a father-daughter relationship or whatever. I pocket the photo, tape the other one of just Bishop onto the bathroom mirror, untwist the overhead light bulb, install a red bulb that I bought at the Party Hearty, and stand inside the red glory. I focus on their red faces, the upcoming kill. I know violence is *never* the answer. I once read somewhere that being happy and living life to the fullest is the best revenge. If she came clean about the shooting, what Jimmy had done to Henry, what she had done to Jimmy, and somehow, she could've tried to get Jimmy help instead of tossing him away as if he was a piece of garbage, then I think there might've been a chance—might've—that I could've reached way down inside and found forgiveness in my heart. Forgive Myrtle. Move on with my life. Be happy. Get a job. Have kids. Pay bills. Drink beer and watch football on Sundays. Now, I don't even know what it feels like to be happy anymore. I think I was happy with Jazz. I think Jazz was happy with me. She made me feel like I still had a chance. She made me want to be a better person, to be a provider, to be more humble and mature and all of that other stuff that comes with being an adult. If that's not love, then I don't know what is. I don't want to turn to violence, but I feel as if I don't have any other option.

Where does one turn when the very people who protect us can no longer be trusted?

Ruby is my failsafe, if I don't make it out of this thing alive. Putting my trust in a person whom I hardly know is hard enough. But whatever faith I still have left inside me, I send it all to him. As far as everybody else, I know what I'm about to do will not sit right with people. I'm going to turn into a talking point, a topic of debate, political rhetoric, even worse, a victim of a personal mental health disorder. I can't say I don't expect this to happen. Eventually, everything that is supposed to happen will happen. *Eventually*, after this crap is over and done with, they're going to point at me with the same hand they jerk off with and tell millions of people streaming or watching TV: "Right there! There's the monster!" Through their screen-soaked eyes they'll act as if they know me. Yet, they're *not* me. They don't know what I'm thinking. They don't know what goes on inside my head.

And the TV people are going to analyze me as this so-called "Lone Wolf," an outcast, a deranged individual. They'll brand me as if I'm cattle: Monster, Creep, Loser, Psycho. Psycho maybe. I *was* crazy—I was, I think, but I'm starting to see things more clearly now. I know they're going to feel much, much better when they label me with these names, the insults, the hoopla. They'll get off when they criticize me or praise me or threaten me or whatever. They'll all run to their computers or their smartphones. Every one of them, trying to "explain" me, and it'll be like tiny echoes lost in an echo chamber, accomplishing absolutely nothing.

As I'm about to exit, I hear a voice coming from behind the shower curtain.

Are you sure about Dwight?

I peel back the curtain and witness Moses lying in the bath-tub; and he's dressed in a black suit, not gray. He looks as awful as he did the last time I saw him.

What the hell do you want?

He doesn't answer. Instead, he mouths off another question: How do you know Dwight won't go to Ayker?

And why would he do that?

He's a cop, remember—

—*Was* a cop. He was one of the good ones who stood by the code: protect and serve.

Moses laughs.

Dwight's a friend.

And how about Valentine?

What about him? He your friend now?

No—

—He was lying.

Lying about what?

Bishop. He was there. He was involved in the shooting.

How do you know?

You really believe word for word what that old man had to say?

Like you have any room to talk.

Moses turns away, doesn't respond.

Soon, everybody will know the truth. You'll see.

I attempt to make my way from the bathroom.

Are you forgetting something?

I stop at the doorway and turn around and Moses is standing just feet away from me.

I don't have time to be doing any favors right now, I tell him.

You'll have time, Moses says weakly. Trust me.

I grab Jimmy's urn from the dresser and as I'm about to walk out the door, the room suddenly goes cave-cold.

What if I were to tell you that you could have your life back, without regrets, without anger, without me?

I turn my shoulder.

Sounds too good to be true, I say as he stands in a slouched posture at the edge of the red room.

All you have to do is a *little* favor. That's it.

His body is covered in red, face too. He looks extremely famished. His red marbled eyes are sunken into the sockets of his skull like a thirsty vampire. He looks almost unfamiliar.

There's a man, Fran Rosalie, Moses says, owner of the Topside Beach Freak Show. I believe you've met him before.

The name rings a bell.

Curlicue, he says. He has something that belongs to me.

The emcee from the Freakspectacular show.

I tell Moses to do it himself.

It must be *you*, he tells me.

I contemplate shutting the door behind me, but something is keeping me from leaving.

A force.

Why me?

Moses says he needs a man of my talents.

If I do this, will you leave me alone?

I witness a smirk somewhere underneath the shadows of his red face.

You have my word, he says.

\\\

As soon as I arrive at the trailer park off Maroon Reserve, I realize I've been here before, as if I'm replaying a past memory.

I park a couple of trailers away, making sure to stay out of sight.

I check the rear view mirror where Moses sits in the backseat, waiting.

Each time he comes around, I notice, his appearance worsens.

I don't know what's going on with him, but I make sure to tell him how awful he looks.

I mean, awful—beyond awful.

He looks like shit—worse than shit.

And he smells, too, as if he just crawled out of a sewer after Cinco de Mayo.

As always, he shrugs off my concern.

Typical Moses.

Then, I do the one thing I hate.

IV

AFTER waiting around for another thirty minutes or so, I finally find my window and make my move. Fran downs the rest of his canned beer and propels out of the lounge chair. I creep inside his trailer, going straight to Ivory's case, which is settled on top of a shelf housing other strange objects, including two-headed frogs and a dead fetus with horns inside of a jar.

As I grab the case from the shelf, I suddenly hear the *flush* of a toilet. Fran is stepping from the bathroom when I bolt out the door.

"Hey," he shouts out, "get back here!"

Before he even has a chance to zip up, I'm already long gone.

V

I locate an abandoned parking lot behind a used car dealership not too far from the shore and burn all the magazines and smut material inside an oil drum full of fire.

I toss the photo of Jazz and Bishop into the fire and watch it blacken and curl until nothing is left but ash.

Lastly, I remove Ivory's head from the case and toss the head into the fire. Clouds of fiery ash shoot up from beneath the old and chewed up wooden scraps at the bottom of the oil drum and fly away through the smoky air like fireflies.

As the flames cut through the first layer of skin, I notice a tag behind Ivory's right ear. I peer closer at the tag and realize it's a barcode, *not* like a tattoo, but an actual barcode with a UPC code and everything. Part of the tag is ripped away.

This is the favor? Are you serious?

It's not until I look down at my callused hands that I realize they're shaking in rage. I ball both of them into tightly clenched fists.

I don't really think about it longer than I should.

Right now, I have other things to burn.

VI

WHEN I break into Yogi's house, he's stepping into the shower. I slip into the bedroom closet without Yogi knowing and do the one thing I hate. If there's one thing I'm good at—except for being a thief—it's waiting. So long, I've been waiting. Waiting for the right moment. Waiting to put all of this crap behind me. Waiting to move one. I'm done waiting.

Ten minutes expire, and I'm beginning to wonder if Yogi's ever going to get out of the shower or if he's going to spend the entire night in the shower, feeding the beast.

As I barely crack open the closet doors, I hear the *squeak* of a faucet!

Between the narrow crack, I witness Yogi stepping out of the steamy shower through the reflection in the mirror. He grabs a burgundy towel from the holder and dries himself off, starting with his hairiest spots. He stands in front of a foggy mirror for a while, checking his belly fat from the side, checking his size, and then applies deodorant and then cologne.

Once he's all done, he ambles into his messy bedroom and as he's slipping into a pair of blue boxers, I open the doors.

My Beretta Px4 Storm is already drawn. My hand is steady. My finger ready.

Yogi's eyes connect with mine; and for a moment, the irises in his eyes go black and swell and then the whites of his eyes go a little whiter. He flinches in a seizure-like pace. He only gets one leg through one of the holes in the boxers before he faces me. The boxers fall to his ankles and he stands there, butt naked. His eyes are opened freakishly wide now. Then, his entire body starts to tremble.

He doesn't say a single word.

Neither do I. Not at first.

I aim the barrel at Yogi's chest.

"Any last words," I say to him.

He stares at me with puppy dog eyes.

Still speechless.

I wait a few seconds and give him a chance to speak.

He says nothing.

I tighten my finger over the trigger. . .

As Yogi suddenly throws up his arms and screams the word *wait*, I blast him straight to hell!

I put two bullets in Yogi's chest. I finish him off with a bullet straight right between the eyes.

After I put down Yogi, I methodically dowse his bedroom, as well as his entire house, with gasoline.

I don't think about what I've just done.

No time to think.

T H E   D A Y • F

JUST as suspected, the two cops, Officer Malone and Rodriquez, are camped in a parking lot across the nightclub. Finally, after several tense moments, they respond to the residential fire off Whitlock Avenue—only a couple of blocks away.

Not wasting time, I do a thorough sweep of the nightclub and check my exits. I don't see Nico's Lambo around. I'm sure he's getting word by now about Yogi—and if he's not, all he has to do is take a step outside and smell the barbeque in the air.

I track down Darius, aka "Babyface," standing at the front of the entranceway while more commotion ensues in the Palace's parking lot, mostly people pointing in the direction of the fire, that initial scatterbrain of thoughts trying to figure out what in the hell is going on. I ignore the clubbers and march directly to Darius, the Beretta concealed underneath my sleeve.

I approach him, and I'm not the least scared or nervous. No time to think. Only time to react. He has his shaved bearlike arms folded across his chest and his bulgy lips display this smile only one can master after years of bouncing. He acknowledges me as I make my way closer, still wearing the same expression on his face, like he's been hitting the gym an extra two times a day this week and he's been looking forward to breaking my neck.

I keep the Beretta concealed until I'm a couple of feet away from him. He unfolds his arms like two clubs peeling from his chest and holds them down by his side, ape-like. His eyes never leave mine as he takes a step away from the line, then his mitt of a hand projects outward, motioning for me to stop or else.

I mimic Darius, only, instead of giving him the talk-to-the-hand gesture, I extend my arm outward and hold out my open palm. The Beretta suddenly shoots from the edge of my sleeve. I catch the grip of the handgun, push aside his arm with my left hand, and place the barrel directly to his chest.

I pull the trigger.

I'm so inside my head that I don't even hear the **KAAPOOW** of the gunshot.

Darius's eyes suddenly glow like tiny embers as an eddy of smoke slowly pours from his mouth. He falls to the ground with a hole in his chest, his glowing eyes fixated on me.

I shoot a glance at the clubbers next to me and some of them are screaming and sprinting away with their arms flailing around, while others are standing there, trembling with fear.

I remind myself that I don't have time for fear. A word such as *fear* doesn't exist in my vocabulary right now.

I direct my attention to another bouncer—*Zeek* is his name. As far as I'm aware, Zeek wasn't involved with the videos, like Darius, or even the shooting. He has a juvenile record but no priors. He was involved in a breaking and entering when he was thirteen, but that's it; however, he is a threat. And there's only one thing to do with a threat. And that's immobilizing it. Zeek comes charging at me. He's not armed. He only carries a fist. I aim for his kneecap and shoot. The knee explodes like a water balloon filled with blood. Zeek stumbles forward and grabs his knee, rolling around like a soccer player on the ground. Zeek's not a threat anymore, but he'll live.

The clubbers inside the nightclub are unaware of the gunshot from the witch house music blasting throughout the club. I shoulder my way through the crowd. Each guard positioned at their proper stations are touching their ears, listening. Then, I read their eyes, their subtle reactions from the recent news.

They rush from their posts to the front of the club; however, the two men guarding the stairs remain stoic and professional.

I remind myself that every bullet counts.

As I prowl across the dance floor, I spot both Flip and Drew in the corner of my eye. Both of them are dancing with a couple of girls, both unaware of my presence. This time Drew is wearing a different color on his cast: navy blue. The cast is larger as well, and runs up his elbow, unlike the other one I broke.

To my left, I spot a frosty guard frantically searching through the crowd!

They're onto me.

Trying not to draw a scene, a couple of other guards are escorting clubbers from the dance floor in a hasty, yet organized fashion, keeping the club from bottlenecking.

In a matter of seconds, the words *shots fired* and then *active shooter* swirl around the club and one by one each clubber follows one another toward the nearest exit. More frantic now, a soon-to-be stampede. Everybody is heading directly toward the front, and yet I'm moving in the opposite direction. The salmon swimming against the current.

One of the guards notices that I'm *not* moving in the correct direction. His eyes hone in on me. Mine hone in on him. He knows I'm looking at him, too, from the way red patches cloud over the top of his cheeks. His jaw drops a notch. He touches his ear. I read his lips.

Got 'em, he mouths.

As he approaches me through a rough sea of bodies, a hand grabs me by the shoulder.

I spin around. Flip. He looks rabid.

"Hey, motherfucka," he says. "You gotta lot of nerve coming here. . . "

He's spitting out all kinds of expletives my way. I keep my composure and turn to the guard, who's closing in on me. Flip grabs me yet again. I react by grabbing his fingers and bending back four of the five fingers on his hand, dislocating them. Flip retaliates by swinging at me. I dodge his wild Hail Mary punch and counter with a spit of a jab directly to his jugular, temporarily incapacitating him. I remind myself that every bullet counts as I feel the guard closing in; in fact, I can feel his presence, his breath, his everything.

I turn.

He's rearing back his right arm, as if he's about to do some real damage on me. . .

With my eyes, I follow a dark, lengthy object gripped tightly in his hand: a blackjack. He's a threat. So, I must immobilize the threat. Instead of bracing for impact and throwing up both of my arms in a shield, I do exactly what Moses trained me to do. I react by removing the butterfly knife from my belt before the guard makes contact with my shoulder and stab him in the forearm. The blackjack immediately falls from his grip.

In one fluid motion, I remove the blade from his forearm and twirl my body tornado-style over the slick dance floor; and while I'm spinning, I hold out my blade and splice him across his abdomen. That puts him down. He's not dead, but he's down for the count as he cradles his gut as if his hands are the only two things keeping his guts from spilling all over the dance floor.

As I remain in my kneeled stance, I spot yet the other guard pushing frantic bodies away. I catch him reaching for an object underneath his armpit. Showtime. He removes a gun from underneath his blazer. I take aim. My vision narrows.

Once I'm in the clear, I fire a shot through the gap of bodies and hit the guard in the shoulder. He falls. However, he's not the only person who falls.

A once even-tempered crowd now turns into a flat out stampede toward the exits after the *ring* of the gunshot. People are pushing other people aside; people are falling, tripping, clawing, kicking, smothering. It's an all-out grudge match. Once mellow clubbers humping one another, now these skittish, almost vermin-like creatures following their most basis instincts, which is survival.

I manage to clear from the frenzied crowd, and I seek out the two guards at the bottom of the staircase. They're both heavily armed with automatics and ready to shoot. I blast both of them away before they can get a shot off. I remove the magazine and reload the Beretta as I make my way up the stairs.

Once I arrive at the second floor, I check the monitors in the surveillance room first. A majority of the club has been cleared out, except for a few stragglers.

The door *squeaks* close from behind. . .

Before I can turn, I'm jolted to the side from a pain rushing through my shoulder. I take a couple of steps back, then reach around and find a ghost of a blade in my back. I follow the glowing eyes behind the blade. Argento. He rears back his arm, which gives me a window to attack. I take aim, but he knocks the Beretta loose from the contraption before I can pull the trigger. The Beretta bounces along the floor until it comes to rest near the leg of a coffee table. He swipes at me, but I suck in my stomach and dodge the teeth of the blade; however, the blade manages to catch part of my shirt, now exposing a sliver of my flesh. He dances around me, blade still in hand, as if he's taunting me to make a move. And he's snarling at me, too, like a dog. His eyes are as mad and revealing as the moonlit night, ravenous for O Negative. He lunges at me, yet again, but I evade the blade and reach for my gun; but he kicks it across the floor. In return, I lower my shoulder and spear Argento into a glass coffee table. The table shatters, shards of pebble-sized glass scrapes along my face and hands. I don't feel any pain, though. The only thing that's singing right now is survival. Argento strikes once more while I'm on top of him, but I evade the blade a second time. I squeeze in a couple of blows to his face before I'm kicked backwards.

I regain my balance as Argento springs to his feet, and we're back to round two.

Knife versus Knife.

I remove the revolver from my belt and let him know that I mean business by showing it to him before I toss it aside. Killing him would be so easy, just point, aim, and pull, then move onto the next one. Right now, I know it's more than survival. This is all for bragging rights. Instead, I draw the butterfly knife and hold it close to me. He dances around me again, tango-style as he's occasionally waving around the blade. He doesn't come close to hitting me. I think it's—more or less—another one of his taunts. He makes one more attempt at cutting me, but I slip around him and cut him along the upper abdomen; however, he doesn't seem the least phased by the cut. I cut him several more times; then he cuts me once along the arm. Nothing life threatening, though. We strike one another at the same time, both of our blades colliding. The butterfly knife suddenly slips from my grip, leaving me weaponless and now vulnerable. He strikes yet again, as if the roles have reversed now and all he cares about is survival. I grab his wrist—the same hand holding the blade—and tug on his arm as if I'm pulling a root from the earth. I pull hard, too, as if the root is in there good. His hand runs underneath my armpit, the blade missing my ribs by inches. I grab his fingers, like I did with Flip; but this time I get my entire hand around three of his fingers and pull back until I hear things *crack* and break. He screams out and releases the blade from his hand, forcing the knife to the floor.

As Flip did with me, Argento retaliates by swinging at me.

As I did with Flip, I dodge the blow. This time I don't return with a punch. Instead, he staggers into my arms and I bite him on the neck like a vampire. A switch is released inside me, and everything about me is violent and vicious. My teeth sink into his flesh, then my jaw clamps down, shaking like some kind of famished predator. I keep sawing away until my teeth pierce through his skin; then, once that familiar yet forgettable metallic taste oozes over my tongue, I pull my mouth away and rip out a chunk of flesh and spit it in his face.

Argento jerks his head away and I come at him again; then he dodges. I come at him again and bite him in the ear. I chew off cartilage as well as soft tissue around the outer ear. I spit it at him once more, cartilage and all, tissue and all, blood and all, letting him know who's the predator and who's the prey. I feel cruel and deadly, nocturnal.

In one swift reaction, he charges at me and slams me to the floor!

The impact momentarily knocks the wind out of me, and before I can catch my breath, I turn my eyes upward and see him striking down at me.

I roll out of the way before he can land a blow and crawl to the Beretta near the foot of the couch.

As I finger the grip, an object passes the corner of my eye, then *crunch*. . . That's the sound of my fingers breaking from the butt of a fire extinguisher crushing my left hand. I've broken something—the extent of the break is uncertain, but it sounds really bad.

I remove my hand before he can crush it a second time. He's now on top of me, pounding on me.

I *retract* the contraption on my right wrist.

With my right hand, I manage to grab him by the collar—the blood from the bite mark dripping all over my head. I extend my wrist backward and release the empty track from my wrist. The track penetrates his throat, causing him to jerk away. He's bleeding now, profusely, from his neck. I've

439

struck an important vein. Panic washes over his face as he backpedals and tries to find something to cover the wound, but the blood keeps coming.

Eventually, he trips and falls to the floor from the substantial loss of blood. His eyes are swimming around in his head, trying to focus on something tangible.

I stand to my feet and collect my weapons, including the revolver from the floor while nursing my left hand.

My whole hand feels as if it's broken from the pain radiating from my fingers down to my wrist; and a couple of fingers appear out of place, mainly my middle and ring finger.

I holster the butterfly knife, slide the Beretta back into the contraption, and aim the barrel at the dying man on the floor.

Argento looks at me as I loom over him. He looks at me and his eyes are begging me to pull the trigger.

Just begging.

I think about putting him out of his sweet misery.

Like every thought, they come and go.

\|\|

THE door to Bishop's office is closed. I check the room. No sign of Bishop or Jazz.

Before I check out the yellow room, I go over all of my injuries: first, my wrist and then my hand. My fingers are as crooked as an arthritic hand.

With my other hand, I run my fingers over my left shoulder blade and remove a handful of blood.

I remind myself it's only a flesh wound.

I ignore the pain and remember why I came here.

I turn to the very last room at the end of the hallway. There's a light on inside; however, the door is closed.

I have an idea of what may be going on inside.

So, I prepare myself.

\|\|\|

\| cautiously enter the yellow room with my gun already drawn.

I peel back the curtain and witness what looks like a crime scene.

Chaos everywhere.

On the floor: an overturned tripod with a camcorder. Pieces of debris from the camcorder are scattered over the floor as well.

I survey more damage to the room: a round hole in the shape of a head in the wall; an overturned couch; a can of Mace on the floor; the mace randomly sprayed all over the floor as well as the wall. I find an earring on the floor. It's the same earring that I bought Jazz at Lassie's. However, Jazz is not here, nor is Bishop. I can smell the two of them in the air, the perfume, the sweat, the chaos.

They were just here.

There was a struggle, and someone was badly hurt.

Suddenly, I hear the curtain opening behind me. I turn and aim. . .

"Dwight?" I say, as my finger nearly squeezes the trigger.

I lower my gun.

Dwight eases into the room, and he's confused.

"What are you doing here?" I ask him.

"I came here to take you in, Robert," he says, looking around at all of the mess.

I ignore Dwight and try to find something that will point me in the direction of Bishop. I pick up the camcorder. Part of the display screen on the side is cracked; however, it still works. I rewind the video, first witnessing the colorful, chaotic scramble on the screen as the camcorder hits the floor and then part of the struggle between Jazz and Bishop. I rewind just moments leading up to the fight. Bishop rushes into the yellow room, telling Jazz that her "boyfriend" is here— *boyfriend*, as in I believe he means me. Jazz is asking Bishop, pleading with Bishop to leave "him" alone, then says that "he" did nothing wrong; then Bishop strikes Jazz across the face with the back of his hand, telling her to shut her mouth. He starts pacing around, looking for something, he's frustrated; then Jazz brandishes a can of Mace from her purse and as she's about to spray Bishop in the face, Bishop grabs Jazz by the neck and violently throws her toward the camcorder, causing it to fall over on the floor. In the staticky blackness, I hear the sound of a struggle, Jazz screaming, a couple of *thuds*, then footsteps trailing farther and farther away.

"We must leave, Robert," Dwight urges from behind.

He knows not to touch me, but he gets close enough to warrant my attention.

"I know where she's going."

"Who?"

"Her name's Jazz," I tell Dwight. "She's in danger."

I make my way to the hallway, Dwight hounding me.

"Robert," he says, "this has gone far enough—"

"—Are you going to try to stop me?"

I turn around and get in Dwight's face.

"If so," I pull out the revolver from my belt, "then go ahead and get it over with. Otherwise, stay out of my way."

Dwight grabs the revolver and looks it over.

"After you," he says finally.

I lead the way, and Dwight follows.

IV

WHEN we reach the first floor, the club has been cleared out—a couple of guards slide like snails toward the main entranceway, gripping their wounds while they leave serpentine-like trails of blood along the dance floor. The smell of gunpowder is potent in the air and a cloud of mist cast from a fog machine next to the DJ's booth lingers above like halos. Next to the bar, the remains of an ice sculpture of a dragon lay all over the floor from where it had toppled over from the stampede. The music is still playing as well, which keeps me more alert.

I look for exits—the kitchen doors, I see, slowly moving back and forth.

I point to the kitchen and tell Dwight to go ahead without me and I'll meet him outside.

"What are you gonna do?" he asks.

"I need to take care of something," I say. Then, I turn to the one door across the club, the one that's always heavily guarded, *the red door*.

"Robert," Dwight says, "cops will be here any second. . . "

I walk toward the red door.

Dwight's still barking in my ear, urging me to leave.

I check the door, and it's locked. I shoot off the lock. Then, I kick open the door with my foot. Rows and rows of tables are lined in the center of the room. Along the walls: stacks of cardboard boxes.

"What is it?" Dwight asks.

"It's nothing."

"What'd you expect?"

I walk over to the table and find powdery residue along the surface.

I run my finger across the table and hold my finger to my lips and take a taste.

Cocaine.

A couple of tables have the same powdery residue along the surface. I can visualize the white mounds of cocaine once piled like tiny mountains on these tables. An entire range of cocaine. All this time, it was there underneath my nose. That's what all of this was about Bishop's business he was nothing more than a drug dealer. I rush to the boxes, carefully remove each box from the stack, and place them on the floor.

One side of the boxes reads: *the* PleasureSaber™.

I open one of the boxes and pull out one of Nico's sex toys and proceed to dissemble it.

"Hold it right there!" Dwight cries out from behind.

I turn around and Dwight has his aim on Nico.

I drop the sex toy.

Nico is aiming a Glock at me.

"Put the gun down," Dwight warns Nico.

Nico ignores Dwight and examines my current state, my left hand especially, and follows with a question: "Where's Bishop?"

I keep my eyes close to the Glock.

Nico steps inside the red room.

"Don't take another step," Dwight says, ready to shoot.

"Relax, Dwight," I say. "He's with me—"

"—The hell I am!" Nico shouts. "Where is he?" he asks once more, but this time more heatedly.

"He took Jazz," I say as I take a step away from the boxes.

Nico keeps the Glock on me.

"You're not going anywhere, you piece of shit," he says, his voice trembling.

Dwight's ready to pull. I tell him to stand down.

I keep the Beretta tucked away as I take another step closer to Nico.

"You're not going to shoot me, Nico. . . "

"Oh yeah!" Nico cries out. "Why the hell not?"

"I know it was you who came back for Foster," I say, stepping closer.

The comment causes his aim to sag, the barrel now pointed at my belly.

I ease closer to Nico until I'm standing face to face with him. He repositions the aim. I'm now staring down the barrel of the Glock.

Nico's face drifts out of focus, like a steamy-mirror reflection.

All I see is black, a tiny black hole peering directly through me.

"You don't know the half of it," he says, his voice is muddy again.

"Maybe not, but I know you." I refocus on Nico. "This isn't who you are. . . "

"You don't know a thing about me—"

"—I know you're not a killer like your father," I say patiently. "You're better than this, Nico. . . "

I hear distant police sirens coming from outside the Palace!

"Robert," Dwight says, "we have to leave now!"

Nico's eyes swell with tears. He doesn't budge an inch as I slip past him.

"Robert!"

I turn to the sound of Nico's voice and I know that he wants to tell me something, but for some reason, he acts as if his words are hard to speak, and we're having this Spaghetti Western stare off. I already know what he's going to say. I decide to leave the words with him. Maybe one day he'll write them down. Maybe one day he'll find the gall to speak them. For now, I leave Nico behind.

Dwight and I rush into the kitchen and head straight to the back door. My eyes come across a gas line.

I frantically move through the kitchen, first grabbing a bottle of Lord® Vodka from the top shelf, then dowsing a rag with the vodka, then stuffing the rag into the half full bottle of liquor.

"Robert. . . " Dwight says, ". . . let's go! Now!"

"Hold on," I tell him.

I place the bottle over the stovetop burner, turn the knob to the highest setting, and light the rag on fire with a torch. Right before we leave, I yank the gas line from the wall and exit through the back door.

While we make our way through the parking lot, the nightclub suddenly erupts in a ball of flames behind me. I admire the flames rising above, but only for a while. Right now, we're pressed for time.

Dwight grabs me by the arm.
He tells me that we have to leave.
A squad of cruisers appears in the corner of my eye.
More chaos coming.
So, Dwight and I leave just in the nick of time.
I tell him to follow me.
"Keep up," I tell him.
Then, we're out.

THE VIDEEOH

ALONG the way to Bishop's, I ride past a fleet of fire trucks and cruisers. I keep my head down and make sure to keep my speed under the limit until I find myself riding on an open road.

It doesn't take me long to reach Bishop's house. I park at a safe distance, Dwight not too far behind. I call Jazz three times, but she's not picking up. Each call goes straight to her voicemail, which isn't a good sign.

Before we move any further, Dwight's itching to know more information on this "girl." First, I ask him he if gave the envelope to Ruby, as I told him to do. He tells me that he did and he's probably at the hotel now as we speak, which means he's gone through the package and now, he's pretty much caught up with everything that's going on, except for the Jazz part.

As we sneak through the backyard, I inform Dwight only on a brief summary of Jazz, how we met, how she's an artist, how I got close to her, then how she got involved with the wrong people. That's all Dwight needs to know, for now at least.

I check the windows in the back of the house before I go any further. I don't see any action inside Bishop's house, at least none that would suggest that Jazz is in immediate danger. Every light appears as if it's turned on; however, I don't see any sign of Bishop or Jazz. The only sign of life, I see, comes from a tame fire burning in Bishop's fancy fireplace.

I turn to Dwight and ask him if he's ready to do this and he's staring at my left hand.

"How's the hand?" he asks.

I look down at my hand and I don't even realize how bad it is until I look it over.

"It's nothing," I lie.

"So," Dwight says over a heavy sigh, "what do you think?"

"She's here," I tell Dwight. "I know it."

"How sure are you?"

"She's here," I repeat.

That's all I give him. That's all he needs to hear.

"Well," he says, "what are you waiting for?"

We make our move.

Halfway toward the house, I get that stabbing sensation again in my gut, like something bad has happened or something bad is about to happen.

A knife in the gut.

Constantly twisting.

I put all of the doubts to bed by focusing on Jazz, reminding myself that she's safe and secure, and that if Bishop is keeping her against her will, then I will do whatever is necessary to make sure he doesn't harm her anymore.

I sneak inside the house via the back door. It's dead quiet inside. Eerily quiet.

I withdraw the gun from the contraption and make my way through the house while Dwight checks my sides for any creepers. I'm not aware of any other henchmen, except for his right-hand man, Argento, who's currently being raped and torn apart by demons. Nonetheless, I keep my guard up.

We make our way upstairs to the master bedroom at the end of the hallway. I'm the first to enter, then Dwight.

Handprints of blood are smeared over the shag carpet. I follow the trail of blood to a naked body lying on the floor closest to the bathroom—*Bishop!*

The left side of Bishop's face, primarily his left cheek and eye socket, is caved in from an apparent bludgeoning. He has deep stab wounds along the upper abdomen, as well as the chest area. Whatever went down here, he went out swinging.

While Dwight keeps lookout, I inspect the room some more. Beside the king-sized bed, which is draped with silk sheets, are sharp knife-like fragments from what looks like a broken glass clock. Blood is everywhere, pooled underneath Bishop's body, sprayed over the bed, as well as the walls, long smears of it pulling away from the nightstand. Blood is even frothy and bubbles from the corners of Bishop's mouth, as if whatever went down here happened not too long ago and he still hasn't completely bled out yet.

"Is he dead?" Dwight asks over my shoulder.

I check Bishop's neck for a pulse. I get nothing.

The cause of his death seems pretty obvious according to his wounds. He either died from the blow to his head or he simply died from the loss of blood.

"Yeah," I tell Dwight. "Dead."

Dwight finds a phone lying on the floor.

"Got something," he says, picking up the phone. "Hers?"

He hands me the phone. It belongs to Jazz.

I type in her password and open her phone.

I read her last chirp.

The chirp reads:

> "BUT EVIL THINGS, IN ROBES OF SORROW,
> ASSAILED THE MONARCH'S HIGH ESTATE."

The verse, I realize, is from Poe's poem, *The Haunted Palace*. Why would she write something like that? I try not to think too much about the chirp. After all, it's only a chirp.

I close the Chatterz app and pull up Jazz's photos. I find a recent selfie taken moments before Bishop picked her up. She's posing in front of a bathroom mirror. Her lips pink and glossy. Her cheeks hollow like a fragrance model. Eyelids heavy with seduction. She's extending out one side of her hips, her hand pressed against the curve of her bottom. I wonder what Jazz's thinking at the time she took the photo besides how incredibly sexy she looks right now. I wonder if she's thinking about me. I scroll through other photos of Jazz, mostly selfies, until I come across a photo of Jazz posing with Moses. What the hell is he doing with her? Her arm is wrapped around his waist. They're both standing outside the gaudy Knight's Bay, both of their eyes bloodshot, both smiling like two Cheshire cats. I scroll through more photos of Jazz and Moses taken at Las Paraíso, photos of them gambling, photos of them hanging around wax sculptures inside a wax museum, a photo of Jazz kissing a waxed sculpture of the famous rock star, Henry the Fif', photos of them strutting down the main drag. In one photo, they're locking lips in front of the Eiffel Tower, *not* the real one but the one in Las Paraíso, the one next to Planet Bollywood. Then, I scroll through more photos: Moses, who's one-less clothing material from being naked, is stretched out on Jazz's bed in her apartment bedroom, her cat, Bob, lying in the crook of his arm, while Jazz's is resting her head over his left pectoral; Moses eating dinner with Jazz at the Cove; Moses washing Jazz's Corolla; Moses playing Frisbee with Jazz on Topside Beach; Moses dancing with Jazz at the Labara Lounge. There's even a photo of Jazz posing for the camera in front of a shark tank. Behind Jazz: a vague reflection of a face in the glass. I peer closer at the reflection, the face.

Before I can make out the face, I'm startled by what sounds like something dropping onto the bathroom floor!

The door is closed, but the light is on. I check the bathroom with the Beretta drawn. I crack open the door. Slowly. Jazz is sitting against the far wall and staring at the bloody tile floor as if she's caught in a trance that she can't escape. Her naked body is curled into a ball and covered with blood, but I don't see any wounds on her body. I assume the blood is from Bishop.

Next to her bare feet lay a shard of glass, possibly the weapon used to kill Bishop.

I rush over to Jazz.

"Are you hurt?" I ask her.

She doesn't answer at first.

The only wound I can find is the one on top of her forehead. It's not deep enough for stitches, but it's noticeable enough to draw attention.

"Jazz. . . " I say closer.

She mechanically rotates her head upward at me. Her eyes look almost empty, like the eyes of an android.

"She's in shock, Robert," Dwight says from the doorway.

I holster the gun, grab a clean white towel from the holder, and wrap the towel around Jazz's shoulders.

"It's okay," I tell her. "We're here now. Everything's going to be okay."

Jazz suddenly snaps from the trance. Her jaw trembles first, then her body starts to tremble like some kind of stray orphan child sitting outside in the cold rain. She lifts her head from my arms and stares at me, her eyes occasionally flicking toward the dead body. Her eyes are jacked open, as if she's been drugged. I look closer at her puffy face and realize, over a thorough study, she hasn't been drugged or whatever. She's frightened of me.

And she's shaking and trying to explain herself, but each one of her words are disjointed and hard to comprehend. I tell her that she's going to be okay.

"*We're* going to be okay," I emphasize.

She stops shaking. She stops talking, and for a moment, it appears as if she stops breathing as her eyes still on mine. For a moment, we're no longer sitting in Bishop's bathroom. Instead, we're standing in front of one of the many computers inside Cyber Jaxx's and we're both watching a video of Lynda Lynx getting raped by a man wearing a black mask.

I peer farther into her murky eyes and she searches deeper into mine.

For a moment, she knows how I found her and it's like all of the terrible acts that had taken place at Crystal Palace are laced upon my eyes like double knotted shoelaces.

For the life of me, I'll never be able to loosen that knot ever again. The knot will always be there, worn tight over both of my eyes, over my bones, over whatever soul I have left.

I hold her close as she finally breaks down and cries. There's nothing I can say or do to erase the awful memory. All I can do is hold her close to me and tell her that everything is going to be okay, even though I know it's not.

\\

\ wait until the water is warm before I let Jazz into the shower. She steps inside as if she's stepping onto ice. She struggles to look me in the eye, and I can't help but wonder if, by her being somewhat intimidated from my presence, it has anything to do with Dwight calling me by my real name or Bishop talking about me to her, as if he knows everything about me. I mean, Jazz has to know who I am, why I'm here, what I plan on doing while I'm here. I get the sense that Bishop has told her everything about me.

I don't even realize how closely I've been watching Jazz until Dwight taps me on the shoulder and pulls me aside and tells me that I need to give her some space. He's right. I've been keeping a close eye on Jazz. I'm just concerned for her. That's all.

While she's in the shower, I grab a couple of things around Bishop's kitchen, including the cotton from a vitamin bottle and a Popsicle from the freezer, to make myself a splint.

I snoop around the house some more. I assume that we have maybe an hour or two before the story catches cold.

While Dwight checks the TV, flipping through both the local and major news channels, I pass a home theatre room. I check Bishop's video collection, mostly porn.

Next, I check out Bishop's office, the next room over. Snoop around some more. I check his cluttered desk, each drawer. I come across some tape to finish my splint. I finish the Popsicle and then lay out the things I need to make the splint: two Popsicle sticks, cotton, and tape.

But first, I have to align the bones in my fingers.

(I read somewhere in the magazine *Med-USA* that adrenaline is added to a number of local anesthetics)

Amazing that we have all of these things already built inside us, like these types of hormones and chemicals, how the human body releases these types of natural responses when faced with peril, even worse, death.

So, I count to three, clinging onto the last bit of adrenaline.

Before I reach three, I snap my fingers in place. I nearly pass out from the pain. I ignore the pain on my left side, even when it wears over me like a heavy coat, by concentrating on the sea. I finish making the splint, and it's a success.

As I'm about to leave the office, my eyes come across something familiar inside one of the drawers.

What are the odds?

Inside the open drawer below is the same DVD from his collection at the Palace. I find a TV with a DVD player and insert the DVD.

I shouldn't be watching the video. I shouldn't even be going near the video, especially with Jazz in the vicinity.

But what was so important on this video for Nico or Bishop to break into my hotel room that one night?

I have to know.

I play the video.

Jazz appears on a bed in some seedy hotel room. She's playing with herself in front of the video. I notice that she appears a couple of years younger, around the same age when the photo of her and Bishop was taken. A middle-aged man— maybe around his fifties or so—enters the frame. I haven't seen the man before. He's wearing next to nothing, only a pair of oversize boxers you'd find at medical emporium. He's out of shape, too, and balding, and he's proudly carrying the belly of a woman on her third trimester. I fast-forward the video until something happens—something bad.

I rewind the video.

The man, now boxerless, starts to strangle Jazz. She's pleading for him to stop, but he continues to strangle her until she's blue in the face. She reaches for something to grab. She finds a beer bottle nearby and suddenly strikes him across the face-neck region. The bottle shatters in half, the jagged neck of the bottle still remains gripped in Jazz's hand. The man shakes off the blow to his head; and then, out of rage, he leaps at Jazz and lands neck-first on the jagged glass. Part of the glass cuts the man's throat. He suddenly jerks backward, grabbing his neck. He's squirming all over the bed. Panicked. Jazz tries to stop the bleeding, but he bleeds out against the wall and the whole time he's staring at Jazz as if he wants Jazz to watch him die, as if by her watching him die is just as bad, even worse, than retaliation.

"What the fuck are you watching?" Dwight says from behind.

My heart skips a beat. Then, I settle down. He steps into the room and watches the rest of the video, Jazz scrambling around the room with her hands cupped over her mouth in sheer horror. Not really helping out the dying man.

I don't have any words. I, too, am left in shock.

"Is that your girl?" Dwight asks.

"Yeah," I say.

"How many other men has this girl killed, Robert?" he asks with concern in his voice. "What the hell have you gotten yourself into? Is she worth going to prison for the rest of your life?"

I stop the DVD.

As I remove it from the player, I notice Jazz is standing in the hallway outside. She's all clean and dressed and her body remains absolutely still, as if it's on pause. She, too, doesn't have any words as she stares at me with this kind of sadness riddled in her eyes. Then, she walks away.

I follow her outside onto the deck outside.

"Do you wanna talk?"

"What is there to say?" she asks, her voice is fragile.

"It was clearly an accident," I tell her. "You were just trying to protect yourself."

Jazz is shaking her head, and she's disgusted by everything.

"Who was he, the man in the video?"

"Just some guy."

"Just some guy?" I repeat. "You mean a 'client.'"

"He said he would take care of me."

"Who?" I say. "Bishop?"

She nods and acts as if she's about to break down again.

"Who else knows about this?"

I show her the DVD in my hand.

"Just Bishop," she says. "Now you and that other guy."

"His name's Dwight," I tell her. "He's a friend."

"Can you trust him?"

"Of course, I can trust him."

"Just asking—"

"—Why was Bishop holding onto this video?"

She doesn't answer.

"I need to know, Jazz—"

"Control," she says finally. "He was gonna go to the authorities, but he didn't. He *used* me. He's been using me. All this time."

"Using you how?"

I get that creeping sensation again, like the one before, telling me that Jazz and I didn't meet out of coincidence or random luck.

"If I told you about me," she says, "you wouldn't have anything to do with me." Then, she squares herself to me and looks directly at me. "Just like if you told me who you are, I wouldn't have anything to do with you."

She knows. She's caught me in the lie. Bishop has told her everything about me. What else did he make her do?

"I don't care who you *were* or what you *did*," she says, struggling to look at me in the eyes. "I know you're not that person anymore. Right? Robert?"

"Right," I say, as Jazz walks over.

She gives me a hug and she tells me that she's sorry for what happened to my brother.

I tell her that I came back here, meaning Topside, because I thought it would help me move on with my life.

I hand Jazz the DVD.

"Now, you have a choice," I tell her.

She looks over the DVD.

Dwight opens the sliding door.

"We have to go," he says. "Story just broke. It's only a matter of time before cops show up."

Behind Dwight, a TV shows a camera crew at Crystal Palace. I walk back inside the house and watch the news. The story has broken over every local news channel, as well as social media.

I get on Bishop's computer and check MyCircle, Photo-Bag, and the Tube. Sure enough, a video, which was filmed by a smartphone, has been posted just minutes ago. I have officially gone viral. The video has already received over forty-four thousand views and counting. I watch the video. The camera steadily pans to the front of the nightclub. Who-ever filmed the video did a decent job at capturing the shot. Then, I enter the frame, stalking through the concrete jungle. The clip shows a side angle of me blasting away the bouncer, Darius. A *boom* crackles through the video! Then, a torrent of shrieks rips through the smoky night air. The video goes shaky and noisy for a moment before pixelating into a fuzzy, muted blackness.

Finally, I check Chatterz. I swear it's like East Providence all over again, the pecking order (blue arrows next to their names, indicating a symbol of approval, as if the Internet has a team of up-to-minute kids somewhere deciding who gets blue arrows), another popularity contest—*Who's currently trending? Who has the most rechirps?*

Now, instead of people saying shit to your face or spreading rumors behind your back, the bullying, all of the name-calling, it's all done by an army of angry fingers. I'm officially trending.

They've already branded me with hashtags:

#MANINBLACK

Another one:

#SHOOTERONTHELOOSE

Another:

#TAKEAWAYTHEGUNS

I read through some of the asinine remarks on Chatterz, kids from all over the world making comments about how sick, how disturbed, how *crazy* I am, as if they know me personally.

The Chatterz kids have even gone so far as to create a brand new hashtag from the already existing club shooter hashtags.

#MENTALHEALTHCRISIS

It's official.
I've been reduced to a hashtag.
Reduced to nothing.
Ones and zeros.
Dwight calls me back over to the TV.
On the TV, I witness what appears to be Moses. He's wearing the same clothes as me. His face is blurry and grainy, but I'm pretty sure it's him. If it is Moses, what the hell was he doing at Grand Valley Estates? The news is airing footage that was taken from a surveillance camera inside the retirement home. Moses, or whoever that is, is storming through a hallway. Then, he turns to the camera in the corner of the hallway. The frame suddenly stills on the unknown man, and then zooms in on his face; however, the face is still blurry and unrecognizable. The anchor is talking about a suspect last seen minutes before Valentine West was "found dead" inside his Grand Valley suite and "if you've seen this man," the anchor says to the people watching, "please contact authorities immediately. He is considered to be armed and very dangerous."

I ignore the strange face on the TV, ignore the TV in general, and face Dwight.

"You don't have to be here anymore," I tell him. "You have done enough."

"I can get you across the border, but that's as far as I go."

Jazz asks, "How about his place?"

"There were surveillance cameras all over Crystal Palace," I tell Jazz when, in fact, I'm indirectly telling Dwight, my way of letting him know that he's just as involved in this thing as me. "I'm sure they have your face on camera."

"What about Bishop?" Dwight asks. "We can't just leave him in there. Our prints are all over this place—"

Suddenly, a *chime* rings throughout the house!

All three of us freeze.

I walk back to the bedroom and find the source of the noise. I search through the blood and chaos. Bishop's clothes. I pull a smartphone from the pocket of his pants, which are laid out in the floor. Dwight tells me not to answer it. I answer it.

I hear Ayker's voice on the other end.

"Where is he?" he asks me.

"Bishop is currently dead at the moment," I tell Ayker. "Can I leave a message?"

"You think this is a game, Mr. Backer?"

"What do you want?"

"Put Luther on the phone."

"I told you," I say. "He's dead."

"Dwight Arlington wouldn't be with you by any chance—"

I turn to Dwight.

Finally, I listen to Dwight and hang up the phone.

"We gotta go," I tell them.

"Who was that?"

"Ayker," I tell him.

I think about the next move. It's easy. Burn the place down. Burn the prints.

I turn to Dwight and ask him, "How much gas do you have in your car?"

"About a half-tank," he says. "Why?"

\\\

WE end up siphoning the gas from Bishop's SUV, as well a vintage Mustang into a gas can.

Jazz tosses the DVD into the fireplace and watches it burn.

"The phone," I tell her. "Throw it in. . . "

456

She looks at me as if I'm as crazy as the Internet says I am.

"They can track us," I tell her.

She turns to the fire. Throws in her phone.

As Jazz watches her sole possessions burn in the fireplace, I dowse the inside of the house with gasoline. I unplug the gas line from the stove and set the trail of gasoline on fire.

Then, we leave.

Jazz rides with Dwight while I ride behind them.

IV

WE make it out of Los Dementes County without getting spotted by any cops. We ride along the Pacific Coast. The traffic is quiet.

I hear a sudden *rev* of an engine behind me!

I turn my shoulder, only to see this black figure looming behind me. I take another look, closer. A SUV without any headlights rams the back wheel of my bike. I'm out of control, zigzagging all over the road. The SUV rams me again, forcing me off the road. I lose complete control over the bike. I crash into a ditch and watch another SUV force Dwight off the two-lane road as well.

Before I have a chance to get back on my bike, a gun is being pointed at my face.

A *thud*.

Then, an electric charge of blood runs through the back of my head.

I feel the coldness slide over me.

Then, you know what happens next.

EPISODE 11

RUBICON

4 R O M   T H 3   6 R A V 3
(R 3 D U X)

CHAINS clink together in darkness.

Blood suddenly rushes to my head, awaking the various spots of pain scattered around my body. My damaged fingers feel as if they're about to form their own fingers, and the stab wound in my shoulder feels incredibly heavy, as if the wound itself is carrying a weight.

I open my eyes, completely. I'm hanging upside down by a rusty chain wrapped around my ankles. I follow the other end of the chain, realizing all of my clothes have been stripped from my body and to make matters worse, the splint has been ripped off my hand and all of the blood is causing my fingers to swell. I lift my weighty arms to my chest, trying my best to release some of the blood from my fingers before they grow into new fingers, but my wrists are tied together with zip ties, and it's not helping ease any of the pain.

I pinpoint the other end of the chain, knotted over a warped rafter above in the blue haze.

The moonlight shines through a couple of perforations in the roof of what looks like an abandoned warehouse, maybe an old factory—I can't tell which—and cast better light over the rafters, which eventually become more clear and visible.

I can't look too long because random dizzy spells force me to pull my eyes away.

And when I come back down, I find myself back in the heavy world where the pain is like a new entity attached to my body. I scan my body for any more injuries without trying not to overexert myself. I don't find any.

Then, I do that thing I do, replaying my thoughts, wondering how I ended up here. I don't know. I crashed. I blacked out. I woke upside down. I try to think of the people responsible for me hanging upside down: either a drug cartel or the cops. This place seems too clean for cops, but I could be wrong.

Suddenly, I hear a grunt over my shoulder.

I turn, causing my body to sway a bit.

Dwight's hanging upside down, as well. And he's starting to wake.

Droplets of blood are dripping from Dwight's forehead and splashing over a forming puddle of blood below Dwight, who's naked as well. He slowly regains consciousnesses. He looks my way; his eyes are wide and bloodshot. The left side of his face swollen with blood.

"What the fuck happened?" he asks.

"I think we were rammed off the road or something."

"All I can remember," he says, breath labored, "some asshole flashing his lights, then I lost control of the car."

"Where's Jazz?"

"Don't know."

"Did they take her?"

"Can't remember," Dwight says, squirming in mid-air. "She was banged up pretty good."

I look around the room for any exits. I don't find any. Only a dusty, gutted room with dark corridors on either side. I think I see some windows, but they're partially broken and boarded with weathered plywood.

"We have to get outta here," Dwight says, attempting to bend the upper part of his body upright. His head only gets to about mid-torso before he decides to give up.

"I've been meaning to ask you, Dwight," I say. "How's Thomas doing?"

"We're about to be gutted like pigs and you want to ask me how your father's doing?"

Something comes over me, and I start laughing. Maybe it's the sight of Dwight squirming around like some kind of bait on a fisherman's hook. Maybe it's the sound of his voice and how much I miss it. Maybe I'm just glad to be with a friend. Even if we're about to be gutted like pigs, Dwight is the one man who I want by my side.

"Tell me, Dwight," I say seriously. "How is he?"

Dwight stops squirming.

"He was upset," he says.

"Of course, he was upset," I say. "His son just escaped from a loony bin."

Dwight gets serious as well.

"Just curious, Robert," he says. "Why they do it?"

"Do what?"

"Why they admit you?"

"I honestly don't know," I tell Dwight. "Maybe because I was out of control. I was going in circles. I always told them that I was going to change, but—" a sudden wash of pain rips through my body and causes me to flex every muscle in my body, "—but it never happened. It was just all talk."

"You have changed, Robert," he says, looking at me. "You might not think so, but you have. I see it in your eyes."

"How about you?"

"What about me?"

"How've you been?"

"To tell you the truth, Robert," Dwight says, "this has probably been the most action I've seen in the past twelve years."

"Twelve years? What the hell you talking about?" I say with a strange sensation building inside my gut. "You're telling me all that time we spent trying to hunt down these scumbags didn't mean anything to you?"

"Of course, it did, Robert," he says, chuckling. "Think that blow to your head gave you amnesia—"

Jazz suddenly screams from a distance!

Then, I hear the *squeak* of a door, then a *thud*, then footsteps closing in. Lots of them.

I hear two men talking.

He's late, one of them says.

Another: *Wait outside for him. I'll handle these two.*

"Showtime," I whisper to Dwight.

"Got any ideas?"

"None," I say. "You?"

"What if we start swinging back and forth?" Dwight suggests. "Maybe we can loosen the chain. . . "

"Save your strength," I tell him.

"You giving up that easily?"

"The fat lady didn't sing just yet."

"You can't talk your way out this one, Robert."

I hear a resonant voice cutting through the darkness.

"Your friend's right," Ayker says, approaching us. "You can't talk your way out of this one, Mr. Backer."

Two of Ayker's bodyguards—the two stooges I saw on TV—surface before the devil himself shows his face.

"How's it hanging, fellas?" Ayker says amusingly.

I ask him, "What did you do with Jazz?"

"Clearly, you're not in the position to be asking any questions, Robert."

"Where is she?"

"She's being taken care of," he says. "She's ah—how should I put it—currently tied up at the moment."

His tone is calm and casual. I'm not sure if he's being figurative or literal, but I know it's a shot at me for what I said about Bishop.

"You know, Robert," Ayker says, "you should've taken my advice when you had the chance. You could've been sitting on a beach somewhere pleasant, but instead, this is what you chose." He walks around us with his hands in his pockets, which, I think he does out of arrogance, his way of telling us that he has pockets to use for comfort, whereas we don't have the luxury of pockets. All we have are our elbows and our assholes. "I can see why you like her," he says, while Jazz's whimpers trail away. "You have a dark side, as well. Don't you?"

"Why don't you let her go and I'll show you how dark I can be—"

"—Tell me, Robert," Ayker says over my voice. "I think we know each other well enough to be going by our first names. Don't you think?"

I don't answer.

"What do you want?" he asks me. "Put your friends aside. What do you *really* want? Justice? Closure? What?"

It's at that moment—as I'm hanging upside down—when the question slices through my abdomen like the blade of a tanto; and for a moment, I'm a ronin doing the seppuku and watching my guts spill out before me. They unravel like a piece of string from a spool; and I realize, at that moment, I will *never* see Jazz again. I'll never be able to talk to her, to tell her that we're going to be okay, to hold her or kiss her ever again; and as much as I want Jazz all to myself, I know I cannot have her, and that kills me. I want to kill what kills me, and I want to kill what I cannot have.

I listen closely to my bad heart and it does all of the speaking for me.

What do I want?

It's not what I want.

It's what I'm going to do.

What I *will* do.

My eyes go twitchy again, me thinking about whether or not to answer the question. I don't give him anything. No answer. No nothing.

"You know, Robert, you remind me a lot of Henry Frick, a young man who bit off more than he could chew," he says casually, as if we're pals. "Then, your brother had to get himself involved in all of this mess. Tell me, Robert. How'd your visit with Valentine go? Did you get the answers you wanted?"

"He told me Myrtle shot my brother."

"Did he?" Ayker says.

"Well, is it true?"

"What do you think, Robert?" he asks me, as if he gets off on watching us suffer. "Do you think it's true? You think Myrtle shot your brother?"

Dwight cuts in, "You think he gives a shit what you think?"

"I don't," he says, shooting a glare at Dwight. "It's a shame what your friend here did to ole Val."

"It was you," I tell Ayker. "You think you can get away with all of this—"

"—Well, according to the news," Ayker interrupts, "as well as every single American watching television, they think you killed Valentine West."

Fuck you.

I mean, really.

You *motherfucker*.

"That's the thing about power," he says closely, "you can do *whatever* you want. You can practically get away with murder."

He gets close to me, too close.

I'm feeling rabid again, like I want to bite off his face.

"I told you to stay out of my business," Ayker says. "Didn't I?" He tilts his head to the side as if he's trying to turn his eyes to my eye level. "Now you're going to die. I'm not going to bury you, though. Not yet. *First*, you're going to watch the ones you love die. How about Dwight? You love him. Don't you?"

Dwight yells out, "Go fuck yourself!"

"Please," I tell Ayker. "I'm begging you. Back off. . . "

"Or what?"

"I'm gonna kill you, you son of a bitch—"

"—Again, Robert, you're clearly not in the position to be killing anyone."

Ayker smiles.

"Before I kill Dwight, why don't I tell you the truth," he says. "It'll be like a confession, a clearing of the air. That's what you Christians believe, right? Forgiveness. Repent. It sounds to me like you already know the truth about what happened to your brother. So, let me tell you what happened afterward. I figure you would want the whole story, right?"

I keep quiet.

I let him talk and have his moment.

Mustache-twirler.

"You see," he says and stands upright and paces around me, "after the whole mess with Henry and your brother, Myrtle went running back to Connie. *But*—and that's a big but— she didn't go back to him to play wife. No. I swear people will do the craziest things when they're in love, even if it means killing another person who you once called your significant other and making it look like a suicide."

I knew it, but, again, it's hard to believe anything that comes out of his mouth.

"I tell you, Robert," he says, still pacing, "she would've made a great cop."

He shakes his head as his eyes drift away from me and then fall to the floor, as if he's watching the old scene play out before his eyes. He pauses, and then starts pacing again.

I wish he'd stop pacing. He's making me dizzy.

"The way she made Connie's death look like a suicide, it was something else."

An image suddenly flashes through my mind: first, Anthony Foster's face, and then Jimmy's face, both faces drenched with blood, both innocent, yet not innocent, *not* completely.

"And. . . " Ayker's voice comes back, this time much louder, ". . . I'm *not* talking about that unspeakable act you committed, Robert, murdering an innocent man. No. What Myrtle did, it worked out beautifully. Quite a show, I must say. Even Shakespeare couldn't write a better ending to Myrtle's story."

What is he talking about?

He pauses, again, and then picks up right where he left off: "What I really enjoy about Shakespeare are the ploys he uses in order to heighten the art of storytelling, such as irony, symbolism, *foreshadowing*. It's as if he purposefully uses these devices to plant seeds in the mind of the reader: Why did the character use that specific word? If so, what was he foreshadowing? And what's next for—"

"—I'll tell you what's next, Ayker," I interrupt his moment and I can tell he's not pleased at all from the change of color in his face. I pull my body closer. "I'm gonna to rip your fucking head off. How's that for foreshadowing?"

If Ayker did kill Myrtle, I'm sure he didn't just kill her. I'm sure he had a "little fun with her" before he put her out of her misery, like torturing Myrtle by telling her all about his love for Shakespeare.

"Anyway," he clenches his jaw, "as I was saying, after Myrtle blew out Connie's brains, I couldn't just let her off the hook. At the time, my loyalty was with Valentine. Sure, I feel bad for killing the geezer. Sure, I feel bad for killing Tony."

Something else comes over me again. I start laughing.

"You're wrong, Ayker," I tell him. "Your boy Tony's still out there."

"You think that's funny."

"Fuck you, man," I tell him.

He pulls out his gun.

"Let's see who's laughing now."

He points his gun at Dwight and shoots him in the chest.

My laughs turn to cries, and I'm cursing at Ayker, calling him every name in the book.

I squirm around, trying to loosen the chain around my ankles.

"Now Jazz," Ayker says. Then, he yells out, "Bring her out!"

"Ayker, I swear to God," I tell Ayker, trying to keep my composure.

I turn to Dwight, and he's taking his final breaths.

"I will haunt you," I tell Ayker, but I don't think he cares but I tell him anyway. "Go ahead! Kill me now! Kill me, you fucking coward!"

Another stooge brings out Jazz, whose hands are tied behind her back. She's tossed to the ground, feet before me.

"Any last words you'd like to say to your girlfriend here?"

Ayker turns to Jazz and aims the gun at her head.

A gunshot suddenly goes off, premature; however, it doesn't come from Ayker's gun!

The shot hits Ayker around the shoulder area, forcing him to take cover behind the other three stooges. He grabs Jazz by the arm, hoists her upright, and takes her with him.

The stooges are blocking Ayker's path as he makes a run for it. They brandish their weapons. Point them to my right.

I'm swinging around as more gunshots go off, and I'm trying not to get hit by bullets screaming by me!

Two stooges are struck; however, one's still standing.

He unloads on the shooter.

Another gunshot, this time much closer!

The shot hits the last standing stooge. Then, he falls to the ground, but he's not completely dead.

Nico surfaces with a shotgun in hand. He pulls out a handgun from his belt. Finishes off each one of Ayker's men with a bullet each in the head. He turns to me, his face blank. Shotgun still smoking. He shoots his eyes upward, aims the shotgun at my feet, and says to me, "Brace yourself."

He shoots the chain above my feet. I fall like a bag of dirt to the ground.

The impact momentarily knocks the wind out of me, but I'm alive. He cuts the ties from my wrists, then shoots Dwight down as well. I catch Dwight and soften his landing. Then gently lay him down on the floor. I check his pulse, but I can't find one. I administer CPR, but Nico touches me on the shoulder and tells me that he's gone. Robert, he says over my shoulder, he's gone.

I know he's gone, but I continue to administer CPR.

Eventually, I stop CPR and close both of Dwight's eyelids. I think about crying, think about how Dwight came back for me, risked his life for me. But the singular thought of Jazz prevents me from crying. I don't have time to cry. She's still out there, still breathing, still kicking.

Nico looks around, searches for any clothes that he can find. He finds my clothes, as well Dwight's, not too far away along the wall.

"He killed Valentine," I tell Nico.

"I know," Nico says, as he hands me my clothes.

I dress.

Check my pockets. Everything is there, except my revolver. Nico and I check Ayker's stooges, first by taking their weapons, including two Glock 19s, a Beretta 3032 Tomcat from an ankle holster; and then, finally, I find my revolver tucked behind one of the guards' belts.

Suddenly, I hear a *screech* of tires outside!

Nico tosses me the shotgun and motions the other way, back to where he came from.

"Let's get this son of a bitch," he says.

I follow Nico toward the exit of what I soon conclude is an abandoned publishing house that's been shut down after I pass this massive printing press that's covered in dust.

I also pass another dead stooge along the way. Must've been Nico's work.

As we're about to leave, I catch a glimmer in the corner of my eye.

As Nico, unaware of the presence next to him, makes his way to his car, another one of Ayker's stooges—a real grease-ball with salt and pepper hair—steps out of the shadows and aims a pistol at Nico's head.

I aim the shotgun and fire.

Startled, Nico turns to his right where the greaseball falls to the ground. Dead. He looks at me. Shocked.

"Thanks," he says simply.

"Consider us even," I tell him.

We rush toward the Porsche 911, get inside, and then follow the clouds of gravel dust.

"If I knew we were about to get into a car chase, I would've brought the Dragon out tonight."

"Just get as close as you can," I tell him.

Nico acts as if that's not a problem, and he guns it and gains some ground behind Ayker's town car.

We continue the chase onto the highway.

After a couple of miles in the chase, Nico manages to close in on Ayker, who's weaving in and out of late-night traffic. Headlights of oncoming cars shine inside Ayker's town car, revealing parts of Jazz in the passenger seat; however, she appears unconscious from the way her head flops from side to side whenever Ayker makes any turns.

I tell Nico to get closer.

"Aim for the tires," Nico says as he swerves into the opposite lane.

He guns it around an oncoming car, the side mirrors nearly grazing one another.

Now, much closer, I get a better look inside the town car and make sure Jazz is still alive. She is. Both of her hands appear as if they're tied to the handle on the ceiling of the car. She starts moving and struggling, even when Ayker is driving straight, no abrupt turns.

Ayker, in return, fires off a couple of shots at us, forcing me to take cover under the dashboard. The bullets bounce off the roof of the car. One pierces the top of the windshield.

I return fire by shooting at the rear wheels, trying to keep the shot away from Jazz. I don't have any luck.

I tell Nico to get even closer. He does.

I reload the shotgun, lean outside the window, and shoot out the driver's side window. Tiny fragments of glass hit Ayker in the side of the face, causing him to swerve off the road. He regains control and accelerates farther from us.

In return, Nico accelerates. I check the speedometer and he just broke a hundred.

The chase continues through the dips and turns of Hillside, Nico having to slow down around the winding curves.

Nico closes in on Ayker once more once we hit a stretch of open road.

Suddenly, the passenger door of the town car flings open.

"Slow down," I yell at Nico.

Jazz glances behind us and then she leaps from the car. Her arms curled into her body, rolling and bouncing along the road.

"Watch out!"

At the very last second, Nico swerves around Jazz. He continues to chase after Ayker. I look back and make sure Jazz is okay. I can't tell for there are no cars behind us. I face front at Ayker, who's feet away from us. Nico's ready to run him off the road. I look back at the dark figure on the road.

I tell Nico to stop the car.

He doesn't.

"Stop the car," I tell him.

"We're gonna lose him!"

He keeps driving.

"Nico," I tell him and point at the flashing sirens below the hill, "he wants us to follow him. Look."

Nico sees the cops and pulls to the side of the road.

I get out and run to Jazz, who's struggling to stand. I check her injuries. She tells me that she's fine, just a twisted ankle. I grab her and hold her close to me.

I'm tempted to tell her that we're going to be okay—an easy line—but, honestly, I just don't want to lie to her anymore.

Of all the sweet rides in here to choose from, you pick the oldest one and not to mention, the ugh—"

"—I need a car that's not going to attract attention."

I grab the keys to the burgundy 1998 Buick Regal.

"You know, Mars is going to kill you if he finds out it was you who took his wife's car."

"Doesn't matter," I tell Nico. "Besides, he'll understand."

Nico holds out his hands, confused.

"Where will you go?"

I turn to Jazz, who's standing outside the garage, both arms crossed like Nico before, staring at a distant skyline of Los Dementes.

"North," I tell him. "We'll head north. We'll be in the clear once we make it past the border. You?"

"South," he says grimly. "Somewhere warm, I guess."

"Listen, Nico—"

"—Don't sweat it, Robert," he interrupts. "It was only a matter of time before the party came to an end. This kind of life, it has an expiration date. I know that. I *knew* that."

Nico struggles to look me in the eyes and when he does, he acts as if he's got something on his mind.

"What about that whole 'living forever' bullshit?"

He lets out a breathy laugh, which is peppered with all sorts of emotions.

"Right."

That's all he says. He seems more impressed than anything, especially me remembering the conversation we had at Trader's Inlet.

Then, after a long pause, he squares himself to me and looks me in the eyes.

"It takes a man to follow a friend into the abyss and pull him back to reality." Nico looks like he's about to start crying, but I know he's saving it for later. I would. "Sometimes, I guess, you don't really know how deep you are until someone comes along and opens your eyes."

"I didn't open your eyes, Nico," I say. "You opened them on your own."

On impulse, Nico bobs his head, sniffling, ready to break.

"You're not gonna start getting emotion with me," I tell him. "Are you?"

"I might."

He lets out yet another laugh, this time a burst of laugh that causes him to nearly break down in front of me.

I walk over to Nico and shake his hand. That's what a friend would do.

I pull him in close to me and hold him close.

"Take care of yourself," I tell him.

"I will," he says, trying to hold himself together.

I take a step away from Nico.

"I hope you find what you're looking for, Robert," Nico says over my shoulder.

"You too," I tell him.

I unlock the doors to the Buick. Jazz gets inside. Then, I say goodbye to Nico and drive away.

And I know that's the last time I'll see him.

\\

ABOUT a minute into the drive, Jazz finally breaks her silence.

"You think he'll be okay?" she asks me.

"I don't know," I tell her.

"We should stop and rest somewhere."

I grab a hold of Jazz's hand. We interlock our fingers.

"We can't," I say. "Right now, we just need to keep moving forward."

I want to stop somewhere, lie down in a cold bed, and sleep until my wounds heal.

I have to constantly remind myself that we're both wanted by the authorities.

\\\

DURING the drive, Jazz and I hardly speak. I know she has a million questions for me. I feel the need to explain myself to her, why I lied about my name, why I came back to Topside.

About four hours on the old highway, which runs parallel to the Pacific coast, my eyelids start to do pull-ups and I know if I drive any longer then there's a chance I'm going to fall asleep. I find a desolate dirt road.

I decide to get off the highway at the last second and make the turn onto the side road surrounded by woods. I drive a few miles in until it dead ends. I park the Regal. Cut off the engine. Loosen my grip from the steering wheel.

As I watch the color finally swim back into my knuckles, Jazz stirs beside me.

"*Robert. . .* " she's first to speak, ". . . what happened? Why are we stopped?"

Before she can finish her thought, I tell her, "I'm sorry I lied to you. Jimmy was my brother."

She looks down for a moment, then looks up, and then asks, "Yes. I know. Bishop. . . " she pauses again and gathers herself, like the sound of Bishop's name on her tongue hurts every inch of her. "He told me." She turns my way. Eyes droopy. "Everything."

All this time, she knew. Yet, she never told me.

She grabs my hand, but I turn away. "Look at me, Robert," she says. Then tells me that she's sorry, that she should've told me sooner.

I ask Jazz, "How long have you known?"

I already know the answer to the question, but I ask her anyway.

"Since before we met."

I don't know why, but I start to tear up a little.

Get a hold of yourself.

"And I'm guessing *you* just bumping into me wasn't a coincidence. Was it?"

Jazz hangs her head. Keeps it there.

"No," she mumbles.

"I want to know something, the truth," I say. "Was it real?"

"Was what real—"

"What we had," I tell her. "Was it real?"

She turns away, crying, gasping. Every breath she embraces is smothered by an overwhelming guilt.

"After my dad passed, I thought I would never love another person ever again," she said, sniffling. "I met Luther one night at the Palace. He made me feel like I was special. He made me feel like there was still a chance for me to love again." With the top of her hand, she wipes the tears from her face; sniffles again. "After I was with him for a couple of months, he started to show his true colors." She shakes her head, more than disgusted. "I should've known from the very start that he was a monster. But I was vulnerable and weak. He saw that in me—the weakness—and he. . . he used it against me. When I found out that he beat up the manager of the Twin, all because I wanted to hang my work inside, I knew what kind of man he was. So many times I just wanted to run away. Never look back at this awful place. I stayed. That's when things got out of hand. He started to give me money for sex. Not just with him but with others. I wanted to leave him *so, so* badly. I was gonna leave him, but. . . maybe I was doing it because it was my way of punishing myself."

"Punishing yourself?" I repeat. "Why?"

She shakes her head again, disgusted to the third power. "I don't know why," she says. "Maybe, I don't know," she turns to me, her eyes dripping with tears, "maybe I liked it. After I lost the weight, I felt like I could do anything. I liked it when guys were looking at me." A strange little smile creeps onto her face, the kind of smile that can either melt a man's heart or turn it to ice. "They were paying attention to me after. . . after all of those years of being *ignored*." She turns to me again but briefly and asks, "What was I supposed to do?"

I don't answer.

I don't think she wants me to answer.

I want to ask her so many things.

I let her talk.

Good cop.

"Then, all they wanted from me was sex," she says, the word *sex* coming from her mouth as if her body is possessed by evil spirits. "And it made me angry, *really*, *really* angry, how a person—a human being—can do that to someone?"

I don't answer. Again, the tone of the question sounds like another question, which is intended to go unanswered.

Jazz's cries calm. She sniffles. She takes in a deep, healthy breath and turns to me. Her eyes are red and watery. "Luther knew I was starting to get close to you. He *hated* that. He hated that I was in love with another man," she says, pointing to her chest while emphasizing the word *I*. "The last thing I wanted to do, Robert, was lie to you." Her tone softens, and she says, "It was real. It *is* real."

I pull Jazz closer and we rest in each other's arms.

"There were times I wanted to tell you about everything," she says against my chest. "He blackmailed me. He threatened me. He said he was going to go to the cops with the video."

"Then why didn't he?"

She doesn't answer.

I don't expect her to.

IV

BY sunrise, we make it to a heavily wooded area surrounded by redwoods as tall as skyscrapers and park in a spot with a pleasant view of a small town below. We keep our heads down and save our strength until we're ready to hit the road again.

V

JAZZ and I take turns sleeping: she takes the first shift, as I get close to three hours of shuteye; and when I wake, she's nowhere around. I frantically search the woods, and just as I start to get that sensation in my gut—that twisting feeling—I stumble across this young woman picking berries in a bush.

"You're awake," Jazz drawls while foraging through bushes. Each berry she plucks from the stem, she places into the bottom of her shirt, which held open like a sack.

"You had me worried for a moment," I say.

"Don't be," she says quietly. "I'm just grabbing some breakfast." She faces me. She looks sickly, as if she's just thrown up; however, the sight of me gives her energy. She

476

holds up a small mound of berries in her hand. "See," she says cutely. "Me and my dad used to go camping. We used to pick berries."

"Berries, huh," I say. "I like berries."

"Who doesn't like berries?"

I find myself doing the one thing she would do.

VI

We eat most of the berries on the way back to the car. We get inside the car and sit in a thick and yet comfortable silence.

"What was it like?" she asks, ending the silence. "Being in a mental institution?"

I don't answer at first

"He told me," she says.

She can't even say *his* name anymore, as if last night was the last night that she'd ever speak the words *Luther* or *Bishop* to me ever again and now he's just an afterthought, another *he*.

"I'm *not* crazy," I tell her.

"I know you're not," she says, her voice as soft as a pillow. "I never said you were. So. . . " she looks at me the same way a kid would look at an adult who's about to tell a story, ". . . what was it like?"

I struggle to answer her question. I really shouldn't, but last night she told me about all of the terrible things she did, even the pleasure she got out of being filmed.

"When I was first admitted to Red Pines—"

"—The mental institution?" she asks curiously.

I nod my head.

"Yeah."

She looks at me again, waiting.

"When I first got there, I felt as if a weight had been lifted off my shoulders," I tell her.

"Why were you admitted?"

"My parents admitted me," I say. "They thought I was out of control with the drinking, the fighting. . . "

I pause and turn to Jazz and once more, she's waiting for me to finish.

". . . The hallucinations."

"What kind of things were you hallucinating?" Before I even have a chance to answer the question, Jazz says jokingly, "You don't see dead people. Do you?"

I don't answer.

Jazz apologizes.

"It's okay."

"What did you see?" she asks.

I remain quiet.

"You don't have to talk about it if you don't want to."

"I do want to talk about it," I tell her. "I want to tell you everything about me."

"What's holding you back?" she asks quietly.

I retrace my thoughts back to the time when we were at Lassie's and it was just Jazz and I browsing through clothing racks. I remember the feeling, how I felt, it was as if the world around us didn't exist.

"I felt free," I tell her, referring to Red Pines. "Like I didn't have to worry anymore, about my safety or other people's safety. For so long, I tried to bring down the people who shot Jimmy. I was the one holding myself down, *not* them. Things that were supposed to be simple weren't so simple anymore. I was making it harder to live with my own self." I pound the palm of my hand against the wheel. "I came *so* close," I tell Jazz. "But every step forward I took, I was taking two steps backwards. I didn't want to think about it anymore. I wanted it to be over."

Jazz rubs my leg and tells me that she's sorry for what happened. Then, as a few seconds of silence pass, I turn to Jazz and she's craning her head above the headrest of the passenger seat. She's now staring at my shoulder.

"What is it?" I ask her from the driver's seat.

She reaches her hand around my neck, peels back the collar of my shirt, and examines my back.

I feel a pinch over my shoulder. Jazz is peeling away a piece of dry skin.

Then, I feel a sudden prick over my back, which causes me to flinch.

Jazz pulls away her hand and shows me the piece of dry skin before she flicks it out the window.

She examines the wound next. Pokes at the wound, as if it's some kind of dead animal.

"Oh God," she says. "You're hurt. . . "

I shake my head.

"I'm fine."

"It'll get infected," she tells me.

"We just need to find another place where we can keep our heads down for a while."

"You need medical attention."

"I'll be fine," I tell Jazz.

Trust me.

VII

BY lunchtime, Jazz and I put California behind us and make our way into the beautiful state of Oregon. I stay out of sight by letting Jazz drive while she hits up a drive-thru restaurant outside Cornerstone Park.

We stop and eat in a parking lot near a rundown strip mall—at least, I try to eat. I can hardly hold down a single bite of food.

VIII

JAZZ decides to stop at a local pharmacy.

She parks in an alleyway next to the store and tells me that she'll be right back.

IX

FIFTEEN minutes pass before Jazz returns with a bagful of supplies. She pockets an item from the bag, as if she's unaware that I'm watching her. I can't make out the object in the rear view mirror. Never ask her about it when she gets back inside the car. Instead, I keep my mouth shut as I rummage through bag containing bandages and whatnot and a lot of organic crap, which smells as if nature just took a dump, then wrapped some kind of citrusy fragrance around it. Jazz tells me it's like a natural antiseptic and it's better for you than the stuff they use at hospitals. She says all of the other stuff will help bring down the fever. She doesn't look too good herself. Her eyes are somewhat bloodshot, similar to the look she had while she was picking berries. Her energy appears extremely low, as well. If I had to take a stab at it, I'd say that all of this mess, the kidnapping, Bishop, the car accident, more kidnapping, all of it has made her sick. Just thinking about everything that we've been through in the past twenty-four hours is enough to make anyone sick. I ask her if anybody was acting suspicious inside the store.

She gets quiet for a moment, then tells me that the cops are looking for Nico. She saw his face on TV.

"How about me?" I ask her.

She doesn't say anything.

I lean into her range of vision, but she doesn't have to say a word. I already know Jazz's answer.

I wish I had listened more closely to what Moses had told me.

X

I keep driving north until I reach Shies Lodge (that's the place where we were going to go when Jazz and I were getting to know each other, you know, before we went to Las Paraíso). It's an ideal place to keep our heads down. So we think.

After Jazz pays for the lodge, we get settled inside. I make sure to lock the doors. I check every inch of the room, making sure it's secure. There's nothing much to it. It has two beds, a bathroom, and a small kitchen area. Right now, it's better than a jail cell.

XI

WE hold off on eating until my wounds are treated. Jazz sets all of the supplies on the nightstand and pulls out a jar of honey. I grab the jar from her hand.

"Really?" I say.

"Really," she snaps at me. "Do you want to heal or not?"

"With honey?"

Jazz nods as she continues to pull out other items from the bag, including boxes of herbal teas like Lady's mantle tea and other medicinal teas which I've never heard of, calendula, which Jazz says is a "Mediterranean plant" used to help prevent infections, as well as these special balms and ointments for the wound, and lastly, a map of Canada.

"We should probably do this in the bathroom," she says and grabs what she needs.

We go to the bathtub and I strip down to my pants. She washes away all of the dried blood, which is caked all over my skin, cleans the wound with sterile soap and water and then dries my skin with a sterile cloth. Afterwards, she breaks an Aloe leaf in half and rubs the gel from the leaf over the wound.

"You would've made a great nurse," I tell Jazz.

"I thought about it once, but I don't know if I could handle all of the blood."

"You would've fooled me."

"*This*," she says, "this I can handle."

As she places a dressing over my shoulder, I turn my shoulder.

"It may scar," she says and stops what she's doing.

"I'll just add it to my collection."

"Quit being so ridiculous."

I grab Jazz by the wrist as she puts the final touches on my shoulder.

"You don't have to be here," I tell her. "You can still leave if you want."

"I don't want to leave," she says.

"Really?"

"Really," she says.

"You'll be an accessory."

She shrugs.

"Maybe." She leans close and whispers in my ear, "I'll just tell them you kidnapped me."

"You wouldn't," I say.

"No," she says as a smile stretches across her face, "I won't have to. Right?"

I nod my head.

"I read somewhere that over twenty percent of Canadians speak French."

"I've heard," Jazz says.

"What about your mother?"

I look over my shoulder and Jazz gets all quiet for a moment.

"What about her?" she says as she places a piece of tape over the dressing.

NO WAY OUT /
FIND A WAY

JAZZ steps out of the shower, smelling like Granny Smith apples.

I crack open my eyes as the other side of the bed shifts. Jazz lies down next to me, her hair still damp and fruity from the recent shower. She turns on the TV, but the volume has been left on MUTE from the last time we watched. I notice they're replaying the same clip of what now looks like Moses walking through Grand Valley Estates, his face much clearer—possibly doctored by Ayker's people. I don't know what to believe anymore. The clip is on a loop, like some kind of trance-induced GIF. That's the whole idea, right? Keep playing the clip over and over until the images sink into people's heads. Like some form of hypnosis. They've even taken a still from the surveillance video and blown the face up on TV. Cleaned up the still.

I was right all along.

Moses.

What the hell was he doing at Grand Valley Estates?

"Turn it up," I tell Jazz and sit upright.

Jazz turns up the volume.

The news anchor is telling us that Valentine West, a former nightclub owner, was pronounced dead when the police arrived at his suite in Grand Valley Estates. The investigators are saying that he possibly died from an overdose of some kind—*heroin*, I realize, thinking about Ayker. That son of a bitch. Investigators won't be for sure until toxicology tests come back.

It's the top of the hour.

The news has even put together some kind of graphic, *Horror on the Coast*.

The headline: MANHUNT IS STILL AT LARGE FOR SHOOTER.

The scroll at the bottom of the screen reads: SEVEN PEOPLE DEAD, FOUR CRITICALLY INJURED.

Then: MASSIVE DRUG RING EXPOSED.

Finally: SUSPECT IS SAID TO BE A COMPETITOR.

Seven people?

I count the bodies in my head: Yogi, Darius, Argento, possibly three security guards. They haven't mentioned a word about Ayker's men. Then, there's Bishop, who I didn't kill.

Seven people?

Where would they pull that number?

I tell Jazz to turn it up some more. Some snarky lawyer from New York is on TV talking about Moses and he's telling the public that this individual, Moses, is a revival drug dealer (false) and he's taking out the competition (false).

Other breaking news is coming in left and right, one of them stating that two years ago Moses was admitted to a mental institution located in the Appalachian mountains of North Carolina for putting a man in the hospital after a violent confrontation. The man, they say, was Dale Rollins. They're also saying that Mr. Rollins hasn't been the same after being hospitalized. He experiences frequent headaches, as well as reoccurring nightmares from the past trauma.

Dale Rollins?

Moses didn't beat up Dale Rollins, didn't turn his face into a bloody pulp. Rollins: that slimeball who ratted me out to cops, the same slimeball who slapped a lawsuit on my parents. Me: I was the one who put that piece of slime in the hospital. I was the one who broke his eye socket. I was the one who broke his jaw into pieces. I was the one who gave him nightmares.

It wasn't Moses.

Or was it?

They're saying that two months ago Moses escaped from Red Pines (fact). Moses did escape from Red Pines. I was right there with him, every single step of the way. I was with him when he stole the key from one of the orderlies. I was with him when he distracted the security guard. I was with him when he stole the outfits from the two orderlies. I was with him as *we* ran to freedom. I saw everything. . .

As I'm watching TV, I feel as if I'm about to turn inside out.

Jazz asks me if I'm feeling all right. She's staring at me too. I want her to stop staring at me. I feel hideous, like some kind of sideshow freak, a monster.

I rush to the bathroom, trying my best to hold in whatever's about to project from my mouth. I close the door behind me, dart toward the sink, and let loose.

Jazz knocks on the door and asks me if she can come in while my stomach punches me in the throat.

"Just a minute," I utter, the words sounding like a cross between a hiccup and a gasp. I belch and dry heave once more. I don't even try to play it quiet. My obnoxious stomach has already made it obvious to Jazz. I splash my face with cold water once my stomach finally starts to settle.

As I reach for a towel, my eyes cross the trashcan next to the toilet.

I pick up a pregnancy test inside the trashcan and it reads a positive sign. I drop the pregnancy test on the floor and when it hits the floor, it makes a thunderous bellow, which shakes the entire room. I hear this high pitch ring in my ears. The noise around me seems distant and muffled. I turn to the mirror before me and stare at my reflection. *Slowly*, I feel the splinters surfacing from my skin. Each pinprick spreading like bolts of lightning underneath my flesh. I feverishly itch the flesh of my face. The itch grows deeper, and the more I scratch, the better it feels. Like I'm unearthing something special and unique. My fingertips dig deeper, now running underneath my flesh. I dig as if I'm a cadaver dog ready to please my master. I continue to dig as if there's a tasty treat at the other end. I dig and claw and scratch away at the flesh until I can feel the bone of my skull. I tear sheets of flesh from my face. The warm and slippery flesh oozes through the narrow cracks of my fingers and falls into the sink below and when the flesh hits the sink, it makes all sorts of splattering sounds. I draw my eyes down at the pile of flesh and it looks like clumps of aged candles that have been melted into a cyclone of hardening ooze. I can no longer feel the bone. Yet, I feel skin. It's new skin, and yet it's old.

Once more, I run my hand across the peach fuzz along my cheeks and realize the hair is no longer thin or soft; yet it's hard and coarse, like stubs.

I suddenly gasp in horror and pull my hands away.

Before I understand what I've done to myself, my entire face has been ripped off and I'm now staring at *my* own reflection in the mirror.

I carefully touch the sides of *his* face and realize, when all of the flesh has shed from my old face, that his face is my face. My thoughts, as clear to me as ever before, travel back in time, to a place that bore neither home nor refuge: his face, I can visualize in my mind, *my face*, glowing with a pale light cast from a boxed TV; every patient around me is dressed in white; one of the patients is watching the same samurai flick with me, a bulldog-like string of drool oozing from the corner of his mouth; then, behind me, I witness, sits a stranger who calls himself Moses; but, as soon as the orderly switches off the TV—the orderly shouting, "Time for bed," from the door-way—the screen slowly dissolves into a grainy black.

As I stand in front of the mirror, I realize Moses was *not* sitting behind me in that very room at Red Pines.

Instead, he was sitting in the *same* seat that I was sitting in.

I can no longer see a vague blur where my face used to be or even the face of a nineteen-year-old kid. The lines on my face run like narrow valleys horizontally across my forehead and ripple outward from the corner of my eyes, like a tragedy fleeing from my eyes which once burned red with passion, the crow's feet.

I can't help but laugh at the sight of my face because it is my face and not his. It's always been my face. Never his. Even my bones feel different underneath my skin. I no longer carry that ache in my joints from when I was a teenager— *growing pains*, as Susannah called them.

Has it really been that long?

I exit the bathroom and Jazz is sitting on the bed. Worried. She's staring at me and biting the inside of her bottom lip.

"Are you okay?" she asks me. "You look a little pale. . . "

I sit on the edge of the bed and Jazz slides closer to me. She looks different, smells different. Everything about her is different. She's not showing, but I know that soon she will.

"I have to ask you a question," I say and look directly into her eyes. "Have you been with any other man after me?"

"No," she says, more worried.

"Are you sure?"

"Yes."

Her eyes trail from mine.

"You saw the test," she says quietly, holding her head downward. "Didn't you?"

"Yeah—"

"—It's yours," she says abruptly.

She interlaces her fingers around mine. She looks into my eyes. She has that look again in her eyes, like she wants to tell me something important.

I ask her, "What are you going to do?"

"What do you want me to do?"

Honestly, I don't know what I want Jazz to do. She has life growing inside her. More than likely, the life inside her shares a part of me. By killing that life, I'm killing an extension of me.

So, the answer is easy.

"When I was a kid, they used to call me Moe." I turn to Jazz. "Short for Moses."

"You mean like Bible Moses?"

"Yeah," I say. "That one."

"Why'd they call you that?"

"They used to pick on me," I say. "They used to make fun of me. I used to make these predictions all of the time and then, whenever they came true, I'd tell them, 'I told you so,' like I was rubbing it in their faces, but I really wasn't. They didn't like that, me being right and them being wrong." I tighten my grip over Jazz's hand and look into her eyes and keep my eyes there until they start to burn. I tell her, "I don't know what's going to happen to us."

She slides her other hand over my left cheek.

"If we knew our fate, what would be the point in living?"

I hold her close.

"I'm scared," I tell her. "I'm so scared."

"Me too," she says.

Once more, I embrace Jazz.

I never want to let her go.

Never.

\ dream about the cops closing in on me, even the Feds, all of them lurking in the dark woods outside Shies Lodge, waiting to make the first move. Each sound I hear somehow seeps into my dream: some barn owl sounding like a wail of a police siren, the *creak* of the bed when I switch positions sounding like blades of a helicopter. They're out for blood. Every one of them. I ease back into the dream, trying to visualize another outcome besides getting caught; however, my thoughts start to run into one another. I try to visualize a future with Jazz after everything blows over; but somehow, I find myself standing over the edge of a cliff with the Pacific roaring below. If I display any kind of emotion in front of her, if I slip up, if I make a wrong move, I know she'll be taken away from me. That's the price, though. Right? If you fall for someone, you do exactly that, you fall; and it's like taking a step off a steep cliff. When you step to the edge, you're terrified. Your mind does this thing where all of a sudden it wants to bail on you. Sorry, buddy, it says, you're on your own. Have a nice life. Adios—*wrong*. And when you finally find the courage to take the first step, you just can't fall with a harness or a nylon-cased rubber band attached to your ankles like a bungee jumper. That's not how love works. Fuck *Peter Pan*. You fall without support, without strings, ropes, or magical fairy dust. It is you and the person who is falling with you. The two of you, plummeting through the madness. To the ultimate demise. But it's that fall that really counts. Right? On the way toward your descent, you fall hand-in-hand and the fall goes by quickly, life rushing by you and death closing in below you; and yet, the fall acts as if it lasts for an eternity and all you're left with by the time you hit the waves are the memories that you both created. Together. The fall will always be the beginning of the end.

After the fall, Jazz and I are tucked away in the corner of the province, British Columbia.

After we settle down, Jazz gives birth to a healthy baby boy. We start a life together, a family. I become the person who I've envisioned myself to be.

After life happens, I wake up.

I check the time.

I've been sleeping for about five hours, mostly drifting in and out of a somewhat decent sleep.

I tell Jazz to get some rest while I keep watch.

While Jazz rests, I sit in front of the TV and on a low volume I watch the news for hours.

The police have released my name.

On TV, the anchor is telling the millions of viewers watching: "Suspect has been identified as thirty-one-year-old Robert Backer from Kuykendall, North Carolina."

Which is true.

"Mr. Backer originally grew up in the Los Dementes area."

Which is also true.

I turn off the TV and keep watch until Jazz wakes.

Then, we change shifts. Jazz keeps a lookout.

I go back to sleep.

Or, at least I try to.

|||

DID you sleep well?

Those are the first words I wake up to as I check the sun in the sky through the window. It's getting darker outside and I'm more or less confused by the time.

I ignore her question and follow with one of my own: "What time is it?"

"A little after six o'clock," she says, as she combs my bangs aside. She tells me that my fever has gone down.

As soon as I shake the horrible nightmare and realize that it was only that, a nightmare, I focus on Jazz and the sight of Jazz is like Sunday morning.

I ask her if she's eaten and she shakes her head no. I check the table and find my revolver open. Next to it is an oily rag and a brush. I'm surprised.

"You cleaned my gun?"

Jazz shrugs.

"Had nothing else better to do," she says innocently.

I thank her for cleaning my revolver. She says that her father used to have a similar gun when she was younger. He'd let her take it apart and clean it.

I grab the revolver and tell her that we won't be needing this where we're going. She agrees, but I know she's just trying to put her mind on something else other than the singular idea of getting busted by police. Susannah used to do the same thing. Whenever she was bored, she'd cleaned. She'd find anything around the house to clean, even if it was already clean.

While Jazz is washing up in the bathroom, I get dressed and organized. I sit down and watch more TV for a minute. My face is plastered all over each channel. I turn to Jazz, who's drying her hands. I turn back to the TV and that's when I get this knot in my gut, not twisting, but something worse. My body turns all warm and sweaty, like I'm having these incredible heat flashes.

Is everything all right?

I hear Jazz's voice, so close yet so far away.

"We have to keep moving," I tell her.

She looks confused, as if she's in no rush to move.

"You really think that's a wise decision right now, with everything that's happening. . . "

"Maybe not."

"I can't live like this, Robert," she says, her voice fragile. "I *won't* live like this. . . "

"Once we make it across the border, we'll be okay."

She runs her hand through her hair and remains deadly silent, as if nothing's getting in and nothing coming out.

I stare into her glossy eyes and ask her, "Do you love me?"

She hesitantly nods her head.

"If you do, I need to hear you say it," I say.

"Yes," she says. "I love you, Robert."

"If you love me, then trust me."

Jazz thinks for a moment. Thinks carefully. Nods.

"Okay," she says, her voice unrestrained. "Let's go."

We go.

IV

JAZZ makes sure it's clear before I step from the lodge.

Jazz decides to drive whereas I take shotgun.

I keep my head mostly toward the ground along the way and try not to make eye contact with any of the guests.

Once we get inside the Regal, we're gone.

BEFORE we make it across Washington State, we run into a roadblock on the 101.

Jazz makes a U-turn and heads farther east into Oregon and finds another bridge, which safely crosses into Washington.

We head north and stay off the main highways.

We drive through the night, taking various detours and driving down side roads to prevent being stopped by any cops.

Now, it's all become a game of Hide and Seek.

We hide while cops try to find us. Then, we seek the border. Then, we hide. Then, we seek. Then, repeat.

By the time the sun rises, we come across yet another roadblock and just as we're about to turn around, a cruiser pulls in behind us and prevents us from passing.

"We're being followed," Jazz says, glancing in the rear view mirror.

"Who?"

"The black car," she says. "I saw that same car when we were leaving Shies Lodge. Can't be a coincidence."

I look through the rear view mirror, keeping my head as still as possible. I see two figures inside the unmarked car. Possibly Feds. Don't know.

"How sure are you?"

"I'm pretty sure."

I notice Jazz's acting suspicious. She's not telling the truth.

"What is it?"

"I made a phone call," she says, biting her lip.

"You did what?"

"I wasn't sure if I was going to talk to her again, Robert," she says.

"Who?"

"My mom."

Shit.

"I just wanted to tell her that I was okay—"

"—Did you tell her where we were going?"

"No," she says. "I just told her that I was okay and not to worry about me."

"Did you tell her where we were staying?"

"No," she says.

"How'd you make the call, Jazz?"

"Calm down."

"Don't tell me to calm down," I say. "I need to know."

"Why is all of this my fault, Robert—"

"—What phone did you use?"

"There was a phone in the lobby."

"Shit."

Double-shit.

"What?"

I look for exits.

I find one.

"There," I say, pointing at an unpaved road that leads into a national park called Gray Falls.

Jazz cuts around the line of cars and drives along the median until we reach the park. She drives safely into the park, keeping the car under the speed limit and driving like any ordinary law abiding citizen, hoping our followers didn't see the illegal maneuver she made, even as minor as it was.

Jazz asks, "Are we good?"

I check the mirrors and then, in a quick turn, check behind us.

"We're good," I tell her, relieved.

Just as I face front, I catch the same black car turning onto the road.

"Wait! They're following us!"

"How many?"

"Just one," I say.

Jazz speeds up and gains distance from the black car.

VI

ONCE we reach the end of the road, we get out and make a run for it through the woods. I get about four strides away from the car before I turn back around and grab the handguns from the glove box that I pulled from Ayker's men, including my revolver as well. I tell Jazz to keep moving. She goes ahead of me while I remain not too far on her tail.

As we make it up a hill, the same black car comes to a skidding stop behind the Regal.

I turn my shoulder, only to find a familiar face at a distance. Shit. Dwight was right.

I turn back to Jazz and tell her to run.

About three miles in, after cutting through the woods, the tip of my shoe snags a swollen root protruding from the earth and my foot bends backward in a ninety-degree angle.

I fall to the ground and grab hold of my ankle in agony. A scream drizzles from the corners of my mouth, forcing Jazz to turn around. She tends to me, but I tell her to go ahead of me.

"Here. Take it." I grab the Beretta from my waistband and hand it to her. "I'll catch up with you."

She's crying and telling me that she's not going to leave me behind.

"It's my fault they found us, not yours," I say and hold Jazz's face close to mine. "Go. I'll catch up. I *promise*. Please. Just go."

"I don't want to lose you," Jazz says desperately.

I don't want to lose Jazz either. I want to fight for Jazz. I want to live with Jazz. I want to survive with Jazz. I want to do everything in my power to keep Jazz alive; but I know with this injury, my story is already set. My ending is closing in.

I grab Jazz by the face and tell her what she *needs* to hear.

"You won't lose me," I say, as I force the Beretta inside her grip. "I promise."

"I can't—"

"—You will." They're both closing in on us. "Run, Jazz," I demand. "Don't look back, don't you *ever* look back, just keep moving forward."

She agrees by bobbing her head.

"Now, go!"

Jazz hugs me one last time and I embrace her as tightly as I can, knowing that this may be the last time I get to hold her.

With the Beretta in her hand, she takes off before I can lose myself in her warm touch.

I hobble to a tree to take cover as they gain ground. Not too far behind them are cops, and they have dogs with them too.

"Robert," I hear Ruby cry out over the pulsating of helicopter blades. "Make it easy on yourself and surrender. . . "

Then, the other voice: *Listen to him, Robert.*

He sounds weak, a tremble in his voice.

A helicopter is closing in, as well.

It feels as if the entire world is closing in.

I withdraw my revolver, open the chamber, pull out the bullet Ayker gave me at the cemetery, and insert it into the chamber. The bullet suddenly bounces off the chamber and drops to the ground for my hands are shaking so badly.

I pick up the bullet and carefully drop it into the chamber. I close the chamber. Conceal my revolver underneath my belt.

I peek around the tree.

They're getting closer.

So, I keep moving forward despite my injury.

I get about a quarter of a mile until my other leg gets extremely heavy from doing all of the work. Jazz is well ahead of me now.

I glance down at the Glock, wondering if this is the end of my story.

Then, as I look over the Glock once more, I hear the sound of water!

I hook a left. I get halfway downstream before Ruby finally catches up with me.

As he enters my range of vision, I force myself through the dense shrubbery and leap into the moving water.

Jazz has already crossed farther up the river, I can tell; and she's now breaking farther away from us.

I let my body go limp and I ride the raging river.

The water gets choppier, the current getting stronger; and I know, not from reading about rivers in books or magazines but from watching them in the movies, the river is about to end.

My story is about to end.

I swim closer to shore and manage to hook my arm around a branch before the river runs off the cliff.

Ruby has already crossed the river, I can tell; and now, he's chasing alongside of me.

I pull myself onto the shore and hobble my way toward the waterfall while the detective approaches me with caution.

"Robert," Ruby says with labored breath, "you have nowhere else to run. . . "

Ruby inches closer. The flap of his chocolate colored trench coat, I notice, once covering his holster, is flipped behind his back as if he's ready to draw.

Behind him, Thomas shows himself. He's hunched over, his breath labored as well.

"Robert," he says patiently, "listen to John. Please, son. . . "

"Do you know what they did to Jimmy?"

"Please, Robert," Thomas says, stepping closer. He turns to the approaching helicopter. "They'll kill you. Do you understand? Our family's already been ripped apart by tragedy! I've buried one son! I will *not* bury another! It will kill me, Robert! It'll kill your mother! Is that what you want?"

I'm holding the waterlogged Glock in my hand and I look at it several times.

Ruby pulls his hands away from his holster and holds them above his head.

"Please, Robert," Ruby says, closer now.

I take a couple of steps back and find myself at the edge of the cliff. I look below at the mouth of the waterfall. The fall would kill me—easily. I don't have the strength or endurance to outrun another man with two healthy legs.

I turn to the gray sky, the police helicopter closing in.

I look down at the Glock.

"Please, Robert," Ruby begs. "Don't do this. It doesn't have to end this way. Just come with me and I will take care of you—*we* will take care of you."

"That's bullshit," I tell Ruby.

"It's not," he says. His eyes are wet too, not from the river. I know Ruby's been talking to both of my parents for a while now. I know all of the missing cases that he works on are personal; but this one, I feel, is different for him.

He tells me that we have enough evidence to build a case on the others involved with the shooting, mainly Ayker and Foster, the two men who are still out there. Foster seems questionable, however.

"We can bring these guys down, the both of us!" he screams out. "Together! Just think about what Jimmy would want you to do—"

"—You didn't know Jimmy!" I cry out, turning to Thomas. "Neither did you!"

The tears brim over Ruby's eyelids as the sun barely peeks from the overcast sky and highlight like tiny jewels in his eyes. He hovers his right hand over the holster while keeping his left hand in the air.

"Don't make me do it, Robert. . . "

My eyes drift from the Glock and land on my own shadow standing before me as the ray of sunlight shines over my shoulder.

I stare at the shadow and the shadow stares back at me. For the first time in a long time, I understand it. I finally know what it feels like to be alive.

I toss the Glock onto dry land.

Ruby breathes a sigh of relief and lowers his left arm.

I turn my eyes toward the woods and I see two pearl-shaped eyes staring at me behind the dark maze of trees.

I suddenly reach behind my back and pull out my revolver.

"Forgive me," I say as I point the revolver to my temple.

I hear Ruby screaming out, "Robert! No!"

As I cock the hammer of the revolver, another gunshot *rings* out!

Ruby's bullet catches me directly in the shoulder, spinning me around like a coin. I lose my bearings. Then, I lose my balance. Then, for a moment, I lose the breath in my lungs.

I'm falling through the waterfall, occasionally drifting in and out of a hazy blackness.

I close my eyes and tighten my body.

In the blackness, a fist comes charging at me and it punches me right in the lungs as soon as I land inside the plunge pool.

A surge of energy comes over me and I'm kicking and punching through the turbulent water.

I try to surface with my good arm, but the weight of the water bearing down on me is too much to handle.

I fight through the pain and try to surface with both of my arms.

Again, the pressure is too much.

Next thing I know, I'm sinking like a rock.

Suddenly, a hand reaches into the water!

I grab the hand and witness the wavy face of Jimmy on the other side of the water.

Jimmy pulls me from the water. I surface, but Jimmy is nowhere around. I use every ounce of energy inside my body and paddle toward dry land.

Once I reach land, my world, once more, goes black.

VII

I'M cold and wet and feverish when I come to; and the right side of my face is kissing marble-sized pebbles.

In the corner of my eye, I witness the helicopter descending over my left shoulder while a pain weighs heavily on my right shoulder, making the stab wound on my left shoulder feel like a bug bite. Even a single flex of the muscles around my shoulder blade inflames the pain, as if the gunshot has its own switch of pain. Each and every move or twitch makes the pain swell into its own entity, a red beast consuming my body. Yet, at the same time, this strange red beast forces me to focus on the light. I do so by honing in on the helicopter as it lands.

I keep these things close me: the landing skids touching down near a patch of land across the river; trees curling backward from the rotary blades; a flurry of leaves in the gusty air; the waterfall running above me.

The waterfall, I notice, is loud and furious and spitting a faint mist over my face.

Not too far away, I hear Ruby's voice. He's arguing with a woman. I listen closer and hear Jazz's voice and she's screaming at the detective.

Soft *thuds* and high-pitch *smacks* play like an amateur drummer with a baby-sized drum kit over the deafening rush of water. I realized it's Jazz kicking and punching at the detective and screaming, "Lemme go!"

The sound of Jazz crying rips a hole in my chest and as much as I want to run to her and hold her and tell her that everything is going to be okay, I cannot move the right side of my body.

I watch a couple of paramedics rush toward me. Their footsteps are getting closer; and the next thing I know, they're on top of me.

Time moves so quickly yet so slowly.

Paramedics hoist my body upright, place me inside a litter, and carry me through the rugged terrain and across a calm body of water. It feels as if I'm seventeen all over again and I'm riding with Jimmy in one of his friends' Jeeps. We're off-roading through the muddy trails of Jacob's Ridge, laughing from each bump and dip of the road.

I hear the sounds of rotary blades getting louder and huskier.

Then, I feel its breath, so violently and deafening, triggering yet another surge of energy.

My body starts to vibrate with the pulsation.

Once again, my world goes black.

Now, I'm not falling through the blackness.

I'm flying. . .

The sound of rotary blades is humming a sweet song, which closely bares a resemblance to something that I once knew all too well.

Like a magician performing a magic trick, the song vanishes into the blackness, and I'm soaring like an eagle through a sky drenched in black.

T H E   D E T E C T I V E

HE *beeping* of machines and the *whisperings* of forgotten phantoms dance all around me as I fall from blackness with a booming thud.

I crack open my heavy eyelids as if my eyelashes are curling dumbbells.

My eyes attempt to adjust to the fluorescent lights above me, causing my eyelids to flutter like wings. I finally hone in on the TV screen above me. I move my eyes from the screen and look around and find myself in the one place I thought I'd never see again.

Worse than Red Pines.

A hospital.

Ruby's leaning over me, and his hand is gently tracing mine; he's telling me I'm lucky to be alive.

I try to move, but it feels as if I have a cinderblock weighing down each one of my shoulders.

The detective tells me to relax.

He has a lot of questions.

So many questions.

I answer all of them to the best of my ability.

While I'm talking with the detective, I look down at my hand and see my wrist handcuffed to the railing of the hospital bed.

\\

DAYS pass like thoughts.

As soon as I'm discharged from Hillary Memorial, I'm treated as if I'm a rock star on my farewell tour.

The paparazzi, news reporters, and journalists all are swarming in front of the hospital like ravenous vultures. Ruby escorts me through the frenzy of a media storm, covering my face from rave club-flashes of lights while reporters squeeze in questions: "Were you responsible for the death of Luther Bishop? What was your motive? What is your connection to Daniel Ayker?"

Each time they speak, it feels as if they're nibbling from my flesh. A question here. A nibble there. Ruby shields my face the best he can with a towel, but there's chaos everywhere.

I can't escape it.

\\\

JAIL is a piece of cake. Don't believe in all of that crap you see in the movies.

You learn a lot about yourself when you're locked in a cage.

While I wait for my trial in Country Jail, I receive two decent meals a day. The guards are like my own personal manservants. They bring food to me, like room service. I can't really complain much about how I've been treated. Whenever the media isn't around and it's just me in my cell, it's not that bad either. It gives me time to process everything that I've done.

Ruby frequently pays me visits and gives me updates on my upcoming trial, but this time he's wearing a special glint in his eye as if he's bringing me a plate of good news.

The door to my cell opens and the detective stands over me with newspapers, both old and new, in his hand.

He hands me the newspapers.

The headline of the *Los Dementes Times* reads: BUSTED!

Another headline: THE VIGILANTE EXPOSES WAVE OF VIOLENT CRIME AMONG COPS.

On the front page is a photo of Ayker being escorted from a quarry outside Fairview, like me at Hillary Memorial, in similar celebrity fashion. Half of Ayker's face is badly scarred. I reckon I had to do something with his minor transformation.

Another photo shows FBI lugging desktop computers, towers, and crates of files from his vacation home in Cape Lucia.

I read about Ayker's arrest, the events leading up to his arrest, how Ruby tracked him down.

"I found him hiding out in the small town of Buford, North Dakota," Ruby tells me. "I followed him to a hole-in-the-wall bar. While he was getting shitfaced, I drained coolant and oil from his engine. I hung around until he left. He got about halfway to his place before his car started to shutdown. He pulled over to the side of the road. Then," Ruby faces me, "I made my move."

The pursuit led to a quarry, Ruby explains. The final showdown. However, as Ruby did with me, he aimed for a limb. But Ayker didn't go down on the first shot. He came at Ruby again. Then, Ruby put one in his belly. Not exactly a kill shot, but it was enough to put him down. I read about how the reputation of the LDPD is in jeopardy and is never to be trusted again. That's the worst fear for any police department: any allegation is a *bad* allegation, especially an allegation with a strong enough base to build a case. Allegations plant seeds of doubts inside the minds of citizens.

With doubts, trust is undermined.

I read about the drugs, the cocaine and heroin, all redistributed by LDPD after the drugs were seized from headline drug dealers. The drugs smuggled across the US/Mexican border like it was nothing. Child's play. Ayker, once a saint, the knight in shining armor who was going to save the city from the corruption, now, a crook poisoning the youth of America.

I read about Border Control Agents who were working with Mexican drug cartels, their own little mules sneaking the drugs into the United States.

I read about the murders of both small time drug dealers as well as Ayker's competitors. All rubbed out. Ayker was behind all of it. Kingpin himself. The Master Puppeteer, the big "Jefe," who thought outside the box. No pun intended. He exploited America's addiction for drugs for his own financial gain. Cocaine was distributed to the nicer areas, such as New Town, the celebrity hoods, the "Hollows," whereas heroin went to smaller communities, even suburbs, or the Point, places where Apple Ripper lived, the rougher areas, hotbeds of crime and murder. Who the hell knows what Ayker wanted to do after Sheriff? What was next for ole Ayker? Mayor? Governor? Who knows? If you have the money and the "power," as Ayker once said, you can buy or do anything.

As far as Bishop and Nico, they were like Santa's elves packaging the drugs inside Nico's product and shipping them across the country. DEA ended up seizing over five hundred pounds of cocaine at *the* PleasureSaber™ manufacturing facility outside San Chino after a bloody shootout. Two agents were wounded during the gun battle, but they'll make a full recovery. Ruby gives me cliff notes on the rest of the story, which isn't in the paper: Over three-fourths of Nico's PleasureSaber website was for major league pushers across the country, he informs me. Each time a new shipment came in from Mexico, the dealers received a promotional code; and that code was used to distinguish who was a "customer" and who was a "dealer." Again, right under my nose. The money was as dirty as Ayker himself; and some of it was going in the pockets of dirty cops, like Officer Rodriquez and Malone, who are both facing trial in the next coming months; while some of it was going to Ayker's campaign for sheriff.

Lastly, I read about Nico and his demise.

According to the article, Nico fled to Mexico after the shooting at the Palace. A couple of weeks later, the local authorities found Nico hanging from a bridge like a human piñata.

"I'm sorry, Robert," he says as I put the newspaper aside. "I know he was your friend."

"He wasn't my friend," I tell Ruby.

The detective sits down next to me.

"Looks like Ayker will be joining you pretty soon," he tells me. "You did it, Robert."

"*We* did it," I say.

I place the paper aside.

"Any word on Foster?"

"I'm afraid not," he says. "There was an Anthony Foster who checked into a hospital just outside North Creek with a gunshot wound to the lower abdomen. Three days later, he disappeared. Nurse said one minute she stepped out of the room. The next, he was gone, like *Invisible Man*. More than likely, he's already changed his name. Sooner or later, he'll have to face the music." Ruby turns to me, nods. "For now, it's time to move on, Robert. It's time to let go. . . "

I think about Bella and how she can finally put Henry to rest, now that she has more closure on how her brother died. Most importantly, I think about the one question that's been sifting through my mind ever since I was locked up in this cage.

"Let me ask you something, Ruby, if you don't mind."

"Shoot."

"Did you miss on purpose?"

"Miss?" he repeats. "What do you mean?"

"Back at Gray Falls, I grew my gun," I say. "You shot me in the arm. Did you miss on purpose?"

Ruby lets a noisy breath from his mouth.

"You know, twice I've drawn my gun during my career," he says. "Twice, I've shot my gun. Twice, I *never* missed my target."

"You could've killed me, but you chose not to."

"That's right—"

"—Why?"

Ruby pulls out an old Polaroid from his coat pocket. He says closely, "In my line of work, you see a lot of things that the average person doesn't see in a lifetime. Sometimes, you see things you want to un-see. As much as you erase the images from your mind, you can't. All you can do is pack them away somewhere inside your mind. They'll always be there collecting dust." He turns to me with a blank expression on his face and leans closer, as if he doesn't want the guards to hear. "Just because you may have lost your mind at one point doesn't mean you've lost your way."

Ruby hands me the Polaroid of me and Jimmy; and in the photo, we're sitting next to each other on the living room floor of our old house, my first house (I don't remember that much about the house, other than we had a play set in the backyard and me and Jimmy used to play on that set all the time, playing make-believe, like cowboys and Indians, cops and robbers). In the Polaroid, I'm playing with *G.I. Joe* action figures and Jimmy has his arm wrapped around my shoulder and we're both smiling from ear to ear.

"After you escaped from Red Pines, Susannah gave me this," he says. "I made her a promise, Robert."

"What was the promise?"

"I promised her that I'd find you and that I wouldn't let anything happen to you." He hangs his head. "When I asked her if she had any recent photos of you, you know she couldn't find a single one," he says, intrigued. "She searched the entire house. Couldn't find one. She had plenty of photos of the family, of Jimmy, your dad. It was almost as if you were cropped out of every photo. Treated like some sort of ghost."

"I was a ghost," I tell Ruby. "If you look at all of the photos, you'd think that I was the one who died, *not* Jimmy."

"After I went through your ah. . . belongings—" he suddenly pauses for a moment, "—it wasn't until I finally put the pieces together when I realized something, Robert. The two of us are no different."

"How so?"

"We both want answers," he says. "We want the *truth*. I just wish. . . " Ruby hangs his head for a moment, sighs, ". . . I wish I could've found you sooner."

"I'm sorry for a lot of things that I've done in my life." I look Ruby in the eyes. "I'm *not* sorry for killing those people."

"And Bishop?" he asks. "Are you sorry for killing him?"

"No," I answer without thinking twice.

"I have one question, Robert," he says after a moment of silence.

I know he's thinking about the other Anthony Foster whose death was ruled as a heroin overdose.

I wait for the question, but it's not one I expect.

"Why steal the prop from Fran Rosalie's trailer?"

I don't answer—not at first.

"I know it was you," he says. "You matched the description. Tell me, Robert. Why?"

I think about the question, and the answer is as clear to me as it's ever been.

"After Jimmy was shot, my mind was consumed with finding the people responsible," I tell him. "I wanted to know the truth. I wanted these people to be held accountable for their actions. That's it. *Then*, after Jimmy passed, I wanted my life back. I didn't want to live in the shadows anymore."

"You're talking about Moses, right?"

"Yes," I say, the sound of the name causing my jaw to loosen a bit. "I heard somewhere—not quite sure where—that sometimes when you lose something in life, life gives you something back. For twelve years, I was hiding from myself. Twelve years angry, alone, afraid to move on." I stop and think about Jazz, what she said to me about living a life of pause. "I never broke any *spell* or whatever when I destroyed Ivory's head, but I told myself that I would. Sometimes, John, we have to live in denial in order to accept the truth."

Ruby bobs his head as he taps me on the leg, as if he approves my answer.

"I'll see you around, Robert," he says and then walks out of the cell.

The door slams shut.

As Ruby walks away, I call out his name and he stops in mid-stride and turns to me.

"I'm not crazy," I tell him, pressing my head against the bars.

"I know you're not, Robert." A thought suddenly pops in his head. "I almost forgot." He places his hands in his pockets and says, "Cedric Gaines was exonerated yesterday. Thought you'd like to know."

Good for him.

"Good," I say as Ruby walks away. "That's good."

"I'll see you around."

"Yeah."

I can't help but think about Cedric Gaines.

It'll be up to *Cedric* where he goes from here.

\V

AS promised by Ruby, Jazz pays me a visit behind the commissioner's back.

The guard, Bobbie, opens my cell for her. I thank him while Jazz strolls around the cell, looks over the blank walls, and then the bed. Her face appears fuller, and she's wearing a red skirt that stretches halfway down her thighs.

"It's not the Fiesta Inn, but it's better than being dead."

Jazz struggles to look me in the eyes.

When she finally does, she steps forward and hugs me.

"You promised," she says into my shoulder.

"I know I did." I hold Jazz tightly in my arms. I whisper closely, "It's not like I'm going anywhere anytime soon."

A smile tries to break through Jazz's face, but it's wounded and her lips are stretched thin from the strain of the smile. She removes herself from my arms, then removes her slippers, and lies down on the bed. I lie down next to her and rake my fingers over her baby bump and ask her, "Will you have another?"

She thinks, but not for too long, as the words naturally flow from her mouth.

"One is enough," she tells me.

I move my eyes away from Jazz's glossy eyes, and I look down at my toes protruding from the edge of the bed. I no longer see ten toes before me but twenty: my toes and Jazz's toes. I rotate my left foot closer to Jazz's right foot and anchor it against the side of her foot.

I can't help but think about Jimmy.

He would've liked Jazz.

THE MUSIC

J @ I L B I R D

THE day I arrived at San Jorge State Prison I was scared shitless, as in I was so damn scared that I was constipated for two weeks straight; and it felt as if I was carrying around a miniature bricklayer inside my gut. A product manufactured from an amalgamation of fear, anxiety, and stress. Of course, I thought the very worst. I thought that I was going to drop dead at any moment. San Jorge was considered to be not only one of the largest prisons on the West Coast, but also one of the deadliest, housing over three thousand inmates, most of whom are considered to be some of the country's deadliest individuals. Of course, I thought about death. I wondered if the thought alone of death could kill a man. If I thought about it long and hard enough, would it eventually come true?

During the first two weeks at San Jorge, I had evolved—or devolved—into the one thing they tell you "not" to be while being locked up: a hypochondriac. Inmates sniff out one like an infection. Lucky me. They never caught onto me, though. After they heard about what I was in for—how I was a major contributor in bringing down a well-known sheriff who happened to be a pillar of the community, as well as a bunch of filthy cops who were just as filthy as the inmates themselves— they gave me very little trouble; in fact, in prison, if you take down a dirty cop, especially a really dirty cop who disrespects the badge—I'm talking like some trigger-happy cop, constantly jacked on some kind of power trip, picking fights or starting shit—you're treated like royalty. Seriously. Free smokes; you get to cut in front of others in the lunch line—in fact, you'll even have an escort, if other fish start to give you shit—they even hook you up with your own personal "bitch," if that's your thing; you're treated with respect. Most of the time. However, prison isn't about earning respect. You're in prison. You have no respect. Prison is about making the best of what you got.

In prison, you're no longer chasing time.

On the contrary, time is chasing you.

And there's no running from it.

Not in San Jorge.

Not anywhere.

Once everything settled down the days went by like any other day on the outside. You wake up. You eat. San Jorge's award-winning breakfast starts at exactly six o'clock—*exactly*, as in everything around here has a time attached to it, no six o'clock-ish or around six o'clock or a little after six o'clock. When they say chow's at six o'clock sharp, they mean it. Chow tastes like shit, not literally, but close enough. I went to breakfast at the beginning, mainly because I didn't want to come off as another bitch. I wanted to show the other inmates that I was the early bird—and you know what they say about the early bird. After a while, I got sick and tired of playing the guessing game every morning. Breakfast was like opening a Cracker Jack box. You never know what kind of prize you may find at the bottom. For me, it was a curly fry shaped pube, a brown toenail as sharp as a razor blade, a week-old Band-Aid stained with puss, or a stud of an earring, which had tooth-breaker all over it. One time, I found someone's ear swimming in my grits. Still intact and everything and when I pushed it around with my spoon, blood oozed from it in a reddish gravy-like sauce. Normally, I skip the breakfast, buy grub from the prison's commissary, and take my breakfast to my cell where I can't be bothered.

After I eat, I head off to work at eight o'clock—right on the dot. That's right. I'm in prison and I'm working! Whenever I get bored, I revert to old habits and pickpocket every now and then (remarkable the *things* inmates carry on their person when it's exactly what they carry that landed them in here in the first place). Old habits never die. Or, is it old habits die young? Whatever. The prison pays me hourly and the wage is about as much as a stick of bubblegum would cost on the outside. It's not much. It's shit, actually. Some poor homeless man makes more money panhandling on the side of the road than a prisoner makes pounding metal. I'm a welder, by the way. I work with all types of metals and whatnot. It's fair to say that I enjoy the work. I've become skilled in making things from metal. The work helps keep my mind busy and that's all that matters.

Work ends right before five o'clock in the afternoon. I piddle around until the showers clear before taking a shower. I clench during the whole excursion. Nothing gets in and nothing gets out, if you know what I mean.

Dinner starts at six o'clock. The dinner is a little better than what they serve at breakfast. I keep mostly to myself. I don't get any lip from the other inmates, especially the brothers.

Once dinner is over, I attend a self-help group called Anger Management. The class is full every time I go. A lot of the inmates have trouble controlling their tempers. A lot of them are frightened from what they'll do when they get out of here. They wonder if they'll go back to their old lives, their old ways or habits. And that's the worst fear, defying nature, trying to change a leopard's spots; and it's written all over their faces too, as if each line on their faces was a mark of what they did back in the day, like that one book, *Scarlet Letter*. The A for Adultery. One cat, Tyrone—Thunderbolt is what all of the brothers call him, or just Bolt—attends the same class as me. Tyrone was, in fact, the one who started the full-scale riot a few weeks after I arrived at San Jorge. He earned himself solitary for a month. I nearly lost an eye. I passed out from all of the smoke; and when I woke up, the side of my face was covered in blood from a projectile. If Tyrone had a word or letter on his face, it's M for Murder; and I feel that I'll be his next victim. I think Tyrone has it in for me. Tyrone's carved up something really sharp to jam into the back of my skull. We call them "shanks" around here, and it's one of many items you get in your prisoner's survival kit. That, as well as a fresh pair of socks, a Bible—if you're into that—and whatever paraphernalia you can smuggle into San Jorge. One item, however, which isn't an item at all but, more or less, something you pick up along the way, like a skill or language. That's a pair of new eyes. And if you practice hard enough, these eyes will save your life. I've learned to grow four sets of them during my time here. Two in front. Two on one side. Two on the other. Then, of course, the two in the back. These are the most important eyes, the ones in the back. These eyes are your sixth sense; and they will work to your advantage. That's why we put locks on our doors or we buy cars with wide enough windows to see our blind spots. You know, sooner or later, someone's going to be creeping up on you.

It's not a matter of who.

It's a matter of when.

At eight o'clock, inmates are able to use the prison phone. I call Jazz and talk to her *every* chance I get. Three years after the trial, Jazz tied the knot with a man named Douglas Beagle. Of all the guys out there to choose from, she chose to marry a veterinarian. I met Doug once during a visitation. Like me, he was scared shitless. Ghostly white. A sudden *boo* would probably kill the man. It almost made me regret taking the rap for Jazz. During the visit, he managed to squeeze in a few words to me. He's—how do I say—nice. Not only that, he has money. He came from money. His father was some doctor or something like that. And I think that's what Jazz needed in her life: a "nice man" who could not only support her, but also our son. I don't sleep much anymore, either. Maybe an hour or two a night, if I'm lucky. I spend lots of nights awake in my cell, thinking about Jazz, wondering if I should just let her go. And that's all it is, really, me just wondering. Reality can be a nasty bitch. I'm in here. She's out there.

At nine o'clock, it's lock up time. During this time, the cells are locked until breakfast. I spend this time writing in my cell, which helps me keep my mind busy as well. I write a lot of letters to my son and my parents. All of the news channels across America were covering my trial in front of millions and millions of viewers. All of the publicity took a toll on Susannah; and she had what doctors call a "mini" stroke, resulting in one side of her body becoming partially paralyzed. She made a full recovery, though, and she's doing much better—so I've heard. I haven't heard from her in a while. She and Thomas also visit me in prison whenever they can. Thomas has a bad hip, but he's still kicking it. He's hoping for a retrial. He's thinking maybe my case will go to the Supreme

Court. I always tell him not to bother. I'm a murderer, I remind him. I'm *not* sorry for being a murderer. It's not who I am, but it's what I became. Susannah blames herself. A lot. She feels as if she could've done more to help me. I have to remind her that it's not her fault. She raised a good kid, so I think. She taught me manners, taught me right from wrong, taught me to follow my heart. I tell her that, even though I may *not* have done the "right" thing, I did what I felt was best in my heart.

Those individuals involved in the shooting needed to pay for not what they did to Jimmy but for what they *didn't* do.

At eleven, the lights go out.

I go to sleep but I don't really sleep.

Instead, I lie in my bed and listen to the sounds of the steel jungle throughout the night.

Then, the cycle repeats itself over again: I wake up; I eat; I go to work; I eat; I sleep but not really; then I follow the same routine.

I live, and I die by routine.

Live and die by routine.

Live and die by routine.

Live and die by routine. . .

‖

PERCY passes by my cell as he normally does after Anger Management.

As Percy normally does, he glides himself over to my cell. A mop in hand. Ready to chat. I've become accustomed to having conversations with Percy, not the typical small talk (*What do you think about the weather?* or *How about them Red Devils?*) but a conversation. Like me, Percy's doing time for murder; however, it's fair to say that Percy had no intention of taking away another person's life. Percy was charged with vehicular manslaughter. The judge wasn't as "lenient" on Percy as the judge was on me. As Percy tells it, he had an argument with his lady friend one night. Went to the nearest watering hole where he had one too many. On the way home from the bar, Percy crossed the yellow line. His vehicle struck a single mother on her way to the first of two jobs to support her two children. Percy carried that one night everywhere with him. He also has a son as well. He was born after Percy was sentenced. He frequently talks about his children and keeps me up to date with all of their progress. Last month, his son, Zachary, who was named after his great grandfather, Zachariah, turned two years old, or what Percy called the "terrible twos." Trying to discipline a two-year-old, he said, was like pulling teeth with a pair of pliers. You can't give them a little pop on the backside whenever they misbehave or act out of line like they did in the old days. You can't use logic to reason with them either. Basically, you point to certain objects that are off-limits and say, "No!" Their brains are like sponges absorbing everything they possibly can. Basically, according to Percy, all they want to do is destroy anything they can get their hands on. He compared him to a much smaller version of *Godzilla*—a mini-zilla. He went through the same difficulty with his daughter who's now three years older than Zachary. Like a storm, he told me, you just have to wait it out until it passes.

At times, I tried to imagine what my son was doing, where he was going, who he was hanging out with, if he had good friends or the bad kind. I thought about him a lot, especially during the time of my trial. I never had a chance to experience the "terrible twos" like Percy. I turned into the father I swore I'd never become: The Ghost of Father's Past. Thomas had gone through the same crap with his father. I didn't find out about Grandpa Backer until a few years after he passed away. He was a cop like Thomas—and not to mention, a lush, too. Every time Grandpa Backer ran to the nearest watering hole, he'd tell the same joke, as if it never went out of style: "What you do for a living?" asked the loner at the bar. As if Grandpa Backer was waiting for the question, he eagerly pulled the joke from his pocket and said, "I tried to become a lawyer, but I could never quite pass the bar?" The comment was usually followed by a long pause of thought. *Get it?* Then, an explosion of laughter erupted throughout the pub as he pointed at the bar. Grandpa Backer later showed up in Thomas's life after he retired from the force, as well as the bar. By then, the damage had already been done. Thomas had already married, had already settled down, already had a life of his own. Then, when Grandpa Backer passed away from cirrhosis of the liver, Thomas buried his father and never spoke of him ever again. The only thing I remember about Grandpa Backer other than the drinking was that he'd never shut up about jazz, as in the type of music. For hours, he'd talk about Coltrane or Davis. He said that jazz was the one genre that'd still exist when we're all fossils. But whatever. I had officially become the makings of the wrong father, another Grandpa Backer, another disappointment. I was never going to show up in my son's life. I never witnessed the birth of my son; never stood by Jazz's side while she brought him into the world; never cradled him in my arms; never reassured him whenever he felt alone in the world; never nurtured him whenever he got sick, like the flu or an ear infection or whatever kids get. I was going to be the father who was "never there."

The Ghost.

The only difference between Grandpa Backer and myself was that I needed my son as much as he needed me.

As Percy makes his way over, I notice he's acting a bit odd. He's not his usual talkative self. His mannerisms, as well as his movements, are off to say the least.

Percy robotically raises his head from his swirling mop. And that's when I realize that the man standing in front of me is *not* Percy. He's someone else, a man twice Percy's age. The more I study his old, scarred face, the more I wonder if he's really an inmate at all. He tells me Percy found another job and he's filling in for the time being. I'm not sure whether I believe him. I look closer at the unscarred half of his face and realize that I've seen the man's face before. Not only have I seen him behind bars, but I've also seen him on the outside.

I ask the inmate, "Do I know you?"

"No," he says, staring at me with a steely-eyed glare, "but in time, you will. . . "

He carefully pulls out a brass key from his right pocket and holds it in his wrinkled palm.

On the cuff of his sleeve is a speckle of blood, which appears fresh.

I tilt my head for a closer look and notice more blood over the side of his wrist.

"It's time to finish what you started," he tells me.

"Excuse me?"

"Does the name *Anthony Foster* ring a bell?"

"How do you know that name?"

Once more, he glances around the desolate cell block, then moves his eyes toward the key below.

"I believe you already know the answer to the question, Robert," he says.

I follow his eyes and feel each groove of the key between my fingertips. My eyes climb farther up his body and settle on the nametag over his breast pocket. The name feels so familiar as the syllable rolls off the tip of my tongue in a soundless utterance; yet, for the life of me, I can't remember where I've heard the name before—*Cap?*

My eyes trace his arthritic hand gripping around the mop, his two gnarled fingers hanging by his waistline.

"What do I have to do?"

The words come out easily, smoothly.

"It's simple," he says, his eyes squinting. "Follow me. . . "

"Follow you where?"

My cell door suddenly opens!

A mischievous smile unravels over one side of Cap's face.

He steps aside for a moment while I stay frozen inside my cell.

When Cap returns, he's carrying a large sling made from a bed sheet.

Inside the sheet are pipes, bars, and clubs with each end fabricated into blade-like points. He sets down the bulky sheet and all of the weapons inside spill out over the floor.

Cap looks up at me with a glint in his eye.

"I didn't say it was going to be pretty," he says.

As Cap hands out weapons to each one of the inmates in my cellblock, I grab the crinkled paperback, *Captured By Light*, from underneath the mattress and slip it behind my waistband. I take what I need and I leave behind what I don't.

\|\|\|

ONCE all of the inmates are armed, Cap, now dressed in prison guard attire, steps over the unconscious prison guard who's already been stripped of his clothes. The guard's bleeding profusely from the back of his head, a small puddle of blood pooling underneath his left cheek. He's not dead, at least not yet he isn't; however, if he doesn't receive medical attention as soon as possible, I feel as if he'll never regain consciousness.

One inmate in particular, Cecil "Cee-Cee" Brown, is dressed in prison guard attire as well and carries a pump-action shotgun in his hands. Like me, Cee-Cee is in for murder; however, he doesn't carry any letter on his face. Only letters Cee-Cee carries around are the letters J and B, which stand for Jamaica Brown.

In another life, in another world, really, Cee-Cee used to be a steelworker. He was raised by a proud generation of Browns who built cities with their own bare hands; a devote Baptist who went to church every Sunday like his father before him. Before he left for work, he used to read the newspaper, like his father before him. Cee-Cee used to have a family until one muggy July night a gangbanger drove by his neighbor's house and started spraying like no tomorrow. One of the bullets grew wings and caught his four-year girl, Jamaica, while she was sleeping in her bed, instantly killing her. Then, after months of carrying out his own investigation, he found the triggerman who had murdered his daughter.

Cee-Cee got his revenge.

All six feet and two inches of it.

Then he got life in prison.

Cee-Cee nods at me—*Ready*.

"Let the madness begin," Cap says as he hits a button on the control panel. All of the cell doors automatically open with that drawn-out, shot clock-like *beep* followed by a track of bars rubbing against each other and then that ritualistic cla-*clonk* of multiple cell doors simultaneously slamming open. . .

One by one, each wide-eyed inmate gradually eases from the cells with metal clubs tightly gripped in their hands.

My stomach lurches, forcing a deep swallow.

Once more, Cap turns to me.

"You ready?"

Am I ready?

The tips of my fingers begin to tingle. My arms go light and feathery, then my thoughts, each thought running into the next: Foster standing among two devils in night darkness, pale moonlight fashioning a flawless halo around his profile; Foster standing on the bridge over Crux River, Jimmy held in his arms; Foster looming over the edge of the bridge, staring down at Jimmy clinging to life, Jimmy's face veiled with terror, a cavity of a bullet hole above his right eye socket oozing with driblets of blood, his lips working through all the frothy blood until they find the one word he can release, a word which had shared no comparison to my usage as whenever I was in the position where I acquired Jimmy's assistance if it was something as banal as tying my shoes or even Jimmy running to nurse me, if it was from falling from my bicycle for the first time and breaking my wrist to rescuing me on the playground by some bully who was on top of me, beating me senseless, then Jimmy swinging from the monkey bars as if he was a cape crusader and rushing to my defense, Jimmy making sure the bully never bothered me ever again: all of these moments in time played out before my eyes because of the constant reminders of a scrappy woman from the small town of Riverdale, California. Whenever Susannah would drop us off at Topside or before she trotted around Moonrise Avenue where she splurged away her paycheck on some clothes or shoes behind Thomas's back (whenever he'd become suspicious of her—after all, he could sniff out a lie the same way a bloodhound could sniff out scent—she'd composedly tell him that she was "only looking" or say that it was on sale or she dug it out of the closet), she'd hold her index finger with her vermillion red acrylic nail inches away from Jimmy's face like a switchblade and tell him, "Don't you dare let your brother out of your sight." She'd give Jimmy a three-second buffer to respond. *"Look after your brother,"* she emphasized. Susannah was the stricter one out of the two, the enforcer who ordered Jimmy to look after me. No matter what he did, no matter where he went, he had my back. That was number one out of the endless list of rules: Look after your little brother. Now, the shoe was on the other foot. Jimmy needed me but I wasn't there to *help* him or to rescue him or to save him, despite the awful thing he had done. My only reaction is to cup my hands over my face and cry, *Oh Jimmy*; and while I picture myself doing this, all I can see is Jimmy's weakened arm reaching out to grab something (*anything!*) as water rushes over his lifeless body in the night darkness—*Ready*.

The word cuts through the tense silence.

I follow with a stiff nod of my head.

I do exactly as Cap says, word for word, and mimic his every move.

When he says, "Stop," I stop.

When he says, "Move," I move.

I stay close to Cap's heels like a canine following its master. We continue down a dimly lit hallway until we reach this long stretch of hallway lit up with fluorescent lights, which have all been recently replaced with brand new bulbs, except for one.

We stop at the intersection of hallways while other inmates break away from us and proceed down another hallway. Everything is clockwork. The guards, now finishing their shifts, leave their posts while the other guards take their places. They're still unaware of the loose inmates. They're still unaware of the madness to come.

As soon as one of the guards crosses the other guards' line of sight, we round the corner and duck into a storage closet without being spotted.

Cap hands me a fresh pair of clothes and tells me to dress.

"You move quickly for an old man—"

"No time to talk," he says with urgency.

"How do you know your way around—"

"I said, 'Quiet.'"

Since time's of the essence, I keep my mouth shut, do as Cap says, and slip out of my prison clothes. The paperback falls to the floor as I remove one of my legs from the pant leg.

Cap picks up the book from the floor and flips it around to the front. He first gives it a once over; then he gives me a once over, but more of an *are-you-serious* kind of look.

Before the words find their way to his lips, I snatch the paperback from his hand. The gesture doesn't sit too well with Cap. His lips pucker with distaste. He turns away, mumbling, "Whatever works for you."

Any disagreement we have dissipates before it has a chance to escalate.

Cap checks the hallway while I change into the casual attire: a pair of blue jeans, a white, firmly pressed shirt, a black leather jacket, which is one size too small, and a pair of Nikes.

Once I'm dressed, I slide the paperback underneath my belt. Then, we're ticking again. Cap unlocks yet another door from his set of keys and tells me to hang back. As before, I do as he says and hang back. I wait for about half a minute until I hear what sounds like a whale's moan behind the walls.

A grumbling sound suddenly runs throughout the complex, sending the building in and out of a volatile state of utter disarray!

The lights above flicker before San Jorge falls to blackness. The silence is thunderous, deathly, unlike those seemingly endless, sleepless nights where the silence comes in the form of a nocturnal medley of coughs, sneezes, snores, farts, or the *clinking* of a restless finger tapping along the bars of a cell. A couple of seconds later the power kicks back on.

Another sound comes forth: footsteps. They're closing in on me and just as I think I'm about to get caught, Cap tugs me into a recess in the wall.

We barely avoid the guard as the guard hooks a right around the corner and heads in the opposite direction from us.

We wait in chaotic silence until the guard is gone; then we're on the move again. . .

Every door Cap walks through, I walk through.

Every step he takes, I take.

Every beat he makes, I make.

Everything about the prison break feels as if it's already happened. Like a hazy dream that lingers around well after I wake up, I can only remember parts of the dream but not the entire dream.

At one point, I even make eye contact with one of the surveillance cameras along the wall. The camera acknowledges both of us; but then, surprisingly, the lens goes black, as if it's turning a blind eye. Cap tells me not to worry about the cameras.

"I've disabled them," he says.

Then, he tells me to keep moving.

So I do.

We keep moving until we reach a main entranceway, which is heavily guarded. Guards still unaware of loose inmates. But not for long. . .

One of the guards rushes from his post. That's when the riot breaks out, when the guard sounds the alarm.

In a matter of minutes, each guard is decked out in Kevlar and equipped with riot shields and masks.

Over the deafening wail a tumult of screams violently ping-pongs throughout each winding corridor of San Jorge.

Cap slips past an automatic door and strikes the first guard who steps in his way with a baton. He single-handedly takes out two more guards before making a clearing for me.

Then, a blast of a shotgun *booms* behind me!

Canisters of smoke are being shot at a drove of inmates, all scurrying from the prison.

Rubber bullets are being fired as well.

While the other guards are trying to corral the loose inmates, Cap and I make our final exit. To say that our prison break was as complicated as depicted like in the movies would be anything short of a lie, although I never had to burrow through any hole in my cell and crawl my way to freedom inside a sewage drain filled with a world of awfulness. I never had to do any of those ridiculous things.

I simply did as Cap commanded and walked straight through the front door without a fuss.

IV

ONCE I reach a navy blue unmarked minivan parked outside San Jorge, Cap tells me this is as far as he goes.

As I'm about to get inside the van, I ask Cap over the blaring alarm, "Who are you?"

Before Cap can answer, a spotlight suddenly dances around us but never quite lands on us!

"Get out of here," he demands.

"Who are you?"

As Cap turns to the opening gates, a clan of guards storm out with weapons drawn.

"Only *you* know who I am, Robert. . . "

Freeze!

Then, Cap cries out, "Now, go!"

I get inside the minivan.

As before, I do as Cap says and drive away.

C L A W   P I G E O ¶

steer clear of the roadblock and drive south through the back roads of Anne-Clara County until I reach the outskirts of Cordova Valley. I come across a deserted underpass covered in an overgrowth of vines. Even the trash and debris that's been discarded from the highway appears as if it's from another time. I park the minivan behind a massive concrete pillar and save the battery cutting off the engine, as well as the headlights. I kick off the sneakers from my feet, grab the paperback from the glove box, and lay down in the backseat. I open Foster's autobiography and flip to the page with the purple "Holy Tour" flyer that Cee-Cee's wife, Odessa, had given him during her last visitation. Like many, Odessa happens to be an admirer of Foster. She's been to one of his shows on the Holy Tour. She's bought all of his books. She's one of the many fools who admires Foster and how he "turned" his life around. I open the flyer and out falls a white crinkled envelope containing a written letter from my son, as well as two photos: one of Jazz holding our son in her arms after his birth and the other one of me and Jimmy, the Polaroid Ruby had given me before my trial.

I place the letter and photos aside and run my finger down each city on the schedule until it lands on the highlighted city, Tovar Bay. I stare at the date, the city. It seems like yesterday I was sitting in the prison library highlighting this one particular date, as well as city. Lots of events have transpired since then. The world has moved one with or without me.

I skim through the other cities, places where Foster has infected and is going to infect with his lies and manipulation. My eyes go weary as I reach the bottom of the list. I drift in and out of sleep, occasionally bolting upright from the jarring rattle of a passing automobile overhead. I don't hear a single police siren throughout the night or the chopping sound of a helicopter ripping through the sky. Strangely, all I hear is the rush of traffic passing overhead, a constant drone that bares absolutely no resemblance to anything living or breathing.

\\

WHEN morning arrives, I'm watching a circular sunbeam about the size of a pea transform itself into a rectangle on the ceiling of the minivan. Inch by inch, half of the ceiling washes over with sunlight, then the sunlight inches farther down the headrest, down the backseat, and finally, splashes over the side of my face with warmth that only a cloudless sun can provide.

Along my belly the paperback book is stretched outward like a dead bird. I pick up the book and glance over the page.

Chapter Eleven: a chapter that I have memorized from start to finish.

In the chapter, Foster explained an incident where he was shot in the upper abdomen during a "drug transaction" in Old Town, which is total bullshit.

According to Foster's fabricated story, the so-called "thugs" stole his wallet, as well as his money, and left him to die in an alleyway.

Sound familiar?

"Next to a dumpster," he wrote, "with the smell of rot lingering in the air." He felt as if he was soon going to "contribute to the rot." He managed to crawl his way to a payphone where he called the one person whom he could trust (Nico). What doesn't make sense in the story is why Nico—of all people—rushed Foster to Presbyterian Medical Center, which happened to be fourteen miles north of Briar Canyon, where he had one of his kidneys removed as a result of the gunshot.

Which is true.

According to Ruby's story, Nico *did* drive Foster to Presbyterian Medical Center located outside North Creek.

Foster *did* have a kidney removed after being shot by Ayker, *not* a drug dealer.

Here's the big, fat hole in Foster's story: Old Town happens to be several hours from Briar Canyon. There are at least four major hospitals between Richport and Briar Canyon. The question was raised: "Of all locations, why Briar Canyon?"

Foster's defense: He was fearful of his life. He thought that maybe these "thugs" would track him down and finish what they started. He had already seen their faces. As far as Foster knew, he was a dead man.

But he wasn't going to be a dead man because none of these things took place. And Nico wasn't alive to recant Foster's story when it was published. Nor was Bishop. Nor was Ayker. It was as if Foster grabbed the story from another story and then made it his own. Even if Ayker was still alive, though, I don't think it would've made any difference. Not too long after he was given life without parole, a prison guard found him dead in his holding cell. The bed sheet had been strategically wound like rope. One end was wrapped around the bar on the window while the other end was tied around Ayker's throat. He didn't even leave a note behind for his wife, René.

About a month after the shooting, Foster wrote that he "fell off the wagon," as in he turned to an old friend, which, inevitably, forced Foster on the streets.

One night he found himself in a bar outside Mexico City. He spent every last penny he had to his name on booze. He could no longer live with the mistakes he had made.

As a result, he drank until all of the pain faded away. He didn't remember much about the night, only the "celestial being" who he described in such vivid detail:

> "As I was being rushed to the hospital, the ceiling of the ambulance split apart in two halves and opened like an elevator door. Within the tedious flashes of amber-colored streetlights dizzily racing over my body, a *tiny speck* of light broke away from the other stars and descended from a starless sky. The light started to approach me, as if it specifically chose me. Of all people, it singled me out. Why? I watched the light fall upon me,

gleaming ever so brightly as it grew in size and shape, each shimmer stretching out into a pair of arms as well as legs until it finally manifested itself into the body of a human. The paramedic touched me on the shoulder and leaned into my range of vision. As he turned away, this light, this celestial being, as weightless as a curtain riding high off a summer breeze, was now hovering over my body. This being didn't have a gender or a race. Its breath was incredibly warm, its face brilliant and beautiful, and when it smiled at me, I witnessed the smile of my mother."

Somehow, after spending over two minutes administering CPR, the doctors found a pulse. Foster found God. Technically, as he wrote in the book, he was dead for two minutes and twenty-one seconds. That Sunday before the book's release, he explained his near-death experience in the critically acclaimed "touching" interview with *60 Minutes*, as well as time he spent in a homeless shelter. Most of the interview wasn't true, but people believed him. Did people believe him or what? He created a new definition for the word *bad*. He was a man who had built the foundation of his brand off deception and greed. The greatest con artist of all time. Yet, everybody was buying it: his merchandise, books, coffee mugs with excerpts from his books, his bookmarks, posters, apparel from his clothing line, TRINITY^{XL}. Foster had played the sympathy card and then once he had supporters wrapped around his little finger, he marketed himself as the "New" Man of Faith. Yet, all of the profit he made from his merchandise, as well as the sold out shows, went straight in his pocket. These types of swindlers usually throw some of their money at a good cause, such as starting some kind of charity or whatever, which usually helps people in need. Foster only had one foundation, the Anthony Foster Foundation and all of the money went straight in his pocket, all to pay for his own private jet, a mansion in Caribou, which cost him millions, a villainous yacht, and an entourage as deep as the Secret Service. I'm not the type of person to tell someone what he or she can buy—but seriously. Foster was a coward, a crook, a con.

And, the *60 Minutes* interview was only the beginning. Every opportunistic producer in Hollywood had dollar signs in their eyes.

About six months later, they turned Foster's story into one of those melodramatic movies called *God's Country*, which aired on the *Lifetime* channel around Christmas every year.

Overnight, Anthony Foster had gone from murderer to miracle man to one of the most successful televangelists in America. I swear you can't even write this stuff in a movie. But they did; however, they left out the most crucial part of Foster's story: *the murderer*. The book, as well as the movie, exploited his crimes, such as a robbery that he committed when he was fourteen years old and then the drunk driving accident in his late teens, which killed a "mother of two children." Foster did a few years in jail, then the coward was free like *Willy*, the beloved orca.

After Foster found God, or as he wrote, "God found him," he started the healing process—hence the Holy Tour, the monthly excursion where he trotted around the globe spreading the word of God, as well as his personal experiences with God, which is all expensed from working class individuals through his foundation. During this so-called "healing process," the first person he reached out to was Samantha Caldwell Beagle. He even had the audacity to televise it and everything in it was an eye-roller of a production; and later, he wrote about it in his book, *Saving Jazz*, which wound up number one on the best-seller's list. He wrote that Jazz wanted nothing to do with him at first. After she was diagnosed with cervical cancer, she turned to God. When God never answered her prayers, she turned to America's greatest con artist. I think she was desperate. I really do. Jazz wasn't the type of person who created attention toward herself, especially with her history and all. I think most people were more or less curious about her "indecent" past in amateur porn. Maybe she felt that if God had been so forgiving with Anthony Foster, then maybe He'd be forgiving toward her. Foster wrote that he prayed a lot for Jazz. He visited her a lot in the treatment center and read Bible passages to her during her chemotherapy. They became close friends, as in what Foster wrote, "a spiritual guidance counselor." The cancer went into remission. Jazz made a full recovery. She was happy, again, with

Doug, with life. Everybody was happy and standing around in circles and holding hands and singing Kumbaya.

To this day, I've been waiting for someone to pinch me and wake me up from this goddamn nightmare.

\\\

\ make a pit stop at the nearest rest stop where I wash the dry blood from my hands.

I check for any injuries but can't find a single one.

After I finish cleaning myself, I'm back on the road. I keep driving south until I reach Rancho de Gio, a small town twenty-three miles east of the populous port city of Tovar Bay.

Before the ramp's exit, I drive past a black billboard with the words THE HOLY TOUR in white hypnotic lettering.

The line below reads: "It's time to start the healing."

Show begins at 7:30 P.M. this coming Monday night at Western Reserve Coliseum.

$ N O W B I R D

ANCHO de Gio reminds me of Topside in that it too hasn't been given a facelift by major corporations or big box stores.

I end up stopping at a diner called Angelo's. I sit in the back and don't make any eye contact with people.

The story has already broken: I'm a wanted man.

Dead or alive.

I manage to hold down some food.

I leave the same way I came in, all hermit-like, and I meet up with Cee-Cee's good pal, Pharaoh "Squid" Jackson, at the salvage yard, Santi's Auto-Salvage, in a rural area called Courtney.

Sure enough, Squid's already waiting on me.

"'Bout time, old man," he says as he checks his watch.

He looks over my shoulder, expecting another person to get out of the minivan.

"Where's Cee?" he asks, holding out his arms in confusion.

"He didn't make it," I tell Squid.

"Didn't make it?"

"Yeah," I say. "Didn't make it."

Squid smacks his gums.

"Let's get this over with," he mumbles.

Then, he walks to the trunk of his smart car and pulls out a small *Dale the Tiger* lunchbox made out of aluminum. He sets the lunchbox on the roof. Opens it. Inside is a Glock 19. I pick up the Glock and check the weight.

"That there belonged to my pops," Squid says. "Had to clean the dust off it and everything. You know what I'm saying?"

"It's perfect."

"Lotta things have changed since you were locked away." He pulls out two boxes of ammunition from his pocket and places them on the trunk on the roof. "These were extremely hard to find. Right before stores shut down, they went like hot cakes."

I pick up one box.

"Just one box will do."

"You sure?"

"One is enough."

"You expectin' to be in and out, huh?"

"Just Foster," I tell him. "After Foster, it's finished."

"Let's just hope you don't have to use it before tomorrow," he says. "Once your face winds up on TV, security's gonna be locked down tight."

"How about this friend of yours?" I ask. "How well do you trust him?"

"Practically grew up with the dude," he says. "Don't worry. He straight."

"How long has he been working at the coliseum?"

"Shit," he says. "I don't know. A couple years? He straight. Trust."

"As long as he did exactly what Cee-Cee told you to do—"

"—Yeah, man," he says. "Straight."

A tense pause.

"So, you and Cee," he says. "You two were close?"

"Yeah," I tell him. "We were close."

"Hard to believe."

What the hell does he mean by that?

"Cecil did a bad thing," I tell the punk. "Doesn't make him a bad man."

"Listen, man," Squid says, smacking his gums again as if it's his common reaction to something he doesn't agree with, "know it ain't none of my bizness, but I have to know. Why go through all of this trouble just to kill some motherfucka who 'bout to die anyway."

"Justice," I tell him.

That's all I got.

That's all I give him.

"Shit man," he shrugs it off. "A'ight. Whatever."

Finally, he pulls out an envelope carrying a wad of cash. He takes Cee-Cee's cut and makes sure to tell me that it's Cee-Cee's cut and *not* his cut. He pockets the cash. I tell him to make sure the money goes to Odessa. He nods, but I know he won't give her a dime. Then, he places a backstage pass on the trunk.

"Last but not least," he says, "that'll get you backstage. You won't have to find my boy, Troy. As soon as make it backstage, you just go straight to the spot and it'll be there waiting for you. From there, you're on your own."

"Thanks," I tell Squid.

"A friend of Cee's is a friend of mine. Word up."

We shake hands.

As I'm about to head back to the minivan, I hear Squid say from behind, "Just curious. When you were in the joint, why'd they call you *Cap*?"

My stomach flinches from the sound of the name, Cap.

I stop, reach in my pocket, and pull out an old Pepsi bottle cap.

I flick the cap at Squid. He catches it. Looks it over.

"Keep it," I tell Squid.

Then, I drive away.

\\

\ drive back into town and stop at a men's clothing store called Grooms and pick out a brownish-colored suit with a black tie to match for tomorrow.

I try on the suit before buying it with the money Squid gave me. The size is much smaller than my normal 40 Regular.

Can you believe it?

I've lost a size.

I try on a smaller size and model it in front of the mirror and it's perfect.

I pay for the suit.

\|\|\|

On the way back to the minivan, I pass by an old lady sitting on a bench. I notice that she's reading the Old Testament. Two kids are both hanging around the bench, up to no good. Both of them are dressed in baggy black clothes, pants sagging well below their waist. One of them is wearing a black bandanna over the bottom of his face like some kind of bandit. The other kid's mocking the blessing by tracing the upright cross over his body, the Father, the Son, and the Holy Ghost. He ends the blessing by pretending to masturbate over the old lady's shoulder. The other one's trying not to laugh with his hand covering over the bandanna; however, he can't hold it in much longer. He lowers the bandanna. A laugh shoots out from his gaping mouth. The other one follows with laughter, causing the old lady to turn her shoulder with a look of disgust on her face.

Nothing has changed, and yet everything has changed.

I stop for a moment, thinking whether or not I should step in and do something.

As I approach the two kids, I see a black spot in the corner of my eye!

I turn to the reflection in the store's window.

There, across the street, stands Cap. He's staring at me with a vacant expression on his face. His murky eyes aimed directly at me.

I turn around and look across the street.

I search for Cap, but I cannot find Cap.

The two kids are laughing again. The poor old lady is shaking her head in disappointment, but this time she's shaking her head at me.

I notice one of the kids is slouched over like a weeping willow, mimicking some confused elderly person. The other kid pats his friend on the shoulder as soon as he catches me staring back at him. They both become still and quiet. I can't draw any attention to myself. I remind myself that I'm a wanted man.

\|V

I decide to walk around the block and blow off some steam.

I pass a Barnes N' Noble bookstore on the way back to the minivan. Behind the storefront window is a display of Foster's NEW YORK TIMES BEST SELLING novel, *The Knockabout*. The cover's done in a similar vein of his debut novel, like a Renaissance-like painting portraying a boy with two identities, the first one, an angelic, translucent-like boy with his arm extended outward as he floats toward an old and weathered door underneath a plush white cloud; and the other, the lifeless body of a boy (I'm guessing the boy's dead body) falls toward a cluster of depraved men and women with their arms stretched out like flames.

V

\ drive past a vibrant motel called Sleep-Inn. Everything about the motel is old and ruined, even all of the lighting, which looks like an attraction from Old Paraíso. I keep driving until I come across a fenced-in construction site. The work appears as if it's been kept on hold for a long time, like many sites I passed that were started but never finished. I break into the site and dump the minivan behind a massive mound of dirt. I wipe down every inch of the inside of the minivan with a shirt. I leave no traces that I was here. Then, finally, I strip the plates, including the VIN number, and toss them in a dumpster.

I walk back to that old motel, pay for a room, and clean the Glock.

Nothing has changed, and yet everything has changed.

V\

\ wake up covered in sweat. I can't sleep again. I switch on the light and grab the envelope on the nightstand. I open the envelope and pull out the letter.

After some careful deliberation, I tear the letter into shreds.

I toss the pieces of paper down the toilet and watch the letters M, S, O, E, S, swirl around the bowel until they're flushed down the toilet.

V\|\|

B</ sunrise, I'm already dressed in my brand new suit and ready to seize the day.

I grab a bite to eat from the vending machine and hang around my room for the better half of the morning, mostly watching news. I flip through each local news channel, as well as major networks. I check each top story, each headline. I can't find my story anywhere on TV.

Surely by now, the news has already broken: PRISON BREAK AT SAN JORGE, INMATES ON THE LOOSE.

I watch TV until noon—*zilch, zip, zero.*

V\|\|\|

\ take the bullet to an upscale business park and after searching through the employees' parking lot filled with smart cars that all look the same, I finally find a real car, vintage, to society's standards.

By now, the employees have returned from lunch and won't leave until past five o'clock at least. When they're ready to leave for work, the show will only be a couple of hours away.

By then, the plates will already be changed and I will be inside the coliseum.

I break into a newer Mustang, black, very sleek, Batman-like.

Not quite the inconspicuous type of car, but I've eaten away too much time searching for a car.

After I hotwire the Mustang, I head to Western Reserve Coliseum.

I cruise around the area surrounding the coliseum, mapping out an exit.

To the right is Southern Bay, a cluttered port, which bares no escape.

To the south is Mexico.

My only option is north.

I park the Mustang closest to the loading dock, face the Mustang north so once I'm finished with Foster I can get the hell out of dodge.

I leave the Glock in the glove box.

More than likely, they'll check for weapons once I'm back-stage.

I can't take any risks.

IX

I slip past a security guard without a problem. I pass another guard and show him the backstage pass worn around my neck.

X

As I'm about to punch in the five-digit password to the stair-case, which will lead me directly to the catwalk, I witness an entourage exiting a dressing room.

In the entourage, I catch a glimpse of Foster, cameras flashing all around him, celebrity-like.

XI

Without anyone watching, I sneak into Foster's dressing room. To my immediate left is a table full of earthy snacks and herbal teas, all meticulously arranged to Foster's liking. I come across a wardrobe case with a couple of Foster's white suits hanging over a clothing rack.

As I'm about to leave, I find a silver pendant of an angel next to a vanity.

I pick up the pendant.

Read the etching: THE SAVING GRACE SHELTER.

I decide to pocket the pendant.

I leave the room before Foster returns.

XII

I take the catwalk to an unused control room in the south side of the coliseum. Below the room suspends a jumbo-sized American flag, which stretches across at least twenty yards in length. I enter the unused control room, like before, using the five-digit password (91879). The door opens without a prob-lem. I blindly move my way through the dark room until I find a black guitar-like case perched against the window. I open the case, revealing a Remington 700.

XIII

FINALLY, the spotlights light up the stage. The show begins with a deafening applause rumbling through the coliseum.

As Foster walks onto the main stage in his flashy white suit with his creamy, flowing white hair—a rather sprightly man for his age—I loosen the collar of my shirt and roll up each one of my sleeves. I set the paperback, *Captured By Light*, next to me.

Next, I pull out two photos from the book, kiss Jimmy, then position the photos upright against the windowsill.

Once the photos are laid out, I reposition myself behind the window by pulling up my pant leg and leaning against the ledge with one foot.

I follow Foster with the scope of the rifle. He acknowledges a couple of audience members seated in the front row.

In return, I acknowledge the audience members.

Suddenly, I see a familiar face. . .

My heart starts pounding against my chest. I remove my eye from the scope and look down at the audience without the scope. I look back through the scope and peer closely.

Jazz?

Next to Jazz sits Doug. Next to Doug are Moses, as well as his teenage son and daughter. There are other people with them as well. Possibly the son or daughter of Doug and Jazz? Did she have more children? Did her children have more children?

I move my aim toward Jazz's head. All these years I was being played, as if I was a part of a brutal social experiment: The consequences of revenge and *what it does to the human spirit*. All those years, I had been treated like a leper by the ones I loved. Not once did Jazz attempt to get me out of prison or build a case against the state. Not once did Jazz come clean about Bishop's death. That's the deal. Is it not? Forgiveness. Confession. All of that religious stuff that they teach you when you're young, tell the truth, cleanse the soul, live without any doubts. She never jumped through hoops or squirreled her way through the many loopholes of the justice system or sought a retrial; whereas my poor mother and father carried my case straight to their graves. Jazz took my imprisonment on the chin. And, to make matters worse, she felt as if I was dragging her along through the gutters and toward a life of punishment. Each time she visited me, she seemed less everything, less interested in what I had to say, less involved, less there, and after a while, Jazz acted like I was some homework assignment or something to be pushed aside. Each time I wrote Jazz, her response letters were shorter and shorter. Then, after she got married, the visitations eventually stopped. The letters stopped, completely. She started her own family and left me in prison for the slow death. In a way, I wanted Jazz to be happy but with me. The fact that Jazz didn't give it her best effort in attempting to reduce my sentence in order to keep me in her life forced me to hate her. All these years I hated her for abandoning me. On top of that, she betrayed me by getting all chummy with Foster. What kind of person befriends someone like that? Either she was doing it on purpose and rubbing their friendship in my face or she had completely forgotten about me, forgotten about what Foster did to Jimmy, to me, to my family. If that was the case, I wasn't even a glint of a memory to her. I was only a phantom who existed in nightmares. After learning that Foster had reached out to Jazz during her treatment, I felt like a stray pet again, something wild or rabid that had turned on its master by biting the hand that fed it; and by doing so, I was dropped off, discarded, and left in a countryside to survive on my own. When you get locked up, the greatest right to man is taken away. I'd take the countryside over San Jorge any day of the week.

But, at the end of the day, I just wanted to be with my family, with people who loved me or so I thought.

Those days were long gone.

I keep my aim on Jazz, then turn it to Doug; and for a moment, I contemplate pulling the trigger.

I pull the aim back to Foster, who's waving at the audience.

I move my aim back to Doug, the man who brainwashed my son, the man who turned my own flesh and blood against me.

I direct my aim back to Jazz. I readjust my grip.

As Foster stands in front of the podium, he thanks the crowd for their support. I take aim at Foster's head. Then. . .

The door opens behind me with a *squeak*!

A voice follows: "Hey! You're not allowed in here!"

I turn my shoulder, only to find a security guard rushing at me.

He reaches for the rifle, but I pull it away.

We play tug of war and struggle and dance. I throw a vicious head butt at the guard, forcing him backward.

During his fall, the rifle suddenly goes off. The shot pierces the window, causing shattered glass to rain down on the crowd below.

Screams cut through the audience!

Chaos.

As the audience scatters to the exits, I turn the rifle upside down and knock out the guard with the butt of the rifle.

I turn back to Foster.

Take aim.

He's already gone.

XIV

As I make my way out of the backstage area, I have nowhere to run. Cops are guarding one end of the hallway while the other end leads to the stage. People are running everywhere.

As the cops try to take control of the chaos, I feel a hand grab me by the arm.

I turn around and find a young man dressed in a Western Reserve collared shirt.

"You Robert?"

I nod my head.

"Troy," he says, out of breath. "Come with me. . . "

I follow Troy away from the cops.

He leads me to another hallway where a group of audience members are racing toward the exits. I lose him in the crowd.

More cops, I see, ahead.

Once more, I look around for Troy but I can't find him anywhere.

I search around for options until I find only one: a *box* housing a fire extinguisher.

With no other option, I rush to the box; and with my elbow, I break the glass door. I pick up a jagged shard of glass from the floor and run the edge of the glass across my forehead. Blood gushes over my face, disguising me.

I stumble to the floor, acting as if I'm being trampled upon. I stagger through a stream of bodies, falling once more to the floor.

A younger man yelling for a paramedic helps me stand to my feet, then ushers me toward the exits.

As we reach the exit, we find a nearby paramedic, who, in return, grabs a kit from the back of an ambulance.

The civilian still hangs around outside the ambulance, waiting for the paramedic to tend to my injuries.

I tell him that I'll be fine.

"It's just a flesh wound," I say.

Yet, despite my greatest effort to get rid of the civilian, he insists on hanging around.

The paramedic finally returns with some sterile gauze to help clean the blood from my face.

As he cleans away the blood, his hands start to shake. His face goes all pale and empty.

He tells me he'll be right back, but I know from the look on his face that he's not coming back—at least not alone. He rotates around.

I find an opportunity and I pick up an instrument from the back of the ambulance and then strike the paramedic in the back of the head, instantly knocking him unconscious.

I turn back to the civilian who's still hanging around—a clingy son of a bitch.

"Don't even try it, Sonny Boy," I say and pull out the pocketknife from my pocket.

The civilian runs to the closest cop while I grab a handful of bandages from the back of the ambulance.

By the time he returns with two cops, I'm already gone.

drive north on Interstate 5.

I turn on the satellite radio.

The story *has* broken.

A broadcaster confirms that there was, in fact, a failed attempt at an assassination.

According to the news, Foster's alive and safe.

The shooter's still at large.

Cops aren't speculating much, but they think it may have been an inside job. They have one man in custody, but they haven't confirmed if it's the shooter or not. Has to be Troy.

Before taking the exit ramp, I decide to get off two exits after Topside.

I stop at a local park where I sit down on a bench, relax, and watch the birds fly overhead. Among the birds, a helicopter rips through the sky.

I've always wondered where helicopters go.

Who are they searching for? Is it a missing person?

A criminal?

For the first time in my life, I know exactly what the people operating the helicopter are searching for.

||

wake up to nightfall. Any minute now, the park will be drizzled with early morning joggers.

I act hastily and find a large rock. I park the Mustang on a sturdy dock, which stretches over a lagoon.

Without wasting anymore time, I roll down the windows inside the Mustang.

I grab the Glock from the glove box.

Then, I place the rock over the gas pedal, switch the gear in drive, and quickly step out of the Mustang's path. The Mustang accelerates over the edge of the dock and crashes into the water.

It doesn't sink at first, as I thought it would. Yet, it floats there like some kind of metal hippopotamus passing gas in the murky water.

Eventually, after a couple of minutes, the Mustang starts to sink below.

Once I ditch the Mustang, I head to Topside.

\|\|\|

ABOUT thirty or so minutes into the walk, the sun starts to peek over the horizon, casting an orange-pinkish hue underneath the thick gray clouds.

I walk for about twenty minutes before I finally arrive at Topside.

Nothing has changed.

I grab a late breakfast at a local dining cart not too far from the beach.

I spend a good amount of the morning thinking about what's next for me.

Where do I go from here?

Once I've exhausted enough time at the diner, I head to the beach.

\|\/

I watch my feet dig into coarse sand, ten tiny, curled, and crinkled toes vanishing before my eyes. I raise my head and turn my gaze toward the great Pacific Ocean.

The beach is sparse with people, mainly due to the overcast skies. About ten feet out, a young man is waist-deep in the water. He carries what looks like a vase in his arms.

As I head back toward Main Street, I catch the young man opening the lid of the vase in the corner of my eye.

I stop and turn around.

I peer closer at the young man. So familiar the young man is, and yet, so strange. He looks down at the sea, then he turns his gaze to the gloomy horizon. At that moment, I realize the vase is *not* a vase. Yet, it's an urn. Inside the urn are ashes, and the young man is about to dump these ashes into the sea. Right before he does, he turns his shoulder and looks directly at me, as if he's aware that I've been watching him all along.

I acknowledge him and remain poised in spite of my severe fatigue.

We both share a long, heavy stare.

I raise my head in a nod, but he never nods back.

I don't expect him too, nor do I want him to for I am an old man who still hasn't found his way back home.

He closes the urn and walks back to the shore.

The temptation of talking to this young man overwhelms me, pulling me every which way until I'm left attached to the beach. One side of me is tempting me to tell this young man that the world hasn't abandoned him as it did me. Another side of me is tempting me to tell this young man that he *still* has a chance, but I know—don't know how or why—I will see him again tomorrow, then the following day, until our paths cross.

When that time comes, he will be ready to talk.

I WILL BE READY TO LISTEN."

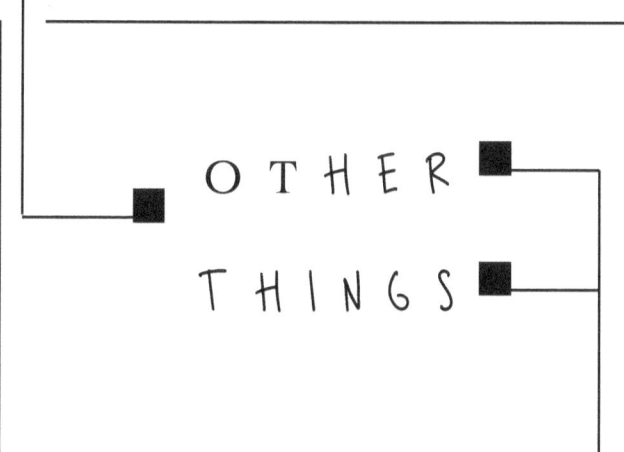

OTHER
THINGS

1   M O E   S T O P   O K A Y ?

watch the wet sand gradually sift through the cracks of my
toes as the tide rushes back toward the open sea before me.
     I take a step closer to the hungry sea, both an eater and a
creator of my darkest dreams. The waves return, like a great
exhale of water that splashes onto the curled ends of my jeans,
which are rolled up to my shins. In that moment, while I embrace a breeze of briny air, the never-ending rhythm of the sea
forcing me to focus on the present, and in that moment, I decide to hold off on dumping his ashes.

Tomorrow, I tell myself.

I will say my final goodbyes to my brother.

With the decision made, I exit the beach.

(I once read in *Mentally Fit*, with an emphasis on "Men" in
the word *Mentally*, that the measure of a Fit Man is based on,
not the decisions he makes, but rather being able to carry and
most importantly, endure responsibilities for those decisions)

Instead of driving, I decide to stroll down Main Street.

I come across another elderly man.

Unlike the one on the beach, he looks like a character one
would discover while flipping through the pages of an Ernest
Hemingway novel.

I'm tempted to ask him if he knows any good places to eat.
As the words make their way to my lips, I witness the furrow,
a pensive line form between his two eyebrows, as though indicating me to stay far away.

\\

HALFWAY down Main Street, I come across a group of wiry people being escorted from the Main Pier, which has been roped off by yellow caution tape.

I keep my head down, make sure not to draw any attention to myself, and carefully scout out the scene.

Four cruisers are idling in a parking lot.

Sirens flashing, however, switched to silent.

Cops aren't saying much to spectators, but rather guiding them away from Main Pier in orderly cop fashion while, at the same time, trying to maintain peace around the crime scene.

When I witness a surfer giving what looks like a statement to a cop, who's jotting down notes in a notepad, I don't get all worked up over it, even though I can feel the slight stirring in my gut, not from the hunger but an overall sense of unease. I remind myself that I'm still in the clear and that I'm okay.

I look around the scene for any other activity but don't find anything significant.

If I had to guess, someone must've found the body.

\\\

BEFORE I grab a bite to eat, I decide to stop at Cyber Jaxx's for a cup of coffee.

As I'm about I log into my account, I feel a sudden urge to use the restroom. Strangely, I don't have to go, as in number 1, 1 being urination, as in take a piss, and then number 2, as in take a shit, then, number 3, as in puke, then, finally, the mysterious number 4, which I once heard had nothing to do with using a toilet.

When I enter the restroom, I'm drawn to the last stall, as in I can feel a force, maybe an intuition, reeling me into the stall.

More cautiously, I look underneath the stall and make sure nobody is occupying the toilet before opening the door.

I open the door, only to find a clogged toilet.

On the left divider wall is a perfectly circular hole. My gut sinks like an anchor, as I soon realize the purpose of the deliberate cutout, especially when I see greasy imprints of two butt cheeks, a splattering of dark stains, as well as the words *Knock 3 Times for a Plug* written in black Sharpie.

All of a sudden, I'm overwhelmed by a sense of déjà vu. I have been here before, not here, physically but mentally.

I return to the Internet café and grab *Joshua'ζ Tree* from my bookbag and flip to the NOTES section behind Chapter 1 and skim through Twiggy's notes until I find the passage about the running shoe TANXX "ᏀᎬᎢ ᏆᎢ ᎢᎪᏁᎪᎪ."

I put the two together *Cyber Jaxx* and *tank*.

More specifically, the words *tissue paper* in one of Twiggy's notes:

"Overflowed with tissue paper."
(Overflowed with tissue paper)

I rush back into the restroom in the back of the café. I enter the last stall and while using a handful of toilet paper as a sort of makeshift glove, open up the lid of the tank. Taped to the bottom of the tank is a plastic bag with something inside.

Warding off the idea of potentially harmful bacteria floating inside the murky water, I roll up my sleeve and reach inside and while trying not to touch the growths of black fuzzy-like mold along the sides of the tank, pull out the plastic bag, which is tightly sealed. Once I bring the bag to the sink, wash it, then dry it off, I empty out the content or contents onto the countertop. Only one object: a silver USB flash drive. I wash my hands with a lot of soap, dry them, then wash them again, then dry them again, then pocket the drive before some horny toad shows up and gets the wrong impression.

I leave in a hurry before things get weird.

With my latest finding, I locate the most private computer in the café. I manage to find one in the very back corner away from any windows and curious eyes. I take a deep breath and insert the USB flash drive into the back of the monitor and the drive labeled "11" appears on the desktop. With the mouse, I double click on the icon, opening the drive.

The window appears, and inside the drive are "449" items. Altogether, there are twenty-three folders, the first one labeled "*Black and White Habit*," then the next, "*Doormats*," then, after I scroll closer to the bottom of the window, I find a folder labeled "*Red Pines*," above another folder called "*Research*." The sight of the folder immediately grabs my attention. I open the folder where, inside, are dozens of videos, some ranging from ten minutes in lengths, while others close to an hour.

Again, I get that feeling in my gut, that anchor planting me to the chair. Yet, despite the feeling of being paralyzed, I feel the sudden urge to run far away from here. Return the flash drive back to the toilet, where it belongs, and scrub any memory of having found the device.

With my heart pounding inside my chest, I hover the cursor over the first video "Exhibit 1."

(I once read in *Bar Code* that exhibits are normally labeled with numbers by a plaintiff in a trial, whereas, for a defendant, exhibits are labeled with letters, for example, Exhibit A)

Instead of double-clicking on the video, I tap the space bar. The video appears on the screen, the camera showing a wide-angle of a frail woman—possibly middle-aged—sleeping on a familiar-looking bed inside a dimly lit room with bars covering the window. I know the room, in fact, know every inch of it, for I have been inside the room, *not* this one in particular, but one very much like it. The door opens loudly, followed by the *jingling* of keys, and in walks one of the orderlies. Startled, the patient wakes from her sleep.

The orderly says to her, "Rise and shine, Twigs."

Twiggy?

Fearful of the orderly, she slides to the end of the bed, her feet reared back. Ready to kick the burly orderly, she cries out for help.

The orderly ends up gagging her with a sock before she can finish crying out "*Help* Me. . . "

Somehow, I already know exactly what's going to happen next. The labels on each one of the folders, exhibits and videos: *This is her design*. After watching only seconds of the other videos, I realize that it's not just the one orderly who sexually assaulted Twiggy, but it's many of them. Altogether, there are eleven orderlies. This is her design. Her way of fighting back against those who stole everything from her.

Physically, she couldn't take on these orderlies, maybe one or two of them, maybe Chuck, who probably weighed a buck-fifty, and she'd more than likely give him a run for his money. But physically, Twiggy was no match for them.

Being that Red Pines is so well guarded and nearly impossible to smuggle inside contraband, I can't help but ask myself: *How was she able to sneak inside a video camera?*

Strangely, I think I already know the answer.

I return to the first video "Exhibit 1" and only watch a few minutes before my insides flex like a fist. I've seen the orderly before, but I don't remember his name.

Feeling sick to my stomach, I exit from Cyber Jaxx with the flash drive containing evidence against eleven—and possibly more—orderlies who work at Red Pines.

IV

AS I continue on Main Street, I nearly bump shoulders with a cute twenty-something who looks at me like I'm a criminal. I ignore her and that expression on her face and kill some time at Jugglers Pizza, where I pay for one grape soda and play two games of a once-popular first-person shooter, *Neo-Cam* (Cam, short for "Camelot," as in that Camelot-Camelot, the one with knights, swords, and round tables).

After I tire out my hands from the joystick, I exit Jugglers. While opening the door, the bell rings above! My eyes catch a round logo of the pizzeria, causing me to pause for a moment. The logo is shaped like a pizza on flames. The similarities of the logo and a CD burning application that I recently saw on the desktop of the computer inside Cyber Jaxx are uncanny. I take note of possibly my next course of action.

V

SOMEWHAT less stressed after slaying base heads and river rats, I hear the blare of a car horn to my right. A pissed-off driver is sticking his fugly mug out of the window and throwing every obscenity in the book at an old man, who, after a closer study, looks similar to the strange man on the beach. He doesn't pay any mind to the obnoxious driver. Instead, the old man waves him off, like an old, tired lion ignoring a hyena whose whoop is much louder than its bite.

As the car peels away and makes quite the scene, I decide, for no particular reason, to follow him toward the store at the end of The Strip. Again, déjà vu is so thick and heavy it wafts over me, leaving me compelled to pick out each detail of the surroundings, first starting with the many flyers covering the side of a local pharmacy. All of the flyers are the same: Promoting this "*upcoming spectacle*" starring "*Fire Juggler: The Eater of Fire.*" The next detail: A hot roller, fried and foiled, chicken flipping on the street corner. Completely zoomed out of his mind. A couple of rocket men are huddled around him, high off the crank as well, dunking invisible donuts inside invisible coffee mugs, then holding those invisible dripping wet donuts high in the air while praising a holy White Boss for their daily trash. One of the chalk-gobblers calls the hot roller "Red," as in the Red Wizard, who, in return, shoos him away like a gnat and cries out to the heavens, "The great light is upon thee!"

Immediately, I'm left with no words for each vivid detail is strikingly similar to her notes. I have been here before. Here. I have, mentally, in this very moment.

I return to *Joshua'ζ Tree*; and sure enough, while skimming through Twiggy's notes inside the novel, I come across a similar, if not, the same tweaker named "Red" whose ranting on and on about a "great light" in front of a bird store.

I watch the old man enter the store, which, after picking up a better look at the yellow sign, I realize is the same store in the notes: One *Stop* Bird Shop.

Even the description in the novel is spot on:

"massive yellow beak protruding from the letter 'P'"
(massive yellow beak protruding from the letter "P")

Has she, as in Twigs, been to Topside before?

During Red's rambles, I pick up one particular word that he utters several times. The word *Doxx*, as in "docks" but pronounced with two letter x's. "Doxx," he rants and raves, "xx, the ole bag of bones, carrier of darkness, scythe-wielder, what do I need to do in order to spell it out! This place is death, do you not see with those camera balls in your head!"

As I walk past the tweaker, I met with his eye, which suddenly appears different but incredibly familiar, like the faintest glow of a cat's eye in the darkness, dumbly robotic and yet, at same time, highly intelligent, god-like.

As soon as he acknowledges my interest, his eyes return to normal and then he continues with his rambling about a great light in the sky.

I ignore the colorful speed demons on the street corner and enter the bird store. The light *ping* of a doorbell sounds. My eyes catch the same "AAA" sign written in her notes next to the door: Like in the notes, the first A in the sign standing for "Accurate," the second, "Attentive," and third, "Awesome."

The owner of the store greets me with a "Welcome to One Stop." He's wearing a black T-shirt with the words *Plaut Hole* above an empty grave with a headstone reading "The Queen of Horror," a shovel leaned up against the headstone.

Trying not to make it so obvious, I piddle around the store, browsing through various feeders and whatnot, until my eyes catch the strange old man standing in front of a row of birdseed in the middle of the center aisle.

While keeping my eyes on products, I make my way into the same aisle. I sneak a glance toward the spot where I last saw the old man and strangely, he's gone. One second, there. Now, poof. Like a figment of my imagination. I walk to the spot where he was standing and first notice a drop of blood on the floor and then I look up and see the shelf of birdseed.

(Even though seagulls are mainly scavengers and their diet consists of eating *sea* food, primarily fish, you know, being so close to the sea and all, I once read in *Birdscape* that seagulls, if given the option, may prefer black oil sunflower seeds)

I don't hear any ping, doorbell, or whatever, which makes me believe that he's still inside the store. I don't know exactly why I'm so interested in finding this one particular man, but I feel compelled to ask him what he's doing in Topside. I check the back of the store but don't have any luck. Sure enough, as written in Twigs's notes, I stumble upon the janitor's closet.

Without any employees or customers watching, I open the closet but don't find anything out of the ordinary.

Before leaving the store, I'm drawn to the restroom. In the novel, Twigs writes about the main character, Joshua, using a restroom, which turns out to be some kind of portal into another world.

Out of curiosity, I check out the restroom, which turns out to be an ordinary restroom. But I'm not alone. I hear someone in the last stall: Sniffling, farting, a *rustling* of toilet paper. I kneel down and see two feet.

In order not to draw any attention to myself, I use the sink and wash up. I hear the sound of a toilet flushing soon after I rip a paper towel from the dispenser.

A man exits the stall, but it's not the old man, but rather an employee of the store.

He looks at me with guilty eyes and says to me, "Fucking burritos, man."

I have no response for him. I'm too drawn to the name on his nametag: "Cal."

That name?

From the novel.

"Take it easy," he says, washes his hands, dries them, then tosses the wadded piece of damp paper towel in the trash, and exits the restroom.

I skim through Twigs's notes, mainly the part in the notes where Joshua discovers a key in the "*fecal-spattered newspaper*" underneath the American Goldfinch cage, and then decide, on a whim, to mimic Joshua's actions. Before making my move, I feel compelled to further investigate the notes written on the DLC section, "Season'z Pass," in particular, the final chapter of the novel, a sort of extension to the main story called *Limbz*. I skim through the notes until I find the name "*Cal Betancourt*" on the back of the page, the name "Cal" immediately catching my eye. I return to the previous page, where Joshua or as he calls himself "Rook," opens an "*aged and dusty trunk*" with the initials "*JL*"—what I assume stands for Joshua Lamb—which later is confused with the number "*13*." Inside the large trunk is a "*lock of hair, strands of both silky jet black hair and blonde hair twisted up in a fine braid*." I don't know the reasons why I'm so drawn to this one particular line in Twigs's notes, but I know it may hold significance, not now, but maybe later, perhaps in the future, and why I feel as if the discovery of a multicolored hair braid is somehow connected to Cal leaves my stomach in knots. I pull myself from the book and make my way toward the Goldfinch.

As I crack open the birdcage, I don't see any keys hiding in the bottom of the cage.

"Excuse me, sir," a familiar voice says from behind. I rotate around and see Burrito Man from the restroom standing in the middle of the aisle "Customers aren't allowed to open the cages."

"Sorry," I say.

Since I'm here and I'm already starting to look like a frisky cat, I buy a bag of birdseed.

VI

AFTER purchasing a bag of black oil sunflower seeds from One Stop, I spot Flip and his animated crew hanging outside the

Galatia. To the right of the arcade is a local bookstore called *E-Z Reads*, which, apparently, for some unusual reason, only features books written by authors with last names starting with the letter "E" through the letter "Z," leaving out the A's, B's, C's, and D's. A bookstore with no Charles Dickens? Or what about Bradbury?

Before moving forward, I'm grabbed by the newly released hardback novel called *Neurobraiding* by author Chase Phisher displayed on a shelf behind the storefront window.

Hair braid? Neurobraiding? Connection?

Then, to the left of the arcade is a video store, Pick-a-Flick, like Fanboys, which, despite the two stores desperately cling-ing onto relevance before their finally liquefied into obscurity by a decadent society that pounded a wooden stake into its once beating heart when it collectively decided to abandoned physical media and proceed toward a slow and painful de-mise, like a kind of suicide cult being summoned by the digital abyss, I can imagine draws a selected crowd that pine for the good ole days when a movie's shelf life is measured by its wear, not the dust it collects: The one disease in America in which the cure is time. One particular 80's-inspired poster for a movie called *The Editors* grabs my eye, and a self-censored wave of nostalgia wafts over me. The poster, from what I can tell, was fan-made and drawn by hand, not a silly prompt where the only creativity required was striking the key on a keyboard. The signature of the local artist is written on the bottom of the movie poster, and I can only make out the name "Jazz."

I make my way toward the group, and of all the frogs, Flip is the first one to acknowledge my presence.

"What's good?" he says and flicks his head in a nod.

"Sup," I say and ask him if he and his friends like to party.

Next, he asks me if I'm holding.

"No," I say, "but I'm looking to score."

VII

THE latest sighting of the old school movie poster has me revel-ing in montages where scenes play out over a Top 40 hit.

While chasing the sun, I practice patterns in a Mad World, where Salamanders and Serpents wage nightly wars in a des-perate attempt to find a way into uncovering and understanding the hands that make me tick, but don't they know that the train has already long departed, *hella*-bullied and nullified, by a manmade thief whose fingers snake into everything we once held sacred, deeply spreading and embedding into the fabric of traditions unforgotten, while providing us futures of great uncertain. The girl from Knowhere sees something in me—she always did, from the moment our eyes connected, but the hollow man wanted to collect *her* soul.

Technically, it is she who teaches me how to kill.

And I kill, not only for him, for Jimmy, but for her.

I kill him.

He kills me.

I kill them all.

Every last one of them.

And they kill every part of me.

The parts that matter the most.

Then, I kill again and again until the truth reveals itself to me.

How much can a doorman pine for the West?

The chamber of the revolver spins like a revolving door.

But I continue to hold open the door.

The rent-a-hot-roller's nose gets redder and redder each go around—is the madness ever going to end?

I can't take it anymore.

I'm ready to listen to *her*.

F O O L   H O U 5 E

watch the wet sand gradually sift through the cracks of my toes, and I can't stand the sight of my feet and what they've become over the past decade. The hammer of modernity has shaped them weak and narrow and boney. Once, I remember, when I was a kid, both my feet were as wide as hands. I used to play outside like a wild animal, in the lawn, on pavement as hot as coals, without any shoes, the soles of my unclothed feet firm, coarse, and molded by the land in which I traveled upon. I used to dig my toes into all kinds of strange and suspicious places: Shady holes or burrows in the ground; the mud; a wetland, which left my feet swollen and infected; nonetheless, my feet endured many inflictions, like bee stings or snakebites or sharp glass or rocks. My feet were liberated. Like my hands. Fingers spread out and free to grab whatever captured my kid-like mind: a spider or a snake.

A *frog*.

When I find myself alone with Flip inside Apple Ripper's house, I aim the barrel of the revolver against his forehead and blow the stoner's brains out. Flip's Merry Band of Frogs rush toward the *blast* of the gunshot. Drew is the first to show his ugly mug. I shoot him dead. Then, next is Chemo, who manages to dodge a gunshot and attempts to pry the revolver from my hand, but I use the top of my forehead and head butt him directly in the bridge of his nose.

(According to *Self D-Fence*, the upper part of the skull is the hardest part, whereas the sides, including the temporal region being softer and more susceptible to injury)

Chemo's nose bursts open like a candy dispenser, strings of blood spraying everywhere.

As he cries out in pain, I put an end to his suffering with a bullet straight to his chrome dome.

What's-His-Name and Wilt make a sudden one-eighty and jet from the house. I shoot them both in the back. Wilt still has some fight in him, as he crawls his way toward the street, leaving behind a snail-trail of blood. I finish him off.

The only person who makes it alive is Apple Ripper, who, despite all of the shooting and killing in front of him, doesn't budge an inch from his shit-stained, jeez-speckled recliner, still gripping his homemade apple-bowl, baked out of his mind, his bloodshot eyes wide and amazed, as if he's caught in a bizarre real-life gun-fu-style anime.

Shortly after the shooting, the cops put out an APB on my description after a witness spotted me fleeing from the Ripper man's house. Days later, after a sweeping manhunt all across Los Dementes County, the cops find me squatting in an abandoned house in The Point, lying in moldy bathtub as naked as the day I was expelled from darkness and thrust into a much darker world where demons greeted you with practiced smiles and flimsy handshakes, moments away from painting my epic Masterpiece along the walls.

Following the arrest, my story makes the headlines. All of the talking heads on TV are speaking about me, as if they all know me, like each and every one of them know what's going on inside my head. They said I shot all those people because it was a drug "deal gone bad." But, strangely, alternative media is starting to scratch the surface as to why I pulled the trigger after news about a massive seizure of drugs, including fentanyl, from the Ripper man's house is buried in the headlines and never, not once, mentioned in the initial reporting. Not a drug deal, but rather more in line with a misguided attempt at vigilantism.

After a prevailing narrative about Jimmy and somehow his death being connected to the shooting in The Point, I turn into a folk hero, if only for a day or two until the next news story.

My story draws the attention of true crime podcasters, who leech off, not only my story, but also Jimmy's, to the millions of subscribers. One of the subscribers is an actual real-life investigative journalist, Stewart Badger, former employee at the pop-culture magazine called *Flashback*. From what I've heard, Badger's quite a bloodhound who possesses a rare patience for keeping his nose to the ground and sniffing out a lead, unlike some attention-whore who's podcasting for *likes* or clicks, but who in the hell am I to judge someone else's hustle in a society where, for most, the only means of survival rests in tricks and trades of the *American Grift*?

In court I plead not guilty even though I feel guilty, but not for the crimes I committed. I don't carry any regrets for plugging those frogs with bullets. But guilty, as in I feel guilty for not acting sooner; instead, I allowed the emotion from the loss of my brother to cripple me to a point where the only remedy was sex, drugs, and alcohol. My own pleasure-soaked escape from reality. Regardless of my feelings, the story is *not* about me. Not anymore. Underneath all of the violence and glamour, the story is about an innocent man named Cedric Gaines, who was sent to prison, and he still remains behind bars even as I head to trial.

After I'm charged with four counts of first-degree murder, stating I, Robert Backer, acted *willfully* and *deliberately* in the deaths of those four frogs, the judge hands out my sentence.

Life in prison.

The trial is televised for the entire country to see. Half of the country scorns me. The other half adores me.

Of all the people who want my story to fade away, Daniel Ayker has a particular interest in deleting my existence from the face of the earth. Sure enough, after Badger learns about Jimmy's story and all of the main players who contributed to his death, the ones who, in another life, should've been pinned and mounted on my wall, a taut red string of yarn connecting each and every one of them, Badger brings a mountain of evidence to a close friend, Dwight, who, in return, surfaces from an early retirement, which mostly consists of fishing on Lake Henderson and reflecting on his Black and White days of beating the pulp out of criminals, daydreaming about capturing his very own White Whale, and seeks help from John Ruby, who finds a *chink* in Ayker's armor: Officer Rodriquez, once a kid from the gutters of El Duero, where streets ran with the blood of gangbangers on a daily basis, nonetheless, a kid who understood criminality at the very young age and the impact it had on *familias*, especially his own, his *hermano* shot and killed by a stray bullet during a turf war when he was only fifteen years old, and then decided soon after high school that he wanted to make sure no *chico* from the gutters ever experienced what he did at such a young age.

With physical evidence showing Rodriquez's involvement in Ayker's criminal enterprise, Ruby manages to convince the officer, who has ambitions of making detective one day, to go on record, basically, "rat out" Daniel Ayker and his partner in crime, Luther Bishop, the owner of Crystal Palace.

The day before Ayker's trial, Nicolas West is found dead in the back of Happy Dragon Spa, fentanyl overdose. From there, each person, including key witnesses, including Jamie, Kim, Yogi, even Rooster, the driver of the Alpine Transportations truck, are "accidentally" killed: An automobile accident or drowning in a hot tub or, in the case of Yogi, death by suicide. His body found hanging from an electrical cord inside his closet, half-cocked. Officer Malone is caught, on camera, picking up Kim. The next morning, Kim's body is found in a dumpster, strangled to death. Despite Malone being the last person who was spotted with Kim, it's still unclear whether or not Ayker ordered Malone to kill all of the witnesses. Either way, I expect a visit from a spineless jellyfish who'll cave from the promise of a shortened sentence. Sure enough, he pays the Reich Bros to snuff me out.

As I catch wind of their latest sock job, which involves me being beaten to death by socks filled with rocks from the yard, I start a fire in the back of the cafeteria; and then soon following the distraction a riot breaks out, rival gangs battling to the death. I take advantage of the smoke and the fights, as well as the flood of guards as cover and use my shank, which I made from the materials that I gathered inside my cell, mainly parts of my bed, to take out each Bro when they're not paying attention. My little stunt results in solitary confinement and when I'm released back into the public, I've earned the respect of the other inmates, including the Beanies, who offer me protection.

Since the contraband-peddling, cigarette-hoarding, Beanie-wearing fat cats have all of the guards in their pockets, I accept their offer, which includes many perks, like the heads of Daniel Ayker and Luther Bishop soon after their sentencing, each served on silver platters in a late afternoon shower, all orchestrated by the prison guards—unlike that crybaby, Bishop, who folds like a lawn chair, Ayker puts up a fight but nothing can match an unbridled anger of losing a brother who was so close to you that you can never imagine a world without him, but I know he's with me, in spirit, my own ghostly warrior shadowing my each and every move, absorbing blows while providing me with enough strength to plunge a faucet knob right through Ayker's eye socket. The offer also includes frills and privileges from the Outside World, for instance, the conjugal visit of one particular groupie who has taken an interest in my story in the headlines: Samantha Jasper Caldwell, but her friends call her "Jazz."

From the moment our eyes connect, I know, in my bones, that she's not like the others. She's incredibly smart, creative, witty, beautiful, and if angels do exist, I reckon that she's sent down by God to spread "Light"—after spending a couple of years in prison, surrounded by men, who closely resemble a rusty tool in a shed, I could probably, with a straight face, find attraction from anyone with XX chromosomes, even though, outside these prison walls, I was a bit more selective. Despite our connection, I'm still skeptical about Jazz, but mostly, I'm skeptical about her motives after she shares with me that she recently started an obsession with a genre called "true crime," says she finds the whole serial killer-thing "as sexy as hell." I want to roll my eyes in front of her and tell her that she's been watching way too many movies, but I find her uniquely attractive and I'm unable to shake her from my head, maybe it's her puppy dog eyes and the way they look up to me or simply into me or the uneven set of chompers, which I find doltishly cute; she doesn't qualify for the glossy mag standards, even though photoshop can edit out her imperfections, but I'd say it's those imperfections that make her beautiful; reminds me of Shelley Duvall's character Wendy from *The Shining*, but with much darker pigmentation, *something* about her that I can't quite put my finger on, but whatever it is, it's magnetic, it's electric, and I say it'd be the *ultimate* crime against humanity if I chose not to embrace her.

(According to *Science Now* serial killers have a reduced gray matter in specific areas of the prefrontal cortex of the brain, as well as the temporal poles, and if that were the case, then I'm a rare and exotic bird who defies Science, since I'm capable of loving and caring for another, like the way I loved Jimmy, and soon, says a tingle deep in my bones, I may be falling for Jazz)

Regardless of whether I agree or disagree with Jazz, I don't want to ruin what we have together, even though the time we spend together is limited. Only one visit per week. Each visit lasts for no more than two hours, depending on holidays. For the next couple of months, we start a relationship. The guards are, in a strange way, rooting for us. Some seem jealous, but not in a vindictive way. During our three-month anniversary, I hook up the guards with imported videos of Giallo films; and in return, the guards clear out the library. For an hour and a half Jazz and I have the entire library all to ourselves.

Two months later, Jazz pays me a visit.

She's acting strange and more aloof.

When I ask her what's wrong, Jazz breaks the news to me and tells me that she's pregnant. I'm excited, but, at the same time, petrified, not for being a father, but being a father who'll never be able to raise his son or daughter. Only two hours a week isn't going to cut it.

(In *Parenting For Dummies*, it compares parenting to a full-time job, and that it's crucial, especially during the first couple of years of raising a child, for both parents to be present)

The thought of dumping all the responsibility on Jazz kills me. Over time, I try to wear her down and encourage Jazz not to keep it. Then I start to think—in prison, you have plenty of time to think—about Jazz's motives. Why start a relationship with a person who is serving four life sentences? Words don't have any impact on Jazz's decision. She eventually decides to have the baby, says the handwritten letter that I receive from one of Jazz's close friends. Said she felt I needed to know. Maybe the mysterious writer hated me so much that the thought alone of being a father and being locked way, unable to see or speak to his own flesh and blood, would be much worse than death itself. I don't see Jazz until two years later after our argument. She tells me that she gave birth to a baby boy, and she named him Moses.

Many years later, when given an opportunity, this old jailbird breaks out of prison, and I head South, where it all began.

\|

\| watch the wet sand gradually sift through the cracks of my toes, and I smile.

Instead of following Flip and his squiggly crew of tadpoles, as I originally planned, I make the last minute decision to shift my focus toward much bigger fish, starting with Mayor Daniel Ayker and while investigating the former cop's involvement in Jimmy's death, I uncover his secret operation, which involves sex trafficking, mostly young women.

One of these women is a former artist named Jazz.

I fall in love with Jazz.

Then, I kill for Jazz.

And she kills for me.

But I take the blame for it.

Then, I kill every last one of them.

Jazz and I escape to the North.

Before we reach the border, I get busted.

After the sentencing, the slam of a jail door closing sounds like music to my ears.

|||

THE song of the sea puts me in a trance.

I think about Jimmy, and the thoughts of my brother are so heavy that I find myself struggling to hold up my head. Before the shooting, he used to compare my wide hobbit feet to fins, like my feet grew the wrong way, width-wise, not length, and I find that observation strange but I don't feel the least insecure about them. Instead, I embrace my imperfections.

As I dig my feet further into the sand, I make fists with my toes, and the feeling of being back home fills me with warmth.

I watch a plastic bag stick to my feet, and I suddenly cringe from the sight of pollution scattered among the sea. I redirect my attention back toward the dusty shoreline and except for a couple of distant bystanders who appear to be drunkenly rocking back and forth like buoys with these helmet-like devices on their heads and a strange old man watching from the dune, the beach is completely deserted.

I leave the polluted beach and while making my way to the street, bump into a guy with tanned skin as burnt, crispy, and cracked as a potato chip and a tattoo of the name *Drew* on his forearm. I ask Mr. Potato Chip about why Topside is so desolate, even though I assume widespread pollution has deterred a lot of people from enjoying the beach and the many amenities and activities it has to offer. He tells me to go fuck off and die already. I'm tempted to punch the old man in the face, but once, in another life, it was considered a mortal sin to strike a person who was your elder, even if he was full of shit. Instead of getting upset, I ignore the bitter old man and it's not until I make it to a VR café called Cyber Jaxx that I fully understand the reasons for his bitterness. Wearing VR headsets, as well as a suction cup device attached to their junk, dozens of men in their prime are propped upright by suspended wires inside the dimly lit café, having virtual sex. The cylinder-shaped devices pump up and down like pistons, and the sight alone causes me to take a step back and rethink my options—*Am I too late?*

I can't help but wonder what Topside would've looked like if I escaped from Red Pines much sooner.

To my left, on the side of a ruined building is a torn billboard that displays the face of the newly elected governor of California, Daniel Ayker, who, despite taxpayer's loathing for him, won by a landslide after his campaign focused on replacing *all* human jobs with artificial intelligence, thus allowing us humans to spend more time focusing on our passions.

(From what I read in the *Los Dementes Times*, Ayker's team was involved in shenanigans during the eleventh hour before the final count, and a lot of fingers point to voting machines, people claming that they were "hacked")

After walking around Topside, it's clear to me that Ayker's plan to replace humans with AI has taken place much sooner than I imagined. I stop by the Cove for a bite to eat.

When I enter the restaurant, I'm immediately greeted by a large kiosk machine, which speaks to me in a voice that, based on my facial recognition and interests, I find soothing. Most, if not all of the tables, are empty, which is alarming, given the time of the day. To my right, I spot only six patrons in the restaurant and each of them is wearing a VR headset, playing virtual games while stuffing their round faces with seafood full of micro plastics.

The only signs of life appear artificially, through *beeps* and prompts of boxy machines strategically scattered throughout the dining area, as well as a conveyer belt that moves a plate of food to a table, as if it's on an assembly line. Even the cook is a machine with two robotic arms.

I soon realize that tracking down those who were involved in Jimmy's death is going to be more difficult than I originally anticipated. I'm going to need a longer gun.

IV

I watch powder sugar sift through the bearded-baker's metal strainer and delicately fall like snow onto a round funnel cake.

I turn toward to my right, where Jazz is also watching on, with a child-like wonder, and the thought of killing Bishop has vanished. I order a cone of Neapolitan ice cream, and Jazz—who has never tried the ice cream before—decides to give it a try. Again, her eyes light up like spotlights.

I never want the moment to end.

Three months later, after we leave Topside, I bring Jazz to the lake where I ask for her hand in marriage.

She says yes.

One year later Ayker tracks us down after a photo of Jazz surfaces on social media. Apparently, without her permission, a random person snapped a photograph of Jazz while she was running at the park and posted the photo on the Internet.

Later that same night, Ayker and his goons show up at the house. Jazz is seriously injured during the shootout. I escape before the local police arrive; and when I later sneak inside the hospital to visit Jazz while she's recovering from the gunshot wound to the shoulder, Jazz tells me that we can no longer be together.

"You bring too much uncertainty," she says.

V

I watch the tears run from Jazz's eyes.

She's screaming and throwing curses at me, telling me how much of a piece of shit I am and how she can't stand the sight of my face.

When she addresses me, she barks the name "Cal."

"Fuck, Cal! You fucking cheater, fucking piece of fucking shit! I hope you rot in fucking hell!"

She's emotional, as she should be.

But I don't regret my actions.

For a second, I can't even remember my own name.

My name is Cal, and what I once loved most about her are stories that she used to tell me about her old man, who played saxophone for the band *The Shift*. But I don't love her.

Not anymore.

She runs out of the Hi-Way Diner.

I don't chase after her.
I already have another love in my life.
Her name is Kelly, and she's pregnant with twins.

VI

I watch wet dirt sift through a sieve, and after I shake and swirl and follow the instructor's advice by dipping the pan into the river and giving the pan one last shake and swirl, a glimmer of light catches my eye.

I reach my fingers into the pan and pluck the grain of gold from the dirt and hold it to the sunlight. All of a sudden, I'm back on the beach, staring down at shrapnel from a bullet inside my brother's ashes.

Shaking away the memory, I turn toward Jazz, who stops sifting for gold, and looks at me with a worried expression on her face and says I look like I've seen a ghost.

A part of me knows that I may never see her face again.
I must return to Topside, where I have unfinished business.

VII

FROM a distance, I watch my own demise.

I feel completely useless walking around Topside with an empty revolver. I secure Jimmy's urn inside my bookbag; and as I make my way back to Cyber Jaxx, I envision another Cyber Jaxx, possibly one from the not-so distant future, maybe a few years from now, when a virtual world has taken over reality, the horror of not being able to unplug from The Machine.

Once I enter the Internet café, I sit at the nearest computer and then log into my account with the username: CLUBHOP-PER69*_*

While checking my feed, I notice a new trend called "Operation Unplug." Users "unplugging" their devices, including computers or televisions, not charging their phones or tablets or mp3 players and allowing these devices to simply die. The ultimate "digital detox." Based on the many videos posted on my feed—which not only contradicts the whole "unplugging" trend, but also undermines it—users even resort to destroying their devices. Before the trend spreads to the Internet café and jocks, whether it be surfers, chatters, hackers, or psycho stalkers, start yanking the monitors from the wall and use them as their own personal wrecking balls in order to release a wound-up tension created by a shitty-ass reality manipulated by a so-cially-awkward, four-eyed brah with a ponytail in gym shorts sitting from his billion dollar mansion in The Hills while bask-ing in the glow of his Full-Metal Laptop, I carry out the one task, which I failed to complete in what felt like another life.

After following the instructions from *Joshua'ζ Tree*, I insert the USB flash drive into the back of the monitor, click on the CD/DVD burner application FYRESC, slide a blank compact disc into the drive, and burn a hard copy of the photos.

Once, maybe in a dream or a delusion, I think that maybe I might've questioned how she was able to smuggle such con-traband into Red Pines, being that all visitors are screened prior to entry. The answer is as certain to me as the sun rising again tomorrow: Twiggy had help from a close friend who paid her a visit during visitation hours. Twiggy's friend, a nun, I don't know her name but I know she wasn't like the Old Testament-type nuns, with the traditional habit and a mile long stare, but rather one dressed in plain clothes, smuggled a mp3 player—a miniature handheld with a high resolution camera—inside the one holy area of her emphasized "*fee*"-for-female body, where guards would never poke or prod around; and when the guard vertically waved his wand over her lower abdomen and picked up a reading on the metal detector, she explained to the guard that she had metal rods in her hip, even showed him the scars from the surgery, and then, with a hint of sarcasm, asked him if he wanted her to rip the rods from her body and show them to him, rods, screws, blood, and all. On any other Tuesday, the security guards wouldn't allow Twiggy's friend to enter the facility, but this time, the vibe was much different, like Twiggy already had a plan B in motion, and that included assistance from someone on the inside. Perhaps another security guard who wasn't so strict about the visitation rules? And if so, what was the guard promised or given in return?

While she visited with Twiggy, she waited until the order-lies weren't watching and pulled out a tightly sealed bag con-taining the mp3 player from her body and then slipped it un-derneath the table to Twiggy.

After the visitation hours were over and Twiggy was es-corted back to her room, it was all about camera placement.

Once the CD is "hot," I secure the disc inside a protective case and hide it inside my bookbag.

On the way to One Stop, I rip off the *Fire Juggler* flyer from the side of the building and pocket it.

Then, after following each instruction, I enter the bird store and distract the employees by claiming that one of the tweakers outside is wielding a knife and plugging pedestrians in his own whacked out rendition of *Hamlet*. The employees, as well as several customers, rush outside. During the commotion, I grab the key from the fecal-spattered newspaper underneath the American Goldfinch cage, as written in Twigs's notes; and as I'm exiting the bird store, two employees have the tweaker pinned to the sidewalk, one of them holding the tweaker in a headlock.

Once I've obtained the key, I stop by DENT STATION.

I walk to the wall of lockers in the back of the train station and located locker 237 and sure enough, the key works.

I open the locker.

Inside is a stuffed animal.

A purple rabbit.

My "Wabby."

I pull the stuffed animal from the locker, and as I touch the foot, I suddenly feel a small yet hard object inside.

Using my switchblade, I cut open the foot and dig through wads of cotton until I find my ticket out of here.

One bullet.

One target to hit.

One last shot at escaping from the house of flies.

H O W   D U H   W E S T   W A S
O N E   &   D U N   S O N

That night, while sleeping in the back of my Civic, I have the most vivid dream.

The violence robs the air from my lungs.

And I wake up gasping, clothes drenching wet with sweat, my wicked heart pounding at what feels like a thousand beats per second. The night darkness helps me find my rhythm.

Despite all of the gore and chaos, I desperately try to piece together the images from the dream before they disappear into the gray. I remember being stuck inside the dank bathroom of a cabin reading two pink lines on a pregnancy test, which belonged to a young and awfully attractive woman.

We were somewhere in the Northwest Pacific, possibly in Oregon or Washington. The atmosphere was damp, the trees a deep green, and incredibly lush. I've seen the young woman before, but, I remember, the feeling alone of being in her presence was so overwhelming, almost smothering, like I couldn't live without her, like I never wanted to lose her, like I'd die if I knew that I could never have her.

As I comb through the fading images, I feel a slight pinch, a pinprick-like sensation deep in my head.

Somehow, I found myself waking up inside another much darker place, climbing from the confines of wires and arms, a large room or lab of some sort, surrounded by dozens of people, perhaps test subjects, each one hooked up to these strange machines, comatose-like, yet their eyeballs racing underneath their eyelids, like REM sleep.

What I do remember as clearly as the night sky before my eyes are the images of me pulling off my face, as in violently tearing off chunks of flesh, revealing the face of a much older man. Or was it total bullshit, and I wasn't pulling off my face, but rather someone else's? Or was it not a face, with flesh and all, but rather a headset or a visor? I recall the similar vision from earlier: the Internet café, Cyber Jaxx, and what the establishment may evolve—or devolve—into years from now.

I put aside the images and focus on the night sky.

While gazing at the stars above, I fall into the black trance. Eventually, I close my eyes and relax.

I tell myself that tomorrow will be the final day.

\\

BEFORE the show begins, I wander around Topside for a majority of the day, making stops at the Galatia to target practice on bass heads or the carnival for a chilidog and once more, work on my shot while playing the game, Water Worxx, and by the fourth game of hosing off mud from alligators, I end up winning a top prize. I look around at the other shooters, first to my left and then to my right, and I see a girl and her dad, both of their aims so awful that they probably can't even hit an elephant if it's charging right at them, but as I watch them, I soon realize the two could care less whether or not they win a prize. Being in each other's company, I realize, playing a silly game together, that's the ultimate prize. I pick out a stuffed animal from the top of the booth. The carnival worker hands me the purple rabbit; and then, in return, I hand the stuffed animal to the girl. The dad thanks me, turns to his daughter, tells her to tell the nice gentleman thank you. Eventually, she manages to speak the words, but they fall to my feet. I'm still left thinking about the dad's comment and how he called me a gentleman.

By the time late afternoon arrives, my clothes, mainly my black and blue flannel, are heavy and they stink, especially my undershirt, and I figure if things go south tonight and I'm going to go out with a bang, then I better do it in style. I stop by Lassie's, a tiny thrift shop on the boardwalk. I pick out some clothes, first a pair of brown slacks, not tight around the groin region in case I need to run or dodge or make explosive move-ments, then a lightweight jacket to match.

Lastly, to complete the look, I browse through a rack of T-shirts, what one may call "vintage," and come across a black Mona's Arch T-shirt. The front of the shirt is a Japanese-like anime close-up of a palish-blue faced woman with red android eyes and a liquid metal tear falling from her eye. On the back is a list of dates from the popular band's widely controversial *Bound and Dangerous Tour.* Apparently, the merch is one of a kind, what one may call an "exclusive." I look closer at the T-shirt and find the signature of the lead singer, Henry the Fif'.

Immediately, I pull the shirt from the hanger, regardless of whether or not it fits. I check the tag, and it's a LARGE, and even though I usually wear MEDIUM, I convince myself that the shirt has shrunken overtime.

After I change in the dressing room, I stop by the front of the store and ask the first employee I see if she has a bag I can use to hold my smelly clothes.

As soon as the employee rotates around, I feel blood rush-ing from my face.

Searching for the right words, I utter the name, "Twiggy?"

She furrows her brow and other parts of her face.

"Excuse me," she says.

"You're Twiggy?"

"No," she says, voice drawn out. "My name's Jazz."

"Jazz, huh?"

I lose myself in her voice, her words, her face, her eyes.

I watch one side of her mouth barely rise, as if she's hiding a smile, as fragile and delicate as a flower ready to bloom from the drop of rainwater or ray of sunlight.

From the moment our eyes connect, I know, in my bones, that she's not like the others.

I find her uniquely attractive, and I'm unable to shake her from my head, maybe it's a glow in her eyes and the way they look into me, or the uneven set of chompers, which I find dolt-ishly cute. She is perfect and imperfect in every way.

"So," I say before the moment turns awkward, "what'daya think? Think I can pull it off?"

I showcase my new outfit.

Jazz gives me a once-over and shrugs.

"Not bad."

"Yeah?"

"I'd say you're dressed to kill."

"Thanks," I say hesitantly. "I guess."

"It's a compliment."

"Umm, thanks."

I glance down at the dirty clothes in my hand.

"So who's the hot date?" she asks, grabbing a bag from the counter.

"Hot date?"

"Yeah," she says and hands me the bag.

Once more, I thank her.

If my math is correct, that's three times I've thanked her.

Again, she asks, "Who's the lucky lady?"

"No lady."

"A guy?"

"No," I say, struggling to hold a thought in my head.

Only one surfaces.

Just ask her, you idiot.

What I really want to ask—despite the most obvious one—is whether or not she was ever admitted to Red Pines.

How do you even broach the subject?

Excuse me, pretty but not that pretty lady. Were you once a crazy chick with Tourette's?

Somehow, waiting for her to burst out in a fit of rage, calling me colorful names, like you DICKLESS IMBECILE who doesn't know what a HOT FUCKIN DATE looks like if she was standing right in front of you, the words slip from my lips: "By any chance. . . "

The words hang in suspension.

Jazz widens her eyes.

"Yeah?"

She waits for me to finish my sentence.

"Forget it," I say, thinking about time and what little time I have left and how I'm in no position to waste any more time on some chick who looks like another chick who's attached to so much pain and suffering.

"Okay," she says, her voice short and somewhat raised.

(The change in a person's voice, especially tone, especially a higher tone, can be a sign of either discomfort or frustration or the person is not telling the truth)

I feel like dying for not saying what I really want to say.

Those words, the other ones, are right there.

Why can't I speak them?

\|\|\|

REPLAYING a previous conversation with the employee at Lassie's in my head, I finally arrive at a massive tent where the upcoming spectacle "Presented by *Freakspectacular*" called The <u>*Dem-on*</u>stration, demon in *demonstration* underlined and italicized, is being held on the end of the boardwalk, in the shadows of the Ferris wheel and a nearby convention center.

Outside the tent hangs a poster with the star of the show, the Fire Juggler himself, Frode Jorgensen, which, at first reading, I mistake for Frodo, as in the little hobbit from *Lord of the Rings*. Another poster shows the cave, which, when taking a step back and looking at it a second time, looks very similar to the tent I'm about to enter. Two menacing-looking eyes glow in the darkness of the cave.

While waiting in line outside the ticket booth, I can't stop thinking about how much she looked like Twiggy, from the videos on the flash drive. Either she has a twin or a double or she wasn't being completely honest with me.

(In Germany, they have a name for doubles called *doppel-gängers*, which rolls off the tongue as cool as an ice cube, and apparently, according to Susannah, who once mistook me for one when she was at the grocery store and then another time, when she was at the DMV, I have one or two, as though they somehow took a wrong exit and wound up in the multiverse)

More relieved not to see any metal detectors at the front of the tent, I breathe easier and focus on the task at hand. I buy a ticket from a super unfriendly attendant, who looks as if he'd rather be at home verbally abusing his parents, and shuffle my way toward yet another long line, which, unlike the previous line, moves quicker.

As the nerves cause my body to tense up, I relax as soon as I enter the tent. Since there are no reserved seats, I pick a seat toward the back of the tent, where I have a clearing at both the stage and the crowd. While making my way to the seat, I spot the same woman from Lassie's. Jazz. Who looks identical to Twiggy. Again, the similarities are uncanny; and when I look at her, I can't help but see flashes of violent acts. With her just lying there. Helpless. With nowhere to escape. Just thinking about what those orderlies did to her causes my insides to flex like a fist. I can't take my eyes away from Jazz. I'm drawn to her wounded beauty. From what I can tell, she's alone.

Right before I take a seat, she turns a shoulder and catches me staring directly at her. Both our eyes connect, but I don't look away. With a blank expression on her face, she holds my gaze. Then, she holds up her head in a nod. I look behind me to make sure she's not acknowledging someone else, but after a quick survey, I don't find anyone looking in her direction. I decide to say hey. When I arrive at her position, she's gone. I search for her in the crowd but can't find her anywhere. For a second, the panic washes over me, causing my chest to tighten like a cave on the verge of collapsing. I cough for some much needed air and reach down inside and take in a deep breath.

Since the show is about to begin, I take her seat and continue to search through the crowd but can't find her anywhere.

I must've scared her away.

What else is new?

Or, worse, I can't help but ask, *is she even here?*

The second suspicion scares me the most—in fact, it scares the shit out of me—and yet, at the same time, leaves me longing to learn more about her. I want to know everything about her: Her favorite food, her favorite movie, her favorites song, her likes and dislikes, her ticks, her bad habits, her everything.

A glare in the corner of my eye draws my attention toward the grassy floor where I find a strange iridescent light, as tiny as a penny, flickering and moving almost frenetically in a see-saw-like motion. I direct my attention upward and spot a narrow slit in the tent, like a tear of some kind, and above the tent is what appears to be the pinkish-purplish-greenish light from the drop tower ride, The Twisted Lighthouse.

All of a sudden, the lights dim to pitch black, and then, just moments later, a spotlight highlights a well in the center of the stage. A reddish-orange light slowly brightens from the well.

A ball of flames bursts upward from the well, revealing the star of the show, Fire Juggler, who ascends from the well.

The audience erupts in applause.

Fire Juggler does his act: Eating fire, spitting fire, juggling all sorts of random objects, some sharp, which he sets on fire, in what I'll admit, with a straight face, is a dazzling display of mega-testosterone, capital A-Alpha energy.

Midway through Fire Juggler's act, his eyes start to glow a fire-red. Appearing more disorientated by a sudden illness, he stumbles and staggers around the stage, struggling to find his bearings. A pair of leathery wings shoots out from his shoulder blades, forcing his assistant to rush out onto the stage and desperately attempt to push the wings back into his body.

Based on the urgency of the situation, I can't tell whether or not the act is part of the show or, in fact, something horribly wrong is unfolding right before the audience's eyes.

Either way, despite the sense of panic by the assistant, the show still goes on, and I'm left in awe and can't look away. A flash of red lights appears from the right side of the stage, then two paramedics, both following the assistant's lead, rush onto the stage.

I soon realize that the transformation is all part of the show as Fire Juggler pushes away the two paramedics and stumbles to the center of the stage and leans over the well as parts of his body swell and freakishly shift out of place, including muscles and bones. His body retches forward followed by the sound of vomiting.

A dense white cloud of smoke rises from below Fire Juggler. Flashes of pink, red, and orange lights flicker from every direction. Above, the bright spotlight, as before, shines down on the well, highlight smoke, as well as the warped shadow of a winged beast that Fire Juggler regurgitates from his mouth.

Sweaty, weak, and exhausted, Fire Juggler falls backward, as the slimy dragon-like creature drops like a thorny turd into the well, causing the audience to gasp and marvel at the grotesque images before their eyes.

The lights go out, leaving the entire stage in pitch black.

Among the blackness, the harsh sounds of fighting fill the entire tent. A violent battle between Fire Juggler and the creature. Lots of shouting and screaming and roaring. The sharp and piercing *clanks* of what sounds like the clashing of swords and metal chains.

Random bursts of flames briefly showcase the struggle between Fire Juggler and the dragon-like beast, wrestling around on stage, fighting to what looks like the death.

When the lights turn back on, Fire Juggler has finally slain the dragon, all thanks to the unlikely hero, his assistant, who captures the creature in a net, which hangs from the rafters.

Once more, the audience erupts in applause and cheers, as Fire Juggler takes a bow, thus ending the "Demonstration."

IV

ONCE the audience has cleared out, I follow Frode, as well as his handlers, to the west wing of the convention center, which is guarded by two security guards.

For the time being, I wait behind a face-painting booth and survey the building and in my survey, search for possible entry and escape points. The front door is clearly off limits. Shortly after Frode enters the convention center, a group—or "crew" of club owners—exit through the front and walk past the body guards. One of the faces among the crew immediately stands out the most. Nico. One of the minions to his left is carrying what looks like a bag of pills.

I'm left with no other choice than to sneak around the side of the building and break into the window of an empty conference room. I twist my ankle in the fall but manage to walk off the pain.

After I exit the conference room and bypass Fire Juggler's security, I track down his voice, which is coming from a room at the end of the hallway. I walk past several employees wearing *Demonstration* T-shirts, too distracted and occupied by their phones to acknowledge me. I swear, despite not caring much for them and the fear of sounding old for speaking in a negative light about *newer* technology, I'd say that phones do have their advantages.

When I arrive at the room, which has been converted into a dressing room, I hear Frode arguing with his assistant about the latest act and how the assistant screwed the pooch and was late in the timing, as in deploying what I can only make out is "the net." I hear foots stomping closer toward me and before the assistant storms from the dressing room, I kneel down in front of a row of stacked black travel cases and with my back turned toward the door, act as if I'm one of those preoccupied employees and rummage through the gear, one particular item being a water cooler filled with packets of fake blood.

I watch the assistant storm away, leaving Frode exposed.

With nobody looking, I pull out the mask cutout from the back of *Joshua'ζ Tree* and slip it over my face. The eyeholes in the mask don't exactly match, but I'm still able to partially see through them.

I enter the dressing room, where Frode is seated in front of a makeup vanity. I count at least a dozen or so scented candles—eucalyptus perhaps—each one lit, which mask a sharp, repugnant smell of burnt garlic and a week-old infection. To my right, I hear a vibrant *hissing* sound, like a mix between a cat and a cobra, inside a rectangular-shaped box covered with a burgundy blanket. Then, not too far away: a duffle bag full of plastic bags containing the experimental flatline pills, which contain ingredients that cannot only stop a person's heart, but also bring a person back to life with a new next level-type of adrenaline kick with a delayed release, more than likely same ones Nico's minion was carrying.

As I brandish the revolver from the back of my waistband and creep farther into the dressing room—Frode, who is much scrawnier than he appeared on stage, still unaware of my presence—my eyes are suddenly drawn to a prosthetic of an upper torso, slightly muscular, with mechanical wings draped over a clothes hanger. Below the prosthetic are several wires and air tubes, which, I assume, create the illusion of a transformation, or whatever in the hell that was, with Fire Juggler regurgitated some kind of winged Tequila worm on steroids.

"*What in the hell are you doing?*"

Startled by the sound of Frode's voice, I face forward, only to find Frode staring at me through the reflection of the vanity mirror. His head lowered slightly with his eyes, not surprised, but keen and narrow, piercing right through me.

"Enough games, Jason," Frode says, as he studies what he believes to be a prop gun in my hand.

"Who the fuck is Jason?" I ask.

Once he hears the sound of my voice behind the paper cut-out mask, Frode rotates around in his chair.

"Not so fast," I say, aiming the revolver at Frode.

"What do you want—" Before Frode can finish his train of thought, he glances over at the bag of pills, "—right. Take em and get the hell outta here before I call security—"

"I'm not here for your poison pills."

"Then, why are you here?"

I hear another *hiss* coming from the crate.

I flick my head toward the crate.

"What the fuck is that thing?" I ask.

Frode's eyes sharpen, as if I hit a sore spot.

"Something that you will *never* understand."

With the revolver aimed at Frode, I take a side step closer to the crate, but I only make it a couple of steps before Frode warns me.

"I wouldn't do that if I were you," he says, his voice trembling. "If you unlock that cage, then everyone in this building will be torn to shreds, including you."

"So, your little act," I say, "it's real?"

"Of all my years in show business, there is one thing that I've learned: an entertainer is *never* entitled to reveal the secrets of a trade, especially in an ungrateful Age that demands transparency—"

"And is that what this is? You think that you're providing a service?"

"You see the look on the audience's faces, mystery man?" he asks but I don't answer. Instead, I readjust my grip around the revolver and steady my aim. "I'll give you one last chance to answer: Why are you here?"

"Justice," I say.

He studies me closer, the blank white-faced mask, my dark eyes.

"You lost someone," he guesses.

"You're getting warm," I say.

"Someone close to you, I suppose, and you blame me for your loss."

"You're on fire."

His lips curl in a devilish smirk.

"You haven't seen me on fire."

To show Frode that I mean business, I cock the hammer of the revolver.

Frode holds up his hands as he attempts to stand.

"Don't," I say, forcing Frode back into his chair.

"You're the boss."

"The pills," I say, "where do you get them?"

"Sorry," he says, hands still raised. "Family secret."

"Don't worry. Your secret won't leave this room."

"Says the man who has a gun pointed at my head."

"So, what? Family secret? So you make this shit?"

"*Warm*," he says arrogantly, as if he's teasing me.

"You sold that fuckin' poison to a doctor, who, in return, used your drugs to experiment on his patients. Does the name William Harcourt ring a bell?"

Frode shakes his head "no."

"Some of those patients died."

"And you blame me?" He holds in the laughter. "Supply and demand 101, amigo."

"Didn't know selling death was in popular demand."

"It's more for a *niche market*," Frode says, while I maintain a strong grip around the handle of the revolver, "but you'd be surprised what people, like your friend, would pay for it."

"Harcourt is no friend and neither are you."

He witnesses the coldness in my eyes and suddenly realizes that I mean business.

I ease away from Frode's pet and while steadying my aim, inch toward a table full of drinks and snacks. Shooting quick glances from Frode to the table, I run through a list of options: first to catch my eye is a can of Green Curry-flavored Pringles, then a two-liter bottle of generic brand name orange soda, and then, finally, a roll of paper towels, each item being somewhat doable for jerry-built suppressors. Considering the weapon in my hand, I soon realize, after the dark fantasy flees my mind, that each one of these items won't work, maybe on a pistol but not a revolver, given the cylinder gap.

Matching the coldness, Frode says more seriously, "In this world, there's no such thing as having too much money. But one day, maybe you'll understand that, once you start making money, you never want to stop making money, and you'll do everything in your power to make sure the money keeps flowing no matter who or what gets caught in the crossfire because at the end of the day someone always gets caught in the crossfire." He bravely stands to his feet, rotates away from the mirror, and faces me, as if he's tired of explaining himself to me. "A river ain't a river without water. And in this timeline," he says, eyes wide and mad, "money's as precious as water. . . "

I aim right between his eyes and pull the trigger!

The blast of the gunshot causes the creature to bang against the sides of the metal cage, rattling it back and forth as Frode's head violently jerks backward, brain matter and blood splatter spraying the makeup vanity.

As Frode falls to the floor, the creature *hisses* soon turn into the low, guttural sounds of a growl. I'm tempted to check out the creature, but I have no more bullets. Plus, the blast of the gunshot will soon draw security; and at any moment, I expect black shirts to swarm the entire hallway.

During the fall, Frode's leg knocks over the chair, which, in return, strikes the side of the vanity, thus resulting in a candle to flip over on its side. An article of clothing catches fire and next thing I know, the entire vanity is up in flames. I remove the mask, pocket it, and then rush toward the doorway; as I predicted, both employees and security guards are scrambling around the hallway, trying to identify the location of the gunshot. I rule out escaping through the same window where I first entered after witnessing a handful of stagehands as wide as top-of-the-line refrigerators standing in front of the conference room doorway, blocking my path. I'm left with no other alternatives than to duck into the smoky dressing room to figure out the next course of action.

I can't leave here without knowing what's inside that cage. Curiosity drives me toward the covered cage, toward the creature, which lets out another deep growl. Only feet away from the cage, my heart starts to race. The fear grips me like a vise. A metal green nametag labeled "Aea" dangles below the bottom of the blanket.

As the fire spreads toward the duffle bag of drugs, my eyes fall below to the carpet where a large white blob of what looks like drool is piled up below the cage. I reach down and run a couple of fingers into the strange substance, which is clumpy, wet, slick, and slimy, similar to what Kit the Horse-Faced Brit calls "ole spunk dat shoots outta ya woody wood pecka," and when I pull several fingertips full from the pile, the substance hardens into a chalky, paste-like gel as soon as it hits oxygen.

Overwhelmed by the shocking discovery, I stand to my feet and remove the blanket and take a couple of steps backward.

The scaly creature slides to the back of the cage, concealing itself in the shadows. The flickers of firelight bring out subtle layers of the serpent-eyed creature, as it coils like a balled fist, ready to strike.

As I take a step closer toward the cage for a better look, the creature reaches out its arm, so quickly that I don't even have a chance to react; and before I know it, the creature slashes the upper part of my forearm with its razor-sharp talons.

I recoil and immediately grab the open wound as soon as I watch the strings of blood racing down the sides of my forearm and try to stop the bleeding by applying as much pressure as possible.

(I read somewhere—Oh, fuck it!)

The fire alarm suddenly blares out!

The creature bangs the side of the cage, causing the rest of the blanket to fall onto the floor.

Even though the dense black smoke helps conceal the creature, I'm able to get a better look at the creature, which looks as if it's a cross between a large lizard, very much similar to a Komodo dragon, a scorpion, based on its tail, which bears the resemblance of a stinger, and finally, a bat, but really, considering the scales, the eyes, the talons, the nicotine-yellow gator-like underbelly, its unique appearance favors more of a reptilian. Despite the comparisons, the four-legged creature is nothing like anything I've ever seen before.

As the fire completely consumes one half of the room and inches closer and closer toward the duffel bag of drugs, as well as Frode's exotic pet, I hear shouting from behind.

I rotate around and as I'm about to make a run toward the doorway, I nearly fall into a deep black hole in the floor.

Frode's blood, so potent and intense, has formed a puddle, which has eaten away at the floor. The upper half of Frode's body is dangling into the side of the hole, which spreads wider and wider, like acid licking its way over the carpeted floor and dissolving everything it touches. One other detail, besides the strange blood, is Frode's skin, which, based on its gray hue, as well as its slimy texture, looks as if it has experienced months, maybe even years, of decomposition. Eventually, as the black hole of a puddle continues to spread wider and wider, Frode's body lifelessly slides and eventually, flops into the darkness.

The shouting is louder, closer.

I suddenly dash toward the door, shut it, and lock it before the security guards can reach for the handle.

With the guards pounding on the door, I set my sights on the black hole in the floor.

As the smoke thickens, blackens, intensifies, and forces me to cover my face with my jacket, I grab a wooden leg from an overturned chair engulfed in flames, break it off, and drop the flaming piece of wood into the black hole.

Cautiously, I lean over the hole but never see the leg hit the bottom.

Behind me, the wall of flames spreads to the duffle bag and then the pills. Flames eat through the plastic bag; then as soon as the flames crisp and blacken those white pills, they release a mustard-yellow smoke in the air.

All of a sudden, a security guard rams his shoulder through the door, causing it to burst off the hinges.

While tightening the core of my body, I step into the hole and close my eyes—*What's it called?* Right. A leap of faith. I fall for what feels like miles into blackness before finally reaching the bottom: An icy body of water. I pierce right through water, that initial sting of the coldness hitting my entire body like thousands of pinpricks along my flesh.

After the shock wears off, I crack open both eyes and look upward and witness a faint beam of amber light shining down on the water, providing barely enough light for me to see my own hands in front of me. I swim to the surface, but both my legs are sore and incredibly heavy. Each stroke feels as if I'm moving in slow motion. The more I ascend closer to the surface, the more I descend further into the abyss, like the water is elastic and the surface is stretching farther and farther away from me. I start to run out of oxygen. So close the surface is and yet, so far away. My vision shrinks into a pinhole. I drift in and out of focus, vision cloudy and blurry, narrowing the world before me. As I reach deep down inside and cling to my last breath, I'm swallowed whole by Darkness, my enemy, my friend, my very own destroyer and savior.

V

THAT amber light returns.

The pinhole of light blooms and cast enough light for me to make out my immediate surroundings, yet the light remains faded, like a sun lost behind a cloud, although waiting for the right moment to shine.

Gasping for air, I open my eyes and find myself lying on a sandy beach-like surface inside a dark cave. The lower half of my body, mostly my lower extremities, including my feet, are submerged in icy cold water. The light, once seen from below the water, no longer provides light from above. Yet, strangely, a similar, if not, the same light shines deep below the water, as if the light is coming from a spotlight on the floor of the water, tempting me to dive back into the mysterious pond or even a lake, which has no end and stretches into the cave darkness.

As I stand to my feet, I feel around my pockets and find an old, damp pack of LEATHER N' LACE matches.

A draft of air pulls me away from the water.

I pluck off the soggy match and attempt to light it, but the match is completely soaked.

I decide to push forward into the quiet, empty darkness. I come across a tunnel, which, like the body of water, looks as if it has no end.

I enter the tunnel; and once more, I'm swallowed whole by the darkness.

The air, however, is much warmer than before and when it presses against my face, it reminds me of being back home. A haunting, almost eerie feeling comes over me, and I suddenly feel as if I'm not alone. The coarse, grating, swishing sound of a match being struck pulls me from the terror of my thoughts.

I rotate toward the source of the sound and there, standing behind a desk, is William. A flame along the tip of the match highlights the bottom half of his face. He brings the flame to a scented candle; and once the flame catches a wick and warms the wax, the aromas bring me back, if only for a brief moment, to Topside, to rich, savory, and sugary sweet smells of a lively arcade, before the aromas decay into the oaky, dusty, moldy, gassy, disinfectant-like stenches of Red Pines.

Guided by the candlelight, William walks over to the set of blinds covering a window along the rough, bumpy, and jagged cave wall; and once he pulls on the cord and opens the blinds and allows sunlight to cut through the darkness, I'm no longer standing in a cave. Rays of pink morning light pour into William's office, and I find myself seated in a chair in front of his desk. I have lost myself, my identity.

As William returns to his desk, he asks, "Would you like a cookie?" He motions his hand to a penguin cookie jar on the desk. This is a first for me. During our sessions, I never saw the jar. "Here," William says, opens the lid, "have a cookie." I remain seated and silent. Losing his patience, William sighs and grabs a cookie himself. "Still don't trust me, huh? Such a pity, especially after all of the progress we've made. I'll *cut* in half. How 'bout that?"

The word immediately leaps off his tongue. Being a doctor who's extremely mindful about the words he uses around his patients and makes sure to stay within the medical term lingo, I find it strange why he used that one particular word. Who in the hell *cuts* a cookie in half?

With both his hands, he *breaks* the cookie in half.

He gives me one half, and he keeps the other.

Before leaning back in the chair, I notice a pack of matches on the top of William's desk. The name on the matches reads "*El Crusoe's*" and yet, strangely, for some reason, I've seen the matches before but can't remember when and where.

To put me at ease, William takes a bite of the oatmeal raisin cookie.

"What's in it?" I ask and examine the cookie.

While chewing, he says through the corner of his mouth, "One cup of butter, light brown sugar, two large eggs—"

"No. . . " I interrupt, ". . . what's in it?"

"Again, with your trust issues," he says and takes a seat on the other side of the desk. "It's just a fucking cookie, Robert. No drugs inside—that is, if you count sugar as a drug, which, to be fair, based on its addictiveness, is worthy of debate. But, to answer your question: I didn't slip anything inside that may hinder or interfere with your judgment."

After staring at the cookie, I finally take a bite.

As soon as I swallow the first bite, William receives a call from his secretary. I can't make out what she's saying through the receiver-end of the telephone, but the only words that grab my ear are the muffled words *start* and *trace*.

Or, is it *art* and *race*?

Art Race?

Art of the *Race*?

After ending the call, William reaches into the top drawer and pulls out the novel, *Joshua'ζ Tree*, and places it on the edge of his desk.

He reads out loud the summary on the back cover: "*In this nightmarish tale of a distorted time in American history, JOSHUA LAMB, a notorious vandal who has a peculiar knack for strategically waging chaos, believes that his deliberate actions of destruction will trigger a catastrophic domino effect, resulting in the inevitable extinction of the human race. One night—*"

"You don't have to read it back to me like I'm an idiot."

"So, you've read it?"

I shrug.

"Most of it."

He finds a paperclip, which I've been using as a bookmark, near the back of the book. He removes the clip from the page. Holds it up.

"You know we don't allow contraband."

"What the hell am I gonna do with little ole paperclip?"

"Gee," William says and places the clip in his top drawer, "I don't know, Robert. You tell me."

"Can I at least have my book back?" I ask him.

He ignores the question and flips to the back of the book, a few pages before the bookmark.

"Since I see you've already taken a lead from our character Mr. Lamb, I'm not going to ask you where you got the pen or pencil," he says disappointedly and returns to the book, "but I am going to ask you this one particular line you circled. And I assume it's your handwriting based on the writing utensil—"

William holds up the open book, his finger pointing at the last line in Chapter 20, more specifically the two-word answer that Joshua says to his new friend, Julia, who asks him about his interests. After observing the commodore of the charitable organization and feeling the sudden urge to better himself, he then replies, "*Personal sovereignty.*"

"But what really intrigues me," William says before I have a chance to respond, "are the notes inside, in particular, *your* notes, Robert, as well as another patient of Red Pines: Medea Clout, or 'Twiggy,' as everybody calls her."

He rapidly flips through the entire novel, starting from the very back to the very front of the novel; then he looks it over, from front cover to back. I replay the flip in my head and find myself holding the same paperback in my hands, rapidly flipping through those pages.

At the start of every chapter is a black solid rectangle and for every chapter, the rectangle moves farther and farther and farther to the right, the standard "left to right" reading direction—or, in this case, since starting from the back of the novel, the rectangle moving toward the left, not the right—thus making the rectangle, not any ordinary rectangle with no purpose, but rather the passenger car of a train which comes alive with each turn of the chapter, like an animation. The faster I flip those pages, the clearer the passenger car moves through the paperback.

Twiggy emphasizes the author's message at the start of the last chapter, Chapter 21, by doodling two additional rectangles that connect to other rectangle, thus making it clearly appear like a train; however, based on the drawings, the train appears to be descending downward like falling off a bridge or cliff, and below, a stick figure man engulfed in flames.

As I once more mentally flip through the entire paperback, I no longer see a train, but rather a potentiometer on a control board. Rectangular in shape, similar to the black and cryptic one at the start of each chapter of the novel, but gray in color, with these tiny grooves to hold the grip of a finger. I stay with the images, and before William pulls me from my thoughts, I see the word *MEMORIES* underneath the potentiometer, and when the operator or engineer places a finger on the control, it slides the control to the right, thus making me remember everything, why I escaped from Red Pines, but most importantly, why I chose to return to such a cursed place where death was only the beginning of a daunting quest to solve the mysteries behind a chamber of secrets.

"*In her notes*," William says, his voice forcing me to focus, "she writes directly to you almost as if she knows you, Robert. But you may ask how would that even be possible, since you two have never met before. I'll tell you how. Your pen pal in here doesn't exist."

I've already figured out all of his tricks.

He's gas-lighting me again and speaking to me as if I'm a squirrel's wet dream (*Uh-oh! Here comes the walrus man!* You know the lyrics), as if that whole saying "*Don't believe what you hear and half of what you see*" is nothing more than some hand-me-down bumper sticker, which has lost its adhesiveness, and really, when you cut through the bullshit, there's no such thing as half of anything, including a cookie.

"She does exist," I say over William. "I have proof."

"What? In here?" he says, running his fingers through the paperback, starting at the back cover and then flipping toward the front.

PC?

Proof copy?

Personal copy?

Personal computer?

A prop, see?

Not see.

You C, the letter C?

The train moves backwards.

All of a sudden, I can't remember the proof. Like one second, pre-flip, the evidence was as tangible as the day. The eye doesn't lie. More importantly, the hand doesn't lie, and I had the evidence in my hands. But now, post-flip, it's gone, faded like a distant memory.

"I wrote these notes in the book in order to free you from this mental prison that you have created for yourself," he says, walking around the very front of the desk. "*Paranoia, delusions of grandeur, profound distrust in other people, social withdraw, isolation, hallucinations, false accusations, feeling constantly on guard,* or *sudden desires to carry out violence against those whom you believe wronged you, as well as those close to you, most importantly, unable to forgive those whom you believe wronged you:* This. . . " he says, holding up the crinkled paperback and then wagging it in the air as if he's a beat away from flinging it at me, ". . . this mental exercise was simply a distraction from *yourself.*"

While he flings a list of all these symptoms at me, I picture distant moments in my life, flashes of vivid images shaped and molded into a glossy glass ball by the flame of time, each and every detail carrying great significance, a collection of a memory, like a snow globe of a scene, from *paranoia* (I picture myself at Topside, running from police) to *isolation* (I picture myself lying in a bathtub, ready to paint my Masterpiece on the wall) to the *sudden desire of violence* (I picture myself on top of a woman, both my hands wrapped around her neck).

I snap out of the trance and focus on William's words.

"*I want you to think about it* for a second, Robert," he says to me. "Do you really think we would allow you, of all people, to possess such a device, of all places, in here?" William says "*in here,*" as in the nut factory. "If you weren't so preoccupied with Joshua and all of his mischief, you'd take out every single person in this building with your little pencil. But you didn't."

Once more, he holds up the "why" in why I didn't hack or slash or stab my way toward freedom.

The book.

His notes, not hers.

The illusion.

Not an illusion.

"Your story begins on that beach," William says, "and it's up to you whether or not you choose to end your story on that beach."

I ask, "*What if* I have no other choice?"

"You have a choice, Robert. You chose to be here, didn't you? You can leave at anytime."

"But in here, I have a purpose."

He nods.

"You do," he says, thinking, "but only because I gave you purpose. But just remember, Robert, if you do go back to that beach, you're going to die."

Flashes of her face appear in my mind. So close and yet so far away. Her beauty haunts me like a ghost, and I'm forever doomed by her spell.

"To love is to die, and I've been to paradise many times," I say, staring up at William as he looms over me. "What's one more trip going to change?"

"*Everything*," he says. "It will change everything."

He walks to the safe below a different painting on the wall, not the *Dark Mountain* one, but rather a black and white painting of a dock on a lake, zips through entering the combination as if it's part of his daily ritual, then cracks open the safe, and pulls out one of those dragon pills. He grabs a bottle of water from the real fridge and hands it to me and then drops the pill into the palm of my hand.

I nod at the painting.

"New piece?"

William acknowledges the painting on the wall.

"*The Last Walk Before I Die*."

"Excuse me?"

"The name of the painting."

"So why'd you change the painting?"

He shrugs.

"I thought it was time to switch things up."

"Nothing strange about that—"

"Time for the real deal, Rob," he says, nodding at the pill.

I open my palm, and the imprint is all wrong. Instead of a dragon stamped logo, it reads the number "101."

Without over-thinking, I pop the white pill into my mouth and before I swallow, I notice William's eyes, which are much different. The irises hazel, eyelashes curled and much thicker, clouded by shadow, seductive. His eyes are not his; instead, they're the eyes of a woman whom I have never seen before.

All of a sudden, the door to William's office springs open!

"You are free, Robert."

Hesitantly, I walk toward the doorway and poke my head into the hallway; and when I turn back around, William is no longer there, as if he has some kind of *trapdoor* near his desk; and as soon as I turned my back, he clicked on a red button.

Somewhere, in my thoughts, I hear Jazz's voice, and she's talking about pushing a big "red" button.

I exit the office, and I only take a couple of steps into the hallway before I feel a sudden urge to not swallow the pill.

"*I've seen this movie before.*"

I spit out the pill into the palm of my hand and while doing so, I notice a scar on my forearm.

The talon of a dragon slices my flesh. Strings of movie-red blood run from the open wound: I suddenly shake away those gory images and return to William's office.

Not William, I say.

Someone else.

Those eyes.

Not his.

But hers.

As I step back into the office, I first notice an object on the edge of William's desk. A purple rabbit's foot. I immediately walk to the desk and reach for the rabbit's foot.

I hear William's voice from the corner of the office, then a clink of a glass.

"*I'll make some exceptions*," he says.

I turn toward the voice and picture William standing in the corner of the office, glass of aged Scotch in hand.

I refocus and return to the desk where I pick up the rabbit's foot, which I recall Susannah giving me during her visit at Red Pines.

With the rabbit's foot in hand, I exit the office.

The hallway is eerily desolate with not a single orderly or doctor or patient in sight.

Despite sunrays pouring in through the windows and striking the recently cleaned tile floors, which appear glossy, I feel a dark presence closing in.

Carefully, I walk past a yellow "WET FLOOR" sign.

Not too far is the exit, which pulls me in closer and closer; and the closer I approach the exit, the more relieved I feel.

All of a sudden, the relief is bludgeoned by a wave of panic as I hear the *squeaky* sound of rubbery soles skidding and sliding on the floor behind me.

I rotate my shoulder.

Moses is charging directly at me.

Feet away.

Inches.

With a menacing scowl on his face, he seethes to me, "Forgetting someone?"

As I try to make a run for the exit, the heel of my foot slips on the wet floor. My feet sweep upward, leaving my body in a freefall. Upon impact, I hit the side of my head on the floor.

Dazed, I gawk at Moses, who, with a blank expression on his face, casually kneels down to the floor.

Intrigued, Moses picks up the rabbit's foot from the floor and holds it close to his ear and shakes it.

I hear an object rattling inside.

Moses unscrews the top of the rabbit's foot and dumps the bullet in the palm of his hand. The scowl returns to his face, haunting, terrorizing. He suddenly pounces on top of me and before I can clench my teeth, slips his fingers inside my mouth and pries it open. He dunks the bullet into my mouth, uses his hands to, not only tightly compress my jaw, but also pinch my nostrils, cutting off all of my oxygen until I end up swallowing the bullet in order to breathe again.

Once I down the bullet with one gulp, Moses releases both his hands from my face, then grabs a handful of my hair, and slams the back of my head against the hard tile floor.

The Darkness greets me with open arms.

What a comfort it is, to embrace an old friend.

S E E D Z & S T E M Z

All around me, everything is black again.

My black dreams carry me to a remote, claustrophobic place in another time, perhaps in another world parallel to my very own, where animated fingers, like the legs of a spider, madly beat the keys of a keyboard and perform a symphony of mayhem, waging unnecessary digital wars while, at the same time, warding off what future custodians of Archives may one day describe as the greatest catastrophe of our time.

Zeroed in on these fingers, I watch two ghostly palish-blue hands, as translucent as a jellyfish, erect from the keyboard.

Once greeted by darkness, the two hands materialize, guiding me to where I belong.

In the pitch black, the hand extends toward me.

I reach out and grab the hand.

A gray wash of light fills the room, then objects appear: A sink, a towel dispenser, a stall, a mirror, a face.

As the light softens, a familiar-looking man is leaning over me and helping me to my feet.

"You aight, man?" he asks, as I stand to my feet.

Confused, I look around and find myself in a strange restroom. Two wannabe alpha-male types, piss-drunk off sauce, are standing by the open doorway, pointing and laughing.

"Ignore those bozos," he says and places his hand over my shoulder.

"What happened?" I ask him.

From a distance, I hear a *thumping* bass of music followed by the *dings* and *pings* and *chirps* from a horde of machines.

"You blacked out when you were washing your hands and I think'ya might've hit your head on the stall."

He points to the stall behind me, and I can make out what looks like a small dent at the bottom of the door.

"I don't remember," I say, trailing off.

"One too many, huh?"

"No," I say clearly. No slur in my voice. "I mean, I don't know. Maybe."

"You good?"

"Yeah," I say, looking him in the eye. "Good."

"Aight." He makes his way toward the exit, then he turns around, and says with a curious flare under his voice, "Say, by any chance, are you with that girl, Jazz?"

All of a sudden, as soon as I hear the name, "*Jazz*," a flood of memories washes over me. I know exactly where I am and how I got here. By car. With Jazz. My date or my girlfriend. I don't know exactly what we are, but I know, in my heart, we are something, and I know, if I play my cards right, I can add the term like "exclusive," as in an "exclusive couple," or simply, "we are exclusive," as in two of a kind, as in a pair.

"Yeah," I say, remembering. "I'm with her," I say more defensively. "Why'd you ask? You know her?"

"Sorry for being so nosy, man," he says. "Back in the day, we used to see each other. Nothing serious."

I take a step closer to him.

"And?"

He holds up his hands.

"Don't worry, brother," he says. "I'm not a threat. I have two little ones now. They're my world." He pauses, his eyes drift in thought. "Reason I ask. . . I just wanted to give you a heads up and warn you. That's all."

"Warn me?"

"Just be careful. That's all." Before I swell up, he deescalates the situation and helps ease the tension by approaching me with open palms, not fists. "Last I saw her she got caught up with the wrong cats. I haven't spoken to her in some time, but every now and then I see her around the Point—"

His face suddenly comes back to me.

"Hold up," I say. "Burrito Man? From the bird store?"

With his eyes wider, he studies my face.

"Oh yeah. . . " he says, his voice higher and more jovial. "Shit, man! I thought I've seen you from somewhere. Crazy running into you like this."

"Small world, huh?"

"Got that right," he says. "What brings you to Paraíso?"

"Jazz and I are here on vacation. It's kind of a spur-of-the-moment deal."

"I see," he says, again his tone more serious.

"And you?"

"Just here with the fam. I work this stagehand gig over the weekends for some extra money. One Stop doesn't pay all the bills, if you know what I mean."

I don't.

"I'm off today," he says. "I'd figure that I take advantage of the opportunity and show my kids where their dad works."

"You were warning me about Jazz?"

"Right," he says, everything about him serious. "As I was saying, just be careful. I'm pretty good at reading folks, and I can tell you gotta good heart and you mean well. Some of the cats she was rolling with were bad news, frankly, not the type of people you wanna get mixed up with. But. . . " he says and shrugs, ". . . she might've changed. Just keep your head on a swivel."

"Sure," I say, deflecting his words as if I have a force field over my body.

"Anyway, I gotta run," he says and heads toward the exit. "Workers here tend to frown upon having kids on the floor. Besides, there's only so much of this place I can handle."

"Not a big gambler?"

"Nah," he says. "But you spend too much time in a place like this, it can drive you fuckin mad."

"Name's Robert," I say.

He walks back into the restroom and shakes my head.

"Cal," he says. "Cal Betancourt."

"Thanks for the heads up."

"No problem," he says. "Have fun."

He exits the restroom.

Shortly after he exits, I follow suit.

During my walk, I can't stop thinking about the name, not Jazz's name, but his name, Cal Betancourt.

Where have I heard that name before?

On the floor of the casino, Cal is greeted by his two kids, twin girls, from what I can tell. Yet, strangely, one of the girls is white with blonde hair and the other is black with dark hair. Watching over the twin girls like a hawk is what looks like the nanny, short and rather stocky, who appears as if she's never been inside a casino before and based on her wide-eyed, slack-jawed gawk, the thought alone of being surrounded by a sea of lights and flesh terrifies her, yet, at the same time, leaves her in a state of awe. I know the look, each and every line and detail of the expression, because, only minutes ago, before I slipped and hit my head, I was looking at that very same expression in the reflection of the mirror.

\|\|

EXCEPT for last night's binge, which left my liver sore and achy and the very back of my eyes feeling like they were one strain-of-a-shit-push away from bursting into gooey pulp after I woke up from my alcohol-induced vampire-sleep, the memories return, and the most recent one, with Trouble calling it a night much sooner than I anticipated and going to bed disappointed, especially in a city that can't emphasize the expression "*You'll sleep when you're dead*" enough, has—forgive the pun—lit a fire underneath my ass and made me determined to put a smile on her face.

(According to a poll on *Lump Sum*, whether you agree with it or not—I certainly don't but whatever—money still remains the "key to a woman's heart")

Thinking that maybe the fall was somehow related to being dehydrated, I purchase a bottle of water, drink the entire thing in three gulps, then leave Planet Bollywood. I walk across the street and stop at Knight's Bay and play the slot machines and fingers-crossed, try to win back what Jazz had lost earlier that night while playing blackjack at the Diamond.

Just my luck, I end up getting three penguins in a row, and the sound of that alarm sounding makes me feel as if I'm float-ing. Eyeballs suddenly shift toward my direction. Some gamblers congratulate me on my recent win—a gentlemen with a curly mustache slaps me on the back of my shoulder, gives me a "way to go, man!"—while the other gamblers scorn me, especially the older sour-faced ones, as drippy as hot melts, who look as if they've been playing slots ever since they spat out a bastard and left it to wander into The Desert of The Broke and The Whacked—which sounds like it'd be a dope-ass name for a movie about a deadly stretch of land, like the main character who consumes and regurgitates everything that Paraíso casts from its wicked spell.

I take my winnings and plan on buying Jazz a gift, something to cheer her up. On the walk back to Planet Bollywood, I stumble upon a small jewelry store called Brackman's, which is probably the size of a walk-in closet, and search through the case of earrings until I come across one in particular that grabs my eye.

I wave down Brackman's son, who manages the store, and tell him that I'm curious about purchasing the golden looped earrings, which he refers to as the symbol, "*Ouroboros*," which, upon further investigation, appears like a snake eating its own tale—in some cultures, he tells me, the symbol represents life, death, and rebirth. When I look at the earrings, all I can see is a reminder of the doom loop, an endless circle jerk of life repeating itself over and over, making the same mistakes, ignoring second chances. I think back moments ago to Cal Betancourt's comment and what he said about Jazz, his warning.

The name suddenly hits me like a sucker punch, and I realize where I've, not heard, but read the name before.

His comment has a reverse effect, and my desire to be with such a dangerous person, like Jazz, grows stronger than ever.

Once a firebug, always a firebug.

\\\

OUR last night in Paraíso starts off with a bang.

Fireworks outside Planet Bollywood.

Jazz and I are having drinks on the balcony of TUG.

Awestruck by the fireworks, Jazz watches all of the bright and vivid patterns fill the night sky, and I can't help but watch the expression on her face melt as soon as she catches me staring at her.

Slightly tipsy, she says, "What?"

"Nothing," I say.

I have no words to explain how I feel about her, except for one, and I fear that even thinking about such a word may ruin everything.

After the fireworks show is over, Jazz and I decide to cap off the night at Knight's Bay. I ask a street performer dressed up as a giant glowing ball to take a photo of the two of us.

Reluctant to hand over the phone to the street performer—which is unusual since the guy looks like he can't even make it a block if he should run off with her phone—Jazz refuses and mentions a photo booth at the Diamond.

"Just one photo," I say, picking up a tremble in her voice.

Eventually, Jazz caves and hands the Ball Man her phone. After the photo is taken, he hands the phone back to Jazz, but during the exchange he accidentally drops the phone.

The Ball Man apologizes and blames the bulky suit.

I reach down and pick up the phone, which isn't scratched or damaged. A blue message box appears on the screen, and I can only make out part of the text, which reads "WHERE DA FUCK U AT????????" typed in all caps before she snatches the phone from my hand.

"Sorry," I say, unaware of how protective Jazz is about her phone.

"Thanks," she says and forces a smile on her face.

IV

BEFORE we arrive at a gaudy, fort-like entrance of Knight's Bay, Jazz receives yet another text message typed in all caps with a lot of question and exclamation marks, and I start to get worried. This time, I can't make out the text, but I can tell, based on her serious facial expression when she reads it, that it demands a reply. I know I should keep my noise-holes zipped shut and mind my own Number Two before it hits the fan. I know that, maybe, my very next words to her may result in an outburst and trigger a fixed series of events that I may not be able to control. I still haven't seen that side of Jazz, but I know it's there because I can sense it, lying in dormant, waiting for that perfect host—me—to come traipsing along and give it a nudge and tell it to the wake the fuck up or else.

As my thoughts scream inside my head, I ask her about the text. The moment the words leave my lips I desperately want to reel them back in, like a fresh catch sullied and ravaged by oily sludge and barbwire.

Somehow, her response is exactly what I expected.

But is her business my business?

Yes and no.

She makes sure that she voices the latter, and the words cut right through me.

Immediately, the tension swells between us, and she struggles to look me in the eyes. I fucked up again.

As the distance grows between us, she receives more calls, more texts. She excuses herself again and again.

In my head, the mystery texter is a haunted lover, a jealous boyfriend perhaps, hell, a dick of a husband who wants her on a tight leash. I even inspect her ring finger and after observing what looks like a pale imprint of a ring, I'm tempted to ask her if she's married but the thought is so jarring and pervasive that it distorts all of my motor functions, and I find myself sinking further and further into myself, into a hyperreal world encompassed by thousand of perverted eyeballs that bare the characteristics of tack hammers beating and beating me down into a corrupted, soulless hellscape riddled with a holy "consume-or-be-consumed" mantra rooted in the whims of wannabe idols, whose vanities often resemble hopeless pleas for power.

As we move our way to the blackjack table, Jazz receives yet another buzz from her phone.

Trying not to lose my patience, I kindly ask Jazz to turn off the phone, but she doesn't.

Then, I ask her to silence the phone.

She doesn't.

Then, after losing my patience, I scream at Jazz.

She freezes in shock.

The phone *buzzes* yet again!

Before she can tend to the phone, I snatch it from her hand and slam it down on the sidewalk, causing the bottom half of the screen to fracture into a spider web-like pattern.

The long expression on her face causes my knees to buckle.

Everybody lingering outside the casino is staring at us with wide-eyed expressions.

All eyes are on me, not her.

I've committed the mortal sin.

Charged and convicted of first-degree murder.

Jazz kneels down and attempts to bring her phone back to life, but the cracked screen makes it nearly impossible to operate.

In a fit of rage, she rips off the earrings, the expensive ones that I gave to her as a gift, and throws them at me. I make an attempt to catch them, but they strike me in the chest, like two curveballs, and fall to the sidewalk.

Jazz storms away.

Hesitant, I reach down to pick up the earrings, but they roll and bounce from my reach. I look back up at Jazz, who's lost in a crowd. I leave the earrings behind and chase after Jazz. I end up catching up with her inside Knight's Bay.

From behind, I grab her by the arm.

She suddenly screams out for help.

Startled, I let go of her arm.

Accompanied by a security guard, who looks like a trained assassin, one of the employees for Knight's Bay approaches us and asks Jazz if I'm bothering her.

She says that she doesn't know me and that I've been harassing her.

The Carolina-blue suited employee asks me to leave, uses a basic de-escalation tactic such as holding up both hands, palm-side up, to show me that he's not a threat, but I try to state my case. I only manage to squeeze out a few words before both of his hands rotate like knives, as he slightly shifts his weight in a defensive posture. He only says it once to me, and I know he means it when his eyes fix on mine.

With the threat of police looming over me, Security escorts me from Knight's Bay.

I walk back to the sidewalk to fetch the earrings, and not to my surprise, I catch a guy dressed in beige khaki shorts and an oversized Hawaiian T-shirt picking up both of the earrings off the ground and then scanning the scene as he pockets them.

As soon as I call out to the thief, he runs away like a deer, clumsily and awkwardly.

I chase after him like a wolf, eyes sharp, determined.

After a couple of blocks, I manage to corner the thief in an alleyway behind the Chateau. He tries to run away. I kick the back of his heel and trip him up. Once he falls face first onto the ground, it's all over for him. I pounce on top of him and start whaling on his face. My fists, his chin: I don't hold back the punches.

One after another, each punch connects to his jaw, causing his eyes to swim around his head, as if he's an eye-blink away from blacking out. A stream of frothy blood oozes from both his nose and mouth.

Among the blood are several teeth, which he spits out between each blow before surfacing through a sea of blood for a
breath of air. I stifle each attempt. Coughing and choking on
his own blood, his eyes widen in panic. A freeze frame of the
face of a man who's moments away from drowning. I ignore
his struggle. I ignore the scaly hand of death as it tries to pull
him into the abyss. His eyelids flutter like the wings of a fledg-
ling. Each blow submerges his head back into that red sea.

Yet despite each blow, he clings onto consciousness. After
his face starts to swell with blood, I realize that I'm no longer
beating him. He's nothing to me but a vessel.

(In some countries, mostly Eastern, from what I've read on
the Internet, including online encyclopedias, if an individual is
caught stealing, then the punishment involves chopping off the
hand—sounds incredibly savage and Backwards with a capital
B, as in millenniums backwards, I know, but right about now,
my blood is on fire)

Somewhere, among his gargles, I hear the word *please*.

I stop punching for a moment and peer closer at the lines,
like deep trenches, along his skin and in that brief moment, his
face appears loose, rubbery, and artificially generated as if he's
wearing the printed face of another person.

I grab hold of his right arm, extend it away from his body,
and stomp on his hand, breaking it. I stomp again, then again
and again, until the bones sound like keys being crushed on a
keyboard. His hand is like a flesh bag of chewed-up gravel.

I'm not beating him, but rather the ghost parasite that has
managed to survive and spread its offspring through a network
so vast that cutting off its food supply would result in the collapse of nations all across the world.

After beating the thief within an inch of his life, I grab the
stolen property from his pocket and then secure the 18k yellow
gold earrings in my pocket. I exit from the alleyway and use
the bottom half of the inside of my shirt to wipe away some of
the blood from my knuckles.

Then, once I return to Planet Bollywood, I locate the nearest restroom to wash my hands. I stop by the bar and order a
whiskey on the rocks from the bartender. I can't even remember the name of the black-labeled whiskey on the bottom shelf;
however, I do remember the logo of a scythe on the bottle.

I down the drink and place the leftover ice cubes inside the napkin and then ball up the napkin and ice my swollen knuckles underneath the bar. My hand still feels like it's buzzing.

Shortly after I order another whiskey from the bartender, a young woman in a black dress sits two stools away from me. I take a look around the bar; and after spotting mostly couples, I realize that I've been marked. She's alone or at least she appears to be alone. Dressed to impress, and she's definitely left an impression on me. First, without making it obvious, I look for a wedding ring as I sip from my drink but don't find one.

Through the corner of my eye, I spot her shooting glances in my direction. I turn and then she looks away, until, finally, both of our eyes meet, the connection of eye contact resulting in her moving to the stool next to me as if we have an unspoken contract that leads to a swift transaction of flesh.

After a few minutes of talking to her, mostly about rigged casinos, I pick up the feeling that she's in the flesh trade.

I don't take the bait.

I can sense that we have eyes on us.

Her pimp maybe?

Employer?

Manager?

Handler?

Whatever you want to call them these days.

Once she gets the hint that I'm not interested, she moves onto another poor sap, a middle-aged gambler with slouched shoulders who acts like he's ready to splurge his life's savings on a complete stranger. While the two talk, he shows her the wedding band on his finger—in fact, she looks like she is the one who points it out—then he makes a gesture indicating that his marriage means nothing to him.

As I watch the two get straight down to business and leave the bar together, I reach down and look inward at my own self and find myself asking a similar question.

If I haven't asked for a photo, then the Ball Man wouldn't have dropped the phone, and if the Ball Man didn't drop the phone, then I never would've seen the text, and if I never saw the text, then I never would've pressed Jazz into telling me the truth. But maybe, the truth would've surfaced if I kept picking and poking at it, like a zit ready to pop.

Again, I ask myself again.

But I don't have any answers.

V

AFTER one more drink to help ease the shooting pain in both of my hands, mostly my right, I return to the hotel room.

As soon as I enter, I smell Jazz's scent in the air.

To my surprise, I see her lying in bed with the lights turned off. Her back is turned. She's facing the window, which overlooks the bright and colorful cityscape of Paraíso. She doesn't budge an inch from my presence.

More quietly, I close the door behind me and approach the bed.

With her back still facing me, she says, "I was going to sit with you at the bar, but I saw you with that woman."

"She means nothing to me," I say, stopping at the edge of the bed.

"What did she want?"

She continues to rest on her side with her back turned towards me.

"Money," I say and gently sit down on the edge of the bed. "Who knows? I told her I wasn't interested."

"You did?"

"Yeah," I say. "I did." I pause. The very next words I'm about to say will either kill her slowly or quickly, but they will kill. They'll kill me. They'll kill anyone who comes in contact with us. "I told her *I'm in love with another woman.*"

I feel the side of the bed shift and then slightly dip. Then, I hear a squeak of bed springs followed by the rustling sounds of Jazz rotating around on her other side. I can sense those eyes burning a hole in my back.

"You don't mean it," she says, her voice clearer.

"I do," I say clearly.

"You don't—"

"But I do, Jazz," I say, facing Jazz. "I would kill for you."

"You wouldn't—"

"I'd tear through an entire army if it stood between me and you—"

"Stop!"

With her eyes beating down at me, Jazz clenches her teeth in a type of anger that only I can understand, as if it's my second language. Her bloodshot eyes swell with tears.

As I wipe away the tears from the side of her cheeks, Jazz moves her eyes to my swollen red hand.

"Your hand." She rolls off the bed and switches on a lamp on the nightstand and carefully inspects my hand. "Rob," she says, "what did you do?"

My other hand is too sore to fit inside my pocket.

"Left pocket."

Jazz reaches into the pocket and pulls out the earrings.

"Some piece of shit tried to steal them," I say and raise my head and look directly in Jazz's eyes. "I figure you could buy at least four phones with those things."

If I hadn't broken Jazz's phone, then Jazz never would've thrown away the earrings, and if I never chased after Jazz instead of retrieving the earrings, then the thief never would've stolen the earrings, and if the thief never stole those earrings, then I never would've broken his face.

She places the earrings on the nightstand and returns to my side of the bed. First, she kisses my swollen right hand. Then, from there, she pushes me onto the bed, removes the clothes from her body, and then the two of us embrace one another. I lose myself in her, her eyes, her everything. I am her, and she is me, and together, we are forever intertwined and bonded by the arms of the sacred sun.

For the first time in a very long time, the world around me disappears, and I'm forever lost in her universe.

I make a wish and in that wish, I wish for this moment to never end.

VI

ACTUALLY, Jazz thinks out loud, she feels much more relieved for not having a phone, at least for one night. I figure it's her way of giving me a pass for my latest outburst.

With our sticky, sweaty bodies soaking wet, she climbs her way through damp bed sheets and grabs hold of one of those ouroboros earring from the nightstand and looks it over.

"Eighteen karats? For real?"

"For real," I say. "Least that's what the seller told me."

"How much were these things?"

"Not telling."

"Eighteen karats?"

"Yeah," I say. "Eighteen karats."

"That's like—"

"I know."

"How'd you get the money?"

"Believe it or not, but I won it from playing slots."

Jazz rolls her eyes toward me until they're fixed on mine.

"Get outta here?"

"I shit you not."

She nudges my shoulder with her elbow.

"You lucky dog."

I make a lame attempt at *barking*, but my voice sounds like crushed gravel from the weight of exhaustion.

Once more, we kiss and embrace each other.

While Jazz rubs her hands through my hair, she suddenly stops and pulls herself away. She feels the back of my head.

"What is that?" she asks.

Following Jazz's hand, I rub the back of my head and feel a small knot about the size of a marble.

"Must be from where I hit the back of my head."

More concerned, Jazz asks, "When did this happen?"

"When I was using the restroom—"

All of a sudden, I hear a *pounding* at the door.

I slip into my boxers and tell Jazz not to worry.

Once I arrive at the door, I peer through the peephole. On the other side of the door stands a man facing in the other direction. As though he can sense me watching, he rotates and faces forward. His face looks like roadkill: Nose twisted with bones, ligaments, and cartilage sticking out, both cheeks, black and blue, are as large as baseballs, and once he cracks open his mouth in a wicked smile, a rope of blood dribbles from his lips and reveals his puffy gums where whatever remaining teeth he has left protrude outward like crooked headstones.

I take a closer look at his face and realize it's the thief from earlier. He leans closer toward the tiny peephole and the sides of his round face balloon outward while his facial features—or what's left—remain exaggerated, either shrunken or enlarged, as though filtered through a fish lens. He rears back his balled up fist and once more, pounds on the door.

Sweating profusely, I wake up the sound of *knocking* on the door, this time less intense.

Startled, Jazz stirs and shortly after I roll out of the bed, I hear a sharp sniffle. She suddenly wakes.

"Who is it?" she asks.

"I dunno," I say, fetch my boxers from the carpeted floor, and slip them on, one leg at a time.

Once dressed, I check out the noise.

Through the peephole, I witness a man dressed in a tacky-looking Hawaiian shirt banging on a door across the hallway. The shirt looks similar, if not, maybe even the same as the one that the thief was wearing. He sways back and forth, and he's yelling out something but from the drunken slur in his voice, I can't make out what he's yelling.

Finally, he staggers away from the door and as he stumbles down the hallway, I mange to get a better look at the drunk's face. Not him. Not even close. Plus, no marks or bruises.

Relieved, I pull myself away from the door and make sure it's locked.

Jazz says from behind, "What is it?"

"Just some drunk," I say and walk back to bed.

As I slide both my feet underneath the covers, I feel several grains of coarse sand along the bed sheets; and strangely, from a distance, I hear the white noise-sound of ocean waves crashing into a shore. I ignore the sand and the sounds and stare up at the ceiling above.

Jazz touches me on the shoulder and says, "I think I might have something that'll help us sleep."

"Yeah?"

She crawls over my body and reaches over me and grabs a baggie from the side pocket of her purse and once she returns to her side of the bed, waves the baggie in front of my face.

"Where you get that?" I ask, as I pull the baggie of darker-than-usual weed closer to my nose and take a whiff of a rotten orange-like odor.

"Just some guy in the lobby."

I feel both jagged and round protrusions in the baggie.

"Lots of seeds and stems."

"We'll manage," she says and pulls out a packet of rolling papers. "I was just about to smoke it before you showed up. I was meaning to ask you earlier. . . " Jazz says and then grabs a glossy magazine on *Paraíso* from the table and then returns to the bed and plumps herself against the headboard and then dumps out the skunky weed on the magazine, ". . . what's the *Art of Contortion*?"

"Oh!" I say teasingly. "So, what? It's okay for you to stick your nose in my stuff?"

"It fell out of your bag," she says, sorting through all of the seeds and stems and moving them into their own separate pile away from the weed. "The title sounds kind of interesting."

"I don't know too much about it—"

"Then, why do you have it?"

"The cover," I say, thinking. "I like the cover design."

"Okay," she says, barely moving her lips.

"But," I say while starting to catch onto Jazz's annoyance in my lack of answer, "from what I've read, it's about this guy named Flip, who tries to bring down a local paper mill that he believes is polluting the air and making people sick, including members of his family—"

"Flip, huh?" She pinches heady pieces of weed, crumbles, and sprinkles them into the folded rolling paper. "Sounds like a good read."

"Apparently, there was some controversy around the book, critics claiming the idea was stolen from another similar story called *The Coop*."

"What idea isn't stolen these days?" Jazz says and finishes the joint by sealing it shut with a lick and finger full of her saliva. "So," she twists the one end of the joint to a sharp point, "what's the meaning behind that title? Exactly how does one contort?"

Having not read the book in its entirety, I think for a moment about the answer.

I say to Jazz, "I dunno, but I think it has to do with trees."

"*Trees*, huh?"

"Yeah," I say. "Trees. But it's not like a traditional book, written in a linear timeline; instead, it's written like a spiritual guide from the perspective of the *contorter*."

Jazz sits in a heavy silence, as if she's patiently waiting for me to further explain myself before she lights up the joint.

"The character, this contorter, Flip. . . " I say, giving more thought to the story and focusing on certain parts I read that highlighted the character's struggle while delving deep into the dark corners of corporate greed and at the same time, desperately trying *not* to abandon his core values, ". . . he must contort himself in order to infiltrate and then eventually, destroy a ruthless company that's making people sick—"

"Contort how?"

"Becoming a tree," I say, waiting for Jazz to hit me with a brutal response like "*What in the holy fuck are you talking about?*"

I wait, but she doesn't say a word. Instead, she holds my gaze and urges me to continue, even if I sound like a rambling fool. "Not literally, but rather more conceptually. Establishing and *planting* his roots inside a company, *contorting* with age, *enduring* the elements, *seeking* out light while being surrounded by darkness." For a second, I glance over at Jazz to make sure I haven't lost her. She seems to be listening, although I can tell that she's itching to smoke that snooze button. I tell myself to wrap it up. "For one to contort is to bend from one's normal shape. There's this term called phototropism—" *or was it photorealism,* "—basically, it's about the way a plant or tree grows based on the direction of the light, let's say, if a tree grows in a shaded area, it'll do whatever it takes to reach a light source—the sun—even if that means bending or twisting its branches in order to find light. But what I'm really trying to say is, life can be complicated at times, and sometimes, people have to do complicated things in order to grow or in Flip's case, seek justice."

Jazz looks at me with heavy eyes.

"Deep." She emphasizes the letter "p" in the word *deep*. "Well, then. . . " she holds out the tightly rolled joint in front of me and says, ". . . let's get contorted."

"Good one."

"Wanna do the honors?"

"Sure," I say and grab the joint from Jazz's hand.

I feel a tremor in my hand the moment I touch the joint, as if I'm holding onto a live cable, and I can feel its energy inside its protective casing. The feeling is similar to the way my red right hand felt moments after I broke the thief's face, the buzzing, tingly sensation, like inside my hand was a hornet's nest. Fearful of tearing the joint, I hold it still and steady. A sudden ripple of nausea deep in my belly forces me to stop thinking so damn much. My thoughts race round and round my head like stock cars, the only way, I tell myself, to prevent a fiery pileup is to focus on my words, speak—say anything.

Feeling the sweat beads pinprick along my forehead, I ask Jazz if she has a light.

"Of course," she says and pulls out a pack of matches from her purse. "Bummed them from some slot junkie."

She hands me the pack of matches.

As my thoughts send me into a dizzy spell, I pull a match from the pack and light it. The presence of fire helps calm me, as well as my thoughts, which suddenly slow, fade, then vanish as if they never even existed.

Thinking more clearly, my eyes are drawn away from the flame to a painting on the wall. I lower the flame and stare at the familiar painting. The flame eventually runs out, burning the tip of my finger. Once I feel the pinch of heat, I wave out the flame.

Next to me, Jazz asks, "What's wrong?"

"That painting," I say and roll out of bed.

I walk over to the framed painting directly across the bed.

"Kind of a strange painting to have on the wall, especially in a place like this," I say, staring at the gloomy painting of a weathered dock stretching and disappearing into a foggy body of water, perhaps a lake. At the end of the dock stands a man with his back turned.

Jazz crawls to the very end of the bed for a closer look at the painting: "And what kind of place is this?"

"You know," I say, glancing over at Jazz "you'd think the hotel would display something less, how do I say, glum."

Jazz sighs, her shoulders deflate.

"Are we gonna get high or not?"

I glance down at the pack of matches in my hand and read the cursive print of a billiards hall, *El Crusoe's*, with the logo of a black eightball in place of the letter "o" in *Crusoe's*, the name underlined with a pool stick, or cue. The last time I saw these matches was at Red Pines.

An orderly—Chuck, I believe it was—said that he and the others, as in the other orderlies, used to hit up the popular spot on the weekends. They were part of a league, I think.

"Robert. . . " Jazz says from behind.

As I rotate around and face Jazz, the tremors are back, but this time they spread over my entire body. After the tremors, the chills hit me. Bullets of sweat drip from my face. Except for the spike in fever, the feeling reminds me of this one time, when I got the jab, a foreign vaccine injected into my body— then, later that night, I felt like I was going to die. Is that what is happening to me right now? Am I about to die?

I look at Jazz, and she looks at me as if I am dying and yet, she can't save me. She wants to save me, but she can't move.

I suddenly hear a mechanical noise to my right. Seated in the darkest corner of the room is a dark figure of a man, similar profile as me but taller, wearing a visor or headset of some kind, with a giant Pacific octopus on top of his lap, the sides of its head pulsating like a heart, while its eight arms cling to the man's lower abdomen. I recognize the bottom half of his face and soon realize the man is Moses.

The tears fall from my eyes and run down the sides of my face.

As the terror leaves me frozen in my stance, I glance over at Jazz and only find an empty bed.

A sharp, stinging, stabbing, shooting pain rushes through my entire body, starting from my genitals to the lower section of my abdomen as if thorny veins are climbing up my veins.

As I feverishly shiver in pain, a sword of light cuts through the center of the room. In the lit doorway stands William, his silhouette as dark as midnight.

With his glassy eyes beating down on me, William says to me, "It's time to go home, Robert."

"No," I mutter, my lips trembling.

Again, I search for Jazz but can't find her anywhere inside the hotel room.

My skin is on fire.

Warm sweat runs down my face and burns my eyes. Each bead of sweat is like a thumbtack prodding into my skin. I can no longer take it anymore, the sharp pain, the blood, the gore, and all of the violence, as well as a low nagging hum of what sounds like an idling engine channeling through my eardrums and devouring my thoughts, only to spit them out, all chewed up, mutated, and gnarly, a thought that doesn't belong to me, a cold, dark, and corrupted thought, carefully implanted, then manipulated by years of constant attention and determination, nursed and curated by those in my circle who selfishly tried to control me. By giving into each strategic incitement, I'm giving them power over me, my body, my thoughts.

As dozens of armed cops rush past William and flood into the room and flank me with their guns drawn, the walls begin to close in all around, suffocating me. I'm tempted to make a run to my bag on the table and grab my revolver from the side pocket, but based on the glint in their eyes, they've been waiting all week—I take it back—these TV cops have been waiting ever since they were shitted out from the Academy to plug the first sucker to reach for his steel.

The hot blood grips a hold of me, the nerves like live wires. I scream out to the top of my lungs until the fire burns a hole in my throat. I dash away from the cops and sprint toward the window, curl my right shoulder inward like a linebacker ready to make a tackle, and charge directly through the glass.

As shards of shattered glass shower over my body, I look down at the twelve stories below and accept my fate and what a relief it is, to finally give in to the madness.

In my grueling descent, I gift myself with the unadulterated path left abandoned, a flawed yet forward path where I long to be touched, spiritually and unequivocally, searching, not only for *her* love, but also figuring out a way to escape the trap that I had sprung onto myself.

No matter what path I take or wherever it may lead me, it always brings me back here, to a place of and for the Forsaken Ones, where briny air clings to the skin like cologne and candied, artificial smells of a forgotten past are wedded by a rich harmony of ageless wonders, a consistent reminder of where I was created and where I will be unplugged, and with a roaring heart, where I watch glimmering light dancing over the face of haunted waters.